EARL THOMPSON'S TATTOO HAS LEFT ITS INDELIBLE IMPRINT ON CRITICS FROM COAST TO COAST

Big Bestsellers from SIGNET

☐ **A GARDEN OF SAND by Earl Thompson.** The big, blistering saga of carnal knowledge in the down-and-out days of the thirties. ". . . brilliant, powerful, sensational."— **The New York Times** (#J6679—$1.95)

☐ **IF BEALE STREET COULD TALK by James Baldwin.** A masterpiece about the love between a man and a woman. . . . **The New York Times** called this bestseller "One of the best novels of the year." A Literary Guild Alternate Selection. (#J6502—$1.95)

☐ **FEAR OF FLYING by Erica Jong.** A dazzling uninhibited novel that exposes a woman's most intimate sexual feelings . . . "A sexual frankness that belongs to and hilariously extends the tradition of **Catcher in the Rye** and **Portnoy's Complaint** . . . it has class and sass, brightness and bite."—John Updike, **New Yorker** (#J6139—$1.95)

☐ **PENTIMENTO by Lillian Hellman.** Hollywood in the days of Sam Goldwyn . . . New York in the glittering times of Dorothy Parker and Tallulah Bankhead . . . a 30-year love affair with Dashiell Hammett, and a distinguished career as a playwright. "Exquisite . . . brilliantly finished . . . it will be a long time before we have another book of personal remembrance as engaging as this one."— **New York Times Book Review** (#J6091—$1.95)

☐ **THE FRENCH LIEUTENANT'S WOMAN by John Fowles.** By the author of **The Collector** and **The Magus**, a haunting love story of the Victorian era. Over one year on the N.Y. Times Bestseller List and an international bestseller. "Filled with enchanting mysteries, charged with erotic possibilities . . ."—**Christopher Lehmann-Haupt, N.Y. Times** (#E6484—$1.75)

TATTOO

«««««««««»»»»»»»»»»

BY

Earl Thompson

Ⓢ

A SIGNET BOOK

NEW AMERICAN LIBRARY

TIMES MIRROR

To Mai Zetterling,
whose existence is an inspiration
and whose personal alchemy
so helped keep me alive
in a mean time

tattōō (tatōō), n., & v.i. 1. Beat of drum, or bugle-call, at 10 p.m. recalling soldiers to quarters, elaboration of this with music & marching as entertainment; *beat the devil's* , drum idly with fingers etc. 2. vi. Rap quickly & repeatedly, beat the devils

tattōō (tatōō), v.t. & n. 1. Mark (skin etc.) with indelible patterns by inserting pigments in punctures. 2. n. Such mark.

—*The Concise Oxford Dictionary*
of Current English

PART ONE

1

THAT Germany had surrendered smacked of yet another damn thing to keep the boy from glory. He hadn't stepped on a crack since Pearl Harbor—a private pagan ritual to insure that the war would never end. When Roosevelt died, he began to panic that it would all be over too soon. For from the morning of December 7 to the present moment, to *Slap a Jap* and *Stun a Hun* had been his most abiding and hopeful ambition, his most certain way of ever making something of himself.

Standing on the corner of Market and Douglass in downtown Wichita in a pair of leaden Levi's, a Falstaff beer T-shirt and run-down brown cowboy boots, he measured his reflection in Kress' plate glass against the image of soldier, sailor, flyboy and the occasional marine who marched so resolutely past, eyes fixed on eternity, turning the admiring glances of bobby-soxers and swingshifters, haunting the longings of wives and Gold and Blue Star Mothers alike.

He was *big* enough. Behind Air Corps sunglasses, the bows bent completely around his ears, he fixed *his* eyes— yet lightstruck after sitting through *Guadalcanal Diary* at the Miller Theater for the fifth time.

Call me "The Chicken," his run-down heels rang out as he marched along, his uniform of the unenlisted and his long blond pachuco pomp clogged with Wildroot Cream Oil turning only the most deprecating eye.

He limped a little, hoping desperately to be taken for a survivor of *something*. In an eyelet of his sweat-darkened Western belt he had screwed the cap device of a marine. Being too young to get in on the only thing in his lifetime that might lift him to a place of respect and reward was a restriction too frantic to bear. His fear of missing his one big chance was greater than his fear of any death that might await behind frozen hedgerow or lurk in steaming

3

jungles with names like sharpened bamboo spears. Yet his fear of death and pain was very real. Particularly the fear of being caught by those goddamned little yellow-bellied Japanese.

He saw himself the marine they called "Chicken" in the film, played by Richard Jaeckel, and felt in his chest the young man's terror. Seeing his own cruel death on the long, cold steel of a Nip bayonet almost moved him to tears.

OK! he resolved. *OK. But give me the goddamned suit!* was his desperate, silent prayer. *Let me live a little. Then I don't care if I do die, do die, do die.*

It was the Germans he had really wanted to fight. He didn't give a shit what they had done to the Jews and all that crap. He would have ripped the blouse off Nina Foch's boobies himself given the opportunity. It was simply that he somehow saw through the bullyboy Nazi bullshit and was as eager to tommy-gun hell out of them as he would have been to blast all the smug caseworkers, cold-nosed teachers, cruel truant officers, juvenile court judges and self-righteous suited citizens who had always found his existence on the face of the earth such an affront. The Japs, however, were frightening, an ultimately foreign mystery. Their presumption in going to war against the United States was insane. And he *knew*, Hollywood to the contrary, that the chances of his running across Paulette Goddard in a black nightie in some stinking jungle were not good.

But if the Nips were all that were left, then the Nips it would have to be. His fear was trebled at least. His possibilities of survival were quite dim—you couldn't even *see* the little bastards! And the spoils of war were something that would have to be postponed until he was home on leave. The world seemed stubbornly committed to deny him every chance of ever getting off relief.

He was ready to fight anyone his own color—the South if it would ever rise again. He was a Kansan, with John Brown's fiery raid on Pottawatomie blazing in a gigantic auditorium mural above the stage at this school. Just thinking about killing Krauts and raping their big-breasted Nazi women gave him a hard-on. The same proposition in Japan made him a little sick. He had no desire to lay hands on yellow skin. The prospect of close combat, hand

4

to hand with some dirty Jap, made him even sicker. The thing to do was lay back and use fucking bombs and flamethrowers against them. He had relished with absolute confidence the idea of going against the German in his goose-stepping hobnailed boots—a canny all-American boy shod by Firestone or Goodyear. The Japanese wore weird split-toed sneakers that made his flesh crawl.

But *BAM-BAM-BAM-BAM!* the heavy lead of his Thompson chopper mowed the mothers down. With a dancing step in sight of a bus stop, he butt-stroked a begging survivor and saw his teeth fly like kernels of white corn from the bloody hole in his face.

Hang on, Audie Murphy, I'm comin! he pledged, swinging up onto a Thirteenth Street bus like a marine paratrooper mounting a C-47.

The plan had taken form a year before. Others had done it. Audie had. Stafford Coleman had gone from a CCC camp into the Marines at fifteen. Staff had been the first man to land on the Marshall Islands. When the boy's grandmother had kept a rooming house on Cleveland, the Colemans had been renters. Staff had been the nearest thing he'd had to a big brother. David Hooten had gone into the Navy at sixteen. He had been on the *Wasp.* His neck and back were a mass of angry red scars. The boy had seen them when David was home on leave. His grandmother cleaned the Hootens' house three times a week.

Mrs. Hooten was busy all the time with the Red Cross, USO and Blue Star Mothers. Mr. Hooten, a veteran of WWI, a tree surgeon, was an officer in the American Legion and an air-raid warden. Their daughter, Rosemary, who looked just like Jinx Falkenburg, was working as a secretary on the swing shift at Boeing. She did not need the money—the Hootens were rich—but she did it out of patriotism. Yet her mother worried, for Rosie went out after almost every shift with one or another of the Air Corps officers that were always around the plant, coming in just in time to grab a bite and leave again for her next shift. On her dressing-table mirror were the photos of *three* B-17's and their crews, lined up beneath a pinup of her and the name "Rosie" painted on the planes' noses.

Mrs. Hooten was also upset by the terrible language David shouted in his sleep when he was home on recuperation leave. She understood it was because of all he had been through, she just wished he would not do it. She had confided in her housekeeper one time: "I feel like this darn war has taken my children and made them so they will never be as I had always dreamed."

The boy sometimes went to the Hootens' when his grandmother was working there. He had found Rosemary passed out in her slip on a downstairs couch, having been too plowed to navigate the stairs to her room, and had breathlessly snaked up the hem of her slip to gaze in hard-on wonder at the beautiful bare Jinx Falkenburg ass for which three B-17's had been named. There was also the certainty of finding a lot of loose change going through the pockets of clothes in the Hootens' closet. But what puzzled him was why the Hootens slept in separate bedrooms. It somehow made all their riches seem not enough. There was always a new chair, bric-a-brac, carpet, game in a leather box, draperies, whenever the boy went there. The house was always being changed. They never wore anything out, yet Mrs. Hooten was never satisfied. He longed for all their fine things and could not imagine having so much money you could leave loose change in a jacket pocket in a closet!

It was the war that had opened the Hootens' house to him. The war was the only possible bridge between the alley in which he lived and the big porched house beyond a broad green lawn where the *Saturday Evening Post, Esquire, Vogue* and half a dozen other magazines came through the mail as if by magic and where Rosie's perfumed and powdered white poo was the great inverted heart of his every Valentine dream.

The war was the greatest thing that ever happened.

There had been all kinds of stories in the news about kids who had enlisted underage by changing their birth certificates. There had been a story about a kid his own age who had been in the Air Corps, the Navy *and* Infantry, enlisting under a different name every time he had been found out. He had been in combat and been decorated too. The boy had intended to wait a little longer, just to make sure, but with the Germans out of it, he simply had to try. Who knew how long the Japs could last? They *said* they would fight to the last man.

God, make them try! he prayed as the bus passed Blue's Dog and Cat Hospital and crossed Emporia.

He stood up and hooked up. The big metal gated hook on the end of his static line clacked onto the polished hand-

rail overhead. It was a daylight drop behind Jap lines, right into old Hirohito's headquarters. Only volunteers were aboard that day. Only the lucky were coming back from this one. He resettled his emergency chute on his chest. The heavy Thompson submachine gun on top glinted dully in the light. On the butt was a pinup and the name "Rosie." *Stand in the door! Chhh!* the doors popped open. Hands on either side of the door. *This is it!*
GERON-IIIIII-MOOOOooo. . . .

Both booted feet hit the sidewalk at the same time. He was loose, ready to roll and collapse his chute. Both feet landed squarely on a crack wide enough to break his mother's back. It was as if he had been shot. He never had any luck. Posthumously he crossed his eyes and spit between his feet, offered yet another faithless prayer, racked his brain for any crazy thing to wipe out the bad portent of that booby-trapped crack. Though he *knew* his superstitions were stupid and worthless as prayer, he had once walked all the way around the block to avoid crossing the path of a smug black cat. He just could not take the chance.

His way home lay up an unnamed niggertown alley between St. Francis and the dirt path called Washington Avenue, that paralleled the Santa Fe tracks. The alley ran behind Ball's Market & Wholesale Meat Company, where the flies swarmed over the waste cans of meat scraps and vegetable trimmings outside the back door and strays came on two feet and four to rustle for food. He surprised an old black uncle bent like an inchworm, tow sack over his bowed shoulder, rummaging in the garbage. The man gave a start, his eyes meeting the boy's. Then he visibly relaxed and silently turned again to his search. The boy felt embarrassed for the old man. There was nothing to say. "Sorry" would not get it. The Depression had not been ended by the war for either of them. That the boy was white and the old man and most of the people in the alley black made the boy's frustration double.

OK. So his stepdad was a jailbird and his mother a whore; so his grandpa and grandma had always been on relief; that didn't mean *he* had to turn out bad. Of one thing, though, he was certain: before he would work at some pissass job all his life and still wind up on welfare, he would take a gun and rob.

7

The war was the only hopeful alternative. The first break in what he had seen until Pearl Harbor as an unshakable system to keep people like him from ever wearing good clothes, living in a real home, owning a car, going to high school and college, having a really nice time. So, as long as they were willing to hand guys like him a great uniform and dough and fall all over themselves in USO's, he was damned if he was going to be cheated out of getting in on it.

Though he had confided his plan to no one, his best buddies, Glenn and Bucky, thought he was too cuckoo about the war. *They* weren't in any hurry to go. They wanted to get out of school and go to work for Boeing, where there was *real* dough and all those lonely cunts chewing the seams out of their slacks. In fact, as they grew older and cunts chewing slacks more available, they saw less and less reason for going to work at all. They were good enough to make walking around money shooting snooker.

Over the years the boy made himself a complete combat kit, including an arsenal of scale model weapons carved from soft pine, so real he had once been stopped by police on the way to the canal bank where he regularly cleared the weeds and cavelike sewer opening of enemy. From a Military Science 1 book he had stolen from the public library, he had copied plans for the weapons and studied the arts of war. From the book, the comics and all the war movies he had seen, he figured training for a snap and a combat commission a definite possibility. It had happened to Audie Murphy.

BAM! he whipped a sniper out of a rattling runt of a castor-bean tree with a single, expertly touched-off shot from his tommy gun. There was a hole in the Nip's forehead the size of a nickel. The whole back of his skull was blown out. Dirt from the dusty, rutted alley grew dark with his blood and grayed his round yellow face.

OK, men, follow me! Swiveling his head in search of other snipers along the treacherous, narrow way, he led men into the mouth of hell.

"Hey, Jackson, you killin them ole Germans and things again?" piped a little brown face peering between broken fence pickets.

The face fronted a narrow, elongated skull like a cantaloupe that had been too long under the heap. It an-

8

swered to the name Arthur. Through the next pair of pickets, lower down, peered the big-eyed, ever-awed, solemn face of his kid sister, Arutha, who never spoke except through her brother who was the only one who had access to her mysterious little mind. Arthur had explained: "She got clef pallet."

BAM! BAM! He plugged them both. They fell in the dirt, holding their starch-distended bellies, Arthur flailing his feet, laughing as if he were being tickled to death.

When he came back from the war, he would bring those two a souvenir.

2

THEY called the chalk gray apparition sagging on its long-gone tires a trailer house, though the only place it had trailed was from the backyard on Cleveland, where it had been built, to the nameless alley in niggertown. It was twenty-six feet long, eight feet wide and had neither a toilet nor running water. The old man had made it when the boy was ten, when it became certain that the church that had inherited the boardinghouse they operated in exchange for two rooms was going to turn them out and convert the place into a home for the more sanctified aged. The trailer was made mostly from scrap lumber and plywood seconds, and the old man had not thought to insulate between inner and outer walls. In winter, with a fire going inside, the walls sweat, blistered and buckled. When spring came, the boy and the old man had lain underneath the thing to tack fuzzy beaverboard beneath the flooring in an effort to keep the linoleum underfoot from being as cold as a rink. Even with the gas burning all night, the windows and the wall beside the studio couch on which he slept still became rimed with ice. In summer the bedbugs ate him alive.

The trailer sat in the backyard of an incredible foul-mouthed old white widow, Mrs. Simmons, who had skidded the rig of her own daughter to live for a year with her daughter's young black common-law husband, a tall, everlastingly drunk blade of a cat called Ralph, whom the widow had never let get out of bed, bringing him bottles of Gallo port wine and flinging the empties out the back door. Daughter, who was half black, had expressed her initial objection to the arrangement by trying to burn down the house one night. She had succeeded only in razing the back porch and scorching the back wall. The sooty shadows of the flames remained. The back door opened onto a three-foot drop bridged by a packing crate and cement block. Forsaking fire for the word, daughter reclaimed her loose property one noon, timing her move when Mrs. Simmons was out for wine. After that, the widow went about in her slip for days on end, bothering the postman, the paper boy, any luckless door-to-door hustler for Watkins or the *Saturday Evening Post*. She had even made a pass at the old man and cast long, frowning, quizzical looks at the boy. For his part, the boy avoided going into her house by regulating his toilet habits so they fell during school hours and always taking a shower after gym to forestall ever having to use the bathroom. She looked at him like one of Toulouse-Lautrec's fabulous old whores which he found in art books in the public library when in search of pictures of healthier female flesh, particularly those that showed a little hair.

The widow opened the back door to let out a steaming big tomcat which shot under the old man's feet as he sat reading the *Evening Eagle*. The cat passed the boy like a turpentined yellow streak and cleared the chicken-wire fence beyond in a bound.

"Goddamned cat!" the old man swore, popping out his paper and carefully tilting back against the tree.

The widow looked after her cat, her breasts the size of peach baskets billowing beneath the tattered lace top of her rusty black slip. Her upper arms were like pale fresh hams. Her Brillo hair was dyed the color of flame. She must be sixty, the boy thought, and in spite of his repugnance at the sight of her, he felt a twinge of shameful desire left from the nights of conjuring about what she had that had held her daughter's man so long.

How many moons, how many Junes, how many bottles of Gallo port wine had flowed across the days and nights of all the changeless years, watering her timeless fleshy dreams? Not war or the prospects for peace altered the patterns of lives like the widow's or the old man's.

"Oh, it's you? Thought it was the cat come back," the old man cracked over the top of his paper. "Where the hell you been and what the hell you been up to?" he demanded, his chair tilted against the weeping willow tree. He wore only relief issue work pants as patched and shapeless as a coolie's over his summer BVD's. It had been the willow that had sold the boy's grandmother on the site. Except for the tree, the entire neighborhood was ashen where it was not sere. All green had long since been smothered under soot from the Santa Fe.

Not waiting for an answer, the old man deduced, "Been sittin in some goddamned picture show, wastin the hard-earned money me and your grandma have to hand out to you. Why don't you get the fuck out and get a job and make somethin out of yourself? By God, when I was your age, I was doin a man's work for a man's pay. Took you in when your good-for-nothin mother couldn't take care of you, gave you a place to sleep, what to eat, bought you clothes, bought you books and sent you to school, and this all the thanks I get. If you had any kind of gumption, you'd do somethin to bring in a little money around here. Picture shows and fartin around with some damn boys—that's all you got in your head. No more goddamn spunk in you than in a wild duck!"

He had heard the old man's words so many times that the pain in his chest was as familiar and somehow perversely cherished as the crescent scar on his right knee, a souvenir of the time he had parachuted from the second-floor landing of the school fire escape with a bed sheet. Yet the words always hurt. They had forged a stubborn rod in him, running his length and making him as angry and unbending in his own way as the old man.

His conviction of the injustice of the old man's indictment continued to fire the inner burning. For the old man had not held a real job in the boy's lifetime. Nor did he consider, whatever the boy's mother might be, that she was his own daughter.

"You haven't given me shit since I knew you," the boy muttered, turning toward the trailer.

"What's that?" The old man craned over the top of his paper, his reading glasses from Woolworth's perched on the end of his big horn.

11

"Nothin."

"You better watch your mouth around here, by God. You aren't too big to have your ass kicked yet."

"Try it," the boy muttered.

"How's that?" The old man made small motions as if to rise, but his butt never actually left the pillow on his chair.

"I said, I'm gettin out. Just as soon as I can. I won't be around here much longer."

The old man snorted, cleared his throat and went back to the news. He had no interest in foolish talk.

The boy took a dipper of water from the bucket beside the little sink just inside the door. He hated drinking from the same dipper as the old man and his grandmother. Who knew what kind of old-age diseases he could get? The entire jerry-built accommodation inside the trailer made him feel vulnerable and on the brink of utter disaster. *Could war be any worse?* he asked himself.

He heard the screen door of the trailer in the next yard screech and bang. He leaped to the window, kneeling on his bed to peek out in hope Mrs. Demicelli was going to take a sunbath.

Out of the corner of his eye, he could see the old man under the tree through the front window. He dug his dick out of his jeans.

Shit! She was going to hang up her wash. Yet.... When she bent to lift something from her basket, her short, rumpled yellow play skirt hiked up her sexy thighs. Her rump was loose and wide. His grandmother thought it was a scandal that Mrs. Demicelli never wore a girdle. She was an entirely average woman with a face so prettily ordinary in spite of constant fussing she lavished on it that the boy could only see it dimly, floating softly around her mocking red mouth when he closed his eyes. Still, she was the nearest thing in his life to the pictures of the women in the "pinup" books he bought secondhand three for a dime and hid behind his bed. He had been in her trailer often in the last year. She liked to invite him for coffee and kid him about his girlfriends and pump him if he was getting any yet. They told each other dirty jokes. He smoked her cigarettes but only barely inhaled. Come back when you're eighteen, she always advised him.

She was married to a little hunchback meat-cutter for Ball's. Her husband came home every day for lunch, which made for much leering and snickering along the al-

ley. Her trailer always smelled of her sweet perfume, cigarettes—she chain-smoked Pall Malls—fresh-cut meat and
come.

The smells came back to him and made the boy feverish
as he knelt on the bed, his cock stiff and throbbing in his
hand.

She hung a big black brassiere beside a pair of panties
on the line. Two clothespins were clipped between her
teeth, her lips open and red. She hoisted the bandanna halter more securely over her big tits with both hands, just as
he saw white below her tan and perhaps the top of a nipple. When she bent, a roll of fat bulged above the waistband of her skirt. He noticed the red chigger bites on her
ankles above the dingy white straps of her wedgies.

The world could have crashed in on him and he could
not have stopped. *"Don't care if I do die, do die, do."* He
jerked his cock, his head swarming with thoughts of how
it would be to be *in* such sexy flesh.

She straightened, hung three pairs of her husband's
jockey shorts on the line and wiped her forehead with the
back of her plump brown arm. Her bleached blond hair,
scraggly with sweat, was tied back with a bandanna that
matched her makeshift halter. She looked right at his window. He quickly leaned back into the shadow.

She walked toward him, looking down at her feet,
toward the faded canvas beach chair in which she sun-
bathed. She sat in the chair, leaning forward to unstrap
her platform sandals. Her near breast mashed against her
shining brown knee and he could see the white globe of it
above her halter. She was going to sunbathe after all. He
stroked himself slowly, saving it. She swung her legs up
into the chair and collapsed against the backrest, facing
him, shifting her hips, rising to the warmth of the slanting
afternoon sun. From the pocket in her skirt she fished a
pack of Pall Malls and lit one with a Zippo lighter. She
unfastened all except the last three buttons of her skirt,
waving the flies away from her heavy, yet shapely legs,
and lay back with the cigarette between her lips, her left
arm thrown across her eyes.

Wait. Wait, he consoled himself. Out of the corner of
his eye, he saw the old man was only half through the paper.

She inched down her halter, first over one spreading
breast, then the other, careful to keep her nipples covered

13

out of some ultimate fractional modesty. She had never had any children. He figured it was because she was afraid they would be hunchbacked like her husband. She flicked fallen ash from her breasts with distaste, slapped a mosquito on her thigh, then raised it to scratch.

Yeah! Yeah! That's it, baby, show it to me. Give it to me. Show me that cunt. Keep that leg up. Oh, yeah, yeah. He could see the shadowed bulge of her colored panties and prayed for another mosquito. She flicked her skirt a little higher, as if she could read his mind and wanted to oblige. She wiped a rivulet of sweat from the shivering meat inside her thigh. Her panties were yellow. He could see through them. *Oh, man! Oh, sweet Mama, don't stop. For christsake, don't stop! Give it to me! Give it to me! Fuck me!* his brain sang, feeling himself going in there—*in* there! He came all over the wall. His ears sang, vision wavered. He felt weak and sick and ashamed, completely desolate. For he had not bridged the distance with his flesh. He wondered if he was crazy. Glenn and Bucky jerked off. But he did not think they had the same thoughts he did. It did not seem to mean very much to them. Besides, they fucked old Vanda Hard-ass-ty all the time and he had not. He had fucked a Mexican girl once the summer before, when he had gone to stay with his stepfather and mother in the Rio Grande Valley, and he had fooled around with his mother those times—but that seemed crazy, as if it hadn't happened and he did not want to think about it. He pushed the thoughts away. Maybe he really was crazy. He was certain he wasn't like all the guys he knew.

He took the blood-dappled rag he kept under his pillow to squash bedbugs and carefully wiped his come from the wall. The rag was stiff with his blood mashed from the stupid flat little bugs and from other comings. He stuffed it down between the bed and the wall. He could look at the woman in the sun now and see where she had stopped shaving her legs at mid-thigh.

What kind of a woman would let a goddamned hunchback fuck her, anyway?

He snapped on the GE console radio that was wedged between the foot of his bed and the curtained closet that ran the rest of the length of the trailer. His grandparents' double bed filled the space between the closet and the back wall. The radio had been the only piece of real furni-

14

ture they had owned since the old man had lost his farm. His uncle had bought it at an auction. It was a magical radio. In ten years of daily use they had never replaced a tube. No one believed it, but it was true. Its veneer had buckled and split like the trailer's walls, but it played perfectly without ground wire or antenna. *They don't make them like that anymore,* he echoed the old man.

Lum and Abner was getting under way. He turned the dial until he found the *Ark-Valley Boys Jamboree.*

"Now, folks, here's a new song from that singin merchant marine from down Oklahoma way, Woody Guthrie—'Reuben James.' And we here in Ark-Valley land all want to thank the good Lord for helpin us to defeat the Huns, and pray we'll soon settle the fish of Immperial Japan, and all the boys like Woody will come sailin safely home soon. Here it is!"

The boy rolled off the couch and dug in the bottom of the closet for a dome-top chest that had once held a small sewing machine. Now it contained what important papers they had left and photographs of his great-grandparents and snapshots of his mother, father, aunt and uncle when they were young, pictures of him as a baby in a tub on the porch of his grandpa's farm. The farm had been lost in the first year of the Depression. Where it had stood there was now a wartime housing development constructed of lumber so green the clapboards were already popping their nails.

Beneath the carbon copies of the court papers granting his grandparents official custody of him, he found his birth certificate. He was careful not to tear it where it had been creased.

... Born to Wilma Wayne McDeramid and Odd Augustavus Andersen, on the 24th Day of May, 1931, a boy, John Odd, 9 lbs. and 10 ozs. Hair blond, eyes blue. ...

His eyes had changed to brown. He remembered when he was in kindergarten and first grade he had one blue eye and one brown. The other kids had called him "Evil Eye" and had not liked him much. He often wondered if his eyes changing color had something to do with his having never felt he was like everyone else.

From the sliding drawer under his bed where he kept

15

his everyday clothes, the guns he had made and the broken balsa-and-tissue paper model of a P-40 Flying Tiger fighter plane, he took the drugstore sack containing the two-part chemical ink eradicator, the blotter, steel school pen and holder and bottle of blue ink.

He had practiced matching the script on his birth certificate a thousand times. He was good in art. The paper of the document was waterstained to begin with. He diluted a drop of ink in the bottle cap until it tested on a bit of scrap to the shade of the faded ink on the certificate. He had already memorized the directions on the eradicator, but he reread them and took a deep breath. Concentrating as he never had before, he dropped a single drop from bottle No. 1 onto the last two digits of his date of birth and carefully blotted it. Then a single drop from No. 2, and the paper became magically bare. He could be anything he wanted to be.

3

MORNING arrived with an importance that made every night in his life forgettable. Euphoric purpose lifted him out of shallow dreams of glory. Desire focused fine enough to burn through all doubt. Drunken, numb on the cheap liquor of his own daring, he dressed quietly, quickly, in clean Levi's and T-shirt. He dipped water from the bucket into the basin and sluiced his face. He carefully combed his wet hair in the cloudy mirror above the basin.

The old man raised from his pillow and asked, "What the hell are you up to? Not goin to get a regular job, I reckon."

"Somethin like that," the boy mumbled.

"Land!" his grandmother exclaimed sleepily, rising on an elbow on the wall side of the old man. Her eyes were inflamed, hayfeverish. "You ain't been up this early of a Saturday since you caddied."

"Probably goin to play some goddamned ball or some

16

such shit," the old man grumbled, turning his back, preparing to catch another couple of winks.

"Don't you want no breakfast?" his grandmother asked halfheartedly. "It's no good to go without breakfast."

"Not hungry."

"Well, when will you be home?"

"Later." He banged out the door.

The slam roused the old man. "Goddamn! Can't he never go out a door without lettin it slam?" the boy heard him complain.

"Just can't never know to expect him for supper or what," his grandmother added.

"Most inconsiderate damned boy I ever seen," he mocked them, going down the alley.

He wished he had shined his boots.

"Hey, Arthur!" he called as the small black boy and his silent sister rounded the corner of their house, eating big slices of sugar-bread, Arutha leading their bony spotted hound and Arthur idly whomping the beast with a battered pan.

"Hey, Jackson!" The boy's narrow face split into a beautiful Hamite conneroo's grin. The kid always sensed when there was a deal to be made. "You bring us some peanuts er somethin from the ball park, OK? Nother of them little bats."

He often hawked peanuts, Cracker Jack, pop or souvenirs at the ball park. Hot dogs were a pain—with or without mustard—you had to wrap them in a napkin. Beer was the best thing, but the older guys had a lock on that.

"What happened to the bat I brought you?"

"Broke it agin a tree."

"Bring you some peanuts if you'll give me a shine," Jack bargained.

"Bag for me un one for Arutha?"

"Yeah."

"OK." He handed Arutha the pan and darted in his back door.

Lest the hound believe whatever crime he was being punished for had been forgotten, sister continued belaboring him with the pan as absentmindedly as had her brother.

"Why are you bangin on that dog?" Jack asked. The

17

soft regular bong of aluminum on barely clothed bone sounded like a distant, muted bell.

She merely stared. He stared back so she would not think he did not care. It was the sum of their communication. The dog accepted his plight as stoically as it was given.

What the hell would become of them? Jack wondered, already feeling himself on his way out of there, toward a better day, one which he saw only in sketchiest outline, distorted by magazine pictures, movies and dreams, but one from which he was determined never to return.

Arthur rushed from the house. His shoeshine box, carried over his shoulder on a leather strap, was chased with bottle caps, a unique handcrafted bejeweled object of his own inspiration and art.

As long as he could remember, Jack had put his left shoe on first—for luck—and it was the left he placed on Arthur's box. Kneeling in the dirt, Arthur applied himself with two brushes, the bristles of which looked bent by a strong wind. Then he slapped brown polish onto the scuffed leather from a can. *Slap-a-slap-a-slap-a-slap.* Arthur danced to the rhythm on his knees. With brushes and expertly popping rag the boy raised a happy shine.

Jack wanted to confide in Arthur what he was off to do but decided to reserve the news until it was sure. That he might fail was a sudden fear. For failure he had no contingent plan. To return to the trailer, where night fartings, the old people's morning breaths and the acrid smell of mashed bedbugs and bacon grease were the distillate of neighborhood air, was, in the light of his hope, beyond his ability to bear any longer. He'd had angry dreams of slaughtering the old people in their bed. By morning light the guilt always made him cranky. He did not want them dead. He just could not live the way they did anymore. He had only one chance. Beyond failure was a void as black as night beyond the moon.

The door of Demicelli's trailer screeched and banged. Mr. D. bounded out with a worried look on his face. His face seemed to grow out of his chest in front of his hump. Late for work again. His wife clutched a pink chenille robe around her and called after him, "Don't forget, bring home something besides goddamn liver!"

When the man passed, Jack said, "Morning, Mr. Demicelli."

18

"Morning," he barked in return.

The boy felt maybe he wasn't too happy about his having coffee with his wife. He and the man were the same height; if anything, Jack was taller. He felt no great fear of the man, only a kind of distasteful wariness.

All he really knew about the Demicellis was that they were from New Jersey, Mrs. D. had been a nudist, and they had been on the way to California when the '36 De-Soto coupe with which they had been towing their trailer had thrown a rod through the block. They had been so broke Mr. D. had let the car go for junk. Mrs. D., who asked Jack to call her "Jan-neece," wanted to get another car. She felt so "confined" without wheels. Besides, she really *had* to get to California. There was a place there called Elysian Fields, where a body could go without clothes all year around and eat oranges right off the trees. She had shown Jack some books that were full of pictures of naked people who'd had their cunts and pricks erased, swimming, riding horses and playing a lot of volleyball. It made him hot when she talked about "nudism," though the way she talked about it sounded as if she were a preacher of some kind of nutty religion. She never talked about fucking or anything when she went on about "nudism." Her eyes got all glowy and farseeing. California was her big dream. She wanted to walk down Hollywood Boulevard, where the names of the stars were set in the sidewalk. She wanted to stand in Carole Lombard's footprints in front of Grauman's Chinese. Though she had never said exactly, Jack felt she had married Mr. D. for the trip. She said he was from Sardinia originally, and called him a Damn Dago, right to his face. Their trailer was a genuine secondhand Lustron. Though it was only twenty feet long, it had both a shower and chemical toilet. It was like a boat inside.

Arthur tapped Jack's boot professionally and looked up with the face of a creditor.

"A whole bag for me and one for Arutha," he reminded.

"Great shine, Arthur. Bring you *three* bags." He started to put out his hand and rub Arthur's kinky head, in which sweat now glistened like drops of dew, then remembered Arthur did not like his head rubbed and drew back his hand.

The boy got up, whipping dust from his knees. In the

19

wonder of the shine, his sister had forgotten the dog, which had collapsed gratefully at her feet.

"Hey, you walkin er takin the bus?" Arthur asked suddenly.

"Takin the bus."

"Oh. If you was walkin, I'd come with you far as town." The shine had inspired him to enterprise. "There'll be a lotsa sojers un sailors round today."

The bus was only a nickel. He had never known Arthur to be *that* short of cash.

"How come you're broke?" he asked, knowing he was about to be conned.

"Rained this week," the boy explained logically. "Un Ma's been sick."

"OK. I'll buy you a token."

"An still bring us them nuts?" He wanted no confusion.

"Yeah."

He turned to the girl. "Arutha, you don go botherin in the house, hear? They's sleepin. An you stay in the yard or somebody *carry you off*!" His voice rose in an intensity that was every bit as frightening as the possibility.

She made some unintelligible sounds. Arthur hoisted his box on his narrow shoulder.

"What she say?" Jack inquired.

"She say you best not forget them nuts," he replied as guilelessly as the soft breeze that blew up the alley.

Though blacks could sit anywhere on Wichita buses, most, particularly the old ones, moved to the back. Not Arthur. He hopped into the nearest vacant seat next to a window, his shine box on the knees of his torn jeans.

Two girls sitting on the seat near the door perpendicular to the route of the bus looked at Jack and Arthur and giggled. One said something behind her hand that seemed to Jack like: "Wonder if that's his brother." He turned red.

Little bitches! They wore North High Redskin sweat shirts that bagged like gunnysacks, the Indian barely bent by their budding pippins. They had knotted identical Randolph Field head scarves under their chins. Their dirty saddle shoes beneath baggy wool athletic socks were covered with other kids' names, pierced hearts and Shmoos.

Short plaid skirts were hiked over their knees. The prettier one's legs were pale and mottled like marble. He would have liked to fuck her. The other was the one who

20

had made the crack. She had on a big button that said KILROY WAS HERE.

If he had been sitting there in the uniform of a U.S. marine, they would have been creaming their jeans—no matter he was with a little nigger boy with a head like a Lincoln Zephyr. Arthur had more brains in his weird dome than those two pigs put together.

Soon the bus was full. Mothers dragging kids, their hair still wet with combing, stiff with wave set, downtown for new shoes, ration books visible in bulging shoulder bags. Men from Boeing, Beechcraft and Cessna, although dressed for town, still sported badges with their photographs on them. A soft hip in flowered rayon swayed lightly against his shoulder. He glanced up at a young woman who swung from the handrail, her upswept red hair like Rita Hayworth's, her eyes staring blankly, the small gold chevrons of an Army T-5 glinting on her collar and her mouth set for the duration. Her old man was far, far away. When the bus swayed again, he leaned in such a way that his shoulder dug deeper into her soft ass. Sitting with Arthur, he felt it might have been embarrassing to offer her his seat. Besides, no one offered anyone a seat anymore.

When the war had started, there had been about forty thousand people in Wichita. Now there were nearly three times that. Crummy, barracklike projects were growing everywhere. Hoover's Orchard, where his "Uncle" Jess and "Aunt" Nellie—actually his grandmother's sister and her husband—had lived for years in a home Jess built around a boxcar core, had been bulldozed away for a project. A whole new town of barracks called Plainview was growing out by Boeing. The only view there was of a mosquito-infested creek and buildings with the sameness of a prison.

In getting up to get off at Broadway and Douglass, he let the back of his left hand come up and graze longingly the soft globes of the woman's butt. And felt the angry heat of her gaze on the back of his neck.

Bastard! he mocked her falsetto in his mind.

"Catch you later, Jackson," Arthur piped, off after two sailors from Hutchinson Naval Air Base. Arthur and Jack's grandfather were the only people he knew who hadn't cried when Roosevelt died.

Jack turned down Broadway toward the post office. He checked his windbreaker pocket to make certain his birth certificate was still there.

21

4

A LINGERING fragrance of spring remained in the air, like the memory of his mother's perfume. Yet the morning sun was already but a single bus stop from summer. Sweat popped between his shoulder blades. A drop broke free and coursed the gully of his spine. He marched, his gut sucked toward his backbone, chest out, shoulders squared, looking neither left nor right. He paraded past Kinney's Shoe Store, where he had once bought a four-dollar pair of sharp, black, pointy-toed oxfords with real leather heels and soles. He made his own money setting pins at the Playmor Bowl just up the street. It had been his first truly grown-up pair of shoes, and they had lasted a month. Their guts had been goddamned cardboard! So there was a war on. There was no goddamned excuse for *that*. He had hated Kinney's ever since.

To set pins at the Playmor, he had gone to the State Social Security Office and sworn on paper he was sixteen—*Five-One-Five-One-Six-Two-Six-Five-Five*, he recited the number to himself. The summer before that he had caddied at the Crestview Country Club.

Caddy house and Playmor locker room came back to deflate him. There was the "pro," who looked like Buster Crabbe, and you had to suck up to him to get the good golfer, running errands for him for nothing, washing practice balls, sweeping up. There were the Navarro brothers, whom you had to risk fighting if you took out someone they considered their regular; coming home at dark, sunburned, bone-tired, sick from too much sun—sunup till dark—two dollars, sometimes three, less your lunch and Cokes. But once there had been an amazing ten spot when Old Doc Zimmerman, who always hit a five iron short of the lake on No. 3, took the three wood Jack offered him, thinking of someone else, and aced the damn thing.

The moment of remembered glory and riches faded to the rank pinboys' room behind the lanes at the Playmor. Three reeking iron bunk beds for the grown men out of work, who drifted in to set pins for ten cents a line, laying down two bits a night for a flop on one of the grimy striped ticking pads. There was an open stall shower with an empty quart bottle that had contained bay rum in one corner and a lidless toilet that smelled like an outhouse. The roller towel had the look of a dishwasher's jacket in a busy cafeteria. Mr. Taves, the manager, had warned him: "You keep outta there, kid, if you know what's good for you." He knew. But Taves didn't want the pinboys loitering around up front. He had to go somewhere. He felt sorry for the geeks and gargoyles who called the place home for one or two nights; they rarely stayed more than a week. He wondered if jail would not have been as good. The walls were covered with the rough sexual fantasies, hatred and despair of ever-lonely men, gouged out of the plaster with pocket knives, illuminated by pencil, pen, crayon. The room was littered with newspapers turned to the want ads, detective and pulp magazines read until their backs and pages were soft as cloth, and dog-eared "pocket" novels. Dead soldiers of all cheap and barely legal brands were kicked into the corners in spite of the order painted the entire width of the wall: NO DRINKING OR OUT YOU GO!

> *There was an old lady from Wheeling*
> *Who had a funny feeling*
> *She laid on her back*
> *And tickled her crack*
> *And pissed all over the ceiling.*

> *There was an old man from Boston*
> *Who bought himself an Austin*
> *Room for his ass,*
> *And a gallon of gas*
> *But his balls hung out,*
> *And he lost 'um.*

THE TIGER'S REVENGE, by Claude Balls.
THE OPEN KIMONA, by I. C. Mohair.
THE RUSSIAN TRAGEDY, by Ivan Kutsyour-
nutsoff

23

were some of the graffiti that stuck in his mind and played like a tune.

> Call me Slake
> Arrived by fast freight
> Got here at 8
> And I ain't ate—
> Burma Shave

was another. In spite of everything, he still had a strange sad fondness for Slake, a small man hunched forward in his jacket, eyes scouting way ahead, who looked as if he were going down the road even when standing still. When his eyes backed and filled and focused on you, they were those of a barroom conneroo who kept cutting glances to either side as if afraid of discovery. A card in his pocket appeared to be only an interesting mosaic of red and blue lines, but it revealed the name SLAKE held flat at eye level. And for a beer or a sandwich, he would make a similar card for *you,* or a plastic ring for your finger out of toothbrush handles, with a tiny photo of yourself in a little window—one day's delivery. He had the small bastard and rattail files right in his pocket along with a small bottle of acetone and a piece of fine emery cloth to polish the finished product. When Slake had a minute, he would file on a ring. Jack didn't see why he couldn't sell the things in stores.

"Mass production, kid. It's all against yuh," he explained. "No chance for the little man anymore. It's the same thing all down the line."

And Slake gave the impression of having been down the line and back more times than the Super Chief.

He slipped a bulky black ring with skull and crossbones in the little window on the boy's finger and said, "Tag along with me, kid, an I'll show you the ropes."

When the boy wondered where Slake was headed, he looked far beyond the crummy room. "The Garden of Allah, Big Rock Candy Mountain where the lemonade springs and Firestone tires grow on vines." He was off to the Gulf Coast and Mexico. "Get a little stake. People can't get tires, eelectric appliances—anything rubber er ee-lectric. Met a guy two weeks ago in L.A. I did time with once. Drivin his own car, pockets *full* of money.

24

Started with four goddamned Firestone tires in Juárez. Sold them that afternoon. And it was all up from there."

Jack never was quite clear how *he* was going to be of help in Slake's climb, but before he could run home and pack a bag, Slake flashed something from his pocket onto the top bunk of one of the beds and asked, "Ever see one of these?"

A Barney Google fuck book. Jack had seen one. Barney's cock like a whole bologna, radiating ee-lectric squiggles and flecking great raindrops of jiss as he galloped at and rammed the thing into the cartoon women with equally electric cunts that looked like toothless mouths in big black beards.

HEY!
HOW ABOUT A FUCK?

THOUGHT YOU WOULD NEVER ASK.

HOTCHA!

GIVE IT TO ME BIG BOY!

JISS ME, DADDY!

OH! I'M GOING TO *COME!!*

WHEE-OOOO!!!

Yeah. Then he felt Slake's cock against his tight ass and his grizzled cheek grazing his own. The smell of Bull Durham and a breath of bay rum.

He had twisted from the encircling, strong, skinny arms.

"Try that again, you sonofabitch, and I'll knock your block off!"

The man's distant, mocking eyes suddenly focused on the present, changing to mean. The words came out of the side of his mouth. "Don't get tough with me, kid. You don't know what you're sayin."

Chastened, scared, the boy had said, "OK. It's only I don't go for that shit."

"Just don't get tough." He stuffed the book back into his jacket. "You forget who you are."

25

"Here." Jack had tossed the ring Slake had given him on the bunk.

"You got a lot to learn, kid." He pocketed the ring.

When the lunchtime bowlers had cleared out, so had Slake, without as much as a "So long."

It was a ten to ten job. Around eight that night, the leagues from the aircraft plants, Coleman's Lamp, Yingling Chevrolet, and Pittsburgh Plate Glass came in. Big bowlers. A league. Real pin busters. He was hopping over the barriers to set three lanes, perching up over the big leather-covered backstops, jumping into the pits, shirt off, sweating like a stoker in a hold. He liked setting pins for the leagues. The lines added up fast. They were bowlers. The balls sizzled down the waxed maple, the pins flying back as from an explosion. Down in the pit, throwing the pins four at a time—his hands barely big enough to span the necks of two pins each—into the rattling metal pinsetters where they lay like shells in a magazine. Racking them down hard, pulling the handle from his gut to make a good set—no wobblers. Too little force and he'd have to scramble out to the gutter to hand-set a toppled pin, while the men up the alley in their team shirts, peering down angrily through the blue cloud of cigarette and cigar smoke, cursed him and yelled, *"Re-rack number four!"* He was a powder monkey in the hold of a battleship. A loader in a tank. Shoving in the ammo.

"ON THE WAY!"

The balls came boiling down, shattering timber, whipping into the backstop with a heavy, padded crump. When the leagues bowled, it was war.

Then, hopping between 4 and 5, he caught a flying pin on the point of his right ankle. The pain shot to his head.

"Rack down on number five. Number five. PINBOY! DOWN ON NUMBER FIVE!"

He had to finish the night. Slake's departure at noon had left them shorthanded. Cleo Sacks, the old black guy who had been a pretty good local welterweight when Jack was a little boy, was setting four lanes, stripped to the waist, still muscled like a horse, his hands like coal scoops. Cleo had killed his wife and couldn't get a job in an aircraft factory or anything like that. Eli Navarro, a cousin of the kids he had caddied with, was setting three lanes. There were a lot of Navarros in Wichita. You couldn't

26

just quit in the middle of a game when it was League Night.

He could barely hobble up to collect for his lines. Mr. Taves said he set lousy. "If you can't do better than that, don't come back."

"Pin hit me in the ankle," he explained. His tennis shoe bulged and throbbed with pain.

"We take no responsibility," Taves assured him. "We told you that when you started."

No one had told Jack, but that they took any responsibility had never crossed his mind. He had never known anyone who had.

"You goin to be in tomorrow?" Taves wanted to know.

"Well, I will if I can."

"That ain't no good. Goddammit, tomorrow is Saturday. You fuckin bastards come in here like a bunch of I-don't-know-whats, thinkin you can work just when you want to. I told you, I want somebody who's regular. Can't get nobody worth a shit anymore cept old Cleo. That nigger is better than all the rest of you punks put together. I gotta know if you're comin in or what. So I can find a boy. It's the Ladies' Bowling League tomorrow!" His voice rose to an apoplectic pitch.

"I can't put no pressure on it. Maybe it's broke."

"Shit!" The war had brought him good business. Now he couldn't get anyone to set pins. He pored over Brunswick catalogs dreaming of knocking out walls and doubling the number of lanes—all with automatic pinsetters. But the war had stopped production on them. If it wasn't one goddamned thing, it was another.

"I'll call if I can't make it," Jack offered.

"Forget it. I'll get another boy . . . somewhere."

Set them yourself, you fat cocksucker, Jack thought. *Sweat YOUR big satchel ass!* He counted his money. "It's five lines short," he reported. As usual when it was busy, Taves thought he could forget a few lines. The man slapped another four bits on the counter.

He had to pedal his bike home with only his left foot. His grandfather cut the laces of his tennis shoe with his knife to get the thing off his foot. It had already grown to the size of an eggplant. In the morning it would be the same color. His grandfather probed it gently with his big spatulated fingers. The boy had seen him handle a calf the same way. He carefully worked it up and down by the

27

toes, his ear bent near to listen for the grate of splintered bone. In spite of the scream the boy loosed, the old man decided it probably was not broken. Would they call a doctor if it had been? Jack would never know. They never called a doctor for anything before. The old man had bathed it with a viscous liniment from a bottle that had the portrait of a man with a beard on it. It stung like hell. His grandmother laid a big piece of bacon rind over it, fat side down, and bound it loosely with a clean white rag she tore from an old sheet. Then she heated the bricks they used to warm their bed in the winter, wrapped them in quilt scraps and packed them on either side of his ankle under a folded blanket. She felt his brow and announced, "He's feverish."

"Well, goddammit, what do you want *me* to do about it?" the old man demanded.

"You sure it ain't broke?" she whispered.

"I don't think so. I don't know. Goddamn boy can't get and keep a job without gettin himself hurt or fired or some damn thing. Goddammit to hell! We can't afford no goddamn doctor. An I don't know where to get one at this hour anyhow. If it ain't better by morning, take him to the county hospital on the bus."

"I'm supposed to be at the Hootens' tomorrow. They are having a big to do. I promised. I just can't let her down. She been as good as gold to us."

"Then I'll have to goddamn take im."

"I can't walk," the boy protested. "I can't go on no bus!"

"Then lay there, goddammit! What you want, a taxi clear across town? By God, when I was cowboyin, not much older than you neither, I had a little sorrel mare fall on me, stove in three ribs. Tied the damn things with some pieces of harness and rode fifty fuckin miles and a doctor never looked at me. Was back doin a full day's work in no time."

He'd walk or lie there.

But the old man had gotten started. "It's always some damn thing with you. Paid down good money for them fuckin magazines you was goin to sell door to door. Didn't sell enough to make the nut. Same shittin thing with your paper route and them fried pies. Had to eat the fuckin things to get our money out. I even *think* fried pie, I want to shit."

28

"I did good with ice-cream bars," Jack reminded him.

"*You* say! *We* never saw anything from it. You'll never make a go of anything, you're just like your fuckin mother! There's not a nickel's worth of thanks in either of you."

"Why don't you let up on him now, Daddy? Let him get some rest."

"It just makes me madder than thunder. Buy him books, send him to school, and he don't amount to a hill of beans. Goin to lay around here spongin off us until we'll never have a chance to have anything. The goddamned allotment the relief gives us for him don't amount to a damn. Couldn't feed a measlin pup on that."

"Soon as I'm old enough, I'll be gettin out," the boy promised. "I don't *want* to be here." Tears burned in his throat.

"Not *good* enough for you! You think you're so goddamn smart and better than the rest of us. Just like your mother. Too damn good to get a decent job and work for a livin. Hell, I was supportin a family of five when I was eleven. And when there wasn't enough for all of us to eat, I got out. Went my own way. I was only twelve when I hit Texas. Makin my *own* way!"

"Now, Daddy, you were awful lucky that that Mr. Chapman took you in on his ranch."

"An I did a man's work for him. Worked from sunup to sundown, seven days a week. An Missus Chapman teachin me to read and write and do numbers at night. I had *ambition*. I *wanted* to make somethin out of myself. By God—"

Suddenly the reality of his circumstances became as vivid to him as they were to the woman and boy.

"I would of *too*, by God! If the thieves, liars and sonsabitches hadn't fucked me out of everything I ever made. The goddamned lawyers, bankers and the Wall Street gang. The kings, the dukes and the czars! The goddamn popes and the Jews, Hoover and Roosevelt—greater thieves never had a gut!" he raged.

"Well," his wife decided, "let's talk about it tomorrow. Let's all get to bed now."

"I don't want to go to goddamn bed!" the old man protested, trying to suck the soggy stub of a King Edward cigar back to life by sheer willpower, it being too short to apply flame safely.

"Take a walk then and cool off," she suggested.

"I'll be a sonofabitch! Can't even be a man in my own goddamn house!" But he went.

"I didn't do it on purpose," the boy told his grandmother.

"I know. And your grandpa feels bad about it, just like I do. But it does seem like it's always somethin, don't it?" She laid a wet washrag on his forehead.

"I can't help it. I try. And you and Grandpa ain't bought me shoes since I was a little boy. I bought my last shoes."

"That's just an example. How long did those fancy shoes last? Throwin money away. You could have gone to Sam Shusterman's and gotten a good, reliable pair of shoes for half what you paid. You could get shoes on relief. But you *had* to have something different."

"I don't want to wear goddamn relief shoes. All the kids know. They tease you about it. Then I come home an been fightin and you give me hell for gettin my shirt tore or somethin. Un Shusterman's are secondhand. I don't want to wear someone else's damn shoes. Maybe a dead man's."

"They're perfectly all right for me and your grandpa. They're *rebuilt*." She sniffed defensively. "Perfectly good. You just always had tastes beyond your means. Your mother was just like you. Too good to eat what *we* eat. Too good to wear what *we* wear."

"Leave her out of it!" he protested.

"Well, it's *true*." The argument was ended, having risen to a plateau of absolute, fundamental righteousness from which there was no appeal.

*The Lord said: On this Rock I will build my Church.
And all the powers of hell shall not prevail against it.*

The only way to be saved was to Believe, Repent and be Baptized for the remission of your sins. There *was* no other way. The Word was God. And Grandma had the Word.

"What about all the people who never heard of the Church of Christ, Grandma?" he had asked early.

"Well, they won't get to heaven unless they do what the Bible tells them."

"But what if they never *heard*?" It didn't seem fair by half.

"I don't know. I only know it says in the Bible as plain as the nose of your face: Lest ye believe in Jesus Christ, the living Son of God, and that He suffered and died for the remission of your sins, repent and be baptized ye shall not know the kingdom of heaven."

"Un what about little babies?" he had wondered.

"They ain't tasted of the fruit of the tree of knowledge. The Lord suffers them."

"Then why don't he suffer heathens just as well?" He really would have liked to understand.

"They've sinned. They live in sin and degradation."

"But if they ain't *heard*, how do they *know* that's what they're doin?"

"Don't matter. They've sinned." Of that she was certain. "They've eaten of the fruit of the tree of knowledge."

That was the key then. "Have I?" he wondered.

"Well, I don't guess you have yet. But you're nibblin away."

"If I died tonight, where would I go?"

"Guess you're kind of betwixt and between. Reckon it would just be in the hands of the Lord. A prayer or two wouldn't hurt. You could ask Him for the benefit of the doubt. You ain't been baptized yet. Lloyd Butler's little girl, Sharon, was baptized last Sunday and she's in your Sunday school class, if you ever went."

Lloyd was the song leader, his Sunday brown suit hiked over white socks by his exertions. Sharon was a stupid little bitch who always came to Sunday school with a hankie pinned to the shoulder of her dress. She wore white gloves and had a white-backed Bible. She thought her shit didn't stink. She read all the eennsy-weensy-goo they handed out in tracts at Sunday school. If she and her family were going to heaven, he simply couldn't understand how there would be a place for people like his own. Maybe there would be a Hoover's Orchard up there, and the old lady could get a job keeping house for the Butlers or doing the angels' goddamn shirts. Or if, as his grandmother said, everyone would be equal there, what the hell were the deacons and elders and all of them who were officers in the First Federal Savings and Loan working so hard to get there for? It had to be a comedown.

So many questions.

31

"Would Mom?"

"What?"

"Go to hell."

"Well. She's been baptized. But she's married a divorced man and she'd have to mend her ways to keep out of it."

"Will Grandpa?"

"Your grandpa most certainly will go to hell if he don't stop smokin, takin the Lord's name in vain, and all the other sinful things he does. And he must follow God's commandment to be saved. He was baptized, though, a Presbyterian."

"That don't count?"

"When God said, 'On this Rock I will build my church,' He didn't say I'm goin to build the Presbyterian Church, nor the Methodist, or Baptist, or Catholic. He said *my* church. There can only be the one."

There was no question that she had found the very number—the Church of Christ! Nothing equivocal about that. She read the Bible as if the words printed in red had been dictated by God to someone taking shorthand.

Still, her church didn't make sense about all those poorass heathens. What kind of God would do such mean shit against people like that? He just didn't believe it.

"Say Grandpa can't go to heaven. Why'd you want to go then?" he had asked.

"I haven't given up hope for your grandpa yet," she vowed. "I'm prayin for him." Then, from that plateau of righteousness: "After that, he's on his own."

Did he detect some hopeful new arrangement in her vision of everlasting glory?

The post office had been built around the same time as North High, the telephone company and the airport. Faintly Egyptian, the scantlings rather Wurlitzer, the building sat almost exactly between immigrant traditions and Hollywood. Enlistment posters in man-high tubular frames mounted guard along the sidewalk. ONLY AMER-ICA'S BEST! From *Saturday Evening Post* cover homes that had wide lemonade porches with cool gliders, sitting above perfect green lawns over which sprinklers bejeweled the grass under the shade of great-grandfather elms.

Hi, Mom. Hi, Dad. Hi, Sally.

Hi, Roger.

32

Say, Dad, can I use the car Saturday night? It's the big prom.

There's a war on, you know, Roger.

Gee, I know, Dad. But it's the BIG PROM!

He has a date with Kathy Jennings.

Aww, Sally. . . .

Let him have the car, Daddy. I can ride with Susan Jennings' car pool to the Red Cross to roll bandages.

Gee, thanks, Mom. You're swell!

Very well, son. I guess I can remember when I was taking your mother to the big prom.

Boy, Dad, you're swell! Think I'll go mow the lawn.

They all looked to Jack like the punk off the cover of a *Boy Scout Handbook*. None of *those* guys ever beat their meat, of that he was certain.

Those posters never showed a guy like himself with a broken front tooth, nor a spade, Mex, Indian or kike. A merely grazing awareness, for the belief in the uniform was so great it was like the Mormon faith—once enlisted, all turned to Spearmint by and by.

FIRST TO FIGHT
ON LAND, SEA, AND IN THE AIR
U.S. MARINES

was the single drum behind which he marched up the glaring stone steps into the cool two-story post office foyer. A pretty woman, her handbag open in front of her, addressed a package at the table just inside the door. He saw it went to an APO number. An old woman at the table on the other side of the entrance was puzzling over her postal savings account. Women and several kids were lined up at the war bonds and stamps window. Above the high window in a WPA project mural, the history of Kansas converged on the great state seal from both wings—*Ad Astra per Aspera*: Humble, prayful Indians accepting Christianity and the flag; John Brown in wrathful parson's black riding before a whirlwind; Jesse Chisholm and the cowboys; sodbusters and McCormick reapers; rail builders, packers, millers, oil and natural gas, helium and salt; into the air age—*Boomtown!* Lindbergh, Wiley Post, Amelia Earhart, Walter Beech—*Yahoo!* The illuminated exploits of the state marched around above the big windows against a mild blue sky where not a tornado or even the

33

portent of one turned a leaf, like a world's fair hatband on a straw skimmer.

Good-bye to all that.

He mounted the stairs to the second floor. Behind the first door on the second floor, the U.S. Marine Corps recruiter awaited, a small sign on a metal standard—gold letters on a red background—announced WALK IN.

He walked in. A sergeant in dress blues looked up from papers on his desk. Red and gold Marine colors and Old Glory flanked him on poles topped by bright gold, preying eagles. His brilliant white garrison cap with shiny black patent-leather visor hung on a dark wooden hat tree. There were crossed rifles under his gold and red chevrons. Two rows of campaign bars under a clear plastic protector blazed above his marksmanship medals. There was a purple heart with two clusters. Above his choker collar his face was as clean as if he had just shaved, as tan as if he had arrived from San Diego that morning. Jack knew why they were called leathernecks. He had read all about everything. A close shock of black hair cut high on the sides and back looked freshly barbered. The boy could feel all the places he had been, sense the things he had done. He *respected* him. Yet the recruiter's gaze up from his papers was more one of wary curiosity than a welcome to the Corps.

"What can I do for you, sonny?"

Sonny!

"I'd like to enlist." He let the words it seemed he had been practicing all his life come out, lowering his voice until it hurt the bottom of his throat.

"How old are you?"

"Seventeen."

"Got any proof?"

"Yes, sir." He dug his lying birth certificate out of his windbreaker pocket and stepped forward to hand it over the wide desk.

The sergeant took it, looked once at the boy and seemed to study every line on the paper. An electric fan on top of a nearby filing cabinet swept back and forth, stuttering at the end of each sweep, the breeze lifting the corners of the onionskin papers on the desk. There was a desk plate with "Gun./Sgt. A. C. Hazzard, Recruiter" on it. Jack felt sleepy. It was like being in church.

The sergeant laid the certificate beside his papers. Jack wasn't sure he trusted it.

"Finish high school?" the sergeant asked.

"No, sir."

"Still in high school?"

"No, sir. I had to quit to go to work." He conjured up the image of a poor boy who quit school to help his poor old grandpa and grandma. "I've lived with my grandparents since my dad got killed," he explained.

"How far you go in school?"

"Eighth grade."

He had thought the way the Nips were wiping out marines in the movies, the only question would be his age. The sergeant acted as if he were trying to *break* in on the war or something.

"Why do you want to be a marine?" The man's eyes bored into his own.

"My best friend, Stafford Coleman, was the first man to land on the Marshalls. He's always been like a big brother." He put a little extra spit on the ball. The recruiter took that bit of news as stoically as if the Marshalls were Newton, Kansas. Then, with sudden inspiration: "An my dad was killed on Wake Island."

"A marine?" the sergeant asked, his eyes narrowing.

"Yes, sir," Jack answered without blinking, praying there was no way to check. He was glad he hadn't mentioned earlier that the damn fool had gotten himself killed driving a brakeless strip-down into the side of a man's tidy Model A on Water Street when Jack was but two. Still he didn't feel the marine believed him. More than a juvenile court judge or anyone Jack had ever met, it seemed the sergeant had a line on the truth that was denied everyone else.

"Height?"

"Five eight."

"Weight?"

"I'm not sure."

The sergeant rose slowly and walked around the desk as if the trip were simply doing the boy a favor. "We've filled our quota," he said. "Only taking regular enlistments."

Jack wanted to be regular.

"Stand on the scale."

Jack got on the medical scale that stood against the wall, stretching as tall as he could, sucking in his gut, his

35

arms stiffly at his sides. The sergeant clamped the measuring rod down tight on the top of his head. Jack nudged it up another quarter of an inch. The recruiter took into account his cowboy boots. He said nothing. He slid the weights on the balance back and forth with a disdainful finger. The sergeant wasn't so damned big, Jack noted. When the bar failed to budge at 130, the sergeant cast the boy a surprised glance and tapped the big weight back to 120. Nothing. A frown crossed his brow. At 110 the bar shot upward. Tapping the small weight back to the right, he balanced the thing at 112.

"You must be hollow." Only then did the man allow himself a kindly smile. "OK." He indicated Jack could step down. He returned to his desk, seated himself. He sighed, picked up Jack's birth certificate and held it out to him.

"We can't use you, son."

Can't use me! The words were like fire in his brain. No maybes. No chance. He blinked and felt like crying.

The sergeant measured the boy again with his eyes, studied his face, looked away from his visible disappointment.

"Just too light. If you want to wait a year or so, try and finish high school, put on a little weight and come back...."

"I want to go now. It might be over any minute," he blurted.

The kindliness vanished from the sergeant's face. "Sorry." He turned back to the papers he had been reading when Jack had come in. He didn't give a damn! He didn't care what Jack had felt and dreamed of as long as he could remember.

He turned to go. He felt numb. Rejected! His legs moved without feeling. It had all turned to nothing. Suddenly stripped of every hope he had ever held, he wondered if it was because the sergeant could see he was lying. Maybe if he didn't jerk off so much, he would have weighed more. He wished his hand were cut off.

"Why don't you try the Navy?" the sergeant suggested casually as he reached the door.

The *Navy*? "I wanted to be a marine," he said, feeling his voice constricted with pain.

The sergeant hadn't looked up from his papers.

They really didn't want him. The *Navy*? He wanted to tell the sergeant all he knew about guns—he could field-strip them in his mind. He knew all about patrolling, killing a sentry with a hand ax or piano wire, infiltrating, fields of fire—he had practiced all that stuff along the canal bank. He could sneak up on anybody. He could crawl on his belly like a snake. He promised himself he would never jerk off again. But the marine did not look up from his papers.

He stood at the head of the stairs. The sound of typing came from the Navy Recruiting Office down the hall. Its placard was white on blue. There had been something in the sergeant's voice—something out of that sense of special knowledge he seemed to have. His mind began working again like an adding machine. Airborne would have been his second choice. No. He couldn't take the chance of striking out twice in the same place. If the Marines didn't want him probably the paratroops wouldn't either. He went toward the Navy office. He had to try. Stafford was no longer his best friend. It was David Hooten who had been on the *Wasp* when it was sunk that became to him like a big brother. His dad could have gone down on a fucking frigate in the North Sea—the run to Murmansk. He walked in.

The sailor, typing with two fingers, stopped and stood up, a smile on his face beneath blue eyes. He had one row of campaign ribbons—no purple heart—and an Armed Guard patch on his right shoulder. There were crossed anchors over his rating.

"I'd like to see about joining the Navy," Jack said without enthusiasm.

"Got proof of your age?"

"Yes, sir." He hauled out his birth certificate again.

The sailor hardly glanced at it. "You're only seventeen. Have you talked this over with your parents? Will they give their permission?"

"Yes, sir," he said.

"You don't have to call me sir. I'm just a Bosun Deuce," the sailor said, though he did not mention what he should call him.

Hatred of the goddamned marine down the hall flared in him. *He* hadn't told him not to call *him* sir. He'd sirred the shit out of him.

The sailor checked his eyes, having him read an eye chart taped on the back of the door.

"Twenty-twenty. Can't beat that." He seemed pleased.

He had Jack stand facing the door and repeat words he whispered from the other side of the room. "Perfect."

This was more like it. Yet he was wary of the moment when he had to get on the dreaded scales he had been eyeing in the corner.

"OK. Let's check your height and weight."

That was it. Now it was all over. He tried to stand *heavy*, thinking down hard on the scales. It balanced at 112. He felt sick. The sailor, however, said nothing.

"OK, mate, let's see how smart you are." He took some papers from the lower drawer in his desk. "Sit over there."

There were three school desks with writing arms against the wall. The sailor gave him a No. 2 pencil.

"Now this is a general intelligence and aptitude test that you will have thirty minutes to complete. Read thoroughly and as rapidly as you can each question and select the best answer from those you will find at the end of each question. Answer all the questions you can in the time given. At the right of the test sheet you will find spaces to mark your answer. Each space is lettered to correspond to the letters of each answer. When you have selected the answer you think is best, find the corresponding lettered space at the right and carefully fill in the correct space with the pencil you have been given. On the end of your pencil is an eraser. If you wish to change your choice of answers or make a mistake, erase thoroughly. Only one answer per question is correct. Mark only *one* space for each question. If two spaces are filled in, even if one is correct, it will be counted as an incorrect answer. Sloppiness will be counted against you. If you are not absolutely certain of the correct answer to a question, go immediately on to the next question. Do not guess. When I say, 'Begin'—not yet!—you may commence. When I say, 'Time,' lay down your pencil immediately. Are there any questions?"

"No."

"OK. The first question is a practice question. I will read the question with you." He read the question.

"D!" Jack was right there.

"That's correct," the sailor said, a bit annoyed. "Now look at the right side of your test sheet, find the space under the letter *D* and carefully fill in with the pencil you have been given the space between the two lines."

Jack filled. The sailor came over and checked it. "Good.

38

Now when I say, 'Begin,' start working right away. You have thirty minutes to complete the test. Ready? Begin!" He sat on the edge of his desk staring at his watch.

Half an hour later he called, "Time!"

Jack dutifully laid down his pencil though he had almost finished reading the next to last question. The reading questions had been a snap. But the arithmetic was tough. He had never been good in math.

"Finished?" the sailor asked.

"All but two."

He looked conspiratorial. "Give you another five minutes. Go!"

Hell of a nice guy. Jack worried over the last two arithmetic problems, mentally counting his fingers and toes. They were problems that could not be solved by anything *he* knew about adding, subtracting, multiplication, short *or* long division. He took a stab at the answers just before his bonus ran out.

When the recruiter laid the grading sheet over the test, he looked disappointed. Jack felt the same sense of failure begin to creep back he had felt down the hall.

"Could have saved the five minutes," the sailor said.

"Missed them both?"

"Yep."

Well, he wasn't going to stay with his grandparents. He would hitchhike to California. Maybe he could get a job in an aircraft plant out there with his forged birth certificate. They hired women, and they hired *midgets* to work in tight places. Get a job, a motorbike, a room, some decent clothes, a girl. He could steal stuff and hock it until he got a job. He was not going to live in that goddamned bed-buggy trailer any longer.

"Not bad," the sailor announced. "In fact, damned good. One twelve. It would have been very high if the arithmetic reasoning hadn't brought you down. You had a perfect score on comprehension and reasoning."

"I passed?"

"You passed. But we have a slight problem. For your height, the Navy's minimum acceptable weight is one fourteen. Like your brain, you only weigh in at one twelve." But before Jack could suffer a twinge of fear, the sailor added, "How soon you want to go?"

Go! "Right away!" he exclaimed.

"We send a group up to district headquarters at Kansas City every month. If you can find a couple of pounds somewhere by Monday, I can send you up on this month's quota. Think you can gain a couple of pounds by Monday?"

"Yes, *sir*! I'll eat a *stalk* of bananas and drink milk shakes."

The recruiter smiled. "OK, buddy. You take these papers home, fill them out, get your parents to sign them and report back here at nine hundred hours, nine A.M. sharp—Monday. There will be others in the office when you arrive. Come straight to me. I'll complete the enlistment forms. At district headquarters in the post office at Kansas City, you will be given a longer intelligence and aptitude test and a complete physical examination. If you are accepted for enlistment, you will be sworn in and given the option of departing for boot camp immediately, or you may return for a week to settle any unfinished business you may have. When you return Monday, bring a handbag or small suitcase containing a change of underwear and socks, a towel and washcloth and your toilet articles. Got it?"

"Yes, sir."

"Oh, you haven't been arrested for a felony, served time in jail or a penitentiary or been issued a summons for anything more serious than a parking ticket, have you?"

He thought of when he had had to go to juvenile court and tell the judge all about how his mother and stepdad had him steal stuff so they could hock it. He had to tell everything so his grandmother could get custody of him. He thought about the times he had been stopped for being out after curfew, about his mother and stepfather in jail so often. He wondered if that would be held against him.

"Once some boys and me got pulled in for throwing a two-inch salute under the squad car of a cop sleeping out on Harry Street." Glenn's dad had come down and got them out, and when they went to juvenile court the next morning, he had also forked over the ten-dollar fine and costs. That had been the only real arrest.

"It's probably nothing. We can check it out." The sailor didn't seem worried. "Nine sharp, Monday. If you're late, you will have to wait until the next group."

"I won't be," Jack promised.

40

Yahoo! He wanted to shout when he left the office. The papers for his grandmother to sign were in his pocket in a U.S. Navy official envelope. *Mate. Buddy.* It was the first organization to which he had belonged. The U.S. Navy. There was an incredible sense of security, elevating fellowship, place, unlimited possibilities—*Join the Navy and See the World!*—citizenship, *patriotism!* He really *loved* his country. All he had ever wanted was a chance to get in on it. He was all right after all.

Hell, he could swim like a fish. The sailor hadn't even asked him.

As he passed the Marine office, a new set of loyalties came into being. He wanted to pop in and tell the *Gy-reen* to shove it up his ass. The Navy guy had been nice as hell. He saw himself in a sailor suit. It was better than nothing. In fact, *Damned good!* He echoed the recruiter's words. *Yeow, man! J. O. Andersen, U.S. Navy.* All the girls at school thought sailors were "cute." Marines got Rita Hayworth and Paulette Goddard. Gobs got June Allyson and Gloria De Haven. Well, Gloria De Haven wasn't bad. And he was *in*—or as good as.

Christ, please let me make it all the way, he prayed.

"How'd it go?"

He turned around. It was the Marine recruiter. An "Out to Lunch" sign had been hung on his door.

"I'm in." Jack beamed. "I mean I gotta put on two pounds by Monday. But I can."

The sardonic smile of one who knows many things beyond and behind the moment flicked across the sergeant's tanned face. "Good luck."

"Thanks."

Man! He was one of them!

When the marine had passed below the stair, his patent visor pointing martially toward lunch, Jack allowed himself a wide grin. Water blurred his vision as he stepped from the cool marble vault into the heat-wavering glare of noonday sun. He wanted to walk; just to keep walking—anywhere. There was no longer any place he could not go with a clear conscience. He felt so good, he wondered if until that moment he hadn't had a headache all his life. The slate was wiped completely clean of every slight he felt he had ever suffered. For the first time he looked at the faces on the streets freely, happily, without fear—a sailor cruising on a buoyant sea of citizenship.

41

Passing the telephone company, he was suddenly engulfed by a flotilla of switchboard operators and file clerks giggling out to lunch as if encircled by Wonder Woman's golden lasso. One pert little half-Mexican girl bumped fully into him. Her proud boobs straining her white blouse were delightful pneumatic swellings beneath his ribs. Her breath was flowery and sweet with Juicy Fruit.

"Hey, watch where you goin, hansome," she said. "You wanta give me cancer?"

"Sorry!" he replied.

The other girls laughed. The little operator stood there on her sturdy short legs, wide of hip, taunting him mildly, letting her eyes go liquid. On her chest was a tiny varnished shingle with the name "Helen" spelled out in alphabet noodles. She pouted her lower lip until he could see the pink flesh behind her dark-red lipstick.

"You look *just* like some movie star," she breathed.

Another girl grabbed her hand and yanked her away amid squeals and laughter.

"Hey! I think I fall in love!" she protested.

"You fall in love the way I use Kleenex," someone cracked.

"Helen, if you tripped and fell, you would bounce until next Tuesday," another offered.

"Sure, everyone knows they're false."

"Yeow, don't you know there's a rubber shortage?"

"She's the biggest little PT in town," a tall girl who reminded Jack of one of the Andrew Sisters turned to advise him.

"I luuuv him!" Helen protested.

"Don't worry, you'll get over it once you get something in your stomach," someone assured her. Which made the whole gang bend over with laughter.

He felt just fine. He ducked into the White Castle, ordered four hamburgers with everything and a milk shake. The burgers were swallowed with only a chew or two. The choc shake was too thick to suck through a straw. He tilted the fluted tall glass back and let the cold pudding slide down his throat.

Amazed at the way the food had disappeared into him, the chubby waitress asked, "You want some dessert on top of that?"

"Ah, yes, ma'am. I think I'll have one of them big chocolate-covered doughnuts and a cup of coffee."

"You'll want cream *and* sugar, right?"

"Yes-um."

She fetched the stuff, shaking her head, whipped her pencil from her cap and noted the additions on his check.

When he left the White Castle, he was struck with a beautiful idea. He would make his grandmother happy and be baptized.

5

"HERE comes a sausage!" Glenn rejoiced when Jack strolled into the Airway Lunch and Pool Hall.

"Hi, sausage," Bucky said.

"Fuck you," Jack said without rancor.

They were playing nine-ball on a back table. Two glasses of beer were racked in a wall holder, sweating icily. Sandwiches on wax papers sat on the table rim. He didn't mind Glenn calling him a sausage. Glenn was good enough to play on a front table if he was hot. With Bucky, Jack could hold his own.

He and Glenn, who was now almost sixteen, had been best friends since fifth grade. Glenn had suffered from asthma and missed a lot of school when he was little. Now he had a thin, beaked Germanic face and an elaborate arrangement of oil-soaked blond curls that broke over an always-upturned collar. He had taken to insisting the other kids call him the Hawk or Cisco, but to Jack he was still the same old Glenn with whom he had measured cocks periodically for years. Bucky was the only other person who could call him by his given name.

Glenn had been suspended from school the last semester after he persuaded Crazy Harry Vise to get in the school's dumbwaiter. He had run Harry to the top, before going off to Metal Shop and leaving him stammering his freckled redhead off up there under the roof. When the bell rang after the second class, Jack suggested maybe they ought to leave an anonymous note near the office. "Don't

43

be an asshole," Glenn had advised. All evening long they would fall down writhing with laughter just *thinking* about Harry. With school quiet, a custodian making his rounds heard the stuttering cries and called the fire department, who had to go through the roof to get him out. He was actually frothing at the mouth when he saw light again.

Though Glenn was small, no bigger than Jack, with legs like a chicken, he was the toughest kid in school. He had built up his torso and arms with a Charles Atlas course (he only paid for the top part) and had arms like a calf's leg. He was good in all sports and could actually throw a curve ball. Just fooling around, Jack could often pin him wrestling, but in a real fight, Glenn never lost.

His mom worked in Buck's Department Store basement in the boys' department, so he always had real Levi's and neat shirts, sweaters and sports coats. His old man pushed a laundry truck and was saving to buy a beer joint. He had told Glenn he'd played for the Chicago Bears. When Glenn found out his old man was lying, he had started getting into trouble all the time. It was then that though he and Jack were the best boys in art in their class, Glenn gave it up as "sissy" and said he thought he would become a machinist or printer. His folks had a small, neat brick house in a new part of town. His mother was always out in shorts working on the goddamned lawn, the blue veins in her short legs like a road map. He had a pretty older sister who he admitted had sort of let him fuck her once, but he would not tell Jack any of the details.

Bucky wasn't really poor either. His dad had been a pilot for early American Airlines and had died in a crash. His old lady was a beautiful, tall, alcoholic brunette who had once been in the *Ziegfeld Follies*. Sometimes when they were over at Bucky's and his mom was stewed, she would show them a picture of herself in a line of chorus girls and do a couple of high kicks to prove she wasn't dead yet. When she did that, Bucky would get angry and stomp out of the room calling her a "goddamned old whore." Most often, though, no matter what time of day they arrived, she looked as if she had just got up and the light hurt her eyes or as if she were wasting with some kind of mysterious disease. She often wore sunglasses, even in the house. There was something of medicine cabinets, enemas and hospitals about her.

Bucky had a genuine German Luger and a box of bullets. He had gone to military school in Oklahoma before coming to Wichita. His mother's boyfriend was a rich old broker about seventy who looked like the little guy in *Esquire* magazine and had a fancy apartment in the Hillcrest. She was always cutting off Bucky's allowance because he let his friends get into her liquor. In the basement was a bar with all kinds of stuff. Though Kansas was dry, she bought booze by the case. She and Bucky lived alone in a two-story stucco house on the way to the airport. You could see the planes coming in all the time.

Bucky was tall, solemn and often disagreeable, with olive skin and long straight black hair he combed meticulously into a perfect duck's ass behind a pompadour that verged on the stratospheric. None of them had cut his hair in nine months. Bucky liked houndstooth check slacks, high rise and pegged tight in the cuff below an eighteen-inch knee. A long gold key chain with a little knife and his house key depended in a lazy loop from belt to knee to pocket—zoot! He wore short-sleeved flowered Hawaiian shirts and had a white sports jacket. His ideals were George and Gus Depolis, two young Greek hoods who always played on the front table for *real* money.

Businessmen, oilmen, guys from city hall, men with tens and twenties in their pockets came every lunch to try their luck with the Depolis brothers. A dollar a ball and whatever on the game George or Gus had nerve enough to make the men believe they could cover. George, who was twenty-two, had been arrested thirty-one times for assault and battery. Gus, who was only twenty, had been booked seventeen times. But everyone was sure Gus would be the first brother to kill someone. He was not only mean, he was crazy.

Only Gus was in that day. George was out chauffeuring around a man who wanted to be governor in a big cream-colored Buick convertible. No one satisfactorily explained what a man who wanted to be governor was doing with George Depolis, but men passed knowing hometown smiles around the baseball and horse tickers and at the lunch counter where beer and sandwiches were served between large bowls of hard-boiled eggs and glass vats of pickled sausages and pig's feet.

Gus' girl was a pretty brunette named Avis Nickel but who more often called herself Jean Porter. She had, according to rumor, gone to Hollywood once and been in a

45

film with Donald O'Connor and Gloria Jean. Now she swung idly back and forth on a stool with her back to the counter, drinking a Coke through a straw, popping something from an aspirin box and nibbling an egg-salad sandwich.

"She's a nympho," everyone agreed with seeming authority. "She'll lay down like that"—snap! "But Gus'll kill anyone who touches her. Say she's got an educated cunt that actually sucks!" The wonder of it all was heady beer for the boy. She often sported a black eye or bruises in testimony to the fact Gus took shit from no one. The men in the pool hall were unanimous in their opinion that if Gus didn't make the pen by killing someone else, he was bound to by killing Avis.

George and Gus had driven several small businesses into bankruptcy—a delivery service, a cleaner and presser and a flower shop. They also ran whiskey into the state for the biggest bootlegger in town, but there had recently been a slight rift between the two. In the pool hall, it was obvious that with George now in "politics" Gus had only his personal, portable cue to depend on. Avis-Jean had taken a waitress job at MacFarlane's Chinese Restaurant, working until midnight. Gus usually picked her up in his '39 Packard roadster he'd had painted with eighteen coats of hand-rubbed metallic blue lacquer at Herb Ray's custom body and fender shop. The upholstery was white naugahyde tucked and rolled, and there were double musical horns on each fender. One played Woody Woodpecker's "Ha-ha-*ha*-HA!" when he pressed a button. When he pressed another, it sounded like "*Gotchercockout!*" He could absolutely make old ladies shit at an intersection with those horns.

Jack had been in love with Avis-Jean ever since she was the prettiest girl in sixth grade at Washington Elementary when he was in third. She had just been Avis Nickel then, who had long black curls, tapped at school assemblies and had a talking crow named Blackie, which came to school with her and sat outside her room on the windowsill, cocking an intelligent eye at the doings inside and piping now and then, "Pretty boy! Pretty boy! Blackie love you." She and her mother lived in a house on the canal, a small yellow house, with a garage and an overgrown garden complete with arbor, fishpond, plaster deer and the seven dwarfs, a jungle of iris, tulips, honeysuckle vines and rose bushes. Once he and Glenn had sat in her darkening arbor with the katydids sawing up the summer night and told dirty jokes until she had let them each feel her soft breasts and given them a single gentle kiss. In spite of her crow, she had never had any real friends. She was the girl Jack had most often dreamed of marrying. In third grade he had given her every Valentine he had bought and made that year and everyone had teased him about it. Now she seemed hardly to notice him, going around with a blank, unseeing look on her face.

When Gus was shooting a sour stick, she would hand over every cent she had as if she no longer knew it was money.

There was such a mysterious, illicit dangerousness added to her quiet, bruised beauty it made Jack's head swim with longing to save her, to make something he could not define aright.

Looking at her swinging on the stool, so slim, soft, fragile, with tan bare legs and curiously innocent, vulnerable knees, he wondered what she thought about. He tried to imagine her going to the can like everyone else. The girl's hair was cut short, a cauliflower of careless black curls around her small quiet face. Though she was very slender, her big soft tits, crammed into a tight pointed bra, bulged like soft tan buttocks at the open collar of her short printed jersey dress. What about her was true? What all had she done since sixth grade? What did she *know*? The questions troubled the boy. He tried to recall the sound of her laughter when he and Glenn had told her dirty jokes, but all he could summon forth was an echo rather than a sound.

She watched Gus dispassionately as he moved assuredly around the table in hand-stitched baby blue pegs that must have cost twenty-five dollars, religious medals hanging out from the open three top buttons of his polka dot navy and white sports shirt. When he had cleaned the two gentlemen, he unscrewed his cue while ten-dollar bills floated onto the baize. He left the money there until he had slipped his cue into its leather scabbard and handed it to the smiling black rackman. If there had been more time, he would have played the men differently, gotten another game or two out of them. He might have spotted them three balls or played them left-handed. The men put on their suit jackets. Gus donned his two-toned hand-detailed

47

sports coat and collected Jean, starting for the exit with one arm around her slender waist and with the other waving to the gentlemen at the lunch counter and the boys on the back tables. As he passed the four rows of theater seats on a platform in front of the baseball and horse boards, beneath the warning ABSOLUTELY NO GAMING, a fat man in the back row plucked at Gus' sleeve. He bent for solemn whispered words with the man. When he rose, he said, "You got it." The man with eyes as dead as snot returned to studying the blackboards, smoking an expensive cigar. He had a diamond ring on his stubby, hairy pinkie.

In the foyer at the foot of the stairs up to the street, Avis-Jean jerked away from Gus, and Jack heard her cry. *"No!* You *promised* you wouldn't anymore!"

Jack lost the game and had to pay for the next rack. He also went to the counter for the beers. The Airway fortified its draft beer, boosting its alcoholic content to, some said, 6 percent, almost double the Kansas legal potency. No one actually admitted the beer was laced, but since the Airway was only a block from the police station and drew a big crowd of off-duty cops, lawyers and city fathers, the boys *knew* it was good beer.

"Guess what?" Jack decided to let the guys in on his secret.

"You got laid," Glenn guessed sarcastically.

"Shee-it," Bucky drawled. "He can't even get into old Vanda Hard-*ass*-ty."

"I joined the Navy."

They rested their cues on the edge of the table.

"Now what kind of bullshit are you tryin to pull?" Glenn asked.

"I did. Go up Monday to K.C. for my physical."

"You can't *join* the Navy, ass!" Bucky insisted.

Jack showed them the papers he had in his pocket. They studied them.

"That don't mean shit," Glenn decided. "Soon as they find out how old you are, they'll kick your ass out so fast—"

Bucky began to mock, his mouth pulled down disdainfully. "Joined the Navy. *Joined the Navy.*" He sang and danced around. "Shit-o-my-dear!"

"Well, I did," Jack said, the absurdity of it beginning to defeat him again.

48

"Hell, you can't even buy beer less you're with us," Glenn cracked. "Rack!"

They played another game. Jack lucked in one ball ahead of Bucky, who was pissed because he lost. Bucky put up his cue.

"You goin to the ball park, Glenn?" Jack asked.

"Aw, I don't know. What are you doin, Buck?"

"I gotta be home for dinner. The old lady's havin Skipper over. They want to talk about somethin."

Bucky got a dollar a day allowance. If he didn't do what his old lady wanted, she would cut him off. He had a lot of expenses.

"Maybe I'll meet you and the sailor later at the Red Ball Inn," he cracked.

Their eyes caught in a knowing partnership that excluded Jack and made the possibility of his actually getting in the Navy as remote as a sausage like him ever playing on the front table or screwing someone like Avis Nickel. They made him feel like a punk kid.

"See you, Glenn," Bucky said.

"Gotcha."

"See you, sausage."

"Fuck you," he replied hollowly. He didn't want to fight Bucky.

There was plenty of time, so they decided to walk to Lawrence Stadium. When Bucky wasn't around, Glenn could still be a good guy. He and Bucky had become friends when Jack had gone to live in Texas with his mother and stepfather, bragging about all the promised good times that were in store for him now that they were doing so well in oil. Glenn, who had always felt sorry that Jack was so poor and had gained a certain superiority by his charity, resented the vision of Gulf Coast beaches and trips to Mexico that Jack had left him with. Glenn had never been out of the state. What neither of them knew was that in Texas it would be the same old business: his stepfather drunk, mean, out of work, the promises nothing but air and a place on the baked banks of the Rio Grande where he could watch catfish die for want of water. Yet when Jack returned, Glenn never quite forgave him. Still, there were times when Bucky wasn't around, that they could talk of—everything—the way they used to; of sun, moon and stars, of tentative speculations on the extent of the universe and of cosmic ventures like turning a stone and marveling at the life they chanced to find there.

"You know, I think that's right, nothin can be destroyed," Jack had offered one night sitting on a curb out on East Douglass, drinking a can of Falstaff, staring up at a harvest moon. "I mean, you burn up somethin you don't destroy it, it just changes into *energy*, and goes on forever. Everything just goes on forever in a different way."

"Yeah!" Glenn saw it. "Seems possible. Like when we die, our energy becomes sort of like fish in a sea of it."

The possibility overwhelmed them, opening up a discussion of reincarnation, which Jack doubted, but which Glenn argued for, and leading to a consideration of what "love" meant, which they decided was the special feeling you had about anything that was so fine you'd never cut your initials on it or want to steal it, something so fine it made you just want to stop and admire.

"Like Satchel Paige pitchin," Jack offered. "Er one of them big old trees in the park. I could just lay under one lookin up all day sometimes."

"Naw." Glenn couldn't see trees. "Jeanne Harris."

"OK," Jack agreed. Jeanne, the head cheerleader, could make him feel it was summer in the park when it was ten-below outside.

Back-of-the-billboards boys, they knew their city the way Michelangelo, in a book of drawings that fascinated them one term, knew anatomy. "Man, he could draw a person from the inside out!" They knew what made the lights go on, where buses slept at night, how the city was fed, where the garbage was hauled. They had an intimate knowledge of what their town ingested, what it discharged and where the process could get hung up.

They had jerked off together, once sucked each other's cocks—only not until they came—and so knew the salty unique taste of the other's flesh. Glenn had a funny upcurving dong. Theirs were both the same size—they had measured—but because Glenn was so skinny, his *looked* bigger.

They had hopped freights side by side, riding from Central Avenue up to the Douglass Avenue overpass, where they hopped off every Saturday and went to the nickel matinee at the Novelty Theater that smelled of cat-shit, mice and rancid popcorn. They had haunted penny-arcade peep shows, silently kibitzed the old men's domino games at the White Way Pool Hall, made wooden scimitars in the YMCA workshop, shot baskets and played handball. They'd had their picture taken together at a Smile-A-Minute.

Once a clumsy kid, Bobby Scrovis, had hooked a freight with them and been swept off the ladder by the IGA warehouse siding at Third Street. His head was crushed under the wheels. They still sometimes stopped to look at the very tie where Bobby's brains had been spewed out like the guts of a run-over cat.

Glenn and Bucky would never share such knowledge and times. But it seemed since Jack had come back, such times were of less and less significance to Glenn. More often than not, it was Jack who recalled what they had done while Glenn became impatient at the memory, wanting quickly to dismiss the subject and talk of something else—usually about beating someone at something.

But they still knew every street and alley in town better than any taxi driver. There was no way for them to get lost. They knew how to sneak into every theater in town, where to rifle parked cars with the most security and where two could eat for the price of one by asking for separate checks and one of them waltzing.

There were all the times they had stolen stuff from stores. And the time they had crouched on the fire escape of the Eton Hotel to window-peek on the whores and their customers. Then the crazy day they had flashed their cocks at a pretty woman in glasses in the balcony stacks of the public library. "You're just a couple of stupid hooligans!" she had advised them, looking straight into their eyes and going to report them. They had fled like fiends, Glenn stiff-arming the old-age pensioner guard who tried to bar their exit, both of them crying, "Gotchercockout, old man! Gotchercockout!" Three blocks away they had collapsed on the lawn of a funeral home, sides aching from flight and laughter. *"You're just a couple of stupid hooligans,"* they mocked the woman. "Showed her our cocks, man!" and "Did you see that old fart's face when I gave him the arm?" "Yeah!" "Whooeee!"

They became friends with a queer who worked for a funeral home on North Market. One night he took them into the room where they embalmed the bodies, whipping a sheet off a fat naked woman as cold as a dime's worth of baloney. They had squeezed her flabby tits and touched the rusty dark hair of her big bush. He said they could fuck her if they liked, but they hadn't.

They were friends with all kinds of people: a photographer for the *Beacon*, named Henry, who showed them how a newspaper was made and let them look at the pictures of movie stars and famous people that were too sexy to print; a guy at Wonder Bread who took them through the bakery, and where they could get broken pies and cakes for next to nothing; a cook at the Lassen Hotel and a bellman at the Riverview who kept them posted on the wild drunken doings of the city's upper crust—all sorts of guys they met at one or another pool hall or beanery.

But then Bucky came from military school with a real German Luger and the tattoo of a python on his left calf. He and Glenn started hanging around on the fringe of Robert Bell's gang, who talked of knocking over filling stations and hitting punchboards. They talked of getting a car. They had gang-banged old Vanda Hard-ass-ty—eight guys—and hadn't invited Jack.

"You know that Navy stuff's a lot of crap," Glenn said as they crossed the Lawrence Bridge. "You come up with a lot of junk like that and the guys think something about you." He sounded as if Jack were an embarrassment to him. Then he confirmed it. "It ain't good for my reputation."

"What'd you mean?" Jack honestly wondered.

"Well, you're always sayin or doin somethin that makes the guys think you're, uh . . . well, you know, not a straight ace er somethin. Kid stuff, you know. . . ." He struggled to express his precise concern. "Like you don't know the score—Shit! I don't know. It's just somethin about you. You ain't made your rep yet. No one's seen you in a real fight since we grew up. I mean, since you came back from Texas. Things are changed now. You got to prove yourself. I can't hang around with somebody everyone else thinks is queer er somethin!"

"They say that?" Jack challenged, suddenly both frightened and angry.

"Well, naw, not in so many words, you know. It's just a feelin. They wanta see you *do* somethin to show em you're all reet."

"How?"

"Well, like whippin some bad ass er somethin. Seems like every time we get in a fight now you ain't around."

"Um, when you ganged Vanda, you guys didn't come get me," Jack countered.

"Well, you was somewhere else. That ain't the point."

"OK," Jack said mildly. "How about Bucky?"

"He'd murder you. Naw, it's just the next time we tangle with some other guys—*be* there!"

"OK," Jack promised. It was stupid. What the hell did they prove fighting? Fighting the Germans and Japs, that seemed worthwhile, you could get something out of that, but starting something with some kids from across town was just pointless. "What does it prove?" Jack asked.

Glenn looked amazed. "Why, who's *best*!" he said, shocked at Jack's ignorance. Honest doubt clouded his yellow eyes. "Now *that's* what I'm talking about. You know, havin to ask somethin like that. Buck or Flash or even Danny wouldn't ask some stupid shit like that."

"OK. I'll fight if I have to," Jack vowed.

"Yeah? Well, you're goin to have to pretty damn soon. Maybe even if it's you and me. And if it is, it's goin to be for real, you can bet your ass!"

The prospect was saddening to Jack. He wanted to walk away from Glenn and never see him again. There was no fun in fighting the way he talked about it. For what? To build some crummy reputation that carried no farther than Wichita? Fuck it.

"And don't say nothin more about goin in the Navy. You ain't goin in no Navy."

"OK, Glenn."

"Reet! Just wanted to get it straightened out. You an me, we've been buddies longer than anybody. I don' like to see any real buddy of mine mess up, you know? I always stick up for you with the guys, you're younger than the rest of us, but if you want to run with us, you gotta do somethin to show them you're OK. You understan?"

"Sure."

Glenn busted him on the arm as hard as he could. The place throbbed. He busted Glenn back, but his heart wasn't in it, for all the real pop he tried to put behind it. Glenn laughed and messed up his hair.

"That's my old buddy. Race you to the end of the bridge." He was off like a shot. "Gotchercockout!" he cried.

Jack echoed the call. That Glenn won by a flying stride was no longer of any importance at all.

53

6

GENE trolleyed around the concessionaire's space allotted to him in a folding tubular wheelchair, the toes of his uncreased black orthopedic shoes always at odd, useless angles on the footplates, his ball cap at a dippy rake. A thirty-four-year-old graduate of Wichita's Paraplegic Institute, he had the pale look of the perpetually crippled. His speech was hesitant, stuttering, as if the effort twisted his spastic tongue like a corkscrew. He dropped words from every sentence the way peanuts and dimes spilled from his barely responsive fingers into the catchall apron over his wasted knees. Turned inward at the wrist in a gesture of eternal chastisement, his hands were just capable of lifting a hot dog to his face and with luck finding his mouth, inadequate either to write or button himself. His large, friendly head under a black crew cut jerked about on his neck. People either lowered their voices in speaking to him or lifted it to one of phony hail-fellow cheerfulness.

The boys had known him for years. To them he was simply Gene. He was eminently fair, a practicing fundamental Christian who carried his New Testament in his carryall on the side of his chair, yet it took real genius to cheat him.

They sat on overturned buckets in the room under the stands where Gene stored his merchandise. He also hawked programs and souvenirs. He had the space next to the main ramp behind the turnstiles. He decorated himself and his chair with National Semi-Pro Baseball Congress buttons and pennants until he looked like a kid's homemade skate scooter after a head on with a hot tamale cart. Two or three times a night, whenever they came back for another basket of peanuts, Jack or Glenn would tidy Gene up, square his cap, retrieve dimes, quarters and four bitses from his apron and stash them in the pouches for him. A minute later he would have twitched

54

and shaken everything around again until he looked like Mortimer Snerd tossed on a penny-arcade vibrating machine.

Between genuinely wanting to keep Gene tidy and beating him out of a dollar or two a night, they could not resist making horrible, shocking, delicious fun of him, acting out his disadvantages in the normal processes of living. Having mocked his tongue-twisted speech, they would both stumble and jutter into some café or other and make the other patrons sick as they tried to feed themselves. They *always* went into MacFarlane's Chinese Restaurant as spastics. It drove the Oriental gentlemen behind the counter and cash register out of their minds. They could move themselves to tears of laughter, spastically approaching a urinal, painfully fumbling out their cocks and pissing all over the room. Once in the bus station they bracketed a middle-aged man at the pisser in tan gabardine suit, cowboy boots and Stetson with their act. The man cried, *"Jesus Christ, boys, you're pissin all over me!"* Twitching around to stammer an apology, they wet both gabardine legs from his knees to his boots.

A kid Jack and Glenn had never seen before popped into the dim little room under the stands. "Hi, guys, I'm Woody. Spastic guy said you'd show me the ropes."

He was an open apple knocker from the West Side wearing plain Monkey Ward jeans rather than Levi's and high-top horsehide shit kickers. He looked as if he had his hair cut at a barber college—a natural sausage.

They flicked an imperceptible, knowing smile between them.

Woody dedicated himself to learning how to put one small scoop of peanuts from the open gunnysack on the floor into a tiny, penny-candy-sized paper bag and, holding the top as if it had ears, spin it into a compact ten-cent package of red-hot jumbos. Jack and Glenn filled their bags to the ultimate nut, which made them hard to close. Woody thought they were just being generous. The filled bags were packed neatly into half-bushel split-wood shopping baskets. They each had a carpenter's apron for carrying their change. Each basket contained fifty bags of nuts, and Gene carefully checked each basket as they started out. They had to provide their own seed change.

The extra boy had been put on in anticipation of a sell-out crowd lured by the promised personal appearance of

Sergeant Joe Louis. He was coming with the Fort Riley Centaurs who were playing the Boeing Bombers in the first game. In the second, it was the Cessna Bobcats versus the Hutchinson Navy Skyhawks.

It was still light when the crowd began drifting in, men recalling for their sons radio broadcasts of Joe Louis' fights as if they had been at ringside.

As soon as they had been checked by Gene, Woody began hawking, "Getcher red-hot peanuts," but Glenn and Jack went to the far end of the lower level and ducked into the men's. Inside, they appropriated the "free" toilet, set their baskets on the stool and water closet and opened every bag. From their hip pockets they took ten extra sacks and filled them from the tops of the others. They worked fast. In fifteen minutes they had made a dollar each. They sold the original fifty bags on a fifty-fifty split for Gene, but the extra ten were all profit.

Fort Riley's band marched across the outfield playing the "Thunderer" march while a rider on a mule mascot galloped around. Then, right after "The Star-Spangled Banner," the announcer called forth: "An inspiration to all the young of America, a gentleman, patriot, credit to his race, the world's heavyweight champion, the one and only Brown Bomber—Sergeant Joe Louis!"

A pudgy, shambling man, no real giant, in poorly fitting khakis, the cap squarely on his head, strolled out to home plate to a standing ovation. Behind home plate a pneumatically lifted microphone rose from a little trapdoor which Joe was facing away from. He jumped as if goosed when the thing swooshed up behind him and then stared at it angrily for a few seconds as if deciding whether to uproot the marvel or not. Flatly, squarely, in a monotone that rolled to the outfield and echoed off the fences, Joe thanked everyone for coming, urged them to buy war bonds, waved once and ambled back into the Centaurs' dugout.

"Is that all there is?" Jack wondered aloud. He had expected to see him move around and throw a few punches of something.

"Hell," Glenn said, "that wasn't nothin. Conn'll cream him next time."

The crowd too was disappointed. "We want Joe!" The chant started out in the Knothole Gang bleachers and quickly spread around the park.

Joe stepped out of the dugout again and waved. Still unsatisfed, the crowd cried for more. After the announcer on the field conferred with the Fort Riley people, Joe came out and hit a few fungoes to the infielders during the Centaurs' warm-up.

"Joe Louis, shee-it," Glenn groaned.

"Getcher fresh roasted peanuts! Red-hot jumbos! Deluxe Spanish double-jumbo peanuts here!" Jack conjured up such succulent pleasure for only ten cents that he himself almost forgot the gunnysack under the stands. "Red-hots here! Getcher red-hots. Get em while they're hot. *Hot nuts!*" That always got a laugh or a grin.

"Hey, boy, I thought you said these were hot?" someone always complained.

"Ten cents, mister," already looking ahead to his next sale. No time to debate. Only rarely was the dime not forthcoming and the bag handed back. It was all the same to Jack. "Red-hots. Hot roasted peanuts here." Catching the eye of a peroxide blonde, her peasant blouse skidding off one shoulder, her peasant skirt hiked high over plump tan knees—from three rows below he could see her fat dimpled thighs go back to where she sat—he cried "Hot nuts!" She giggled and nudged her aircrafter boyfriend or husband.

"I like hot nuts," she distinctly cracked.

"Here, boy!" the aircrafter reacted, tearing himself away from an easy out, short to first. "He ain't got no hot nuts," he joked with the woman. "Just some little ole goobers."

"Betcha he has. Doncha, honey?" Her face looked like a new catcher's mitt with a blobby little nose stuck on it.

"That's twenty cents, please."

The aircrafter was drawn back to the game by a towering pop fly that Jack didn't even turn around to watch. He gave the man a nickel's change from his quarter. The dumb blonde fell back onto her cushion as if the sky-high pop might actually have fallen for a hit. Hell, Fort Riley had Pistol Pete Reiser of the Dodgers out there. What did she think?

The unnatural daylight of the stadium kliegs drove back the prairie night so they all existed in a special time and place of nine innings. Jack was appalled at how many of the crowd were really rubes about baseball. Of the world that existed under the stadium before the lights came on

57

and was there when they went off, he had a license to shortchange the clucks every chance he got. Caught, he would play dumb and fork over the correct money.

Up on the roof, reached via a stairway guarded by a man in uniform, was the exalted aerie of the press box, where both KFH and KANS had their banners hung out to show they were carrying the game on radio.

Joe and an Army major with an especially pretty girl in a tight summer dress and high-heeled shoes passed so close Jack could have touched them on their way to the press box. Joe looked a lot bigger up close. But he still didn't seem as if he were having a good time.

"You'll say a few words during the seventh-inning stretch," the major explained. "The radio people may ask you a few questions. Be sure to get the pitch for war bonds in. Both stations will interview you. Since it's going to the same places, try to make your answers a little different. OK, Champ?"

"Yeah, sure," he drawled. He had the distracted, pro look Jack had seen in some of the big-leaguers that were playing for service teams. Their minds always seemed elsewhere. There was a kind of anger or unhappiness about them, and they did not blink as often as ordinary men, of that he was certain.

Under the end of the stands where the Knothole Gang bleachers began, Glenn had Vanda Hardasty backed into the shadows behind a steel girder.

"I'm with Joy Ann and these two sailors she knows," she was explaining earnestly. "I *can't.*"

"Hell, you can," Glenn assured her. "Joy Ann can go with Jack Andersen."

"You know I would if I could, but I just *can't,*" she squeaked.

Glenn had set down his peanut basket. He had her backed against the silver-painted steel.

"Come on, Vanda," he purred. "You know you want it."

"I *can't,*" she said again as if in pain.

Glenn cupped her right breast and ground his narrow hips against her. Cutting a quick look, she let him kiss her, winding both arms around his neck.

"Whew!" she exhaled dramatically when he leaned back grinning. She glanced around again to make sure her date hadn't seen her.

"Meet you here end of eighth inning, reet?"

"You know I would, if I could . . ." she pleaded.

"Be here, bitch!" he snapped.

"Glenn, I *can't!*"

"OK. Fuss you, sisser," Glenn said, drawing himself up. "We're through."

"They're only here until tomorrow afternoon. Come over tomorrow night," she bargained.

"Fuck it! Tonight. Yes or no?"

"I *can't!*"

"See ya." He turned abruptly away.

"*Gl-enn* . . ." she called after him.

He gave her the finger without looking back.

Glenn waited for no cunt.

She went toward the bleachers, a perfectly medium girl in every way; neither ugly nor what anyone called "pretty," medium of breast and hip, she already had the gayless look of someone's wife: medium plump, ordinary brown hair and, according to Glenn, only a medium good screw. Those who didn't like her said she only did it to get guys.

At the beginning of the seventh inning of the last game, Jack and Woody bumped into each other up high behind home plate. Cessna was leading the Skyhawks 8 to 1. More than half the crowd had left. Those who hadn't moved down to better seats except for a few kids and their girls who were necking in the shadows on the highest row under the roof.

"How'd it go?" Jack asked.

"Real good!" Woody enthused.

"Usually ain't so good," Jack assured him.

"Wish I could sell all the time."

"Match you a nickel," Jack offered.

Wanting to be a good sport, Woody reluctantly agreed.

They flipped nickels, catching them and popping them into their left hands. It had been a good night. Jack had sold a hundred and twenty-three bags with over two bucks grifted for himself.

"Gotcha!" Jack called.

Woody collected his nickel. Jack already had another out. "You get me." Woody won again. They matched for about ten minutes, moving up to dimes. Woody was ahead by about thirty cents when Glenn came up.

"You cleanin this sausage?" Glenn asked the new boy.

"He's got me down three dimes," Jack explained, sounding worried.

"He's easy," Glenn confided to the hick. "Let me get in on this." He flipped his dime. "Took him for five bucks last night. Odd man wins."

They all three came up tails. They flipped again. Woody won.

"He's too damn lucky. Think I'll quit," Jack complained.

"The hell! Don't be a piker."

Jack reluctantly let himself be coaxed to play.

They had practiced the skill so if they flipped their coins one with head up and the other with tail up, one or the other would win most of the time.

Before Woody became discouraged after the stakes had been generously raised to quarters to let him have a chance to catch up, they had trimmed him of almost three dollars. He never figured it out.

At the end of the eighth inning they went to settle with Gene. Splitting what they had taken from Woody, they left ahead of the crowd richer by almost ten bucks each—a big night. They lifted two bottles of Pabst from a concessionaire's cooler and went out the players' gate with a happy "Good night, Jake," for the old guard. They stopped in the parking lot to pry the tops off the beer on the bumper of a car.

They finished their beers on the bridge, walking in the trickle of people who had been sitting atop boxcars along right field, seeing the game for free. They sailed the bottles out far over the river, saw them splash in the dark water reflecting the stadium lights.

Ahead, they saw Vanda and Joy Ann with their young sailors. The girls were wearing the sailors' caps. The sailors had their arms around the girls' waists. They were all laughing at some stupid something.

"Fuckin pig," Glenn grumbled.

They stepped along to trail behind them. Glenn said, "Hot Springs tonight, reet, Vanda?"

She shot him an annoyed glance over her shoulder, then clearly looked pleading.

Joy Ann snarled, "Get lost, crud!"

The sailors hadn't yet decided the extent of their responsibility.

"Gotcherself a cinch there, mate," Glenn told the sailor knowingly.

"You guys better shove off," the sailor advised.

"Yeah, no one pulled *your* chain," Joy Ann sniffed.

"Rrrrr-ough!" Glenn growled and feigned terror.

"You lookin for trouble?" the sailor asked.

"Naw, I ain't lookin for trouble," Glenn told him, the fun gone from his voice. "I'm lookin at you, ass. I don't think that's trouble."

"Yeah?" He made a move to disentangle himself from Vanda, but not move enough to escape from both arms she had clamped around his right arm, digging her rubber-soled shoes into the sidewalk.

"Don't pay them no attention. They're just actin smart. Let's cross the street. Come on." She tugged him.

"Yeah?" the sailor asked again, eyeing the casual pachuco rooster whose eyes never left his clean face.

"They're the worst boys in school," Joy Ann explained.

The sailors let themselves be started across the street.

"Yeah?" the sailor still wondered.

"Something *smells* around here," Joy Ann sniffed.

"Guess we know what *that* is," Glenn cracked. "They both suck cock. Kiss em and you'll know what every dong in town tastes like," he advised the Navy.

Vanda wanted them just to ignore it.

Joy Ann cried back, *"Up yours,* Glenn Frisch!"

"Up yours, sister! If you had as many stickin out of you as you've had stuck in you, you'd look like a goddamn porkypine."

The disapproving eyes of family men and their wives glared at them all.

Vanda and the sailors ducked into the Riverview Coffee Shop.

A city street sweeper came by, big circular brushes cleaning the gutters, jetting water out behind from a bar of nozzles, leaving the asphalt gleaming like patent leather, raising an invisible steam that smelled like the soul of summer night in the city.

"She-it, man, we should go plow them fuckin swab jockeys," Glenn said, smashing the knobby fist in the palm of his hand. "I just want to *feel* it! See them pretty boy faces fucked up, man. I *want* it, man. Come on." He grabbed Jack as if to start back.

"Naw, forget it," Jack advised. "Fuck it."

Glenn reluctantly let himself be persuaded, shaking his head as if the effort were enormous. "When I get hot like that, I just want to *bust* somebody."

"Yeah. But they ain't nobody."

"Yeah. I guess you're right. I coulda got them cunts for us. I saw Vanda at the game. They'da gone with us like that." He snapped his fingers. "Fuck er. Got a box like a garbage can."

"They missed some trash." A dumpy little woman about fifty in a print housedress, her lardy upper arms sunburned, sniffed at the boys. She walked with a thin old man whose coat and trousers didn't match, who was carrying two folding campstools and a gallon Thermos jug off the boxcar bleachers.

"What's that, old lady?" Glenn whirled on her.

She drew herself back into several chins. "Just go on," she said.

"I want to know what you said," Glenn demanded.

"She didn't say nothin," the man said.

"You just go on and leave us be," the woman scolded.

"You didn't say nothin about trash or anything like that?" Glenn persisted.

"You go on now," the woman repeated.

"She didn't say nothin," the man insisted.

"She said *somethin*." Glenn was certain. He grabbed her by the billowing left breast. Her little mouth flew open, speechless, gulping air.

"Well, goddamn!" Her old husband was amazed. "Here! You turn her loose."

Glenn brushed the sparrow away. With his lower lip caught between his long teeth, he twisted the woman's tit until it looked as if her eyes would pop, forcing her onto her toes up against the concrete bridge railing. "Tell me you didn't say anything, old cunt. You wouldn't say anything bad about us, would you?" He gave her tit another twist.

The old man dropped his campstools and wound up to brain Glenn with his jug. Jack stepped between them just as the husband swung, deflecting the jug upward, spinning the old man around and giving him a shove that sent him sprawling off the curbing, his jug rolling across the bridge, jingling broken glass inside.

Glenn shoved his right hand between the woman's fat legs, cramming her dress into the big cleft of her sex. Her terrified face turned red. Sweat popped, and her skin shone. Her little mouth opened and closed.

"Lookit her. She's gittin all hot and bothered," Glenn crowed.

The husband gathered himself and made another rush. Jack easily caught him and wrestled as gently as possible with him. The old man was strong. His thin arms were like cords.

"But him!" Glenn commanded.

Jack couldn't hold him much longer.

"*Bust* him!"

Jack hit the old man a straight left on the nose that made him blink and come in head down, flailing both arms. He hit him with a right uppercut, as the old man's fists flailed blindly around his head.

"Goddammit, *hit* him!" Glenn shouted. "Bust his old ass."

Jack hit him with another right that dropped the man to his knees. There was blood around his mouth and nose. He looked furious, hurt. Jack felt sorry for him. Gamely he tried to get up and come on again. Glenn turned the woman loose and stepped forward and smashed the old man left and right as he tried to rise. He went over backward, his arms outspread, his thin body bent over his legs underneath him. His head thonked the pavement sickeningly, as his wife screamed and dropped to his side.

"Let's cut!" Glenn spat. "Think I coulda killed im."

They bolted to the end of the bridge, darted up the first alley.

"We're in this together, man," Glenn puffed as they flew.

It was all over. *Had to end in some shit like this,* Jack thought mournfully as he ran. They heard a siren— couldn't be sure from which direction. *God! God! God! Dumb, mean, stupid bastard!* He wasn't angry with Glenn. But his disappointment was total. *No sense in that shit. None at all.* He still heard the woman yelling "Police! Police!" It rang in his brain like a goddamn alarm clock.

Past the John Deere tractor company they turned up an intersecting alley and stopped to rest in the dark among the ghostly parts of old farm equipment and splintered packing crates with sisal dripping from them like Spanish moss. A cat shot out of a box, and Jack leaped with fear. His heart felt as if it had actually stopped.

"Sonofabitch!" Glenn exclaimed.

Jack looked at the other boy breathing heavily beside him against the wall. He really didn't know what went on behind those yellow eyes. All confidences they had shared no longer lived in there. He was simply squinting ahead, looking determined. He wasn't even what you would call poor. What made him so mean?

Glenn caught him looking and reminded him, "We're in it together. All the way."

"Yeah."

"You damn right, boy! Come on."

They no longer ran. Then, thinking they would look more suspicious if they were spotted in the alley, they decided to get back on a street.

"Maybe if we split up, we'd have a better chance if they're lookin for two guys," Jack suggested.

"Naw. You stick with me," Glenn said suspiciously.

"Just thought we could meet somewhere."

"Naw."

On Douglass again, they went into a café that boasted in stuttering red neon in its bug-stained window: HOMEMADE PIES. Windrows of locusts lay dead and dying in the lee of the building. The bugs crunched under Jack's boots. Maybe they would hear something. People crossing the bridge after them would be stopping in the place for hamburgers and coffee.

They sat in a booth where they could watch the street by stretching their necks a little. They both sat on the same side.

A girl in a limp, stained uniform took her pencil from her hairnet and scribbled their order on a pad that hooked onto her belt. When she bent to mop the tabletop with a gray cloth, Jack could see a tiny bit of pale thigh above her stocking top in the gap between uniform buttons. It made him feel excited. As she walked away, he saw her hose were laddered up the back and one seam was turned in, the other out. She had wide, square hips like Vanda Hardasty's and the same color hair. Then, studying his feelings in view of their circumstances, he thought he really must be crazy.

The burgers tasted ersatz, dull, greasy, probably had pork and lamb trimmings in the meat, horse, mule, monkey—who knew what the hell was in meat anymore? Since the war, only Kings-X and White Castle could be counted on, and they had raised their prices and shrunk the patties. Candy bars had become half their former size and no longer tasted as good. Then there were all those new bars without any chocolate that looked and tasted like glued, sweetened sawdust. Hostess cupcakes changed their frosting and called it a new invention. Longing for the old flavors came back to Jack.

"You think when the war's over, they'll go back to makin stuff like before?" he asked, chewing a bite of burger.

"Huh?"

"I was thinkin about how good Hershey bars and Hostess cupcakes used to be when we were little."

"What are you talkin about?"

"How things used to taste."

"Jesus Christ! I probably killed some old fart, and you're thinkin about candy un cake."

"We could call the hospitals and see if they brought him in to emergency," Jack suggested.

"Oh, sure! You never heard about tracin a call?"

"We could call from a booth, put a handkerchief over the mouthpiece. You know, just ask like we was his son or somethin."

"That's the dumbest goddamn thing."

"We could call Danny. We can trust him. He could sort of get some information from his brother."

Glenn thought that over. "Yeah, maybe that would be an idea."

"I don't think you killed him," Jack decided.

"Listen, I hit the shit outa him!" Glenn insisted. "I can *hear* it. Made a sort of noise like his life was goin out of him." He imitated an airy, deathly rattle in his throat. "His head hit the sidewalk then, boy, like a dropped melon. Didn't you *hear* it?"

Jack shuddered. He heard it.

"If he ain't dead, he's almost." Glenn was certain. He threw a short punch in self-admiration and wonder. "Sheit. . . ."

7

ROWS of locusts like photos of dead banzai assault troops were heaped in rows along the sidewalks. The rows grew slightly less thick as they got farther away from the river.

There's an art to carrying a clutch bag—

Where the hell did that come from? Odd things like that—phrases heard or read often sounded in his mind at inappropriate times—spoken so clearly in a woman's voice that there might have been a radio in his head.

Probably came from one of his mother's magazines. She was as crazy as he was. She pretended to be just like everyone else, a mother like any other—gloves and good posture, no swearing, and goddamned women's magazines from which she clipped recipes and poems—while selling her ass, rolling drunks, papering some dinky burg with little old ten- and twenty-buck hot checks. Then fleeing the insane recall, the time he had spent with her and his stepdad seeming so unreal, he sometimes wondered now if it hadn't been a bad dream, knowing all the while it had been true, beginning to realize that no juvenile court judge's order could ever wipe out how it had been with a writ taking him away from her forever. Last he had heard she was going to Albuquerque to wait for his stepdad to get out of jail.

Sound of skirling fiddles and whining electric guitar spilled out of the Red Ball Inn where red neon painted the windrows of witless dead locusts in Technicolor blood.

Bucky sat uncomfortably across the booth from Avis Nickel. He looked relieved when they walked in and waved them over with an enthusiasm that was not at all like him. He hadn't wanted to be caught alone in a booth with Avis if Gus Depolis walked in.

Don't be caught booking. The voice clear and feminine spoke a curious warning in his head. The warning was perfectly sympathetic, utterly wise, without urgency. Its meaning was portentous, though in no way understandable. Yet, when the voice spoke in him, he felt his heart stop. The voice filled him as if his body were a cathedral with echoes beyond his ken. When it spoke once, it might speak several times in the space of an evening, then be gone for days or weeks. He thought he remembered it speaking to him when he was a baby, before he could speak himself. Often it came as he slept, merely calling his name until it awakened him. He was certain he had more than once answered, "Yes," aloud. Why it was always a woman's voice puzzled and troubled him. It was the most beautiful voice in creation. For all the fear and doubt it sponsored in him he hoped it would not go away and never return. Initially he thought it was his mother's voice. But it was without accent—clear and beautiful as a stone thrown into clean, still water, radiating perfect rings to either shore. It could have been the voice of Jesus' mother, but he didn't believe that.

Bucky raised his arm and half rose in the booth. He had on his white sports jacket. From the obvious anxiety he had felt before their arrival, Jack knew he had learned a lot about Bucky he hadn't realized before. It made him grin inwardly, though what he saw also saddened him. It was like topping a rise and discovering a valley he had never known existed. The world was instantly larger, truer, and yet a less secure place. Everything he was learning lately had such a quality.

He wondered if Glenn and Bucky ever had such thoughts. Once he had been sure Glenn had. Then they grew up. Now he was ashamed that such ideas wormed through his brain. He worried because the voice in his head was a woman's. Was he down deep some kind of queer? He wanted just to be a straight ace like his buddies, live in a real house, have some neat clothes, punch someone's head off, man—be done with soft, punky fuckin thoughts—sleep, get up— What? *WHAT?* Do what?... Man, he didn't want to do all his days like Glenn and Buck.

He felt giddy, so weightless he might float up to the stamped metal ceiling in the barnlike bar—up there with the fuzzed, dead old propeller fans that were now just decoration. An atmosphere for Glenn and Buck. Their natural arena. Bigassed bullshitters lined up at the bar, drifting back to the shuffleboard table with one another or with some sorry cunt in a print dress who carried a little sweater in anticipation of the air conditioning. "Play that 'Yellow Rose of Texas' on the juke, honey. I sure like Bob Wills and them Texas Playboys."

A man at the bar was grinning at a woman perched on the imitation red leather of the high stools, her foot bobbing in high-heeled strapped shoes, legs stained tan because of the stocking shortage. Jack saw through it all. Getting between those skinny painted legs seemed suddenly so simple a trick he felt sorry for the roughneck who was making such a boring big deal of it.

Lordy Backeroo, the woman's beautiful voice in his head tagged his amusement, laughing with him. So pure. Oh, he loved her. She was half of him. Worth a million Glenns.

It could have been the air conditioning, but his eyes watered. He felt happy, sad, sweet and wise as a sonofabitch.

While Glenn jigged and jabbered yet another line, dropped a shoulder and spoke of cooling the old man on the bridge and Bucky half stood as if ready to take his beer and move off with them to another booth, Jack slid into the seat beside the girl and said, "Hi, Avis."

Plainly she was certain she knew him, though there was nothing in her eyes to indicate her certainty was based on any specific recall.

"Buy you a beer?" he offered. A nearly empty Coke bottle and a glass in which the ice cubes had almost melted sat in front of her.

"I'll just have another Coke," she said.

Without touching her, Jack felt a physical awareness of the young woman's slender softness. Something more than warmth radiated from her thigh across the four inches of air-conditioned plastic between them. Jack's face felt warm. A sort of unspecific assurance and daring made him lock out Glenn and Buck as if they were children.

Glenn slid in beside Bucky. He no more than acknowledged Avis' presence. For once he did not run a line of shit the way he always did for the benefit of any woman, young or old, pretty or plain. He talked to women in a way so that they would invariably think of him as "cute" or "a devil" joshing and teasing, figuratively waving his cock. Toward Avis he directed a kind of careful, solicitous respect as if she were a nun in a religious order to which he was a recent zealous convert. It was funny. Jack had never seen Glenn so mushily floppy. He might have been visiting Avis in a hospital.

"How's Gus?" he then asked, affirming his loyalty, though Glenn was no more to Gus than one of dozens of skinny pachooks who played on the back tables of the big-time pool halls. "Hi, kid," was Gus' greeting for Glenn, Bucky and Jack alike.

"We're through," Avis said flatly, looking at nothing.

Jack's heart leaped.

"Whadya mean?" Glenn asked. The news made him look even more worried than before. He and Buck exchanged glances.

"I'm not taking his crap anymore," Avis explained. "He can't treat me like just some pig. The golden Greek! Ha! He doesn't even like girls. Just his big fat mama."

Glenn and Buck looked shocked. They didn't want to hear such blasphemy.

"Aw, Gus is *great*," Glenn said. Clearly Avis didn't understand about a real man. A dizzy, sentimental cunt. They were all alike. "It'll work out," he assured her like a brother.

"*You* live with him," she offered. "Asshole, that's what he likes."

Glenn visibly recoiled. That kind of talk was simply too dangerous to touch.

"Naw, naw. You're just a little upset." He forced a tiny laugh. "Tomorrow you'll kiss and make up."

"I wouldn't let him kiss my foot."

"You don't quit on Gus." Bucky took the hard line, sneering at her presumption.

She looked at him coolly for a long second. "You aren't tough, you know. You're just mean. All of you guys think you're so damn tough. You're just mean. You're all like Gus—mean mama's boys. Didn't any of you have a father?"

"I'm not mean," Jack offered.

She really looked at him for the first time. She smiled and laid her right hand trembling and warm along his cheek.

"You're a baby."

Glenn and Buck hooted.

"I'm going in the Navy," he protested. "Got to gain two pounds by Monday."

"He thinks because they let him take some papers to fill out he's goin in the Navy," Buck explained while Glenn described dizzy circles around his right ear with his finger to let her know Jack was not quite all there, just someone they tolerated.

"I changed my birth certificate," Jack explained. "I passed all the tests. I'm a couple of pounds underweight, but if I can gain them by Monday morning, they'll send me to K.C., and if I pass there, I can leave for boot camp right away." He liked saying "boot camp." And Avis looked truly interested.

"He ain't goin in no Navy," Glenn said. "Let's get some beers here." He turned to summon the waitress. "Beer, Avis?"

"I'll just have a Coke."

"Reet. Three beers for three engineers with the foam on the bottom," he instructed the waitress who had sauntered over from her station in the middle of the bar.

She shifted her gum back and forth between her jaws and banged her tray softly against her knee like a tambourine.

"What did you guys ever *engineer?*" she would have liked to know.

"Choo-choo you around the bend any day," Glenn cracked.

"Whooo! You and whose army?" the woman hooted.

Glenn made a move to run his hand up the back of her short black uniform and caught her tray on his knuckles hard enough to gong.

He shook his hand in merry but real pain and blew on the knuckles.

"Keep your hands off that, buster. That's special reserved stuff. And closed for the duration."

"That ain't what I hear," Glenn sneered.

"You hear with your patoot, curlylocks. When my guy comes back, he's going to know he's had a virgin for the duration."

"Yeah? In which ear?"

"Wise little bastard, ain't you? *I* wouldn't wanta be you punks when the boys all come home."

"When the boys all come home!" Glenn mocked, falling back against Buck in mock terror. "Save me!"

"There ain't no savin something like you." She turned abruptly away.

"Make them schooners," Glenn called.

"And a Coke, please," Jack added.

The waitress looked like Jack's Aunt Elfie. A small, compact, black-haired woman who drew on her eyebrows, strong and short of leg, a feisty, round little ass which she swung with a chin-up "Eat-your-heart-out-buster!" between booth and bar.

When the drinks were on the table, Avis took an aspirin box out of her purse and popped a couple of tiny pills into her mouth, chasing them with Coca-Cola. Glenn and Buck shot each other knowing glances.

"What was that?" Jack asked her.

"Dexedrine."

"What's that?"

"Keeps me up."

"How they make you feel, drunk?"

"Unh-unh. Just sort of high. Keeps you awake is all. Makes your heart kick faster. Feel."

She took his hand and placed it beneath her left breast on her small rib cage. The depending weight of her breast rested along the top of his hand. There was a rush of blood to his head. Her ribs felt small and fragile as a child's. Her hand holding his trembled as if a slight tremor, a nervous purr shook her entire body. Her heart pounded like a little engine about to burst. He had been pulled close enough to smell her hair and a faint lemony perfume.

"It's goin like hammers," he exclaimed.

"I don't like to get drunk," she said.

"Does it hurt you?" he wondered after she gave him his hand back. She shrugged.

"Can I try one?" he asked. Glenn and Buck looked shocked.

She looked at him carefully. "Why?"

"I'd just like to see what it feels like." He figured if it didn't kill her, it wouldn't kill him.

"Go ahead, give him one," Bucky encouraged.

She fished out the Bayer aspirin box and handed him a tiny pale-pink pill shaped like a toilet-wall drawing of a cunt—a rounded-off triangle with a crease across its heart. He popped it in his mouth.

"Pussies pop pills," Glenn reminded him. Men drank.

He chased it with beer and waited to feel something. They all stared at him. He didn't feel any different.

"You don't feel anything right away," Avis explained. "They really aren't anything."

"What about this old fart you cooled?" Buck asked, having lost interest in Jack's experiment with dope.

"Man! I chilled him. He could be dead. I mean, I really pasted that old cock." He kept cutting glances to see the effect of his words on Avis. She wasn't listening.

"Do you dance?" she asked Jack.

"Not very well."

"Well, dance with me."

Jack found himself standing up with every intention of dancing with the girl of Gus Depolis in the Red Ball Inn. Glenn was a great dancer, could really jitterbug. Buck was OK. Jack had never learned.

Avis' hand was small and warm in his own. She seemed warmer to the touch than anyone he could think of.

"Catch this." Glenn jogged Buck with an elbow. "The sausage is goin to dance."

They wouldn't have been caught dead dancing with Gus' girl. Avis led him onto the small rosined dance floor and fit herself against him so perfectly it made his head swim. There was no sort of tug-of-war and bumped feet as with other girls.

"Don't hold me so loose. I won't break," she explained. "What do you have in your pocket?"

"Ah, uh baseball."

She leaned back to look at him. Her pelvis and belly were more noticeably against him. She smiled, almost biting her lower lip. Her eyes shone with a film of water. She looked happy for the first time since she was in sixth grade and Jack was in third. He smiled back and blushed. She laughed lightly and in touching her cheek against his gave him a small gentle kiss under his right ear. He could feel her sooty black eyelashes brush his cheek.

He stepped on her toe; not heavily, more just a bump, he danced carefully, quick to keep his feet off those of his partner.

"I'm sorry!" he said quickly.

She tightened her arm over his shoulders in a little hug to let him know it was OK.

"Glenn's a real good dancer," he offered.

"Shhh." She sang along with the music. Her voice was good. He thought it was better than the woman's on the record.

"You could be a real big-time singer," he complimented her. She shook her curls that she could not.

"Did you really go to Hollywood and make a movie?"

"If you blinked, you missed me. Mom thought I would be the new Gloria Jean."

"You're better and prettier than her," he assured her very seriously.

She said, "You're sweet."

"I *mean* it. You're *beautiful*!" he insisted.

She laughed and gave him a hug. "Say beautiful again."

He said, "Beautiful."

"You say *be*-yoo-tee-ful."

He didn't know what was wrong with that.

"I love it," she said.

When the song was over, he was ready to go back to the booth. She held his hand and waited for the next record. It was Count Basie's "One O'Clock Jump." He couldn't jitterbug.

"Just do what I do," she told him.

He stared at her feet and tried to ape her movement, always at least a beat behind, until he felt so tied in knots and stupid he could hardly move at all. He knew Glenn and Bucky were breaking up in the booth.

"Let yourself go. Do *anything*." She smiled, grabbing both his hands and swinging him from side to side. "Let go."

He felt suddenly very good about it. Hell, it didn't matter what anyone else thought. Dancing with Avis was fun. There wasn't a prettier girl in the place. She wasn't embarrassed for him. He started shaking from the shoulders down, letting his feet go, his dusty cowboy boots slapping the boards, coming down on his heels, sliding around on his toes, jigging, jiving.

"That's it!" She laughed, flinging herself back to the full extension of her arm, her head thrown back, curls dancing. She trucked back toward him, chin lowered, looking into his eyes, her knees splayed, pelvis swinging between her hips. He threw her out again, yanked her back against him, did a couple of bops together, spun her away, jumped up off both feet and spun her underneath the bridge of his arm, doubled her arm behind her back when he came down and spun her in the opposite direction. Her skirt had worked halfway up her thighs.

73

"Lookit the sausage go!" he heard Glenn call.

People had made a little space for them in the middle of the floor. He knew he wasn't doing it right, but Avis could make anyone look good. She locked him into her with her eyes so he could tell pretty well what to do next. When he misread, she covered for him immediately. Once when he flung her out and her hand slipped from his, she made it look as if it were intentional. Trucking back toward him, forefingers pointed toward her heels, shaking her juicy boobs, she winked at him.

He loved her.

For a finish they caught hands, went under the bridge together and then back, and she jumped astraddle of him, her skirt sliding so high he could see her white panties. His baseball jumped out and bounced across the floor. He heaved her away, and she landed on the floor and slid into a perfect split. He yanked her up, and she fell into his arms, kicking up her right heel, laughing. He laughed too.

"Man, I was sooo bad." He laughed.

"You were *be*-yoo-tee-ful."

He heard a tall blond guy with a wave-set duck's ass pomp explain to his chick in a skirt, light sweater and bobby socks, "That's Gus Depolis' girl."

Jack was puffed by the quiet awe in the guy's voice.

"Hey, fireballer. Think you dropped this." An old air-crafter with badge and tool chits on a ring on his belt called to him and tossed him his baseball the way someone does who hasn't thrown a ball in a long time.

Jack snagged it in the air with his left hand without taking his right from Avis' slender waist.

"Thanks." He tipped it at the man and stuffed the ball in his pocket. He wiped his forehead with his hand and said, "I need a beer!"

Avis fanned herself daintily with her hand and blew her breath up over her face.

"Don't ever let anyone tell you you can't dance again." She smiled.

"Aw, it was you. I couldn't of done anything with anyone else."

They held hands all the way back to the booth.

"I never seen anything like that," Glenn squeaked. He and Bucky were curled in the booth with laughter. "You dance like Gene the Spastic screws," he told Jack.

"Give him another of those pills and he'll fly," Bucky put in.

"—An when that fuckin ball jumped out of his pocket—man, I could of *died*!" Glenn was lying virtually on his back, kicking his feet in the air. "Never saw anything so goddamned funny!"

Jack drained his schooner of beer. "How about another round here, Bea?" he called to the woman at the bar.

"And a Coke?" she asked.

Avis shook her head no.

When the music started again, Glenn stood up and said, "Come on, if you really want to dance."

"No, thanks. I've got to be going soon." Avis looked at her watch.

To cover his rejection, Glenn hitched up his Levi's and said, "Think I'll shake a little dew off the lily then." He turned toward the door beyond the dance floor marked HIS. Next to it was a door marked HERS and then one marked OURS which led to the storeroom. A hand-lettered poster was taped to the door:

LIVE BAND
NEXT FRI. & SAT.
NITE
JELLY (RED) HASKELL
and his
SWINGSHIFTERS
($2 cover)

Jelly (Red), eyes of blue, tomorrow never comes, and I love you. He smiled over his schooner at Avis. On the seat between them she squeezed his hand.

"You waitin for Gus?" Bucky asked, pointedly.

"Two hours ago, maybe I *was* waiting for Gus. It is rather a habit, you know. I'm not waiting for him anymore . . . ever."

Bucky knew better. He grinned and lowered his eyes like a wise cat. She was *Gus'* cunt. It could have been a city ordinance. It never worked the other way around unless some guy went pussy himself over some cunt. Gus would tell her where to put her chair. He picked up her gold cigarette lighter—a gift from Gus—and rolled it meaningfully up and down his palm.

75

When Glenn returned to the booth, Avis checked her watch again. It was past one.

"I've got to be going," she announced. She dropped a pack of Philip Morris into her purse and took her lighter from Bucky.

"I'm goin, too," Jack blurted. "Can I see you home?"

She shrugged. "If you want to."

"You don't know what you're doin, boy," Glenn warned very seriously.

Jack just grinned. He told himself he was just doing Gus a favor—seeing his girl home at one in the morning. Anyone with any decency would do the same. He honestly did not dare consider he had any other motive. By the time they were on their feet he was convinced Gus would not only understand, but would thank him, if it ever came to that.

"What you want us to tell Gus if he comes lookin for you?" Bucky asked.

"Tell him I joined the Navy," Avis said.

"See you guys," Jack offered.

"Umm," Glenn grunted. He and Buck already had their heads together.

At the door Jack heard Glenn's braying laugh.

It didn't matter. He had never felt so sure of himself. He wasn't afraid of Glenn, Bucky or Gus Depolis. He wasn't afraid of falling into the hands of the Japs. Outside, he did a little jitterbug step, half swinging Avis away on the sidewalk. The locusts crunched under his boots. Avis did not share his fun. Now she seemed worried.

"You don't really have to do this, you know. I can get home alone."

"Wouldn't think of it," he mouthed a line from some movie.

"I'm going to stay at my mother's," she said. "It's clear across town."

"I'll get us a cab." He turned to search the empty street for a taxi. A Black and White sped across Water Street. His whistle did not catch it.

"Let's walk awhile," Avis suggested. She linked her arm in his. She seemed happier then.

She was a funny one all right.

"Penny for your thoughts," he offered.

She shook her head and smiled.

"How old are you really?" she asked.

"Sixteen," he lied. "How old are you?"

"Nineteen."

"Gee, you seem older."

"Oh, *thanks*!"

"I didn't mean it like that. I didn't mean you *looked* older or anything. I just meant you, uh. . . ."

"Been around, right?"

"Well, no. . . ."

"But you've heard things, right?"

"Aw, nothin, you know. Just. . . ."

"What?"

"Stuff. Nothin."

"What kind of stuff?"

"Well, everyone talks about when you went out to Hollywood. I don't know. I can't think of nothin special. It's just like everyone knows some big secret. I don't know." He couldn't honestly think of any specific thing anyone *had* said, except that she was a nymphomaniac. He wasn't sure exactly what that meant. It was like she had some sickness. And they said she took dope. He realized she honestly didn't know what everyone said about her. She was still the mysterious, beautiful little girl in sixth grade who could tap and sing and had a talking crow.

"What happened to your crow?" he suddenly wondered.

She laughed. "He's a star. They gave us a thousand dollars for him in Hollywood."

"Wow! No shit?" He thought what he could do with a thousand bucks. It seemed a fortune.

"Mom bought us fur jackets and we came back on the Super Chief," Avis explained.

He was disappointed. What anyone wanted with a fur jacket in Kansas was beyond him. He would have bought a car and driven back.

"I was only just fifteen when we went out. You see those movies with sweet Judy Garland and all that. You think those are just apple-pie kids, don't you? Well, believe me, they aren't. And the producers, directors and agents—you wouldn't believe those old lechers with their saggy tans. They don't respect nothing. Least of all talent." She shuddered. "Oh, I guess they do recognize *real* talent. They wanted Blackie."

That her crow had been sold for a couple of fur jackets

77

and a ticket on the Super Chief saddened him. "That was a damned smart crow," he remembered.

"It was Mom. I didn't want to sell him. But we were broke and needed the money. And by then it really didn't matter." She shuddered again. "Let's talk about something else. Why do you want to go into the Navy?"

They had turned onto Douglass. If Gus came cruising by in his car, there was no way he would miss them. It was almost two miles to where her mother lived near the canal. He was very conscious of her arm linked in his. He had shortened his stride to match hers. They walked in time with each other. Now and then her hip bumped him lightly. Her breast squashed softly against his arm.

"I wanted to go in the Marines. I was too light. And they aren't taking many guys now anyway. So, I tried the Navy and passed."

"But why?"

"Oh, you mean— Well, I don't like being poor all the time." He had never had to explain it before. Still, for some reason, he knew he could tell the girl anything. "I gotta live in a goddamned crappy old trailer house with my grandpa and grandma in niggertown. My mom and stepdad are always gettin in jail, gypsyin from one place to another. I can't live like that, an I can't live like grandpa and grandma. Glenn and Bucky always talk about hittin some punchboards or knockin over some gas station—shit, I stole more stuff for my stepdad to hock when I was nine and ten than they'll ever get with a gun. Buck's got this German Luger. I just feel like I got to *do* somethin. I don't know how to explain it. I just feel like if I don't get out of here now, I'm really goin to go nuts or somethin real bad is goin to happen. I wanta get in on the war. I don't know why, I guess."

"I know," she said. "I think we are a lot alike."

That pleased him.

"I've seriously thought about joining the WAVES. Maybe I could make a new start. I could be a nurse or something. Maybe they would even let me entertain. I've thought about it. Maybe I'll do it."

"Yeow! That'd be great. Maybe we'd meet up someplace. Be all sharp in our uniforms." It was a scene from a movie. "Boy, I'd like that." And he would sail away at dawn for some secret place he couldn't tell her about. But she would know it was dangerous. The Big Push. She would cry. They would kiss. She would wait for him. In his locker on his tin can or PT boat would be her picture.

She smiled at him. "When is your birthday?" she asked suddenly.

"May twenty-fourth. Why?"

"*You're kidding!*" she cried, stopping in the middle of the street they were crossing.

"No I'm not."

"*So's mine!*"

He hadn't known that. "Well! I never met anyone with my same birthday."

"I haven't either! It's *fantastic!*" She threw both arms around his neck and hugged him tight against her. Then she leaned back and looked at him. He was grinning like a fool. Her eyes shone. "Oh, I'm so *happy!*" She squealed and hugged him again. "We're cosmic twins."

He didn't know what that meant. But he knew he didn't want to feel like her brother.

"That's why we both have such unhappy lives," she explained as they walked on. She clung to his arm with both hands. "We're Geminis."

That was it. "Oh, my mom always reads them horoscope magazines," he admitted. "She always said my life would be hard but that I could triumph er somethin. I never paid much attention. But I felt like she thought I wasn't quite like everyone else. You know. Always said I was *special.*" He sneered at the assumption.

"That's it. We have dual personalities. I even have two names. One for each."

"I don't want to be special," he said.

"Well, you can't help it. I think it's great! And I'm so happy. Things like this always happen to Geminis, you know. I mean, why you? But here we are. And against astronomical odds."

"Um. But I don't want to think about you like no sister," he blurted.

She laughed and stopped again. She grinned crookedly. "How do you want to think of me?"

He looked into her gently quizzical, faintly mocking eyes. "Well, like a girlfriend or somethin," he mumbled.

"You're sweet." She gave him a chaste kiss. Her lips were so soft. Her mouth looked small. Yet when she kissed him, her lips seemed full.

Locusts, moths and June bugs crashed insanely into the

streetlights. In the doorway of a small shop with a FOR RENT sign taped to the torn brown paper mask behind its windows he spotted a green Lucky Strike pack, wadded and discarded—how long ago? He wondered at seeing it there.

Lucky Strike Green Has Gone to War.

The place at various times had been a hopeful diner, a barbershop and the draped trap of two gypsy women who called to men from just inside offering to tell their fortunes but seeming to promise so much more. Sometimes there had been a grubby little gypsy baby playing on the linoleum. One of the women had been very young and pretty, one older.

Though he had been tempted, he had never had guts enough to step inside when one or the other beckoned with a meaningful jerk of her head toward the curtained back, mumbling something that he thought was more than an invitation to have his palm read. And Glenn had told him it would cost him at least five bucks.

"What was your mother?" Avis asked.

"A waitress mostly. Sometimes she worked in a drugstore. She liked to say she was a 'cosmetician.' Sometimes she was a whore."

"Really?"

"Yeah. She really did."

She shrugged to let him know that news didn't faze her in the least. "What's a whore anyway?" she asked. "All those little virgins getting married who think their ass is pure gold, they're just married whores. Selling it for a ring and rose-colored promises."

He had always sort of felt that way himself but never actually said it. He liked Avis. There was more to her than anyone thought.

"No, I meant what was your mother's sign."

"Oh, you mean on the horoscope. I don't know what you call it. It was the one with the scales."

"Libra. That's a very good sign. Is she beautiful?"

"Well, yeow, she's pretty. She was prettier, but got her nose sorta broken. But she's not as pretty as you."

"Do you love her very much?"

Her questions made him itchy. "I guess so."

"I'm sure you do. You are just embarrassed to say so, aren't you?"

"Well, I know in spite of everything, she did the best

for me she could. And I don't blame her for nothin! You know?"

"That's how I feel about my mother. But she's a Capricorn and very mercenary, very self-centered. I'm sure I'd like your mother better. It's really incredible. I feel like we are related from way back before the earth was born." She hugged his arm. "My cosmic other half."

Whatever that was, if it kept her left tit squashed against him like that, he was for it.

"Hey, you know what?" she asked. "I'm starving." A block away a White Castle was lit up on the corner. When they got there, he pushed open the door and handed her inside. He could feel the warm deep gully of her spine beneath his hand. He saw her again on the auditorium stage of Washington Elementary doing backbends in the red spangled suit she wore to tap, twirling her top hat on the end of her cane. Blackie, her crow, cawing from his perch onstage, "Pretty girl. Pretty girl. Bravo! Bravo!"

He loved her the way he loved the woman's voice in his head.

He waited until she ordered a hamburger, "No onions, please," then did the same. They had orange juice and afterward big hot mugs of White Castle coffee. She took hers black. He used cream and sugar. With her coffee she opened her purse, took out the aspirin box and popped another pill into her mouth. She did not offer him one. When she took the pill, a sort of illicit furtiveness blanked her face, a bit apologetic, yet totally defiant, as if no power on earth could stop her. He felt witness to a rite so personal he really oughtn't to watch. Neither commented on it.

The counterman, a thin red-haired young man, his face pocked and freckled beneath his paper White Castle cap, gave Jack his change, but his eyes were all for Avis. Jack figured he was working his way through some course or other. A 4-F if there ever was one. He had glanced at them from time to time as they ate.

"Say, ain't you Avis Nickel?" he blurted. "I went to Roosevelt with you. Eldon Green."

"Oh, sure," she acknowledged, not really remembering him.

"Yeah. You're in the movies er something, ain't you? Changed your name. You back for a visit?"

"Something like that."

"Well, it's sure good to see you."

81

"Nice to see you."

They escaped outside. Jack realized again he was in the company of a celebrity. It made him feel dizzy with a pleasure that left him nervous with longings he dared not define. He was just seeing her home, but he did not want the walk ever to end.

He had never felt so intimately alone with a real girl, a beautiful girl who was not some sniveling, adenoidal adolescent like Vanda Hardasty or her friends. Avis Nickel-Jean Porter was Big Time. Ever since the garbage on the bridge with Glenn and the old couple he had felt increasingly alien in his own hometown, no more truly with it and of it than were his mother and stepfather, a transient, a drifter, but with a paper in his pocket to Join the Navy and See the World. When he returned, it would be on different terms. He wouldn't have to take anybody's shit. All loyalties and local frustrations were finally canceled out. He just wished he could explain it to Avis, help her get out.

"Will you write to me?" he asked.

"What? Oh, sure."

"When I'm out there, I'd like to get letters from you."

She laughed. "OK. I'll write."

"And send me a pinup picture?"

"To my darling . . . you know what? I don't even know your name."

He was shocked. "Jack!"

"I'm sorry." She hugged his arm and kissed his cheek. "I'm awful about names."

He was hurt.

"I'll send you my very favorite photo," she promised. "And you can be sure I'll never forget the only person I've ever met who has the same birthday as me."

He felt better.

They were only a couple of blocks from her mother's house. At the canal he blurted, "Glenn said you used to go down the canal bank with a lot of guys. Did you?"

"I don't know," she said flatly. "Everything seems so long ago."

"Glenn said you were the first girl he ever did it with."

"I don't remember, really."

The idea that Glenn had put his cock in her infuriated him. He wanted to know. "How many?"

"What?"

"Guys?" he squeaked.

"Oh, hell, I don't know. Why are you acting like this?"

"I don't know," he cried. "I just feel—I want—" The thought of Glenn, all those faceless other guys—it gave him a headache. "Will you with me?" he mumbled.

"What?" She hadn't quite heard.

"Go down the canal bank with me? . . . Please, Avis . . . Jean?"

She stopped, placing her fingers lightly on his lips. "Baby, baby," she said sadly. "You don't want that."

"Yes, I do," he insisted. "I want you. I love you."

"Shhh. Don't love me. Don't spoil everything."

"I *do*! I have ever since I was in third grade. How could that spoil anything? Remember? I gave you all my Valentines. . . . You was in sixth. You kissed me and all the kids made fun."

"Please . . . Jack . . . listen. . . ."

He grabbed her and tried to kiss her, roughly, awkwardly. She turned her face away.

"Don't you even want to kiss me?" he asked, choking.

"Sit down. Let's have a cigarette."

She sat down on the curbing. He spread his windbreaker for her to sit on. She sat on the baseball in his pocket, laughed and shifted to one side. There were no sidewalks along that street. The lawns went up to small bungalows perched above tiny terraced lawns. The houses were all dark. They sat in the shadow cast by a big elm. A flower bed nodded behind them. There was always a breeze along the canal. Leaf-dappled moonlight played across Avis' face. He found a bent packet of matches in his pocket and lit her Philip Morris. He had taken a proffered cigarette, though he did not inhale. She blew out a long flume of smoke.

He grabbed her left shoulder with his right hand and tried to kiss her again. She quickly put her left hand on his chest to hold him off as he forced her backward.

"Wait a minute, lover, listen. . . ."

"I just want to *kiss* you," he argued.

"And then what?"

"I don't know. I just want to. Please, Avis, let me." He sneaked up on her left tit. It was so big for such a small girl.

"Don't. . . ." Her face looked pained.

"Why? I *want* to. You let everybody else—" He hadn't meant to say that. "I don't mean that," he apologized.

"It's just, I . . . I want to, Avis . . . Jean. Let me. . . . Just a kiss. . . ." He hadn't let go of her breast. She had quit trying to take away his hand. He unbuttoned the top of her dress, fingers shaking. She did not stop him.

"I wish you wouldn't," she said.

He dug under the top of the brassiere, pulling and kneading her warm, flaccid flesh. He tugged her bra up over her left breast and dropped his face into the spreading, elusive pillow, finding the small nipple.

"Just be sweet," she said, laying her hand on the back of his head, fingering the long hair at the back of his neck.

For some reason, it suddenly crossed his mind that maybe she had the clap or something. Maybe that was her big secret. Still he did not care. He had a rubber in his wallet.

"I don't want to be sweet," he said. He tried to get as much of her breast in his mouth as possible.

"Ow!" she cried.

"Sorry," he apologized. "They're so big when you're so small."

"Have you had a lot of girls?" she asked.

"Some."

"How many?" she asked, stroking the back of his head.

"Uh . . . well . . . two . . . three."

She smiled and raised his head to her shoulder. The perfume at the juncture of her neck and in her hair was like fresh lemons and flowers. Their cigarettes were two bug's eyes in the grass.

"Who was the first?" she asked.

"My mother," he confessed honestly, softly in her hair. It hadn't occurred to him to lie to her. She was the only one he ever told. He held his breath in silence. She seemed to have quit breathing. He became afraid he had spoiled everything. He raised up to look at her, ready for her to say something horrible and hurting.

She asked, "Is that true?"

"Yes," he said, eyes closed tight.

Then her arms were around his neck. He was pulled down swimming in a kiss that had no definable dimension. He felt a smear of come inside his shorts against his leg. He quickly shifted his right hand from her breast to between her legs, going straight for her sex. Even through her white cotton panties he could feel it was wet. He worked his fingers under the tight leg opening of her pant-

84

ies and between the deep, clinging lips. God! She felt hot in there, like a furnace.

"If you do that, I can't stop you," she breathed against his lips. Her eyes had rolled back under the lids until only half the dark violet pupil showed. She opened her legs a bit, lifted her bottom and drew his fingers inside her. Heavy, clinging flesh. How could so slender a girl be like that? Her arms were tight around him, almost hurting him. She fucked his fingers, rolling her ass, thrusting, squirming, twisting, all so strongly.

"Can I take off your pants?" he asked.

She did not answer.

"Can I?"

"Tell me about your mother," she insisted. It seemed important to her.

He was afraid. He didn't want to talk about it. "You think I did somethin really bad, don't you?" His voice was thinned and strained. He did not understand her interest. He was afraid she was going to leap up and damn him.

Yet his fingers were still in her. She continued to move deliciously around his fingers.

"No. Please. Tell me."

"It just sort of happened. The old man was always in jail. We almost always only had one bed. It began when I was little. Just messin around. She sorta let me. I don't know why. When I was little, she let me suck her boobs. Said it felt nice. Then once, later, when she was sleepin or playin asleep, I just put it in her . . . once. It went in easy . . . you know?"

"Um."

"Then, a couple of times when I was bigger, I guess she actually let me do it. She was doin it with all them other guys for dough. I just wanted to, and she let me. But she always acted like it was a big mistake . . . like she didn't know what she was doin. I don't know, it almost don't seem real now. I don't know. She always looked so pretty to me. She was around with her clothes off or dressin or undressin all the time. . . ."

"But how *was* it? What did it *feel* like?"

"OK. . . . I don't know. Not like this. She didn't feel like you. She never hardly moved. . . ."

She pulled his head down and kissed him, running her tongue deep into his mouth, doing with her tongue in his mouth what he was doing with his fingers.

"Take off your pants," he again asked.

She shook her head. "Unh-unh."

"Why?"

She did not answer but kissed him again. "My little boy," she crooned.

He removed his fingers from her. Her sex seemed to hang onto them to the very end. When he had gone, she gave a small sigh of disappointment. He reached up and grasped the waistband of her panties.

"Don't," she said, dreamily.

What the hell? "Yes. I'm going to," he insisted, tugging at the soft cotton cloth. He had been surprised she wore simple white cotton panties. He had expected something sexy.

"Raise up a little or I'll tear them," he warned.

She tried to draw him over her.

"I'll tear them off . . ." he warned again. Threads popped.

She lifted herself slightly. "I wish you wouldn't."

He got her pants over her left hip. Then he knelt in the gutter and tugged them with both hands underneath her lifted rump, down over her slender legs. Her bare belly and fine dark bush were raised to the moonlight. He worked her panties carefully over the low-heeled shoes she wore for working.

Her eyes were closed as if she were sleeping, but she opened her legs that he might kneel between. Kneeling on the dusty leaves in the gutter, he unbuckled his belt, pulled down his pants and underwear. He wanted to feel his belly against hers. Feel everything. He fumbled out his wallet and with his forefinger fished up the single condom he had carried so long there was a ring imprinted in leather of the stamp pocket in which it had been hidden. The foil was crinkled and tattered. He had never used a rubber. He had put them on before, had even jerked off in one to see what it would feel like. Hands shaking, he started to roll it on. A thin blaze of the fluid that came before but which was not come glistened and plastered the fair hairs on his thigh. The place felt cool in the night air.

She lifted her head and asked, "What are you doing?"

"I don't want to give you a baby," he explained.

She grabbed his cock and snatched the rubber away. "I don't like that. I can't have a baby." Then she held him, lifted herself and rubbed the head of his cock along the heavy wet lips of her sex, exciting herself again.

"Like that?" she smiled.

"Um!"

"My little boy. Come here. Kiss me." She guided him into her, rising and twisting as it went into her. He felt a foot long.

He was in Avis Nickel—Jean Porter. Either way, he was IN HER! It was wonderful. She kissed him, moving, twisting, turning, making sounds that excited him even more. Her small fingers clawed his back, grabbed and raked his bottom, holding him tight against her, straining upward to grind against him. He was amazed at her strength. He was constantly amazed at how strong women were. They looked as if they hadn't muscle-one. Then she released him to slide to the very end of his sex, seeming to hold it just by the end by some kind of suction, then drew him deliciously back into her. He moved and moved, feeling himself coming. She became a frenzy. He felt himself squirting deep inside her, only then the heat of his sex matching the warmth that surrounded him.

"Ummmm," she crooned in his mouth.

Unlike jerking off, unlike the times he thought he had fucked before, it was not over. She continued to move slowly again, marvelously, deeply, lingeringly, shallowly, around and around, in and out. He stayed as hard as he had begun. His heart pounded as hard as did her own. He learned to move in a complementary way with her as they had when dancing. He felt in all his life there might never again be another like Avis . . . Jean?

"I love you," he pledged beyond all he had meant when he had given her his Valentines, and all he had said before, kissing her with a hunger he had never known, a delight so excruciating death would have been blessing, though he did not, by any means, want to die.

She laughed happily beside his head, kissed his cheek, nibbled his ear.

"Does it feel so good to you, too?" he wanted to know.

"Ummm," she buzzed. "My cosmic brother. My eternal twin."

"Avis?"

But she had gone somewhere beyond her eyes. She began to move wildly again. He clutched her twisting bottom to which bits of grass clung.

She wrapped both legs around him and began bucking like a horse. Her face looked a sprinter's. Her eyes were open wide, staring into his own so he could see her as a little girl, a baby, everything she had been and become. It was like looking too long beyond a star in a summer night's sky. Neither blinked. The stare was more profound than any kiss.

"Are you goin to come?" he asked.

"Yes. *Yes!*"

"Me too . . . AVIS!"

Her mouth opened wide in what looked like a silent scream. A tiny vein in her beautiful forehead stood out like a small worm beneath her skin. Then she closed her eyes and smiled, arching herself upward deliciously, clamping his head between her upraised, straining arms, winding them around his shaggy head like snakes, pulling him down into a kiss that felt like sinking.

He came and came and came again. Going blind, the night a kaleidoscope of carnival colors. Still she moved beneath him, drawing on his penis with every heartbeat. It seemed their hearts beat in time.

It was true! he thought. Her cunt *sucked!* It was amazing. He only hated that somehow it had become such common knowledge, the stuff of pool hall jokes and asshole humor. He wanted her forever only his own. Then, as suddenly, he worried maybe she did have something. What if he got the clap and couldn't get into the Navy? There *had* been sharp, tiny pains in his balls the second time he had come. They felt very tender. She had reached down and was gently fondling him.

"Avis?"

"Um?" She smoothed his face with her other hand, giving him little kisses. He still hadn't gone soft in her.

"You ain't never had VD, have you?"

"*What?*" She let go of his balls. She squirmed to get from beneath him, even while her sex continued to squeeze him with a will of its own.

"I just *asked!*" he assured her. "Me neither."

"What the hell do you think I *am?* Get *off!*"

"No. I'm sorry. I love you. I didn't mean nothin. *Honest!*" He resisted her efforts to get free. "Avis. Cut it out! I said I'm sorry. I didn't know. I was just afraid."

"*Get off me, you motherfucker!*"

"AVIS!" Tears filled his eyes. He moved in her, trying to take her mind off what he had said. "I *love* you!" he insisted. "I'll prove it. Avis? I'll marry you. We can go to Arkansas. Avis? Please, don't go away. Say somethin!"

"Will you *please* get off me?"

"No. I don't want to ... ever. I love you. We're twins, like you said, remember. I can't help it if I'm stupid. I don't know anything. Just listen. I love you."

"Stop loving me," she commanded. "No!"

He continued to move in her, and she began to quit trying to get away. He was aware of their come, dried and cool on their bellies, stiffening their hairs. "I don't ever want to be out of you." She stopped struggling.

"I thought you were something very special," she said sadly. "Aren't you finished? I'd like a cigarette."

"I want to *be* somethin special ... for you. I never wanted to before. Now I do. I love you. I really do." He tried to kiss her. Presently, she reluctantly gave him her lips.

She moved with him again, sulkily at first, but he sensed it was all right, she wasn't too mad at him anymore. He wondered if he could do it again. His balls ached.

She looked at him quizzically. Then she half smiled.

He could. He could!

They heard the car at the same time. The sound purred through the moment. He became intensely aware that they were at the foot of someone's yard, fucking in a gutter, wide open, practically in the street, his bare ass shining like a moon. He turned his head and saw the tail of Gus' metallic blue Packard roadster cruise slowly beneath the light hanging over the treelined intersection at the corner, sliding into the tunnel of elms toward Avis' house, two houses from the corner. She saw it too. He was out of her. It was over, and he felt that an important part of him had been neatly, painlessly extracted to go with her forever. Not cock. Something more personal than cock. It might have all been a dream. How to hold her? How to keep her for himself? His brain spun.

"He didn't see," he assured her. "We're a good two blocks away. Don't go, Avis."

She was getting herself together fast. Her panties went on so adroitly it seemed an affront to everything he felt, was trying to say. Was that all there was going to be?

"You don't have to go," he said, reluctantly buckling his belt, kneeling on the curb. If they could go somewhere before Gus got done checking her house. "We could go down the canal bank," he virtually begged.

She knelt on her knees on the lawn, brushing her clothes, picking bits of grass from her hair.

"See anything?" She offered herself for inspection.

"You're OK," he said gloomily.

She shook herself. Gave him a quick kiss.

"Can I see you again?" he wanted to know.

"Um. We'll see."

He tried to hold her, wrapping both arms around her waist.

She gently removed his arms, glancing both ways up the street. "Really, I must go. Call me." She slipped away.

"Will you write to me?"

"*Call* me," she told him in a loud whisper. Then she was across the street, trotting on her beautiful legs beside a dark board fence. At the corner she touched her hair with both hands and slowed to a walk.

When she had gone, he could not believe he had actually fucked her. Avis Nickel or Jean Porter, she was Gus' girl. He turned down and walked along the canal bank.

8

BETWEEN dream which was sweet as truth and memory marked by doubt, wakefulness hovered. Then he opened his eyes, grasped his cock and balls in both hands and realized only: *Man, I fucked her.*

His grandmother would be coming home from church soon. He had wanted to get up early and go with her. It would have given him a good chance to talk to her under conditions in which she would have been most agreeable. He sat on the edge of the daybed, staring at his naked feet on the scuffed linoleum. He thought of trying to call Avis Nickel. He tugged the phone book from under the telephone on the radio at the foot of his bed. The relief let his grandmother have the phone in the hope it would bring her employment. It was, however, a four-party line. They shared the line with three black families. He flipped through the directory to the *N*'s and located Avis' mother's number. He turned down the page. He looked under *D* for Gus Depolis with whom Avis lived. There was no listing. He replaced the book under the phone and flicked on the radio.

The old man in his work pants, BVD top and house slippers, was outside in his chair under the widow's weeping willow, reading the Sunday *Eagle*. Jack pissed in the little trailer sink and dipped water from the bucket next to it to flush down the yellow stain. He held his dick in his hand for a moment, studying it, recalling once more the clinging, hot cunt of Avis Nickel.

Boy, that had really been something. Something so much his own he would never tell Glenn or Bucky about it. That so curious a little hose could extract such feelings, such improbable delight from being inside a woman's body was a wonder to him of cosmic proportions.

He returned his pajawonk tenderly to the pouch of his jockeys, and moved across the floor throwing a left and right hook at the vision of a tall, ducked-ass Greek. Bang-bang!

She-it!

He rolled up his bedding and stowed it in one of the big drawers underneath the bed. His old Levi's felt cool, soft, familiar as he drew them on over his legs. Any other trousers were just a pair of pants, but Levi's became something altogether your own. They never felt better than they did first thing in the morning.

Barefoot and shirtless, he took half a pound of bacon from the dinky old icebox. In the winter they didn't take ice, keeping milk and stuff outside a window in a crate. There was coffee in the chipped enamel pot on the three-burner gas plate. He lit a low fire under it, and a cockroach scuttled away.

"Goddamn things!" he swore aloud. Barefoot, he watched the bastard speed under his bed. "Cocksucking sonofabitches are smart," he mumbled. Them and little old ladies like his grandma would inherit the earth, he was certain. How many old farts like his grandpa did you see around? he argued, throwing the bacon into an iron skillet older than most people alive on the face of the earth. It had been his grandmother's mother's. It was the only thing she had left from her "trusseau" as she put it. She had

91

taken it on the trail when her husband had been a "cattleman." She had fried mush in it over a fire of cow and buffalo chips out in western Kansas in a sod house when the old man got out of cattle and went to homesteading. If all the poor-do gravy that had been stirred up in that iron pan was poured end to end, the stream would rival the Big and Little Arkansas rivers.

He forked the overdone bacon from the pan directly to waiting slices of "day-old" Bond bread, which was the bread the trucks brought back unsold from the stores and Bond retailed at half price at their bakery. The grease seeped into the bread, softening it. He broke two brown eggs into the hot grease in the pan. They bubbled wildly and spat fat. Blue smoke rose from the pan and fogged the trailer. His grandmother always said he cooked over too high a fire. But he liked his eggs french-fried. The edges quickly became crisp brown lace. He flopped them and saw the golden yolk peeping through the brown. In a minute they were done. He gave two more slices of bread a second or so on top the eggs, then lifted the lot with a spatula onto the waiting other halves of his sandwiches. Carrying the plate to the table, he placed it on the oilcloth where a bottle of milk waited beside a tall jelly glass with a picture of Pluto on roller skates on it. He pulled out one of the two folding chairs and sat down to breakfast. He shook the bottle of milk vigorously to get all the cruddy curds mixed up and poured himself a glassful. Into the milk he dropped two heaping spoons of Bosco and stirred the mixture until almost all of it, except for a few chocolate trails at the bottom of the glass, had become chocolate milk. He couldn't drink the shit without Bosco in it. He ate his breakfast quickly, watching the sunlight play through the thin clouds of smoke wafting through the trailer. He wondered what kind of food he would get in the Navy. It was a considerable concern. He doubted there would be bacon and egg sandwiches, real hamburgers, Bosco, chili, hot tamales. Would there be enough bananas to sustain him? If he didn't have a couple of bananas a day, he was certain he would perish.

Well, there was a war on. He guessed if thirteen million strong could take it, so could he. And full of sandwiches and Bosco, he belched acid bacon grease. The fear of starvation passed.

He heard or sensed the approach of his grandmother

and saw her in his mind's eye huffing up the alley, silently chewing over old or new grievances, mentally rummaging the icebox and cupboard for Sunday dinner.

"Law! I hain't the slightest notion what we can have for dinner," she announced, hopping inside the trailer. In her left hand was her New Testament and an oft-mended pair of white gloves which had gotten washed with a pair of red socks and were now more pink than white. "Here's the church paper if you want to look at it. Guess you don't care about what them who went to Sunday school with you are doin no more, though. Boyd Box's killed in the war. You might like to know. They announced it at church this morning."

Boyd Box's old man and older brother were deacons. They owned a drugstore. Boyd was a pharmacist's mate in the Navy. How the hell could a penis machinest get killed? The war was getting rough.

"It was on one of them islands—Tin—somethin or other."

"Tinian?"

"That sounds right."

"Must of been a corpsman with the Marines." Jack was impressed. Boyd had always been such a candyass sort of punk—boy scout and all that.

"Boyd was always very nice to me. Always made a point of comin up after church, and if it was rainin or snowin, many's the time he offered to drive me home," she remembered.

"Ummm." Boyd was an asshole with the airs of a shoe salesman with sore feet. Smiley, like a cat eating shit. Always washing his fat, pale hands together while he talked to you. Fingers and cock were useless on the boy. A third stringer in every way. A drudge. What right did *he* have getting himself killed on Tinian? Hero's ass.

"Grandma, I joined the Navy."

"How's that?" She was unpinning the hat that always made him think of flat, broken cake. Even the artificial flowers looked dead. Her stockings were different shades. They had come from the Hootens. She had to turn the toes way under to wear them. The Hooten women were tall. Her hem dipped unevenly, her upper arms hung down like wattles, and seeping eczema inflamed her ankles.

"I joined the Navy. I can go up to Kansas City for my final physical and everything Monday if you'll sign the papers." He got the official envelope from his jacket and smoothed the papers on the table for her to read.

"You're too young to join the Navy, son."

"I changed my birth certificate. I passed all the tests here, and they said I could go up Monday if you'll sign the papers."

She looked over the documents on the table. He showed her where the sailor had made an *X* at the line on which she was to sign.

"But they'll find out you ain't old enough. Maybe you'll get into a lot of trouble."

"No, they won't. David Hooten went in when he was sixteen or something. Stafford Coleman joined the Marines when he was just fifteen out of the CCC's. They don't check if you will sign the papers."

"But you ain't hardly fourteen."

"I passed the tests. I only got to gain two pounds by Monday."

"Well, I don't know. . . ."

"I want to, Grandma. I gotta go. I don't want to stay here like this."

"Guess this old trailer and me and your grandpa ain't fine enough for you," she sniffed.

"No, Grandma. That ain't it. I just want to go. They say you can learn a good trade in the Navy. An I feel like I'm imposin on you here." It was a favor he was doing *them*.

"Hmm. Never knowed you to be so concerned about imposin before. First you ever mentioned it." She had been around conneroos all her life.

"Well, I *did* feel like it. All the time. I just never said anything. Will you sign?"

"Well, I don't know. Then if you get into trouble over it, *I'm* responsible."

"No, you aren't! No one's gettin into trouble."

"I'll have to speak to your grandfather."

"If you don't sign, I'll forge your signature and go anyway," he threatened. "Hell! You never want me to do what I want to do. What you want me around here for anyway? You and Grandpa are always complainin that I ain't no good and eatin you out of house and home. Here's a chance for me to do somethin, make somethin of myself. Hell! I was even goin to be baptized. I thought you'd be happy. I passed all the tests. . . ."

She laid her dry, calloused hand on the top of his head. "Son, son. You always had ideas too big for your breeches."

"But I can *do* it, Grandma!" he insisted.

"We'll have to think about it."

"What the hell's there to think about?" he squeaked. "All you have to do is sign the fuckin papers."

"I'm not signin anything if you're goin to talk like that."

"I'm sorry. I just want to go. The war's maybe goin to be over soon. I want my chance. I don't want to lay around here and grow up like Glenn and Bucky and all those guys. I want to *do* somethin!"

"Yes. Ever since you were a little boy, you always wanted to *do* somethin."

"Well, will you?" He held out the papers to her.

She wouldn't touch them, only gave them a sidelong glance. "I'll fix us a nice dinner, and then we'll talk about it with your grandpa."

"If it's OK with him, will you sign?"

"We'll see."

That meant it was almost as good as done. He carefully put the papers back in the official envelope.

"I'd like to go to church with you tonight," he said with all the contrite wholesomeness of Boyd Box. "I been thinkin I ought to be baptized ... you know in case somethin happens to me out there."

"Somethin you've been thinkin about for a long time, I reckon." She smiled.

"Well, yeow. I think about things, even if you don't think so. Hell, I thought you would be happy."

"I'd be happy if I thought your decision was a true call to Christ and not just another scheme to work me for somethin you want."

"Oh, for christsake! You never believe me about *anything*!"

"I wonder why."

He took his windbreaker, shrugged it on over bare shoulders and went outside, letting the screen door bang.

Arthur was standing in the alley silently peering at the old man under the tree reading the Sunday funnies. The old man in turn had discovered the small dark lad with the weird dome like a Lincoln Zephyr and was peering back through his spectacles over the top of his paper.

"This young fella says he has business with you." The

old man chuckled. Arthur was independent as a Kansas Democrat. Nothing or no one intimidated him. Through his skinny, long-faced, narrow-headed mother the blood of ancient kings and queens flowed in him. Man or boy, you dealt with Arthur as an equal.

"Hey, Arthur!"

He nodded. "Come for them peanuts." He had waited half a day.

Jack had forgotten. "We sold clear out," he quickly covered.

He wasn't conning Arthur. Skepticism narrowed his eyes. "You said two bags. One for me and one for Arutha."

"Well, we sold out. Listen, I got somethin else. Look." He dug out the baseball that had been knocked over the fence. He held it out to the boy.

Arthur approached it like an East Douglass Shylock. Peanuts were what he had been promised.

"It's a genuine leaguer," Jack touted the ball. "Pete Reiser hit it out in dead center field. It's worth two fifty anywhere."

Arthur examined the ball, clearly wondering on what bigger boy he might unload it and for how much.

"Arutha was sure set on havin her some peanuts," he hedged.

"OK. Here. Here's a dime. Get yourself and Arutha some candy."

Arthur hadn't expected that. He hid his surprise, pocketing the ball in one voluminous pocket and the dime in the other. His trousers had been cut down into knee shorts from a much larger pair of pants. The pockets peeped below the chopped-off legs.

"Wait." Jack had another inspiration.

Arthur wasn't budging.

Jack went into the trailer. He dug out all his stuff from the drawer beneath his bed: the model guns, his old ball glove, some clothes, a pair of beat-up baseball spikes with a pitcher's plate on the right toe, a ball cap and shirt he had worn when he pitched for the junior Civics, a barlow knife, a stock of comic books—*Superman, Batman, Tarzan, Captain America, Fighting Heroes, Plastic Man, The Spirit, Sheena Jungle Woman.* He bought the books secondhand, five cents each, three for a dime. The titles had all been taken off. He carried the stuff outside and piled it into Arthur's arms.

Only walking to the alley did Arthur wonder why.

"I'm going to K.C. tomorrow, Arthur. I joined the Navy. I'll probably leave for boot camp right from there. So I guess I won't be seein you and Arutha for a while."

"You kiddin."

"No. I signed up yesterday."

"In the real Navy?"

"Yeow."

"You old enough to do that?"

"I lied a little. They won't find out. When I come back, I'll bring you some Jap ears or somethin."

"Real ears cut off some head?"

"Sure."

"Umm-um." *That* ought to be worth something! "You won't forget like the peanuts?"

"Promise."

"Yeah, you promise peanuts too."

"Cross my heart. One pair of Jap ears."

"Shake on it?"

"OK." He reached under the pile of stuff in the kid's arms and found his small brown hand. It was hard as a rock.

He couldn't wait to tell Arutha.

"See you, Jackson."

"See you, Arthur."

From a distance Arthur's dusty little legs looked like gray weathered sticks.

When he returned to the trailer, there was the sound inside of round steak being pounded with a heavy butcher knife. Getting on the trailer hitch and reading the sports section of the Sunday paper, he decided not to bother the old man about the Navy until dinner was ready.

The old man knew something was coming. When the boy asked for the third time if he would care for more gravy, he was certain. He took the gravy, but that didn't mean he was about to fork over a penny-one.

There was steak, pounded, breaded and fried in bacon grease with onions that always made the boy think of the half soles the old man tacked on his shoes; biscuits with bacon grease for shortening that had the consistency and

97

weight of hockey pucks; fried potatoes and gray pan gravy floating bits of browning and onion. There was lemonade to wash down the steak, which tasted of nothing at all once the grease and onions were chewed out.

"You goin to tell him?" his grandmother asked.

"What's that?" the old man asked, sopping up gravy with a bit of biscuit.

"I joined the Navy, Grandpa. All I need is for Grandma to sign my papers cause she's my legal guardian now and I can go up tomorrow morning."

"Tomorrow morning?" The old man didn't seem quite to get it.

"Yeow. I passed the physical here and the tests. They said if I can gain two pounds by tomorrow morning, they'll send me to K.C."

"They let him do that?" the old man asked his wife.

"Don't ask me! He has these papers. He changed his birth certificate to show he's seventeen. I don't know what he's doin. That's how come I wanted him to speak to you."

"What the hell you want to do somethin like that for?" the old man wanted to know.

"What?"

"Joinin the goddamn Army!"

"I joined the Navy."

"Mounts to the same shittin thing."

"You always said I'm not doin any good around here. I can learn a trade in the Navy. See the world."

"What kind of goddamned trade? Killin some other poor sonofabitch to keep the goddamn kings, dukes and czars in power? Goddamned assholes! If the fuckin people'd had enough gumption to vote that fuckin, Jew-loving, sonofabitch Roosevelt out of office, there wouldn't of been no goddamn war. It's that sick sonofabitch's war. It ain't poor folks war. It's between the kings and the dukes and the czars, the goddamn money interests, the international cartels, the Fords, Rockefellers, DuPonts and Rothschilds. All this cryin about the goddamn Jews. The goddamn Jews are the cause of it."

"That's what Hitler says."

"THE HELL IT IS!" The old man exploded, banging the table, making the crockery jump. "I'm tellin you how it is, by God! Hitler's one of them! He's just sayin what them Krupps and other big German industrialists want to

98

hear. There ain't no more difference between Hitler and Roosevelt than the two sides of a mule's ass. Goddamn idiot. Tellin *me* I'm sayin what Hitler says. That just shows what the hell you know about anything. Go in the fuckin Army if you ain't got no more sense than that. But you ain't seein me goin. An you ain't seein Son goin. I wouldn't go in World War One, and I ain't goin now, and no one with any sense is goin. I told Kenneth, stay out of it. Let the other dumb cocksuckers go and get themselves killed. I told them during World War One when they came to get me—'I ain't goin. I'll fight right here. I'll fight you and anyone like you. But I ain't goin.' And I didn't neither, by God!"

"You was too old," the boy said softly. "Once they found out your real age." The old man's records had been lost in Tennessee. He had left home at eleven and gone to Texas, where a rancher took him in. He was ten years older than his wife believed when they got married. She found out his real age when they tried to draft him. Though he always looked much younger than his years, she never let him forget he had lied to her.

The old man sputtered a moment, found his theme again. "That don't matter. I wouldn't of gone nohow. My heart was in the right place. And they knew it too, by God. John MacDeramid wasn't goin to their goddamned war. I told them then and I'd tell them now, as old as I am. I'll fight right here. For what's right. The poor folks ain't never had a chance in this world, and they ain't goin to have one long as goddamn fools like yourself keep wantin to go off and fight the rich man's wars. Look at the way I have to live—me and your grandma—why, goddammit to hell, we made this country what it is—us and folks like us—we done more to make somethin out of this land than all the Carnegies, Mellons, Astors, Goulds and Lodges rolled into one. And look at the thanks we get. Live like goddamn niggers! We're all niggers cept for a privileged few. Only no one can see it. Goddamn such a goddamn way of doin!"

He was finished. Jack had heard it all ever since he could remember.

"But can I go?" he asked quietly.

"Go! I don't give a good fart what you do! You ain't no damn good around here for me and your grandma. Readin them damn funny books, playin ball and runnin around, that's all you think of. Don't try to help us out. Make something out of yourself. Don't care no more about us than your mother did. I don't give a shit if she is my own daughter. She ain't worth the powder to blow her ass to hell. Go, if that's all you can think to do. Good riddance. But *I* ain't goin! I didn't before and I ain't now."

He heaved himself up from the table and went outside. He let the screen door bang.

"Nobody can do anything around here without an uproar," the boy said. His dinner burned in his stomach. He felt as if he had been beaten.

"Well, I knowed he would have to blow off some steam about it," the old woman said.

"Well, will you sign now? He don't care nothin about me."

"Now that ain't so. That's just his way. He's just against war. And so am I. But I guess if you have your heart set on goin, there ain't nothin but to let you try. But if you get out there and don't like it, don't come cryin for me to get you out."

"Don't worry."

"Wouldn't be the first time."

"Well, it won't be this time!"

"Let's get this mess cleaned up; then we can think about it."

He left the table.

"You could help me with the dishes," she whined.

He was already out the door. For once he didn't let it slam.

He slipped around the side of the house and went up the alley. At the corner of Thirteenth and Washington there was an old black man with a wagon of vegetables and fruit. His incredible, swaybacked, piebald horse, shaggy, rheumy of eye, shoulders rubbed bare from his collar, stood sleeping in the traces, his nose in an old oat bag.

Jack bought two dozen giant bananas and let himself be touted toward a watermelon.

"Sweet as honey," the old man assured him, giving the melon a knowing thump with a weathered long brown finger. "Let me plug it for you, son." While the boy hesitated, the old man cut a neat pyramid from the melon and offered it to him on the tip of his knife which had been ground down over the years until it was thin and sharp as a scalpel. Stores and markets would never plug a melon for you anymore. "Taste that!"

The sweet red meat tasted of sunshine and sugar, transporting him to some satisfying place outside memory.

"How much?"

The old man hefted it on one hand. "Let you have this one for six bits. . . . Cause it's Sunday." The old man chuckled.

"If it was Monday, would it be any more?" the boy joshed back.

"Oney if you was a big shot white man in a big ole black car. Then this melon be a dollar any day of the week."

"I sure like watermelon." The boy grinned.

"That's one thing we got in common then," the old man said.

"I'll take it."

"Knowed you would." Before replacing the plug, he neatly carved a bit off and popped it into his mouth with the tip of his knife. "Um, you got yersef a good one, boy."

As Jack walked away, the old man rang a small tinkling hand bell and called softly, because it was Sunday: "Fresh fruits and vegetables. Got peaches, plums, dee-licious apples, ripe red melons, honeydews, got beans, okra, lettuce, bess garden produce—I given them away!"

When Jack came back up the alley, the melon under one arm, the bananas under the other, Mr. and Mrs. Demicelli were sitting outside their trailer in striped canvas chairs. Mrs. D. had on white shorts and a flowered halter. Her humpbacked husband wore a Hawaiian sports shirt and a pair of shiny yellow slacks—the kind that wrinkled as soon as you sat down. They took the *Beacon*. He had the paper spread around his chair. He was reading the sports. She was reading the funnies. A pot of coffee and big Sunday cups were on a folding table between them.

"Hi!" Jack called, slowing a bit.

"Hi!" Mrs. D. replied. Mister looked up over his paper.

"What was all that noise over there awhile ago?" Missus wondered. "Got us up."

Stay in bed over there to the middle of the day, it's indecent! his grandmother's voice spoke in his head.

"Aw, it was Grandpa. Told him I'd joined the Navy and he hit the ceiling. He don't think anyone ought to go." He jerked his head to show them he knew the old man was cracked.

"You did what?" Mr. D. asked narrowly.

"I joined the Navy. Go up tomorrow for my final physical and everything."

"*I* didn't know you were old enough to join anything," Mrs. D. quickly interjected. She and her husband were looking at each other in a funny way. He seemed almost angry. She looked surprised.

"I ain't quite. I changed my birth certificate. But I passed. Only got to gain a couple of pounds by in the morning." He showed them the bananas.

"You going to eat all those by tomorrow?" Mrs. D. laughed.

"Going to eat 'em all just before I go in."

"Boy, are you going to have a bellyache!"

"I read how other guys did it. Anyway, I *like* bananas."

She smiled, but it didn't look as if they were going to invite him over for coffee. Her belly looked round and nice in the white shorts. There was a slight, shadowed depression that was her bellybutton. She had a big one.

"Well, we'll miss you around here," she said. Her husband, who had gone back to his paper, popped the pages loudly in turning them. She cut him a sidelong glance and winked at the boy that he shouldn't pay him any mind. She cocked one leg up on the edge of her chair.

Goddamn! She knew what she was doing! He felt himself turn red and started to get a hard-on.

"Know what they say about them little Chink girls?" She grinned.

He knew, but he said, "No."

She made a horizontal line back and forth in the air and laughed. "You'll drive them wild in your sailor suit, I bet."

"I don't know." He blushed. "Always went for blondes myself," he lied, dropping his eyes, but they kept straying back to what she knew she was showing him. *Prickteaser!* he thought without rancor. He lifted his eyes to her own. Wordlessly he vowed: *I want to fuck you.* It was she who looked away. She lowered her leg.

"Well, I'll be leaving early in the morning, so I'll say so long now."

"Maybe you'll go to California!" Mrs. D. exclaimed.

102

"Send us a postcard. We may be out there soon. Right, honey?"

"Hum? Oh, yeah, sure," Mister mumbled.

"So I'll see you," Jack said.

"Bye. Take care." She cut a quick look at her husband and blew Jack a kiss.

He grinned. "Maybe I'll see you when I'm on boot leave."

"Oh, do!" she exclaimed. "Gotta see you in your uniform. I think sailors are the cutest. Love how their little pants fit."

"See you, Mr. Demicelli."

"Hm? Yeah. See ya." He never looked up from his paper.

"Give them hell, honey," Mrs. D. called after him.

He promised over his shoulder, "I will."

He heard Mr. D. tell her, "Fuckin kid's nuts."

"Oh, I think he's sweet," Mrs. D. said.

"He's a creep."

Fuck him! Hunchbacked 4-F freak. He'd show them. He'd show her, too, when he came home on leave. Prick-teasing bitch. She wanted it. He'd give it to her. Fuck her big ass dry, man! He'd cut Avis Nickel. She would be a snap. He saw himself unsnapping his thirteen buttons and her sprawling all over her bed in her trailer dying for it. He'd show them, by God. All of them.

"Want a piece of good melon?" he asked the old man.

"How's that?" he grumbled, still bitter from the dinner uproar.

"Got a melon on the corner. It's a good one. The man plugged it for me."

"Well, I guess I could eat a little melon."

"Grandma, want some watermelon?"

She came to the door. "Where'd you get that. And what on earth are you goin to do with all them nanas?"

"Goin to eat them in the morning before I go up."

"*All* of them?"

"Sure."

She laughed. "Remember when we was livin on Waco an you wasn't five years old, you took fifty cents from your mama's purse and bought a bunch of green bananas and sat down outside and ate so many you had a bellyache that you'd thought you'd die. Oh, you was sick! Recall I was goin to give you an enema, only by time I got it all

103

rigged up you were so scared and cryin I didn't have to give you one after all."

He remembered. He hadn't had an enema yet.

The old man just shook his head. He took out his pocket knife and deftly split the melon in two. It was a good one, thin of rind, red evenly from the heart to the edge.

"Well, it looks like you got a good one all right," the old man allowed him, brightening perceptibly. "Buy it yourself?"

"Yeow. I worked at the ball park last night. Did pretty good."

His grandmother came outside. She pulled up an old chair that had a faded pillow on it, the wood rotting where it was joined.

They ate watermelon, bending over to spit the seeds on the barren ground.

"Guess I'll put this other piece in the icebox," his grandmother said. "That was good melon."

The old man belched and tipped back in his chair against the tree, put his feet up on a box, covered his face with his newspaper and prepared to take a nap.

Jack followed his grandmother inside. "Will you sign the papers now?"

"Oh, I guess we might as well get it over with. You sure this is what you want to do?"

"Yeow. I'm sure." He spread the papers on the table, showed her where to sign. He got the ink and pen. "You don't have to read it all," he advised her.

"Never sign nothin I don't read. Can't make head nor tail of this anyhow. How come they got your name backwards?" she asked as if it was a plot of his own.

"That's how they do it in service," he explained. "Last name first, first name, middle name," he recited as had the recruiting officer.

"Well, it seems a darn dumb way of doin to me." She signed her name in shaky, old-fashioned script where he showed her.

When she was done, she put down the pen and wiped the corners of her eyes with the hem of her dress, being careful her slip covered her knees. "Darn hayfever's so bad I can hardly see."

"Thanks, Grandma." He gave her a kiss on the forehead. He blew on the ink until it was dry, folded the papers carefully and put them back into the envelope.

"Think I'll lay down for a little," the old woman said. She prepared herself a damp washrag to put over her eyes.

He turned the radio on low. There was a doubleheader between the Cleveland Indians and the St. Louis Browns. He listened for a minute. Hell, everyone good was gone. Feller was a gunnery officer in the Navy. Boudreau was gone. The Browns had a guy with *one* arm named Gray playing the outfield. The war was the only game going. He turned off the radio.

"Think I'll run uptown for a little, Grandma."

"Then you won't be back in time for church."

"Yes, I will. I promise."

"No, you won't. You'll meet some of them boys and not come in until all hours."

"No, I won't. I'll be back."

"I'll believe it when I see it."

"OK. Don't believe it!" he snapped. "But I will!" Hell! For the second time in one day he was careful not to let the door slam.

Uptown he stopped in the Hollywood Candy Kitchen next to the Wichita Theater. Kids who had been to see the matinee filled all the booths. The juke was nickeled up several times over. Hamp's "Boogie Woogie" came on. Some kids at the back started to jitterbug between the booths. The harried Syrian with his syrup-stained apron hurried from behind the cash register to tell them for the hundredth time there was no dancing allowed. The kids cordoned off the way, for a moment isolating a gum-chewing hep kitten who could really jive and her hep cat while other kids got up in the booths to boo.

"I close up! Everyone out!" the fat manager threatened. "I don't need this business. You wanta dance, you go where there's dancin. No dancin here! Out! Everyone out!"

"BOOOO!" they called. But the dancers sat down, glaring at the man.

"I'm no kiddin. Any more dancin an everyone goes out!"

Vanda Hardasty and her sailor from Hutchinson Naval Air Base were in one of the booths. He caught her eye, but she ignored him. He was sitting at the soda fountain. Two of the prettiest girls in junior high came in and took the stools beside him. One was Jeremy Ferrell and the other Jeanne Harris. They were rich. Jeremy's dad was an oilman, Jeanne's an orthopedic surgeon. He used to see them, brown and blond, happy and beautiful, around the country club pool when he caddied. Jeanne was going to be a champion swimmer and diver. Jeremy already played golf better than anyone her age.

He said, "Hi."

"Oh, hi," Jeremy said in that way that always made him feel he ought to have a badge or something to establish his right to live.

"Been to the movies?"

She turned again from Jeanne as if interrupted. "Yes." She turned back.

Their sweaters were cashmere. Each wore a tiny real gold heart locket on a chain around her neck. Their hair was cropped short, sun-streaked from swimming. He knew they wore clean, fresh, white panties. He would have liked to reach up Jeremy's skirt and touch her pussy. Those clean, slim brown legs. They both had stuck-up little round asses.

"I'm goin in the Navy tomorrow," he said.

"Did you *say* something?" Jeremy turned to inquire.

"Said I was goin in the Navy tomorrow."

"How interesting."

"What did he say?" Jeanne asked.

"He says he's going in the Navy."

"Yeow, I am." He leaned around to speak to the other girl.

"You aren't old enough, Jack Andersen," she sneered.

"I changed my birth certificate," he explained. "Go up tomorrow."

They whispered something and giggled.

"Yeow, we'll leave for boot camp right from Kansas City."

Jeremy turned toward him. "Everyone knows what a big liar you are. Just who do you think you're trying to impress?"

It was like a slap.

"Well, I am. Don't give a damn if you believe me or not."

106

big ribbons in their hair giggled at him. He turned and bowed from the waist.

"Ladies," sweeping off an imaginary wide-brimmed zoot fedora. They whooped and jumped in their saddle shoes, jabbing and slapping each other. A tall black kid named Ronald Reed grinned at him.

"Goin to the Navy tomorrow, Ron. Hep. Hep." He pointed his finger at him the way the black guys did.

Ron pointed back. "No goofin, man?"

"You know it."

"Hey, watch your ass."

"Jus truckin on down. Truckin on down."

Ron laughed.

"Hey, there's my bus!" He sprinted to the stop, weaving through the Sunday evening people on the street, pretending he was carrying a football. On the steps of the bus he lofted the ball to Ron who made a leaping catch, tucked it in his gut and sneaked around the ticket booth of the theater.

He took the seat beside a disapproving portly old doll. She wore shoes like his Aunt Nellie and had legs like a piano.

"You'd never think to look at me I'm half Negro, would you?" He leaned close to ask the woman.

She scootched as far over in the seat as she could, clutching her big alligator purse to her ample bosom with both arms and sniffing audibly.

He realized he was feeling freer and happier than any time he could recall. He chuckled to himself, almst laughed aloud. Tears filled his eyes. All the way to his stp he sat loose, his legs sprawled wide apart so every lurh the bus made his left leg bump the old clutched doll. Eah time she would sniff and try to plaster the left cheek of her big butt tighter against the wall.

9

ON a board in the vestibule of the church were some two dozen names of members of the congregation in service. After four of the names was the notation KILLED IN ACTION and a decal of a cross and a lily of the valley. The black enamel and decal after the name of Pharm/mate 3d C1 Boyd Box was shinier than the other three.

Dead out there on a sunny island called Tinian. Would they send his body home? the boy wondered.

The church had been bought from the First Presbyterians after their war-increased prosperity permitted them to move uptown and challenge the First Baptists, edifice for edifice. It had come with a mighty pipe organ—a handsome brass copse rising to the ceiling behind the pulpit. The Church of Christ had the thing uprooted and stuffed down in the cellar before they would set sanctified foot in the place. It was their cardinal belief that you could only get to heaven *a cappella*. Their faith was founded on the fact that nowhere in the New Testament was there a reference to instrumental music in the church. That and an insistence that only baptism by total immersion was valid were the rocks from which they intended to climb to heaven to the exclusion of all others. In place of the organ a baptistry was niched aft of the movable pulpit in a paneled cove of some medium-toned wood—perhaps pecan—rising to the roof with all the character of a new, unbespoke brown suit.

The totally uninteresting panels made the boy uneasy. Simple, shining hope had somehow become smugness. If the church's contention was right, acres and acres of heaven were going to be without flocks. Since the congregation had become slightly more prosperous, the church had acquired an atmosphere of the First Federal Savings and Loan, of which some four deacons were officers.

In fact, the whole of his grandmother's faith struck him

as a savings and loan operation, or of having been put together out of junked parts—like the jitneys of the thirties. Neither Willys-Knight nor Nash, not Ford V-8 or Freewheeling Chevy, it befogged the air with hatred for the long black Cadillac of Catholicism, the doughty Plymouth of the Methodists, Presbyterian Dodges, First Baptist Buicks, Second Baptist Chevies, and Evangelical Reformed Midget Austins.

The church had disseminated at one dollar a copy a pamphlet exposing the *Secret and Evil Practices of Catholicism,* supposedly written by an ex-nun at the risk of her life, which was forbidden reading for any unmarried Christian under the age of twenty-one. His grandmother kept her copy in a place he had futilely turned the trailer house inside out in an effort to discover.

When he had first been taken to church, it was a cracking pale-yellow stucco job a few blocks beyond a bus stop, as straightforward as a pipe. You went up the steps and inside and you were there. In summer the simple narrow windows were opened and funeral home fans on sticks were handed out. In winter, if the only seats left were near one of the heaters along the walls, not even a visiting evangelist or a missionary just back from darkest Africa with slides or all the marshaled powers of the Holy Ghost could keep even his grandmother awake ten minutes into the sermon. Now, the new place, for all the hiding of the pipe organ, still *felt* First Presbyterian. Air-conditioned, centrally heated, carpeted thick enough to sneak up on a wide-awake jackrabbit. The ushers began going around on tiptoe, and everyone took on airs. Even the kids had quit sliding down the wide stone balustrades that flanked the broad entrance.

"Brothers and sisters, a matter has come to our attention." The head deacon stood below the pulpit to address the congregation. "As you know, we are blessed in being able to minister to a young Christian gentleman who has had his faith tested a hundred times over since birth by a physical affliction that would have tried the souls of anyone of us beyond measure. And he has triumphed with the help of God to become a worthy citizen, husband and beloved member of this body of Christ. I'm speaking, of course, of our dear brother Gene. Now he has never asked for special treatment, shouldering his burden not only manfully, but happily, as all of us who glory in his

111

acquaintance are well aware. So much so that we, too much with ourselves or indifferent, perhaps, in these perilous times that try our souls, did not realize how difficult it is for this young man merely to mount the stairs into the House of the Lord in his unflagging effort to hear the Word and testify for Christ. Gene hasn't missed Sunday school or the Sunday service in several years! So the deacons and elders, having become aware of this young brother's gallant struggle, have met and propose to set aside whatever monies is necessary to build a ramp alongside the north steps to make his way to Christ somewhat easier. In keeping with the bylaws of this congregation we now ask you to indicate by show of hands whether or not we will help this worthy brother or not. All in agreement. . . ."

Not a hand remained unraised. Even Gene, parked in his wheelchair off to one side, lifted his shaking, spastic mitt, flashing a grin all around which kept twisting into an angry grimace in spite of his will.

At the old church the preacher had been a Brother Dykes who had resembled a cross between Charles Atlas and young Franklin D. Roosevelt. Out of Abilene Texas Christian College, he had played semipro baseball and wore pince-nez glasses on a cord even after rimless had become the fashion. There was an intelligence and humor to his evangelism that was obvious even to the boy. Jack missed Brother Dykes.

Elvin E. "Dub" Jones, the new guy, came by way of something called Southeast Oklahoma Bible College. He resembled a South Broadway used car salesman on one of those lots unsponsored by a legitimate manufacturer, hustling a '38 Pumpkin Straight Eight which he *knew* had a transmission and rear end packed with sawdust. Crinkly black hair capped his face, and a greasy blue shadow of beard showed on his lotioned jowls. He smelled like a barbershop, but he moved as if he had foot trouble. Supporting this theory, he wore tight white cotton socks. He liked to tell the teen-agers how he had played tackle for Southeast Oklahoma, working his experiences into some asshole parable of elephantine effort.

Between Brother Dykes and Brother Dub an ineffable something had definitely changed.

It was Dub's second sermon of the day. Sunday morning was most often a gentle lesson to illustrate one of the

Ten Commandments. Sunday night was when Brother Dub got after the sinners.

Where Brother Dykes used to stand calling softly during the Invitation, Brother Dub had to work like a mule to move someone off his ass, out of his pew and up to the mourners' bench. Down out of the pulpit, onto the floor on the level of the congregation, waving his Bible like the ultimate weapon—it was Come to Jesus or Else!

The congregation stood and sang "Almost Persuaded."

"—You who are lost in sin out there. *You* know who you are. The Lord knows, too. Each and every one of you. You who have never stood up and pledged yourself to Christ. You brothers and sisters who have backslid. You who say to yourself, 'But it was just a *little* sin, Lord.' The eyes of the Lord are never off you. There's no sin too small to go without notice. No mercy too great for the sinner who repents. God *never* sleeps. There's no hiding. No postponing. No putting off the Lord. There's no bargaining with God. No hiding place. No alibiing. You can't sneak out of sin. You can't buy your way out. You can only with the grace of God pray your way out. Oh! I know it's *hard*. Hard to stand up before your friends and loved ones and say, 'Yes, Jesus, I've sinned. I've taken your name in vain. I've lied and cheated my fellowman. I've been unfaithful to my wife—to my husband—I've not been a good Christian model for my dear children.' It's *hard*! Lord *knows* it's hard. That's why in His infinite mercy He *guarantees* you not ten percent, not fifty percent, but *one hundred* percent mercy! One hundred percent forgiveness! You have but to take one step for the Lord and He will come all the way for you. When you *know* the nature of the Lord, how can you then sit there wretched and lost in sin. How many of you, if you died tonight, *know* there's a place prepared for you in the kingdom of heaven? How many of you *know* when the sheep are divided from the goats that your way isn't the downward path to the eternal fires of hell? *Oh, my brothers and sisters* ... how much *harder* is the way down. How much more painful those eternal fires. Those aren't *figurative* fires. Those are *real* fires! The Lord is as real as the nose on your face. He isn't talking about *figurative* salvation. He's talking about *true* salvation. Christ didn't suffer *figurative* pain. That was *real* pain. You think the pain of yourself who are also the children of God is going to

113

be any different? I'm here to tell you that it's not! It's going to be *real*. And you will BURN! Burn forever without consuming. Burn forever without consuming." His voice took a pitying dive. "Think of that, brothers and sisters, think of that. There is no *middle* way. There's only the way of the Lord.

"Oh, the suffering, the weeping and the gnashing of teeth! Oh, how sweet is the mercy of Our Lord Jesus Christ. Come now while we sing. Just a step. Take a step with me. I'll meet you halfway. Can't you come halfway alone for the Lord?"

Asses stirred on the hard seats, but no one was making a move to rise.

"Stand where you are." Brother Dub switched tactics. "Raise your hand," he pleaded. "Raise your hand and bow your head and say, 'Jesus, I've sinned! I am lost in sin. But I just can't get up and come to you. I'm too weak. The spirit moves me, but my flesh is too weak.' You who have backslid from the teachings of Christ, raise your hand where you are. Raise your hand and show the Lord you believe He died for your sins. Show the Lord you are sorry and beg His forgiveness. The Lord will understand. He will help you. Raise your hand! *Amen!* I see you, Brother! Praise the Lord. Amen.

"One more time. Let us sing one more time. Hang out the latch cord to the Kingdom of His Holy Word. One more time. Almost persuaded! Almost persuaded. How sweet the sound. *Almost ... persuaded*. How close you are to the eternal loving bosom of Christ. One step. Don't be *almost* persuaded. Take that step, you who have never been baptized, into the body of Christ. Don't be *almost* persuaded. If you believe Jesus Christ died for your sins and are tired of living a wretched life of sin, come forward now while we sing. . . . "

Jack was up. He didn't look at his grandmother. He felt electrified. Not by anything Brother had said, but by his own daring. He was up and moving, eyes fixed on Brother, who had the sudden look of an angler who had hooked something he wasn't sure was a keeper or not, and him without a tape measure.

"God bless you, boy," an old man wheezed behind him as he made his way out of the pew.

"Amen. God bless," an old maid Jack had always teased whispered with genuine relief as he slid in front of her.

"Oh, praise God, Jack Andersen. I've been praying for you." The songleader's sniveling asshole little daughter Sharon plucked his trouser leg.

"Oh, I feel the power of the Lord is *great* tonight!" Brother Dub exclaimed, raising both arms and his New Testament toward the rafters.

Jack's trousers had sweated and were trapped in the crack of his butt. He couldn't very well reach back and snatch them out with the eyes of two hundred and fifty-seven Sunday-evening Christians on him. Did he hear a snigger from the boys in the back row?

"Praise God. Come on, son. That's the way. Just one step at a time," Brother Dub went on manfully. The ways of the Lord were strange and not for us to question. What the Lord dredged up, Brother would immerse.

"Sit right there, boy," he whispered out of the corner of his mouth. "What's your name, again?"

"Jack Andersen."

"That's right!" Dub congratulated him upon knowing his own name. "Have you come forward to testify for Christ our Lord?"

"I'd like to be baptized," Jack explained his mission. He had thought Brother would have been tipped off.

"Yes indeed." Brother dropped quickly to his knees, placed his hand on the back of Jack's head and pulled him forehead to forehead against his own.

The songleader led the congregation in yet another rendition of "Almost Persuaded."

"Do you believe with all your heart and soul that Jesus Christ suffered and died on the cross for the remission of your sins?"

"Yes, sir."

"Do you recognize that you are lost in sin and without the blessing of the Lord for all time to come and that you will suffer the eternal fires of hell?"

"Yes."

"And do you repent with all your heart and after sober and painful reflection, seek forgiveness for your sins? Now be sure."

"I do," Jack squeaked. He almost giggled. It was as if he were being married. If Brother hadn't a breath like an old tennis shoe, he would have giggled. He would have agreed to *anything* to get out of Brother's goddamned headlock. What he had been afraid of was that he would have to cite all his many sins in *detail*. Who the hell could have told Brother Dub he had pronged his mother? *That,* he had decided he would keep to himself, even at the risk of invalidating the whole show.

"And now, do you accept Jesus Christ as your Saviour and vow when included in His body to go and sin no more?"

"I do."

"Then praise the Lord."

Then he was gone, standing before the congregation.

"God in all His mercy has seen fit tonight to bring to us Jack Andersen, the grandson of Sister MacDeramid, whom we have all known and loved as a good Christian woman for many years. He says God has come into his heart and he has come to beg His mercy and accept Christ as his eternal Saviour. He has professed his belief in Jesus Christ and repented his sins and would now be baptized. If there is any brother or sister who would offer testimony against this young man, let him speak now or forever hold his peace."

Jack held his breath, fully expecting someone to stand up and say, "Just a minute there—"

"Praise the Lord. Everyone pray for this lamb come to the fold, while we go and prepare. Amen."

Several "amens" rose as an echo around the congregation.

One of the young men who had served communion and taken up collection came over and knelt down by Jack. The songleader was saying, "Now let us all sing number one hundred and eighty-four."

"Weary prodigal, come . . ." they all sang.

"You have to fill out this card with me," the guy who was kneeling beside him said, showing him a small four-by-six card. He knelt with pen poised. He was the son of a deacon named Harvey Beech-Maple, an officer of the First Federal Savings and Loan. He had never liked Jack, and Jack had never liked him. Jack answered his questions with the distinct feeling that the guy didn't believe for a moment that he'd had a legitimate call to Christ. It was as if Jack's desire to join the church was going to dilute the quality of the congregation.

What the hell were they all afraid of? What was it that made them get all itchy and testy? Then it hit him. *Fear!* All of them afraid. *Ashamed. Hypocrites. If what he had*

116

experienced the night before with Avis Nickel was fucking, then whatever he'd done with his mother really hardly counted. And that was it! All that counting! Measuring. Weighing. THAT was where everything got screwed up. The revelation filled him with a pure draft finer than winter's cold dry air. His brain felt illuminated! He might reach up and grasp a comic book light bulb burning above his head.

Then he wasn't so sure. Illumination dimmed. He felt he had been surely on the track of something splendid; then it trickled away.

"You don't work, do you?" Young Beech-Maple virtually sneered. "What is your father's occupation?"

"He's doin twenty to life for bein a habitual."

"I'm sorry."

"Nothing. My grandmother is my legal guardian. She's on relief. I'm goin in the Navy in the morning."

The young man shot him a look of disbelief.

"Yeah. Put down that I'm goin in the U.S. Navy tomorrow."

The guy dutifully wrote it in, but he was clearly not convinced.

Then he led Jack up to a door at the left side of the baptistry. There was a small closet in which there were three different sizes of white trousers and shirts hanging on pegs. Beech-Maple selected a set and handed them to Jack.

"These ought to fit. I'll step outside. When you've changed into these, knock softly on the door."

Jack stripped and put on the whites. There was no belt, so he needed to hold the pants up with one hand. He tapped on the door. Beech-Maple came in.

"OK. In a minute I'll tell you to go down. Through that white curtain you'll go down some steps into the water. Brother Jones will be waiting for you." He handed Jack a washcloth from a stack on a shelf. "Hold it in your hands like this." He lifted Jack's hands to form a penitent cup before him, chest high. "When Brother Jones says, 'I baptize thee,' don't resist him. Let yourself go. He'll immerse you and raise you up. The thing to do is be relaxed."

"But if I hold the cloth *this* way, these pants are goin to slip." They were already just hanging on his hips.

"Nuts! You don't have a pin?"

"No."

"I don't either."

On the other side of the curtain there was some splashing.

"Too late now. Just be careful," was Beech-Maple's advice.

Jack stepped through the curtain. The place smelled of chlorine. The water was warm as piss. Brother waited, all in white, the tails of his white suit billowing out around him in the water. Jack held the washcloth as he had been instructed, trying to keep his trousers up by clamping his elbows tight at his sides.

The backdrop to the baptistry was a tepid painting of an Egyptian river with palm trees and camels beside its banks, along with some Arabs who weren't taking any notice at all of the miracle that was occurring downstream. The lights were out in the church. Someone had rolled back the pulpit. He couldn't see anything. Over Jack's head there was a bar with yellow and pink lights that were so hot they felt like sun lamps.

Brother caught him by the back of the neck with his left hand, raised his right and his countenance toward the lights above the baptistry and crooned:

"Having accepted the Lord Jesus Christ as his undying Saviour, repented of his sins and stated his desire to be entered into the rolls of the blessed and this congregation of the Sacred Body of Christ, I now baptize thee, Jack Odd Andersen, in the name of the Father, and of the Son, and of the Holy Ghost."

Dub placed his right hand under Jack's and forced the washcloth over his mouth and nose. Down Jack went under the water.

He hadn't closed his eyes. Looking around below the surface, he saw that Brother Dub had on nipple-high green Red Ball waders beneath his holy shirt and white jacket to keep from getting his big butt wet.

Just as Jack was beginning to wonder if Brother'd had a change of heart midway along and was about to drown him, he was hoisted up and the congregation broke into the hymn "Amazing Grace." It was a song that always gave him goose bumps.

Climbing the stairs, he felt his trousers, the pockets full of water, start to go for certain. He snatched a belt loop front and back.

Dressed, he combed his still-wet hair in the tiny mirror in the dressing room, carefully shaping a wave behind each ear, flicking with his little finger a curly fall in the center of his forehead.

When he stepped from the little room, the lights were all on and people were milling about the aisles, brothering and sistering each other. He felt he had probably made their Sunday. That exit from the Nile with his pants bagging over his butt ought to have given them a giggle.

Mrs. Lloyd Butler, the songleader's wife, who had been Jack's Sunday schoolteacher the last time he had attended, came fluttering up. A rather pretty woman with heavy but attractive legs and very small feet, she wore glasses that were shaped like bird's wings set with rhinestones. Her auburn hair was stiff with permanent gunk. Jack had always liked watching her write something on the blackboard because her big bottom rolled with her roundy-round hand. But she was not what you would call fat. She threw her plump arms around him quickly and kissed his cheek. She had nice soft lips. He was aware of her big tits, soft as her lips, pressing against his arm, which he had instinctively raised between them as she swooped.

"Oh, I am so *thrilled!*" she exclaimed. "And your grandmother explained you are going up for your final physical for the—Navy, isn't it?"

"Yes, ma'am."

"Well, I just think it's marvelous. She is so happy, and I want you to know we are too." She gave him another squeeze, mashing her fine boobs flat and turned away to yoohoo at somebody she wanted to have a word with.

Her daughter Sharon shook his hand. "I've prayed for you a lot," she said, so piously he almost believed it. "I always knew you were good underneath."

He ducked his head shyly and mumbled something.

"Want to come have Cokes with some of the kids?"

"Well, I gotta see Grandma home."

"Maybe another time? We're having a picnic and swimming party next Saturday."

He scanned the little bubbles beneath her sweater. She had begun to wear a bra. She was aware of where he was looking, but she didn't flinch. When he looked up, she was smiling as broadly as before. Maybe he had figured her all wrong. Maybe it wasn't that the dolls in the church were so tight-assed; maybe it was just you had to be one of them. He rather regretted not being able to hang around to check it out.

"I'm leaving for the Navy in the mornin."

"So soon?" she groaned. "Darn! I was so hoping we would be able to see a lot of you now."

He shrugged.

"Anyway, we'd like you to have this." She gave him a black-backed New Testament. "It's from our Sunday school class. It's the custom," she explained. "God bless you ... Jack." She took his hand again in a tight grip; only this time she carried it quickly to her bosom and gave him a peck on the cheek. But she had distinctly and on purpose pressed the back of his hand against her little right knocker. There was no doubt about it. His face and hers were red when she skipped away. She turned once to wave and ask, "Sure you won't come have a Coke?"

"Can't," he called.

She made a disappointed moue.

"I just hope you mean this and take it seriously," his grandmother said as she approached him.

What the hell did he have to do to please her, grow flapping wings?

However, all the way home on the bus she was satisfied that his high spirits were the Glory of the Lord shining through him.

Christianity was just like anything else—a snap.

When they got off, he turned and lifted his hand to help her down. Maybe at least it would improve his manners.

Thinking of how both Mrs. Butler and little Sharon had taken him to their bosoms, he was ready to concede there was more to Christian fellowship than he had ever supposed. Yesterday he couldn't have touched them with St. Peter's relic.

"Praise the Lord!" he shouted in the alley.

"Don't show off," his grandmother cautioned. "You ain't to heaven yet.... Not by a dang sight."

10

BOYS who had never owned anything swifter than mongrel rat terriers were arguing which was faster—a greyhound or a whippet.

From the corner of Twelfth Street and Vine the mellow brass voice of a black woman came through the window like a mama cat whose curiosity had been satisfied long, long ago.

Kansas City blues, thought the boy sitting on the sill. He knew what that music was all about, though he could not have explained it if his life hung in the balance. He had seen New Orleans, Mobile, Gulfport, Pascagoula, Biloxi, Port Arthur, Shrevesport, Houston, Galveston, Corpus, the border from Rio Grande City to Brownsville, from San Pedro de Roma to Matamoros. He had drifted, scuttled, hustled and hitched that way with his mother and stepfather; so far from *The Eyes and Ears of the World,* the only news that they could ever use was passed by word of mouth—rumor of a job, a place to flop, name of a lawyer willing to take a case for a hundred down and speculation, tip on a leadpipe cinch. A low-grade current, the voice from across the street flowed into him with a feeling like love. Only everyone *said* love was a happy thing. Moon, June, spoon, croon—everyone was full of shit. It was sad. Sad without any pity in it, so low-down even your good time had a claw. Yet it was all right. It was . . . just a million miles from war.

Soldiers and sailors prowled the street below. They might have been a foreign army of occupation. To *Slap a Jap* and *Stun a Hun* might have a kind of beat, but down below *they* didn't have to go to war to slap or stun anyone, or to be slapped and stunned.

A white soldier, his shirttail out behind, his cunt cap crosswise on his dome, staggered along happily, held up by a chunky black whore with an enormous Hottentot can in a bottle-green slit skirt and a fuchsia satin blouse. She was pointing him toward some promise the soldier saw as an enormous joke. The strain in her face told you she wasn't working *that* hard for fun, Henry Aldrich.

"A whippet'll beat a greyhound every time," a guy named Gowens from Fort Scott insisted. He was a blond with a crew cut, almost six feet, with a turned-up nose you could look into. "*E*egyptians trained them to chase gazelles," he elaborated.

"That was a different dog," Gorilla Gerela said.

"What damn dog?"

"The kind that can't bark."

"What the hell kind of dog can't bark?" Gowens wasn't going to be funned.

"Ben-something-or-others," Gorilla said. "Anyway, that's what they chased gazelles with."

"Barkless dogs." Gowens and his shit kickers had never heard of such a thing. "Dog's got a pair of balls he barks," he said very loudly. "Maybe you got *barkless* dogs in Wichita. None in Fort Scott."

Gorilla's buddy, Al Edwards, looked over the top of his *Startling Detective Stories* and observed, "Balls haven't anything to do with it. The dog that barks the most is usually the one with the least to bark about."

"Whatdya mean by that?" Gowens demanded. "You mean somethin by that?"

"Only telling you what we've seen to be true in Wichita," Edwards said blandly.

Al and Gorilla had enlisted together. They had been friends since high school. A recruiter had dubbed them Abbott and Costello, and they did remind you of them once someone said it. Edwards was a tall, long-faced fellow without being angular and sharp. He combed his hair straight back from a high forehead. He had the muscular softness and pale look of a commercial traveler. There was an atmosphere of cheap hotel lobbies about him. Though he was only about twenty-two, the attitudes and manner of a man over thirty had already begun to settle upon him. Jack could not imagine his ever being a little boy. At their physical he had seen the beginning of softness around his lower back and hips. His skin was white as milk; his legs were hairless. He did not like standing around without anything on. He held his records in front of his parts, trying to look casual.

Gorilla would have gone innocently naked in front of Mrs. Roosevelt. A torso like a keg and with no more cock on him than an American Beauty Rosebud. Gorilla's legs were shorter than his arms, which, because of his heavy upper development, were carried six inches out from his sides. Moreover, he was knock-kneed so when he tried to march, he rolled and swayed like an angry duck. Gentle of face as a bear, before enlistment he had pushed a refrigerated meat truck for Armour's and could carry a quarter of a beef on one shoulder. He wore a size 17-½ collar and found buttoning it uncomfortable. Naked, he looked like a big man cut off at the knees. He took the razzing that naturally befell someone who resembled a cross between Lou Costello and an ape with a forbearance and good humor that could make one think he was dumb. This suspicion was further fed by the fact that though old enough to vote, he was still an avid reader of comic books. But close examination would reveal that of the six funny books he kept under the pillow of his bunk, two were *Classic Comics*. He never pretended to intellect, but he was no one's fool. Edwards never teased him, always solicited his opinion and desires before making a combined move and generally waited upon Gorilla like a doting uncle with a nephew prodigy. Though it wasn't immediately obvious at what Gorilla excelled, Jack accepted Edwards' point of view and fought every inclination to bait the fireplug himself.

As soon as they met in the recruiting office in Wichita, Jack had attached himself to Al and Gorilla. They had both been to Kansas City before. And though they both knew he was too young to be going into the Navy, they found his audacity interesting. They listened to his elaborate lies—by the time they had got on the train Jack had invented a history for himself that had his stepfather doing time in prison right enough, but for something quite acceptable, like illegal oil leases rather than being nicked with an indefinite sentence for being an habitual petty criminal whose main forte was papering the country with a gang of little bitty old twenty-five-dollar hot checks. His mother was a cosmetician in a ritzy shop in the desert. She had a '41 maroon Cadillac roadster. Before his old man had been salted away, he had attended TMI, an expensive Texas military academy. When he was unable to go back, he decided to enlist. Whether they believed him or not, Gorilla offered him a funny book and Al dubbed him with the nickname Muskrat.

Gorilla, Al and Jack had bought a bottle of Early Times to celebrate passing their physicals. Gowens and his crowd had sneaked in a fifth of Four Roses. There were sixteen bunk beds in the room. Four were empty; the fellows that had been in them had flunked. Gowens insisted one of the guys had been bumped for a case of the clap.

Gowens had been a know-it-all right from the beginning. Since he'd had ROTC in high school, the recruiters let him be in charge on the way from Wichita to Kansas City.

The hotel had been a fleabag—a single floor in a building above a cheap luggage store and a pawnshop. There was no lobby. A sailor sat at the bottom of the stairs to hand out mattress covers, pillowcases and blankets and to make sure no one tried to sneak up a woman. Liquor too was forbidden, but the sailor didn't search them.

Gowens' farmers were everyone not from Wichita. With all the rejectees falling out of the Wichita group, it left the farmers with eight guys to Wichita's six, with one of the leftovers being a slender young man, beautiful of face and with very good clothes, who had done a year at WU and wanted to be a hospital corpsman. Edwards claimed it would give you a hard-on just to march behind the guy from the hotel to the post office.

Gowens had played fullback for Fort Scott. He had a '32 Ford roadster with a '40 Merc motor, ported and relieved, milled heads, a quarter-race cam, chromed all over, and God-knows-what-all. He had a registered quarter horse; fought in the Golden Gloves; fucked every girl within two hundred miles of Fort Scott; killed all kinds of game with an arsenal of exotic weapons; and could shovel more wheat and shit in one day than any mortal man could weigh. Al dubbed him Superclod and predicted, "Somebody's going to slap a button on that flap."

When Jack had finished processing earlier that day, his name was called out and he was told to report to the chief's office. Gorilla and Al had looked at each other knowingly. The Muskrat had been caught out. Or he hadn't passed. Jack was more afraid it was the former possibility because the names of all those who had flunked their physicals had been called right away and the group had been hustled out of sight. The recruiter hadn't said

124

they had failed, but everyone knew. By the time the rest got back to the hotel the rejected guys had gone.

"Good luck, Muskrat." Gorilla patted him on the back as he stepped out of line.

"Knew he would never make it," Gowens said, as if the Navy had consulted him personally.

The chief looked incredibly like Randolph Scott, not at all like a sailor, more like a lonely forest ranger. Jack's papers were alone on the blotter of his desk. Behind the chief was the forbidding dark poster of a ship sliding into the depths of a midnight sea. In the foreground the periscope of a sub cut a shark's fin wake. A SLIP OF THE LIP CAN SINK A SHIP!

"You're just on the borderline, son," the chief informed him. "You're a bit underweight. . . ." He let it hang as if something else was more truly worrying him.

"I weighed enough in Wichita before I came up," Jack said. "Right on the nose." He had eaten the two dozen bananas before he had been weighed on Monday and had tried to hold the edge with milk shakes and banana splits the two days he had been in K.C. The expense had been so great his pocket money was almost gone.

"Maybe we aren't feeding you well enough," the chief offered kindly.

They had been given meal tickets redeemable at a couple of restaurants near the post office, where the choice for ticket holders was meat loaf, mashed potatoes and green beans or chicken a la king, mashed potatoes and green beans. At that, Jack had never eaten better in his life. He couldn't understand why everyone bitched about the food. *They* couldn't understand how he could waffle up everything and cast longing looks at the plates of those around him. He *liked* meat loaf, and ketchup was free.

"How bad do you want to be in the Navy?" the chief had asked.

"Real bad, sir. It's all I've ever wanted since my dad was killed."

"He was in the Navy?" the chief asked.

"A pilot on the *Wasp*, sir," Jack lied, letting his hatred of the Japs begin to well up in him. "He was killed in action."

The chief had flipped a page of his papers.

"That's my stepdad there," the boy quickly said.

"What was your father's name?"

"Lieutenant Gus Andersen, sir."

"I was on the *Wasp*," the chief said.

Jack's heart had sunk. A slip of the lip. . . . "Did you know him, sir?" he covered hopefully.

"No. A carrier is a big ship."

"I just want to get back at the damn Japs," Jack threw in out of some movie he had seen.

"What do you intend to strike for?"

"How's that?"

"What do you want to do?"

"I'd like to fly, sir. Maybe be a gunner on a TBF, a belly gunner." He had hoped to impress him with his knowledge. And he had heard that was a job for which lightweight guys like himself were often selected.

"That's a dangerous job."

"The important thing is I do whatever the Navy thinks I'd be best at," he had added piously.

Jack had the feeling the chief wasn't buying any of it. The chief slowly selected a large rubber stamp from a battery in a holder on his desk, moistened it on a deep scarlet ink pad, hesitated and looked at the boy again.

"If I approve this, you think you can keep up?"

"Yes, sir!"

He banged the stamp down on the top of Jack's papers. When he lifted it there was in red capital letters across the top: U.S.N.R. ONLY. He put the papers on top of others in a basket on his desk.

"Don't let me down."

"I won't," Jack had promised.

Only then did the chief smile wearily, not without his doubts.

"Reckon you're young. You'll fill out."

"Yes, sir!"

Hell, that chief knew he wasn't old enough. And he was in! All that was left was to be sworn in at 0900 the next morning.

Jack had been a little high before, but he had never been truly drunk. He took a big slug from the bottle lest they think he was a piker and chased it with a pull at the Coke Gorilla offered him right behind it. Gorilla and Al glanced at each other with amusement.

Gowens was still going on about goddamned dogs. Now it was hunting dogs. He had the best brace of bird dogs in the county and possibly the entire state.

Some of the guys got up and went out to look for a movie. From the hall they heard someone discover:

"Hey! There's a real *burly*-que here!"

"No shit?"

"Hey, let's go see that!"

After a while Al leaned over out of his top bunk and asked Gorilla below, "You want to go see the burlesque?"

"Naw." He turned the page of his comic book. When he read, he concentrated, his eyes like a child's, his lips perceptibly forming the words.

"Why not? We ought to get out and do something."

"I seen one."

"I *know* you have seen one. So have I. Would you like to see another?"

"Naw."

"Why not?"

"The candy."

"The *candy*?"

"Yeah."

"What about the goddamned candy?"

"They never put more'n three or four pieces in the box."

"You don't have to *buy* the candy."

"You do if you want to get the wristwatch er fountain pen set."

"You know that's just a come-on to get you to buy the effing candy. There aren't any watches and fountain pens in there."

"That's just it."

"*What* is?"

"Why I don't wanta go."

Al flopped back and took up his detective magazine. "Gorilla, sometimes it is hard to talk to you."

"Um." He had not taken his eyes off his funny book.

Presently Al leaned over again and asked, "How about taking in a movie then?"

"Naw."

"I know—he's seen one!" Gowens butted in. Both Al and Gorilla laid down their magazines to stare at him. He had crossed over into the Wichita side of the room, carrying his bottle with him by the throat. He hooked an arm over the foot of Al's bunk. "Ever hear that one about the pussyfoot caught in the draft? The sergeant asks him, 'You smoke?' An the pussyfoot answers, 'Nope, tried it once and didn't like it.' Then he asks, 'You drink?' Feller says, 'Nope, tried it once and didn't like it.' And he goes on like that. To everything the sergeant asks, the pussyfoot says, 'Nope, tried it once and didn't like it.' So at the end, the sergeant says, 'You have one kid, I take it!' "

Jack laughed.

Al and Gorilla remained absolutely silent. They didn't even smile. They picked up their magazines.

"You guys heard it before," Gowens accused them.

"Yeah . . . once," Gorilla said.

Then they smiled. Gowens went back to his side of the room.

When Gorilla finished his funny book, he lifted his legs and gently jostled the sagging shape overhead.

"Whadya say, Al, let's go out and get a sandwich or somethin?"

"OK."

They got off their bunks. Jack watched them prepare to leave. At the door they hesitated. Gorilla said something to Al, then turned back.

"You comin with us, Muskrat? Get a sandwich or somethin."

"OK. Sure!" He bounded off the windowsill after them.

Twelfth Street had looked ordinary enough by early morning light when they had come out of the hotel to go to the post office, a paper blowing down it, the joints closed, garbage cans on the curb, cats looking for breakfast. By night, everything changed. The Jungle Club, Muff's & Brown's, The Leevee. Servicemen: No Cover, No Minimum. NO MINORS!! A shotgun boite called The Shaft, barely wider than its doorway, was guarded by a black bouncer the size and shade of a Pacific & Great Western fast freight engine tilted on end.

"Got a dozen lovely girls inside dyin to meet ya," he confided in a whisper that made them think the building had spoken or the guy could throw his voice.

"Got girls in there?" Gorilla upped to the dark mountain and asked.

"An even dozen beautiful girls," the engine rumbled. "They sent me out here to look for *you*. If you don't find what you like, you come see me. Step right in, gentlemen." He opened the door a crack, though it had no handle outside they could see, enough for Gorilla to peek around him and inside.

"Dark as pit in there. Can't see *anything*."

"Things goin on there, boy, we don want jus anybody to see. They'll find ya. Don' worry. They carry little flashlights."

"How about it, Al?" Gorilla asked.

"Wouldn't go in there with a miner's light and a pistol," was Al's opinion.

It was all the same to the bouncer. The crack closed.

Though Jack would have liked to see what a dozen beautiful girls had to carry little flashlights for, he was down to his last two singles. He reckoned two bucks wouldn't go far in a place like that.

Ahead on the corner a Katz drugstore was a fluorescent oasis of soothing milk shake ablutions and limeade springs toward which they were drawn—a little bit of home in the heart of Baghdad. But not even Katz had gone untouched by its neighborhood. Sheiks and Trojans, Rameses and Durex were racked beside the pharmaceutical cash register casually as chewing gum, and the chemist overlooked a help-yourself garden of flowered douche bags, vaginal salts, economy quarts of Lysol and Listerine. He had the eyes of a cash-and-carry abortionist, clearly satisfied he had missed a higher calling.

A tuna salad sandwich on toast and a double thick chocolate milk shake which had been less thick by half than an ordinary shake back in Wichita had bored a sixty-cent chunk out of the boy's reserves. He now stood with a dollar forty to blow between that moment and San Diego.

Standing in front of the burlesque with Al and Gorilla, he saw he was a dime short if they decided to go inside. That he was willing to lay down his last cent to trip the chrome stile there was no question. Three times larger than life, even in one dimension, Chiquita, the Mexican Wildcat, stood astride the entrance, casting a wanton shadow that reached all the way back to the collection of secondhand pinup magazines he had hidden under his mattress at home. Sears, Roebuck catalogs of sexual fantasy. And there she was all alive, alive-o, *just inside*. A private fever gripped him. He would gladly go hungry to see her. He feigned indifference.

The stile was controlled by a woman with the face and figure of an angry Winston Churchill beneath a flame wig. She was locked inside the ticket booth behind glass that looked bulletproof. Above a perforated speaking hole which made her voice sound like an ancient tiny recording, hung the satin banner of a Blue Star Mother.

"Well, we goin in or not?" Al wondered.

"Might as well, can't dance," Gorilla said.

At the cashier's he turned back. "You comin, Muskrat?"

"You guys go on. I'm a dime light."

"Hell!" Gorilla pushed through another dollar and a half for Jack's ticket. Nor would he let the boy give him the money he had in his pocket once they were in the lobby. "You're with us," he explained easily.

"I'll pay you back," he promised.

Gorilla waved the notion away.

Jack felt warmly that he had found brothers finer than any he might have had through blood.

TITS! Great God almighty—the TITS! Venus Darling, taller than any girl in the slough-footed chorus, blond hair spilling down to her enormous inverted Valentine ass, white thighs writhing with pythons beneath the powdered skin, lifted and offered her breasts as if they were babies of her own birthing. Her scarlet-tipped fingers touched those big boobies as if a fingernail might cause the delicate skin to burst. Lavender-sequined cones covered her nipples, tipping the Jello-filled pillows with dangerous aggressive points. There was not a freckle or mole on her. Only a nickel-sized vaccination scar high on her left thigh marred living flesh as awesome as an unbroken field of new snow. The sequined lavender pouch below the white acre of her belly became almost insignificant to the boy so entranced was he by the overwhelming totality of the woman.

Woman, he found himself silently forming the word in his mouth. He licked dry lips and swallowed.

She was so clean. More beautiful than any movie star. When she opened her mouth, her teeth were perfectly white in a wide, antiseptic mouth, her tongue pink and shiny as paint. The idea that such a woman might be fucked like any other, suffer a cold or any other common complaint, was beyond his ability to imagine.

Gorilla nudged Al on his left. They both turned and grinned at the boy, who was staring openmouthed at the performance on the stage.

When she lifted first her left tit and kissed it, then her right, and, peeking coyly over both, mouthed a kiss the

130

boy was electrified to think of as his own, he was transported beyond belief into something close to love.

Venus Darling was the voice that always spoke in his
head! He was certain.

Then she was gone. The chorus came back in red, white
and blue costumes, carrying white wooden rifles over their
shoulders, and stumbled through a tap number to a
medley of military anthems. "Anchors Aweigh" raised
gooseflesh on the boy, though the girls were giggling and
making asides to one another. No three were ever long in
step, their rifles canting at raw boot angles, their taps
sounding more like a disorderly cavalry rout than rhythm
dancing. Popping a fusillade of bumps, they aimed their
rifles at the audience in a twenty-one-gun salute. Skipping
offstage, a bouncing little brunette visibly goosed a beefy
Teutonic girl in front of her, to the delight of the girls yet
behind.

The boys were sitting in the front row. The sad-looking
musicians ducked into a little door under the stage while a
barker came out and challenged everyone in the audience
to prove they were gentlemen, good sports, and not rubes
at their first burlesque show by buying a box of hand-
dipped French chocolates, in which one might find "A
genuine Barker pen and pencil set or one of the world-
famous twenny-one jewel-like Elger wristwatches."

The musicians had left the little door open. Jack could
see one of the baggy-pants comics tipping up a pint of Old
Crow in the low, bare-bulb-lighted passageway. He looked
ancient, angry and oblivious to the half-naked squad of
girls flitting through the passageway. Venus Darling appeared out of a door off the hall, a stained pink dressing
gown over her shoulders, open down the front. In the un-
tinted light her skin looked mottled. There were bruises on
her thighs and her ankles were dirty! Her face was layered
with a thick pink makeup that crinkled in long lines when
she spoke and squinted her eyes. She too looked angry.
Offstage she slumped, and her tits hung halfway to her
belly button.

She reached for the comic's bottle, which he yanked out
of the way by pure reflex. After he passed it to her, she
tilted it up under the flyspecked bulb in the passageway
and drank from the neck like a man before making a face
and handing it back. Then, as if conscious eyes were

watching her, she gathered her robe around her and returned to her room, slamming the door behind her.

The boy felt robbed. She hadn't been the woman whose voice spoke in his head after all.

There was a busy little brunette, all bounce and black ruffles, garters, long black stockings, high-heeled shoes, who performed on a French-looking chaise longue, fucking it every way but flying. She had three vaccinations and a heart-shaped beauty mark beside her pouty red mouth. There was Rusty the Texas Whirlwind, a redhead, tall as the Gulf Building in Houston of whom Gorilla said, "Stick a stirrer up her big butt and she could make butter. Looks a little like ole Jean, don't she?"

"Yeah, a little," Al conceded. "She's got ten toes."

And so she had. Jack counted. And feet larger than his own.

Jack liked the blackouts. The sadass comic he had seen in the passageway beneath the stage was so funny he often made the straight man and the girls in the skits break up with genuine laughter. Jack was amazed to find a lot of the innocent routines of movie comics had their origin in raunchy burlesque skits.

Wanna buy a duck? Only in burlesque did it make sense.

After a buildup worthy of the Second Coming alive and onstage, the Mexican Wildcat appeared in a lap of a vaguely Aztec god ten feet high. She was oiled to the color of new bronze and was sprouting a fantastic feathered headdress that divided into wings attached to her wrists. The upper half of her face was covered with a hawklike golden mask. Matching golden spurs were fastened to her ankles with black and white bands of feathers. She did a lot of swooping back and forth across the stage and was hoisted on a wire to fly out over the audience before getting down to stripping off mask and feathered tunic and offering herself, tits, mouth, cunt and bung to the god, while thunder, lightning, jungle cries and tomtoms for a moment turned a little bit of Kansas City into a place where virgins might be flayed so that dark gods could parade in their skins.

Outside, Jack felt dull, flattened, surprisingly disappointed. It had been too much, and yet not enough. Each girl had stirred and pointed his desire, then was gone, the comics between somehow driving her from his mind. By the time the Mexican Wildcat appeared he had become a critic.

If they had little private cubicles where you could jerk off while they were doing it, he thought. *And some way to get out afterward without everyone seeing you.... Nothing* was ever perfect. Everything had a goddamned hook.

"Gowens gone out to get us some gash," announced one of the farmers sitting on the edge of his bunk in solemn, boozy anticipation. "He's goin to whistle outside when he's got er and we'll lower the fire escape. You guys wanta chip in on it?"

"You can't bring a woman up here," Al said.

"The hell!" the farmer said belligerently. "We need some pussy!" He rubbed his blue-jeaned basket vigorously. "My ole pecker's hungry for some old K and C *dark* meat. I'm first after Gowens."

"Holding his brains," Al mumbled to Gorilla and Jack.

"How's that?" the farmer asked.

"Said I'm going to pass."

"How about you, Goriller?"

"Naw. I even became a vegetarian when I found out what you farmers did to livestock."

"Shee-it, man, you don't know what's *good!* Ain't nothin nicer than a tight little heifer, mare or sheep, or clean sow—is there, boys?"

"Um-umm! No, sir!" they chorused.

"Shee-it, I got a cousin who even fucked a chicken ever time he had to wring one's neck for dinner. Says there ain't *nothin* like that dyin quiver," he cawed, slapping his knee. He spat a stream of tobacco juice into an empty Coke bottle.

When Gowens and the guy who was going to be second went out for whiskey, they had come back chewing great chaws of Beech-Nut chewing tobacco, amusing themselves by spitting as close as possible to the saddle shoes of the pretty boy from Wichita who was going to be a medic. He had taken his kit bag and scooted. It was Al's guess he had rented a room somewhere for himself.

"I feel plumb sorry for you poor Wichita fistfuckers, bein deprived of growin up without an ole cow, sheep er sow er somethin."

"I suppose it is a cheap date," Al agreed. "But don't your sisters get jealous?"

"Whadya mean?"

"He means we fuck blood kin," a kid with an Adam's apple running up and down his scrawny neck croaked just this side of tears, his cheek bulging with a chaw to prove he was one of the boys.

"That's what *they* do in Wichita," the farmer assured everyone. "Got nothin to fuck there but their fists an their sisters an mothers. I'd rather fuck a cow any day than some stuff like that."

The way the guy said it fell so close to the truth for Jack it seemed a personal attack.

Forget it, darling, the sweet voice in his head said, a cool palm on his brow.

"Can you imagine what ole Goriller's sister looks like?" another careless yokel strove for applause.

"Betcha she's a hairy little monkey," the one who was going to be second cackled.

Jack has seen Gorilla's sister at the station. His whole family had come to see him off. She was a pretty, happy-faced girl about thirteen with long dark-blond hair and the promise of being as pretty and buxom as her mother, a kind, merry woman taller than both Gorilla and his father. His dad had stuffed some bills in Gorilla's pocket and kissed him good-bye without a second's embarrassment. Then the others piled on him and Al, with kisses and hugs and good luck. Jack had envied Gorilla his family and bought a fistful of candy bars at the depot stand to fill the ache of having no one to tell him good-bye. Then Gorilla called him over and introduced him. His father shook his hand with genuine warmth. Any friend of his son's was aces with him. Mrs. Gerela gave him a quick hug and told him to be careful. His sister, Gloria, asked, "Is he *old* enough to be going into the Navy?" Gorilla had told her to shut up, but everyone laughed. "I think she's interested." Mrs. Gerela smiled. "I'm sure she would love to write, if you wanted to," she explained.

"Mom!" The girl had blushed. But Jack saw in the girl's eyes that her mother was right.

If Gorilla wanted to clean those loudmouthed farmers' plows, he was ready to help him.

Gorilla took a drink and handed the bottle to Jack. He took a big drink that made his eyes water. He gagged on the taste, and Gorilla quickly handed him a bottle of warm Coke.

"Drink up, Muskrat," Al encouraged. "You're in the Navy now." He took a drink and passed the bottle back to Jack.

A piercing whistle from the sidewalk below sent the farmers scrambling for the windows.

Just outside the shadow of the wall Gowens and a farmer stood on either side of a black woman as tall as they and wider than both. When she looked up, Gorilla's face became aquiline by comparison.

"Um, *man*, that's an ugly woman!" someone agonized, swallowing a little too much tobacco juice.

"But look at them boobs on her!" another took a more positive view. "Bigger than your head!"

"Bigger than two bushels!"

"Hey, Gowens, who got you there, Aunt Jemima?" someone called down.

"Shut up, dumbass!" Gowens hissed.

The woman's lips moved, counting the heads hanging out the window. There was an animated conference between her and Gowens with much gesturing on her part with an arm that looked hooked to her shoulder with a whole ham. The conference ended with her adamant, hands on elephantine hips, her chin stuck aggressively in Gowens' white country face.

Al and Gorilla could not believe it.

"If that's what *he* calls gash, I'd hate to send him after help," Al mused.

"What did you do, go all the way to Fort Scott for that one?" Gorilla called down.

"You guys be quiet up there er she ain't goin to do it," Gowens hissed, bending near the woman for further persuasive argument.

"Holy cow! That clown thinks he got a goddamned debutante down there!" Al could contain laughter no longer.

"Look at her, man." Gorilla giggled. "I've never seen anything so all over ugly in my life!"

"Go look in a mirror," a farmer advised testily.

"Yeah, you fistfuckers are just jealous," another claimed.

"Them big black mamas got muscles in their twats," the one who was going to be second assured them wisely. "An you don't have to put no pillas under *her* butt!"

"I'll say," Al said. "You'll need a scalin ladder to get up to it once you get her on her back."

"Shit, you guys got no call to mouth off if you ain't in on it," a farmer complained.

"He's right," Al conceded. "Gorilla, you and Muskrat stop thinking all those nasty things about that poor unfortunate creature. Look at it from *her* point of view."

They all three collapsed in laughter. They needed a good stiff drink.

The bargain down below having been renegotiated to the woman's satisfaction, the problem now was to convince her to climb that rusty fire escape.

Grumbling, she began climbing, with the guy who was going to be second tugging her by one hand from above and Gowens and the other guy, shouldering a cheek each, boosting from below.

There was an awful moment when she was wedged in the window, one huge black leg, head, tits and both arms inside, one gigantic haunch and leg out on the fire escape. The two behind her gave a great heave and she popped into the room like a big cork.

Adjusting her skirt of some material that shone like patent leather and tugging a skintight striped pullover down over her forty-pound tits, she sniffed, "Usually when I visits some genemens, they show me in by way of the door."

"That's what you get for goin with boys who were born in a barn," Al suggested.

"Now, that's sure nough for damn sure!" she agreed. "I oney doin this cause that blond one say you boys all join the Navy today. I gotta soft spot for servicemen," she explained.

"Where's the spot, Mama?" a farmer wanted to be shown.

"I show you where."

"Yeah! Baby! You show us!"

"Show me the ress uh my money firss."

"You're a real patriot."

"Yeow, it's another buck each to you guys," Gowens advised. "She wouldn't go up that fire escape for less than forty bucks on the nose."

"I coulda broken a heel uh ma shoe. There's shoe rationin, y'know. Jes look, I done got a runner in my stocks." She showed them a ladder in the dark brown hose that cut into her darker dimpled flesh.

"Just so there ain't no rationin of pussy," a farmer called, already waving his additional limp dollar.

Gowen levied the surcharge and handed it to the woman.

"OK, les get this show on the road," she said, fitting action to word, kicking off her shoes and slithering out of her skirt like a hippo crawling out of a slick pit. When she removed her perpetually strained black bra, a farmer scooped it up and whirled it around his head, making small jumps as if it were a double canopied parachute. The flesh hung on her in soft brown folds deeper than a hand. Beneath the fourth fold of her belly a wide, coarse black wedge of curls peeped from the junction of her elephantine thighs.

The farmers had dropped trousers and doffed shirts all over the room. Two fell on the woman to weigh her tits. She slapped their hands away.

"One at a damn time, an don think I can't count," she warned. "No seconds and no warm-ups neither." She set forth her working conditions.

"Gowens is first," the one who was going to be second announced.

"Then, Mr. Gowens, whichever you is, less get goin, I ain't got *all* night." She placed her purse beneath the pillow on a bottom bunk across the room, lay down and spread her thighs. Gowens stood beside the bed trying frantically to raise a hard.

"Gimme that little ole thing," she snorted, pulling him to her.

Jack was fascinated.

"Pour it to her, Gowens!" someone cheered.

"Show her how they do it in Fort Scott!"

"Fuck her big black ass, man!'

"Save some for me," the one who was going to be second cautioned.

"Nough there for the *whole* Navy," Al suggested.

"Man, look at old Gowens go!"

"How is it, boy?" someone wanted to know.

Gowens didn't answer. He even fucked like an asshole. His bare butt looked selfish and stupid. He was going like hammers, but mama never shifted gears. She rolled like a soft southern sea.

"Thass it!" she announced, tapping Gowens on the back. "You got it, honey. Nex?"

The one who was second had a trick. He kept slippin his cock out to make it last longer. Mama didn't scold.

She had a trick of her own. She smothered the farmer's head between her big tits, looped one big leg over his ass, gave a scootch and a twist to her works and the trickster was going to be done in a minute or smothered.

"Nex."

She did them all in half an hour flat by Al's watch.

"Someone git me a towel," she requested, still asprawl.

"Sure you Wichita fellas don't wanta little?" Gowens turned pimp. "S'good stuff."

"No, thanks," Al said.

"They're too good," someone said.

"They're fags," another sneered.

"I'd *give* a dollar to see Gorilla ride that mother."

"How about you, Muskrat?" Gowens asked.

"Can't afford it. I'm about broke."

"Yeah! Let's see that Muskrat on her!"

"Hey, Mama, you wanta pop a real cherry?"

"How's that?"

"We got this kid here. He's cherry. Just a baby. How about lettin him go for a discount?"

"I ain't no bargain basement, honey. Cos him same as y'all."

Off behind a bunk the one who had been second and another were whispering.

"How about a drink, Mama?" Gowens suggested. "Who's got the jug?"

"Here it is. Have a snort, Mama."

"For christsake, get a glass, ass!" Gowens yelled. "I ain't drinkin after some ole nigger whore."

She accepted the tumbler of whiskey cautiously. She had already hitched up her stockings, twisted them into a knot above her knees and was feeling with her feet for her shoes.

The one who had been second snatched her purse from under the pillow and lofted it across the room to the farmer behind the bunk. He was full of tricks.

"Now jes what you call that?" the woman wanted to know.

"Fuck you! Think we're about to pay good money for an ole black cunt like you? Shee-it!"

"Heh, heh! Now you boys quit'cher funnin me." She chose to take a positive view. She had on her shoes and was reaching for her underwear, her eyes following her purse as it was tossed from one farmer to another. "I

138

know you all *good* boys. Jes high-spirited an havin your
fun. I gave you a *good* time. I ain't no USO. I gotta live
too. Live and let live, thass my ole motto. I *know* you jes
funnin. Wouldn't beat a hardworkin woman like me outa
her bread. Now. No *real* sailor boy *ever* do that."

"We ain't funnin, bitch," the one who had been second
assured her. He held her purse tauntingly just beyond her
reach and opened it. "Bet you got a fortune in here."

"Gimme that!" She lunged for it.

And caught a splat of Beech-Nut full in the face. It
stung her eyes. She looked like King Kong about to weep.
She snatched for the towel she had swabbed herself with
after they had done and felt blindly for a spot with which
to wipe her eyes.

"Let's make her suck cock!" someone suggested.

"I want to fuck'er tween them big tits!"

They leaped on her. She went backward on the bunk
which bowed beneath the thrashing weight. Bare white
asses, elbows, heads and feet—she was buried beneath the
pile of farmers, her huge black legs in laddered brown
stockings and broken-down patent heels thrashed in the
tangle of pale knobby limps. A black fist came out of the
heap and grabbed a handful of lank hair. The farmer attached to it screamed.

"Bitch bites!" someone cried from underneath.

"Tie her down!"

"Calf-rope the cunt!"

Two detached themselves and wrestled one leg apiece.
They stripped down her stockings, gave them a turn
around her ankles and finally succeeded in fastening her
feet to the iron railing of the bunk. Then they tied her
arms to the head of the cot.

"Stop yer goddamn fightin," Gowens warned her.
"Relax and enjoy it!"

She never ceased struggling or uttered a single word all
the while. Only mighty grunts, heaves and snortings came
from her as farmers piled on her and were thrown off in a
mighty heave of her belly.

"Make er suck yer cock," another demanded of
Gowens, who responded by grabbing a handful of kinky
hair on either side of her head. When she spit on his tool,
he took it as the supreme insult and busted her in the face
with his fist.

"We was just teasin you, you cunt, but now you're really goin to get it."

"STOP THAT!" Gorilla was out of his bunk in his jockey shorts and rolling across the room. Al, more prudent in face of the odds, was a minute or so behind.

Gowens dropped his chin behind his left shoulder and shuffled his feet as if he *had* been in the Golden Gloves. He stuck out a left which was like trying to stop the rush of a grizzly bear with a switch. Gorilla flicked it aside and swung his right arm like a club alongside Gowens' head. Gowens quit shuffling his feet and looked sick.

The woman was forgotten as all converged on the squat fury that was among them. Gorilla grabbed Gowens around the waist from behind with both arms and carried him before him like a shield. Gowens' face turned purple, the veins stood out on his head and neck and his eyes bulged as though he could no longer see. His legs and arms dangled like a corpse's. He'd swallowed his tobacco.

Jack leaped on the back of the one who had been second, wrapping his legs around his waist and his arms around his neck. When they went down on the floor, he whipped him on the back of the head with the whore's high-heeled shoe. Al was taking on two of the others, and for a soft-looking man he sure knew what to do with both his hands and his feet. Gorilla hoisted Gowens by the gullet and crotch and put him painfully across the steel railing of an upper bunk before wading into what was left of the others. They swore later they saw nothing but the top of his head and a windmill of fists.

The sailor on watch downstairs came running up, opened the door and quickly closed it again.

Left on her own, the whore got one hand free and then the other. She untied her feet, snatched the shoe from Jack's hand in midair, found the other one and pried them on her feet. Not bothering with stockings or underwear, she skinned into her skirt and pullover, kicked the two guys who had Al down and grabbed her purse. Armed, she tarried long enough to swing it at the head of one of the farmers. She must have had a pound jar of cold cream or a brick inside, for he was out on his feet, falling as if she had jellied his bones. Then she made for the window, grunted over the sill and chugged down the fire escape.

Within five minutes the room was ablaze with light and full of Shore Patrol and Kansas City police.

140

They were lined up at attention down the middle of the room. Gowens stood bent over as if ruptured. The evidence was gathered. One sailor found the farmer's bottle, and another collected the other one.

A policeman flicked mama's black panties from under the bed with his nightstick and held them up at full stretch for the wonder of all. Shore Patrol and cop alike shook their heads in disbelief.

"Sir?" the one who had been second began meekly.

"Shut up!" snapped the young ensign who had arrived with the Shore Patrol. "So far you men have broken enough regulations to keep you in the brig for a year. This *is* a U.S. Navy installation. Have these men been sworn in yet?" he asked the sailor from downstairs.

"No, sir. They get sworn in tomorrow."

"Nevertheless, you are technically under our jurisdiction. I've never seen a more disgusting, disreputable bunch of boots in my life. I'd just as soon turn you over to the police officers here and be done with you. The Navy would be better off without your kind. How did they get the woman up here?" he demanded of the sailor from downstairs.

"I don't know, sir. They couldn't have snuck anything *that* big in under a blanket."

The other sailors and cops grinned. The ensign did not think it was funny.

"I'm placing you all under arrest and order you to remain in these quarters until it is decided what we will do with you. As you haven't as yet been sworn into the Navy, those of you who wish to may step forward now and I'll let the police officers here take charge of you. But I want you to know, if you stay, I'm going to personally see every one of you gets your ass burned and burned good. I want these men's names." He handed the sailor from downstairs a clipboard.

"Jack Andersen," the boy said.

"Last name, first name, middle initial," the sailor snapped.

"Andersen, John, O."

"What's wrong with you?" the ensign demanded of Gowens.

"I think somethin's busted inside," Gowens piped.

"Stand up when you address an officer and say 'sir.'"

"I can't, sir," Gowens said. He tried manfully and made it until he could see the officer's shoulder boards.

The officer turned to the sailor in charge of the billet. "I want this room put in order before any of these men hit the sack. I *mean* I want it scrubbed down and the bunks made for inspection. I don't give a damn if it takes them all night."

"Yes, sir!" the sailor snapped.

On their way out one of the cops observed, "Guess you're scrapin the bottom of the barrel with this bunch."

The officer said, "Punks like those were just kids when the war started. They think it's some kind of joke," though he looked barely older than the men in the room.

The sailor brought buckets and mops, brooms and brushes.

Scrubbing the floor side by side on their knees, the one who had been second told Jack, "This ain't the end of this, you little bastard. I'm goin to get you if it's the last fuckin thing I do."

Gorilla, who was following in their wake with a mop, swished it across the farmer's bare feet.

"Any of you guys ever touch Muskrat or Al again, you'll answer to me."

There wasn't a sound save for the swish and scrub of brush and broom.

"You guys ought to know Gorilla was an all-state wrestler for four years," Al offered for the edification of all. "I've seen him take on a professional twice his size at a carnival and not only stay in for the three minutes to win the twenty-five skins but pin him."

No one expressed a doubt.

When the room had been inspected and lights were out, all painful possibilities that faced them on the morrow imagined and discussed, and everyone quiet in their bunks, an occasional groan still issued from the curled form of Gowens.

"Reckon he's all right?" one of the farmers whispered.

Another answered, "Shee-it, he's just actin."

Then Gorilla, Al and Jack knew they could close their eyes and sleep.

11

THEIR records must have been flagged from the beginning. For whenever there were brooms, swabs, brushes, holy stones or buckets to be used, garbage hauled, something cleaned, polished, chipped, painted, lifted and shifted, it was more often than was fair—"Andersen, Edwards and Gerela!"

Immediately after being sworn in, they were handed buckets and swabs and set to cleaning the deck of the hall. On the troop train to San Diego, a creeping collection of Southern Pacific day coaches that hadn't seen service since the days of Pancho Villa, it was: "Andersen, Edwards and Gerela to the mess car."

The train traveled a route of such low priority, being sidetracked day or night for anything from a handcar up, that the recruits began to call from the cars to kids along the crossing. "Hey! Is this country still at war?"

By the time they cleared Kingdom, Barstow and Needles all hands were flying laundry from the windows which was hauled in dirtier than when it had been hung out. There had been no ice for three days. Water from the cold tap came boiling hot. Men marched about the coaches naked as jaybirds while their last pair of blue jeans and a shirt flew in the train's sooty slipstream.

A kid from Iron City, Missouri, saw his only pair of Levi's whipped from his grasp and go tumbling down the track like half a scarecrow in a whirlwind. Having ditched his only other trousers and his underwear a few days earlier, he stood in desperate fear of arriving in San Diego with nothing but himself between his sockless shoe tops and his shirttail. Though he canvassed the train from end to end, his last dollar bill in hand, humor had either become more precious than dough or there was not a spare pair of trousers aboard the train. A lot of the guys had sent all but a change of underwear and socks home before boarding.

"Fellas, I can't show up like *this!*" He desperately went from seat to seat, his single hopefully in hand.

Gorilla succumbed to sympathy and rummaged in his bag. He looped a scarlet tie with the head of a horse painted on it around pantless Jones' neck, deftly folded it under his grimy, wrinkled collar and lashed it expertly in a flaring windsor.

"What the hell good is a tie?" the guy wanted to know.

"Stand behind somebody, maybe they won't notice," was Gorilla's earnest advice.

Sandwiches grabbed from station platform vendors were scalped for upwards of two dollars each, a warm bottle of Coke was a buck, a bottle of Bud two fifty, an apple or orange four bits. The Army Transportation Corps cooks on the train had run out of everything except powdered eggs, beans, fruit cocktail and bread. The bread had begun to taste like someone's abandoned socks. There was talk of mutiny, intimations of riot. Men slept with their hands on negotiable property. A foraging party took off from a siding half a mile from a Fred Harvey's at Needles, fully intending to eat or know the reason why, and were left waving madly along the right-of-way until someone providentially yanked the emergency cord under threat of court-martial to give them time to clamber back aboard with nothing to show for their effort but half a box of Hershey bars that had at one time or another been too long in the sun.

Halted outside San Bernadino next to a first-class civilian train at dinnertime, they watched citizens and military on leave sit down in the dining car before crystal, silver and napery and order from menus. A gray-haired businessman waved a dripping forkful of something in a gesture of good luck, and a thousand bellies growled angrily. The man's female companion stared across the distance as if the boys were some kind of prisoners of war. The other train moved ahead, starting slowly out of deference to the diners. In the Pullman section an Air Corps colonel in a compartment with a very blond woman was drinking champagne.

People truly did live like that! Jack Andersen was amazed. The disparity between the colonel's accommodation and his own made him sad. Here he was in the

144

Navy—living a delicious, illicit, underage dream—and nothing had really changed *that* much. Across the chat of the rail beds the gulf was as wide as ever.

So they reached San Diego and disembarked with a single strangled cry: *"When do we eat?"*

Lined up in three hungry, meandering ranks, they were shepherded by clipboard-carrying seamen with white stars on their lower left sleeves. The star-sleeves simultaneously bawled out names from the rosters on their clipboards, and in the babble, Andersen, Edwards and Gerela were irrevocably separated from Gowens and the farmers. Once aboard the gray Navy buses, the entire levy rocked the vehicles with the stamp of feet, chanting, *"We want to eat! We want to eat!"* The star-sleeves screamed no bus would leave until the chant ceased.

In the middle rank, with others collapsed inward upon him, Pantless made it undetected onto a bus.

They were driven directly to a base mess where cooks already cleaning up after breakfast were commanded by the chief to serve the new boots. The cooks angrily forked and spooned up chow, slapping creamed chipped beef on toast onto the men's trays with a hatred that caused the gravy and oil to part. Baked beans were hurriedly heated and gallon cans of applesauce hacked open.

Pantless was between the beans and applesauce when an indignant mess cook stopped the line, refusing to serve any man in *his* mess who was not wearing pants. Gorilla's necktie had gotten the man that far. Rather than make an issue of it for applesauce, Pantless would have gladly passed on to the coffee and been done with it.

The seamen with stars on their sleeves responded to every crisis by blasting on their whistles—indoors or out. Indoors, the sound could make your fillings hurt. Not a fork moved. Starving men sat poised with food an inch from their mouths while the star-sleeves and a chief rushed to the chow line, where Pantless drew himself starkly up to attention and offered the converging gentlemen a desperate, terrified salute.

"Just *what* do *you* purport to be?" the first man there screamed.

"I don't know, sir," Jones stammered.

"Are you trying to make a fool of the Navy?" the second demanded.

"N-n-no, sir."

"What is your name?" a third star-sleeve demanded, searching his clipboard.

"Jones, John P."

"What's this now? What's this?" The chief, a tall, tired man in grays, sailed cautiously alongside, as if the incident were but another shoal placed by mysterious, perverse chance to foul his way toward the safe harbor of dignified retirement.

"This man hasn't on any trousers, Chief," the first star-sleeve reported.

"Nor skivvies either," another put in as proof of his superior vigilance.

"Jones, John P.," the third read from his clipboard.

"What's the P. for?" the chief asked warily.

"Paul, sir."

"That's what I was afraid of."

"If you're trying to pull the Navy's leg, boot, you'll wish you were never born!" the first star-sleeve warned.

"That's his name, sir," the man in line behind offered.

"Why is it you haven't any trousers, son?" the chief asked gently.

"They go-g-got away from me on the train," Jones said, still holding his shaky salute.

"Got away from you on the train," the chief repeated, plainly not desiring to pursue the matter further.

"Yes, sir."

"You, uh, didn't consider it would have been preferable to let the tie escape, I take it?" The chief spoke, lifting the tail of Jones' haberdashery to better see the head of the hand-painted horse.

"Answer the chief!" a star-sleeve commanded.

"I thought maybe nobody would notice," Jones squeaked.

The chief pursed his lips and silently nodded his head as if that was a perfectly understandable contention.

"That man can't chow down like that, Chief," the head mess cook insisted. "It ain't sanitary."

On the other hand, neither could he safely be set outside somewhere to wait.

Just when it looked like a stalemate, the chief consulted the first star-sleeve's clipboard.

"Andersen, Edwards, Gerela."

They had learned by then merely to raise a hand or say, "Here," was not the response the Navy expected of them.

"You get the feeling, Al, there ain't anyone around but us?" Gorilla asked, already on his feet.

"You three men. I want you to form a convoy around this man. You stick to him like paint. You breathe when he breathes. If between here and issuance of your gear as much as a single personnel notices this man's condition, you all four might as well have been naked. Is that clear?"

"Yes, sir!" Andersen spoke for them all.

"But he can't eat in *here*," the head mess cook insisted.

"Let him eat in the head," a star-sleeve suggested.

"That's good." The chief brightened. "You three men escort him to the head and go get him when you are through."

The chief started to leave, then turned and returned Jones' salute though it pained him worse than lumbago to do it.

"You are off to a very poor start, Jones. A *very* poor start."

"Yes, sir."

And three for the next shit detail had become four.

TAKE ALL YOU WANT. EAT ALL YOU TAKE!! a sign the width of the mess line invited. FOOD IS AMMUNITION, DON'T WASTE IT! ! a poster over the single garbage can on the way out reminded them. A hard-eyed warden assayed every scrap of garbage and sent those whose criteria differed from his own back to eat what they would have otherwise thrown away. "Eat if it makes you puke, boot! Nothin goin in this can but picked bones, peelins and rinds!"

From the mess they went directly to the barbershop while boots along their route, already in their second to eighth week of training, were permitted to hoot, "You'll be sorry!"

The barbers were all civilians. "This is the only free one you'll get," Jack's barber told him, holding up a mirror for him to see his pale, bare, knobby skull—naked and defenseless as an egg.

"If I had to pay, I'd sue," Al assured his man.

"How about a hot towel and a facial?" Gorilla asked in his chair.

"Look what wants a facial!" Gorilla's barber laughed. "Something escaped from a zoo."

"Eight chairs, gentlemen, no waiting," the head barber

147

joked in a faintly Italian accent. "Tell the barbers on which side you want your part."

Then it was medical inspection, shots, dog tags stamped and on chains around their necks, and on to the clothing store, where Pantless Jones quickly disappeared into the ranks of the identically garbed.

A white canvas sea bag, hammock, ditty bag, toilet articles, stencils for marking clothes, socks, skivvies, work shoes, dress shoes, dungarees, leggins, whites, blues, pea jacket, gloves, sweater, watch cap, wool swim trunks—better than any Christmas in the boy's memory, the stuff came snowing down—brand-new, smelling of clothing factories, stiff with sizing, his name and serial number stenciled on it forever, making it for that moment and evermore his own:

ANDERSEN, J.O.
343-9024

For the purposes of training the seaman first with the star on his sleeve was to be addressed as Mr. Smiley or sir. Although selected from a similar boot company only three months before, Smiley rolled when he marched as if his feet had been so long wedded to a deck he was unsteady on solid ground. His face was freckled beneath his sunburn, and an undershot jaw like a lake fish's gave agonizing lie to his name.

While half the company shivered under blankets with vaccine-induced fevers, it was once again: "Andersen, Edwards, Gerela, fall out and fall into the head." Only this time the detail also included: "Jones, J. P."

First instruction was how to roll, stop and store their clothing. There was a chart on every bunk. When the clothing was ready and laid out according to the chart, in came Mr. Smiley. Shaking a limp roll of whites beneath a terrified boot's nose, he bellowed, "This is limp as a dead horse's cock! It's gotta bounce!" He demonstrated by dashing the roll onto the floor where it landed with a sickening, bounceless thud. Fingers were worn raw stretching and tucking and rolling the new cloth until each item bounced to Smiley's satisfaction.

"Excuse me, sir," Al ventured. "But where does our laundry go? There's no place on this chart for dirty clothes."

"YOU WILL NEVER HAVE DIRTY CLOTHES!" He had touched Smiley's most sensitive nerve. "Is that understood, boot? This is a scrub brush." He lifted the very number from Edwards' display. "Every evening after training you will take this brush and any dirty gear you have and scrub them at the wash racks. You may have one pair of skivvies, one pair of socks, one suit of dungarees and one chambray shirt on the line, one outfit on your person. There will never at any time be dirty gear in your sea bag. Is that perfectly clear?"

"Yes, sir!" they chorused.

They were instructed in the drill for wearing leggins so that from polished shoe top to squared round white cap they individually and collectively formed a measured, trim military line. Then they marched off to draw weapons.

The rifles were *toys*! Wooden replicas of Springfield '03's you could get in a department store for a couple of bucks.

Jack felt cheated. "Mr. Smiley, why aren't we issued real rifles?" he ventured to ask.

"If the Navy had wanted you to have real rifles, it would give you real rifles. As far as you are concerned, this *is* a real rifle."

But try as he might, it simply was not the same. "Wish I had gone in the Marines," he whispered to Gorilla. Walking guard along the area fence, he imagined a landing party of Japs coming up through the swamp from the bay and saw himself standing there, sounding the alarm and going "Bang! Bang!"

Some Navy.

Four weeks later he was whirling around in a gunnery hall almost flat on his back, tracking Zeros and Zekes across a motion-picture sky, the tracers going out and the sound quite real. It was better than any penny-arcade shooting gallery.

"Edwards! You are shooting at your own planes!"

"Jones! *Jones!* Two bandits at four o'clock. *Four o'clock*, John Paul, not *nine!* Too bad! You've just been blown out of the water!"

"Andersen and Gerela—good shooting! That's four point oh!"

Members of the company recognition team as well, Gorilla and Jack were almost certainly bound for gunnery school.

That possibility, however, cut no ice with Mr. Smiley. After they had moved into real barracks on the weekend of the company's first liberty in San Diego, when the entire company was scrubbed, shined, out in the sun in dress whites, it was once again: "Andersen, Edwards and Gerela . . . and Jones, you will change into dungarees and report to Mess Hall Number Nine. . . . On the double."

From the other direction on the street in front of No. 9 pounded Gowens and three of his gang—on the double.

"Christ, we ain't caught nothin but pure-dee shit since we been here!" Gowens breathlessly said. "How's it been goin for you guys?" He showed not even a glimmer that they might figure *him* to bear the lion's share of the fault for the harassment that dogged their steps forever.

"You stay away from us, you goddamned Jonah," Gorilla warned.

"Hell, if that's the way you feel about it, OK." Gowens sulked. "I was all ready to shake and call it square."

"Keep me from killin him, Al. Keep me!" Gorilla begged.

Going into his golden glover's dance, Gowens began cycling his fists. "Go ahead, turn him loose. Turn him loose."

The head mess cook took that moment to open the door and show them inside.

"Fuck-offs! Why don't they ever detail me anything but fuck-offs?" he moaned.

Navy mess regulations called for a spotless deck off which one would gladly eat. On hands and knees the boys scrubbed the zillion pale tiles. Cooks climbed steel step-stools to taste from the bubbling liquors inside great stainless vats. Lettuces like taken heads were quartered by two apprentices with brand-new cleavers. Dough was worked and folded in a Mixmaster large enough to bathe in. Nearby a mess cook with the girth of Falstaff lopped off precise measures of dough and delicately formed them into sweet rolls with a hypnotizing efficiency that caused the boy to tarry and watch.

"That's pretty neat," he admired.

"This ain't nothin," the cook explained. "Once when I was on an old DE during the invasion of Africa, I was makin bread. The can was rollin and pitchin as the captain dodged torpedoes and bombs. There wasn't no air conditionin. Had my shirt off, stripped to the waist. Mixer was out. Down there sweatin, floppin the dough against my bare belly and lettin it fall back on the board. Floppin it against my belly and lettin it flop back down on the board. And who should pop her head in? *Mrs. Roosevelt!* 'My goodness, sailor, isn't that unsanitary?' she said. 'Hell, lady,' I told her, 'if you think *this* is unsanitary, you ought to be here when I make doughnuts!' " He laughed, his belly shaking.

All cooks are crazy, the boy recalled someone's warning.

The head mess cook, also a portly man though in no way jolly, ordered, corrected and somehow moved all operations toward a convergent goal to which he alone held the key under his high chef's linen crown. His authority seemed more absolute than Nimitz's, and he alone in all the Navy appeared to reserve the right to flog.

Gowens and his gang were up to their rolled sleeves in deep sinks where enormous crusty bake pans that had held pineapple upside-down cake, barbecued ribs and candied yams were stacked row upon row as high as a tall man could reach. Another gang from first platoon ran lunch trays, crockery and silverware through the steaming, yet ever-gleaming caldron of the dishwasher.

Gorilla carried hundred-pound sacks of potatoes from the storeroom to an enormous peeler the size and power of a concrete mixer and dumped them in under the watchful eye of a cook apprentice.

Pudding was measured in gallons of milk, pounds of sugar, dozens of eggs.

This was only one of more than nine mess halls where other men were doing precisely the same things. All the bases and ships at sea. The logistics became overwhelming. Creeping along the floor beneath the vats, the boy began to feel like a denim bug. *The money it must cost!* The picayune struggle of his people to make ends meet seemed insignificant, meaningless by comparison. One day's mess might keep them forever. He would write them and try to communicate his awe. But how could they *imagine* a hundred dozen eggs? A Niagara of coffee? Tons of bread? There was nothing in their experience with which to weigh it. He knew his own view would be forever altered. Somewhere there was un unending cornucopia and no reason

151

for anyone to ever have to buy a mere dime's worth of bologna again.

Dinner had come and passed; everything once again was cleaned from beginning to end, the deck scrubbed and swabbed. But the head mess cook did not tell them they were through. Instead, he led them into one of the long halls that fed stores into the kitchen. Down the center of the hall, a long metal table with sides sloped slightly down to a built-in double deep sink at the end. Overhead daylight fluorescent ran the length of the hall. Shadowless, outside measured hours, they faced a phalanx of barrels heaped with carcasses of five thousand naked, fresh chickens, replete with heads and feet. It was 10 P.M. civilian time. When the chickens were cleaned and the hall shipshape, they could leave.

Gowens and his gang formed on one side of the table, Gorilla and his on the other. On Gorilla's side, Jones took chickens from the barrel and opened their vents. Andersen and Gerela reached in the birds and pulled out guts, giblets, gizzard and craw, salvaged hearts, liver, and shoved the birds to Edwards, who lopped off heads and feet, split the breasts in two, rinsed them and placed them skin side up in one of the huge baking pans on the trundles drawn up like a miniature freight trian alongside the windows.

Distaste and weariness built to anger as table and deck became slick with poultry slime.

Jack's right hand was cold and wrinkled from reaching into the body cavities of chickens. The dead poultry smell would cling to him for days, invade his dreams.

Across the table one of the farmers sliced his finger, his blood staining the waxy, yellow skin of the poultry. Jack turned and puked in the barrel of guts beside him. It kept coming up until he was empty.

"He's got a delicate stomach," his counterpart across the table chided. "Little bit of chicken guts turn your tummy, candy ass?" the farmer sneered. It was the one he had fought with back in Kansas City.

"Fuck you," the boy strangled.

"You got a big mouth when you got your buddies with you, ain't you, Muskrat? One these days I'm goin to get you alone and see how tough you talk then."

"Yeow?"

"You better believe it!"

A few minutes later the farmer found something particularly bloody and disgusting in a hen's egg sac and thrust it across the table under Andersen's nose. The boy automatically recoiled, knocking the reeking mess in the man's hand away. It landed and ran down the farmer's shirt front. The farmer swore and winged a handful of guts in the boy's face. And the great chicken fight of Mess No. 9 was on.

Jack swung a bird by one foot and caught the farmer climbing over the table alongside the head.

"No knives! No knives!" Edwards yelled, going down on the slippery deck, Gowens trying to smother him with half a broiler. Gorilla waded in, flailing away with a chicken in each hand. One of the farmers was firing handfuls of guts as fast as he could dip and throw. Jones swung birds around his head to gain velocity and let them fly. A mess cook came on the run, skidded on half a chicken and disappeared under the table like a man down a fire chute. The head of Jack's weapon separated from its frame. He grabbed another. The beak had left a deep peck beneath the farmer's eye. It *hurt* getting hit with a damn chicken. The farmer's bird burst over Jack's head, the giblets running down over both the boy's ears. He countered with renewed fury, fully intending to beat the bastard to death with his bird. Other mess cooks came skidding in and joined the slippery fray, trying vainly to separate the battling boots.

Only the head mess cook, arriving with two guards armed with nightsticks and shouting, "ATTENTION!" as if the Secretary of the Navy himself were standing in the door, drew the men apart. They formed two bedraggled ranks along opposite walls.

"I want every one of these men's names reported to their training companies," he instructed an assistant. "Fuck-offs. All they ever send are the fuck-offs," he went away muttering.

The two sailors with clubs remained at parade rest in the doorway until the chickens were all dressed and the deck, walls and overhead had been scrubbed and scrubbed again.

When the boys left the dining hall, it was beginning to become light. Fog rolled up the streets, smelling of the bay, tasting of salt and the sea. They were too tired to talk, too tired to complain.

They showered and collapsed in their bunks, figuring to sleep until roused by someone in authority. They slept deep into the afternoon.

While they slept, on the island of Tinian a black and orange bomb was hoisted from a special pit in the airstrip loading area into the belly of a B-29 called the *Enola Gay*. The plane took off alone late in the afternoon. The bomb was dropped at eight fifteen the next morning over the city of Hiroshima, where people were busily on their way to work. At least seventy-eight thousand citizens were wasted in the single brilliant blast. Another hundred and twenty-five thousand were wounded or missing. Four fifths of the city's people would never go to work again. Eight days later the war was over.

12

WASHED along on the tide of people, kissed by women and girls giving their lips with fearful urgency to any man in uniform, the boy was at once overwhelmed by the impersonal attention and secretly sad that he had lost his chance at his cherished war. For the kisses of milling nameless women he was paying the full price of glory. So he gorged himself on kisses.

Someone yelled that Lili St. Cyr and the girls of the burlesque were going all the way to celebrate VJ-Day. It was open house, first come, first served. But no way to get within two blocks of the place. So the girls came outside and stood overhead on the marquee, raining down garments on the cheering mob below. A human pyramid formed below, and the gob on the apex garnered a kiss from Lili that went around the world. Then her G-string fluttered down, and for a split second she was the motionless alabaster perfection for which everyone had been convinced they were fighting. The next day it would be the same old grind.

There were drinks in the street. Drinks on the house.

Drinks offered from the windows of parked cars. The boys were towed up the stairs to a small downtown apartment by two well-dressed women and offered glasses of champagne and a single deep champagne kiss from each. There were elegant little sandwiches from which the crusts had been neatly pared.

"Man, we've really lucked into something," Gorilla whispered to Jack. "These are real fancy whores or something."

But champagne and sandwiches were all they were laying on for the occasion.

The street teemed with willing mouths, tits and buns.

Another well-dressed young woman wearing Air Corps wings on her collar kissed the boy more passionately than he had been kissed except once before. Then, as he tried to pledge his undying love, turned him over to her best friend, who breathed, "Love you, darling! Just *love* you!" before twisting deftly away.

In her place stood a dowdy old crone like his grandmother, holding two American flags in a V in her left hand with the patience of one wearing gum-soled canvas shoes. A Gold Star Mother's pennant hung from its golden cord around her neck. In her right hand she held a stiff hand-tinted Smile-A-Minute portrait of a sailor wearing an Armed Guard patch.

"Would you have ever met my boy?" she inquired.

"No, ma'am."

"Well, God bless you anyway. I just wondered. He was on one of them Liberty ships. We haven't heard from him in years. He went in right after high school graduation. Him and his best friend, Chuck Dawes. That very day. He was always a good boy. If you'd ever met him, you'd say so too."

"I'm sure we would," Al said.

"Well, I just wondered."

"No, ma'am. But he sure looks like a fine boy," Gorilla said.

"I just want you to know how proud of you all I am," she said.

"Thank you," they all said.

She shuffled off, a slow, still little island sailing below the crest of the crowd.

"I just wanta say thanks for all you fellas have done." A drunken aircrafter in a safety hat and sporting a Lock-

155

heed badge straddled the way before them, holding out a sweat-worn wallet. "Take whatever you want. I only wish I coulda gone myself. I tried, but they said I was too old. A young man's war, they said. Go on. Take anything. Nothing's too much for you guys."

They declined with thanks.

Veterans had hauled out their uniforms to get in on the fun. Sea scouts wandered in twos and threes in whites, hoping to be mistaken for Navy. Two marines caught a tall, acned kid in khakis bogusly adorned with emblems of the Corps and stripped him to his penny loafers on the spot.

"Kill the sonofabitch!" an irate middle-aged civilian shouted again and again. *"Kill* the sonofabitch!"

The marines turned the terrified kid over their knees and spanked his ass and sent him fleeing through the crowd.

"You fellas should have killed that phony sonofabitch." The civilian came up and caught the marines by the arm. They wore Third Division patches. There was some very respectable shit on their left breasts. They shrugged the man's hands away, looked at him until he blinked and then walked off.

In a hotel lobby crammed with people, two well-dressed women were borne above the crowd over the shoulders of a tall Navy pilot and a shorter Marine major. They kicked their legs and pounded the men's backs in protest, giddy and wondering when the joke would end, their skirts rucked up over stocking tops, tanned square hands gripping the pale flesh above their stockings. Bottles and drinks were lifted to toast their passing. The officers bore them resolutely up the wide carpeted stairs from the lobby.

The boys were hauled into a green Plymouth full of young girls and driven through the clogged streets, kissing mouths tasting of chewing gum and whiskey, squeezing tits beneath sweaters, groping under skirts between bare, plump young thighs, getting a finger or two in someone's happy pie. Then the car was stopped by half a dozen sailors, the boys hauled out and the willing, screaming girls shanghaied, other servicemen piling on the car's hood and roof.

Gorilla had lost his cap. Jack ran his middle finger under Gerela's nose.

"Got my finger wet," he bragged.

Gorilla pushed it away. "Probably had it up your own butt in that mess."

"Where the hell are we anyway?" Al wondered, looking for a familiar landmark.

"Welcome to San Pete!" a young woman cried in reply and kissed him slowly as if they had been lovers all their lives.

Her girlfriend came on at a trot. "Hey, Bea! Lookit this one! Ain't he *cute*!" she squealed, bending over Gorilla like a cross between one of the Andrews sisters and a preying mantis.

Bea tore herself away from Al long enough to observe, "He ain't but titty-high to you, honey."

"He's a teddy bear!" she insisted, bending Gorilla over her knee as in a tango and kissing his mouth and face like one of those toy drinking birds run amok.

"We got a real nice place, me and Lee," Al's woman said. "Why don't we go there and fix up something to eat and have some drinks? We got some good records. We can dance."

"OK with me," said Al. "Gorilla?"

"Sure."

"Then what are we waiting for?" Bea wanted to know.

"Well, listen, how about gettin a girl for Muskrat here?" Gorilla suggested.

"Oh, gee. I don't know about that. You know anyone we could scare up, Lee?"

"Naw. Not *now*! Less maybe Marty. She works at the phone company," she explained.

The other consulted her wristwatch. "But she's gotten off now."

"If she's off, it's too late." Lee was certain.

"He's too young for her, anyway," Bea said, peering closer at the boy. "Why, he ain't even dry behind the ears!"

"He's dry!" Gorilla laughed. "Sure, he's older than any of us. He began smokin as a little babe, and it stunted his growth."

"Hee-hee. Marty wouldn't want anybody who'd been *stunted*!" Bea giggled. "Would she, Lee?"

"Naw, she wouldn't if I know her. But it's too late anyhow. He's welcome to come along if he'd just like somethin to eat," she offered, hooking her arm in Gorilla's as if he were her property.

"How about it, Muskrat?"

"Aw, I don't know, fellas, why don't you just go on?"

"We *ain't* the world's greatest cooks anyway, are we, Lee?" Bea giggled, nuzzling Al's jaw, both arms clamping his right wing.

"Listen, Muskrat, if you want, we'll just wait until we can find three?" Gorilla offered.

"Naw, you guys go on." San Pedro did not look to be the hunting ground that Diego had been. It was after two in the morning. Only a few strays and gangs of bobby-soxers locked in unbreakable chains prowled the littered street, swerving to avoid drunken servicemen trying to keep the party going forever.

"You sure?" Gorilla asked again.

"Sure."

"OK then. You be careful. We'll see you back at the base. Right?"

"Right." As they headed off, the boy called, "Hey, Gorilla, let me know if they can sing."

He looked up at the two dogs. "I see what you mean."

He was across the street from a curtained stone and glass block bar called the Fouled Anchor Cocktail Lounge & Inn. Four giggling bobby-soxers swooped around him, one offering a puckered little mouth to kiss, while another tried to cop his white cap. He saved his cap. They darted away already in the possession of headgear from all branches.

A drunken torpedoman third class stumbled up, his belly showing between his jumber and the top of his filthy, unbuttoned white pants. He looped a heavy arm over the boy's shoulders.

"Howya doin, mate? Ever seen so much gash?" he slurred. "Ain't seen a couple of tall broads look like Abraham Lincoln, have you?"

"They went thata way," he said, aiming the torpedoman up the street.

"Hot damn!" He went weaving off, squaring his cap.

The boy stepped out into the street bound for the bar from which Charlie Barnett's "Pomptom Turnpike" was followed by "The Girl from Twenty-nine Palms." A woman in a fur coat staggered out precariously on high-heeled open sandals that were nothing topside but thin patent straps.

Birds do it and fly, a woman's voice sang in his head so clearly it made him shiver.

She stumbled and caught herself with one hand against the wall. Jack ambled after her. He wasn't sure what he had in mind, but he was determined. At the corner she turned off the main drag onto a dark street that quickly became residential.

Aware she was being tailed, she turned and yelled, "Get lost, you lousy sonofabitch!" and stepped out in the street, walking and waving for a nonexistent cab. She seemed to be crying.

He stopped a moment, then went on, caught up with her. "Can I help?" he asked.

"Oh! *You* ain't the one!" She squinted at him.

"Who?"

"Nothin. Push off, sailor. I want to be alone." She turned and began walking again in the street.

"Just looked like you needed help." Jack followed her. "Don't think you'll get a cab."

"Look!" She turned and faced him angrily. "I don't need your help. Go find yourself some other girl."

"Just looked like you could use a little help. So——"

"There the bastard is." She saw something behind him that made him cut a frightened look. She clamped his arm in her own and dragged him back onto the sidewalk. He was still trying to see over his shoulder. Nothing there but the empty street, some cars along the curb beneath the leafy trees, fog beginning to roll in turning the street light to a halo of diamonds.

"Just walk with me a little way. He's followin me."

The boy cut another look. "Nobody back there, ma'am."

"He is. Behind one of those cars. Oh, he's sly. The goddamn creep."

She made *his* skin creep.

"Tried to rape me," she explained as if that had been the least of his offenses.

"Well, he won't bother you while you're with me," the boy offered shakily.

She quickly glanced at him with a skeptical smile, more wanting him for a witness than for protection.

"OK. But it won't do you no good. I mean if you're lookin for something, forget it. You aren't goin to get it."

"I'm not lookin for anything," he said.

"HA!" she snorted, stumbling on a piece of broken pavement. He caught her and hauled her upright. She hiccuped in his face. She had a little round hat topped with two long, waving black feathers. She braced her palms flat on each of his shoulders.

"You're very young," she belched. "But you're kind of sweet." The top of her head came just to his nose. He was turned so he could watch the street behind between the feathers of her hat. She sort of lay against him, looked up at him. He had his hands under her coat, steadying her. It was VJ-Day. He drew her to him and she automatically turned her face up for a loose, boozy kiss. He could have held it forever. She was no damn girl.

"Umm!" She pushed him away. "Not after anything, indeed!" she hooted. "Like hell you aren't! You're all the same."

"I thought you were likin it, ma'am?" he apologized. "I sure was."

"I noticed," she said sarcastically. "Look, sailor." She fiddled with the tails of his neckerchief. "Really, that's all you can hope to get. You're just wastin your time. Go on and have a good time. Tonight's a once-in-a-lifetime thing. I feel bad, takin you away. Don't waste your time on me, hunh?"

"I'm seein you home, ma'am. I ain't lookin for anything you don't want to give."

"You *are* sweet."

He tried to kiss her again. She put her hand over his mouth. "Unh-unh. I mean what I say."

"OK."

"You'll get nothin from me but a couple of kisses and maybe a little feel. I'm not fuckin."

He had never heard a white woman use that word so unselfconsciously. California was sure an interesting place. But she certainly protested a lot about his intentions. Sometimes she seemed very drunk, then the next minute sober and mean.

"OK," he agreed. "But I sure do like the way you kiss."

"You aren't so bad yourself . . . for a kid." She grinned.

"I'm not such a kid," he protested.

"The hell you're not. You aren't even old enough to be in the Navy. What did you do, lie about your age?"

Shit, she knew everything! She was experienced. He felt good to be with her, even if—

She suddenly stopped again and clamped his right hand with her own, trapping it under her coat on her medium right breast.

"Goddamn sailors are all *hands.*"

"You said," he protested.

Suddenly she laughed. "OK. If you get your kicks feelin my tit. How old are you anyway?"

"Seventeen."

"I'll bet! You probably aren't even *in* the Navy. A kid dressed up in his big brother's uniform out wolfin chicks."

"No, really, I'm in," he protested.

She lifted his cap. "Yeah. I guess you wouldn't ask anyone to do *that* to you. Just out of boots?"

"Yes, ma'am."

"What are you going to do?"

"Belly gunner on a TBF. Aerial gunnery school's what I put in for."

"My—" She caught herself.

"What?"

"Oh, I knew a guy who flew TBF's once. Look, you can twist that off and it ain't goin to do you any good. Just cut it out, OK? It makes me nervous."

Through her dress and slip and bra he had isolated her nipple and was squeezing it between forefinger and thumb, rolling it until it became hard.

"You know all the tricks, huh?" she sneered.

"No, ma'am." He had gone back to simply kneading her breast. He wanted to ask her why in the middle of August she was wearing a fur coat.

"Are you a movie star or somethin?" he asked.

"A what?"

"In the movies."

"Come on, honey, that line's got *whiskers*! You can do better than that."

"No. I mean it's because of the coat."

"The coat?"

"Yeow."

"Shucks," she pouted. "I thought it was because I was so *glam-or-ous.*"

161

"Well, you are. I just meant— With the fog comin in, it *is* kind of chilly, though."

"Where are you from?"

"Kansas."

"KANS-ASS! Oh, wow! This is really *my* night!"

"It's not a bad place," he offered feebly.

"I know, darling," she soothed. "Lots of sunshine, sunflowers and—"

"Sonsabitches," he leaped in. He'd heard it before.

"You said it, not me. Listen, would you let up on that or change sides or somethin, that one's gettin sore?"

"Mind if I change sides?" He switched to the other side of the walk.

"Hell, no. Be my guest. Just forget I'm here."

"I like you," he confessed.

"That's nice. I was beginnin to think it was only my body you were after."

"Well, I sure wouldn't kick it out of bed," he leveled with her confidentially.

She groaned and muttered to herself, "Kansas, for christsake." She clutched her coat at the throat and rubbed her chin in the collar. A big engagement ring and diamond wedding band caught the light.

"You're married," he observed.

"How'd you guess?"

"Your rings."

"Very observant," she congratulated him. "Won't have to worry about a bright boy like you findin your way back."

"He in the service?"

"Just see me home, sailor, or push off, OK? No questions."

"OK. I'm sorry. I understand if you don't wanta talk about it."

"GODDAMN!" She stopped, threw up her hands and screamed.

He caught her wrists. She was a small-boned, soft woman with sort of shallow pocks in her powdered cheeks and a soft, almost invisible fuzz along the sides of her jaw.

She looked at him hard, angrily, then began to leak tears and collapsed against his chest.

"I'm really sorry, ma'am. I didn't mean to upset you or nothin."

"I know. I know. You're really very sweet. Just shut up, OK?"

He shut. He pushed her little hat back to keep the feathers from tickling his nose. She looked at him, her face streaked with tears.

"Poor little swabbie. Just out lookin for a little fun and hauled up crazy, crazy me." She frowned as if stabbed by a pain. "Kiss me! Hold me *tight*!" She almost squeezed the breath out of him. She shoved his tongue out of her mouth with her own and pursued it toward the back of his throat. Her tongue filled his mouth. With a tongue like that she could have more than touched the tip of her nose. He could gently chew it, tasting the tobacco and sour liquor. Against her warm, round belly he almost came. He was dizzy. She kicked up her right heel behind her, raising and balancing on her left toe, curving against him. She slowly withdrew her tongue, touched the tip of his own, ran it all around his lips, gave him a soft ordinary kiss and an extra squeeze. She reached up and, blotting carefully under her eyes with her forefinger, sniffed.

"See, I ain't such a tough old bag."

"No, ma'am! I *never* been kissed like that!"

She grinned crookedly, gave him a mock punch on the chin. "You're so *young*. Great God, I thought, can *anyone* be that young? And you taste good. Like my first boy friend."

"I don't really smoke."

"Regular boy scout. No bad habits. Help nutty, drunken ladies to their door." They had resumed walking. "Except you have rovin hands." She placed his hand firmly on her belt.

"See, I made myself a promise. When the war was over or he came home, I was goin to put on his favorite dress, the sexiest black underwear I could find and this coat he got for me our last Christmas—didn't matter if it was the hottest fuckin day on earth—and we were goin out and have ourselves a time. Only he ain't here." She looked as if she might cloud up again.

"That's a tough lick."

"Ain't it, though?"

"He Navy?"

"Navy? Shit, no! He was a marine. Up for captain. Went on a mission over Subic Bay. One of the fellas in his squadron came to see me. Said the last he was

163

seen his plane was low over the jungle. Said he didn't look as if he had been hit. Shit! I just wish I *knew*."

"Sure," he sympathized.

"I pray. Would you believe it? Me? I get down on my knees and pray. Hell, I won't pretend I've been the faithful little wife by the book. I was being humped by his best pal the night his squadron shipped out. I'm a tramp. He *liked* a tramp. The only thing he really loved was the Corps. He was going to be a career man. Thirty years. He loved the war. Crazy, huh?"

"No, ma'am. I feel like that. Well, I did. I tried to join the Marines."

She patted his hand. "Yeah, I bet you did." She studied him. "He was a little like you. Young. So young. Sweet, dumb. Would you believe I got his cherry? It's true! He was eighteen. Don't ask me how old *I* was. But it wasn't eighteen. So goddamn sweet, I just bawled and bawled. He proposed that night. I told him he was just excited about losin his cherry and all. I've been told I'm pretty sensational in bed, so I guess it's so. But he insisted. Even when he found out I was sort of a joke around the officers' club at the base, he just brushed it aside. Insisted we have a real wedding in the base chapel, crossed swords, dress blues, his folks flew out, I was all in white with a train, the whole *schmeer*. Then would you believe it? I began to want him to love me, really love me. Love *me* more than the Corps. Serves me right for being such a tramp, I guess. But it was a long time, I just did it to make him jealous. I guess I came as near lovin him as it's possible for me. So that's the story, sailor. Sorry. If it was any other night.... You just picked yourself a loser. This night's for him."

"It's OK."

"I just hope you can find yourself a girl."

"Heck, I'd rather kiss you than do anything with any other girl," he said.

"Have you ever *had* a girl?"

"Sure!"

"Oh, a lot of girls?"

"Well, not so many."

"How many?"

"Um, I can't exactly remember."

"The hell you can't! At your age you can remember everyone who gave you a little smell. How many? One, two, three? A little blond girl back in Kansas with a turned-up nose and white cotton panties?"

He wasn't talking.

"I'll bet *you're* a cherry!" She puckered her lips and gave him tiny, teasing kisses. "Cherry. Cherry. Cherr—" He grabbed her and stopped her with another real, long kiss.

When he let her go, she straightened her hat with both hands, breathing audibly through her nose. "Whatever your status, I must say, you have natural talent." Then she looked sharply again over his shoulder. "He's still there," she whispered.

He spun, ready to fight. A cat darted from beneath a parked car and trotted across the street. He saw nothing but the fog, the trees, parked cars, windshields beginning to sweat.

"You see him?" he breathed.

"I don't have to see him. He's *there.*"

It gave him the creeps. On the other hand, she did not seem unduly worried. She took his arm, put it around her waist.

"You'll protect me." She snuggled.

Maybe she *was* a cuckoo. He looked again. He didn't see a *thing*! He had the feeling it was all some kind of elaborate act. But he was going to have some of her fancy, crazy ass. . . . He was sure as hell going to try. Maybe she *wanted* to be raped.

"Well, this is as far as we go, sailor," she said at the corner. "I live over there." She indicated a stucco bungalow on a tiny lawn surrounded by a shoulder-high, neatly clipped hedge. There were lights on. He could hear music, a woman's laugh.

"I can't ask you in. I live with a couple of other girls. Guess they have some guys from the base in. Officers."

"Oh. Well, I'll see you to the door anyway."

"You don't have to. This is fine." She closed her eyes and moved her face close to be kissed.

He declined, taking her arm firmly and guiding her across the street. "Said I would see you home. I'll see you home."

"My boy scout. *Kans-ass.* You aren't for real."

They went up the walk, and she stopped on the step and turned again. "Really, thanks. You don't know what a savior you've been for me."

Now he was ready for that kiss. He had both arms around her beneath her coat, locked around her waist above the soft jut of her bottom.

"One more, then it's good-night, right?"

He made no promises. Again she gave him her incredibly long tongue. Then all sensation of taste disappeared. Under her coat he sneaked up the back of her skirt, massaging her fancy soft can. When his fingers touched the warm flesh above her stocking top, she said, "Unh-unh!" and made a grab for his hand. He captured her protesting hand in his right and twisted it up behind her back; her left was trapped in front by the circle of his arms.

"Don't, dammit! I *told* you. You've been sweet. Don't spoil it now. *Please! You are hurting me,* in case you're wondering."

"I'm sorry. I just want to touch you a little. You're so soft, so sexy. I've never had a woman like you. Just a little. I don't want to hurt you. Honest." He found the way up to where lacy underwear felt almost spiky over her warm skin. She had said it was black. Hadn't she said it was black?

"Any other night, sailor, really. I like you. But not tonight, please. Understand," she begged. "Don't! It isn't goin to do you any good. Believe me, you're just workin yourself up for nothin. Really, baby, I gotta go in."

He stopped her mouth with another deep kiss. This time he had to chase her tongue into her mouth. Over the waistband of her panties he plunged his hand down over the clasping lacy frame of a garter belt and found the smooth, dimpled globe of her bun. Standing on the step below her, he felt his hard-on poking her belly at the juncture with her thighs. He rammed it against her hard, ground it against her.

"Now, listen, I'm really tired. You've only got yourself worked up for nothin. I'm sorry."

For an answer he dove for her lips again. She wrenched her face away. But that threw her in more of an arch against him. He shifted his grip on her waist, dug his cock out with his free hand, yanked up her dress in front and fed it between her clamped, wriggling thighs. She tried to kick him, and he yanked up the lock on her arm until she cried out, but not too loud.

"*You lousy, little bastard!*" she hissed. "If I yell, there'll be some guys out here that'll kill you."

"I don't care. Go ahead and yell." He truly did not care. But something told him she wasn't about to yell.

He shoved the crotch of her panties aside and guided himself against the warm fold of flesh beneath the tangled hair. He unlocked his knees, shifted a little down, forward, up and *in!*

"Oh, shit. . . ." She dropped her head onto his shoulder, turned her face to rest her lips against his neck and relaxed, letting him do what he wanted. She even began to move.

Back in the shadows of the honeysuckle vine closing the small porch he saw an upholstered glider. He was aware of the party inside the house. A woman laughed all the way up the scale. He began to move the woman toward the glider, carefully, making sure he kept himself at least a little way in. She clung to his neck with both arms. He almost carried her, her toes just grazing the stone floor. He reached down and tugged all the cloth between them to one side and sank fully in, withdrew to the very tip, then viciously rammed it home again, causing her to catch her breath in a tiny stifled cry. He repeated the maneuver, teased her with just the tip until she was lifting her bottom for him, then drove her into the cushion on the glider. He lifted her left leg and bent it toward her ear.

"You're no cherry," she sneered.

"Neither are you."

"Touché! Oh! I'm such a tramp." She began to really move her ass.

"I think you're wonderful," he told her.

"I'm a tramp. A fuckin, worthless tramp! Tell me I'm a tramp!"

Her nails bit into either side of his naked head; she drew his face down in the dark toward her own. "Fuck," she whispered against his lips. "Fuck!" And devoured the lower half of his face with her mouth.

He came, driving hard into her, fast, the goddamn glider squeaking like mad. Yet he heard Fred Astaire singing inside, "The Bridegroom's Last Night Out." The music seemed very loud. Someone broke a glass. There was a crash as if someone had fallen, followed by laughter. After he came, she held him tight in her and ground away at him more vigorously than before, all alone, got it, shivered, let out a feathery, airy sigh, part relief and part inward pain. Then she lay with her head nestled in the collar of her fur coat, her face turned away from him.

Tears glistened in the dark beads of her lashes. Her lips and chin quivered. He bent and kissed the pulse in her throat. There was a tiny gold chain with a heart on which there was a Marine Corps emblem.

He said, "You sure do that good, ma'am. Thank you."

Her belly gave involuntary heaves. The tears came for real. He quickly got out his handkerchief and, reaching between them, slowly withdrew into the folded handkerchief. He quickly buttoned himself, stood up and pulled down her dress. She lay there, staring in the dark at nothing.

"You all right?" He bent and asked, "Ma'am?"

"Scram!"

He was as anxious then to get away as she was to be rid of him, yet he couldn't just walk away like that. He glanced at the door to the house.

"Listen, I didn't want to make you feel bad. I just had to, you know. I was just too crazy to stop."

She suddenly sat up, burying her face in her hands on her knees. "Shit! Shit! SHIT!" she cried. The last was almost shouted. He looked again quickly at the door, poised, listening for footsteps inside. Old Fred was singing "Bridegroom's Last Night Out" over again. They had forgotten the record. No one would want to hear *that* more than once.

"What are you waitin for?" she looked up and demanded. Her hat had fallen over one eye. She angrily batted it back with a swipe of her hand. "You got what you wanted. Go on, shove off, Kansas. You've got yours. Go back to Diego and tell 'em how good it was . . . and how easy it is. . . ." She dissolved into tears again.

"I'm sorry." He touched the top of her head, tentatively.

"No!" She sat up, sniffed loudly and wiped her nose with the back of her hand like a little kid. "I'm sorry. Forget it, sailor. I'm just a crazy dame. A real crazy dame. You did the right thing. OK?" She offered him her hand. He took it, and they shook. "Fair and square," she sniffled, forcing a smile.

"You're OK now?"

"Well, I ain't four oh, but I'm OK. I've got to go in."

"Thanks again."

"Yeah. Happy VJ-Day, Navy."

"Good night, ma'am. I think you're swell."

"Of course. G'night."

He went down the walk before she had found the key in her purse and let herself in.

Shit, that place could be a cathouse, he thought. What the hell *was* her story?

Then, crouched behind a flag bed in the shadow of the side hedge he saw a sailor, his cap off to better hide himself.

"YOU - SONOFABITCH - WHAT - THE - HELL - YOU - DOIN - THERE?" he bawled from the bottom of his guts, shaking, his fists clenched until his nails dug into his palms, a bomb, a tiger.

The sailor jumped up and ran. He flew!

"DON'T - YOU - EVER - COME - ROUND - HERE - AGAIN!" the boy yelled after him.

Then he was aware of how tightly he had been coiled, how fierce he had sounded.

Man, he cut! he told himself, amazed. "Shee-it," he said aloud and giggled like a girl.

13

THEY had gone into blues the day before they began boot leave. Their seabags checked through, they waited in the open palm court of the Los Angeles depot for the Super Chief. When the boy walked, he affected the pigeon-toed roll of an old salt. Watching him accompany Gorilla to the newsstand, a tall black girl perched on three-inch wedgies in a short-skirted, pinstriped Joan Crawford suit shook her head and smiled knowingly at his passing. She had seen a lot of boots.

At first the boots had hung together out of habit, but as trains were called and time passed, other guys broke off or drifted away until Gorilla, Al and Jack waited alone.

In the line before the gate to the train, a little boy in a sailor suit, tied to his mother by a harness hooked in a leather leash, turned a face like a small Charles Laughton up toward Jack and challenged, "You ain't in the *real* Navy." He tugged his leash to get his mother's attention. "He ain't in the *real* Navy, is he?"

"Don't say 'ain't,' precious," she instructed him.

"But he *isn't,* is he?" Precious persisted.

"Here we go, darling," she trilled. "We're going on the choo-choo train now."

The kid stuck his tongue out at Jack.

Gorilla and Al laughed. Behind the woman's back Jack bent down, cupping his right hand in his left as if showing the kid a trick. When he had riveted his attention, he whipped away his left, giving the kid the finger.

"Brat," he hissed.

"Mama! Mama!" The little boy tolled his leash like a bell rope. "See what he did to me?"

"Shh, precious. We are going to the choo-choo in just a minute. We are going to see Grandma. Don't you want to go see Grandma? And the kitties?"

"He say me 'Brat.' He do me this!" Precious showed Mama the gestures.

"Really! Walter. I told you if you would be a good boy until we were on the choo-choo, I'd give you some bubble gum. Mama is disappointed, darling." She shot Jack a furious, cold look.

"I'm going to tell my daddy!" the kid promised. He stuck out his tongue.

"Stop that!" his mother pleaded.

"Probably an admiral's kid," Al whispered.

Jack, all innocence, flashed the woman a goofy grin. "Cute. Does he bite?"

Her eyes flashed. "Well!" she huffed. Yanking Precious on his leash, she pushed by a heavyset black lady carrying a stuffed shopping bag in one hand, a small carton tied with cord weighing down the other, her ticket clenched firmly in her teeth. "Pardon us. Pardon me, please. We have reserved seats."

Gorilla and Al found seats together. Jack searched for one next to a window or a pretty girl.

"Is this seat taken?" he inquired of a sexy bleached blonde, a fashion magazine balanced on her bare, tanned knees.

"Sure is, sailor," she snapped.

"Seat here," a man said behind him.

"Thanks." Big help. He tossed his ditty bag in the overhead and took the seat beside an Air Force sergeant.

"If you'd like the window, I don't mind the aisle," the sergeant offered.

"Naw. Thanks. This is fine." He saw a rat-ass Army corporal in the fucking Signal Corps slide in beside the blonde. Plainly he and the blonde had never met before.

"Too bad, buddy." The sergeant beside Jack smiled. "Sometimes that's how it goes."

Jack relaxed. The sergeant seemed a regular guy. He reminded him a little of Stafford Coleman—more a cross between Staff and Dick Foran, when he looked closer. There was a ruptured duck sewn above an aerial gunner's wings and three rows of fruit salad. His campaign ribbons were so covered with battle stars it was hard to discern the theaters. He had been in both Europe and the Pacific.

"Looks like you got around, Sarge."

"A bit. You just out of boot camp?"

"Yeow. Guess it shows, huh?"

"A little."

"You're goin home."

"Yep. All done."

"Guess you're glad."

He quit turning his *Life* magazine and looked at the boy. "I honestly don't know. Would you believe, I'm so scared I could pee in my pants?"

"You? Scared?" He jerked a thumb at the man's chest.

He waved that away. "I was only eighteen when I went in. All I've known for six years is the Air Corps. All this *terrifies* me."

He spoke like a man with a good education.

"Oh, I'm Larry." He offered Jack his hand.

His hand was large, but soft and moist with sweat. The boy figured he had probably seen a lot to sweat about.

"Jack."

"I'm very pleased to meet you, Jack. To tell you the truth, when that blonde you admire got on, I was so afraid she would take this seat I was ready to do to her what she did to you. *Everything* about this civilian life makes me break out in a cold sweat."

"Guess you seen a lot of action, huh? I was goin to gunnery school. I was in for it." He showed the sergeant the target sewn on his lower left sleeve. "That's for being the best marksman in my company. Had the highest score in

171

aircraft recognition too. I was a cinch for aerial gunnery school. I'm a good size for belly gunner on TBF's. They only have a life expectancy in combat of like nine minutes or something, they say, but I didn't care. Only now they're only sending Regular Navy to gun schools. So when I come off leave, I'm just going to the fleet."

"I'm sure you would have been a hell of a gunner," the sergeant said sincerely, smiling.

"What was it like?" Jack eagerly asked. He felt as if he had known the sergeant all his life.

"Of course the right thing to say is, 'It was just a job.' " The sergeant let his gaze drift and stared out the window. They were clearing the L.A. suburbs. There were the strings of humpty houses covered with fake brick asphalt siding, tar-paper roofs, laundry flying from rickety back porches. Some raggedy black kids and Mexicans rose up along the right-of-way to wave at the Super Chief. Then some threw fist-sized rocks which landed short of the train.

"Ambivalence," the sergeant said to himself.

"How's that?"

"Nothing. First those kids waved at the train, and then they threw rocks. And I confess, after six years at war, I don't know what *anything* is all about." He shook off the thought and smiled. "What were we talking about?"

"The war."

"Oh, yes, the war. You asked me what it was like?"

"Yeow. But if you would rather not talk about it. . . ."

"No. I don't mind in the least. In fact, I'd rather like to. In Europe my squadron was in B-Twenty-fours. Cows. Hard to fly, slow. But they could be shot to pieces and stay in the air. Flew over forty missions. Some big ones. I was young and full of it. There was a kind of camaraderie, you know, real gung-ho. If I don't come back, kiss em for me." He smiled again. "Then a lot of guys I knew *didn't* come back. When the squadron was sent back to the States toward the end of it there, I thought I was done. But we were put in B-Twenty-nines, trained and sent to the Pacific. Our general, Curtis LeMay, said we were being honored. Where are you from, by the way?"

"Wichita, Kansas."

He smiled. "I thought so. You sound like you are from Kansas. We trained at Salina."

"No shit?"

172

"It gets *cold* in Kansas! We were in uninsulated barracks with just an old-fashioned potbellied stove at each end. So cold I didn't see myself bare for a month. Had to break ice in the wash racks to shave. *Brrrr!* But one thing, Kansas and California have the prettiest girls anywhere."

"Hey, that's what I've been trying to tell a bunch of Missouri, Iowa and Oklahoma meatheads since I've been in. They won't believe me."

"My theory is that most of the kids in California being from the same stock as those from Kansas is what makes them so healthy and handsome. So many people went West during the Depression."

"Sure, I had an uncle and his wife and my cousins went out. Had an old truck they built on a Hudson. There were cops at the state line and they turned them back. Wouldn't even let them in. When they finally got home, that old Hudson just collapsed in the front yard. Gave up the ghost. Uncle said he didn't know what held the thing together the last eight hundred miles, but he's sworn by Hudsons ever since."

"Have you read *The Grapes of Wrath*?"

"No."

"You ought to. Great book. I think it would mean a lot to you."

"I'll read it," Jack promised.

Just before the train began really picking up speed, the sergeant turned to watch an old stewbum humping along the far track under a weathered felt hat, his bedroll over his back, headed toward L.A. "Amazing," he said. "So what happened to your uncle?"

"Oh, he junked for a while. He never went on relief like we were. He was too proud. Did a little bootleggin for a guy. Then the war came, and all the plants opened up, and he went to work for Beechcraft."

"And he got himself a new Hudson." The sergeant smiled.

"Naw. That's a funny thing. He got a Chevy and liked *it* so much he's been drivin' Chevies ever since."

The sergeant laughed aloud for the first time. "Let's have a drink." He hauled a silver flask from a pocket inside his blouse. "I don't think you'll need a chaser. It's sloe gin."

Jack took it straight. It tasted like syrup and burned like sin. His eyes watered.

"Want me to ask the porter for a chaser?" the sergeant asked.

"Naw. S'fine."

"Stout lad."

"So tell me some more about the war."

"Well, as I said, we were honored by General LeMay with full-scale daylight bombing of Japan. We were based in the Marianas. A lot like Salina." He grinned. "Only not so cold. . . . And the girls were definitely not pretty. It was always very high-altitude bombing. We had been told to expect the skies to be black with Zeros. That they would come at us with a fury we had never seen. We were bombing Imperial Japan. Our first raid was the Musashino Aircraft plant about ten miles from Hirohito's palace. More than one hundred B-Twenty-nines. They were supposed to have five thousand fighters just waiting for us. That was why we were coming in so high—twenty-seven thousand feet. That was what the planes were designed for—to get above their fighters. But hardly any came up to meet us. We dropped two hundred and seventy *tons* of bombs. Recon said only forty-eight bombs hit the factory. LeMay hit the roof. He really chewed out the bombardiers. But that was how it went. We kept coming in at over twenty thousand feet and knocking out about two percent of our targets. So LeMay decided to hell with the bombsight. It suddenly dawned on Air Corps command that most of the buildings in Japan are made of wood. They have such frequent earthquakes they decided long ago the cheapest way to rebuild is with paper and wood. So we went to incendiaries. LeMay himself led the first raid. They say he kept walking around all day before, rubbing his hands together, and muttering, 'Dresden. Dresden.' I'll never forget it. We went over Japan at night at five to six thousand feet. It was like Europe all over again. Lots of flak, searchlights, some fighters. We were laying *nothing* but fire bombs. I could see them tumbling from the bays of the other planes."

"I saw the newsreels."

"Yeah?"

"Tokyo."

"That was probably March ninth. That was the biggest. Three hundred and thirty-four of us. Then we burned Osaka. We were going somewhere over Japan every night. Burned their six biggest cities. And for the really big

174

boom, we found a couple we hadn't hit. Hiroshima and Nagasaki. Guess for the purposes of evaluating atom bombs Intelligence wanted *clean* targets."

"Wow! Were you in on that one?!"

"*No!*" He took another drink before thoughtfully offering the boy one.

"I sure wish I could of been along," the boy dreamed. He looked at the white target sewn on his navy blue sleeve. "Yeow, I wish I had been along. I missed it all. If I had only been a year older, I could have seen some action. I wish I was you."

The sergeant choked on that one. "I was just sitting here wishing I were *you*."

"Why?" He couldn't imagine such a thing. He would have all that fruit salad on his chest. There was an air medal there.

The sergeant waved his cigarette. "Maybe I wish I had never been . . . at all. Well, here's to war." He offered the boy another drink.

"You shoot down any planes?" the boy asked.

"Um. Yeah, I got some. Hey, isn't it about time for lunch?"

Jack said, "I don't know. I haven't got a watch."

The sergeant consulted his own. It was a hefty chronometer. It looked gold.

"Thought my stomach was telling me it was time for chow. How about it?"

"Sure."

Passing back to the dining car, Jack stopped at Gorilla and Al's seats. "You guys goin to chow?"

They sort of looked the sergeant up and down.

"We're goin to wait until the second sitting," Al said.

"We're goin now. Sarge says first sitting's better."

"Yeow? That's what Sarge says?"

What the hell was eating him? Jack wondered.

"Your buddies?" Larry asked.

"Yeow. We're all from Wichita."

"They sort of look out for you, right?"

Jack hadn't thought of it like that. "Well, *they're* real friends. We just sort of stick together. They're OK."

"I'm sure they are. After a while I quit having close buddies. Guess after Europe I never had a buddy that was really a friend. On Twenty-nines, if you're in the tail, you're sort of isolated."

At lunch the sergeant insisted Jack have a complete meal when all he had intended to have was a club sandwich. A damn sandwich cost a fortune.

"It's on me," he insisted. "I know how little you get. I'm loaded with flight pay and mustering-out pay, terminal leave. Really, I insist."

He was not awed by the array of silverware, the different glasses. He unfurled his napkin and placed it on his lap. Jack watched and followed suit.

Jack caught the sergeant watching him and blushed. "We never had napkins and all this at home," he confessed. "Hell, the old man eats nearly everything with his knife."

"Tell me about your home," the sergeant encouraged, truly interested.

"Well, we've always been pretty poor. . . ." Jack told him the story of his life, leaving out or altering only that of which he dare not speak.

"You really aren't old enough to be in the Navy, are you?" the sergeant said. "Don't worry, you can trust me. I'm not a spook."

"Well, not quite."

"I didn't think so." He told the waiter to bring them some kind of wine. When it arrived in a silver bucket with a napkin around its neck, two women and two men at the table across the aisle looked impressed.

"This is good!" Jack realized, quaffing the wine as if it were beer.

"You ought to come to Chicago with me and I'll show you how to live."

It was great being in uniform. Everyone treated you like a friend. The boy ate his soup with the big spoon after crumbling crackers in it, but noticing how the sergeant did it, he dipped it out of the back of the bowl instead of the front and was careful not to slurp. He learned how to put a curl of butter on his plate rather than directly onto his bread, how to break a roll instead of cutting it. He dropped his fork into his lap, shifting it from his left mitt to his right before forking a piece of meat. The sergeant pretended not to notice.

"A little more wine?"

"Yeow, thanks. This is really goin first class."

The sergeant laughed. "Listen, why *don't* you tag along to Chicago with me?"

176

"Huh?"

"Come to Chicago. We'll have a fine time, I promise you. First class all the way. The truth is, I'm not a little anxious about seeing the family again. I've been sort of toying with the idea of getting a great suite at the Edgewater Beach and living like a king until I'm broke. If you'll come along with me, I'll do it. We'll have a ball."

The boy's brain swarmed with the possibilities. A hotel suite! Every meal like the dining car. The girls! He understood how the sergeant felt. At least he thought he did. When David Hooten had come home after being sunk on the *Wasp,* he didn't trust himself to be alone and brought a buddy home with him from Texas who hadn't any family. They slept in the same bed in David's room. So when David called out in the night, Mack could wake him and tell him it was all right. Jack was deeply touched. In spite of the sergeant's smile, there were flickering haunts in his eyes.

"Gee, Sarge, that's damned nice of you. I'd really like to. Only I wrote my grandparents and they're expectin me home."

"You can send them a wire. You can send one from the train."

"You can do that?"

"Sure. I'll call the conductor."

"Naw. I better not. Anyway, once you get near home, you'll want to see your mom and dad."

"I haven't told them I'm coming home. They're rather old. We were never close. I have an older sister. She's a nun."

"Oh. Well, I'm Church of Christ myself."

The sergeant smiled and looked at the boy through the light wine in his glass.

"I like you, Jack."

"Well, I like you, too. I think you're swell, Sarge. This was the best meal I ever ate. Thanks. But can't I pay my share of the bill?"

"No way!" He looked at the check and laid some bills from a fat wallet on it.

"Listen, I'm serious about Chicago. I just don't know what I'm going to do. I'm more frightened about going home than I was on my first raid. You have to believe me."

"I can't imagine you bein *that* scared, Sarge."

"Please, Jack, call me Larry. I'm out now, remember?"

"Roger . . . Larry."

"Good boy. It's just that I've changed so much. No one will understand. They expect me to go back to school. I'm twenty-five-years old. The idea of school seems so young. I was going to study drama. Can you imagine?"

Jack wasn't certain what "drama" meant.

"I'm sure your folks will understand." Jack tried to cheer him up. "They sound like swell folks."

He smiled, looked at the boy again through his glass and said, "I don't think they will, my friend. I don't think they will."

He waved for the waiter to keep the change and got a wide Cream of Wheat smile. "I sure hope you gentlemens enjoyed your lunch. *Yessir.* I'll save a place just for you at dinner. You ask for Sam." He gave Jack's shoulders a flick or two with his napkin.

"Thanks, George," Jack said. He felt expansive.

In the vestibule the sergeant said, "It's very rude to call a porter or steward on a train George. It's patronizing. You must either find out and address them by name or simply say porter or steward. And never, never call them boy." He grabbed Jack by the scruff of the neck and gave him a friendly shake.

"All the guys always call them boy or George," Jack offered in his defense.

"Well, let's hope you aren't going to be just 'one of the guys.' Just because someone is black or different from you, it doesn't mean they have no feelings. How'd you like it if everyone called you *George?*"

"I'd like it fine! Shit, they call me Muskrat as it is!"

The sergeant threw back his head and laughed and laughed.

"Oh, my!" He held his side. "Do you know, I haven't laughed like that in so long I think I've hurt myself. Really, Jack, you *must* come to Chicago with me. Whatever you want, we'll do. Anything your heart desires. You want a blonde like that one up there?"

The boy was seeing the suite. There was the blonde.

"I'll get you half a dozen."

"You could do that?" The boy liked the sergeant. But half a dozen seemed a lot.

The sergeant hauled out his wallet. It was packed with

dough. Most of it in hundred-dollar bills. "We'll blow it all."

"Gee, I'd really like to. . . ."

"Do it. We'll send a wire."

He thought of his grandparents taking the bus or a cab and coming down to the station in the middle of the night to meet him. He couldn't do that to them. Then he had to show off his uniform a little around town. He couldn't miss that. There were too many people who had to eat a little crow.

"Naw, I just gotta go home, Sarge."

"Larry."

"Larry."

He shrugged. "OK." Then he had a thought. He peeled a fifty-dollar bill out of the wallet and stuffed it in Jack's jumper pocket. "You go home, see your grandparents. If after a couple of days you want to come, wire me at the Edgewater Beach. I'll write it out for you. Hop a plane and come on. I'll meet you at Midway Airport, a blonde on one arm and a bottle of good wine in the other."

"I can't take this!" He tried to get the fifty out of his pocket.

The sergeant caught his hand in his own and held it fast. He was strong.

"If I didn't want to do it, I wouldn't. Quit acting like a hick or you'll make me mad."

"OK."

"Then it's a deal?'

Jack wasn't sure to what he was expected to agree. The sergeant put out his hand, and Jack took it. This time the sergeant hardly squeezed at all.

Just then Gorilla and Al came sidling along toward the dining car.

"How's it goin, Muskrat?" Gorilla asked.

"Hey, guys. Fine! Listen, this's—" But they didn't stop to be introduced.

"Looks it," Gorilla cracked as they went past.

Al jerked his head over his shoulder. "Real buddies. To the end." He and Gorilla exchanged their private look.

Jack looked at the sergeant. "Don't know what's eatin them."

The sergeant raised both eyebrows and shrugged.

After lunch the sergeant insisted Jack sit by the window. They had some more sloe gin. Jack read the sergeant's *Life* magazine. He knew about everything. Baseball, books, more goddamned history than Jack had heard in eight years of school.

"Why weren't you an officer?" Jack asked.

The sergeant laughed. He fingered the cloth of Jack's sleeve. "I never wanted that kind of power. Nor that responsibility." He started talking about: "Once one has drank from the well of power, a cup, a bucket, an ocean of it is never enough. . . ."

Jack nodded off, the sergeant's measured words lulling him along with the clack-clack of the train. He dreamed of a Paramount hotel suite and of the blonde across the aisle who was slumbering on the signal corpsman's chest, her fingertips just in his shirt beneath his tie.

When he awoke, it was dark. He had been sleeping on the sergeant's shoulder. He sat up with a start.

"Sorry, Sarge. Should have given me an elbow."

"You sleep *hard*. I didn't mind. It's dinnertime."

"Boy, I must have really slept."

"Sloe gin's sneaky."

"Guess so."

They stopped in the washroom and washed for dinner. Dinner was even more elegant than lunch. They had filet mignon and an expensive red wine, which the steward brought lying in a basket on its side as if it might explode. Amazingly, it was as smooth and dry as something not even related to booze. After dessert, the sergeant bought them cigars and brandy with their coffee. They tarried in the car until nearly all others had gone.

"You take your time, gentlemens," Sam told them. "You just take all the time you want."

Gorilla and Al came in and and were shown to the tiny table just inside the door of the car. When the sergeant had paid and he and Jack got up to leave, Gorilla caught the boy by the wrist and yanked him close.

"Muskrat, you know what the fuck you're doin?"

"Sure . . . what do you mean?"

Larry had gone on ahead.

"That guy's after your ass, Muskrat!"

"*What?* You're nuts. He's a tail gunner. Seventy missions or more."

"He's a tail gunner," Al said. "He's queer as a nine-dollar bill."

They were pulling his leg. "Come on." He twirled a big cigar.

"Tell him, Gorilla."

Gorilla looked up. "Naw. Hell, let him find out for himself. He's a *big* boy now."

Even if they were kidding, it really pissed him off. When he got back to his seat, his face was red.

"What's the matter?" Larry asked.

Jack coughed on the cigar. "Nothin." Larry thumped his back. Jack stared at the stogie as if coughing had been *its* fault.

"What did your friends say about me?"

"Aw, nothin."

"We're buddies, right? A buddy levels with a buddy?"

"Aw, they were just foolin around. They like to worry me."

"Tell me. What did they say?"

"Ain't worth repeatin."

"Tell me."

"Hell, they tried to make out you were a damn queer," he blurted, wanting to get it out and be done with it. "Ha! They're always sayin somebody's a queer. Told me once Randolph Scott was. Now ain't that a crock? Imagine, a guy like you who's flown all them missions, shot down Jap planes."

The sergeant was laughing. Jack began to laugh too.

"I don't know about Randolph Scott, but about me, they're right, Jack."

"Huh?"

He patted the boy's knee. "They're right."

"The hell!" Jack was still grinning. "Now *you're* tryin to kid me, too."

"I wouldn't kid you, Jacky. Never. I am."

"But, but all them missions. Those ribbons. What about that?"

"That's all real. Everything I've told you is true. That has nothing to do with any private watch we keep."

"I don't understand."

"Maybe we ought to wear some kind of badge. I'm sorry. I've disappointed you. But we aren't all effeminate nances. Is this what you thought?"

Jack wasn't sure at this point what he thought. He felt sick. He looked for someplace to put out the damn cigar.

The sergeant took it from his fingers and stubbed it out in the ashtray by the window.

"Really, Jack, I don't apologize for what I am. It happened. I was only eighteen when I went in the Air Corps. I came from a strict home. I'd had an experience with a teaching brother at my school. I reported him and hated myself. Lord, the penance I did. I'd never really had a girl. I tried. I'd go out with the guys on the base, but they were like wild animals or something. Most of the time I would go to a film or find a library. I *lived* in a USO." He laughed. "I wasn't alone. I don't mean I ran with queers. I wasn't sure then. But there were other good boys. We had girls. Put their pictures up in our lockers, wrote regularly. But we didn't whore around. I've always liked to read. Well, I got this 'Dear John.' Didn't break my heart. She was just a friend. Married a guy we were with as freshmen at Northwestern. A well-known actor now. But it was sort of cutting the last tie. Then, there was this big armorer sergeant. Career man. Always kidding around with us younger guys, pinching our cheeks, patting our ass. Saying things. Anyway, I had to go there to clean guns as extra duty for something. We were alone in the back of the room. I felt this ham of hand on my shoulder and turned around. He was standing there with it out. I felt like there wasn't a muscle in my body. He said, 'This is what you want, kid. I knew it first time I saw you!' I wanted to protest, tell him he had made a mistake. I couldn't even squeak. It was awful!

"I didn't go to chow for days. I went on sick call. Then we were alerted. Maybe that's why I never minded all the missions in Europe. I didn't care if I did die. But when we got shipped to the Pacific, I began to hate flying. I still wasn't afraid, but it was just all those goddamned bombs, so impersonal, going down without a sound. I couldn't hear all the people screaming—old men, women and children—but I could hear them in my mind. All alone back in the tail, it made me sick, truly sick. I wondered if Japanese scream as you and I would. Up there I could never know. And all I wanted when I got back from a mission was to find a man. That's why I don't want to go home. I don't understand it. I tried to go with women. I went with a whore. An Oriental. She took off her clothes, and all I could see was her burning, her flesh ugly and peeling off her bones. I puked in her peter pan. I ran out of there.

There was a native boy. I remember his breath smelled of garlic. I—"

Jack said, "Excuse me!" Clapped his hands over his mouth and plunged toward the head.

People along the aisle not asleep nudged each other and laughed.

"Not got your sea legs yet, swabbie?" a wag cracked as he just made the door. Lunch followed dinner into the stainless-steel bowl. Everything came up, then pure, bitter, yellow bile.

Outside, he washed his mouth out in one of the little sinks. He ran cold water over his face and head. When he stood up, a patient porter held out a towel. When he had dried his face and combed his short hair, the porter was pouring Bromo Seltzer back and forth between two glasses.

"You drink this, young man. It fix you up quick. It settles your stomach fine."

"Thanks." He took the proffered glass and drank it down.

He belched. The porter giggled in an affected Amos and Andy way for Jack's benefit.

"Thank you, sir," the boy said. He fished four bits from his pocket and handed it to the man. It disappeared without the porter's seeming to turn a muscle.

"You needs somethin else, young man, you just come to see Your Uncle George. Yessir."

He weaved his way back to his seat. On the way he got out the fifty the sergeant had given him to come to Chicago.

The seat was empty. Where the sergeant had been was a paperback book. He didn't touch it. He took the aisle seat to wait, the fifty in his hand.

When an hour had passed and the sergeant hadn't returned, Gorilla came up and said, "Where's your boyfriend?"

"He wasn't *my* boyfriend!" Jack shot sparks.

"Shove over." Gorilla started to sit down. Jack moved the book and the sergeant's wristwatch was underneath. It was a Benrus, "21 Jewels, 18 carat gold" it said on the case. On the back was engraved:

To my son,
Love, Dad.

"He dropped his watch." Jack showed it to Gorilla.

"Think he left it, Muskie. He grabbed his kit up there when you went to the head and took off toward the end of the train."

"Well, I ain't keepin it," Jack said.

"Damn good watch," Gorilla said, examining it.

"Why the hell would he leave a watch like that from his dad?"

"Great watch."

"You keep it."

"Not me, ace. I got a watch."

"I'll give it to the conductor," Jack decided.

Gorilla shrugged and handed it back. "What's the book?"

It was a dog-eared paper copy, the kind that came in Red Cross packages.

Grapes of Wrath.

Gorilla thumbed through it. "He didn't write nothin in it."

"Well, I'm goin to find the conductor."

He found the man in the smoking room of the head figuring something in a small leather book.

"Excuse me, sir. But there was a sergeant sitting back there. Air Corps. He changed his seat but musta dropped this watch. Fella said he saw him goin toward the rear of the train."

"All right. We'll see if we can find him. Looks like a good watch. He'll probably be looking for it."

"That's what I thought."

"What you want," Gorilla asked, "*Captain America* or *The Spirit and Plastic Man?*"

"*Plastic Man.*"

They read the comics until the aisle lights went out overhead. Gorilla curled up in the seat, his head hanging over the arm as if his neck were broken, and began to snore. The boy watched desert and mountains slide past. The dark and shadowed space outside the train became filled with newsreel sounds of sirens and bombs. Silently screaming Oriental men, women and children stood along the right-of-way on fire. Their hair flamed and lit their faces. Pubic hair, cocks and cunts were burning. Their flesh peeled and sloughed off their white bones. Their skeletons stood screaming. The train sounded its whistle

184

and plunged into a tunnel. A foot away, the wall rushed by at a hundred miles an hour. His face, reflected in the pane, was distorted by horizontal streams of water. He wondered where the water came from. It hadn't been raining. The engine or the air conditioning, probably, he decided.

He wished his leave was over and he was already on the way to join the fleet.

The lights came on. "Wichita. This is Wichita," the conductor came down the aisle, softly calling. It was the middle of the night. In Wichita it was raining.

Gorilla's dad, mom and sister and Edwards' dad were waiting out on the platform when the train came in. Jack was forgotten in the kissing and hugging. He looked around. Maybe his grandparents were waiting inside.

"Your people meeting you?" Gorilla's tiny father came over to ask.

"Well, I don't know. The buses have quit running. Maybe they couldn't get a cab. I'll wait a bit. They're always late," he lied. Both of them would rather miss a seat at the Last Supper if they had to arrive late.

"We'll be glad to drive you home," Mr. Gerela offered.

"Thanks, but I better wait."

"Give me a call tomorrow, Muskrat," Gorilla said.

"I will."

"But not before noon! I'm goin to sleep until I wake up."

"No way," Jack promised. "Me too."

Mrs. Gerela said, "I can't get over how different you all look! And grown! Goodness!"

She turned, her arm around her son, Gorilla's dad struggling with his sea bag. "Please, Muskrat, do come over," she said. "You're just like Gorilla and Al now. Our house is yours."

"Thank you, ma'am."

After they had got into their cars and left, Jack humped his bag outside and tossed it in a cab.

14

RAIN was not kind to the neighborhood, neither washing its dirty face nor softening any of its corrugated and tar-paper angles. An odor of something like smoldering compost from the soybean plant across the tracks hugged the heavy air, an infuriating industrial fart, killing all sweet rain smell. Graceless yards ran brooks of gray mud into the gutters, backing up in a small alluvial flood where a drain was plugged by a partially burned crib mattress. The houses so long in need of paint were soaked far down their shoulders as if standing in cheap raincoats. The place seemed smaller, more rickety and less rooted than ever before.

Rain or no, not patriotism, bribery or common decency was going to get the vet behind the wheel to turn his taxi up an unlighted niggertown alley at half past two in the morning even if he did still sport the patch of the fight-ingest division in the U. S. Infantry on the right shoulder of his unpressed Ike jacket.

"We are only supposed to go on bon-ee-fide numbers, sailor," he explained with an air of outraged fastidious-ness. "It's the law," he snapped. No one *he* knew, and his social standing was not *that* high, had any business up there, and he wasn't going.

"You can let me out here." The boy paid the fare, hoisted his seabag out into the rain, shouldered it and set off up the alley through the mud.

No light burned for him in his grandparents' trailer. But since they were people with nothing left to lose, the door was never locked. Holding open the screen with his back he forced the sticking rain-swollen door and as quietly as possible pushed his bag inside.

"Who's that?" the old man asked, fumbling for a light, and for the first time the boy realized the old man felt fear. It was in his voice.

"It's Jack," he said, torn between savoring the old man's fright a second longer and putting it to rest.

The light snapped on next to their bed. The old folks sat up, blinking sleep from their eyes.

"It's Jack," his grandmother told the old man, who was squinting and feeling for his eyeglasses.

"I can see! I can see," he insisted. Then, getting his specs hooked over his big dewflop ears, he asked, "By God, is that you, boy?"

"It's me."

"Don't *look* like you." He peered, hanging his neck out like an old turtle.

"He's in the Navy now. That's just his sailor suit," the old woman explained patiently.

"I know what the goddamn hell he is *in*!" he turned on her. "Act like I'm some kind of damn fool."

"See he hasn't gentled much since I left," the boy said.

"Been fumin around here for days. Your Uncle Kenneth got laid off out at Beech. And he was a leadman too. Been there six years. All the plants are layin off."

"That's what the cocksuckers think of you! Work your guts out for six years, start to get a little ahead and they give you the slip."

"He wasn't in the union," the old woman said.

"*Union!*" the old man raged. "The union don't mean shit no more. They're all in cahoots since the war. Anyway, they're layin off union too. Son said."

"Well, it's just a shame," the old woman sighed. "Elfie is just sick. They got new furniture last Christmas. Nobody thought the war would be over so soon. Kenny went down and traded in on a used Chevy. The old one was just fallin apart. He needed it to get out Beech. They don't know how they're goin to keep the payments up. They're still payin on their house too, you know."

"I told Son, he ought to get himself a gun and go clean them cocksuckers out," the old man said.

"You told him the war wasn't goin to end, too," the old woman accused.

"Now blame *that* on me!" He turned on her again. "You don't know nothin! If Roosevelt hadn't of died, it would *still* be goin on. *He'd* of found some shittin way. Truman knew what to do!"

"Wish he knew what to do about Kenneth," she mused wistfully.

"It ain't Truman!" the old man insisted. "It's the goddamn Roosevelt Congress. He spoiled em. Congress ain't goin to do nothin! Never mounted to a hill of beans anyway. Never did! Just do what their special interests tell them. Don't represent the people. Never did! That's the lie I been tryin to expose to this country since I began," he railed as if he were standing for election sitting up in his old long johns in bed. "Represent nothin but the goddamn vested interests and the thieves, liars and sonsabitches—Like this sonofabitch here just yesterday—I still got the paper. I want you to read it and just see what kind of goddamned thinkin runs this country—president of one of the plants here. . . ." There was a slip in the old man's thought during which he visibly searched for a name, waved it away in the air with his hand. "One of them. Don't matter. They all *think* the same. Said right in the paper: 'Too much money in too many hands!' That was *his* fuckin economics! Said: 'Periodical layoffs are *good* for the country. Clears the system of waste.' *That's what they think of you! That's what they think of Son! That's what they think of us! By God, there ain't nothin plainer than that!* THEY THINK WE'RE SHIT!" The veins stood out on his forehead. His big fists were clenched. The trailor shook with his anger.

"Daddy! You'll raise the neighbors," his wife hissed.

"Don't give a damn if I do! Let em hear! Time they waked up to what the government's doin to them! Don't matter they're niggers! I've said it once and I'll say it again, when they can treat us this way we're all by God niggers cept for a fuckin privileged few! Let em wake up and learn! All them smug, egg suckin Christian sonsabitches you go to church with, all them people you clean and sweep for who ain't quite feelin the pinch, let 'em hear *too*, by God! They're all niggers, too! They ain't just woke up to it yet. Long as they can get a little more than the next man, they think they're doin *good!* No more future in their way of thinkin than seein past the end of their cocks—and if them rogues sportin around your church are any example, that ain't far at all! All them out there sellin each other *insurance! Shee-it fire!* If it wasn't killin me, I'd laugh."

"Daddy, it's near three in the morning!" she advised him.

"Well, it just makes my craw burn. . . . How you been?" he asked the boy. "They treatin you all right?"

"Yeow. Fine."

"Hell of a time to be gettin in." He looked at the boy's muddy shoes. "You walk?"

"Cabdriver wouldn't come up the alley."

"We'd of met you," his grandmother said. "But you never said what time you was gettin in. Been expecting you since yesterday. See? I done made your bed."

Sheets she had sewn from flour sacks, a blanket and pillow awaited him on the narrow couch.

"She made it up for you two nights in a row," the old man added.

"Said in my letter I would be comin in today on the Super Chief," the boy said.

"Couldn't make head nor tail of your letter. Looks like goin to all that school you coulda learned to write a better hand." The old man had always been proud of his handwriting, though the boy could never remember his ever writing a letter or receiving one addressed just to him. He would fill the borders of his newspaper after he read it with his name and the names of all his kin in pointed, old-fashioned script amazingly like that of Abraham Lincoln. If anything, he wrote a better hand than Lincoln.

"I told Dad it was tonight you was comin in. I was goin to call and see if they'd tell me the time. . . ." She sort of trailed off.

They were getting very old, the boy suddenly realized. They oughtn't to be living there alone. They could burn the place down and themselves with it. His grandmother had always been very careful with fire, however. But there were cigar burns in everything the old man wore, including his underwear.

"Well, then Mrs. Hooten called," his grandmother went on as if there had been no pause. "David had a wreck in his new car. Think he was drinkin," she said as if sharing a secret. "So she asked me to come over and fix dinner so she could be at the hospital. I didn't get home till after ten. By then it had started to rain. I figured if it was tonight you was gettin in, you'd know your way home. . . . Ain't that right?" She laughed.

"Sure. No sweat. How's David?"

"Oh, he's fine. Fractured his collarbone and near cut off

189

his ear. But they sewed it right back on. Amazing what they can do nowadays, ain't it?"

"Yeow."

"Hope you ain't hungry or anything?" she asked cautiously. "I don't know what we got in the house to eat."

"I had somethin on the train."

"Bet that costs a pretty penny," the old man said.

"Sure does!"

"Well," the old woman chimed in, still back in her thought. "You always been so picky, I just thought I'd wait until you got here before layin anything in. Hate to fix you somethin nice and you turn your nose up at it."

"Sort of thought I'd take you and Granddad out to dinner one night," the boy said. The idea, which had made him feel so good in thought, faded now to a charitable chore to be gotten over as quickly as possible.

"Didn't know bein in the Navy made you rich," the old man joked. "Don't guess you'd like to send me and your grandma some of that right along?" He laughed.

"Sixty-five a month ain't rich."

"That's what they pay you? Reckon you can afford that big dinner?"

"I reckon." They always had to find out what everyone made and how it was spent. His grandmother never went to the store without returning and pricing every item out of the sack and recalling what she had paid for it ten or twenty years before. The old man never *went* to the store.

"Guess they feed you good enough, though," the old man observed, sizing up the boy. "You've filled out some."

"Pretty good."

"Can't say a lot for their barberin, though." He chuckled. "Not enough hair on your head to give shade to a dyin flea."

"That's the idea." The boy grinned, riffling the stubble.

"Guess it is," the old man agreed.

"Well, he's here now." The old woman sighed. "Let's all get to sleep and talk in the morning."

"Guess I better get up an pee." The old man yawned.

The boy began to undress. His grandmother lay back staring at the flyspecked, buckled plywood ceiling, waiting for the old man to put out the light. Her small eyes seemed to be seeing through the ceiling ... or maybe she was seeing nothing at all.

The old man swung his cadaverous-looking feet out

190

from under the covers, the toes turned up in anticipation of a cold floor. He tested them against the linoleum like a woman testing the temperature of a flat iron. In long, yellow-stained BVD's he padded the two steps to the slop jar that was mounted on a low stool set on a newspaper out of respect for his failing aim. He lifted the lid and pissed a noisy stream.

"Got to get up two, sometimes three times a night," he said. "It's hell gettin old. Comes from all that cowboyin I done. Ridin all day, breakin broncs, ruins a man's bladder in later life," he explained, shaking his once-proud meat, dropping it back into his sagging underwear, no longer bothering to button up in view of the frequency of the call. The acrid odor of the pot touched the back of the boy's throat and made his nose try to close, his eyes water.

The old man toddled back and sat on the edge of the bed. "You're all right then?"

"Yeow. Fine."

"Like it OK, do you?"

"It's OK. Sure."

"Learnin a good trade, I reckon?"

"*Daddy,* for goodness sake, get in bed and let him get to sleep," the old woman pleaded.

"Just waitin for him so's I can blow out the light."

"Well, let's talk in the mornin."

The boy got into the rough, seamed sheets. The old man turned out the light.

In the dark, his grandmother whispered, "Daddy, you still got your glasses on."

"Guess I do."

Fumbling for the lamp switch. Then the light was back on. He had to sit up, carefully remove his specs one bow at a time, fold them just so, lay them in their tin box, snap it shut, and locate the spot on the dresser next to the bed where he wanted to place them—but it was odds on that someone would have to find them for *him* in the morning. Once his covers felt right, he again snapped out the light.

After a long moment the boy's grandmother said, "Good night."

"Good night," he replied, the word sticking in his throat.

He dreamed without sleeping of bombs. Bombs of fire which no brilliant maneuver might avoid. Bombs which no very brilliant maneuver was required to apply. A bomb of ultimate destruction. The final say. No word would survive the blast. The old man's ranting and all the screams would be so much yelling on the winds of fire, the silence, the quiet of non-sense. Gone all tyrannical gods. Gone all pic-ayune and grandiose plans. No private voice would ever speak again in his head. Stupid. Absurd. Then even sad-ness would be gone. Pity forever blasted. Gone. He dreamed of being dead and so drifted into the shallows of sleep.

He dreamed of the beautiful woman who spoke in his head. Smiling gently, she stood more still inside herself than any schoolteacher or nun. He tried desperately to dis-cern her face, the true color of her hair. She smiled and loosed her robe with a single tender toll of a cord at its throat. It fell with the silence of parachute silk upon his caught breath. She had never revealed herself before. She was merely perfect. She held out her arms. His every touch deepened her smile, and when ecstasy came, it came without glimmer of meanness, doubt of pain. All joy. But he could not define her face, measure or weigh her breasts or limbs or say for certain if her hair and perfect bush were any color at all. She was all feeling.

Welcome home, honey, she said. Or had he silently mouthed the words himself?

Awake in the dark, he was ashamed of pursuing her elusive dimensions in his need to define her.

Then he felt the wetness plastering his skivvies to his thigh. Christ! He hadn't had a wet dream in years. Jerked off too much for that. He felt rather proud. He rolled the skivvy leg up to keep it off his skin.

The boy peered through the dark to where the old man and the old woman snored; she softly, curled on her side facing the wall, he flat on his back with his teeth out, his mouth like a pocket in a pool table.

He was awakened again by his grandmother bustling around to get ready for church.

"Guess you wouldn't want to get up and come with me?" she whined.

"I'll go with you tonight," he said, turning toward the ruptured split ply wall. The day had dawned with a bright September sun which fell in a hot beam through the glass. His head ached.

"Guess you've just forgot all about bein a good Chris-tian," she sniffed.

"I'll go tonight," he said.

"Thought I'd kind of like to show you off in your uniform." She partially laughed.

"I promise, I'll go tonight." He covered his head with the pillow.

"It ain't the same," she said, grabbing her New Testament and breaking for the bus. By her faith, the Sunday morning service had at least half again as many heavenly merits as the one that evening or Wednesday night prayer meeting.

Presently he could stay in bed no more. He arose, and, holding his nose against the unlidded stench, relieved himself in the old man's jar. The old man snored like a drowning horse. Drop a tennis ball in there on the intake, and if it didn't kill him, he'd put it over a building. Some old horse.

He dipped water from the bucket at the other end of the trailer into a chipped enamel pan they'd had as long as he could remember. The pan was mended with a washer and bolt through the bottom around which a chancre of rust was persistently growing. He thought maybe he would buy them a new pan. On second thought, he decided, fuck it. He threw his slops out the door. He would have to heat some water and shave before he went anywhere, he determined, stroking the soft hairs on his chin. Dressing in dungarees, he cleaned and shined his shoes before the old man woke up.

The old man had a great head. Even with his teeth out, it ought to be on money, the boy thought. Still thick, long white hair that made the boy think of a forge's pale flame rose above his broad, deeply lined brow. For all the old man's anger, disappointment and incontinent hatreds, the furrows in his face were yet more of amusement and concern than of bitterness. The contradictions made the boy wonder what the hell all the old man really knew; what was bullshit, what true?

As he watched, the old man awoke, broke wind beneath the covers, stretched and swung his feet carefully out to test the floor for snakes.

He again addressed the slop jar, leisurely relieving himself, yawning, scratching his hairy prat through the gap in the back of his long johns, wondering at the end of the yawn, "Reckon we can get a little breakfast around here?"

"I'll fix something," the boy volunteered. "Soon as I empty that jar."

The jar had been his task before he enlisted. He wondered who did it while he was away. He would lay odds it wasn't the old man.

He carried the pot outside and up the loose boards that served as a walk to the widow's back door.

"When the hell'd you ever have to knock?" she crowed as soon as she recognized who it was, letting him in. She might have wrapped him in a smothering hug if it hadn't been for his making sure she regarded the jar. A tatty black slip billowed around her, the lace of its hem loose and hanging. Her hair reminded him of a huge worn-out orange plastic pot scrubber. Dregs of yesterday's lipstick stained her seamed old mouth; hose rolled to her sagging ankles; the entire apparition stood in new beaded sheepskin scuffs.

"What the hell they do to your hair?" She riffled his combed and agonizingly parted crew cut. "Feels like a kitten's fur. But you're lookin fine." She stepped back to appraise him better. "Growed, ain't cha?"

"Some." He turned toward her toilet with the pot. Cats on her kitchen table ate from the stacks of dirty dishes, sniffed open jam jars, stalked a sack of bread. Her entire house smelled of goddamned cats.

"Sure got a cute little old butt on you. No wider than my hand," she said following him into the can. She reached forward and squeezed his tail. "Hard as a goddamn rock. You young fellas are all muscle and cock and hair triggers. You'd be surprised at all the young fellas after me when I get fixed up nice. It's true!" she insisted before he had time to harbor a doubt secretly.

Her toilet had a cracked wooden seat and an overhead tank that sounded when flushed as an elephant might if you fed it alive into an enormous meat grinder. The surface glaze had long since gone from her tub. It looked gritty.

When he turned around, she was leaning against the open door. Old as his grandmother, she was slowly, coyly, sneaking the ragged hem of her slip up her pale, mottled thighs, until her entire bush was exposed in all its flaming glory. She dyed the damn thing as well.

It was more as if she were favoring him with a peek at a naughty keepsake than making him an outright offer.

194

"How about that, huh?" she asked.

He was not certain whether he could comment without risking a personal commitment or not.

"Pretty fancy," he hazarded in a mumble.

"Damn right, boy!" She dropped her hem. "Don't think I can't ring your bell, buddy," she added aggressively, though he hadn't offered a challenge.

He hoped he might take her word for it and escape. "Well, the old man's waitin for breakfast. . . ." He offered to pass.

She stepped aside, reaching out and cupping his cock and cods in her plump, liver-spotted hand. Her hands were adorned with a ransom of dime store rings, and ragged, lacquered, pasted-on nails. "You come see me before you go back," she advised, breathing against his face. "I'll show you what this sex stuff is all about."

"Bet you could," he vowed. He didn't want any argument.

"You bet your little dandy! I'm versed in all the arts," she confided. "Just gobble you plumb up."

He made the kitchen door. If she jumped him outright, he might brain her with the pot.

"I'll french," she promised so there would be no misunderstanding, running her tongue obscenely around her lips as the screen door snapped between them. "You come have a snort with me before you go back, you hear now?" she called through the door. "I'll treat you right."

—*Treat you right,* a voice out of time past. Young Loretta Young to Spencer Tracy in a shantytown movie of the thirties? Treat you right. Mae West.

French my foot, he thought, his stomach quite unsteady. Crazy old woman.

She ought to be in a home, was his thought. *In any other neighborhood she would be put away as a public nuisance. In any other neighborhood they would* all *be a nuisance.*

Shaved and in dress blues, the boy went up the alley. He kept to the edge to avoid the still-soft track.

The door of the Demicelli's trailer was closed. There was no sound of a radio within. It was still as sleep.

Arutha was out in her backyard trying to get their old fart hound to chase a stick. A faded red coat sweater with holes in it the size of softballs depended below her little

195

cotton dress. She wore a pair of her mother's pumps from which both high heels had been knocked off, giving the pointed, turned-up toes a kind of Persian aspect. The dog lay belly down in the dirt, peering balefully over his paws, rumbling at the stick the little girl waved in front of his dripping nozzle. Her hair had been severely parted in eight distinct sections, each section being secured with a bit of colored cloth. She barked two indistinct commands that might have been "Fetch! Fetch!" She flung the stick.

Dog pointedly turned his head away with an expression of weary disdain. She scampered after the stick, running oddly from the uphill cant of her shoes, retrieved it and carried it back to Dog. She explained the game again in her labored, unintelligible way, punctuating the tirade with raps on the beast's head with the stick. He shifted sideways and lay one paw over his flea-eaten flat head to avoid the raps, grumbling and narrowing his eyes. Whatever the animal's ancestry, it seemed to the boy he had the fathomless dark character of an old black whose final sanctuary was his calculated worthlessness. Dog did not want to be bothered, not one way or another. Only that and shreds of doggy loyalty kept him from savaging the child. She again flung the stick. Dog did not want to know about it. She trotted after it and came back spewing homicidal imprecations. Dog had had enough of that game. He got up and shook his scabrous hide, creating a small dust storm, out of which he slunk off, his tail between his legs to protect his retreat. It was the way the boy had always seen him. Dog hadn't had anything to wag his tail about since he was a pup.

"Hey, Arutha," the boy called. "Where's Arthur?"

She poised in her turned-up shoes as if to fly. Then she relaxed and backed toward the house, idly nibbling the end of the stick.

"Is Arthur home?" he asked.

She nodded her head ambiguously, still backing.

"Is he?" he insisted. "Don't you remember me?" He lifted his cap that she might better recognize him.

Partial recognition warred with all her horrors of being carried off, but she still backed toward the security of her door.

A tall, narrow-headed woman, distinctly Arthur's mother, appeared at the back door, holding open the screen for Arutha to slip inside. Arutha peeped around the woman's thighs, clasping her with an arm around her legs that twisted her short skirt up well above her birdlike knees. She was a pretty woman of unique build, all of it bunched up on top of those long, skinny legs, like a big-assed bird. From her knees down to her long feet, her legs were like two pipestems. Face, breasts, arms and fingers, everything seemed squeezed into elongated line. Like Arthur and Arutha, "black" did not catch her shading. She was the color of fresh liver, good cordovan shoes, an expensive baseman's glove. Arthur called her Mama.

"What you want?" she inquired guardedly.

"Is Arthur around?"

"Arthur how much?"

"*Arthur,* your little boy."

"Oh. . . . He ain't here. He gone away."

"Gone away?"

"Yeah. He gone away. Who you?"

"I live up in that old trailer. I'm a friend of Arthur's."

"Um." Plainly she knew no friend of Arthur's who wore any kind of uniform. "Well, he gone now."

"When will he be back?"

"He don't be back. He gone away."

"Away?"

"Yeah, that's it. He gone away." She let the screen close, then stood behind it silently until he went on.

Away? Man, there was an impenetrable finality in that that could mean anything. He saw in his mind's eye a tube as long as a pipeline with a little bit of blue sky at the end of it.

"Jackson!" The voice spoke from a tiny grove of sunflowers and hollyhocks next to a falling-down chicken coop. In the wire-covered abandoned chicken run Arthur's face was back in the shaded tall stalks.

"Hey, Arthur."

"You bring me some Jap ears?"

"Jap ears! Shit, Arthur, I just got out of boot camp."

"You ain't been to the war an kill no Japs er shit?"

"No. You have to go through boot camp first. Think they just give you a gun or somethin?"

"I don't know about that. You just say when you come home you bring me some Jap ears cut off some head, man."

"I meant when I came back *next* time."

"Oh, you mean *next* time."

"Yeow. But the war's over now, Arthur. The Japs surrendered."

"That mean you don't bring no ears."

"I don't think they'd let me just lop a set off some citizen."

"Well, I goin away anyway."

"Your mother said you'd gone."

"Yeah. I see her talkin to you now. So I come down here to call. I'm livin here now."

"Why?"

"Got in some little mess, see." He bowed his weird head. "So I livin here. Police come lookin for me, I ain't there. No one sees me here. So many kids here comin and goin no one notice another'n."

"What the hell you do?"

"Don't do *nothin!*" His eyes glinted with angry lights. "Just stole some ole tire an wheel off some car and sell em to the junkmans."

"One ole tire and wheel that serious?"

"Not *one* ole tire, *some* ole tire!" Arthur's pride was hurt.

"Some how much?"

"Um, maybe ten, eleven, maybe some more . . . like that."

"Oh."

"Yeah. They don't *catch* me, see? They catch these two cats an my name come up and the police come lookin. Say, Mama, they send my ass to *ree*-form school. Not me! Regular school starting soon, then they find me sure. So I goin away."

"Where?"

"Buff-low, *New* York. Goin live wif my aunt. She got oney one girl. She almost rich. Say they got a *good* school there. Not some little tacky nigger school. Got *real* school. Yeah. Goin live there."

"Soon?"

"Soon's she send the ticket. Any day now."

"You're glad then?"

"She-it, yeow! This cousin, see, she ain't got no clef pallet like Arutha. She some kind of pretty, Mama says. Thirteen, she. An Mama get real mad about them tires an goin around wif some cats t'see that Missus Simmons." He laughed.

"What do you mean, Arthur?"

"What you mean what you mean? Messa guys always goin around there. She crazy! Whooooeee! Let you fuck her ole red pussy, butt—she suck a cock all day, man. She get kinda nervous when they let some us short stuff go along, but she *crazy*, she don know what's happenin."

"You do anything?" Jack asked the boy, who seemed frail whatever his age.

"It's there for doin, ain't it?" he answered, but Jack could see it was at least a half-empty boast.

"Been busy since I left."

"Yeah, shoeshine ain't for shit. Get five dollar sometimes for a good tire an wheel. An we had plans . . ." he added mysteriously.

"How old are you, Arthur?"

"Why?"

"I just forgot."

"Mos ten."

"Hope you like Buffalo."

"Sure, I like it. Don't like it I come back."

"Well, I'll see ya, Arthur."

"Yeah. See ya. Look sharp in that suit, man."

"Yeah. It's OK."

"You ain't seen me, check?" The smaller boy wanted it understood.

"Gotcha, Arthur."

"You get a chance for them ears you owe me. I tell everybody about them ears. Make me look bad now, man. No ears."

"I'll keep an eye out."

He slipped along the chicken run and was gone.

Dropping a nickel in the slot of the telephone, he anticipated contact with a saner place than the alley. The distant mechanical insistence lifted his mood. He caught the eye of the girl behind the soda fountain and smiled. She smiled back.

"Hello." Mrs. Gerela's voice was warm and pleasant in his ear.

"It's Muskrat, Missus Gerela, is Gorilla home?"

"Hi, Muskrat!" she said cheerfully. "How are you?"

"Just fine."

"Gorilla isn't *up* yet. I'm going to let him sleep until he wakes. It might be next Tuesday." She laughed.

"I'll call back later. I promised him I would call today."

"I'll be certain to tell him. But as soon as he *does* wake up, we are going to his grandmother's over at Coldwater. You know how those things are."

"Yes, ma'am."

"But I know he and Al are scheming something a lot more fun. I'm sure they will want you to go along. So why don't you give him a ring tomorrow? Gorilla *should* be up by then. His father has gone upstairs half a dozen times and he just stands there looking at Sleeping Beauty, then comes down shaking his head in disbelief. I swear they gave me the wrong child in the hospital." She laughed again. "Look, Muskrat, we want you to come over for dinner next Sunday. Al will be here. We are taking some pheasant out of the freezer. I mean you are welcome anytime. But next Sunday's sort of special. Can we count on you?"

"Sure! Thanks. You sure can."

"OK. And I'll tell Gorilla you called when he wakes up."

"Thank you."

They said good-bye. She sure was a nice lady. Anyone who could happily call her son Gorilla and find nothing extraordinary in his having a buddy called Muskrat had to be something special. They weren't rich or anything. The old man was a salesman for Armour's. Mrs. Gerela worked for Cessna in the office. But, by God, they were happy people. If the old man fooled around a little on the road for Armour's, as Gorilla hinted, it wasn't anything to trouble Mrs. Gerela's mind. They weren't churchy. They just liked one another. Everything was relaxed. They never gave a damn what anyone else thought or spent a moment congratulating themselves on the fact. They had fun.

He swung up on a stool at the fountain. The girl in Rexall orange and blue swished the Formica in front of him with a damp sponge and smiled again. "Hi," she said.

"Hi."

"What will you have?" She flirted slightly, tilting her head toward her right shoulder.

"Oh . . . a tall lime Coke," he decided. He had intended having a sandwich as well, but inexplicably he did not want to make her build him one. Syrup and bubbling water was how he liked her to go.

"You live around here?" she asked.

"Yeow. Well, my grandparents do."

"You didn't go to North, did you?" She was cute without being pretty. An almost baby face with large eyes and wide full lips. She was dark enough to have a touch of Indian or Mexican blood.

Hairy little monkey, he thought. Dark brown hair was tucked and pinned up off her starched collar. He noticed the fine dark hair on her sturdy arms. A cheerleader's can raised a shelf of her uniform behind.

"East," he lied.

She made a face. "Didn't think I'd ever seen you around North. Do you know Karen Whiteside at East?"

"No."

"Bobby McGruder or Chuck Zanders?"

He had heard of Zanders. A rich kid who always had a new convertible whose dad got arrested once for hunting jackrabbits with a Thompson submachine gun he had sneaked into the country from Mexico. Chuck was a cocksman. If she knew Chuck, she wasn't a cherry.

"I only went to East a year," he lied. "Then I went TMI—Texas Military Institute. My mom and dad live in Texas."

"Oh. You on leave?"

"Yeow."

"Having any fun?"

"Just got in last night. Seeing you has been the best thing so far."

"Ah. Ah." She wagged her finger at him. "You sailors always have a line, don't you?"

"I'm serious!" he insisted.

"*Sure* you are."

"What time do you get off?" he asked to prove it.

"Work fast, don't you?" she teased.

"What time?"

"Not until ten tonight." She pulled a face.

"Maybe I could take you home."

"Don't think my boyfriend would like it." She waved a massive class ring on her finger wrapped with half a bolt of adhesive tape to keep it on. "Going steady, sorry," she sang.

"You know sailors aren't bothered by those little technicalities." He smiled.

"But I am." She smiled. "He was All State last year."

"At what?"

"Football!" she exclaimed as if he were really from out of town. What else was there?

"What's he play?" He began to feel jealous of the guy. Had to be a big bastard to wear a ring like that.

"Guard. Edwin Bogue. Maybe you heard of him." Clearly if he had not, he was the only person on earth who hadn't.

"Edwin?" he sneered.

"Everyone calls him Eddie, smarty-pants."

"Oh. Well, how's the team, still getting creamed by East?"

"We are going to be Ark Valley champions this year!"

"Never happen."

"You'll see. We almost beat East last year. If they didn't have all them niggers, we would have. We *will* this year."

"No way."

"Poo on you."

"Boyfriend come take you home?"

"Yes! . . ." She seemed to change gears again. "Only he's out following the wheat harvest to get in shape."

"Well then, it's settled. I'll pick you up at ten."

"Don't you dare!"

"Sure. I'll be here at ten."

She studied him a moment, a small frown between her beautiful thick eyebrows. "You have a car?"

"Uh. . . . No. I sold it when I went in the Navy," he lied.

Her momentary interest was gone.

"Your boyfriend have a car?" he asked.

"Sure!" She said it in a way that made him feel naked being caught in public without an automobile.

"What kind?"

"Thirty-four Ford. Red," she said.

"If this was Texas, I'd take you home in a real car," he boasted. "My mother has a Forty-one Cad convertible . . . maroon. It's the same as mine. She hardly ever uses it."

She was not much impressed with distant Cadillacs. Little bitch. He paid for his limeade and swung off the stool. He leaned across the counter and motioned her to come closer. She cautiously edged over.

"What?"

"I was just checking you out. I'm an old friend of Chuck Zanders. He told me *all* about you."

202

"He did not!" She turned red. "Anyway, there's nothin to tell."

"You tell Edwin that."

"What do you mean?"

"Nothin. Maybe you better meet me here at ten and we can discuss it."

"What does Chuck look like?" She got cagey.

"Blond, wavy hair, short, rich as hell. Old man buys him a new car every year. I know Chuck."

"What did he say about me?"

"You know what you did."

"Oh, yeow? Who was with me?"

"Chuck just went into detail about you. I'm not going to play games with you. Just be here at ten. I'll have my granddad's big Packard. It's like a bed in back," he said meaningfully.

She stood there, her mouth opening and closing like an angry puppy.

"Beats the back seat of a Ford anytime." He winked. "Ten o'clock."

He left her fuming and went back to the phone. He looked up a number in the book and dropped in his nickel. The little girl stared at him, trying to figure out how he had come to haunt her life.

A woman who sounded like one of his relatives came on the wire.

"Is Vanda there, Missus Hardasty?" he asked.

"Why, no . . . she isn't. . . . Who is this?"

"Jack Andersen. Just got home on leave from the Navy and thought I would give Vanda a ring."

"Well, she got married."

"She did?"

"Why, yes. Three weeks ago. Married a boy from the base at Hutchinson."

"Well. . . . Well, give her my best wishes."

"I sure will. What did you say your name was?"

"Jack Andersen."

She repeated it. Then she sort of laughed. "She just up and surprised everybody."

Jack said good-bye and hung up. Vanda Hard-ass-ty married. Poor chump. He felt sorry for the guy. Probably got a little surprise herself.

The girl had come from behind the counter. "Listen."

203

She laid her hand on his sleeve. "I really want to know what he said about me."

"Forget it," he advised her. "It isn't important. You just made me a little mad with all that All State crap."

"Please tell me." She stood a little closer and looked up at him pleadingly.

"I'll tell you tonight."

"I *can't*. . . . Honest," she agonized. "Tell me."

He shrugged. He flipped her pouting lower lip with his finger. It made a tiny "pop, pop" sound. He toyed with the locket in the V of her uniform. The back of his fingers brushed her tawny skin. She shot a quick look at the manager.

"Don't. . . . You got to tell me," she begged.

He went on. "Ten."

"Oh, all right," she gave in. "But just straight home. . . ." Then she saw the weakness of her demand. "OK?"

"We'll talk about that, too," Jack promised.

He went outside as if he were Gene Kelly and might break into a tap dance. Out of sight, for want of wheels, he slumped inside himself until he wished his blues had pockets in which to carry his hands. He thought of his mother and wondered if he ought to get on a bus and go to Albuquerque and see her, though the only address he had for her was a post office box number.

Passing Ball's market, he noticed the fluorescent light burning overhead in the wholesale meat department. The windows had been painted with an advertisement higher than a man's head to keep people from looking in and seeing the meat being butchered. He leaped up and saw Mr. Demicelli carving away at a loin of beef, stacking up thick steaks on the butcher's block. His hump lifted the back of his long white coat.

The boy took a deep breath and went through the Demicellis' gate. They had planted flowers in boxes along the brick walk Mr. D. had laid, and a miniature orange tree was in a large pot beside the door to make Mrs. D. think of California.

He tapped lightly on the door. Presently her face appeared in the porthole. She did not look happy to see him, but she opened the door.

"Thought I smelled coffee." He smiled.

"Then you must have the best sense of smell on earth," she grumbled. "It's cold as ice." She indicated what was left in the glass pot from Mister's breakfast.

"What the hell was all that racket over there this morning?" She had a short yellow terry-cloth robe wrapped around her. Her feet were slipped into a pair of dirty white wedgies, the straps unfastened, twisted under her bare heels. She poked at her hair.

"I got in about three. The old man started yelling about my uncle gettin laid off out at Beech," he explained.

"Well, one of these days, if he don't watch it, someone's going to call the police on him," she warned darkly.

"Sorry he disturbed you," Jack offered. It wasn't going at all how he had hoped coming up the alley.

He stretched to his full height, sucked in his gut. She seemed smaller than when he had left. She sort of bent inside her robe as if cold. He wondered if he might put his arm around her playfully as he had before.

"Stop posing and sit down," she said. "I've had a good look at you. Still you don't look dry behind the ears yet. But that uniform suits you."

He slid into the tiny dining nook. "I gained almost twenty pounds and growed two inches," he announced proudly.

"Every little bit helps," she said. She noticed he was looking in the loose gap at the top of her robe and pointedly gathered it closer with her left hand while setting the Silex on her electric plate, dipping in measures of fresh coffee.

"Excuse me a minute." She went into the trailer's small toilet.

He glanced at the magazines strewn on the shelf behind the nook and pulled out a copy of *Sunshine & Health* from the pile. He studied the photographs. So many different sizes and shapes of people. In a smiling line of half a dozen men and women and children, he found himself thinking of photos of concentration camp victims being herded naked into gas chambers. Individually, each woman might have not been bad-looking, but in a bareass bunch one's imperfections seemed to draw his eye to another's. These were people the same as any club or lodge or church group on a sunny picnic—they had those same simpering, "ain't we got fun?" expressions. Then there were the pale blurs where their genitals and pubic hair

205

had been burned away by retoucher's chemicals. They appeared ridiculously unconcerned victims of a fiendish ray and made him think of Hiroshima and Nagasaki.

He flipped to the center of the magazine and a photo of a professional model. That she only took her clothes off for money somehow made her more real than all those around the volleyball court and crummy pool. She knew every way to turn her body to make it look good. Her smile went beyond her eyes into your dreams.

"California is great," he said.

"Um," the woman said from inside the closet.

"Thought about you out there. Saw Hollywood, everything. Only I never went to a nudist camp."

The little toilet flushed. She came out. Without makeup she looked both younger one way and older another. Her bare face made him nervous. It was too naked—something. He liked her happy and teasing. Her personality was absent.

She leaned forward to study her face in the mirror, touched the corner of her open mouth with the tip of a pinkie.

"Caught me on my growly side," she said. Her terry wrap would not stay tight without a true knot in its belt. In the mirror, as she leaned forward to examine her back teeth, he saw the inner hemispheres of her heavy breasts halfway around the southern poles. He glanced softly so as not to draw her attention to the condition of her robe. Beneath the low unmade bed across the end of the trailer he saw the gossamer wad of her pale-yellow panties. A big black satin brassiere hung from the handle of her clothes closet. The trailer had been shut all night. It smelled of stale cigarette smoke, perfume gone flat, dirty clothes, sex and coffee. She took a pack of Pall Malls from her robe pocket and lit a cigarette. She laid the pack and her Zippo on the dinette table.

The poor were curiously saddled with so many feminine diminutives: *Dinette, Kitchenette, Roomette, Couchette—Superette, for christsake! What the fuck was a Superette?* The boy would have liked someone to tell him.

The coffeepot boiled up in a rush into the top half of the maker and bubbled over, sizzling onto the electric plate. She made a lunge for it to set it off the heat. She was not a light woman. Jack thought she had said she was of Polish "extraction." He loved how people said they were of this or that "extraction"—like something squeezed from a wiener machine. But there were larger bones in her ankles and wrists than he had seen in any of the women in his family.

While the coffee steeped, she sat on the bed, cigarette dangling from her lips, and smeared some lotion on first one leg, then the other, with a cotton ball. The crap smelled like Pluto Water. She rolled each meaty leg over to smear the backs well above her knees. Her tits rolled around in the loose top of her robe. She tucked the top tighter before rucking up her sleeves and smearing the stuff on her arms.

"What is that?" he asked.

"Hair remover. I got big pores. Shaving just makes them bigger," she explained.

"Smells like—"

"Yeah, don't it?" She left her cigarette burning in a big ashtray on the bed and, holding the tails of her robe slightly away from her legs, tiptoed comically to their tiny toilet and shower. "Just be a minute," she said.

He heard the water in the shower raining on a plastic curtain, followed the change of the sound as the spray was muted by her body. A bar of sunlight over the bed boiled with the smoke of her cigarette and tiny bits of floating dust.

"Want me to wash your back?" he called.

"What?"

He moved to the door and called again, "Want me to wash your back?"

"Ha-ha!" she said wetly, not laughing.

He went back and sat down at the dinette.

The shower stopped. He heard the curtain rings clatter back.

"Ow! Damn," she exclaimed in the little closet.

"What's the matter?" he asked.

"Not room enough in here to dry your ... big toe. I bumped my head. I *usually* dry off out there."

"Be my guest," he offered.

"Ha-ha."

Presently the door opened a crack, letting out a tumbling cloud of perfumed steam. The humidity in the trailer went up a thousand percent instantly. A smooth, dewy arm and naked shoulder appeared in the crack, waving its hand aimlessly toward the rear of the trailer.

"Honey, will you hand me that tall bottle on my dresser, the one with the gold top?"

He didn't see it.

"Says lotion pour dee corpse on it," she instructed.

He didn't see anything that looked like lotion for any corpse.

"Oh! Maybe it's on the floor under the bed." She laughed as at a naughty memory. He shot her a look. She had stepped out with the narrow mirrored door for a shield, hanging around its edge, exposing a fraction of her bare right flank from shoulder to showered pink toes. She covered her right breast with her left hand, cradling it tenderly. She had large, soft hands. "Stop gawking and look under the bed," she said, ducking farther behind the door.

He got down on his hands and knees. He lifted her panties with thumb and forefinger and dropped them on the unmade bed. There it was. He could just reach it. It was a long smooth glass bottle without shoulders, almost exactly the size and shape of a 30 millimeter shell. Its gold cap made it look even more like ammunition. He brushed a puff of dust from its sticky sides and bore it toward her as if it were a gift.

"What do you use *this* for?"

"What?" It was as if he had challenged her.

"Looks like a cannon shell," he said.

"Oh? Yeah?" She laughed nervously. She took the bottle. "Makes me smoooooooth all over." She bugged her small eyes at him.

"Be glad to smear it on you," he offered.

"Got a one-track mind, don't you?" she asked. "Thanks, but no thanks. Find something to play with for a minute, will you?" She closed the door.

Maybe she fucked herself with that corpse lotion bottle. He would like to see *that*. He liked to believe there was very little a pretty woman who would stoop to marrying a hunchback wouldn't do.

She came out of the closet with a blue towel twisted into a turban on her head, her short robe again cinched tightly around her. She gave the belt another tug for good measure and sighed. "Whew! *Now* I feel better." She even smiled. She smelled good. "Feel." She offered him the smooth surface of her forearm for inspection. "Nice?"

"Yeow! Smoooooth."

She laughed. He felt her calf. "Smooooth." She let him

slide his fingers just over the back of her knee; then she squealed and yanked it away.

"Just wanted to see how far it goes," he reasoned.

"*It* goes all the way, buster. But *I* don't."

"Oh?"

"Um!" She left her lotion on the edge of the dinette table and poured them two large mugs of coffee. She set sugar and a can of condensed milk out with them.

"Shove over." She slid into the nook beside him. "So tell me all about what you've been up to," and prepared herself to listen.

He told her about boot camp, making it sound like the hell they had all convinced themselves it had been. He got a laugh out of her with the tale of the boot named John Paul Jones who had lost his pants.

"And the Navy's *clean!*" he told her. "We had a guy get a three six eight, an undesirable discharge for being dirty."

"That's the worst kind," she cut in.

"No. Dishonorable's worse," he explained, his mind back on the sunny grinders of Diego.

She closed the gap at the top of her robe with her hand and laughed aloud. "Yeah. You're right!"

He rambled on about his accomplishments and honors. "I was the tops in gunnery in our company," turning his left sleeve around to show her his award.

She forced herself to regard it very seriously. Her near breast was pressed against his right arm as she reached across him to examine the tiny white target. The perfume of her shampoo and lotion mingled with the dampness of the turbaned towel. "Regular little shot, are you?" she asked in that way she had as if she were always insinuating something else.

"Sure," he said.

"How sure?" she teased, her bare face close enough to kiss.

"Pretty damn sure—" He made a lunge with his head toward her lips. She deftly recoiled out of range, clamping her hand strongly around his wrist on the table top. She laughed and stuck out her tongue.

"Maggie's drawers that time sure shot," she taunted. "The little boy shot, but he missed . . . her come-plete-ly," she teased. It was a line his stepfather had often used and found great mirth in, though Jack had never learned the joke.

He tried to twist his left arm free. Her big boobs shifted liquidly, barely caught in her gapping robe.

"Strong, ain't I?" she said.

"For a woman," he granted.

"Phooey! Handle a guy like you any day." It became a test of strength. They clenched their teeth.

Inch by inch he lifted his arm until they were even over the table. Then he began to force her back, turning until just the tensed right cheek of his butt was still on the seat. With her left hand she again gathered her robe close and blocked him by raising her knee. He saw a puff of dark hair peeping from the squeezed tight junction of her thighs.

"Um? *Now* what are you going to do?" she asked. "Think you're going to rape me, do you? Better men than you have tried."

"Yeah?"

"Yeah."

Bearing forward with his weight merely carried him up on her upraised knee.

"If I wanted to, I could ruin you," she told him, tapping him gently between his legs with her toes. Then the knee in his chest went limp, but as he fell forward, she twisted out of the booth and his chin caught the edge so hard it made their cups and spoons jump. She howled with delight. He sat up, rubbing his chin. She secured her robe once more and showed him her muscle, hauling up her right sleeve in a parody of a male showoff. It was very impressive.

"Still got some to grow, sailor, if you're going to handle me," she said, hauling down her sleeve.

"Didn't come to wrestle," he mumbled, still rubbing his chin. He had bitten his tongue a bit as well.

"Oh? And what did you come for? ... Coffee?" She smirkingly refilled his cup. "You come back when you're man enough." She resumed her place beside him in the booth. "We naturists keep in shape."

"I'm man enough." He turned and scowled.

"Oh. Did I hurt your feelings?" She feigned sorrow. "I'm sorry. I'm *sure* you are . . . almost man enough."

While he sulked, he idly stroked her lotion bottle, feeling the vaguely oily sides slide between his middle finger and thumb.

"Two falls out of three?" she offered brightly. "Stop

that!" She snatched away the bottle. "Makes me nervous."

He jerked his head. He hadn't been aware of what he was doing. She clasped his hands in a prayerful attitude between her own.

"Friends?"

"Sure."

"Show me a smile."

Dutifully he smiled.

"You go back to California from here?" she asked.

"Yeow. Then I get a ship."

"Boy, I wish I were going." Wistfulness dissolved into a frown. "He's afraid he can't find such a good job out there. Hell, we got the money now for the trip. And they screw him here. Don't pay him anything what he's worth. Always asking him to work over and come in on Sunday. They don't give him any money for it, you know. They don't know about overtime. Think because he's not like everyone else they can treat him like dirt. It destroys his confidence. That's why he drinks. I've had him come home because of something someone has said or done and cry in my arms like a baby. Makes me so mad I could just *kill* them sometimes."

He did not like to know she had such feelings for her old man.

"Yeah," she went on, braiding her fingers idly with his own. "They look at him and all they see is his poor hump. They don't *see* the man. Well, I can tell them— He's a *real* man!" She fixed him sternly with her gaze, making him guiltily feel she counted him as one of "them." "You better believe it!" Then she turned shy. "Do you know, we have been married eight—almost nine—years, and I haven't been unfaithful to him once?" She blushed as if ashamed of the statistic.

"Not once?" he asked, his voice rising to a slightly desperate note.

She drew his hands between her own toward her until they prayed in her warm cleavage. She extended her face over them, lowering her lids sexily. She was so close he could feel her breath on his face. "Not . . . even . . . once, . . ." she said, softly emphasizing each word, her upper lip barely moving. She let him come closer. Without touching yet, he felt an electric tension between their flesh that made him wonder if the human body wasn't encased in some kind of thin magnetic field. Then she went. *"Puh!"*

211

puffing a soft jet of breath up his nose. He jerked backward, blinking his surprise. She really thought she had done a funny, laughing at the expression on his face. "Silly boy," she chided him. "You really have small hands!" she exclaimed, measuring his left palm to palm with her right.

"They aren't so small," he protested, trying to make his fingers longer than her own.

"Mine are bigger," she judged.

"About the same. You have big hands."

She slapped his upraised palm. "I do not! You have *small* hands for a man." It was a condition she made sound less desirable than having a hump. "I like a man who has large, strong hands," she cooed, and shivered at the thought. "Know what they say about a man with large hands?" she asked.

He knew.

She teasingly bent his middle finger down across his palm. He strained for another quarter of an inch. She marked the spot with her thumb, let him extend his palm wide again and measured the distance to the tip of his middle finger, spanning it between the soft pads of her own mature forefinger and thumb.

"Not bad," she granted condescendingly.

"That don't mean nothin," he said. "I got seven inches. I measured."

"Seven inches!" she hooted. "Where did you *measure* from?"

"Want me to prove it?" he challenged, his face very red.

Still laughing, she got up and carried their cups to the trailer's tiny sink and put them in. She glanced at him and began laughing again.

"I can prove it," he insisted.

She shook her head. "Not today you can't. You've got to scoot so I can get dressed. My husband will be coming home in"—she glanced at the clock—"half an hour and I gotta get dressed and fix lunch."

"Does he have to go back to Ball's after lunch?" he asked.

"Yeah, I think so. Why?"

"Can I come over again?"

She pointed toward the door and gave him a swat on the can. "Enn . . . ohhh!"

"How about tomorrow when he's at work?"

"Just for coffee?"

"Well . . . yeah. Right. Coffee."

"Maybe." She had been caught by her reflection in the mirror and stopped to study it. "I ain't such a bag, am I? You should see me with an all-over tan. I'm fair, but I never burn."

"Tomorrow," he said at the door, opening and standing in the step, leaning back to hear her answer.

"I just remembered, tomorrow's Bargain Day."

"Then the *next* day."

"Um . . . OK."

For christsake! She was looking at herself in the mirror and fluffing up her cunt hair with her comb.

He shut the door. When was it ever Bargain Day for him?

He rounded the corner of his grandparents' trailer, feeling as if every hair on his body were bent in the wrong direction. Maybe the Demicellis had mites or crabs or something—he itched. Before he had time to scratch, he looked back and saw Lloyd Butler, the songleader from church, and his wife coming carefully up the rutted alley behind the windshield of their well-kept airflow Chrysler. Mrs. Butler saw him and leaned toward the windshield, poking her hand out the side window to wave gaily. His grandmother was on the same side in the back seat, leaning forward slightly as if she had been talking. Sharon, the Butlers' asshole daughter, was also in the back seat.

He didn't want them to see the crappy old trailer where he lived! His grandmother didn't have any damn pride.

"Hi, sailor!" Mrs. Butler called as the car stopped. "Didn't see you at church," she clucked reprovingly, not even glancing at the trailer.

"I got in real late and just sort of slept in."

"I guess we can excuse *one* morning in that case." She smiled.

"Woke me up too, but you see I got up and went," the old woman said righteously, like a child getting one ahead of a naughty brother.

Sister Butler offered Jack her hand through the window. Brother Butler was surreptitiously studying the ratty trailer with the eyes of an appraiser. Sister hauled Jack down and gave him a peck on the cheek, whispering, "We've been praying for you. I most specially want you to

213

turn out to be a fine, fine Christian. You'd of never guessed, but you were secretly always my favorite bad boy. I always believed in my heart you could do it. You won't let your old Sunday schoolteacher down, will you?"

"No whisperin now," his grandmother chuckled.

"Jack and I have a secret. Don't we?" She winked.

"You bet." He winked back. Better to play along than start a big discussion. He looked at her open, smiling, good-as-gold face and thought of the woman behind thin walls not five yards away, a woman now standing in front of a full-length mirror combing her bush with a big plastic comb. He felt suddenly as if he had been in a fight, conscious of every small hurt and bruise. Yet he liked Sister Butler even if she didn't know shit. She wore a perfume he liked better than any he had ever smelled. There was nothing churchy about that scent. A sweet, dark, very feminine fragrance. On a little girl would make him sick.

"Your perfume," he blurted.

"What?" She blushed. She looked as if perhaps something were wrong. She sniffed.

"I remember you always wore that perfume even when I was a little boy."

"Oh. Isn't that nice?"

"It's called Arpège," Sharon offered from the back seat. "It's very expensive." Jack was aware of the shock in her eyes in seeing where he lived.

"Sharon!" Her mother laughed. She smiled again. "It's my most extravagant vanity." She blushed again. "Anyway I hope it isn't a sin."

"Well, I always liked it," Jack assured her.

The conversation was making Lloyd edgy. He hadn't cut off the engine. He gripped the wheel with both hands. Jack thought of him sitting there with his little pitch pipe in his pocket. Maybe Sister cut his hair to pay for her expensive perfume. It was almost as short as Jack's own. He wondered why Lloyd had never been in service.

"How long are you home for?" Sharon asked.

"Ten days."

"Good."

"Yes," Sister cut in. "We were just talking on the way over here about how Sharon would like to take you to meet some of the kids. I mean, you know most of them, but they've all grown since you attended Sunday school

214

with them. And we thought that being a member now and all you might like to sort of get back into the swim, so to speak. To tell the truth, Sharon was so disappointed when you didn't attend this morning, I don't think she heard a word of the sermon or much else."

"Mother! That's not true!"

Sister Butler winked again and nodded assurance that it was so.

"Well, sure . . ." Jack said. "I'd be glad to, uh, get back in the swim of things." He caught Sharon's eye, and she quickly started picking at the ribbons in the white New Testament on her lap. He could see she was blushing. She wore a hat like a small brown scuttle banded with a purple velvet ribbon that framed her face prettily. What his grandmother called a "princess bodice" tightly encased her from the waist up, fastened with a tiny glass button every half inch all the way down the front. The top two buttons were undone and a string of pearls peeped out. Her fingers picking at the Bible ribbons were encased in good tight tan leather gloves. She wore real stockings and almost grown-up high heels the color of her gloves. She wasn't bad. Then through the back window he saw Mr. Demicelli coming up the alley.

"So we'll see you tonight then?" Sister Butler said.

"Sure! Yes, ma'am," he corrected himself.

"I'll get him there tonight if I have to drag him," his grandmother promised. She opened the door and put out her foot in its mended shoe and the stocking she had salvaged from someone's rags. Her perfume came from Kress'. The smallest bottle cost ten cents. For all that, he was very solicitous handing her out of the car. It was such a surprise to her she gave him a queer look.

"Bye," Sister chirped.

"Bye," Sharon said.

"Good day, Sister Mac," Brother said, reaching for one of those low baritone notes. "Jack. Nice to have you home even if it is for such a short time."

"Thanks."

When the car drove away, not one of them looked back. The boy could *feel* their sighs of relief.

"Charity's such a tiresome chore, ain't it?" he asked bitterly.

"Now just what do you mean?" his grandmother asked.

"*Them!* Couldn't get out of here fast enough. Shit, he

couldn't have taken it another five minutes. And her! Blabbing on like we are just like anyone else, pretending not to see."

"Now that's just not so. They were *happy* to bring me home. They did it because they wanted to see you."

"Bull! Why didn't they get out and come in? I'm sure Lloyd and Granddad would have hit it off just fine. I could have walked that Sharon around and shown her the neighborhood sights."

"Now that just ain't so! They ain't like that. They are good, decent Christian folks. They know we ain't rich. That don't matter. Looks like you would be glad such people take an interest in you."

"Horseshit! Christian's ass! Good God, can't you *see?* They were about to puke!"

"Now that's just how you want to feel. You're just like your mother. Can't stand it for someone to try and do somethin nice for you. Treat you decent and you just turn your nose up at them. Not everyone is too proud to accept the Christian fellowship of well-meanin folks when it's offered. I'm not ashamed we aren't rich. Neither are Brother and Sister Butler. Not everyone thinks so narrow and selfishly as you."

"Rich!" The way she sniffed the word made him want to yell, laugh, cry. *"Rich!"* He waved helplessly at the visable manifestations of their circumstances while she stubbornly stood her ground, her small chin tilted righteously. Rich to her meant two thousand dollars a year. Beyond that was simply a world of folks with more money than they could do with, the object of her mirth and a righteous conviction that their wealth would be no comfort to them in hell. "We aren't talking about rich," he agonized, struggling to find words to give voice to the claws of frustration and anger that ripped the inside of his chest. He felt dizzy as if he had held his breath too long. *"Rich!* Oh-shit-oh-my-dear! They were about to puke! Invite them *in* next time! *Invite them in!"* he raved hysterically and began laughing.

"They wouldn't hesitate a minute," she insisted. "And I *would* have," she plainly lied, looking away, the words sounding suddenly soft and tremulous. Her chin quivered. "I just can't never invite anyone in cause I never know if you'll be out of bed."

His laughter was bitter and hysterical. He could just see

216

them when a bedbug or roach crept out to test their faith. Prisspants Sharon would flat scream!

"Go on and laugh. You ain't so smart. You don't know everything. Everyone don't think like you do," she sniffed.

"I know what they think." He was certain.

The old man was tilted against the willow reading the Sunday paper. "What's all that?" he demanded.

"Brother and Sister Lloyd Butler were kind enough to give me a ride home after church, and now he's tryin to make out like it's a sin for them to do me the favor."

"Their kind of charity is no goddamned favor!" the boy exclaimed.

"Oh, you just think like your mother that everyone's as dead rotten as yourself," the old woman snapped.

"Boy's probably right," the old man mumbled, not looking up from the news. "But you quit devilin your grandma, hear?" he warned the boy.

"You're two of a kind!" she cried. "Hell won't have either of you!" She stomped inside.

For the first time, the boy felt proud to have been likened to his grandfather. He followed the old woman inside and sat on the couch-bed. Some leave.

"Grandma, I've been thinking I'd sort of like to go see Mom. Thought maybe I could catch a bus to Albuquerque tomorrow or next day."

She was very still for a moment, then sighed deeply. "Now what do you want to do that for? Guess you just don't like seein me."

"No, I just kind of would like to see her. I'll be shipped out soon as I get back."

"Well, you just can't."

"What do you mean?"

"Oh, you might as well find out. She's in jail again." She sat down wearily at the table, staring blankly out the small window at Demicelli's trailer.

"How do you know?"

"Well, I know because she wrote asking me and Daddy for the money to get a lawyer to try and get her out. That's how I know."

"I don't believe you," he said suspiciously, though as soon as he said it, he knew it was probably true. "You just don't want me to go, just want me to parade around at church," he added irrationally.

"That's as little as you think of me," she whined. "Well, I don't lie!"

"Sometimes you do," he challenged. "If you don't want me to know somethin."

"Maybe I stretch the truth a bit, but I don't lie."

"I got two letters from her in boot camp. She said she had a good job demonstratin cosmetics, living with another girl, fixin up a nice apartment—went into great detail about it. Said she was goin horseback riding a lot. Said she was through with Bill, had learned her lesson and just wanted to get her life straightened out. Said she met a forest ranger who flew his own plane who was a great guy and really wanted to meet me."

The old woman sighed. "That's just some more of her make-believe. She made me promise not to tell you. She said she was too ashamed. But I just never seem able to stay party to a lie. Somethin always catches me up." She sighed again.

Sanctimonious old fool! he thought. Then he thought about his mother making up all that shit she wrote him. "What's she in for?"

"Same darn thing I reckon. Hot checks. I told her when she married that good-for-nothin Bill, a divorced man, she was heading for everlastin trouble. But she wouldn't listen to her mother. Oh, no, not to me! Like you, she knew better than me. She had big ideas. So she married that fast talker and just look at her now."

"You send her the money?"

"No, I did not," she said primly. "Oh, I thought about it. I guess I could of gotten a loan from First Federal. Brother Beech-Maple would of probably let me have it. They all know me and know I'm good for it. But I talked to Kenneth, and he said, 'Well, Mom, you do what you think is right.' He would have been glad to sign the note with me if I asked him. That was before he lost his job. But he knows as well as I do she'll just go and do the same darn thing again! She's done it before. She don't care nothin about me and her father and the family until she gets into some blame trouble. Then she sees the error of her ways and is full of promises. She's just no darn good. Not since she married that cussed Bill Wild."

"She's OK. She does the best she can," he muttered.

"Well, it's a pretty sorry way of doin, if you ask me! Just look where it got her. If you think she's so blame nice, *you* send her the money. I scrimped and saved to raise you when she didn't care enough about you to think a single minute before runnin off with that Bill. But you never cared nothin about *me*. You always thought more of her than you did of me." She began to cry.

"How much is it?"

"She wanted two hundred and fifty dollars. I don't have it. I'd of had to borrow it. Go into debt. You got that much?"

"No."

"I didn't think so." She seemed gratified.

"Well, shit!" He leaped up and stalked the length of the trailer and back again.

"Now cussin and carryin on ain't goin to do no good. There's nothin none of us can do. She wouldn't listen to me. She'll just have to take her medicine."

"Oh, shut up."

"Now-you-listen-here, you can't talk to me like that! It ain't my fault."

"Then who the hell's fault is it?" He would really have liked to know.

"Well, it ain't mine!"

"Bullshit!" He grabbed his cap.

"Where are you going?"

"I don't know! Out!"

"Ain't you going to have dinner? I got a nice chicken at the Jew's. I was goin to fix nice chicken and gravy. You always liked that."

"I don't want any goddamn dinner!" he said at the door.

"That's just what I thought. Try to make somethin nice for you. Have a decent meal in peace like folks, and this is all the thanks I get for my tryin."

He wanted her to cry. He wanted to hurt her.

"You don't care nothin about how *I* feel. *You're just like her!*"

"That's right!" he snapped, clamping his cap on his head.

"Nobody cares how *I* feel," she blubbered. "No matter how hard I try, nothin ever comes out right. What am I goin to do with this chicken now?" she wailed.

"Shove it up your ass!"

15

HE ORDERED a hamburger and a 7-Up at a North Broadway diner. While the burger sizzled on the griddle, he telephoned Glenn. He explained he had only got in from San Diego that morning, told him where he was and left the next move up to Glenn. He said he would be right there. He had sounded really glad to hear from him, Jack decided after hanging up.

He skarfed the hamburger and the drink. Within fifteen minutes Glenn and Bucky pulled up at the curb in front in a '36 Ford four-door, shined within an inch of its life. It was Glenn's old man's car, though it looked as if Glenn had been working on it. A foxtail flew from a Greyhound hood ornament that had lighted blue eyes.

Glenn charged inside the diner like a madman. "You lousy son—" he yelled, yellow eyes flashing, drawing the stares of citizens having Sunday dinner and a cop sitting around the end of the counter over doughnuts and coffee.

Having spun around on the stool, Jack was speechless, his face drained with fright. He felt paralyzed. Glenn's fist whistled past a quarter of an inch from his nose. He hauled Jack off the stool.

"Now you're going to get it!" he raged.

"Here! You boys!" the fry cook called.

Glenn threw another roundhouse left. Jack's head snapped back. The sound of the punch was like a shot. He hit him three more shots, each one loud and sharp. Then Jack fought back, winging lefts and rights that sent Glenn falling about rubber-legged. They stood toe to toe, their punches coming faster than the eye could follow, the impacts like gunshots.

"Somebody *stop* it!" a woman screeched.

The cop started to get up.

It was a trick they had perfected in junior high. Barely

missing each other, the other sharply clapping his hands while all eyes followed the murderous swift blows. They fell around snorting, cursing and crying out in pain in their old mock fight. They collapsed in each other's arms. The thing only took a couple of minutes. People were half standing in the booths. One guy with his family was resolutely forking meat loaf in his mouth, not about to look or get involved in something that was not his business.

"Get out of here with that garbage!" The fry cook came and shook his spatula at them.

They were laughing. The fry cook was not amused. "Go on," he grumped. "We don't need that kind of nonsense in here."

"We're goin quietly, Officer!" Glenn trilled at the cop, who grinned at them shyly.

They tumbled outside. Glenn snatched Jack's cap.

"Man, you looked worried!" Glenn taunted. "Thought I was really after your ass, didn't you?"

"Looked like he was about to pee," Buck said without humor.

"Well, I wasn't sure," Jack admitted.

"You were about to crap," Buck said.

"How'd I look as a sailor?" Glenn bent the cap onto the back of his head. Jack took it and squared it over Glenn's wad of greasy curls just above his eyebrows. There was a small scar, a mere nick, across his right brow.

"Look great."

Glenn bent to see his reflection in the car's Simonized finish.

"Naw. . . . Hey, I don't look bad, do I?"

"Great," Jack said.

Glenn gave him back his cap. He whipped a comb out of his hip pocket and bent deeply at the knees to rebuild his elaborate hairdo in the car's waxy shine. They had to wait until he was through. It was no petty enterprise. Glenn had to have his hair just so.

"How you been, Buck?" Jack asked the sullen dark young man. "Been gettin plenty?"

"More than you." He made it sound like a challenge. Asshole.

"Yeah," Glenn cut in. "Guess bein shut up in boot camp you ain't had a lot of time to go after the gash."

"Only VJ-Night," Jack said. "Man, did I luck into somethin that night!"

"Yeah? Here, too, man! We borrowed some of Rich's brother's Air Corps officer's uniforms. He was killed over Germany, you know. We picked up these three married broads. One was twenty-eight, one was thirty and one was thirty-*four*! Man, they just ate our asses up. Kept changin around all night. Huh, Buck?"

"Yeah."

"Hey, you look like you've grown, man," Glenn said. He had to measure. He stood back to back with Jack and measured across their heads. Even with his pile of curls Jack was a couple of inches taller. "Put on some weight too, ain't yuh?" He slapped Jack's belly hard with the flat of his hand, knocking a bit of breath out of him. He laughed. "Don't guess you feel big enough to *try* my ass though."

Jack smiled and shrugged. "That wasn't what I called you up for."

"Naw, I don't guess you'd do that." Glenn laughed. "Want to feel a calf's leg?" He hauled up his sweater sleeve and made a muscle like an ad for a Charles Atlas course. He had an arm on him indeed like a calf's leg. The muscles were corded and knotted upon themselves. "Feel that rock," he demanded proudly.

Jack could barely span the bicep with both hands. He dutifully shook his head in wonder and admiration.

"Damn right! Dynamic Tension," Glenn explained.

Jack mumbled he would look into it. Glenn wore only a smart soft yellow V-necked sweater over his dynamic torso. Buck had on a shirt with quarter-sized polka dots, a suede-paneled coat sweater and light-colored pegged gabardine slacks with hand stitching down the seams.

"Got the car looking great," Jack observed.

Glenn and Buck got into the front seat. "Yeow. You notice I dropped the rear shackles? I been takin care of it. Old man says I can have it. Got me to go back to finish school. Says long as I go the car's mine, and if I graduate, he'll give it to me and pay my first year in college. Shee-it, can you see *me* in college? !"

Jack wasn't too sure.

"Well, I'm goin to do it. I'm going to make it. Hell, I can do that stuff when I try."

Buck cut him a look and grinned.

"Fuck you!" Glenn turned and spat. "I can do it! Can't I?" he asked Jack.

"Don't see why not."

"Fuckin-a-do! I'm through with all this fuckin around. I gotta look for my future. With all these goddamn veterans comin back with their GI Bills there ain't goin to be shit soon for a guy without an education." He recited what Jack knew his dad had told him. He laughed. "Anyway, the old man said get ass back to school or get out and get a regular job. Beats workin. So, what do yuh want to do? This is your night." He generously made Jack the gift.

"I don't know. Thought we might get some beers or somethin. Maybe scare up some cunt."

Glenn and Buck looked at each other as if they had made a bet on what he would say.

"You popped your cherry yet?" Glenn asked, bulging his tongue in his cheek and winking at Buck.

"Hell, you weren't listening. I told you there was this great cunt in San Pedro on VJ-Day. Not that she was the first, though I let her *think* she was. She was a lot older. Real grown-up hep cunt. Old man was a Marine pilot."

"Oh, yeah, you did mention somethin, didn't you? But you know we weren't there."

"I'm tellin you," Jack explained. He sat on the edge of the back seat to lean forward on the back of the front seat between them. "She was real crazy. But, man, she fucked like a greased mink!"

"Fucked her, did yuh?" Glenn asked loudly as if he hadn't been listening.

"Yeow, I did," Jack insisted.

"What he say, Buck?" Glenn asked.

"Said he did," Buck shouted.

"Fuck you both," Jack grumbled. They never believed anything.

They laughed. "That's all right, little buddy," Glenn promised. "What say, Buck, think we ought to fix him up right tonight?"

"Whatever you say, man."

Jack wanted to tell them about plugging Avis Nickel the night before he left when he had walked out with her leaving them in the Red Ball Inn. They were so goddamned smart. Then he decided to hell with them He wouldn't cheapen the experience by telling them. They wouldn't believe him anyway.

As if reading his mind, Glenn's question made him jump. "You hear about what happened to Gus?"

"I sort of heard he got arrested or something," Jack admitted.

"Dumbass had a sack of pot—whole fuckin gunnysack full—tryin to cure it in Avis' old lady's garage and it caught fire! You ever hear anything so goddamned dumb? But they couldn't really hook him too bad for it. His brother, George, had been fartin around with this guy Woodward who wants to be governor. Gus copped a plea. Got ninety days or something, on the Pea Farm."

"How's Avis?" Jack wondered.

"Oh, I don't know. Think she got off with probation or somethin. Somebody said she'd gone up to Larned State Hospital to have her head checked. And someone else said she and Gus were goin to get married or somethin as soon as he gets out. You know, she was the first cunt I ever banged? Down on the canal bank." He took one hand from the wheel and rubbed his crotch at the memory. "She-it, if I only knew then what I know now," he dreamed. "Man, she's got one of them cunts that *suck!* That's why she can't help herself," he added wisely. "She's just got to have it, man! She's got no control."

"I'd admit that," Jack admitted.

"Yeow. Take it from me, it's true."

"How's old Vanda Hard-ass-ty?"

"Got her scummy ass *married,* man!" Glenn crowed. "Yeow, hooked this dumbass swabbie from Hutchinson. *Married!* Whoee! Think of livin with the ghost of all the peters that have been in her. They were in town a couple of weeks ago. Ran into them in front of the Candy Kitchen. She still goes for my ass. I tell her to squat and piss and she'll ask where and how much. We fucked her! Yeah, me and Buck. Told her *sailor* she was goin to see a girlfriend one afternoon. We drove her ass out into the toolies, and she let both me and Buck fuck her pregnant ass. Right, Buck?"

Buck nodded silent corroboration.

"Hell, the kid could be mine anyway." Glenn puffed out his chest.

"Or a hundred other guys," Buck said.

"Oh, yeow, but she really *loved* my ass!" Glenn insisted. "She didn't give a shit if I came in her. Anyway, she still can't fuck for shit," he sneered. "So I made her suck my cock. And I didn't even wipe it off neither. She didn't want to do it with Buck watchin, but she got right down in broad daylight standin outside the car, me layin back in the seat and gobbled the goop." He laughed at the picture. "Then old Buck comes around and plugs her dog fashion while she's goin down on me. That's a funny sensation, man."

"Threw her guts up," Buck said.

"Yeow, well, that's because she was pregnant and gets morning sickness," Glenn explained seriously. "She was a little mad, but that don't mean shit. All I gotta do is snap my fingers and that stupid bitch will come on a trot, pregnant, draggin *two* husbands—she loves my ass, man!"

Maybe she did. "She isn't in town now?" Jack asked.

Glenn laughed. "Ain't seen her. You, Buck?"

Buck hadn't seen her.

"Well, guess we'll have to let him in on our good stuff," Glenn said. "We been takin out these two nurses. Me and mine are like that!" He held up two knobby fingers crossed. "But Buck's havin a little trouble with his. Won't give him smell. These are *good* girls, man. Yeow, they only do it for *love*. No shit. And does mine *love* my ass!" he crowed, rubbing himself again. "Tight as a glove. Almost a virgin before me. I really had to talk some shit, man. She *cried* the first time! No shit. She cried. . . ." His voice dropped with the wonder of it, became so sentimental Jack thought he would sniff back a tear at the recall. "That really got me, man. Hell, she's twenty-*three*! That's no snotty damn kid, man. She's all woman. I was really the first one. Had this crummy cousin or somethin who'd stuck his cock a little way in, but they're Catholic and he got scared. It was cherry, man. Twenty-three! That means somethin to a guy," he vowed. "Buck goes with her roommate. He can't get into her *no* way. Funny, cause she knows what Linda and me are doin. She's been in the other room when I stayed all night. Thought it would help set her up for Buck. But these are funny cunts. Real religious."

"Piss on her," Buck said.

They drove out North Broadway to Twenty-first Street, past the livestock yards and exchange where the head of a golden life-sized longhorn steer glittered above the white-columned entrance. Some cowboys were around, carrying stock whips, their pants tucked into their boots, wearing Stetsons. One actually had on chaps. A couple of yard nags were tied at one of the truck loading gates. Because it was the weekend, only a few head of cattle were bawling in the holding pens beyond the tricky board fences. The smell of the stockyards, of Swift's, Cudahy's and the Wichita Desiccating Plant, was a sweet, sour, rotting-hide, burning-shit odor all along the street. Glenn whipped into the bumpy dirt parking lot in front of a dive called the Stockyards Saloon & Recreation, a low, one-room heap of boards held together by tin beer and soft-drink signs.

Inside there was a small, rough stand-up bar, a pocket pool table, its baize mended with two-inch widths of adhesive tape under a tin-shaded light, and a vintage Wurlitzer in which a dozen dead flies lay about on their backs, their little legs in the air, oblivious to the gay, faded bubbling lights that played in their musical mausoleum. Conked by one rendition too many of "The Yellow Rose of Texas" or "That Waltz You Saved For Me."

"Three Hamms," Glenn ordered for them all, turning to study the juke's offerings. "Got a quarter, ace?" he asked Jack.

"Sure."

He dropped in the quarter Jack handed him. "Anything you want to hear?"

"I don't care."

"Nothin but fuckin cowboy shit." Glenn punched up the quarter and the small room was filled with fiddles and steel guitars.

The cowboy behind the bar, dark sideburns neatly angled off below his ears, set the bottles on the bar and popped the tops with a giveaway opener tied to the bar with a length of binder twine.

"You guys want glasses?" he drawled.

"Not me." Glenn said.

"Naw."

"No glasses." The cowboy looked more friendly.

"Not much business today," Glenn observed.

"Well, it is a little slow," the cowboy allowed. "Picks up later when the drovers start comin in to get in line for market in the mornin."

With the cattlemen would come the Twenty-first Street floozies from the dilapidated old walk-up flops along the streets, both floozies and flops operating behind false fronts phony enough for the sets of a Western movie. When

Twenty-first Street picked up, it was as down-and-out tough as any place the boys had ever been.

They tipped up their beers.

"What say we get a bottle?" Glenn lowered his voice to ask Jack.

"Sure. OK with me."

Glenn leaned conspiratorially across the bar to speak to the cowboy. "Can you let us have a bottle?"

The bartender automatically assured himself there was no one else in the bar. "Pint or fifth?" he asked, barely moving his lips, not really looking at any of them. Buying whiskey in Kansas was still an illicit enterprise, locking seller and buyer in crime.

"What you got?"

"Glenmores or Early Times."

"Early Times."

"That's five a pint or ten a fifth."

"Let's get a fifth," Glenn suggested. "And six beers?"

"Can't let you have it here," the cowboy said. "You'll have to go around to the back."

"OK. Let's drink up, gang."

At the back door Glenn patted his pockets. "I'm a little light. OK if I catch you later?" he asked Jack.

"Sure. Forget it. Let me get the jug."

"Hey! That's straight ace!" He clapped Jack's back. "Anyway, we're gettin the girls, aren't we?" He grinned. Then righteously, evening it all up: "An I got the car, right?"

Jack felt a flash of total recognition, recall and prophetic vision. Glenn made Jack feel as he had around his stepfather—a master barroom conneroo who would afterward deride those who always stood him a drink or a beer out of some pitying respect for what he might have been rather than for how clever he thought he had become. In the moment Jack saw his first true friend becoming such an obviously sly barroom child.

"Me and Buck'll get the beers," Glenn offered generously, flourishing a wilted dollar bill. He collected Buck's single and Jack's ten to hand to the cowboy who opened the door and quickly handed out a brown grocery sack with the warning: "Don't hang around with that here."

"Keep the change," Glenn cracked and collected the sacks as if it had been his treat.

They cruised around, drinking from the bottle with beer

227

chasers until eight, when the nurses got off duty. Glenn had telephoned his girl and assured Jack. "It's all fixed up." Then he leveled like a very real and straight good buddy: "I can't guarantee. I mean, I told her not to get no dog or anything. She'll do her best. I told her you were this real good-lookin swabbie home on leave and wasn't, you know, lookin to hold hands." He chuckled. "Built you up good."

"Thanks," Jack said.

"Yeow. Well, you know, these are high-class cunts. You got to talk shit to them. Sell em. These ain't goddamn high school kids. Anyway, I told her to be sort of choosy. I just don't want you to blame me if it don't work out. I mean, if you don't get laid or somethin."

"Sure it will be all right," Jack assured him.

"Hell, yeah!" He reached back and jogged Jack's arm on the back of the front seat. "I guess you can take care of yourself now better than you used to, even if you still ain't as old as me and Buck. I just don't want any hard feelins, you know, if you don't get laid or somethin."

"I know . . . ace," Jack assured him. He sat back in the seat like a passenger. *Fuck em,* he thought, feeling a nice buzz from the booze. *Let's see these great damn girls.* He convinced himself he did not give a damn one way or the other. What had once seemed imperative had been yammered by Glenn into passing curiosity. *Just along for the ride, ace,* he told himself. *Just killin time.* He had a thought and giggled to himself.

Bucky cut him a look.

Glenn grinned. "What's so funny?"

"Just thought. You ever know a pet duck not named Elmer?"

"A fuckin *what*?"

"Everyone always calls a pet white duck *Elmer!*" It really struck him funny.

"What's he talkin about?" Glenn asked Bucky, beginning to laugh in spite of himself.

Buck didn't know. "He's gettin crocked."

"Hey, listen, you gotta be straight when we get these girls," Glenn cautioned very seriously. "Don't wanta make me look bad to my moose. She's goin out of her way for you."

"Naw. No, I'm not drunk, man. I just realized, everyone's ever had a pet duck they call it Elmer. You know, all these millions of gaggle-headed damn ducks runnin around in that ducky way they got, goin quack-quack, and they're all named . . . *Elmer!*"

Glenn began to nod, seeing it. "Yeah, yeah, yeah." He began to laugh.

"See in the paper this morning that a pet duck got kicked by a horse and broke his leg. They stuffed him in a stovepipe joint for a cast and put a pair of kid's rubber boots on him to keep him from paddlin around—lookin out of that pipe in that dumb ducky way. . . ." He could not explain for laughing. "Didn't you *see* it?"

Glenn was pounding the steering wheel with both hands, stomping his feet on the floor, making the car lurch forward as if it had hiccups, which set off even more hysterical laughter. Even Buck was laughing in that silent way he had.

"Oh, yeow," Glenn howled. "Quack! Quack!" They all began to quack.

"The way they *look*, man!" Glenn was deep into it. "You ever *look* at one of them Elmer pet ducks? Looks like a little kid with his first football . . . just before you kick his ass and take it away from him and play a game with it."

"They *look* like a goddamn Elmer!"

"Shit-oh-my-dear! 'Ever know a pet white duck?' "

They sailed through the stoplight at Broadway and Harry. Jack had wondered why they were going the wrong way from St. Frances Hospital. At the corner on South Broadway where sidewalks ended, a small-wheel carnival, the last of the season, truculent as a gypsy beggar in its faded, tattered flies, too poor to lay its own sawdust, had set up where the big carnivals had been. A few people had parked to idle along the brief midway where the Ferris wheel sporting several burned-out lights slowly turned.

"We'll take them to the carnival!" Glenn decided before whipping into the parking lot of the 400 Club, bouncing through it and pulling up in the drive of a shade-drawn little bungalow on the corner. He stopped and cut the lights but kept his engine running.

"Guess we'll need another bottle."

Jack's mother had once worked at the 400 as a hatcheck girl. His Uncle Kenneth, in Levi's, a straw cowboy hat and reversed hide high-heeled boots, came from the bungalow's back porch and approached the car.

229

"Evenin, boys," he said, perfunctorily flashing a small flashlight through the car.

"Kenny!" Jack said. "It's me, Jack."

The spare, not really tall man, with the same kind of Lincolnesque face as his old man, leaned to look closer into the back. Jack poked his head out of the window. His uncle was plainly embarrassed to have Jack see him peddling bootleg booze. Though everyone in the family knew what he did at night, they all operated under the fiction he merely "parked cars."

"Well, damn. Mom said you was comin in."

"Got in at three this morning."

He shuffled his boots on the gravel. "It's sure good to see you." He chuckled, shyly. "Don't look the same somehow, though, in that there sailor suit. Cut all your hair off."

"Yeow." He liked Kenny, though his uncle had always spoken as if words were a penny apiece and he was saving up for some secret loquacious toot. Jack's grandmother had always said, "Son never talks much cause Daddy never gave him the chance."

"Grandpa woke the neighbors this mornin when I came in cussin about how you got laid off at Beech."

Kenneth just smiled.

"Reckon you'll be out to see us," he drawled. "The boys been lookin forward to you comin home."

"Yeow, I will."

Another man appeared at the closed-in back porch. "You OK, Ken?"

Then a tall, pale, red-haired woman in a flowered kimono came and leaned on the man on the porch. She was a head taller than either of the men. A big girl. About a yard and a half of sheer black stockings were clamped in the nickel-and-rubber jaw of a garter strap halfway up her big white thigh. "Come on, Ken-nee. It's your *de*-all."

"Get back in the house," Kenneth said. Then he told the man, "It's OK, Pete. This is my nephew, Jack, my sister's boy. Just got home from the Navy."

"Oh. Hiya."

"Hi."

"This ain't such a good place to talk," the boy's uncle drawled.

"Yeow," Glenn said. "We'd like to get a bottle."

230

Kenneth's eyes narrowed as if he were thinking about it for a couple of beats. "OK. What you want?"

"Some straight bourbon," Glenn said. As long as *he* wasn't buying, they might as well go first class. "That OK?" he asked Jack.

"Sure."

Kenny studied Jack for a bit and then seemed to decide he guessed if he was old enough to serve, he was old enough to drink.

"Old Crow be good enough?" he grinned.

"Hell, yes!" Glenn crowed.

Kenny went to the back porch and brought out a fifth.

"I thought we'd just get a pint, cause I'm light," Glenn said. "That stuff's expensive."

"It's OK," Jack said, hauling out his wallet again. He handed his uncle two fives. "That right?"

"Aw . . . shit." Kenny took just one of the fives. "But don't come around here again," he told Jack. "There's other places if you want to buy whiskey."

"Sure, Kenny."

"All right. You have fun, but be careful."

"We will."

When he turned to go back in, they noticed the handle of a flat, black leather sap peeking from his Western pocket.

"I didn't know he was your uncle!" Glenn exclaimed. "Man, you see that sap in his hip pocket?" He was impressed. "He don't say much, but you can tell, man, you don't wanta fuck with him."

"He will go a long way to stay out of trouble," Jack said.

The blackjack wasn't for the cops. There was a case or two of booze just inside the back porch so they wouldn't have to work too hard when the sheriff's men staged their periodical raids. They hadn't surprised Jack's uncle or the man he worked for in a dozen years.

"Guess that woman wasn't your aunt?" Glenn laughed.

"Wish the hell she was!" Jack said.

"Yeow, man!" Glenn rubbed his cock. "I'd like me some of that. Your uncle always dress like?"

"Yeow. He's been playin John Wayne all his life."

"That goddamn duck in a stovepipe." Glenn chuckled. "Remember how we used to laugh our ass off at Woody Woodpecker and Elmer Fudd or that crazy little two-gun

231

guy with the red whiskers that Bugs Bunny just drove *wild*—What the hell was his name?"

Jack could not think.

"What *was* his name? Anyway," he told Bucky, "ole Jack and me used to laugh until we were fallin out of the seats. He can do that Tweety Bird. Do Tweety," he requested.

"I think I saw a putty tat," Jack dutifully replied.

Glenn chuckled. But it wasn't the same. Bucky spun around in his seat to look at Jack. The corners of his mouth turned down disparagingly as if he had caught Jack doing something completely off base. Glenn caught Bucky's look.

"Heh-heh. Yeah. Well, that was then. Don't seem so funny now." He cleared his throat. His voice took a deep dive until he sounded just like his big bullshit of an old man. "Let's get these cunts and get the show on the road."

Jack sat back again in his seat. Shit. Why did they have to have all these stupid ticks? As many fuckin petty rules as a goddamn lodge. Why can't anyone just enjoy something? Always got to put up some kind of front.

Jack's girl was a little fat and had freckles all over a sort of flirty chipmunk face. Her name was Nina. That at least seemed hopeful. She was perfectly willing to squeeze in the back on Jack's lap, while Buck and his girl doubled on their side of the seat.

"Hope I don't squash you." Nina giggled.

"You watch him," Glenn warned. "He's just back from six months at sea and you're the first woman he's seen."

"Oooooh, really!" She wriggled her big bottom into his lap. It was tightly encased in a girdle so it was an unyielding mono-rump, with less fleshly warmth than a medicine ball. "I'll have to watch it then."

"Really? Where have you been?" Glenn's girl, Linda, turned to ask.

"No. He just said that. I'm home on boot leave."

"Come on, woman, give your ever-lovin daddy a kiss," Glenn said before starting up. He snapped his fingers. She narrowed her eyes but gave him a perfunctory kiss.

"I taught you better than that," he growled. He bent her head roughly over the back of the front seat and kissed her long and roundly. He cupped her small breast. She covered his hand and hummed "Nnnnnnuh," but did

not let it become a test of strengths. Her nurse's cap became dislodged, and she had to reach back to hold it on.

Glenn broke it off with a flourish.

"Show off!" she snapped.

"Aw, you know you *love* my skinny ass." He preened for the benefit of those in the back seat.

"Ha!" she snorted.

"You don't love me?" he dared her.

"Just go on."

"Not until you tell me you love me. I mean we can just end it here."

"Oh, for Christsake. OK. I love you. *Now* can we just go?"

"I don't like the way you said it. Say it like you do when we're alone and I got you so hot you can't see—"

"Gl-enn!" she screeched.

"Say it!" he insisted.

"For God's sake!" She leaped up with both knees in the seat, yanked back his curly country satyr's head and breathed languidly in his face. "I luuuuuuuuv youuuuuuuu. You drive me wild."

"That's better," he agreed.

She flopped back onto her side of the seat, angrily crossed her arms and stared out the window.

He started the car. "She's got a temper, man. But I like a women with lots of spirit. . . . Don't I, honey?"

"Drive," she said.

He reached over and loudly slapped her thigh.

"If it's going to be one of *those* kind of evenings"—the dark-haired girl on Buck's lap arched—"I'd just as soon stay home and wash my hair."

"What do you think of my sweetheart?" Glenn asked over his shoulder.

"Beautiful!" Jack dutifully exclaimed.

"Hear that?" he asked her. "See, I told you you were beautiful. Maybe now you'll believe me. Jack's very intelligent. Reads all kinds of books. Comes out with them *big* words sometimes, like you."

"If he's a friend of yours, I wouldn't believe a word he says," she sulked.

"Hey! This ain't how I wanted this party to be. What's got into everybody here? Come on. Let's all be friends." He hoisted up a bottle and passed it around. "Look, what I got, real straight bourbon."

233

Nina was ready. She took a dainty drink and coughed, them snuggled down, tweaked Jack's turned-up nose and said, "I think you're cute."

Buck choked on his drink. "That's the word, baby. *Key-ute!*"

"What's *his* trouble?" Nina wondered.

"He needs a high enema," Buck's girl, Grace, snapped. "Like all the way up to his brain."

"Enema *your* ass!" he growled, hauling her down and going for her tits.

"Come on, honey." Glenn became suddenly pleading. "Don't sit way over there in the cold."

"Believe me what I feel right now is not cold," Linda said.

"Then come over and give me some warm."

"That is not what I meant," she said, but she slid over in the seat until she straddled the gearshift. Glenn took his right hand from the wheel and put it around her shoulders, steering with the death's-head joy knob. Soon she rested her head on his shoulder.

Buck was kissing Grace, so Jack gave Nina a kiss. She kissed fat, though it was pretty nice with a lot of spit in it . . . an initial, passionless kiss of a girl who went on dates expecting to neck. A meaningless, nameless thing . . . not even peanuts with a cold beer. With their tastes in each other's mouths they touched foreheads. "Nice?" she said.

"Good."

"You too."

He knew with absolute certainty that she would go. In the awareness there was a tension that told her he knew. They gave a sort of muted short cry. She heaved down and twisted around, wrapping a heavy freckled arm around his neck and snuffled into an honest kiss.

For a good-size girl, she had very small tits, and most of that was padding.

"Sure you haven't been six months at sea." She smiled, her chipmunk face close to his own.

Suddenly, he felt quite sorry for her. "Where are you from?"

"Great Bend," she said. "Why?"

"Just wondered."

"Yeow," Glenn said over his shoulder. "They're just little country girls. Come to the city and fell into a rough crowd." There was the sound of him slapping Linda's bare thigh above her stocking top. "Like that virgin country stuff!"

"That's enough!" Linda took a wild slap at his face. He deftly caught her wrist in midair.

"Too fast for you. Got those quick reactions." Glenn laughed.

"He sure loves himself," Nina whispered.

"She's worried about what you'll think," he said over his shoulder. "Hell, baby, we aren't children. Everyone *knows* I'm gettin into your pants like gangbusters."

"Glenn! For God sake!" she yelled again.

He winked. "She don't like that crude language." He smirked. "Except sometimes, huh?"

"Glenn I'm warning you!"

He laughed. "What did I tell you? She's got a temper, huh? Didn't I tell you she was a real good girl? A real woman?"

"Why don't you take out an ad?" she snapped angrily. "Let the whole world know."

"Listen, when I take out an ad, it'll be to announce our engagement."

"That'll be the day!"

"Uh-uh. She's mad, man. See, there's this guy in the Coast Guard who's had a thing on her ever since they were little kids. Writes these deadass letters to her—"

"Can you imagine someone who would get into your personal letters and *read* them?" She turned to solicit an opinion. *"He* did."

"Hell, when a woman's my woman, we don't have no secrets," he said. "Anyway, that's all over now. He wants to come home and marry her. Only now there's me. Yeow, you'd never think to see *me* so crazy about a girl, huh?" he asked. "Man, it's serious!"

She just shook her head, not mollified.

She was not really a pretty girl. A nice, ordinary face full of small-town stillnesses and anxieties. The thin bangs that accentuated her rather long nose gave her a sort of Irish setter look. Yet she had a creamy complexion, nice, large eyes and a bearing of maturity that most of the girls they had gone with did not possess. Her best feature was her ass. Even in her starched white uniform, it flipped. She was so swaybacked she seemed mildly deformed, her small breasts elevated like antiaircraft artillery. In the little

235

Catholic town in eastern Kansas from which she came, St. Paul, she had been a drum majorette in the school band.

"Yeow, she's goin to straighten me out," he confided in that phony, sentimental way Jack supposed he actually believed passed for conviction. "Going to buckle down and get this high school crap over with. Then we're goin to get married and she's goin to put me through college. Right, honey?"

She stared at him with frightened eyes. Jack wondered if she had ever heard him outline their future before. Whatever hope for them she harbored was wrapped in pain and some disbelief that she was there at all.

"Oh, yeow," he blabbed on. "Never thought you'd see the day Cisco fell in love, did yuh?" His corny sentimentality imbued the word with the quality of candied, glazed fruit—all sugar and no essence. "Too good for me. Haven't I told you you're too good for me?" he asked her. "Don't know why she puts up with me, randy, badass hood." He pronounced it "Whoo-d." "But love ain't no respecter." He wrapped it up, brightening perceptibly. "An we're really in love, ain't we, honey?"

She did not answer. He put out his hand, a pleading, doggy look on his face. She let herself be drawn closer. Then she gave in and threw her arms around his neck and buried her face in his neck, whispering something. "Sure," he crooned and patted her head. "She's a *registered* nurse!" he exclaimed.

Bucky wrestled with his girl on his side of the seat. She had clamped her arms at her sides and twisted to press tight against him to keep him from her breasts, crossed and entwined her legs until he could only bother the top of her right thigh with his left hand. When he would work her uniform up above her stocking, she would yank it down reprovingly. She was the prettiest of the three. She had dark hair, wore black-rimmed glasses, had a soft face with good bones, a wide, full mouth. Her lower lip looked swollen. She reminded Jack of Kathryn Grayson. Had those same big forty-inch knockers up front. Her name was Grace.

The car smelled of antiseptic and rubbing alcohol. They were driving under a tunnel of trees beyond which large old houses sat on deep lawns. Once the homes of bankers and kings of cattle and wheat, they had been divided into housekeeping apartments. On the lawn of one of the houses, where a blue neon VFW post number hung above the door, there was still a fenced corral into which people threw rubbish for the wartime scrap drive.

The girls had run into their houses to change while the boys waited in the car. Glenn passed the bottle around.

"How's it goin with that Nina?" he asked Jack.

"Fine."

"Yeow, she's sort of fat, ain't she, but I was watchin in the mirror. She'll go, man. You gotcherself a cinch piece of tail there, boy."

"Seems like."

"Sure," he said expansively. "Told you old Cisco would fix you up. My girl and Buck's don't run around with her usually. Linda says she's a regular punchin bag. But like I told her, you only got a little time home, right?"

"She's fine."

"What do you think of mine, huh? Man, she gets a few drinks in her and she can't get enough of my old pajonk! You want to find yourself one of these twenty-three-year-old virgins, man. You get their cherry, they just love your ass to death. Did I tell you, the first time she cried?"

"Yeow, that's what you said."

"Yeow, and that cunt is so smooth and tight. Um ... um." He jerked his thumb at Buck, sitting sulkily in the corner of the seat. Buck hit the bottle hard.

"Buck's still ain't let him get his finger wet. You must be slippin, stud."

"Kiss off, cock!" Buck grumped.

Glenn laughed.

"Piss on her," Buck said. " 'Oh, don't Bucky. Please, be nice.' " He mocked the girl in sneering falsetto.

"They got those high religious defenses," Glenn said. "Took me a solid damn week. But I *wanted* her ass! Hell, I even bought her a bunch of flowers! *Me!* But you guys ever let *that* get out and we'll go to dukes." He suddenly leaned over the back of the seat, caught them both behind the necks and shook them up. "Not two other guys in the world I'd rather be around with. Who's a bunch of bastards?"

"We are!" Jack joined Glenn in an old cheer. Buck went deeper into a blackass sulk.

"That's all right, old buddy." Glenn laid his cheek

against Jack's as they had when they were younger, posing for a Smile-A-Minute together. "We got *ours!*"

They all had another drink.

"Shoulda got that Nina," Glenn told Buck.

"You want to trade, Buck," Jack offered, "you let me know. I sort of like that Grace's looks."

"Go fuck yourself, punk!" Buck snapped with inordinate fury.

"Uh uh," Glenn cautioned. "We're just all good buddies tonight. No grudges. Clean slate."

"Aw, that fuckin uniform don't change shit," Buck said. "Once a punk always a punk."

"Look, I was doin you a favor," Jack protested.

"Don't you *ever* do *me* no goddamn favors ... *punk!*" The word was a definite challenge.

"Come on, Buck. Knock it off," Glenn said. He reached back to give Buck a friendly jog. Buck shoved his hand away.

"I called him a punk. Anybody that'll take that will take this!" He grabbed his cock, making motions as if to wave it.

"No, I wouldn't, Buck," Jack said, screwing down tight on his anger and fear.

"Shit! Look at him! You ever *see* such a punk? Shittin his blues. Pissin his pants. You're yellow as baby shit, Andersen."

"No, I'm not."

"Prove it ... *punk!*" He swung a backhand which Jack just slipped.

Glenn dived over the seat to get between them.

"Let me get at that fuckin punk!" Buck pleaded, trying to get around Glenn. He shoved Glenn too roughly. Glenn pushed him onto the back of his neck in the corner of the seat.

"That ain't him you're messin with! This is *me!*"

"Then tell him to get his ass out of the car. I *want* some of his phony sailor's ass! I *want* him, Glenn," he begged.

Glenn looked at Jack, shrugged. "Didn't want to see this," he said. "Looks like it's on, man."

Buck racked down the handle of the door on his side and bailed out.

"He's higher than you," Glenn whispered confidentially. "Keep circling to his right and stick, stick, stick him," was his advice. Jack nodded that he understood. "Maybe he won't hurt you too bad," he added hopefully.

Buck was waiting for him, chin tucked behind his left shoulder, peeking over his cocked right, lazily exercising his jab.

Jack came out of the car circling. He shot a short, very tentative left over which Buck threw a whistling right that brushed the tip of his nose as he leaned quickly backward. Buck followed with a left hook Jack just ducked under, Bucky slipping on the grass and falling over Jack's back onto the grass. He leaped right up and displayed his fancy footwork to show it had been a slip and to get used to the footing.

"He's serious now," Glenn warned darkly.

Buck came bobbing and weaving, feinting, as Jack, doggedly following Glenn's advice, circled to the darker boy's right. He'd had boxing lessons in boot camp and a little judo. With sixteen-ounce gloves he had held his own in his weight class. He buoyed himself with the memory, slipping Buck's left leads, catching a right off his forehead. He dipped inside another right and hooked Buck hard just under the ribs, got stung with a left and right on each ear and caught Buck with an overhead right on the mouth, and to everyone's surprise, Buck was on the seat of his hand-stitched slacks.

"I slipped, you sonofabitch!" Buck snarled.

"Don't let him get up!" Glenn hissed.

Buck touched his lip with the back of his forefinger and saw a little blood. He came up throwing.

Jack circled again, but Buck rushed him and rocked his head with rights and lefts.

"You let him get up, man." Glenn sighed.

Jack went backward, hiding behind his arms, bent to offer Buck only the top of his head. Buck threw rocks off his skull. An uppercut banged Jack's own fists hard into his mouth. His arms felt without muscle-one.

"Punk! Punk! Punk! Punk!" Buck whipped his head.

Jack felt he had backed as far as he could. He lunged forward. The top of his head connected with Buck's chin. Bucky's leather-bottomed, expensive blue seude shoes slipped again on the grass. Jack threw a blind left hook as he sensed Buck going down and caught him on the side of the jaw. He felt the jolt all the way up his arm. He stood there rocking with the beat of the blood in his head.

Bucky was stretched out on the grass, his cheek cradled on his left arm as if taking a nap. Then he stirred and got to his hands and knees.

Jack heard himself say from a long way away in a frightened, punky voice, "You OK, Buck? It was just a slip. You had me whipped."

One of the girls exclaimed behind him, "Oh, *God!* Now they're fighting!"

"Naw, naw." Glenn moved to calm them. "It's cool now. Just a little argument. Been comin for years. It's all copacetic now. All over now."

Jack offered Buck his hand. He slapped it away and swore, "Nothin's settled, *punk!*"

"You won, all right?" Jack asked.

"Yeow, it was a lucky punch. You slipped. You had his ass whipped, man. Everyone knows it now." Glenn came over and wanted to get them all in the car.

"I'd just as soon go right back upstairs," Grace said. "If this is how the evening's going to be." She and Linda had put on skintight faded Levi's rolled to just below their knees, tight sleeveless sweaters, and had matching cardigans loosely over their shoulders.

"Hey, I thought this was supposed to be a *friendly* party," Nina cracked. The other girls hadn't told her what they were wearing. She had a zebra-striped dress with a low square neck and full skirt held out with a stiffened underslip. She wore stockings and high heels.

"It is!" Glenn insisted. "Come on, clowns, or I'll deck you both. Shake and make up for the rest of the night, OK?"

Jack put out his hand. Buck hit him a shot in the gut that doubled him over.

"That's it!" Grace said. "I'm not going anywhere with him! They're drunk."

Glenn threw Buck up against the car. "You shape the hell up, boy! I mean right now!"

"I just want to *plow* his yellow ass!" Jack heard Buck beg. He sounded about to cry.

"Forget it! You won. You know it. I know it. He knows it. You hurt him. I mean forget it."

"He ain't hurt. He's just too yellow to stand up like a man. Sayin I won don't mean anything. You know that! You know that!" he pleaded. "Just let me cream him."

"Yeah. Yeah. I *know* how you feel, man. Don't I know?

But *not tonight!* *He* bought the bottle. Now, tomorrow's another day. But any more shit tonight and you're goin to have to whip *my* ass! But that don't mean I don't *understand,* man. OK?" He shook Buck until he reluctantly agreed.

"Well, all reet!" He turned, rubbing his hands together eagerly. On the grass he executed a perfect handstand and kip-up to clear the air.

"Hey, where's Grace?"

Linda stood in the drive, her arms folded beneath her breasts, a disgusted look on her face. "She went in, Glenn. She isn't going. You're all half blind."

"Aw, naw. We're just fine. Sure she's goin! You run in and get her. Tell her it's all cool now." He slapped her hard on her tightly encased faded denim bottom.

"She won't go!"

"Sure she will."

"No, she won't! She won't go with him. I know her."

"Aw, that's nothin. See, no one's with nobody. Yeah!" He congratulated himself upon the beauty of his solution. "No one's with nobody! You go tell her. You ain't with me. She ain't with him. Nina ain't with Jack. We're all just together! Go tell her."

"It's just crazy," she said. But she went back into the large, doughty old house.

"I ought to go and put on something more casual," Nina suggested.

"Naw, naw," Glenn assured her. "You're just fine." He grabbed her and danced her around in the drive, whirling so fast she squealed. He plunked his hands on her wide hips. "Lots of women here! Listen, if I'd of met you first. . . ." He leered.

"I'll bet!" Nina simpered.

Linda came out again, followed by a reluctant Grace.

"Hooray!" Glenn cheered. "Now there's a good sport! I told everyone you wouldn't spoil it all. OK, let's have a ball!"

"Ha!" Grace rolled her large dark eyes behind her glasses. "Some ball!"

"Everyone in the car!"

"I'm not getting in with *him,*" Grace indicated Buck, slumped and ostensibly sleeping in the corner of the back seat.

"OK, now who's riding in front with me?" Glenn busied

241

about getting it all worked out. Nina hovered breathlessly near. He did not see her. "I got it!" He steered Grace and Jack to the other side of the car. "You ride on his lap. He said he really went for you," he whispered to her. "He's a great guy."

She eyed Jack suspiciously.

"Yeah. That's it, in you go." He dashed around and led Nina toward the other door. When he opened it, Buck's knee fell out. He lifted the bottle from the cradle of Buck's arms. Nina looked at Buck doubtfully. Glenn slapped his knee until Buck stirred. "Sit up, ass. Got a present for yuh."

"You want me to sit on him?" Nina asked.

"You on him or him on you. In you go." He boosted her, giggling, inside.

"Hi! I'm Nina, remember?" She giggled. "Nobody's with nobody now."

"Hi, Nina. They say you like to punch," Buck slurred.

"Oh, wow! Is *he* bombed!" she groaned. "Thanks a lot, pal."

Buck hauled her down and stopped her mouth with a kiss, her stiffened underskirt lifting her dress like a sail.

They started off. The other girl felt good on Jack's lap. There was a definite warmth from her bottom that he had not felt with Nina. Her large right breast joggled nicely against his chest with the movement of the car.

"Raise up a little, pud, you're bending my lily," Buck slurred. Nina lifted herself up so he could reach underneath and sort himself out. He gave her a thumb which made her squeal and bump her head on the headlining. "Christ! What you got on, a girdle?" Buck asked.

"That's for me to know and for you to find out," she whispered coyly.

He hauled her back down into a sloppy kiss. "That bitch over there kisses like a goddamn fish," he told her, meaning Grace.

"How you doing back there?" Glenn asked.

"Oh, *lovely*," Grace said.

"That's good. Don't do anything I wouldn't do."

"Fat chance!"

Buck tried to get his hand into the top of Nina's dress.

"Don't!" she pleaded. When he did not stop, she said, "You'll be sorree. . . ."

"Charming," Grace said.

Jack felt she was probably a bit jealous. Even though she did not like Buck, it was not easy for her to see him mauling another girl. He was a handsome guy.

"Hey!" Buck fished around in the top of Nina's dress like a kid feeling for the bottom on a sack. "This bitch wears falsies! She ain't got titty-one!"

"Oh, marvelous!" Grace clapped her hands.

"Piss on your sister!" Buck spat at her. "You got what you deserve. Go on, kiss the punk."

"You stink!" she snarled back.

"You watch your mouth, you tightassed pig. I'll bust your fuckin lip for yuh. Candyass there won't be of any help to you neither. Look at them!" he instructed Nina. "You ever see two more punky sausages?" He laughed. "Laugh!" he charged her. "When I laugh, you laugh."

"I don't feel like laughing," she cooed.

"The hell!" He began tickling her under the arms, and she erupted into a flurry of dancing knees and hysterical laughter. One of her high heels came down on Jack's instep. He raised himself and Grace off the seat.

"Oh, sorry! . . ." Nina howled with laughter. "Please no more," she begged.

Buck stopped for a moment and looked at Jack. "You lookin at my girl, punk? You know what a punk this sailor boy is?" he asked Nina. "That's how you tell a real punk. Ain't that right, punk? See, a punk don't *mind* being called a punk."

"Whatever you say, Buck," Jack said in a dead voice, saving just enough pride to convince himself he was sacrificing the rest for the sake of everyone's good time.

"Fuckin-right! We got a date, little boy blue. Before you go back."

"OK, Buck."

"Ok, Buck," he nanced in a high voice. He laughed. "Go on, let's see you kiss that punk," he challenged Grace.

She and Jack looked at each other. "With pleasure." She lowered her lips onto his, closed her eyes behind her glasses and wrapped her arms around his head. Her lips were soft and full. She opened her mouth, but he could not find her tongue. What the hell had she done with it? Swallowed it? There the little rascal was! It was tipped up against the roof of her mouth, baring its muscular, defensive back. To reach it raked the string under his own tongue on her sharp lower incisors. It was like walking around in a dark room empty of furniture. Presently he gave up. She sighed and snuggled her big boobs against his chest.

"What's a punk?" Linda asked Glenn, her head on his shoulder.

"Shh. I'll tell you later."

Buck began tickling Nina again.

"Oh, don't! Please! I'll pee my pants!" she howled. "I can't *stand* it!"

"You could make her have a fit." Linda turned to warn Buck seriously.

"Cronk, you fat bitch!" Buck commanded the helpless big girl, bearing down until tears coursed down her chipmunk cheeks.

"Uh! Uh! Uh!" She fought for breath.

"He could hurt her," Linda told Glenn.

"She's all right." He determined with a glance. "We're almost there."

Buck stopped. Nina lay across his knees helplessly limp, her heavy legs slightly asprawl. Buck passed a hand in front of her eyes. "Laughed her fool self blind." He chuckled. He began slapping her face. "Hey, cunt!" Wake up and piss, the world's on fire!" She feebly stirred and twitched one hand to protect herself, frowned as if asleep. Buck turned his attention to her knees, flipped her skirt and underskirt up over her face and plunged his hand between her sweaty, fat legs.

Grace snuggled her head in the corner where she could not see and wanted Jack to kiss her again. He wondered if he might go for one of her tits.

"She's a rubber woman!" Buck cried, pushing Nina's clothing back further to reveal a perforated pink rubber girdle.

"Nunnh ..." she mumbled from beneath her upturned skirts.

Buck pushed her back down."You keep out of this. Go back to sleep."

"There's still a rubber shortage, you know," Linda turned to remind him coldly. "A girl can't always get a two-way stretch. That's just mean!" She turned away.

"Hey! Look at this!" There was the sound of three little snaps letting go. Then three more.

"Don't," the girl said weakly from under her clothes. Too late.

244

Linda turned around and saw the rubber snap-out crotch of Nina's girdle dangled before her eyes. She clapped both hands over her mouth to stifle a cry or a laugh. Holding the thing between thumb and forefinger, Buck jiggled it, making it jump obscenely. Linda squealed and squeezed shut her eyes.

"We don't need that." Buck flipped the flap out the open window.

Linda began to laugh in spite of herself.

Nina struggled feebly under her clothes, trying ineffectually to cover herself. "Don't do anything to me. ..." Her voice came drifting up as from a foggy depth.

Everyone except Grace began to laugh. Jack had the distinct feeling Nina had returned to the real world, such as it was for the time being, quite some minutes before.

"Just going to play with your pussy," Buck scolded, pushing away the limp hand with which she offered to cover herself. "I'll take care of that. You just hush up now."

He lifted her dead right leg with both hands and set it down with her knee against the front seat. Linda peeked between her fingers, choking back laughter.

"Don't look," Grace whispered to Jack. "Kiss me."

Buck cupped his hand to his ear listening at the turned-up layers of clothes. "Shh . . ." he whispered. He gave a downbeat.

"Don't do anything to meeee ..." the frail eerie voice moaned.

Linda exploded with laughter the way a fire hose does blowing a connection. *"Oh! Merceeee!"* she howled, pounding the back of the seat with both fists, raising such a dust old Nina sneezed. Then they all blew into high, roaring laughter. Even Grace laughed.

"Poor girl." She laughed.

Sneeze or not, if Nina was just acting, she had gone too far into it suddenly to spring to life. She made only a few, futile movements to protect herself.

"Why doesn't someone *do* something?" Grace wanted to know.

"Maybe she likes being the center of attention," Jack offered.

"It's ghastly."

"Oh. Oh." Her leg began to inch closed. She stirred as if she might turn onto her side on Buck's lap. Buck smartly nudged her leg back to where it had been, slapped it as if it had been naughty and it went even more convincingly limp. Buck lifted Nina's right arm and let it fall. It came down like a limp lead rope. He nodded wisely and slid his hand between her legs.

"Dooooooon't," she groaned.

"Aw, shut up!"

By the time they pulled up at the carnival Buck was jobbing her with a fury that rocked the car. Linda leaned back and flipped the girl's skirts down.

"Oooooooh," Nina moaned. "OH!"

"Hey, lookit," Buck said. "She's goin to come!"

"OOOOOOOHHHHHHH!" she cried in rising intensity.

Jack could feel Grace breathing with excitement in spite of herself. Nor could she stop watching. They were all silently watching. Jack reached around Grace's back and just got his hand on her large left breast. She gave a slight jump but did not try to move his hand.

"OH! OH! NO!" Nina yelled. She clamped Buck's hand tight between her legs and thrust furiously against it.

"Go, cunt, *go!*" Buck encouraged her.

"Oh, *gawd*. . . ." She shuddered and moaned. Then old Nina came, socking it home like a man. Bam! Bam! Bam!

"Wonderful!" Linda squeaked hysterically, no longer laughing. In the carnival lights playing over her face, Jack saw a vein swollen and throbbing in the middle of her brow. "In the category of the best unconscious orgasm of the year by an Irish registered nurse, I nominate—Miss Boom-Boom Brennan!"

Nina was crying. She had buried her face against Buck. "What will everyone think of me?" she blubbered.

"Don't," Grace said and removed Jack's hand.

Glenn passed the bottle around. Buck tried to get Nina to take a nip. She would not show her face.

"She all right?" Glenn asked.

"She's goin to be better," Buck promised. "Just leave us that bottle here."

"Here's where I came in," Linda said. She opened the door and bounded out of the car.

Outside, Grace wondered, "Are we just going to leave her here?"

"Oh, don't be a goose, Grace!" Linda told her. "You want to stay and hold her hand?"

"I feel like an accomplice or something."

246

"She doesn't *need* an accomplice."

Buck was already shifting Nina around on the seat to get on top of her. They heard her say as they walked away, "I wish you wouldn't. . . . What's everyone going to think of me? . . . I don't care if it's that kind of party," she assured him. "But this isn't *fair!*"

"I don't see how she can be like that," Grace said, allowing herself another quick look.

"I think Grace is a little sorry she missed her chance," Glenn joked to Linda. Grace overheard.

"That's all *you* know, creep-o!"

"Yeow? I don't know. You're sure worked up about it."

"Well, for goodness sake! Why, what if the police come along and catch them?" she raved. "They'll find out we were with them. How will *that* look at St. Francis?"

"Oh, Grace, come on." Linda sighed.

"I just don't see how you can take a mortal sin so lightly."

"I have an understanding confessor. Grace, what do you think Glenn and I are doing when he stays over? For heaven sake, you're in the other room!"

"I don't listen," she said primly. "And, anyway, you're going to get married . . . aren't you?"

"Well, not *tomorrow!* Or next week."

"You've changed, Linda," Grace said seriously. "You really have. You've grown *hard.*"

Linda said, "Shit!"

Glenn laughed. "How you like goin with nobody so far?"

"Beats goin alone." She laughed.

They locked arms and began to skip.

Halfway down the midway, Jack saw Linda open her small purse, holding it between herself and Glenn, and gave him some money.

They rode all the rides. Glenn won Linda a Kewpie doll spilling the milk, Jack won Grace one shooting the guns.

"Hey, Jack," Glenn called, standing in front of the freak show, "let's get tattooed."

"Over my dead body!" Linda tried to haul him away.

"Now, wait a minute. A sailor ought to have a tattoo," Glenn argued.

"I don't care if he gets one, but not you. You're not a sailor."

"I might be." He clamped on Jack's white cap. "Huh?

247

What if I just knock you up and run off and join the Navy?"

"Bite your tongue!"

He did a little dance, hoisting his trousers fore and aft.

"Very cute. Come on, no tattoo."

"Now wait a minute, Linda. You don't understand. I want to buy him a tattoo. It's sorta a good-luck thing, for a buddy going away, you know. It's the least you can do."

"Do you *want* to get tattooed?" she asked Jack.

"Guess so. Sure. Why not?"

She began acting like an ape. "Make-um decision like-um good buddy Glenn," she growled deep in her throat. She put Jack's cap on her head and began walking around with her can poking out, doing the fore and aft bit with her hands. *"Bell-bottomed trousers, coat of Navy blue—"* she sang. "Hey! Let's *all* get tattooed!"

"Linda!" Grace screeched. "Are you drunk? You wouldn't!"

"Umm ... sure! Why not! A small tasteful butterfly here." She peered down and touched the slope of her left breast. "Or perhaps here." She turned out her right leg and tapped high inside her thigh.

"Linda!" Grace was shocked.

"Yeah ..." Glenn drawled thoughtfully.

"There?" she asked, pushing out the small mound of her tummy and touching between it and where the seam of her Levi's cut into her soft sex. "Or *bluebirds!*" she cried gaily, turning around to poke out her behind, peering over her shoulder. "There and there."

"Naw." Glen couldn't see bluebirds.

"How about a python slithering up my leg?" She slithered the way with her hands.

"No snakes!" Glenn was definite.

"Snappy sayings!" she wondered. She outlined a gruff sign across her chest: "Post No Bills!" Lower down, with a roll of her eyes and twist of her hips: "Please Pay Toll ... Straight Ahead."

Glenn shook his head no.

"Fifteen Minutes Standing Only?" she tried.

"That's the hell!" Glenn exclaimed.

She ignored him. "How about, 'Don't Trod On Me!'? I think that would be very practical," she said.

"Hey! Why don't you?"

"I beg your pardon!" She looked shocked and tried to cover herself with her hands.

"Sure! I'd like a little butterfly or maybe a bee!" He advanced to pick the spot. She shrank back in terror. He was *serious.*

"Touch me and I'll scratch your yellow eyes out!" she warned.

"There!" he cried, stabbing her in the hollow between her right hip and pelvic arch.

She covered the place with her hand as if it might leak blood.

"You *are* nuts!" she discovered. "Have this fair body tattooed to sate your perverted lusts?"

"Yeah—What do you mean, *perverted?*" he bridled.

Linda threw herself on Grace's shoulder. "You were right, honey, I have definitely dipped beneath me this time."

"What the hell you mean by that? She say that? You butt out of what we got goin!" he ordered Grace, hauling Linda away from her. "You mean that?" he demanded.

"What?"

"What you said."

She too became suddenly quite serious. "I don't know."

"What do you mean you don't know? *What the hell is this?*" He cast about as if seeking an answer from someone else.

"It's just I can't believe that I—me—I'm standing here actually arguing with someone who wants me to get *tattooed!*" She shook her head at the insane wonder of it.

"What's wrong with that?" He truly would have liked to know. "Lotsa women get a little tattoo ... when they love someone like you do me."

"Good Lord," she whispered.

"What?" He searched himself for whatever it was that she was staring at.

"Nothing." She shook off the feeling. "Sorry."

"I wish to hell you would clue me as to what's goin on here?" he requested heatedly.

"Nothing. No. Go on get a tattoo, if you want one."

He brightened. "It's OK with you?"

"Um. ... Didn't you say it was good luck for a friend to buy you one? Let me pay for yours." She opened her small purse.

"Sure it's OK with you?" He wanted to be sure. "I

wouldn't want to do somethin to, you know, make you not like me or somethin."

"What *could* you do?" she asked. "How much does it cost?"

"Uh, five skins, I think. That's about the cheapest *good* tattoo."

"Well, you be sure and get a good one." She slapped a five in his palm. "Five skins."

"You gotta come and pick it out," he said.

"No way!"

"Aw, it won't be the same then."

"Well, if it isn't, it isn't, but I'll be damned if I watch you get tattooed."

"Man, I don't know what's eatin her," he confessed to Jack. Happy to have the fin in his hand and his mind flipping at the prospect of getting tattooed, he did not try to pursue her problem. "Some great nurses!" he sneered. "Afraid to watch someone get a little tattoo."

By the flip of a coin, Jack was first in the Tattooed Man's chair. Jack had picked a five-dollar design from the catalog of "traditional" designs, a fouled anchor surrounded by thirteen stars, emblazoned with his first name and U.S.N.

The man made double sure he had the very number. A tattoo left no room for a subsequent change of mind. Then he shaved a place on Jack's forearm, washed it with rubbing alcohol, found a glassine stencil in the drawer of his cabinet and transferred the design to Jack's arm. He buzzed his electric multiple needle machine in a shot glass of alcohol to sterilize it. He dipped it in a pot of thick blue ink, held Jack's arm securely in his left hand and touched the needles to his skin. After the first little jump, it was just a hot tingle between a low-grade electrical shock and a not-intolerable burning.

"What's it feel like?" Glenn asked, glancing from his search of the man's panels of designs for the one that fitted him.

"Not much. Between a tickle and a burn."

"That's nothin then. Hell, I ought to stand a ten-dollar job."

"Oh, you ought to be able to go for a fifty-dollar job. 'Washington Crossing the Delaware' in one go," Jack suggested. The old, illustrated ex-pug grinned.

Then Glenn found the very one. But it was ten dollars.

"Let me pay for the other half," Jack requested. "Linda and I will be partners. Ought to be twice as lucky."

"Hey, yeow!"

Jack began to understand how a man *might* get himself tattooed all over. Once you started there was still a lot of uncolored skin. The electric searing was insidious, something you might get to a point of being unable to leave alone. Then a tattoo was there, indelible, altering familiar symmetry forever. You might get another on the other arm for balance and the process would never stop.

The tattooist laid a gauze over the newly carved anchor, securing it with a one-fourth-inch adhesive tape. "Leave da bandage on for a day-two. You clean it wit rubbin alcohol, booze, anaseptic, like dat. When it's all scabbed nice and tin, den yousé ca'take a shower, get wet."

There was a cautiousness about the man, a weariness. He did not look directly at anyone. Jack could tell from the man's voice and ways he considered everyone who came to be tattooed a wise guy, every work of his art potential trouble.

"Don't feel a thing, huh?" Glenn got into the man's chipped, portable medical chair.

"You'll like it," Jack promised him.

He did not like it. "Take a break a goddamn minute!" he told the tattooist. Glenn was sweating. His ten-buck selection was two-thirds as long as his forearm. "Hey! Let's knock off for a second!" he bent to shout at the man.

The pug cut off his machine, looked up from underneath his green eyeshade. He gave Glenn a couple minutes' rest, then switched on his needles and bent to work.

"He's hittin nerves er somethin!" Glenn protested. "Feels like a fuckin *thing* is crawlin along eatin my arm!"

"Told you you would like it," Jack grinned.

"Fuck you, Jack! I never liked needles, man. Dinky old fin job. *Look* at this mother! You know what it is?" He had figured it out. "I've built up my arms, see. So all the muscles have pushed the nerves all up close to my skin."

"That must be it," Jack agreed.

"Shit, yeow! If I had arms like you, I wouldn't feel nothin either. Ain't that right, mister?" He solicited an expert opinion.

"Whatever yuh say, sonny, you're in da chair."

"See." Glenn offered his witness. "That's it."

251

"That took long enough," Linda said. "What did you get for your money? The Sistine ceiling?"

"Naw. Anyway, I got a ten-dollar one. Here to here."

He measured the length of his tattoo, a swelling, bandaged bulge under his sleeve.

"Good Lord!"

"His is like this." He held up forefinger and thumb about four inches apart.

"Poor boy!" She patted Jack's hand.

Glenn looked at his fingers and got the joke and laughed. "Well, you know me," he puffed.

"He didn't get a life-size portrait of *that*?" she asked.

"Got a hula-hula girl. When I tense my arm, she does a dance."

"You didn't! Did he?" she asked Jack.

"He wants to surprise you," Jack told her.

"Did it hurt?" Grace asked.

"Naw, not much," Glenn said. "But because of my muscular development, my nerves been all pushed up into my skin, and it hurt me more than it did him."

"Can't you show us?" Grace asked.

Jack raised his sleeve and lifted the bandage. His forearm had begun to swell. The design seeped tiny beads of blood.

"You must be careful of infection," she observed professionally.

"How about this?" Glenn carefully unveiled his masterpiece.

A bloody dagger pierced a bleeding heart across which there was the banner DEATH BEFORE DISHONOR.

"We each own half of it," Jack told Linda.

From her horrified stare, she turned her face toward Jack with a look of definite, unspoken conspiracy. Whatever Glenn had in mind, Jack knew his old buddy'd had his last stand with Linda.

"What'd yuh think?" Glenn insisted.

"It's perfect," she said. "Suits you."

Nina was sitting alone in the front seat, staring angrily over the waxed hood. When they came up, she began weeping hysterically. Buck was sprawled in the back, the empty bottle cradled on his chest. The car smelled of drunken vomit.

"What must all of you think of me!" Nina wailed.

"Look what he did on me!" Buck had puked all over her front. "He called me terrible things," she cried. "I wish I were dead!"

Linda soothed her and covered her puked-upon front with a sweater.

"He didn't take any precautions with me," Nina confided, then became quite hysterical again. "He promised he would, but he *didn't!*"

"Sit in the front with us," Linda told her.

"I'm not getting in there!" Grace said.

Jack said, "Look, Glenn, we'll just catch a cab."

"Well, OK. Sorry, man, about all this. So we'll see you at Linda and Grace's."

Jack looked at Linda and Grace. The party was over. "Naw. I'll just go home. I'm really beat. It's been a long day."

"Well, all reet. Call me, OK?"

"Sure."

"Nice meeting you, Jack," Linda said, offering him her hand. There was again a flash of their conspiracy, their curious partnership. Her hand was smooth, small and warm.

"Good luck," he said.

She smiled. "Don't worry." She gave his hand a private squeeze.

It had always been a goddamned bore. He was amazed he hadn't realized it before. Going up the alley toward his bed, he knew there had never been a time since he and Glenn had been going with girls that he had come home without feeling less satisfied than before—no matter how the time had gone.

He thought of Grace, her big soft breasts, virgin sex. He thought of how it might have been if he had stuck with poor Nina. He thought of Linda, the mystery of how such a girl could ever have taken Glenn into her bed. He thought of other girls. He thought of his mother in prison in New Mexico, under rough blankets on an iron bed in a cage among other women. Passing the Demicellis' dark trailer, he thought of Mrs. D. and her hunchbacked meat-cutter in bed just beyond their thin wall.

The light was on in the widow's kitchen, though his grandmother had left no light for him in the trailer. He remembered Mrs. Simmons showing him her flame-dyed old bush, grabbing his cock in her glass-bejeweled, liver-spotted plump hand, and heard again her obscene promise: "I'll French. . . ."

He went through her sagging gate, up the plank walk to her back door. The world was a goddamn freak show. He peeked beneath the gap in her shade on the back door. Dirty dishes were still on her kitchen table. Cupboards were left open. Cats were on the table among the dishes. There was a low light in the living room near the floor.

He knocked and waited breathlessly, then knocked again. Afraid someone might be with her, in which case he planned to just be coming in to use the toilet, he turned the loose knob and pushed open the door. Cats bounded off the table. Roaches prowled the dirty plates and her sink. A drawer of rusty cutlery was spilled on the filthy linoleum floor. He had come to fuck her old head. Blood rose and throbbed behind his mask. His left eye twitched uncontrollably. All that old flaccid pale flesh. She was old as his grandmother! He was certain he was truly insane.

She sprawled on her back on the living-room floor. A table lamp had been knocked from a stand next to her sagging couch. Her laddered black hose were rolled and knotted above her fat knees. Her fleshy old body was pale as scalded fresh pork. She lay there naked, except for stockings, a kitten playfully pawing at her grizzly red bush. Another lapped at the puddle of blood in which lay her staring head. Her throat had been cut from ear to ear. The wound was a gaping, obscene fun-house grin. The butcher knife had been plunged to the handle in the center of the spreading flab of her big white belly.

He stood frozen with terror, the hair actually lifting on his head. He cast about in panic that the murderer might still be there. Then he fled.

Police had turned the widow's house into a site arrested in time, sanitized it within their signs and the corded boundaries of their custody, giving it an importance it had never had among its neighbors. The place had been ransacked. The police decided someone thought she'd had a secret small fortune. Gawkers drove slowly past in their cars. The postman delivered the old woman's light bill and some magazines, tiptoeing upon the porch, passing a word with the cop at the door, tiptoeing away, looking back over his shoulder, solemn for the futility of his mission.

The neighborhood had the whispering pall of a hospital emergency room, in which everyone huddled to examine fears and reflect upon the chance horrors of life.

All the young men in the neighborhood that could be found were being questioned. Jack had given the police a statement, awed by the suspicion in his interrogator's eyes. There was not a black kid in the neighborhood who had *ever* been inside her house. No, sir!

"She was just askin for it," was their parents' opinion.

Mrs. Simmons' daughter and her black blade of a husband came to make arrangements for her funeral and lay claim to the property.

Walking up the alley, Jack saw Arthur gathered with several other young kids in the backyard where he was hiding out with another family. He stopped at the chicken-wire fence until Arthur saw him. They stared at each other. Neither spoke. Then Arthur looked away, laughed and began talking animatedly with the other little black kids. Jack walked on. Neither he nor the police would ever know who killed Mrs. Simmons. In his grandparents' eyes he had seen the fear that they considered him perfectly capable of having done it.

PART TWO

16

IN THE timbers of the Oakland jetty the boy could already smell China. Where storied and obscure ships had touched there was a ghostly scent of the Orient. No one else, though, seemed to sense it. Amid the levee's catcalls against the unknown, and its grabass, he felt an unspeakable tie to shanghaied sailors, whalers and pigtailed tars. History but vaguely glimpsed, distorted by cinematic eye, tipped by hint of sandalwood, rum, jasmine, spices, oils, and tea, was a teeming mystery akin to spring's fevered ache when he had stared to the horizon over waves of a wheat sea. A boy forever of the Middle Border. For all that, he must have looked pensive, even grim.

"Homesick already?" Al saw his mood. Al had not seen his home.

Homesick was only a bastard relative to the thing he felt. It was more the feeling that he, of all those there, was leaving nothing any of them would ever have thought of as home for places beyond the Bay Bridge he knew he could never call his own. It was all right. Just something he did not feel grabass about.

Across the bay at Treasure Island they loaded their seabags onto trucks and clambered after them. The trucks were hooded with canvas so only those with seats near the tailgates could follow their route.

They unloaded again under the roof of a long covered wharf. The boy looked for the ship, uncertain except for the smell he was near water. Rails ran in there to deadmen at the end. Sailors driving forklifts shuttled busily behind a barrier of temporary wire hung with the warnings KEEP CLEAR GANGWAY. The lifts moved through distant doors into what the boy took to be an adjacent warehouse. On the floor in a corner, guarded by an armed marine, were thousands of barrels that looked like the metal kegs for draft beer. Other fork trucks were carefully moving flats of the

259

kegs into the warehouse. On some of the kegs the boy could see a skull and cross-bones and the words POISON GAS stenciled in bilious yellow paint.

On the other side of the wharf, through the open doors, lay sun-glint water floating bits of wood and rubbish, scavenged by gulls. Still, there was no ship.

Hurry up and wait.

Their names were being called off. All were present.

"At the head of the gangway sound off your last name, first name, middle initial and serial number," the bosun in charge bawled. "Left face! Column of files from the left. March!"

But where was the ship? They passed curious, questioning glances at one another.

The one thing their training had not prepared them for was a ship. There had been actual ship's compartments constructed ashore in which they practiced fire-fighting, rescue with breathing apparatus, shoring bulkheads in simulated battle damage. There had been gun pots of all kinds, mechanically articulated quad-40's, even working turrets with twin five-inch 38's. They had lowered whaleboats from dockside davits and made away; popped life rafts in a swimming pool. They had landed with their toy rifles on a sand beach from P and M boats to attack marines firing blanks. They had handled lines on a phony fo'c'sle; rigged cargo nets and worked booms hung from a ship's mast set firmly in concrete. But not a landsman in the levy had ever been prairie-close enough to an actual ship to have measured its length with anything but two joints of a single finger.

The gray warehouse next door was the side of a ship!

Up to that moment the grandest thing afloat on which any of them had ever set foot was the Oakland ferry.

They hadn't known it would be *that* big. They had memorized tonnages, feet, class and silhouette, but a ship was bigger face to face than damn near anything! Big as anything in Wichita. It went *up*! Up, five or six more stories! Lowering over the roof of the shed, the overhang of its flight deck blotted out all but a brilliant blue chink of sky where dirty harbor gulls wheeled.

From the door through which they were boarding, fifteen, twenty feet above the waterline, the boy could not see anything but the curvature of the ship on either end. He had pictured himself joining the fleet topside, coming

260

smartly up a gangway like a gentleman, saluting, everything out in the open beneath a clear good-bye sky. Even officers and gentlemen crept in and out through huge side doors. There was a quality perfectly elephantine about the aircraft carrier. Unlike photographs and airbrushed posters, its hide was not smooth but made up of great plates fastened with enormous welded seams, the painted metal rough as something hewed from a solid block.

Up forward there was a slightly smaller door with a gangway for officers. Around the end of the gangway clustered a couple dozen officers, their wives, children, pretty girlfriends, all laughing, touching fondly, kissing, calling final remembrances.

A band marched in the open end of the shed to the rattle of a cadence drum.

Farther aft, stores were being loaded under the direction of cooks in aprons and caps. Still farther, the flats of kegged poison gas were carefully being run aboard under the direction of a cargo officer who harangued the fork-truck operators constantly to watch their asses. "One of those split open and everyone in this shed is dead!" he shrieked at a particularly casual operator who wheeled his truck with an individual country art.

The band began to play a jazzy, military version of "The Girl from Twenty-nine Palms," followed by "Home on the Range" for all the sons of the Middle Border struck silent in their awe. Would Billy the Kid have not felt the same?

The captain and his wife arrived in a two-star admiral's limousine. The band swung immediately into "The Michigan Fight Song" for either the captain or the admiral. Everyone around the officers' gangway snapped to attention. They were quickly put at ease. The captain and the admiral shook hands with many of the officers. They exchanged pleasantries with the women. The atmosphere around the officers' gangway was very like that outside a football stadium before the big game. The captain's wife was a tall dark-haired woman, taller than he was. She wore a dove-gray dress and matching coat with a fox collar and a little hat with feathers and short veil. She was older than the other women, and they clearly deferred to her seniority. With the air of a bishop or cardinal she bestowed kind words and familiarities. It was funny how the women too had a way of sort of coming to attention.

On the PA throughout the ship a single voice speaking on many horns announced, "Now hear this. Now hear this. The smoking lamp is out throughout the ship. The smoking lamp is out."

When the other officers' women threw their arms around the necks of their men, the captain's wife offered him her cheek to kiss. Though the tension of their parting was no less than that of the others, the boy sensed it was something they had done many, many times. The captain remained quite jocular, casual. He had almost a holiday air.

"What's the name of this ship?" Gorilla asked one of the marines guarding the gangway.

"The *Tippecanoe*. Keep moving."

"Turn right at the first passageway and follow the ladders down until someone directs you to your compartment," a seaman nearby amplified mechanically. "Step lively. Keep it moving."

Rolling their sea bags down the ladder, they came skidding down the handrails, hitting a step between each deck to break their elated slide. If a plummeting sea bag wiped out anyone on the ladder ahead, all landing in a heap on the deck below, all the more fun.

Stowing their bags on bunks in compartments in which the ship's aircraft divisions had once slept, they raced topside to attend their departure from the vantage of the flight deck. There were no planes aboard, except an old unarmed pontoon scout plane. The hangar deck was huge, empty and echoing. The slightest breeze made the vast, planked plain of the flight deck windswept. Their trousers whipped about their ankles. Neckerchiefs escaped from pea jackets and snapped around their ears. Already the radar towers were turning. Large as a town, the ship throbbed with internal life that turned steel, pipe, wood into an enormous, living thing. The boy felt the life through his feet; then it became part of his every molecule. It tickled his heart—a genuine sensation—a unique, not unpleasant vibration of all viscera, then a nervous intermuscular itch too deep to scratch.

Lines fore and aft were slackened. Imperceptibly the big fellow eased away from the shed. Six huffy tugs moved around its flanks, looking to offer nose.

All lines were cast off. A tiny spontaneous cheer rose from those in the doors of the shed. The band began to

262

play "Anchors Aweigh." The small clutch of women and children drew in upon itself. Mothers touched their children. There were tears above shining, brave smiles. They waved handkerchiefs. The boy felt it had always been this way. A drama more powerful than religious ritual.

The band began "Now Is the Hour." The captain's wife lifted a gloved hand.

Soon they were in the bay. They passed Alcatraz. The boy could see prisoners working about walls. He thought of his mother in a New Mexico prison, of his stepfather locked up in Texas. He felt personally fortunate. Going beneath the Golden Gate, the antennas atop the ship's superstructure seemed but a dozen feet from the bridgeway. On the deck where the wind was not a force against which they might gently lean they could see the expressions on the faces of those who had stopped to watch the carrier go out. A pretty girl with a face as open as the sky behind her threw kisses with both hands. For the first time in his memory, the boy felt he had escaped the shadow of prison walls forever. He felt like a full citizen in the world of the happy girl above who made as if to leap into the uplifted arms of the cheering sailors below.

Their mess was small and pleasant. Their berths large as those in sick bay or chief's quarters. But the boy was too excited to eat. He had no desire to sleep. The sea slipped land tints for fathomless blue.

The ocean did not *go* anywhere. It was just there, heavy, yet cresting with the finest salty spray. A god like the ocean was not the petty, snippish, stingy Uncle Sam-ass of a Christian old man. Sexless or perfectly sexual (it came to the same thing within his ability and language to think about it), earless, blind, deeper than conscience, the great sea rolled. Pacific, its name had to mean peace, not an illusory peace with ever-present danger and chance but the peace known truly only by those who were not strangers to physical pain.

He gloried in the ship, feeling a sense of possession and affluence beyond anything he had ever known. Having changed into dungarees, he roamed the ship from bow to stern after the others had gone to their bunks to read or, as the sea began to come up heavier, to lie ashamedly rigid while nausea ripped their guts. Few were going to mess that first evening. The boy felt the heave of the ship

263

but not so strongly that he was going to go below and miss his first storm at sea.

He saw the lip of the flight deck plunge and elevator up. In the storm glow of evening, light spray broke back from the lip of the deck like fine windblown rain. As on the prairie, he could see the dark army of rain sweep slowly out of the east, seeming to trample and quiet all beneath it. Beyond the seething thunderheads clouds of snowiest white rose faster than an artist's brush could catch them, higher than the Alps. Then, on toward the west, the sky became a Biblical print of God's majesty; highways of sunbeams solid enough to carry chariots drove shafts through the clouds. Still farther beyond was a depthless sky of pacific blue. The sunshafts opened like a Japanese fan. The boy wanted words he did not own to mark the moment; beneath his wonder and joy he felt anxious, bereft for want of someone to share his feelings.

Before his eyes, the fan slipped past the clouds and vanished below the rim of the sea.

As if waiting for strategic night, the wind and sea rose until, in the strange, electric dark, the boy could see the ship sailing into a thunderhead of Neptune himself. Sky-high and miles wide. It gave him great pleasure.

"Blow, you old fart! Blow!" he hollered into the wind. The words whipped from his mouth were sent tumbling aft like scraps. Leaning on the wind, he went forward on the deserted plain of the deck. His clothing whipped and filled with wind until his shirt buttons strained. Spray plastered the cloth wetly but without chill against his chest and thighs. He opened his mouth and wind filled and fluttered his cheeks. He swallowed the wind and spray. He tasted the salt. Ecstasy of a quality so perfectly independent of any sensation he had known before made him wish for ever more lashing winds and sea. He wanted to breast the force as a figurehead, withstand it, stand to it until its fury was spent and it slunk away—done. That it might tear him away was part of his glory. But he put his cap inside his shirt to keep it safe.

He went forward, then down below the lip of the flight deck to stand between the twin quad-40 gun pots, his hands gripping the steel flange of the bow. He rode the pitch and fall of the ship, convinced he could stay that way forever. The act alone moved him ages beyond his kin. He had come through a pass in his heritage to regard

264

himself as incomparably fortunate, geniuslike in the discovery that to live a moment in such self-awareness was superior to the realization of any desire he could imagine. While he clung to the plunging bow free from the anxious lust of wishes, the moment alone seemed to justify his having been born. He was convinced he could be swept off into the sea with no good explanation for his survivors, and it would be equal in some unwritten history with anything he or anyone might ever do. The argument of a hermit masterpiece never subjected to critical review, the thought of an explosion known only by subsequent evidence in some distant galaxy filled his mind as the bow soared upward again.

Down the bow plowed more violently than before, driving steeply into the sea with a kind of muted metallic scream. He was lifted off his feet. Clinging with all his might to the steel breast-high wall, thrust headlong into a wave higher than the deck overhead, he was afraid he would indeed be pitched into the sea.

He saw the fish, large as a torpedo, zoom toward him, saw its large frightened eye; he ducked as it flashed past his head, silver and midnight color with tints of green and gold, and huge!

There was no sound save the crash of the enormous wave and perhaps the muted groan of the ship. Over his shoulder he saw the fish bang into the bulkhead behind the guns. Then he was soaring up from underwater into the night. The next wave was nothing in comparison with the last. Nor was the next.

He made his way hand over hand along the rim of the bow toward the shelter of the bulkhead. The fish, a great tuna larger than himself, more sleek and solid of flesh than any beast, struggled between the rotating gun platform and the deck, caught in the mechanism, half dead from the collision with the bulkhead.

In his fear he stopped for an instant to regard its large eye and to wonder what it saw, what it might think. He felt it too knew fear. He was certain he saw anger and accusation there, a wall-eyed bitterness in face of death. Soaking wet, he felt suddenly chilled and shivered violently inside his skin. He hurried to get inside and below.

Those in the compartment not sickly oblivious were mockingly curious as to how he had got so wet, finding in his reply, "I was just out on the bow," cause for knowing glances and tolerant smiles.

"They piped word half an hour ago for all personnel to stay off catwalks and open decks," Gorilla advised him.

"Well, I didn't hear," the boy said.

"The salt," someone crowed. "What we hit a bit ago, a wall?"

"Little Boy Blue, you can come blow my horn," another in skivvies cracked from an upper rack.

He stripped and dried himself with a towel. Warmth luxuriously filled the exhausted places in him, making him drowsy. He felt clean all the way through. When he licked his lips, there was still the taste of salt. As he stood naked facing his berth, the wag from the upper rack observed, "Muskrat, you sure got a lot of woman in you." Others laughed. "Got legs pretty as a girl."

Quickly, he put on clean underwear. He hopped into his bunk and pulled up the blanket. From beneath his pillow he took a dog-eared paperback copy of *God's Little Acre* and a Butterfinger candy bar. He peeled the bar and prepared to read. But he could not concentrate on the words for thinking of the fish caught in the gun mechanism on the bow.

"How old do tuna fish get?" he asked Gorilla, reading in the rack below.

"Huh? I don't know. Why?"

"I just wondered."

Al was already asleep. He looked sick even in sleep, having surrendered totally to the pitch and roll of the ship. He had a towel handy in case he could not make it into the head.

No one really knew anything about tuna.

"There's a real big one caught in the forties up on the bow," he offered.

No one cared.

The compartment tilted and rolled. Bunk chains slacked and strained slightly with the heavy movements of the big ship. When the carrier plowed into an especially large wave they could feel the screws break free of the sea and propeller wildly, the entire ship shuddering, as someone said, "like a dog passing peach pits." It was amazing to realize that but for the power of its engines the ship—a thing as large and with more integrity than a village—

would be no more to the ocean than flotsam—no more than a chip.

Pacific days of shirtless sun, time passed in sport, the ship's more intimate exploration, gunnery thoughts, reading and speculation. Interminable games of hearts and poker wore out a cache of Bicycles, red-backed and blue. They rendezvoused with a tender to take on fuel, mail, and exchange motion pictures. After an alteration in course, the weather became less tropical. There was a rumor they were bound for the Aleutians. They met a destroyer on a blowy gray day to take aboard a sick man who was dollied across the dangerous sea between ships in a litter on a running line like tenement laundry. In exchange, they sent back cans of ice-cream mix for the tin can's crew. Then it was warm again. Languorous days passed in lazy talk, furtive masturbation—the beginning of an itch to get where they were going.

17

BEING merely passengers, not of the crew, they stood no watches. There was very little for them to do. To make work, they were detailed to paint the chain locker. The anchor chain was hauled and bent into half an acre of massive lengths on the hangar deck. Each link would have filled a large trunk. A chain so huge threw one's perspective out of whack, so those who had never been to sea before approached it with the awe of boys regarding their first elephant. They touched the monster links, heaved at one, guessed its weight, argued whether or not Charles Atlas might lift it. Hook a chain like that on a nearby star and you might anchor the earth.

The locker was a steel bin the size of a four-story building. Three dozen men were sent down into it where they stood on tiers of scaffolding pecking paint from the walls with ubiquitous chipping hammers. The din was so enraging that soon every man would have driven his hammer into the brain of his closest friend to escape, his way barred only by the invisible weight of lawful authority and the stubborn reluctance to be the first to admit intolerable misery. In the hellish swirl of rusty dust, choking beneath makeshift handkerchief face masks, each man grew to hate his neighbor, feeling in the relentless industry of the other an ignorant collusion toward his own irrational discomfort. Every moment was a choked-back curse against the consuming desire to throw down the hammer and scream—FUCK IT!

The boy chipped and looked repeatedly, longingly at the hatch overhead. He glanced at the face of Gorilla's dusty watch and knew he could not last until lunch. They had been in the bin little more than an hour. He felt sick from the dust and heat, drunken. Pains shot threw his shoulders, neck, brain. He would have gladly seen all those in there with him dead if the noise and dust would only stop.

After the first half hour all joking and healthy bitching had ceased. After the second hour the man next to Gorilla, a burly weightlifter named Tompkins, from Portland, barely literate but always quiet, never any trouble, smashed his only buddy, a tall, extremely goosey Finn with feet so big the Navy had to provide him with special shoes, in the face, knocking him off the tier.

"What the hell you do that for?" Finn yelled up from the dust below, more truly puzzled than hurt.

Tompkins looked as surprised as Finn. He searched the others for an explanation, embarrassed not to have one of his own. Then his tiny eyes flared. It came to him. *"I didn't like what you were thinkin!"*

Finn seemed to accept that. He climbed back up onto the tier and began chipping.

Thirty times within the hour the boy had decided he would just climb up and tell whoever was in charge he was too young to be in the Navy. He rehearsed it many times in his mind, hoping he could get away from the moment of confession and off the ship without seeing his friends. Maybe they would put him in sick bay or even in the brig. Bread and water would be all right. Countless times he was going to chip one more chip and go.

Then a seaman named Porter pitched backward off the middle tier across the way and went headlong onto the sole of the locker. It was inches deep in chipped paint and dust. His body displaced a billowing rusty cloud that feathered upward and outward from where he fell.

"Hey, Porter!" someone yelled.

By degrees hammers stopped until only a couple were chipping beyond the ringing in the men's ears.

"There's a man passed out down here!" someone yelled. Others began to loose dry yells.

Two men who had been chipping beside Porter dropped into the dust below. One held the man's head up out of the dust. The other pulled away the handkerchief covering his face. With his ear next to Porter's slack mouth he said, "He ain't breathin." He passed a hand before his eyes and looking scared. *"There's a man hurt down here goddamn bad!"* he yelled.

"Artificial respiration!" the other decided.

"Someone go get help!" the man nearest the ladder said, then, realizing where he was, scrambled up and out himself.

"Help! Help! Down here!" others continued to shout.

The face of one of the fo'c'sle ratings appeared in the hatch overhead.

"Man's not breathin down here!" Finn hollered up.

Two men in the bottom of the locker hoisted the limp man onto a lower tier, lay his dusty, streaked cheek upon his forearm and one got astride to offer artificial respiration. The man's eyes were wide open, blind as marbles.

"We got to get him out of here!" the other man shouted up to the rating. "This air's not good to be pumpin into him."

The rating, a bosun deuce, clambered down the ladder with the bight of a sturdy line in his teeth. He quickly fashioned a professional sling around the man, beneath his arms and between his legs, the knot a large heartlike lump on Porter's back. He yelled for those above to haul away. Porter hung lifeless in the sling, rotating slowly as he was hauled up, his feet dangling down pitifully. He seemed to have stretched several inches, so his pale ankles were visible between the bottoms of his dungarees and the top of his socks. He bumped the bulkhead and the ladder. The bosun got on the ladder to guide Porter up. Porter's head lolled upon his chest. His mouth hung agape. His face made the boy think of the embryo of a child he had once seen displayed in a jar of alcohol.

When Porter had been hauled out and the hole was

empty, the men looked at one another. A couple of eager beavers began to chip once more.

"I'm getting out of here," the boy said to Gorilla.

Gorilla turned to those on the tier barring the way to the ladder and said, "Let us past if you want to stay down here. We're getting out of here."

Tompkins and Finn and a couple of others let them pass. They were already out of the hole when a young officer came and shouted down. "Everyone out of there! On the double!"

Outside, Jack's lungs still burned. The fresh air made him aware of the taste of chrome.

White-clothed corpsmen appeared. One took over the artificial respiration from the bosun.

"We need a Pulmotor," the young officer decided suddenly and went to a telephone on a distant bulkhead to call for one.

The Pulmotor arrived with two more corpsmen and a doctor who seemed very angry, as if he had been called away from something more important or interesting. He knelt and roughly searched for the man's pulse. Then he became more gentle. He flashed his little penlight in the man's eyes. He did not look hopeful. He wielded the mask of the Pulmotor himself. Porter's chest moved up and down as if breathing. Hell, it looked as if he were going to be all right. But after a while the doctor removed the mask, and Porter's chest never lifted again.

"This man is dead," he told the desk officer. A corpsman closed Porter's eyes.

"What's the problem here?" The executive officer had come from the bridge. A way was made for him through the crowd.

"Man's dead," the doctor said.

"What are these men standing around here for?" the exec demanded of the young deck officer.

"They just came up out of the chain locker, sir. They were detailed to chip the chain locker."

"Get them away from this man!"

"Yes, sir! You men, get away from here. Go over by the bulkhead."

The exec looked as cold as Porter, though his face above his starched khaki collar was very red. The corpsmen loaded Porter in a wire litter and went off with him.

The doctor and the exec went down to look into the locker.

"These men should not work in there without dust masks and proper ventilation," the doctor said. "We must watch all these men for signs of metal poisoning."

"Who is in charge of this detail?" the exec demanded.

"I am, sir," the bosun snapped, coming to attention.

"Did you rig for this work?"

"Yes, sir. . . ." He looked at the lieutenant for help.

"I okayed it, sir," the lieutenant said.

"You will have a full report on this to me"—he consulted his watch—"by fourteen hundred. Is that clear?"

"Yes, sir," the lieutenant said.

"Bosun, see that these men are taken immediately to sick bay," the exec ordered. He and the doctor walked away together. The exec made a hopeless gesture with his left hand.

Only a couple of them were kept in sick bay—men who confessed to a history of childhood respiratory complaint. They were all examined and X-rayed. They did not go back into the chain locker that day. The day after, when they did go down again, they were given dust masks. Hoses had been rigged with fine spray nozzles to lay the dust as they chipped, flooding the bottom of the locker. The debris was sucked up, out and over the side through a portable pump. Even then, a corpsman with a resuscitator was stationed up top, and the detail was given fifteen-minute breaks out of every hour. The young deck officer wore a raw look that reflected the ass chewing he'd had and the unfavorable notation that had gone into his file. They caught him staring at the rigging of the pump and hoses, clearly bewildered why a bright fellow like himself had not thought of all that before.

Services for Porter were held 0900 hours Saturday on the starboard elevator of the hangar deck. His body, lashed in hammock canvas, rested on a plank between the sawhorses beneath an American flag. The chaplain had a purple religious sash over his shouders. He was a tall Yankee to whom the waxy, hymnbook atmosphere of churches clung even when, in sweat shirt and khakis, he joined in a spirited game of touch football on the flight deck—officers versus enlisted men—the ball filled with ka-

271

pok rather than air to keep it from bouncing over the side. But the chaplain played hard—all Yankee elbows and knees. That was what Jack thought about during the brief service. The only other officers there were the captain and the lieutenant who had been in charge of the detail. Nor were many of the men there who had been in the locker the day Porter died. He had no one close buddy. Everyone had decided he had some kind of lung condition which he had kept from the Navy. The chaplain said the prayer committing Porter to the deep, charging the Lord his soul to keep. The plank was lifted by six seamen from the crew, three along each side. A bosun's pipe sounded over the PA system. The men came to attention, and Porter's shrouded lump slid from under the flag and shot feet first into the sea. The seamen folded the flag expertly.

When the detail was dismissed, Jack, Gorilla and Al went topside to look back where Porter had been dumped. There was nothing to see but the ship's wide wake curving far behind.

"They put weights in the bottom so he sinks right away," Al said.

In the boy's mind, he saw Porter sinking feet first past fishes, perhaps sunken hulks, into the deepest part of the sea where no light penetrated. He had read that morning in *The Tippecanoe Target* that the ship's position that day was over the Great Pacific Trench. From *National Geographics* he knew there were weird neon fish down there strung with lights of their own. He thought maybe Porter would be crushed by the pressure, his canvas envelope split open. He considered what his folks would think. It seemed a long way from anywhere to be dumped into the Pacific Ocean.

When they went back below, the carpenters were building a strong chute of boards on the wide door from which Porter had been jettisoned. Two men were stringing lines hung with KEEP OUT signs across that area of the hangar deck.

That afternoon they were detailed back to the hangar deck. Strong pine boxes with rope handles on either end were being brought up from a magazine below and stacked in the cordoned-off area. Stencils on the boxes indicated they contained ammunition and shells in all calibers and millimeters. As the ship proceeded slowly along the deep trench below, they were instructed to carry the boxes to the wooden chute and slide them into the sea.

"Why are we doing this?" Al wondered on the other side of a box, a taxpayer's concern reflected in his voice.

"Ask the chief," Jack suggested.

"Ammo gets high if it's stored too long," the chief, a heavyset fellow who cocked his billed cap at a bus driver's angle up and off his face, explained. "Handle it carefully. Some of it, I guess, is just surplus. Or it's been improperly stored. I don't know. We just have to dump it."

Most of the boxes were stenciled with dates before 1942. Still, it seemed a waste.

"How much you reckon all this is worth, Chief?" the boy asked.

"Oh, I don't know. Figure at least a hundred clams a box."

At that rate, before they were through they had jettisoned a million dollars' worth of ammunition into the deepest part of the ocean.

DEAR GRANDMA & GRANDPA [he wrote a letter that night in the crew's library near their compartment]:

Today, I helped dump a million dollars' worth of old ammo in the ocean. *A million dollars!!* Think what we could do with that!! Couldn't help but think what Grandpa would say if he had been here. He'd gone crazy. The money just running a ship like this costs so much you couldn't believe it. Course I don't see much of it—ha ha! Tomorrow we dump poison gas. Even though gas was outlawed since WWI, the USA was making it. Just in case, I guess. Makes you wonder don't it? Sure Grandpa would have plenty to say about that too.

Oh, one of our gang, named Porter from Coffeyville, died on another detail we was on chipping paint in the chain locker. We buried him at sea. Makes you feel funny to just dump a guy into the ocean.

Everything is fine with me. But I'm growing so fast I'm going to be out of my clothes soon. We're having a boxing smoker next week. They weighed me and I gotta box at 135 pounds. I ain't fat neither!

It's like summer here now. Getting a good tan on

273

deck. Guess it's icy and snow there. Be careful walking.

Love to you and all. Don't know where we're headed yet. They say we're going to stop at Okinawa soon and maybe we will pick up some mail there. Sure hope I have some.

Love, your grandson
JACK

Two men handled each barrel of gas, tilted it on its side and carefully rolled it onto the wooden ramp and let it go. The cans were seeded along the Pacific Trench like depth charges.

"What happens when the barrels rust?" the boy asked. "Won't it kill all the fish?"

"It's going so deep, by the time it comes open it will be so diluted it won't be dangerous," the chief assured him.

Still he did not like dumping that stuff in the ocean. How could they be sure?

"Don't worry about it, Muskrat." Gorilla laughed. "This old ocean is so big whole islands and countries have disappeared into it without a trace."

The gas was something called phosgene.

"A drop of it is enough to kill you," the chief said. "Nerve gas."

It was not hard work, rather fun, dumping the barrels over the side. But the detail left the boy feeling nervous, touchy. He wondered if perhaps microscopic particles of the gas clung to the outside of the barrels and if that might not be what was affecting him. When they were released by the chief, he did not want to be with the others or go to chow.

"I'm going up for a breath of air," he explained.

In his investigation of the ship he had discovered places where there were all sorts of hidey-holes. There was a room off the catwalk where the flight deck jutted out to accommodate the portside elevator formed of the supporting superstructure. It had a steel mesh floor where one could lie and look through the mesh at the sea passing below. It was only about ten feet square and four feet high. Someone had put a couple of mattresses in there, and a battle lantern. In a bracket on the wall someone had wedged a *Strength & Health* magazine.

It was the quiet time just before supper. The sun was

still a couple of hours from setting, glancing at a low angle off the water, plating it with silver. The rush of water away from the deep knifing of the ship's hull roared beneath the catwalk.

He stuck his head into the room. There were two men in there. He almost said, "Excuse me!" A young white corpsman was on the mattress, his trousers off, being fucked in the ass by a large, very black mess man, who had his whites and skivvies down to his knees. He had only a skivy shirt on top. Sweat stood visibly on his dark face, glazed the bunching muscles of his narrow buttocks and the enormous arm that went around the smaller white man's waist, where he jacked the corpsman's cock in time with the thrusts he made into the boy's pale bun. The corpsman groaned just like a girl. His face looked very feminine, his lips so full and red the boy wondered if he didn't have lipstick on. The black guy's dong looked enormous. He could not imagine having something like that shoved up his ass. He and his oldest cousin had cornholed each other when they were little and beneath the notice of another cousin named Dolores, who would sometimes let them play with her boobies and even once showed them her pussy. For the first time since being at sea, he would have really liked to have a girl. Backing carefully away from the place, he felt his face go hot. The corpsman had looked so like a girl, he thought he might have liked to fuck him if he had the chance and he could be sure no one would find out.

He went along the catwalk and crossed the flight deck and dropped down on the other side. As far aft as he could go, he climbed into the stacks of life rafts hung under the edge of the deck. Their canvas-covered cork rims were smooth with layers of gray navy paint. In the rubber bottom he snuggled down to watch the sun sink into the sea. He thought of how easy it would be to smuggle a girl in there and keep her in one of the superstructure spaces or in a raft. It would be great to have a native girl there.

From his pocket he took two worn letters, the last he had received before leaving the States. The first he opened was on heavy blue paper with deckled edge. The envelope was lined with thin white tissue paper. A bunch of lilies of the valley was printed in the corner of the paper. The writing was large and back-slanted with tiny *o*'s instead of

275

dots over the *i*'s. The lines were as straight as if they had
been ruled. His own letters had a tendency to drift downward toward the right-hand corner of the page if he didn't
have lines.

DEAR JACK,

I was very surprised and certainly pleased to receive your letter. Of course I shall be happy to write
to you. I too am sorry you were unable to attend
services during your leave. (I looked for you.) But I
will try to understand how the tragedy in your neighborhood upset you so. But maybe if you had brought
your cares to the House of the Lord and trusted in
our fellowship you would have found peace and
strength to overcome your low spirits. It really is
true, Jack, if you trust in God, there is no trouble He
will not help you bear. And please believe me, where
your grandparents live and how poor you are, doesn't
matter to me in the least! I hope I am a better Christian than that! If you put your entire faith in Christ
you can overcome what you call "your past." You
truly must believe this, Jack, or your testament to
Christ means nothing. (Enough preaching for now.)

As for your being "a bad guy" and "not good
enough" to write to someone like me—balderdash!
The Lord said "If thy brother ask thee to go a mile
with him, gladly go ten." (I should have looked that
up. I'm afraid lately that at Scripture I'm a disappointment. I started East this year and it takes so
much of my time.)

I'm writing this in study hall. It is strange to be sitting here seeing the familiar trees outside the window
and "speaking" to someone so far away in foreign
climes. Please be sure to write about all the faraway
things you see so that I can share a little of your experiences with you. Our Sunday school class will also
be interested. I figured out you are a year younger
than I am! I was sixteen in March. (I hope you don't
mind my mentioning it.) It just seems so *scary* to
think of you out there. Praise God the war is over! *I*
sure couldn't do what you are doing. And when I
look at the boys our age, you seem so grown-up in
comparison. (Maybe *too* grown-up?)

No, I don't have what you would consider a

"pinup" picture of myself, I'm afraid. (I hope the enclosed snap will do.) It was taken at our last picnic. You will recognize Sybil and Betty. (That's me in the middle in case you have forgotten what I look like. I think you really must have if you think I am "beautiful.") Also, you must not think of me as a "princess." I am just ordinary flesh and blood as we all are, praying to God every day to give me strength and guidance to grow into a good and worthy Christian woman. So, please don't flatter me with pretty words, kind sir. (Vanity is a terrible temptation for me. I made straight A's this term and that worries me almost a much as if I had gotten D's. And I must confess, I am glad you always thought I was "beautiful" even if it isn't all true. Though I must say, you certainly hid your feelings well, while we were growing up. You were *horrible* to me! Haha.)

This year we are exchanging Wed. night prayer meetings with a Negro Church of Christ on Moseley. It is wonderful to go and see how these people who have so little (they have a little poor church. We give them one collection a month to help them), demonstrate their love for Christ. And they sing *so well!* Father loves leading them in song.

I hope you are able to attend services where you are, but I suppose it isn't likely you will have the ministry of a true brother in Christ. Still, you can read your New Testament and I will send you our church paper and some literature. And from now on you can rest assured I include a special remembrance for you in my prayers—and think of you often.

Your friend in Christ, always,

SHARON

He had written her from California while waiting for orders. He held the snapshot in his hand. Three smiling young girls on a blanket in Sim's Park, with summer dresses tucked over their knees. Sharon was by far the prettiest. She knew it, too. Her hair was down around her shoulders. She wore more lipstick than he remembered. Her dress had a sort of square peasant neckline. She was really getting a pair of knockers on her. Maybe she was going to have tits like her mother. But her face—so goddamned *Christian*—denied she ever had to go to the can like anyone real. He could not imagine such a thing. He tried to think about fucking her in the ass, seeing her in the position of the corpsman being buggered on the other side of the ship. Man! He'd like to do that to her, hear *her* moan. Then he saw the big black mess man doing it to her and became both excited and furious. He had to wipe the vision away. How could he even approach a girl like Sharon with such things on his mind? She had sown all approaches with shallow Scriptural mines. Yet she was ripe. In her protests there was that awareness. She could be sitting right there in the photo on a Kotex, smiling like an advertisement. That killed all desire he had been harboring of jerking off looking at her picture. Her letter made him feel cheap about the one he had written her, and his requesting she send him a "pinup." Cunt! All those kind of people had a way of making you feel they were doing you a favor. She probably showed his letter to her mother and asked permission to answer. He looked at the little church paper she had sent, wadded it up and threw it over the side. But he returned her letter to its envelope.

The other letter was from his mother. It was in an envelope with a PO box number in Albuquerque printed on it. The handwriting was neat, plain as a penmanship diagram, leaning slightly in the direction of the letter's flow. The letter was on the cheap, lined paper of a small tablet.

DEAREST DARLING,

I have the picture you sent of yourself in your uniform right here as I write. My, you look so *grown-up!* So handsome too! You don't know how much you look like your father when he was young. Do the other boys call you "Swede" too? Bet they do. It makes your old mother shed a tear to think of her baby so grown up. Guess I can't call you my baby anymore. You never did like that did you? Even when you were tiny you wanted to be a little man.

I just hope, dear, you don't think too badly of me for—everything. I will never forgive Mom for telling you where I am. Of course it is a darn frame-up! And all Bill's fault. You can believe me when I tell you this time I am through with him for good. I just want to do my time and get out of here and go somewhere and try to start my life over. I don't think it's too late, do you? I still have my health. I'm still young enough. I don't look *too* bad, do I? The picture is of me and my roommate here, Maria Sanchez.

They were sitting on a wooden bench before an institutional wall. His mother had lost a lot of weight. She looked great. She and the other girl were holding hands and laughing. The other was a small, rather neckless girl with a narrow Mexican face beneath a kinky bush of black hair pulled severely back from a very low brow. She wore a short-sleeved sweater and a short skirt. Her knees looked dusty. His mother had on a light blouse and short dark skirt he remembered. The skirt was navy blue. One leg was crossed over the other knee. She had legs as good as Betty Grable. The buttons of the blouse were strained over her breasts. There was the shadowed hollow where her throat came down so femininely into the soft, white v of her collar. She was a soft woman. In a photograph her edges always seemed slightly blurred. There was a soft, invisible fuzz along the back of her cheek, but she was otherwise so smooth her arms and legs seemed hairless. In even the most difficult times she would take care of her hands and feet and concentrate on her makeup and clothes. Only in the last days he had seen her, when she had been drinking for more than a week with his stepfather, did he discern in her the potential of being a slattern. Her hands were fine and held as dramatically as a saleswoman's in a perfumery, a job for which she often applied. Only a slightly pushed-in nose and eyeglasses so thick they made her temples appear notched kept her from being truly pretty. Prison seemed such a ridiculous place for her to be. She was harmless.

I think Maria is in love with you, too. Every day she must look at your picture. She wants me to ask you if you would like to write to her too? She is also very lonely here. She is only nineteen. She's Mexican but a very sweet girl. We have become like sisters. She's had a very rough deal, and would sure appreciate hearing from you. She's a lot prettier than her picture, too. I won't be *too* jealous!

Well, honey, things never did go for us how I always dreamed, did they? I just hope and pray one day you will realize that I tried to do the best for

279

you I could and you won't think too bad of me. With all my love, I tried to give you all I had to give. I've thought about that a lot here. And I know my motives were not entirely pure. But in my heart if Jesus walked in, I know He would understand and forgive. I think when you are older and things are not so black and white you will understand too. I really love you as much as any mother can. Maybe more than most. I'm not ashamed.

One thing you learn in a place like this, is what you think has happened only to you, is the story in only slightly different ways of so many others. And the world doesn't cave in. You just try to keep from going too nuts and try to go on. The stories I could tell! If I had a good education I could write a book. I always wanted to, you know. I read a lot here. There's a good library. It's funny, you have to go way back to the old books to find writers who knew and cared about people like us. Although the guy who wrote *Knock on Any Door* does pretty well. I also finished a book called *Crime and Punishment* and now am reading a story by Victor Hugo about some urchins who live in the statue of an elephant in Paris. Maria says she and her whole family lived one year in a culvert beneath a highway. Fixed it up real nice too. Only in winter they put in a stove and someone saw smoke coming from their flue and the sheriff came and kicked them out. So I guess it wasn't all hard times for us, was it? We never lived in a pipe or an elephant. Though I guess I can think of a couple times when they might have been better. But we had some good times too, didn't we?

I just get so blue here sometimes. Bill writes me, but I am not going to answer. I've fallen for *his* line for the last time! So you are the only one I have to pour my heart out to. My only fella.

Oh, I would like to go to a nice beach somewhere where there was hardly anyone else and talk about books and such things with you! It seems like in all my life since high school you are the only one I have ever been able to talk to. You wouldn't have to be ashamed of me. I've really lost weight here. In all the right places! I wouldn't be afraid to put on a bathing suit. Wouldn't it be fun! We could take a picnic. But

I guess now you could go with so many pretty little girls, you wouldn't have time to waste a day on the beach with me—huh? But what I wouldn't give to go out for just one night and have a good dinner and go dancing! We can have a portable radio here and sometimes we girls get so hot to dance we dance with each other. It ain't the same, McGee.

Glad to hear there is a chance for you to learn a good trade while you are in the Navy. I always knew if you got the breaks you could go far. If your father had lived he would have too and our life would have been different. Well, no use crying over spilt milk, right? It is just up to you now. I know you can make it.

Please write me as often as you can. I really need your letters, darling. I feel so alone. You give me something to live for, lift my hopes that it isn't too late to pull myself together, maybe meet some good understanding man who can give us a home and life we can be proud of. But no more liars and boozers! In the meantime I want you to know how proud I am of you. Maybe because you had to be a man so soon, I've helped you a little bit to be one. It gives me a warm feeling as I write this to think that. It makes me feel what I did was somehow right after all, and makes me wish I had understood enough to make it nicer. If that's awful, I'm sorry, but that's how I feel. Now when I think of the last few days we were together I want to cry. I was so selfish and stupid and hurt you so deeply. Bill just always had this hold on me. But *no more!* I promise I'll make it up to you. Now that you are grown-up I think it is time I grew up as well. I'm thirty-five now, you know! I won't try to lie to you anymore, ever. I only did because I thought you were too young, and I didn't want to hurt you. And you were right. I should have left Bill then, a geek in the Rio Grande City jail, and never looked back. But I'm not that way. I just couldn't. Though if I had I wouldn't have landed in here. Well, it's over now. New Mexico let him be extradited to Texas, and Kansas wants him when he gets out of there. I just want to get out of here and settle down someplace where you can come see me whenever you want and be happy. I've never wanted anything more. It really doesn't seem a lot to ask. I wonder why it was always more than I could ever achieve? That's all Mom ever wanted too, and she never really got it either. Neither did her mother. It's funny. Do you suppose there is a family curse? Our men were all smarter, handsomer, stronger—even Bill basically—than thousands of others, but for some reason they never were able to make a go of a thing. Stubbornness and too proud to kiss another man's patoot to get along was the problem our family's men all had in common. Our curse was always that that was the kind of man we women loved.

Sometimes I think our clan was meant to live in olden times out of sight of God. I've often dreamed of sitting in a kind of cave, sewing clothes out of skins. I've told you that, haven't I? It always makes me very afraid, as if I had died. Mom is there cooking something in a pot same as she is now. We all look the same in this dream, only it's in ancient times. Dad is the same. Like he is in summer when he goes around with his shirt off and his suspenders down, his old patched pants hanging on his hips, only in the dream his pants are patched skins. We have an ox and Daddy uses it with a wooden plow to make a field. Your father is away on a long journey. I feel very lonely because he has been gone a long time. And I sing "Bye, Baby bunting, Daddy's gone a-hunting," the way I used to to you. But then the next thing I know it's *you* who is coming back! You are all grown-up. Your hair is long and curly and you have a short beard. You have this beautiful girl with you who has inky black hair. She is very wild and frightened and speaks some foreign tongue. When I look closer she is your grandmother Andersen! Only just a girl, or a girl just like her. And Mom says, just clear as day, "You can't keep her here!" Then I always wake up. Isn't that an odd dream? What do you make of it? Anyway, it seems like we all have been in that place forever. It feels just like home.

Well, I'll close now. I figured out if you only do eighteen months in the Navy, we'll be getting out about the same time. Maybe we can have a little celebration together. Oh, I hate to ask you this, but if you can spare it, could you send me a little money now and then? I don't need much. Just enough for cigarettes (Yes, I finally began smoking in here), stationery, stamps, some decent soap, Nescafe, things like that. $5 or $10 when you can spare it.

And you watch out for those little slant-eyed girls over there! I'll bet you'll just drive them crazy. But, seriously, honey, do be careful what you go with. You could get a disease. Also, I've heard some of them put razor blades in their—you know whats—for revenge. I guess the Navy tells you all about things like that though. I just worry because I love you. Write soon. All my love.

YOUR MOTHER

While he read, he heard her voice as clearly as though she were there in the raft. Time spun crazily without a single cog. The breeze riffled the papers in his hand. He was aware of where he was and of the sound of the ship cutting the sea. A flying fish either flew or was blown onto the high catwalk outside the raft. Its skin made him think of light seen through a broken Christmas tree ornament. He reached out and flicked it off the catwalk back into the sea.

Worlds existed one within another in an entrancing babble and rush of sound. To choose one to the exclusion of the others seemed a stupidity he would not order his mind to perform. It was better, more thrilling than any movie. Let er roll! They were all speaking in the raft as if one could not hear the other, but he could hear them all. His mother's voice, soft and slack as a cat's skin, with—for all she had seen and done—still more of a bubble of insinuating gaiety than whine beneath her jailhouse blues. Her words touched and teased him in places that quickened. Did she do it consciously, or as a mother tubbing a baby? In a sunny room, her voice crooned him to her body, which he knew more intimately than his own, then held him at arm's length to pretend to scold. What had she promised him? *"I'll make it up to you, sweetheart. Make it nicer."* Or he understood how out of her caged loneliness she reached out in her letter to fasten on him. She was a whore, and she gave what she had to give. They weren't like other people. Maybe they never could be.

18

FIRST there was a native fishing skiff, a small scabrous white chip with a tattered sail of patches. The two brown-skinned men aboard did not wave. Then the boy noticed the birds, fast, lean interceptors who barely grazed the waves out at the farthest reach of land smell. The water became paler, with tints of green. Someone sighted the tops of palms ahead. The island.

Could thirty-six thousand Americans and one-hundred thousand Japanese have died for that? was a question that sank claws in the boy's brain. He had expected something more. What *had* been the place's importance?

An island of no obvious charm, sixty miles long and two to eighteen miles wide, Okinawa was the last land battle of the war, and probably the bloodiest of all. The cost worked out to about one hundred dead per square mile, counting Japs. Bury them all like citizens equally distributed over the ground for which they had fought, and there would be no place one might walk without real risk of desecrating a grave.

Viewing it that way, the boy began to wonder about war. He had not thought of it in actual numbers of dead before. The bit of island which he saw through a slight early-morning fog had cost as many souls as the entire population of Wichita. He felt an incalculable fear that had nothing to do with his personal courage.

They steamed slowly into Buckner Bay. In the shallows the masts of smaller ships rose above the glassy surface. A Turk's-head ventilator on a pipe aft of the mast of a sunken DE spun idly in the light breeze. Down on a point a destroyer had run aground.

The boy glassed the scene and the beaches with Navy binoculars. He had seen the war in picture show and newsreel, and now his binoculars became the luscious matinee dark of a theater where his thoughts were freed in air-conditioned anonymity. Again began the constant bombardment of the island by a newsreel fleet. Dragons' tongues of flame roared from the muzzles of naval guns. An unknown sailor stood outlined against a Pacific sky where pompons flowered against the blue in patches that made the heavens look as if they had burst into deadly black blooms. Planes careened like dark insects within the patterns. A plane spun a dying smoke trail, screaming soundlessly down into the sea. The camera followed the entire dying plunge.

He lowered the binoculars, sad to have missed the fighting. What good was it to be in the Navy if there was no one to fight? It made him feel he was an impostor.

"Any girls on that island?" Gorilla waddled up behind and chimed.

"I didn't see any," the boy said.

"That why you look so sad?" He took the binoculars.

"I was just thinkin. I would have liked to at least gone through *one* goddamned battle. I'd liked to been on this ship when it was last here. Or been a marine. Half my life, about, there's been war; then in the end, I just miss it. It ain't fair."

"What's the Muskrat pissin about now?" Al came over to ask and take a turn at the glasses.

"Says it ain't fair he missed seein some action," Gorilla explained.

"Yeah? Now *that's* somethin I can hardly sleep nights myself for cravin." Al shook his head. "Anyway, Muskie, you're young. Just stick around."

Away from brutality and meanness, courage grew in the boy faster than he was growing out of his clothes. Though he was years younger than his shipmates, nothing of ships and guns, unknown lands where tongues were incomprehensible, or the mores of benighted heathen were as terrible in his mind as any Saturday night of his civilian memory. Neither was the contemplation of any war as frightening as the fear of pain, disfigurement, and death with which he had lived before. He would fight against any nation—gladly—a small price to pay for the end of fear.

Standing higher than a three-story building above the glassy bay on the fantail of the carrier, he paused a moment to inhale the Pacific joy of his courage before jumping in for a swim. He could see deeply into the clear water. A single mackerel-like fish drifted through a tinsel of minnows. Two pale greenish jobs with undershot jaws prowled like a couple of Texas cops. Barracuda. A shark watch had been posted, two marines with Springfield .03's. Men counseled each other to watch out for the 'cuda.

The boy leaped far off the rail as if executing a standing broad jump. Feet first, holding his nuts in both hands, he dropped. A simple thing. Yet how many people on earth had done it? was a thought as he fell. His life was being irrevocably changed by a train of such small adventures. Unlike the minds of his older shipmates, his had not already been glazed by an alternative reality of any appeal at all.

The rush of bubbles surged around him as he sank like a bolt into the crystal water. He had never been in such clear water. He could see for yards in all directions. The fish—amazing. Then he turned. He felt as if he had cried out. He was deep enough to see the enormous propellers of the ship, and a good distance along its huge, scummy bottom. It loomed like a steel cloud, darkening the sea beneath it to a great depth. Fish large and small lurked in the shade, close up and under the hull. A ling as large as himself lazed there in total stillness. When, in less time than it took to blink an eye, the fish went from lolling indolence to full speed ahead, the boy felt a shock of terror that was the more electric for being thirty-five feet deep in the ocean. And after the terror came an exhilarating joy that had him laughing underwater as he swam up toward a new kind of sky, dappled and shifting, a definite goal beyond which there was breath.

A bosun with a red beard, both arms tattooed, built like a professional wrestler, was putting on a diving exhibition off the flight deck, about sixty feet above the water. He was not pretty, but he swanned, jackknifed and twisted from a hell of a long way up until he entered the water like a bomb. Amidships others were swimming, diving off the hangar deck near where M-boats and a launch were moored to a rigged boom.

The boy repeatedly climbed the Jacob's ladder from the water to the fantail and jumped back into the ocean until he hardly had strength to fight his way back to the surface after a plunge. It was one of the best days in his life in a succession of such days. He guarded his delight lest authorities discover it and cancel the Navy or something.

He and Gorilla decided to try a real dive, one daring the other. They mounted the rail side by side, grinning at each other. Diving, they went deeper than they had by jumping. The boy was aware of the turbulence around Gorilla a few yards from him as they plunged deep. When he turned and the water became clear, he saw someone trying to swim under the big ship from one side to the other. There were two of them. One was almost clear on the port side. The trailing swimmer, seeming to tire, bumped the bottom of the hull. Then he rose and remained pressed against it, struggling to crawl along. His movements became frantic. Gorilla saw it too and grabbed the boy's arm and pointed. There was no question that they could help the man. They swam toward the surface. As soon as they could command breath, they began yelling about the seaman trapped beneath the hull. Up the ladder they explained what they had seen. One of the crewmen went to a telephone and called someone. Soon word was being passed for all of them to clear the water. No further swimming was allowed. Better swimmers were delegated to dive and see what the problem was. The man who had swum beneath the ship was hoisted out. Official ship's divers donned masks and breathing apparatus and swim fins and went over the side on the end of lines. A lot of time had passed. Finally they brought up the man who had been trapped beneath the hull and laid him in the launch moored to the boom. They signaled that he was dead. Mechanical resuscitation was useless. There were scrapes on his back. His elbows and heels seemed rubbed bare to the bone. The thought of dying like that was suffocating.

The next day, when swimming was again permitted, it was restricted to an area off the hangar deck created by rigging cargo nets to form a sort of net pool. The man who had swum beneath the ship was officially reprimanded, but among the men he became something of a hero and was known for as long as the boy was aboard as the one who swam under the ship.

A marine guard had killed two Japs during the night. He had caught them trying to tunnel into the commissary stores. They had dug thirty feet under the wire perimeter of the area and come up next to the concrete floor of the hut. When they had tried to run rather than surrender, the young marine guard had killed them both with bursts from his Reising.

The bodies were left there until the commander could get the photographer down to take pictures. It was bound to make *Life*.

On the way to chow the sailors drifted over to see the Japs.

The sailors had been put ashore to await reassignment to ships which were expected in the bay any day.

"Hungry-looking sonsabitches," Gorilla observed of the corpses.

"They ain't much, are they?" the boy said.

They weren't anything like the stealthy masters of jujitsu with calves like marathon runners' that leaped from the toolies onto big John Wayne's neck. They did not impress the boy as being as dangerous as most of the people, girls included, who lived in his alley back home. Neither was much over five feet. Their faded mustard-colored uniforms were made of very poor quality cotton, with little attention as to fit. They looked like soldiers from a war that was fought before he was born. Each man was skeletal from hunger. Their jackets and trousers had been opened. To show their wounds, the boy supposed.

"Fuckers are so hungry they're eatin each other out in the boondocks," a young marine corporal in a pith helmet explained.

One wore those little old-fashioned Jap eyeglasses. His lightless eyes stared unseeing beneath the lenses at the morning sun. Flies had begun to blow the corpses. The guard and an officer from public relations took turns shooing them until the photographer arrived. Neither Jap carried a weapon other than the entrenching tool with which he had been tunneling.

There were still Japanese soldiers hiding out in the cane and caves. Marines went on patrols hunting them.

"I don't see how little guys like that could have dreamed of conquerin the world," the boy said.

"Best jungle fighters there are," the marine said.

More than ever the boy wished he had been a marine and seen some action against the Japs. How in the hell could they have whipped anyone?

"I'd of liked to got me a few of those," the boy mused.

"We run a sorta souvenir safari," the young marine beside them confided. "Twenty bucks and you can keep all the crap you find."

"What do you mean?"

"You wanta go huntin Japs, see Sergeant Stigers, Second Battalion. But don't blab it around." He moved away.

The photographer arrived with the marine commandant. Spectators were pushed back.

The big .45 caliber slugs had made bruised, nickel-sized holes in the emaciated, jaundiced-looking flesh of the little men. The perimeter of each hole was enflamed and swollen. But there was very little blood. When the photographer had finished, the commandant rolled the Jap with the eyeglasses over onto his belly with his boot and lifted his jacket with the swagger stick he carried. There were two holes in his back the size of saucers. Flies were already at the wounds.

They were late at the mess hall. The mess cook at the door with a mechanical head counter in his hand glared at them as if they were the enemy.

On a bulletin board the menu was posted: Fluffy Scrambled Eggs; Pennsylvania Scrapple; Kadota Figs in Syrup. . . .

Which in translation meant watery powdered eggs, something that tasted like greasy fried oatmeal and canned figs.

"I don't feel like chow," the boy decided.

"Me neither," Gorilla agreed.

The boy had a box of Mounds back in the tent. Gorilla had a box of Hershey's almond bars. They could buy beer and sandwiches later down at the beach beer garden.

A platoon of marines were doing close-order drill on a dusty bare grinder decorated only by a white-painted flagpole from which a new American flag idly lifted on the breeze. The backs of the marines' shirts were dark with sweat. At the far corner of the field they could see where a baseball diamond had been worn into the dirt.

The marines' area had a certain sort of military elegance. Whitewashed stones described small, swept-earth gardens on either side of Quonset hut doors. In the gardens around orderly rooms, flowers were being encouraged to grow. An elaborate marine mural of painted stones was angled in front of headquarters. Marine prisoners in fatigues with white *P*'s stenciled on them were tend-ing these enterprises under armed guard, bent and patient as gardeners.

Already the heat was starting to slow down even the flies. Light off the whitewashed stones was blinding. It was an effort to put one foot before the other, so suddenly low was the store of energy.

Out in the bay the *Topeka* and a Navy transport swung on anchors. M-boats skated around. The captain's gig from the cruiser was a bit of meringue coming across the water. Two PT boats were tied side by side down by the jetty. Dungareed crews were doing minor maintenance on their decks. The M-boat ferry service to Ie Shima was preparing to leave the dock with a couple of Army officers and a load of stores.

The boy yet harbored the dim hope of getting assigned to one of the PT boats. He and Gorilla studied the papers posted in the glass-fronted bulletin board outside the headquarters Quonset of their tent area. Their names were not among those going that afternoon to the *Topeka*. Nor were they listed with those bound for duty on the transport. A cruiser, particularly one named after the capital of their home state, would have been good duty, they agreed with mutual regret. Nor were their names posted for anything. They had to muster at reveille and at noon. If they were not on duty or on a roster to move out, they were free to do pretty much as they wished.

Jack had found a lucrative market for sketches of his mates, getting a dollar each for life-sized charcoal portraits and two dollars for those in pastels on tan paper. He also copied photographs of the guys' girlfriends. From magazines he would draw movie stars, naked, with beautiful puffs of pubic hair and amazing nipples. Tompkins gave him five dollars for a bareass Betty Grable in color, which he was reluctant to let go at any price. What Tompkins did with the drawing, no one knew, for they never saw it again. Tompkins was weird. In the six days they had been on the island, the boy had earned thirty dollars from the drawings. The paper and colors were free at the rec hall. The Red Cross girl in charge of the place told him he had a lot of talent. He told her when he got out he was thinking seriously about studying art.

She was a broad-beamed, rather bowlegged young woman with short, copper-colored hair and sunburned freckled arms beneath the jacket of a seersucker suit, on the left breast of which, riding on a large, shapeless tit, was the nameplate: Miss Dissen ARC. She walked with an athletic stride, which prompted *sotto voce* speculation regarding the possibility of her guts falling out. Gorilla, tooling a leather wallet nearby, took the contrary view, that it was those mincing, close-legged girls who had to worry. When she leaned over to observe Jack's progress on a picture, she inadvertently or perhaps even purposely rested her right boob on his shoulder, causing his face to become flushed and his hand to falter.

"Very nice! Very, very nice!" she breathed intimately. Her voice had the metallic shadings of her hair. A strange accent. She said she was from Long Island.

They noticed a different officer called for her every day to see her to lunch, and often another came in the evening when the hall was about to be closed.

"Pig never had it so good," was Al's observation.

For all the limited delights of Okinawa, the young woman did seem to be having the time of her life. "Peppy" was the teeth-grating adjective that best caught her spirit. Every man there wanted the stocky girl, though most hated the idea and circumstances of their desire.

"I wouldn't fuck her with *your* dick!" was the consensus. "Anywhere except out here."

That the chances of fucking her at all were as remote as waking to a foot of snow made her jolly, untouchable, schoolteacher's attitude toward them all the more annoying. Only a few guys—churchy, teacher's pet types or spooky solitaries like that tall, dark sailor who had appointed himself her unofficial dogsbody, *happy* for any errand or mundane word—hung around the place all the time.

What *was* his hope, how insane his fantasy? The mope fascinated the boy. He looked at the dumpy woman with such sadass longing the boy considered mercy killing as a gift.

"Gorilla, let's go hunt Japs," the boy suddenly suggested.

Al had to be convinced. He didn't *want* any souvenirs. Nor had he been interested in arts and crafts. He spent most of his time on his bunk, reading a paperback book which he then traded for another, the books going around, the pages becoming dog-eared, particularly those folded at places one could jack off over. Al was more interested in a good mystery than books with a lot of fucking in them.

There was absolutely nothing Al really *liked* to do, nor did doing nothing seem to make him noticeably happier.

"You *like* to go huntin and fishin," Gorilla reasoned.

"Then let's go fish for Japs," was Al's suggestion.

"You like to hunt pheasants," Gorilla insisted.

"Do Japs fly when they're flushed?"

"Aw, come on," Gorilla urged.

"Your muscles will get soft always lyin around," the boy added.

"His muscles always been soft." Gorilla warned the boy he was on the wrong track.

"You get to keep all the souvenirs you find," the boy offered.

"Anyway, come with us to talk to the marines," Gorilla asked.

"Just to keep you two out of trouble," Al reluctantly agreed.

It was about time to go for their three beers anyway. Each had a beer ration card good for three cans a day for a month. Guys who shipped before their cards were used up were able to sell them for five dollars or so to marines. None of the sailors expected to be on the island for a month. They were supposed to turn in the cards, but with the end of the war, discipline in such things was relaxed except for the occasional hardhead who wanted to write down a man's name for any small forgetfulness. Even so, with everyone on his way home or just coming out, the taking of names rarely resulted in any punishment.

Seabees and Army engineers were busy turning the island into a permanent U.S. base. Stateside type bungalows were already going up for dependents of permanent personnel who would be sent out in the future. Most of the work was being done by Okinawans. They cleaned up around the mess halls, hauled the garbage, scrubbed the cans and pots. Each marine hut or tent had its dog robber. Okinawans only a few months from Japanese occupation could work up a spit shine as if they had been born to it.

Still the marines complained. The Okinawans, it seemed, had not been all that overjoyed in being liberated. By blood the people were about half and half, a mixture of Japanese and Chinese, both nations that had long controlled the island. But their sympathies were predominantly Japanese. Such allegiance was a confounding puzzle to country American minds that had known nothing of the Japanese other than the fear and hate that had been taught them in school and dramatized in film, photo and cartoon. For the American's safety, liberty was strictly limited to one day a week, between 1300 and 2200. The boys had not yet been offered liberty.

Cards and crap games were the central outlet for passions. The marines ran the best crap games. There was a big floating game that ran twenty-four hours a day, every day of the week. Hot high rollers were said to have paid another up to one hundred dollars to pull duty for them. Everyone had a rumor of someone who had won thousands of dollars. Wristwatches, portable radios, good pen-and-pencil sets blossomed and disappeared with the tides of fortune. The boy had yet to understand all the side betting with its odds, so only gambled in friendly, small games.

An offshoot of the gambling was a five-dollar-for-ten-dollar loan-sharking business which left a rump-ordained Southern Baptist minister from Oklahoma on his way to being a rich Christian. His fear of any printed word other than the New Testament was absolute. A Pocket Book tossed on his bunk could as well have been a serpent. His expression became that of angry hysteric who would have beaten the book to death if he had a stick handy. He wore Air Corps sunglasses, combed his hair into a gelatinous country pomp and tithed his pay and tithed the vigorish on his sharking. Any effort at debate always ended in his angrily insisting, "Lest thee be washed in the blood of the Lamb, all the ways of thy life are death!"

His name was Skeens and his mission in life, beyond guarding his roll of money, was to bring Tompkins to the Lord. Tompkins, being hardly able to read or write, appreciated the attention. He would lie on his bunk with his hands behind his head, an inert and unquestioning lump of muscle-bound, moldable human clay, while Skeens crouched on his metal rail reading him lessons and verse. They caught Tompkins in the head comparing his reflection in the mirror to the pen-and-ink drawing of a sallow, riddled face atop an orange tract against self-abuse which Skeens had given him.

"Grow hair in your palm, big boy," Al had razzed him.

"Strike you blind," Gorilla warned.

"Hair on his thumb," Jack amended. Tompkins had

such a peeny pecker he'd of had to lope it with forefinger and thumb.

Skeens convinced Tompkins not to drink beer, then made a deal for him to sell his beer card for five dollars, and took no commission for either himself or God. By that act alone, he had come nearer to bringing Tompkins to the Lord than even he had dreamed possible.

They found the sergeant in a squad tent drinking from a coconut. From the strange light in his eyes, they wondered what was in the nut besides milk.

"It's ten bucks each to go," he explained. "Twenty if you get a clean shot at a Jap or if you take any souvenirs. We'll also buy exceptional items from you if you don't want to keep them. Or, I can show you some number one souvenirs if you want to save yourself the trip."

Fitting action to word, he hauled a Japanese rising sun flag from a locker and threw it like a silk merchant over his bunk.

"Flew from Shuri Castle," he assured them. "Those are real bullet holes. A one-of-a-kind specimen. That's one hundred dollars."

It seemed a lot for a flag. So he tricked out an almost identical twin for fifty dollars, bloodstained from having been wrapped around the belly of a banzai officer whom the sergeant had personally sent to his ancestors. For a hundred he would throw in the officer's own samurai sword, a personal memento he would relinquish most reluctantly, and only because he had dropped a lot of loot in a poker game and needed the cash to get well. The sword had the tinsel look the boy associated with prizes at a carnival spill-the-milk.

"You can shave with that blade," he promised, and did manage to scrape a few hairs from his wrist.

On a shelf was a small human skull with a hole in its forehead and a cigarette jammed in its yellow teeth. Fifty dollars. The sergeant had two others without a bullet hole for thirty dollars.

Guns. He lifted the boards from the floor and displayed an arsenal that included two Nambu pistols, very rare now, half a dozen Arisaka rifles a yard and a half long stocked with something that looked like pulpwood. Each came with a twenty-one-inch bayonet. The boy eagerly worked the bolt of the one the sergeant offered him.

"Forty bucks," the sergeant said, not looking at any of them.

The boy handed the rifle back. Then the sergeant opened a little Oriental casket and pulled out something that looked like a couple of dried apricots threaded on a dogtag chain.

"Jap ears. You won't be seeing many of these anymore," he assured them to justify the tweny-five dollars a pair he asked. He held up another pair for comparison.

Looking close and seeing the fine hairs still in the leathery shells, the boy remembered his promise to Arthur.

"All this stuff is only going to go up in value. It's an investment. You can get your money out any time you want. I'd buy back next week at these prices what I let you have today and make a profit." He took another pull at the coconut.

There were also a machine gun on bipod and a Japanese knee mortar, but these he did not even offer them, clearly items for serious collectors.

"You won't find a better collection of stuff or better prices on the island," he vowed.

When they were interested in hunting for their own, he asked for the full twenty dollar price each immediately.

"If you don't get to shoot at a Jap or find any souvenirs, you'll get half back," he explained, counting and smoothing the bills before wrapping them around a roll even more impressive than Skeens'. "You be back here in a hour. We'll furnish guns and fatigues. You'll go out with a regular patrol, so you'll have to take other guys' names. There's no real danger, unless you shoot one another. You're in luck anyway. There are reports of several Japs being seen in the paddies and cane south of Naha. And the guys usually stop for a few beers in Naha on the way back."

They had the feeling they had thrown away twenty dollars.

"It's a racket," Al insisted. "We'll never see that bastard again."

That sponsored anxiety.

"Don't you think we can trust him?" the boy asked.

"Those holes in his flag looked burned with butts to me. Probably gets the ears from a local mortician."

They drank their beer ration at the mess tables set above the beach behind a sign: NO BEER BEYOND THIS POINT! Though the stuff was 3.2, those who had acquired others' rations were managing a beery Saturday afternoon drunk.

Along the road they saw a gray Navy jeep with three young officers and Miss Dissen bound for the seclusion of Officers' Beach. She wore a black one-piece bathing suit beneath a loose white robe. She turned on the seat to lead the two officers in the back in singing some song.

"Think she gangbangs or takes them all three at once?" Al wondered.

"Is that possible?" the boy asked.

"What?"

"Taking all three at once?"

"Figure it out."

He thought about it as the jeep disappeared down the road.

They had become so convinced that they had thrown away their money that their happiness at seeing the sergeant made him wary lest they had got drunk in the hour they had been gone. He had yet another coconut from which he took a sip before directing their attention to the gear heaped on his bed. Three pairs of marine fatigues, cartridge belts, canteens and M-1 rifles.

"You'll be Jones," he told Al. "You, uh, Willowithe," he dubbed Gorilla reluctantly.

"Willowithe?"

"Yeah. That's a bitch, ain't it? But a very tough little guy."

"Cline," he told the boy. "That's with an Irish *C*, not a Heeb *K*."

The sergeant himself was not going on the patrol. When they were dressed and armed and Al had been refreshed in the drill of loading an M-1, he took them to a Quonset hut where a truck was parked and a dozen marines were gathered around a tall sergeant named McCarthy.

"We use the buddy system. Each of you will stick with a marine. You do what he tells you."

The boy's buddy was a kid with a twisted mouth who said he was from "West-By-God-Virginia," as if it were a challenge. His name was Stanley.

Also on the truck besides the rifle squad were two flamethrower teams of two men each and an old Chinese with a bullhorn. He wore shoes without socks, issue khaki trousers several sizes too large held up by a marine web belt, a dingy white shirt and a stained Panama hat. He was obsequious to men young enough to be his sons and so fawning when cadging a smoke the boy had to look away. His teeth were rotted, tobacco-colored pegs.

"Hey, Lun," a marine hailed the old man. "We're all going to stop in Naha on the way back and fuckee your daughters."

The old man giggled as if that were the funniest thing he had heard.

"You guys know ole Lun is the father of half the whores on this useless island?" the loudmouth went on. "No shit! He sold—how many Lun, six? Nine?" The old man giggled, bobbing his head at the absurdity. "Sold his daughters to the madams. You know Ching-Ling with the gold tooth who really *likes* to suck cock? That's his oldest living daughter. She told me. When she spits out a load of your come, she does it in a way to damn Lun's soul in the hereafter. Ain't that right, Lun?"

He giggled again and held his stomach in mirth while feebly denying the marine's contention.

"Old crud's the biggest opium smoker on the island. That's why he sold his daughters, to get money for fuckin opium. You likee the pipe, huh, Lun?" He cradled his cheek on one palm and pantomimed smoking a long pipe.

The old man had never seen anything so funny. If what the marine said was true, there was not a shadow of regret in his eyes.

"Gooks don't have consciences like we do," Jack's "buddy" explained. "Life don't mean nothin to them. They'll sell their wives, daughters, kids, like goddamn livestock. I don't know what the hell we were doin fightin for them for. I really don't."

Stanley's only battle had been Okinawa. He had landed in the first wave, he said. The boy wanted to know what it had been like, as the truck rolled along Route 1 toward Shuri Castle.

"Weren't no Japs on the beach. We were a couple miles deep the first day. In three days we held a beachhead three to ten miles wide and fifteen miles long. They'd all dug in around Shuri. The heights and Naha were completely leveled by air. But still the bastards were able to counterattack us. Every Jap was told to take at least one American with him. They came in banzai bayonet attacks, firing fuckin mortars point-blank in your face. We fought with flamethrowers, pistols, every fuckin thing. Lasted two days, day and night. When it was over, about fifteen thousand of the fuckers were dead. They say it was the bloodiest single battle in the war."

They were rolling along a coastal plain where there were kamikaze mosquitoes, rice paddies, canebrakes and fields of pineapple.

"They use human shit for fertilizer," the marine explained. "That's why everyone is diseased. Should wipe the sorryass crud from the face of the earth."

They went through Naha, a washed-out heap of sticks. Jerry-built bars advertised HOSTESSES, one poet going so far as to pledge FOR YOUR LOVING PLEASURE. The people trotted along under loads, often seeming to shift a hundredweight of rubble toward a place where the same thing they were carrying lay about in abundance. IWO BEER was the people's choice in those parts.

Then they were into some rugged hills that looked wasted by a recent forest fire. Broken trees and dark craters made the boy think of the teeth of the old man smoking now behind unseeing eyes. The hills were chewed, tracked, pocked, scorched by blazes of jellied gasoline all the way up to where the boy could see the ruin of the castle. Yet here and there were shoots of young green. Along the road were posted signs warning of unexploded shells and the possibility of confronting the odd, starving Jap.

They were on a track just wide enough for the truck, the road raised and shoulderless. When they met a two-wheeled cart pulled by an ox and led by a bare-legged, barefoot man under an Army helmet liner, the truck driver without slackening speed began honking and flashing his lights. The ox's eyes rolled wildly. The herdsman flitted about trying to calm the beast and slow the truck with his upraised hand. Finally, he had to lead the ox hurriedly off the edge of the road. In the process the truck clipped the end of the cart, causing it to tip onto its side. The ox driver babbled an outraged cry and waved his arms at the receding tailgate, a dim figure in the dust.

Lun's face remained impassive, as if he had not seen a thing.

The landscape was now steep, going up through

298

plateaus marked by signs of battle. On each plateau were caves.

They came to a small hamlet, perched on the base of the heights. There Lun talked to a handful of villagers who reluctantly came forth and accepted American cigarettes. A young bare-legged boy with a shock of short-cropped hair led them out of the village along a path that went around the heights to an outcropping of overgrown rock in which there was a cave large enough for a small man to wriggle into. On the left of the path was a field of cane about shoulder high. The cave opening was blackened from jellied gasoline. Lun said three Japanese had been seen there recently.

The sergeant deployed them along the path to prevent anyone in the cave from making a break into the cover of the field, while Mr. Lun, speaking Japanese, called for anyone in the cave to come out and surrender. He promised them good treatment and a speedy return to Japan. The alternative was certain death.

The boy stared at the tiny opening in the hillside, and his grip on the stock of his rifle became sweaty.

When there was no sign of life from the cave, the sergeant waved a grenadier up to toss a couple of smoke grenades into the hole. After they had popped and the mouth of the place breathed white phosphorus plumes, they saw the dark and bare shoulders of a man wriggle out. He held a scrap of white cloth in his left hand.

The boy had seen them do that in movies, then spring a machine gun or sack of grenades from behind their backs. He lifted the rifle and sighted it on the man's head as he emerged from the smoke. He had only to squeeze the trigger and the man would be dead.

Mr. Lun ordered the man to turn completely around once he stood before the hole. He wore a kind of knee pants held up with a leather belt. He was barefoot.

"Tell him to take his clothes off, all of them!" the sergeant instructed Mr. Lun.

When the prisoner had complied, he was ordered to come slowly toward them with his hands over his head. He was very thin. The boy could count every rib. His buttocks were wasted, the bones raw-looking. His eyes were as frightened and wary as a child's.

The sergeant gave him a cigarette. When he had taken a couple of cautious puffs, the marine told Lun to give

299

him the bullhorn and have him tell his buddies to come out of the cave.

Through Mr. Lun, the man protested he was the only one in the cave. The sergeant knocked him to his knees in the path with a stroke of his Reising. He went down without a sound.

The sergeant kicked him in the face, sending him curling fetuslike on the path. His bony, bare ass looked pathetic. The sergeant continued to put his boot to the man, who received each kick with a grunt and low moan but did not cry out. Amazingly, when the sergeant grabbed the man by the hair and yanked him flat on his back on the path, his penis was fully erect. The marines laughed. The sergeant tried to turn the man's condition to an advantage, whipping out his sheath knife and threatening to cut the man's prick off if he did not admit there were others in the cave. He wanted to know how many there were and if they were armed.

The prisoner insisted he was alone. There was not a flicker of concern across his face for the impending loss of his member.

The sergeant swore and gave the man's dong a nick with the blade of his knife. The man winced upon a deep, wet suck of breath. Still there was no anger in his eyes toward his captors. His dick quickly became limp.

The sergeant stood up and waved a flamethrower toward the pathetic hole in the hill. A man with gas and compressed-air bottles on his back went forward while his partner covered him with a Reising gun. They knelt a few yards in front of the hole. The operator squeezed the gas-air trigger. A sticky lizard tongue of jellied gasoline found its way into the opening. There was a pop as the operator touched off the igniter match and heavy yellow flame raced with a roar from the fist-sized conical tip of the gun along the jelly string. The fiery stream dipped deep into the hole.

"THERE'S SOMEONE TRYIN TO COME OUT!" a marine cried.

The burning head and torso of a man appeared in the opening. Its expression was that of an incredulous human prairie dog. He was black and shiny as new tar and black curls of flesh peeled upward from his arms and chest, revealing for a moment a white, porklike layer of subcutaneous fat. The boy could see his ribs, the red meat of

300

heart and lungs. Incredibly the burning man lifted his right arm, palm up and forward. Down the line Gorilla puked on the ground.

The sergeant who was standing on the path near where Jack crouched turned and grinned. "Put him out of his misery, kid." He gestured that the boy shoot. It was a gift.

He raised the M-1 and sighted on the center of the burning man's chest. He saw the man through the heat waves that boiled up from the napalm. He squeezed off the shot—shocked to the core when the rifle actually went off, the recoil a kick against his shoulder and jaw. The human torch in the hole took the bullet as something already dead might.

"Now you're a killer." The sergeant teased him with the playfulness of a professional.

The boy noticed that Al and Gorilla were looking at him with a disapproval that came close to anger.

I killed a man. The boy felt different. The act had added a new dimension to him. He thought of his mother, of lying beside her sleeping body, lifting her gown and tremulously touching her naked flesh. *That's two things,* he assured himself with a kind of selfish hardness that amazed him. *That's two things.* But he felt as alone as he had ever felt in his life. It was as if the security he had known since enlisting had been abrogated by shooting the burning Jap. There was no pride or other kindness in the sergeant's congratulation. He remembered the day he had cooked a pet turtle in a can of burning oil out of idle summer curiosity. Yet he did not feel entirely bad. There was the unique knowledge of having shot the man, a knowledge akin to illicitly touching his mother. Sentiment aside, the experience was worth *something*. Nothing heroic, only something his very own.

They went cautiously forward to examine the smoking corpse. The man seemed hardly larger than a child. The boy was amazed by the delicacy of the bones.

With the folding metal stock of his tommy gun, the sergeant nudged the head of the man. It snapped off and tumbled toward the feet of the naked prisoner. Only then did he cry out and do a little dance to avoid being touched by the blackened loose knob of his buddy. The marines laughed.

The sergeant took the boy's bayonet and went after the

head. He bore it back impaled on the blade and offered it to the boy.

"Boil it out and you got one good Jap. Take it," he insisted. "For a souvenir. Hell, you may have fired the last shot of the fuckin war, sailor. Killed the last Jap."

He let the sergeant press the bayonet upon him. Their hands touched in the transaction. The sergeant's hand felt hard, still and somehow very old, like his grandfather's. It was lined and nicked with small scars. The nails were short and square. Freckles were under the sandy hairs on its back. It was completely dry. A passing vision of the hand holding a pencil or crayon to draw a picture made the boy feel weak, feminine, a fake man against the sergeant's grazing touch.

"What you want that thing for?" Gorilla came alongside to inquire, the rifle the marines had lent him now a burden he wished he was without.

"The sergeant says I might have shot the last Jap of the war," the boy explained, glancing with the beginning of defensive fondness at the blackened skull.

"He would of died of burns anyway," Gorilla reasoned. "Throw the damn thing away."

"I want it," the boy said.

"What for?"

"I don't know. I just do. It's mine." He racked his brain for a better excuse. "Maybe I'll make a lamp or something out of it."

"Jesus Christ!" Gorilla dropped back to walk with Al.

The boy did not think they were envious. What the hell was *wrong* with wanting the head of maybe the last Jap killed in the war? Especially since he had killed him. Even if the man hadn't *felt* it when he killed him, the boy was positive he had been alive when he had shot. He was sorry it had not been more clean-cut. So many of his life's victories seemed so narrow as to be debatable. Just once he would have liked to score the winning touchdown, saved someone's life, done the clearly heroic thing. But the farther he carried the charred head, the more he became determined to keep it, no matter what anyone said.

Political differences no longer pertain was one of those curious statements that often sounded in his mind, out of nowhere, nor for any reason he could understand. And there the phrase was, as if out of thin air. He rolled it over in his mouth and felt a sense of having learned something important, though he hadn't the vaguest idea what.

The prisoner squatted on the floor of the truck with his hands tied behind his bare back. Naked, he withdrew into himself and seemed beyond embarrassment, fear or expectation.

The boy sat next to the sergeant; in his mind, the head he held on his bayonet formed a kind of spiritual tie between them. He told the sergeant he had tried to be a marine, and that when his Navy hitch was up, he might try again. The sergeant was hardly interested. Mr. Lun sat across from them, smoking, his eyes as inward-looking as the prisoner's. Recalling what memory? Whittling what profitable scheme?

"Did he really sell his daughters?"

"Huh? Lun? Sure. Why not?" the sergeant mumbled.

There was an almost dreamy lassitude among the others. The mood was like riding in from a hard job with roughnecks, or harvesters, or a team after losing a game. No one was talking very much. No jokes. Most talk had turned to promises of what each would do when they got home.

"First thing I'm goin to do," the man on the other side of the boy vowed, "is drink me a whole gallon of *real* ice-cold milk."

The thought made the boy's stomach seem empty.

"Hey, Sarge, we goin to stop in Naha?" someone asked.

"Just for a beer," he replied. "We got the prisoner."

"How long you been in, Sarge?" the boy ventured.

"Six years," he said flatly.

"You don't look so old," the boy said.

The sergeant snorted. "Went in in Thirty-nine when I was fifteen."

"No shit! That's how old I am!" the boy exclaimed. He and the professional were alike.

But the boy's eager revelation had the opposite effect on the sergeant. It seemed to make him angry and lowered his estimation of the boy, which had not been *that* high in any case. He coughed, looked at the kid for a second, frowned, sucked spit back between his teeth, looked down at his boots, then up, out at the passing landscape.

To rekindle the sergeant's interest, the boy tried asking him about his war experiences.

"Bet you killed a lot of Japs, didn't you, Sarge?"

"Look, kid, let's don't get married," he growled.

The boy felt he had been slapped.

How did you become a guy like the sergeant? he wondered once the sting of the rebuke cooled. What did a guy have to do to be one of them? He looked down at the rifle, its butt resting between his dusty boots, the wooden forearm smooth, warm and smelling faintly of linseed oil against his cheek. The grip where he had held the rifle was still darkened by the sweat of his palm.

When he looked up, Mr. Lun was impassively studying him and his grisly trophy, the one thing no more in his view than the other.

Same-o, same-o, the boy thought.

"You have a cigalette for me, prease?" the old man asked, as if *that* had been all there was on the mind behind those tobacco-colored eyes.

He fumbled for his pack and shook out a butt for the Chinese.

"Ah! Velly good, Rucky Stlikes," he beamed approval, daintily removing one. His fingers tapered too delicately at the tips, and for all his cast-off wardrobe, his nails were long and filed to points—a man who did not work with his hands. After he had shifted the cigarette to his other hand, his obsequiousness became a disgusting, fawning thing devoid of all dignity, as spineless as something the old man might hawk up and spit on the street. "Prease, you give me one cigalette fol rater, OK?"

There was no way to refuse his wheedling self-abasement. But in granting the old man's request, the boy felt unforgivably intruded upon, somehow violated and diminished by the beggar's disregard for himself.

The sergeant rose and stood leaning on the cab of the truck to look away from the transaction.

Old Lun's grin as he stored away *both* cigarettes for later caused the boy to want to grab the opium-smoking son of a bitch and make him smoke one then or blow off his ugly head.

Lun bowed his thanks, the pleasure of his coup already dimming in his eyes as his thoughts turned to other designs.

Not once during the ride did Lun or the prisoner so much as glance at each other.

They hauled the prisoner with them into the low ramshackle bar on the edge of Naha. A marine had tied a cord around his neck and dubbed him Stud. He led the man into the bar with little tugs on the cord.

A small, bandy-legged whore in a purple satin Hong Kong dress slit to her hipbones threw up her hands in mock surrender when the first marines came through the door with their guns.

The prisoner's guard made him squat again on what was a small crude dance floor between the rough tables, tying his lead to a table leg. His penis and balls hung down below his bony, raw buttocks. He bowed his head in the embarrassment of being presented in such a way before women.

Like Lun, the women pretended the prisoner did not exist. It was *more* than just pretense. Somehow, though they might have to walk around the tied, squatting, naked man, he was not there. They did not *see* him.

Everyone quickly bought one of the large bottles of strong and very good Iwo beer. Half a dozen girls were busy trying to get the marines to buy them a drink. The marines seemed to know all the girls, calling them by name, making intimate jokes about their bodies and sexual abilities. Soon a couple of marines and girls were going out back.

"Make it fast," the sergeant warned them.

"Him quick on the ord tliggel." A little whore giggled, slapping a big PFC a third again her height on the belly.

Gorilla and Al were at a table talking earnestly with a couple of marines. The sergeant leaned at the bar. The boy's assigned "buddy" was busy with his hand under the dress of a girl who sat on his lap with his soft cap cocked on her head. The boy found himself standing alone near the door where he had leaned his rifle, a quart of beer in one hand and his trophy in the other.

A woman older and more beautiful than the others in a sky-blue embroidered cheongsam, her hair piled in sleek Dragon Lady coils, saw the boy and began complaining angrily.

"No! No! No! Go! Go! No *good!* No good hell!" She had a gold front tooth. The lipstick, thick on her widely painted mouth, was cracked and dark as veinous blood. But she was beautiful as a poison flower.

"Ching-Ling doesn't want you to bring that in here." The sergeant laughed at the boy.

"No! No! Ugry! Ugry ting!" She clung to the sergeant's arm.

"Worst kind of gook luck," the sergeant tried to explain. "The body'll come out looking for its head or something. Better take it out."

"Would they have a sack or something?" the boy wondered.

"Sack. Sackee." The sergeant drew a picture with his hands. He turned to old Lun, who was sipping something green in a small glass in a corner by himself. "Get a sack."

Lun moved as if he had only been waiting for the request. He spoke sharply to the pretty woman, who turned angrily and went away without answering him. The boy remembered the marines had said Ching-Ling was a daughter he had sold. The boy had the feeling the old man had an even greater interest in the establishment than that. He had noticed he hadn't paid for his drink.

"Better take it out," the sergeant said. Two of the girls at the bar were clinging to each other, staring fearfully at the blackened skull on the bayonet.

Lun brought him a cloth sack that had held U.S. Navy dried beans. The boy slipped the head from the bayonet into the sack and twisted a knot into the top. He stored his prize under the folding bench seat along the bed of the truck. A query of urchins stood across the road staring at the truck and the men in the bar.

"You have one cigalette fol me?" Lun asked, as if he had never seen the boy before.

"What? *No!*" the boy snapped.

Lun merely turned away. Nothing ventured. . . .

The boy went back inside and crossed to lean with those at the bar near the sergeant and Ching-Ling. The sergeant had his arm around her. She had her fine hairless arm around his neck.

"You come see Ching-Ling this night?" she leaned her forehead against his and asked. Her gold tooth was a warm beacon.

"Yeah, don't be busy."

"I save me jus fol you."

"You do that." The sergeant grinned skeptically.

"I have rove fol you," she insisted. "You bling something flom Pee Exx fol Ching-Ring," she wheedled.

"Yeah, sure."

"You bling me, sure?"

"I bling you."

She hugged him and gave him a little kiss, pursing her lips like one for whom kisses were an acquired, unnatural talent.

She was the only one the boy liked. She was longer and more shapely of leg than the other, with a high, rolling feminine ass and no sign of underwear beneath her wrinkled satin.

"You buy me dlink?" A small direct hand stole between his legs and squeezed his peter and balls with mechanical insistence. Barely reaching his shoulder, a broad-faced, dark-skinned girl with the stance of a coolie stood hopefully before him.

When he guessed not, the hand stopped as mechanically as it had begun and she moved to the next man with an identical grope, query, inflection.

Compared to the woman with the gold tooth, the others looked as though they had been hit in the ass with a shovel. If he got the chance, the boy promised himself, he would come back to see Ching-Ling.

"Hey, swabbie!" One of the marines who had taken his beer outside stuck his head in to yell at the boy. "A kid's runnin off with your head."

The boy hurried to the door without actually running. He saw one of the bare-legged urchins in a large olive-drab T-shirt sprinting up the road with the bean sack held by the knot, banging alongside.

"Hey! Hey! Stop!" he yelled. Then set off after the little thief.

The kid glanced over his shoulder, then cut to the right between a couple of buildings and into a narrow alley barely a yard wide that twisted back between little two-story hovels. An open sewer, merely a trench, ran alongside the alley and under the road. A few yards up the cool, ever-shaded passage, an old woman squatted in her doorway, tearing with her fingers what looked like the guts of a rat from a gray fur carcass in her hand and washing it in the fast-flowing little trench. She looked up and blinked at the boy like an old rat herself. The little thief was nowhere in sight. If he had torn past the old woman, there was no sign in her face.

He wasn't going up there.

Walking back he passed a sidewalk vendor with his

store set on a box. He had loose packs of cigarettes—Luckies and Camels—chewing gum and Hershey bars, Lux soap and Pepsodent toothpaste, playing cards and glassine wrapped sepia prints of battle scenes of Okinawa.

When the boy returned Al and Gorilla were ready to be buddies with him again. The adventure would come to be known as "the day Muskrat lost his head."

They regaled each other imagining the little bastard's surprise and terror when he opened that bean sack. He would never forget the moment as long as he lived. The boy wondered how such an experience *would* affect a kid's life. And what would happen to the Jap's head? As for himself, he had witnesses. He'd had the head. His witnesses were from his hometown. It was probably even better than having the evidence. He hadn't relished the idea of boiling that thing to get the skull.

There had been a picture in *Life* magazine of a pretty blond girl in Arizona writing her boyfriend in the Pacific at a table on which there was a picture of her hero and a human skull he had sent her: *"A good Jap!"* The boy wondered if the dreamy, custard-faced girl and the guy who had sent her the skull had gotten married. What were they like to each other? Did they still live with the trophy? How would something like that touch an ordinary American town in Arizona?

That night he wrote both Sharon, who for want of an alternative he now considered "his girl," and his mother that he might have been the one to have killed the last Jap of the war, eagerly describing the day's adventure in fulsome detail.

As it turned out later, Sharon thought the adventure "simply horrible" and offered him Scriptural consolation and an even more fulsome account of the hazards of her high school debating club. His mother did not believe a word of his tale, though she was tolerant of his imagination. "Tell me about the fun things you do," she requested.

An extension of his civilization into the Pacific, bound for Asia, what were his responsibilities, his purpose?

"Be like the big dog," Gorilla advised. "If you can't eat it or fuck it, piss on it."

Political differences no longer pertain, the boy thought, though he hadn't the dimmest notion why.

19

ALL hope of glory died when their names were read off for assignment aboard the USS *Retreat*. They had not dreamed of such a gunless possibility. Why would they put three of the potentially best gunners in the fleet on an unarmed hospital ship?

They inquired anxiously of the scribe who read off the orders. It had to be a mistake.

The idea of painting that big white elephant stretched their future colorlessly before them as they lowered their gear into the M-boat that would take them out to the ship. Besides the boy, Gorilla and Al, Tompkins, Finn, Skeens and four others had drawn the unmanning duty.

Looking at those with whom they shared assignment— an illiterate, a goosey Finn, and a crazed come-to-Jesus-or-else lay preacher of a most fundamental and cruel faith—they realized the Navy's estimation of themselves was considerably below their own. Or, someone, somewhere, had it in for them as far as it would go. There was no other rational explanation.

The ship was *all* white, from stack to waterline, with but a waistband of green and two large red crosses on either side. Deck apes worked in *whites*, not dungarees. There was not a joke in the boat. The boy watched the big white ship come up as they crossed the bay, glumly wondering if he hadn't been so close to Gorilla and Al if he might not have done better.

Drawing nearer, they saw that the upper decks were lined with hundreds of Army nurses. They turned in wonder toward one another. Hundreds of them. Yet not even that was enough to cheer them up.

A short-cropped, husky blond nurse cupped her hands around her mouth and hollered, "You'll be *soooorrr-reee. . . !*"

A jolly mustang officer, still sucking his lunch from his

teeth, his gut rolling over his belt, mustered them on the fantail and said, "Welcome to the *Retreat*. This is an easy ship. A happy ship. You will get along fine as long as you remember that all female personnel aboard are officers and abide accordingly."

He smiled like a man who had found his own personal heaven.

He explained the ship was divided into Deck, Engineering, Communications, Administrative and Medical divisions. There were opportunities for them in all divisions. Being an engine officer himself, he jocularly suggested his line was the one which would be most profitable both in a naval career, should they decide to pursue it, or later upon return to civilian life. He read each man's name off the record jacket a scribe handed him, appraised the new man individually and asked what rating he wished to strike for.

Tompkins, amazingly, had been an electrician's helper before joining the Navy. He was put down for E Division.

If *he* was an electrician, so was Jack.

"Have any experience?" the officer asked, searching his records.

"My stepfather was an electrician. I used to work with him," the boy lied. It seemed like clean work.

Gorilla looked at him as if he were mad, barely able to contain his laughter.

But he too was put down for E division.

"I'd like to learn air conditioning," Al said, inspired. He had often said that was the coming thing. He was put down for air conditioning and evaporators. He explained he and Gorilla intended to start a business after their hitches were up. It was news to Gorilla, but he was game.

Unforunately there were no other openings in A & E.

How would he like to be the ship's battery mechanic? the officer wondered, checking a list on his clipboard. It struck Gorilla as better than chipping and painting.

For the same reason most of the others agreed to strike for other below-decks ratings. A couple of fellows they barely knew had wanted to be corpsmen. They were the only really happy ones with their assignments. They sprung superior grins. Even the officer was curious to see how they walked. Skeens, out of love for his Saviour, the boy guessed, became a carpenter apprentice.

"We are bound from here to Japan to deliver five hundred Army nurses we have aboard; then we are to relieve the USS *Hope* on permanent station at Shanghai," the officer informed them.

He explained the ship had been built at Bethesda, Maryland, the hull having been laid down as a tanker in 1939 but finished as a hospital ship when the war began, which explained why the stack was so far aft. It was the most modern hospital ship in the Navy.

"It also carries the largest naval gun afloat," he riddled them a riddle. Down in the bilges for ballast, there was the tube of a 16-incher originally turned for some dreadnaught that was never built. "But you younger fellas"—he grinned at the boy and sucked his teeth—"are well advised to spurn any offer by one of the old chiefs to show it to you." He wished them luck.

A scribe with their records would show them to their quarters and introduce them to their division chiefs.

"You'll want to have all your jumpers put in the tailor shop," the scribe said. "To have them changed from right arm to left arm rates." That meant instead of the fighting white braid around his shoulder, the boy would be wearing fireman's red around his left. Instead of the proud guns on his sleeve, he would sport a globe with magnetic grids.

"What about those dames?" Gorilla wondered.

"Forget it, sailor," the scribe advised. "No way!" he insisted. "They're strictly officers' territory."

Their racks were back by the ship's laundry, actually the last berths aft on the ship, available because the others in their compartment had moved as far away from the screw as possible.

The division chief was a bandy little petty officer first class named Egan, a draftee over forty, whose short graying hair above a mournful Irish face grew in strange wayward tufts as if he perpetually had his finger stuck in a 220-volt socket. Beyond all bell-bottomed vanity, he wore his dungarees low under a little pot, bagging over his fleshless butt, dragging the deck with their frayed hem. He put on his white cap as if donning a fedora, so it sat squarely on his head in a strange fore and aft oval instead of in the conventional crosswise flare. He had the slouched bearing of the boy's alcoholic stepfather shuffling between drinks; a man of irrevocable shuffling, a civilian bent from a lifetime of bench work and installations in places with a low overhead.

It took him two minutes flat to discern the boy did not know an ampere from his elbow. He handed him the Navy's primer on electricity to study, a long wooden box of light bulbs of all possible sizes, a sectional aluminum stick with a springy rubber gripper on one end, and went away muttering to himself.

A big, soft, smooth-skinned, friendly fellow from Elizabeth, New Jersey, with the name Keating stenciled on the raggedyest acid-eaten dungarees in creation, peered through a pair of Navy glasses on the end of his large nose and explained the boy's duties.

"You're the bulb snatcher. You go from one end of the ship to the other and change any burnt-out bulb you find."

"That's all?"

"How'd you like to learn to run the movies?" he asked hesitantly, as if it were something illegal. "You get ten bucks extra a month for it. Work every other night. And the day you're on movies, you get the afternoon off to prepare the film and play records."

Sounded great to Jack. Keating was the battery mechanic, but he was being promoted to second class and was tired of batteries. He and a man who wanted out of it shared the movie duty. He would train Gorilla for batteries and Jack as a projectionist.

How *had* he been so lucky? the boy wondered. What could be better than showing movies? That was right up there with airline pilots in his estimation, the epitome of what everyone meant by having your cake and eating it too. And he got paid extra as well! He thought he should have been required to fight someone for a deal like that.

"When we get the films, you have to edit each reel for breaks and splice them. When the film breaks, the guys really give you hell. Sometimes they'll throw stuff and you have to close the front of the projection booth until you get the film fixed. That's why no one wants the job."

"Oh."

"I'll show you this afternoon. It's not hard. I'll take care of adjusting and replacing the arcs. You just want to check the film really well, and for God's sake be sure to get the reels in the right sequence. They're supposed to come rewound, but they come ass-to and every whichaway. Don't worry. It's easy."

In a small compartment next to the radio shack was Keating's battery locker. There were racks of heavy-duty batteries in there bubbling up a recharge. The room smelled like batteries. The racks and rubber mat on the floor had been splashed with acid.

"Don't touch anything," he warned. There was an enormous hole in the right thigh of his dungarees and another in the seat. His cuffs and shirt sleeves looked as if he had moths.

"You'll go through a pair of dungarees in a month," he promised Gorilla. "I've been trying to get a supplemental clothing allowance, but they haven't done anything yet. Some damn deck officer is always stopping you and chewing you out for the holes. But they sort of steer clear of you. You'll feel like you have leprosy. But then you get left alone. Everyone sees you and they think acid, like it was catching." He was casually topping up the batteries with an enormous rubber-bulbed glass syringe, splattering the clear liquid between rubber container and the batteries like a mad professor, peering through his glasses on the end of his nose, dribbling the liquid on the left leg of his dungarees. The boy pointed out the danger, expecting to see the cloth and leg eaten to the bone. The stuff did not seem to eat human flesh, whatever it was.

Catching Gorilla's concern, Keating assured him, "It isn't dangerous. You have to watch they don't blow up on you. You don't want to get it in your eyes."

"No," Gorilla agreed. "Breathing the fumes don't do anything to you?" he asked as casually as possible, peering closely at the big guy who was beginning to look more and more like a nutty pelican in a high tail wind.

"Oh, no," he said. "You just have to be sure to keep the captain's gig and the liberty launch running and you'll have no trouble. You're on your own."

"What about the nurses?" the boy wondered when Keating had locked his bubbling batteries safely behind steel.

He shrugged as if they had never crossed his mind. "I try to think of them as men."

"Yeah?" The boy looked back to where a lanky brunette and a short blonde with a Lana Turner hairstyle were doing deep breathing and touching their sneaker toes. Their backs were toward the sailors. The flared legs of their GI shorts rose in back when they bent, to reveal two

pair of definitely unmanly cheeks hanging out of strictly
nonreg panties. He rolled his eyes at Gorilla and glanced
questioningly at Keating, who was going ahead of them
down the ladder.

He was breathing *something*.

20

THE wind blew, the shit flew, and there stood Egan. Over
his shoe tops in water in the electric shop, his Irish mug
aglow with medical alcohol cut with canned grapefruit
juice, he was in his underwear, swabbing the shop deck
and trying to wring the swab into a bucket that was afloat,
washing back and forth with the pitch and roll of the ship.
A Charlie Chaplin turn: he wrung the mop more frequently back into the rising flood than into the bobbing
bucket. They weren't shipping sea water. The freshwater
tanks in the hold were overflowing in the storm.

Typhoon. The word called up visions of Dorothy La-
mour and John Hall up to their eaves in an Oriental flood.
Everyone assured one another the wind was a hundred
miles an hour and the waves between trough and trench a
hundred feet high. As soon as it had started, they had
hauled anchor and made way to keep from being torn
loose and driven upon the beach. A couple of destroyers
had run aground and broken on the point of the island.
The boy curiously thought of Ernie Pyle lying in his grave
beneath a memorial on Ie Shima, the grave lashed by the
rain and the wind. Someone on another ship would write
about the storm and sell the story to the *Saturday Evening
Post*.

Mountains of green water with a lot of weed in it
roared up in the lights. Safety handlines were strung in all
passages and on all open decks. Lobbies were crossed
hand over hand on a web of safety lines. No one was allowed on open decks without special orders. Seamen were
posted at all double waterproof hatches leading on deck.

A mess cook was scalded trying to make coffee. Supper was sandwiches and canned fruit juice. Already sick, anyone who had a cache of anything alcoholic was washing down their Dramamine with it. It *could* have been how the world ended.

All the Army nurses were seasick, dizzy on Dramamine, drunk, or all three. The ship's medical crew who were not sick themselves were busy getting the nurses out of their quarters and into the passageway, where they secured them against the roll of the ship with bunk straps under their arms and over the handrail. Each was given a container of some sort to vomit in. The ship was losing steam, and the captain had cut the air conditioning and nonessential power to run the outside illumination. Other Army nurses and bands of sailors roamed the ship like drunken looters Jack had seen once after a tornado at Blackwell, Oklahoma; that hell-won't-have-it look in their eyes as if authority were as frail as country outhouse walls gone in the first real wind. Their laughter and banter were like the chatter of human crows. Those who had jobs were too busy to bother with them.

One of the lifeboats, a huge steel thing capable of carrying sixty passengers if necessary, was twisted loose from a davit. It hung by its stern wire, banging the side of the ship like a hammer of hell. A corpsman decided they were sinking and ran shrieking through the Army nurses' passageway chased by two muscular corpsmen from the padded ward. A deck gang was sent out to do something about the lifeboat before it did knock a hole in the side of the ship. The lowering winch was twisted and jammed. A seaman had his left arm crushed trying to cut the boat loose by sawing through the cable. A coxswain finally got some explosive, put it on the cable and blew the boat loose.

Then the ship lost steam and the lights went out. The telephone began to ring in the electric shop. While the black gang tried to get up steam, the ship was lighted by battle lanterns and emergency equipment. Passageways had the eerie, shadowed quality of fabled ships in shipwreck movies. With the blowers cut off, sounds and voices that would not ordinarily have been heard provided strange echoes in the eerie spaces. The roar of the storm outside was a banshee howling itself hoarse.

"There's a power failure in Number One Operating

Room," Keating announced, hanging up the phone. Egan was beyond caring. He continued to swab as the water rose halfway up his shins. Everyone else was either in the engine room or rigging submersible pumps in compartments that were shipping sea water.

"Come on, kid." Keating grabbed Jack and hung a coil of heavy-duty cable over his shoulder.

By the blackout curtains in the closetlike space between the double watertight doors off the quarterdeck which they had to pass through to get to the hospital area, a tall black sailor in whites was fucking an Army nurse up against the bulkhead. Her feet were clear off the deck, wrapped around his narrow, thrusting hips, her pale face a blank ecstatic blob over his left shoulder. The second lieutenant's bar on her collar a gold glint.

"Oh. Sorry!" Keating apologized as they slipped past, locking the inner door behind them by spinning its wheel.

"If we were shipwrecked on some lost island," the boy dreamed, "we might start a whole new race." It seemed an appealing possibility.

"That guy's not waiting for a shipwreck." Keating grinned.

Army nurses in pajamas, in robes, in their underwear, sat in the ward deck passage too sick for pride or caring. A Navy nurse and a corpsman tended them, wiped their faces with a damp cloth, administered whatever pills were available.

His own ears ringing with Dramimine, the boy hurried after his tattered mentor.

The chief surgeon was stitching a flap of skin over the fresh stub of the seaman whose arm had been crushed by the loose lifeboat. He worked by the light of battle lanterns held by a corpsman. The senior surgery nurse, a tall woman with large breasts, reminded the boy of Mary Astor, Barbara Stanwyck, one of those. Keating claimed she was the surgeon's girlfriend. There was a lot of blood over the table and the sheet and on the gowns of the doctor and nurse. His rubber gloves were streaked with gore. In a stainless-steel basin on a frame hooked on the side of the gimbaled operating platform was the seaman's arm. It bore an anchor tattoo similar to the one Jack wore on his own arm, and the name ROY. The boy felt strange, though not sick. It was a heightened sense of his own good health and completeness. White splinters of bone stuck

316

through the arm's red meat. He could see the hairs on the severed arm. There was a gold wedding band on the ring finger of its hand.

He wondered what they would do with the arm. Did they just chuck it over the side with garbage?

Man, he did not want to lose any parts.

Keating opened a large junction box on the bulkhead and quickly tested the fuses. He found the defective one, pulled it with the fiber fuse puller, inserted another in its jaws and snapped it in place. The room was brilliant with shadowless light. The nurse glanced at them and seemed to smile with her dark eyes over her mask. A corpsman blotted perspiration from the surgeon's face. Medical instruments had been dropped on the deck and slid about as the ship pitched and rolled.

Out in the passage they met two men from the engine room supporting another between them who had been burned by live steam. Corpsmen hurried them into an emergency dressing station.

"How soon you getting up steam?" Keating asked one of the engine men.

"Be about an hour," he called over his shoulder. "It's a bitch down there. Hotter than a fresh fucked fox in a forest fire!"

Sweat was dripping off the end of Keating's nose, and his glasses were steamed. He wiped his own brow with his sleeve.

Keating was a funny guy. There was a sort of "auntie" or librarian quality about him, though he was only twenty-two. He was not fat, but there was an almost feminine softness about his body despite his six-foot height. His forearms were as smooth and hairless as the boy's mother's. His face was so smooth beneath a shock of short black hair; you wanted to chuck his cheeks. Yet there was nothing prissy or nancing about him.

The surgeon and nurse came out.

"We'll use Number Two if there are any more," he told her. He was a medium-sized graying man with forearms like a blacksmith. There was a science in his face that superseded his military rank, an impersonal, professional aura about him that made the still-boyish freckles on his face and arms as enviable in Jack's eyes as Red Schoendienst's. When he passed close, his energy was palpable.

"That's a tough bastard," the boy whispered to Keating.

"How are you feeling?" he heard the surgeon ask the nurse.

"I feel all right."

"Well, get some rest."

She looked after him as if she expected him to say something more. He did not look back.

As the ship plunged onto its port bow, the nurse lurched toward the boy, looping one arm around his neck, and they fell back against the bulkhead.

"Excuse me!" she breathed, her face close enough for him to smell her warm breath and see the small pores of her sweat-glazed cheek.

There was a momentary awareness of her breasts flattened against his chest. In her low, rubber-soled shoes she was as tall as he was. He gripped her waist with both hands to steady her. There was a softness over the tensed muscles above her hips.

"Are you OK?" She smiled crookedly, pushing herself away.

"Yes, ma'am," he stammered. He had not been aware how far removed he was living from actual awareness of a female body and touch. Fantasy had given the illusion that "women" were close by. In the honest touch of one, the boy realized he was thousands of miles and countless days from where he might catch a shopgirl's eye or share the electric awareness of each other with an attractive woman in an elevator or bus. Touching the nurse, whose dark eyes amusingly mocked his embarrassment, made him feel a deep pang of loneliness—a more civilized and sad emotion than the solitary anger of deprivation he had always felt before. She must have sensed something of what he felt, for a soft question lived for an instant in her eyes. He felt as if her hand had all but started to touch his cheek. It *was* like looking up and meeting the interested gaze of a shopgirl or waitress, only wide and hushed as a comfortable, deeply carpeted room upon which shades had been drawn against the sunlight to save the cool. In his mind he heard the woman ask "Yes?" with the genuine sweet concern of the beautiful feminine apparition that often spoke in his head.

She smiled crookedly, gently mocking. "Thanks for the dance."

Then she spun, her short, boyishly cropped hair lifting on her neck, and walked briskly away.

She wasn't what he would have called "sexy" or "cute" like some of the nurses he had seen aboard. There was a bruised, sardonic look about her, a wry, quiet humor in her direct brown eyes. She spoke softly and did not kid around with the younger nurses except in the reserved manner of an older sister. Yet she was not brusque like some of the nurses in charge of wards or dressing stations. The boy thought when she was older she could be one of those women like Mrs. Roosevelt or his elementary school principal, Miss Rebstein, who had gone on a lone safari in Darkest Africa in the days when the Johnsons were doing that! You would never have thought to look at her that she had been out there in a canoe on the Amazon or whatever it was with a trio of nearly naked black studs, armed only with her old German movie camera. Once a year she showed her film and slides in assembly. There she was, tall and beaming in a Sunday print frock in some native village with her arms linked with those on either side in a line of half a dozen black women who just wore little grass skirts and had necks stretched weirdly by brass rings, all as shy and happy as a graduating class. Some of the women, the boy recalled, had perky apple tits with nipples like the tiny roofs of conical huts, while the tits of others hung down like Lister bags.

What the hell *was* that river? The Nile? There were so many things he suddenly wanted to know. He had seen the ship's library. It was as large as the one at school. To be on a ship with such a library made him feel happy, confident and now at home.

"She's the nicest nurse on this damn ship," Keating said, as she walked away, stopping a second to bend down and pass a joke with a corpsman on hands and knees in the passage wiping up a puddle of his own vomit.

Jack thought he detected a wistfulness in Keating's tone that made him look closely at the tattered heap and wonder if he had a rival in fantasy.

"They're doin it all over this ship!" an old chief machinist, so fat he wore farmer's overalls instead of dungarees, told them in the passage outside the chiefs' quarters. "Let me show you our big gun, honey." He leered and pinched Jack's cheek, bellying him against the bulkhead in the narrow passage. He was over six feet, resembling a beardless Falstaff. They called him Farmer Brown. The boy had been warned the first day, "Never turn your back on him." He had over twenty years in the Navy, had been going ashore alone for years and disappeared almost as soon as he was off the ship. There was nothing that he did not turn into a greasy, corpulent, insulting sexual allusion.

"Keep your filthy paws to yourself!" the boy said, being pressed with incredible strength against the bulkhead by the man's enormous belly, trying to sound mean.

The chief just laughed—a malevolent, evil Santa Claus. He backed off laughing at the ten-inch blade of the Navy sheath knife the boy had slipped from his belt and pressed into the man's gut.

"I'll *have* your sweet ass now, sweetheart." He rolled his eyes. Quickly he clasped the boy's head between his big fat hands and kissed him wetly on the mouth. He pirouetted away like a dancing elephant. Laughter more crudely sexual than any primitive scrawl on a public toilet wall racketed along the passage.

The boy wondered why he hadn't stuck the knife in the crazy old crud. He wiped his mouth vigorously with his sleeve. Still, the strong, wet tobacco taste remained. He wanted to wash his mouth, to rinse it out with unsweetened grapefruit juice laced with medical alcohol.

"He touches me again, I'll cut his fat gut open!" he vowed. He was trembling.

Keating looked uncomfortable.

The boy felt either he should not have pulled the knife or he should have used it. The relentless sound of the typhoon, the heavy tossing of the ship had gone on too long. Keating complained that the change in pressure affected his breathing. The boy felt his nerve endings extended through his skin, waving like invisible hairs. He itched. His hair ached. He felt shrimpy and ugly.

Egan, Huffman, Gorilla and Al, who had come to the electric shop from watch, were sipping grapefruit juice and medical alcohol from coffee mugs when Jack and Keating got back. They poured some for themselves. They all sat like apes along the workbenches to keep their feet above the flood that sloshed in the hold.

"Got to get a submersible pump in here and pump it out." Egan stared at the water on the deck. No one jumped up to go find one.

"Think they're all in use, Egan," Keating said.

320

"Wheeeeeeee!" They all froze at the sound of a high, giddy feminine voice from the ladder down into the hold. They searched one another's faces for the meaning.

When they heard a loud splash and soft thud, they waded outside to see what was happening.

The blond nurse they had seen doing calisthenics with the dykey-looking brunette thought she was on a cruise and had found the ship's swimming pool. She was stroking away in barely a foot of water, happy as a seal. She rolled over onto her back and began backstroking toward the bow with a wide froglike motion of tan, glistening thighs. She spouted a small geyser of water from her mouth.

"Whee!" she cried again. "Come on in, fellas, the water's fine." She bubbled happily up at the electricians standing around her.

"She's drunk outa her mind," Gorilla observed.

"Thinks she's Esther Williams," the boy added.

"Come on, Esther." Gorilla went after her as the ship's rolling worked her toward a bulkhead. He snatched her by one ankle, hauling her underwater but saving her from breaking her blond noodle.

She came up sputtering as Gorilla braced her against the bulkhead to keep her from slipping.

"Steady there, Esther!" he encouraged her.

"Connie," she slurred sulkily. Her bleached blond hair hung wetly in her face; her khaki shirt and skirt were plastered to a body that had less shoulders and more hip and boob than Esther ever showed.

She suddenly announced, "I was Dogwood Queen of Lake of the Ozarks!" Then as if that were a sad memory: "Anybody got a drink?"

"We sure do," Jack offered eagerly.

The others looked at him sharply. But they finally helped her into the shop and put a mug in her hand. They got her on a workbench where she leaned back seeking the bulkhead and nearly slid off again onto the deck. They propped her up, and she squinted drunkenly at them, laughing at some private joke and lifting her mug.

"Here's to sin." She knocked back half the mug. They could see her soft throat ticking the stuff down. She gagged and looked as if she were going to be sick. "What is this?" she squeaked, making a funny ugly face.

"That's gyro juice," Egan informed her with haughty scorn.

"Fuck *me!*" she exclaimed, staring cross-eyed at the mug.

Huffman muttered something about its being a pleasure.

She suddenly seemed to realize she'd had a swim. Flapping her wet hem with her free hand, she bubbled, "I got alllllll wet. ...." Then she set down her cup and began determinedly to take off her skirt, fumbling for the button and zipper.

Egan looked suddenly very frightened. "Uh, Lieutenant, you really hadn't better do that. Ma'am?" He glanced furtively toward the brightly lit space beyond the shop.

She stood weavingly in water halfway to her knees and let the skirt fall.

"Lass one in's a rotten egg!" She went down on her bottom in the water and slumped over on her side. Gorilla hauled her head out before she drowned.

They all looked at the nurse sitting in the water on the deck and at one another.

"Maybe someone will be lookin for her," Egan warned.

"We could put her in the IC Room," Huffman suggested, his voice breaking.

"I don't want to know about it." Egan shook his head absolutely. "Whatever you do, I don't want to know." He took his big can of grapefruit juice and waded off toward the storeroom which contained a mattress on one of the bins on which the duty electrician could catch a few winks.

They tried to lift her. She was slippery, and they kept getting in one another's way. Finally Keating lifted her by the shoulders, and Gorilla got hold of her legs at the knees like a man wheeling a barrow. Jack grabbed her skirt. All their eyes were drawn to the dark triangle beneath the wet, sheer white panties she wore. No one dared speak.

Huffman had the IC Room open when they turned the corner across the hold between the ship's brig and the portside ladder. They all felt aware of the presence of the silent door to the brig as they stepped with their load through the IC Room hatch. On the door was stenciled DANGER! KEEP OUT! OFF LIMITS TO ALL BUT AUTHORIZED PERSONNEL! *They* were authorized. The nurse was not.

She lifted her head as they crossed the threshold. "Did I mention, I was Queen of the Dogwood Festival at Lake of the Ozarrrrrrs. ...." Her head went slack again.

"Yeah, you told us," Huffman said, reaching between her legs to slap the softest part of her thigh.

There was a folding canvas cot and mattress on the last tier of automatic telephone circuits. Huffman locked the hatch and hurried to haul down the cot. The hatch itself was high enough to keep out the water.

Huffman and Jack set up the cot and placed the mattress on it.

"You guys think of the trouble you could be gettin into?" Al asked.

They lay the nurse on the cot. Only then did the realization of what they all had in mind become more than a lark. Her face was slack as a child's in sleep. Drunken breath feathered between her lips. She raised a little snore. She had skinned her knees slightly diving from the ladder. She grumbled a bit and frowned and groped with her right hand to cradle her sex. Her fingers curved innocently over the soft mound.

"What do you think?" Gorilla asked Keating.

"I don't know," he confessed, staring down at the girl.

Jack still held her skirt. "She *wanted* to take her clothes off," he reminded them.

"Yeah!" Huffman said. "We ought to get her out of those wet clothes anyway."

"Count me out," Al decided. "If you get caught, they'll burn your asses forever. You know what they'll do to a GI who rapes a nurse?"

"We ain't *rapin* her!" Gorilla insisted.

"What do you think *they'll* call it?"

"We'll ask her!" Huffman had a brainstorm.

"Let me out." Al went to the door.

"I wish you'd stay," Gorilla said.

"Nope. I don't need some drunken fuck *that* bad. But if anyone comes down, I'll try and ring the IC Room, though I don't know where you'd stash her in here."

When Al had gone and they had locked the door, Huffman bent and asked the passed-out nurse, "Would you like to get out of those wet clothes, ma'am?"

The sound of it struck the boy so funny he laughed aloud.

"Shut up, Muskrat!" Gorilla snapped disapproval.

Very seriously Huffman bent and shook her by the shoulder and asked again. This time she mumbled something and frowned at the hand which shook her.

"What she say?"

"Sounded like um-hum," Huffman reported.

"That mean yes?" Jack asked, still touched by the giggles.

"You say yes, ma'am?" Huffman bent and shook the young nurse again.

"Mmm," she said.

"That sounds like yes to me," Huffman said seriously.

"Sounded like," Keating agreed.

"Could have been," Gorilla agreed.

"That was a yes if I ever heard one." Jack giggled.

She scratched her sex where her wet panties were binding her.

Huffman and Keating began stripping off her shirt. They sat her up. Her head lolled forward onto her chest while Keating fumbled at the catch of her brassiere. The back of her neck over which her wet short hair had parted looked girlish and helpless. Jack felt a rush of tenderness toward her and some wonder if they were after all doing the right thing.

Her breasts, so white in contrast with her tan, spilled out under her slack chin and hung over the rim of her ribs. Both arms and hands hung helplessly at her sides on the mattress. They lowered her back on it as a long breath escaped from her. Then there were only her panties. With shaking hands, Huffman tugged them off her hips and over her bottom and off her still-damp legs. They all paused to look at her.

"She's pretty, ain't she?" Jack said.

"What did she say she was queen of?" Gorilla asked.

"Dogberry festival or something," Huffman said.

"Dogwood. It's a tree," Keating supplied.

Only a small appendix scar marred her otherwise quite lovely body. Her pubic hair was dark brown, curly and healthy-looking. In spite of the visible signs of her breathing, she seemed as helpless as a corpse.

"Any of you guys ever screwed a girl who's passed out?" Gorilla asked.

None of them had.

"I have," he admitted gloomily. "We ought wear rubbers," he suggested. "You know, so she don't get a kid."

They all agreed that would be the fair thing to do.

"Who's going to be first?" Huffman wondered.

"Guess we better throw fingers for it," Keating suggested.

Over her softly snoring naked body they threw fingers until Huffman was first, Gorilla second, Keating, then Jack. The others went around to the other side of the shielding bank of IC circuits to wait. Keating decided to turn off the overhead lights, then put on the red battle lanterns. The three of them huddled around the gyro compass, passing a can of grapefruit juice and alcohol. They all had an inferno glow in the red light. The sound of the storm and the creaking of the ship made the sound of the cot muted, distant.

Huffman came around the telephone circuit bank buttoning up his dungarees, looking more sad than Jack had ever seen him.

"How was it?" he asked.

"Dead." He shrugged. "She can't feel nothing."

They all turned to look at Gorilla. He started off, carrying a foil-wrapped condom—a sliver of silver in his hand.

Huffman went over, put on a headset and began plugging in to the ship's telephone lines.

"Captain Butts got seasick on the bridge and had to go to his cabin," he announced. "Puked all over the bridge. Lieutenant Cheatham's calling for the surgeon."

"You know Butts is filing to run for Congress?" Keating asked. "He's going to give up the Navy to go into politics."

"He wouldn't get my vote. The schnorrp!" Huffman promised.

"Can you imagine an asshole like that? Lieutenant Cheatham says he has even joked about running for President someday."

"That *is* a joke!"

"Can you imagine a guy like that as President? President Foggy Butts. The Great I Am!"

Gorilla came back. Keating went behind the telephone bank.

"Ow!" the nurse cried out. "OW!" Then: "Oh! Oh! *OH! ...Gawd-damn!*"

They hurried around to see what Keating was doing to her.

He was just fucking her. His big bare white ass shone pinkly above the girl's spread knees. She moaned and squirmed a bit. Her arms were wrapped tightly around his neck.

Keating surprisingly had an enormous whang. The thick

white shaft of the thing was pumping in and out of the girl's body. There seemed no end of the damn thing.

They went away.

"Christ, you would never know to look at him," Gorilla said.

Keating was always so self-conscious about his large, soft, almost hairless body with its rather feminine breasts, he rarely showered when others were in the stall. None of the electricians had ever noticed it before. Or limp, it had not been that impressive. He always came from the shower with his skivvies on or a towel wrapped around him. No one had actually *looked* at him for fear of embarrassing him.

"He's got the biggest prong I ever saw on a white man," Gorilla said in honest admiration.

"He ain't Jewish, you know. He's Catholic," Huffman curiously added.

"*He* woke her up, whatever he is," Jack said.

"*Can somebody bring her a drink?*" Keating called from the cot.

They all three took the can. They were both sitting on the edge of the cot. The nurse had her arms locked around Keating's neck, her face buried in his chest. He supported her with an arm around her bare waist. He hadn't even taken off his glasses.

"No more," she slurred against his shirt. "Just you. . . ."

"Sure. You're fine. Here you go. Want a drink?" He held the can for her and touched it to her lips. The smell made her head jerk up. She looked blankly at the others standing there, squinted her eyes and frowned. She put her hand on Keating's to steady the juice and drank, closing her eyes.

"*Oooooooh. . . .*" Her head swiveled around in drunken circles. "*Ooooooooooh . . .*" she groaned. She clung to Keating's neck as he lowered her back onto the mattress. "Jus you. . . ." It was a fading plea.

Keating looked embarrassed as he stood up and buttoned his trousers. He did not look any of them in the eye. Gorilla clapped him on the back as they went with him to the other side of the tier.

Jack dropped his dungarees and skivvies, looking down at the young woman's body. Her skin was white where she had worn a two-piece bathing suit. He gave his dick a couple of jerks to get it hard and with both hands rolled on the rubber.

Her lips looked bloodless in the red light. He got between her legs. The back of his knuckles grazed a damp place on the mattress beneath her bottom as he guided his dick into her. The hair between her legs felt stiff as sisal. In spite of the lack of air conditioning her skin and sex felt cold. He had to push and move around a lot before he worked himself into the loose warm center of her body.

She opened her eyes once then and murmured. "You aren't the one. . . ." She trailed off, her eyes rolling around as they sank beneath her closing lids.

He came in her unresponsive body.

"She's still out," he went and announced to the others.

"We better get rid of her," Gorilla suggested.

Jack had a vision of them throwing her over the side.

She was harder to dress than she had been to undress. She was completely out. There wasn't a muscle working anywhere in her body.

"Let's get a stretcher!" Jack suggested. "It will look better."

He went and took one from the ladder well. It was an ordinary canvas one with wooden poles.

They carried her along the portside quarterdeck, then down to the hospital area.

Lieutenant Commander "Mother" Chaffee, the chief of nurses, was on deck, starch-stiff in spite of the heat and smell.

Keating said, "This one fell down one ladder into the forward hold, ma'am."

"Right in here." She swung open a door to a receiving station. "Is she hurt?"

"We don't think so, ma'am. Just drunk, I think," Keating said.

She shot them a fierce look as if they had challenged the entire officer class.

"I think that will be *all*," she snapped.

"Yes, ma'am," they said in unison.

She looked up from her examination of the nurse to the men who were backing from the room.

"None of you touched her, did you?" she demanded.

"No, ma'am!" they chorused.

"There are ways to tell, you know." She squinted.

"Well, ma'am," Gorilla said, "if she's been touched, it

327

was before she fell down *our* ladder. She's been out like light. We just got her here as fast as we could."

"All right. Uh . . . dismissed."

"Yes, ma'am."

Back on the quarterdeck, yelling onto the wind, Huffman asked, "Can they tell it was us?"

"They can't," Keating assured him. "We all wore sheaths. There's nothing they can check."

"What if she remembers us?" Huffman wondered.

"She won't remember anyone for certain," Gorilla said. "Unless she remembers Keating. She might never forget him."

They laughed. All except Keating.

21

THREE small boys down on the jetty were whirling bullets on the end of strings, exploding them against an iron bollard. There was no joy in their play as they skipped to avoid the weak trajectory of the projectiles. Their clothing was a crazyquilt of patches overlaying patches. The basic garments, if there ever were such out of a common cloth, had long since disappeared in a maze of remnants.

Between shipside and the jetty something small and milk-white floated in the garbage-laden water, as it rose and fell. It wasn't a rat or a drowned cat, the boy decided. Yet it had limbs. Bleached and bloated, he thought it might be a hairless monkey. Then he saw it was a baby. The shock was visceral, filling his brain until he felt it pressed painfully inside his skull. He had been long enough in China to be neither surprised nor enraged. Rather, he felt an ineffable sadness, a hopelessness that reached back to a time when *he* was new from the womb.

Some sort of murky grouper, a gnarled-looking scavenger for which the citizens of the bumboat colony avidly fished, slipped out of the shadowed depths beneath the jetty and took a quick tug at the infant corpse.

The boy snatched a light bulb from the box beside him on the deck and threw it. There was no weight to it, and the ugly little fish came back for another quick nip. He snatched the electrician's insulated pliers from the scabbard on his belt and threw them with inspired aim. But soon the fish was back. He could heave everything in his scabbard, bomb the fish with everything he might tear loose from the ship and make not a dent in the inevitability of the river in that patched land.

He raced down to the quarterdeck and told the duty officer what he had seen. The bosun was dispatched with him off the ship.

The three boys who had been exploding bullets against the bollard scampered over to beg, "Hey, Joe! No mama, no papa, no chow-chow. You give me cigarette, chewing gum, chocolate?"

"Beat it!" Jack waved the urchins away.

Still they persisted. "No mama, no papa, no chow-chow, Joe!" They plucked at the sailors' sleeves as they knelt to peer in the water between jetty and ship. The bosun sent one sprawling.

"Fuckum somebitch!" the kid screamed.

They would need a net or basket. The bosun went to get something.

"No mama, no papa, no chow-chow, Joe," the two remaining boys pleaded. They had looked over the edge of the jetty, but what they saw was of no importance to them.

Jack dug three cigarettes from his breast pocket and threw them as far as he could. The three had to race an old man squatting impassively in his rags in the sun for the weeds, beating him out only by their willingness to dive headlong onto the splintered planks for them. The old man said something to them in Chinese clearly reprobation. They replied in tones that had never learned a moment's traditional respect for the aged.

The bosun returned with a bucket on the end of a handline. After several tries they were able to scoop up the tiny corpse and hoist it onto the jetty. By then a few seamen and some nurses and officers had gathered above along the rails. Some of the nurses covered their eyes and turned away.

Jack stripped off his shirt and laid it on the jetty. The bosun poured the baby out onto it as gently as possible. It

329

was a boy. His tiny penis was like a small tuberous flower beneath his distended belly. A wormlike length of pale umbilical cord remained. The tiny face was puffed in sleep that would never have an awakening this side of the womb.

He hated China. And he did not believe in God or the hereafter.

When he handed over the bundle to a corpsman, who wrapped it again in a bath towel, he gave away something of his own. He felt as aged and impassive as the old man still squatting in the sun on the dock.

He and the bosun were sent immediately to sick bay where they were given boosters to their cholera, typhus and tetanus shots. Death was more common in Shanghai than crumpled cigarette packs in the gutters back home.

He had become inured to death. That is, its only visible effect on him was a slightly grim set to his mouth and a deepening of the squinting facial flinch with which he had lived all his life.

The Army engineers had patrol boats at the mouth of the Whangpoo to intercept and fish out the rafts of lashed-together bodies that came floating down. It was not clear if the rafts were sent by the rebels or as warning to the potential rebels within the city by the Nationalists. Whatever the intent, one of the effects was to drive the virtually worthless yen to even greater depths.

Only coolies dealt in single bills actually worth less on the open market than the paper on which they were printed. Shopkeepers and people of any capital at all traded in tightly bundled cubes of bills three inches square. A wheelbarrow load was required for a transaction of any substance.

On the black market, the only market worth dealing in, the common currency was U.S. Military Script and dollars printed in Hawaii. Yen was more valuable as souvenirs sold in glassine envelopes than it was as legal tender.

On every main thoroughfare horribly wasted people lay along the walls and gutters, wrapped in pathetic rags, a begging bowl or cup beside their heads, lifting a stump, if able, at passersby. Many were too weak to lift a thing, begging only with their eyes. Others lay, past begging, death filming their stares, faces and limbs half-eaten away, flies blowing mortifying flesh you would not touch with a pole. And no one—not church or state—offered a hand.

Early in his life he had acquired the dread of passing

from this world in a skid row doorway—*Unknown male Caucasian. No known address.* He knew no greater fear.

"Aw, fuck it, man," his shipmates counseled. "They're gooks! They aren't like us. They haven't any respect for life."

But there was Chiang Kai-shek in his cape, with the missus on his arm, going up the steps of the White House. Wasn't he a gook? What the hell were *his* plans? Shaking hands with Harry and Bess Truman, General Chennault and his sexy Dragon Lady. Flying Tigers. *Ding-How!* Shee-it.

Ask the whores. Even the Japs were more humane.

No mama, no papa, no chow-chow.

Someone was doing a shitpot of lying about China somewhere.

Still, people streamed into the city from the country. If there was no work that paid enough to feed even one, there was at least a better chance for graft and theft.

The boy had asked himself which he would do: haul a boat up the Yangtze in harness like a donkey or try the streets of Shanghai? The answer was obvious. He had been a thief but a few years earlier, stealing stuff his stepfather and mother could hock, stealing his clothes, stealing the toys to make himself a Christmas, a birthday. After the initial thrill of free riches, it was too lonely and nervous an occupation to consider as a career.

Except for a well-organized few, the pickings in Shanghai looked thin to him. Even the shopkeeper to whom he sold his cigarettes at twenty dollars a carton had to finger his abacus like a maestro to eke out a few pennies on the transaction.

The streets were so crowded that he was merely able to shuffle and jostle along in a river of anxious humanity that overflowed into the gutters. There were so many people you practically had to crawl in on hands and knees to buy a Chinese fuck, except in the more spacious houses run by the enterprising White Russian madams. Yet, in the aftermath of war, the city was a mecca offering anonymity for those of the countryside who saw a chance to escape warlords and generations of debts that might bind them forever. In disorder, the boy supposed, all poor might hope to rise on criminal dreams of freedom.

In the International Settlement, the British, French and Americans clung to their walled outposts, and Chinese had to show passes proving they were servants to get past the stoic Sikh mercenaries. All the Sikhs were over six feet tall and bearded, with dull turbans wrapped around their heads. They mounted watch outside the roughest sailors' dens where enticing hostesses in cheongsams beckoned from the doorways. Neither hostess nor sailor could lure a Sikh inside, be it rain, sleet or snow. Armed only with nightsticks, they displayed a mystical intransigence and unassailable stoicism that gained them the respect of everyone.

The boy had seen a single Sikh who spoke no more Chinese than he did settle a small war between half a dozen pedicab and rickshaw boys without breaking a head or disturbing his turban. In fact, the only time Jack had seen a Sikh lose his calm was when a merchant seaman tried to snatch the giant's turban and make away with it. He was arrested in flight by an arm as long as a cattle barrier, hoisted clear off the ground and shaken like a cur while being lectured in Hindi. When the seaman was set down, he ran half a block in white terror, then stopped and vomited against a building.

The detachment of Sikhs who guarded the dock area were billeted in a barrack behind a bombed warehouse. They did their own laundry, hanging it from tiers of clotheslines strung from the upper windows to forestall theft. No women were ever seen around the barrack, and it was rumored they were homosexual. Their sole entertainment seemed to be spirited volleyball games over a rope strung between two poles in the small courtyard beneath their laundry. They had cleared the space by banking rubble around the adjacent walls. They kept strictly to their own and would not be lured into international sport by a contingent of Japanese ex-soldiers who lived in the bombed-out warehouse, under very loose Chinese guard, seemingly forgotten by the commission for the repatriation of prisoners. But the Sikhs did let the Japs occasionally use their court and ball.

The Japanese in the warehouse puzzled the boy. Some of them had women and children, presumably Chinese, whom they had met during their occupation of the city. There appeared to be more than fifty of them living in the skeletal ruin, feeding communally from steaming stuff cooked in oil drums. The Chinese guard eventually stopped being posted, yet the Japanese, many still wearing the remnants of their uniforms, never strayed except when marshaled to go in a body to unload a ship, evidently driving the cost of longshoremen to a price where even the coolies finally rebelled, setting off a dock war that lasted until the Nationalist police arrived and saved the Japs' asses by shooting more than a dozen Chinese and breaking some dozen more Chinese heads. The going rate for a coolie longshoreman was the equivalent of two cents, U.S., per day, and any coolie caught pilfering was flogged on the spot by a gang boss and kicked off the jetty.

Jack tried to write to his grandparents, to his mother, to the girl Sharon whose photo he had taped in his locker some idea of the things he saw and felt. Their replies seemed to accuse him of trying to shock them in an effort to enhance his self-importance. It was as if he were seeking out the worst things to tell them so he could disturb their own lives, which, in the case of his kin, were desperate enough as it was; Sharon simply chalked it up to imagination. She had listened to a lecture by a missionary of the Church of Christ who had just come from Chungking, and he had nothing but praise for the Chinese whom he had brought to Christ. He had shown slides of happy, smiling people who loved God and in no way resembled those in Jack's letters to her. She sent along the address of a mission in Shanghai and suggested he visit the brother in Christ who ran it. "You must learn to look for the *good* in your fellowman. We are all children of God," was her advice. He began writing only of what he hoped to do once he returned home, and of his longing for the things of America.

The difference between his daily experiences and the sensibilities of his conditioning began to produce a strangely subtle alteration of character which, for want of better explanation, everyone simply called "going Asiatic."

The most obvious sign of "going Asiatic" was a desire to go on liberty alone. Not that he did anything differently by himself from what he might have done in the company of his shipmates. It was simply a more personal experience. The sights and sounds and smells of the city became intense, unfiltered by joke or Stateside voices. The Navy warned against going ashore alone, for hardly a week passed that a sailor was not fished out of the Whangpoo. The body was always sent to the *Retreat* for autopsy and disposition. Invariably he had become separated from his shipmates, robbed, often stripped and dumped into the river. Yet, after a time, even that fear whetted a perverse confidence in Jack as he was hauled through the streets in rickshaw or pedicab or made his way afoot in the jostling throngs.

Overlaying the subtle hint of sandalwood was the ever-present smell of a strong Chinese onion, more powerful than garlic. The nearest thing to it in the boy's experience was a nasty wild onion in the States called ramps. It came from the cooking stalls along the jetty and streets. In a crowd it was the collective odor of shuffling humanity.

"You rike-a girr, Joe?" the pedicab man asked. "Nicee crean girr."

"Chinese or White Russian?" the boy inquired automatically. He had a definite destination in mind.

"Chinese girr. Velly young, Joe. Nicee, crean. You see?"

He had a face as guileless as a Chinese Mortimer Snerd. The color of old, junked piano keys set in sockets of pitch, his teeth grew and overlapped one another at cruel angles so he could not actually close his lips. There was an innocence in the man's eyes and eager offer that told the boy his experience with women was probably less than his own. His pedicab too was a dull worn machine with some sort of jerry-rigged solid front tire in the place of an easier-going balloon.

Out of a sudden shallow pity and curiosity to see what lay at the end of the poor man's limited hustle the boy asked, "How far?"

"Five mintues!" the man assured him eagerly, already mounting his seat.

There was not a cathouse in Shanghai that was more than five minutes by pedicab from wherever one was solicited.

"OK." He grinned and sat back in the double seat against the asphalt-colored cloth over the thin cushioning.

The man wore trousers that ended above his knees. His calves were enormous, hairless, tapering to delicate ankles above feet shod in oft-mended cloth slippers of the kind made in the country by women. The soles were layers of rags sewn to thickness in thousands of tiny stitches. Even the common soldiers of the Nationalist Army wore the slippers, their calves wound tightly at the end of their ill-fitting faded uniforms in ragged cloth puttees. The man's entire body strained with the effort of pedaling. His bare calves became glazed with sweat. The turning of national fortune in war had lifted the boy from a hopeless alley of twisted souls at home and carried him to where he was one to be obsequiously solicited and gladly hauled around by the straining body of another human being.

Fifteen minutes or so later they turned into a narrow alley between the two circular OFF LIMITS shields on the houses at the mouth of the entry. Then there was a widening—not a true courtyard—where there was a communal water tap.

He gave the driver fifteen cents in script. It was more than he would have had to pay if he had haggled in yen, but he no longer took any pleasure in beating down a price by haggling. A nonsmoker, he had sixty dollars in his wallet from the sale of cigarettes. He always sold his cigarettes now to an old silk merchant with shrewd gray whiskers of wisdom who ran a small shop in a street just off the Bund. Haggling was kept at a minimum, and then only over the odd carton of Old Golds or Raleighs the boy had to take along with his ration of two cartons of Camels or Luckies. The old man had long since stopped trying to palm off yen on the boy, dealing only in script or Hawaiian dollars. The boy let most of his pay ride and lived off his sale of cigarettes, drawing only enough each payday to convince the Navy he was a frugal sailor with spartan tastes and eye toward the future. With interest, his savings were approaching one thousand dollars. When he was ready to get out, this, along with his mustering-out pay, would give him a tidy sum to carry back to civilian life.

A smiling madam with gold teeth bowed him inside. It was a new place, not yet well known. There was the anxious eagerness of enterprise that had yet to make its nut. A gesture from the madam and a very young girl, perhaps no more than twelve, was pushed forward from the muster of lasciviously smiling whores. Her face was a wanton cosmetic mask that made him think of the tiny *sam-san* girls, some no more than three, hauled from bar to bar by their parents, a brother or a sponsor who had bought them and trained them to play the single-stringed instrument that sounded to Occidental ears like something terrible befalling a cat. The little girls were tarted up like the souvenir dolls one saw in shops. Sailors assured one another such children could be bought outright for around three hundred dollars. But the only time Jack had tested the theory by offering such a sum to the young boy who was hauling the little painted *sam-san* girl around the bars, he fled with her as if he had seen the face of the worst devil of Oriental imagination. It was also rumored the little girls were trained to suck cock, and that merchant seamen bought them and kept them aboard ship, selling them eventually in some distant port where they might wash up broke.

It was true that children could be bought and sold in China, as it was true that children could be hired to suck cock or submit to other abuse, but Jack had, until that moment, always preferred the pleasures of grown women with deep full-formed bodies and the unsubtle minds of full-fledged whores. Most often he frequented the White Russian houses that seemed caught forever in a faded decadence.

Even on tiptoe in Occidental high-heeled shoes, the girl did not come to his shoulder. She wrapped her thin arms fiercely around his neck and nibbled it with little cupid's bow lips, leaving scarlet lipstick tracks along his collar.

"I rove you," she vowed. "You rove me? You likee me? You rikee fuckee-suckee?"

He looked over her head at beckoning, more fleshy merchandise.

"Young girr, Joe," the madam assured him. "You rike. Armost vilgin. You rike. Fi dorrars. You rike!"

"Too much," he said. The child's perfume was so strong he could taste it in the back of his throat. She lifted herself clear of the floor and hung from his neck, nibbling his face. She weighed nothing. She was so thin.

"What you say, Joe?" the madam bargained.

"Two."

Even the child pretended to be insulted by the offer. She ceased nibbling and let herself slide back to stand on the floor. Still, she kept a lock around his neck.

"She young girr, Joe. Crean—"

"Yeow, almost a virgin." He reached up to loose her grip. Her face became sad, pleading.

The going rate, no matter how intense the haggling, was two bucks, and every sailor except those pulling their first liberty knew it.

"Foo-ul dorrar, Joe. You rike. I plomise."

"Three." He held up three fingers. The girl was squirming eagerly against him.

"No. No, Joe. Foo-ul." The madam held up four fingers. "Fuckee-suckee, foo-ul dorrars. OK, Joe?"

"OK, Mama."

Then everyone laughed. "OK, Mama." The other whores giggled and hugged each other. The child kissed him passionately on the mouth. Behind the taste of her lipstick and the smell of the perfume in which she had been drenched there was the taste of those goddamned ramps. Going up the ladder behind the girl's small, round bottom, he wondered why he was doing it. He had no desire for her. There had not been the hot, thick rush to the back of his brain he felt when he had looked over her head at the wide-hipped older whore who had beckoned him with her eyes. A whore of perhaps thirty with belly and big tits straining her tight blue cheongsam. He had gone Asiatic. There was no other rational explanation.

They crawled into the second tier on hands and knees. The girl slid shut the paper-paneled door. It was a space about six by seven feet lined with flowered cotton cloth-covered pads that felt suspiciously like Navy mattresses. There was headroom to sit. The girl unzipped and slithered out of her dress. She wore nothing underneath. Kneeling, his head bumped the overhead. She protested slightly when he stripped as naked as herself.

"No, no. SP's," she cautioned, as if just removing his trousers would better facilitate his chance for escape. He no longer feared the SP's. Most of them knew all the men off the *Retreat*. It was the only ship on permanent station there, and they would not take a man's liberty card unless they caught him off limits twice in a single night. Everyone off the *Retreat* was Asiatic anyway. It was common knowledge that caused the Shore Patrol to treat them with sympathy.

The low room was very warm. There was no air. The girl's perfume was intoxicating in the space. The light filtered through the paper was mellow. She was very white. That Chinese had yellow skins was nonsense. The girl was more the color of young ivory. His own skin, tanned and with an underlying ruddiness, was darker than her own. Only her small face seemed shadowed and indistinct. The clown's circles of rouge on her cheeks and the cupid's bow mouth came up as a grotesque mask of something less than human—it sponsored the feeling he had when being hauled in a rickshaw or pedicab, an urge to kick or whip the driver to greater effort, even as he suffered pity for the man turned beast. Often others, when drunk, did drive the rickshaw boys and pedicab boys like donkeys in great, raucously exuberant abuse.

Perhaps she sensed something in him. Her eyes seemed wary. When he stretched beside her on the pad, there was a tremble in her childishly thin body. He was not so far from childhood to know they were half again as sensitive to things as their elders.

With mechanical eagerness and an intensity born of inexperience she began kissing his face and mouth, vowing, "I rove you, Joe. I rove you. You rove me?" while tugging his peter in her small hand with a painful monotony that would have drawn milk had he been a cow.

"Easy. *Easy!*" he suggested. He stroked the smooth length of her delicate spine to give her the idea. But she only squeezed tighter in lieu of a positive reaction in her hand and yanked all the faster. He caught her thin wrist and tried to show her a rhythm more likely to achieve her goal. But as soon as he released her wrist, it was all yank-yank-yank.

He rose on his left elbow forcing her back onto the cushion and kissed her truly as he might any girl. She merely opened her mouth wide and let his tongue prowl the interior, watching him warily all the while, unblinking, trembling, beginning to sweat through her makeup. Her skin now felt warm and damp. He caressed her budding, small hard breasts. The nipples were no larger than his own, set in tiny pink aureoles. When he covered one small breast with his mouth, she shuddered and looked very scared.

"Whatsamatter you, Joe?" she inquired, honestly puzzled. The mechanical hand was getting her nowhere. "You dlinkee too much?" she wondered.

So slight was her experience, she was not aware he had not been drinking at all. Perhaps she had never been with a sailor who had not been drinking. Only solitary sailors who had gone Asiatic went to cathouses without first getting bombed.

Her belly sunk between her narrow hips was a small mound he could span with his open hand. Beneath the soft skin her stomach muscles were tensed. Only fine sparse black hair covered the solid small mound of her sex. He

338

stopped her hand and lifted her body against him, kissing her again. His cock then began to rise against her body.

"Suckee, suckee," she offered, making an O of her small mouth and describing a circle around it with her forefinger.

He lay back and watched her bend to the task. She sucked as mechanically and unimaginatively as she had tugged upon him. She was a single-gaited child who had yet to learn speed did not always equal efficiency. Her hair had been wound up off her neck in a too-mature style for her face and stuck with a decorative sprig of white flowers that hung like tiny bells from its stem. The flowers danced with the relentless bob-bob-bobbing of her small head as her mouth slid up and down his shaft, her lips at least skillfully shielding her teeth. The naked back of her neck and the S curve of her clear back as she bent over him were beautiful. Her right arm curved over his belly and down his right thigh where her hand lay passive, small and very pretty. He stroked her back down to her buttocks and slid his fingers under her left buttock to graze the tight, narrow slit there.

He lifted her away from her work and lay her back on the cushion. Her face was flushed from her futile exertions. The flush spread down her chest. Frightened lack of understanding filled her eyes as she rapidly searched his face. Her frail body was glazed with sweat. He felt a bead of sweat run from the side of his nose to the corner of his mouth. She opened her thin legs wide as he got between them. She seemed so very small. He felt large and coarse and thought he must appear quite ugly and foreign in her eyes.

She guided his penis against the lips of her narrow slit. Hadn't they told her about lubrication? Or was it part of her advertisement as an "almost virgin"?

There was a tapping on the sliding door. The madam called, "You finish? You finish now."

"No!" he replied, his words sounding loud, almost a bellow.

"Yes! Yes! You finish," she insisted. She slid open the panel a bit to peer in. He reached for the trailing edge and slammed it shut. He heard her chattering wildly in Chinese outside.

He withdrew from the frantically working child beneath him. She was dripping with sweat. Before she knew what

339

he was doing, he flipped her onto her belly. She began protesting wildly.

"No! No! No, Joe! No! We finish. We finish!"

He knew she was afraid he was going to screw her in the ass. With his right hand beneath her he lifted her sex clear of the pad and held her there, fingering the tiny bud of her clitoris while he entered her sex again from the rear. She cried out more in wonder than pain. Her cheek was turned and flattened on the cushion. Her frightened eyes stared unseeing. He fucked her roundy-roundy, gently, slowly, until he slid easily into her narrow passage. Rubbing her little clit made her thin body jerk and tremble other than mechanically. But there was only fear and something like loathing in her face which had become smeared with her lipstick and rouge. The stem of the tiny flowers in her hair had become broken and hung pathetically in the now-disheveled coil on her pale neck. He held her belly off the pad with his left hand and could feel his cock inside her through the wall of her thin body. Her pretty, pale bottom squashed and filled against his lower belly. His cock looked thick and dark going into her. Her mouth was open, and she muttered something repeatedly in Chinese. When he came, he clutched the child to him, thrust deep inside her. He loosed a low cry. He felt himself coming through the wall of her body beneath his hand. He heard her give a small cry too. Of surprise. Certainly not of pleasure. He was so dizzy the room spun.

His prick felt very tender as he withdrew it. It looked red as hell. The girl sat upon the cushion and openly looked at his still-erect penis. Then, realizing he was aware of her look, she glanced away. She called out something in Chinese.

She and the madam below held quite a conversation between the paper walls before the panel slid open and an old woman thrust in a basin of warm water pink with pomegranate. The girl dutifully washed his prick with a bar of Lux soap and the disinfected water. Then she squatted over the pan with her back to the sailor in the low room and washed herself.

She asked him, "Prease," indicating he could zip up her dress, though she had not once met his eyes with her own.

He realized suddenly she had been the first girl he had fucked in China without wearing a rubber. He knew in that, if nothing else, he was certainly slipping. It was nuts!

He would have to get immediately to the prophylactic station at the Red Cross Club. From his wallet he slipped a small dollar in script and pressed it in the girl's hand.

"For you. You keepee," he insisted. She closed her hand on the bill.

Down the ladder the madam told him, "You bad man. Give me nother dorrer."

"That's your ass, Mama." He smiled at her.

"What ship you?" the woman demanded.

"The *Retreat*," he said.

She had guessed as much. She had only been fooled by his boyish face. She explained in Chinese to the girls the problems of entertaining anyone off that unholy white ship that had sat so long in the river. "Awrr sayohs on *Reatleet* no-good-somebitches!" was her heartfelt judgment.

He laughed and patted her generous bottom. Some of the younger whores looked horrified. A couple giggled. The one who had first caught his eyes pushed between them to walk him to the door. She hung onto his arm with both hands and pressed her soft left breast against his arm.

"Next time you see me," she offered.

Slipping through the curtain, he saw the new little whore dutifully hand over the bill he had given her to the madam as if she had never harbored a thought of keeping it for her own.

He hated China.

Yet, walking up the alley, feeling light and satisfied after having his ashes so surprisingly hauled, he loved the scent of the city's rot and scorned fear in its dangerous shadows. He felt secure within himself, and walked up the middle of the narrow, dark alley relishing fearful possibility.

Don't care if I do die, do die, die, he sang to himself, feeling as far from death and wasting disease as a young man could feel. But on a main street he hailed a pedicab and told him to make for the Red Cross Club "chop-chop!"

The Red Cross Club was near a famous Buddhist shrine, though he had never been inside. It was a spooky place guarded by two immense ugly gods around the feet of which burned long tapers of incense sticks.

After going up the broad steps of the club he made directly for the basement men's room. From a bin just inside the door he took one of the small brown paper packets and went to the trough urinal over which there were mounted water taps. He dropped his trousers and underwear. He tore open the packet and removed a soap-impregnated coarsely woven little cloth, wet it and soaped his genitals thoroughly with it. Then he rinsed away the soap and dried his parts with a paper towel. He then opened the small tube of ointment that came in the packet, lifted his penis, squeezed it to open the urethra and inserted the end of the tube into his dick, squeezing the ointment inside, working it back by massaging the shaft of his cock, saving a bit in the tube to cover the glans and shaft. Another man near him was doing the same thing. Men just in to urinate took no notice. With the bit of tissue in the packet he covered his now-medicated parts to keep the salve from staining his underclothes. Where the ointment touched white cloth, it turned black when laundered. There was nothing on the packet to tell him what chemicals he was squeezing up his cock, but used properly, immediately after intercourse, it most certainly prevented VD.

The film slipped through his fingers as he wound it from one reel to another, feeling for broken sprocket holes and bad splices. There was magic in film, yet a bothering crudity. That it was necessary to show continuous motion in the split-second increments of frames seemed an enormous complication which science must one day certainly simplify. Television, a system he had read about in *Popular Science*, seemed hopeful. Constant pictures through the air, waiting around the clock for you to tune in. History, travel, stories, everything at your beck by the flick of a switch. Would half the world jerk off in the privacy of television whenever Ann Miller went into her dance, or was that merely his own feverish inclination? But it could change the world. Surely when you could have all that adventure and knowledge right in your home, home could never look so good again. Wife and husband would have to get their asses up there with Ann Miller and Tyrone Power or it was all over. Who would want to go to work when they could stay at home and travel to Tibet? Real *Buck Rogers* stuff. He had little doubt that within his lifetime he might travel forward and maybe backward through time, live in any chosen moment.

"You're never satisfied," he heard his grandmother chide him wearily in the hot steel booth.

Well, there it *was!* He was in China, and she spoke as plainly as if she were standing beside him. Wouldn't *she* be something in China? He smiled at the notion. His grandmother Mac standing there in her everyday housedress, arms glazed with slime from reaching into a chicken, the smell of singed pinfeathers so real he glanced around the booth to be certain something was not burning.

Science impressed him as a crude, disorganized bunch of stuff. Every *Popular Science* magazine promised a marvelous world of moving sidewalks, personal helicopters, meals from a centrally supplied cooking machine at the touch of a switch, citrus and strawberries in the heart of winter, alternative interior decoration at the touch of a button, education while you slept, libraries and all the great pictures of creation at a wish, highways under the seas, fast ocean liners that flew on the water, intercontinental passenger submarines (the idea of making love to some beautiful modern girl in the face of a bewildered fish had a particular appeal) and earth satellite farms and farms on ocean beds promised a world without want, interstellar homesteads, garbage gobbled up at your sink and whisked by pneumatic tube to a central processing plant to be mulched into fertilizer for those ever-bearing strawberries and citrus. Everyone in *Popular Science* illustrations was the natural offspring of Dick and Jane, who had been in the readers he had been given in school. *Popular Science* promised the world, while outside his booth everything seemed still to be dying and more raggedyassed than ever. For want of science.

And there was never anyone to talk to about it.

He had begun to live two lives. Then he realized that was how he had always lived. From the time he was a baby until the present moment, there had been the face he showed others to satisfy *their* expectations and the one that lived in wonder, disappointment, fear and discovery, of secret courage and feminine sensitivity behind the movie set false front. A boy with the boyo's, he was eager in their interests and skillful in their sport and entertainments. But alone they all seemed of a dark and dying world. He felt like some monster by-product adrift in the brackish unillustrated backwash of *Popular Science*.

Books had become his gyro stabilizer. There was H. G. Wells putting lie to the stuff pooped out by publishers and dropped on his school desk. Not that the history he was taught in school was wrong; it simply was not right enough. There was more history in *The Outline of History* than he had supposed from school it was possible to know. From church and school he had taken their word that the world had been sitting around with its fingers up its butt waiting for Christianity to show it the way and America to free the slaves. The world hadn't been waiting for a thing. Even in a short history, Christianity and America were but a wink.

Wells made him feel a sense of the people rather than just the rumors of kings. Why schools didn't use Wells' book instead of all those others was a puzzle.

He thought he ought to introduce Wells to his grandfather and had written the old man a long letter about it.

The old man had written back in his Lincolnesque hand, complaining about the boy's own handwriting being impossible to make "head nor tail of." He wrote:

> Books are OK if you learn something besides. But books don't amount to a damn if you don't know what the folks who make the world what it is are about. I've read books. Far as I'm concerned 99% of them book writers ought to have to go back and work and listen to folks. They don't know shit from Shinola when it comes to all us who worked like niggers all our lives and are treated worse today than old nigger slaves when they got old and couldn't go hoe. All the goddamned books in the world ain't changed that one whit.

Whenever he thought of his grandfather, he saw him in his everyday trousers, which were as patched as any coolie's. The haunting similarity between the old man's pants and those of China called into question everything in between. Yet try to talk about such things, even to a close buddy, earned him nothing but a quick platitude and a stare that told him he was showing definite signs of going Asiatic.

Outside the routine of the ship, his duties, the grabass and loyalties of camaraderie, there were only the books, his crazy thoughts for which he had not words to speak except to himself and the whores. Find someone aboard who seemed interested, and he either ran out of patience or was more truly interested in sucking his cock or poguing him. It began to seem that everyone who was interested in anything except preparing for a good job, fucking, sports or some hobby was queer. And *their* interest was always, ultimately, secondary to their needs.

Even his duties were ones he did alone. He spent most of the day wandering about the ship, poking into every compartment and space, changing light bulbs. He stood solitary watch on DC generators, isolated by sound from the figures of the machinists in other parts of the engine room. Running the movie every other night was a solitary task. But with books and the whores he felt a little less lonely than he had before.

Being only nominally an electrician, he was often detailed by the division chief to go on work parties to fetch supplies. This had the advantage of giving him first crack at boxes of books destined for the ship. He always passed them on after he had read them, but he might take half a dozen for himself from the box.

He was always on the lookout for a book with some sexy stuff in it, a lot of real talk. Erle Stanley Gardner and James M. Cain seldom disappointed him. He liked Bret Harte and Jack London. John Steinbeck had become a favorite, though he thought Theodore Dreiser wrote truer stories. Steinbeck always seemed to be writing about people a notch up from Jack's own, or else his own were a truly criminal clan who were lucky they had not been totally stamped out. He felt Dreiser would have felt right at home up the old man's tin-can alley. The people of Erskine Caldwell's *God's Little Acre* were close too, but too simple and one-track. He felt he really knew Harry Morgan and his wife in *To Have and Have Not*. They could have been his stepfather and mother. If Bill had had a boat and not been afraid of guns, he might have done something like that. Bill never really wanted *that* kind of trouble. Harry's wife going for his handless stub—that was really something. He'd read it again and jerked off in the hot, locked privacy of his projection booth.

Then he found a book of short stories by a Russian named Andreyev, whose people might have really been his own. There was a story about a young boy and girl walking in the woods. They were in love. They passed some woodcutters. In the forest they stopped to kiss and make love. The woodcutters came and drove the boy off and took turns raping the girl. The boy could do nothing. In his frustration he came to hate the girl, though he loved her very much, still. Even the sexy parts of the Russian's story were so true he could not honestly enjoy jerking off over them. It was the same with Dreiser, though he was not nearly so sexy. He looked and looked for other books by that Russian, but he never found another.

When the film was rewound and the first two reels threaded into the projectors, he switched on the record player that was hooked into the loudspeakers beside the movie screen. Nurses had begun to come up for shuffleboard and sunbathing in an area around the stack screened by canvas for that purpose.

Only from his booth could one see over the canvas.

He set the needle on the record.

"Hi, fellas! This is your best gal GI Jill with her GI jive for all you lovin soldiers, sailors, airmen, coastguardsmen and marines out there from Kiska to the bottom of the world. A special hello and a big smackereenie today for the fighter jockeys at Fürstenfeldbruck. Hi, fellas [loud kissing noise]. You know you really send me into a spin. OK for all of you from your best gal me, here is that sentimental gentleman of swing, Mr. T.D. Hope you like it, fellas. . . ."

He had always thought GI Jill was actually broadcasting when he heard her before. It was a great disappointment to discover that she was all on records. He would watch guys in the mess chowing down, listening to a GI Jill record they had heard a week before, their eyes telling him they still believed there was a blonde at a mike somewhere with the legs of Betty Grable and the chest of Lana Turner and a face like that girl who was always going to the malt shop with Donald O'Connor and Peter Lawford, talking just to them.

By opening the panel in the front of the projection booth just a crack, he could peek out and see the sunbathers beyond the screen. Most wore two-piece bathing suits or shorts and halters, only unfastening their straps when they lay on their stomach. There was Lieutenant Plumb, whom he had caught one night between the blackout curtains in the double doors off the quarterdeck with Lieutenant Cheatham. He liked Cheatham. He was glad if someone was cutting Lieutenant Plumb it was him. That way it was almost as if he were too. But, of course, he wasn't.

She wore white play shorts rolled as high as she could roll them behind the safety of the screen. She pinned up her dark hair and lowered her halter strap and tucked them into the top of her halter. She smeared herself all over with a concoction of mineral oil and iodine the nurses made up for suntan lotion. A tall mannish redhead whose own skin was lobstery from the sun left a card game to slap some lotion on the small brunette girl's back. The other cardplayers said something that made them all laugh except the redhead.

Lieutenant Plumb glanced at the sun and spread her towel at a three-quarter angle to where the boy stood peeking from the booth. She lay on her back with her feet toward him and covered her eyes with two little dabs of cotton. When she spread her legs slightly, he could see up the rolled legs of her shorts. She wore white panties. He got the 7x50 binoculars he kept there for just such moments. Turned on edge in the crack of the booth's panel, squinting through one lens with his left eye, he could zero right in up her pants' leg and see the fine black hairs peeking from the elastic of her underwear. He dug out his cock and slowly, lovingly masturbated. When he was finished, his shirt was wringing wet.

He wiped up his semen with his handkerchief and stowed it in his pocket. He put the binoculars back in their case and stashed them in the cache where he had the stack of flimsy, poorly printed pornographic stories you could buy on the streets of Shanghai. Tales of a lad who climbed over a wall into a harem. Stories by Marquis De Sade. Stories where women were fucked by all sorts of animals and machines and took on five men at one time. They were beautiful, elaborate stories with all kinds of information about eating, architecture, powerful governments of princes and lords, clothing, customs and manners. For the most part they told him more about things than most of the regular books he read. And, you really couldn't help jerking off over them. They made you want to. He even believed a lot of it was true. He was skeptical about all those guys running around with cocks a foot long and balls like two avocados. But they ate stuff and smoked stuff and took stuff in their wine that made them see things and fuck the clock around. He was certain somewhere in a place like Shanghai, if nowhere else, such substances must be available. De Sade wrote about things Jack had thought only he imagined. The girl served up in the center of the table at one of those De Sade dinners often looked a lot like Lieutenant Plumb. She was born to be carried off to some spooky castle and trained like a beast. He daydreamed of hanging her up by the wrists and whipping her until she did not know her name and was ready to do anything.

When he read stories or saw films about the treatment of women in concentration camps by the Nazis and Japs, he always hated the bastards for the envy he felt in wishing he were there sharing their cruel fun. Great burly Nazis, pigs, using those beautiful, large-eyed Jewish women. Using them until they were shit, then breeding them with apes, trying to make them pregnant by lower species to create a slave race. The bandy-legged little Japs, like apes themselves, lining up to fuck some beautiful, large Caucasian woman, thirty at a time, leaving her so sodden and defiled she lived only for vengeance. And when their salvation was at hand by the approach of the Allied heroes, the women could not return to real life and always threw themselves upon their former captors in one suicidal rush of revenge.

He opened the door and sat outside on a folding campstool. Lieutenant Wentz, the senior surgery nurse, and three of her friends were playing shuffleboard on the navigation deck below. She looked up and smiled.

"What's the movie tonight, Muskrat?" she called.

"*Saratoga Trunk* with Gary Cooper and Ingrid Bergman."

That made them very happy. Everyone liked Gary Cooper and Ingrid Bergman. They all promised to save each other seats.

Gary Cooper, Tyrone Power, Clark Gable, Humphrey Bogart, Spencer Tracy, James Cagney, Jimmy Stewart,

Henry Fonda, Ingrid Bergman, Katharine Hepburn, Bette
Davis, Loretta Young, Gene Tierney, Paulette Goddard,
Lana Turner, and Betty Grable, even Maria Montez, they
were fathers, mothers, husbands and wives, brothers, sisters, uncles and aunts, in a way somehow more real than
blood kin. Tiny pictures catching split-second motions. GI
Jill, sending kisses to guys from Kiska to the bottom of
the world, on a record. It was funny. The movies came in
cans from a factory like tinned salmon. And like salmon
for the price, they were a bargain.

Being a projectionist, he felt closer to the stars, but he
also felt they had somehow played him for a boob before.
He would never be able to lose himself totally in a picture
show again.

22

ALFONSO CASTRO was the first person who caught
your eye among the replacements. What set Castro apart
from the others was his expensive, tailor-made blues.
Eighteen-ounce serge, sculpted to his lithe Mexican-American frame, they had twenty-one-inch bells and a built-in
swagger. He would never pass a captain's inspection in
that outfit, but he moved in memory of the figure he cut
on old Perdido Street.

The replacements were greeted with a solicitousness reserved for survivors of disasters and frail aunties. Men
with points enough to go home rushed to relieve the new
men of their sea bags lest they strain themselves between
quarterdeck and muster on the fantail. Then they hovered
about the rails back there or busied themselves at meaningless tasks, slyly measuring their chosen man. A deck
ape and a machinist literally shadowed the bewildered little Mexican to muster, all but snapping at each other over

possession. Pete Peterson had Alfonso Castro's sea bag, but Yablonski had his records, hand baggage and a souvenir samurai sword the lad had been sold by an enterprising marine on some atoll at which the troopship had put in.

Alfonso had himself rated for guns, and his disappointment in being assigned to a noncombatant ship was as real as had been Jack's own—though more vocal than shrewd.

"Where I go to put in for transfer off this fuckin meatball?" his voice shrilled over the levee on the fantail. "I put in for a transfer today! They make some mistake with me." His voice rose to where Jack leaned on the rail a deck above. Jack had points to go before he would take a personal interest in replacements.

"I show you!" Alfonso Castro promised skeptics on either side who advised him to shut up. "I don't stay on this fuckin big white meatball! I ship over Regular Navy—today!"

He had the right idea. The only way anyone ever got off the *Retreat* was either to fuck up so badly they were up for an undesirable discharge or to extend their enlistment to request reassignment.

Huffman from E Division was down there doing his own hopeful personnel work in search of a graduate of electricians' school or an apt striker he could help advance as quickly as possible. He had been trying to get Jack to study for third class, offering tuition, promising to get a copy of the test to study before the examination. But as important as Ohm's and Faraday's laws may have been to the world, they made dull reading to Jack. Huffman was three months over in points enough to go home. Each month he would hurry to check the bulletin board outside the personnel office and see his points higher than a winning blackjack hand when men were going home with only eighteen. They told him he was "key personnel."

"No electricians, huh?" Jack observed in anticipation of Huffman's complaint, staring beyond his gloomy face over the river where the late-morning ferry was leaving the Bund. It was so loaded with Chinese and their bundles that young men clung outside the rails with their toes in the scuppers. The doughty old three-decked, high-funneled tub lumbered along, its antique engine laboring mightily.

Where the hell were they going? the boy forever wondered. Wherever the ferry went, it came back later as loaded as it had been when it chugged out. People fought and shoved for a place aboard. Riots broke out. Old women were moved to curses, and young women with children wept. *One of those is going to capsize someday,* he was certain.

"You have no goddamned ambition!" Huffman accused bitterly. "You . . . bulb snatcher!"

Jack had long since given up any notion of a more glamorous assignment. He no longer envied the men on cruisers, destroyers and submarines that tied up out in the river. Their guns always looked trained for an official photograph. There was no one to shoot at. He knew on one of those there was all kinds of horseshit discipline. As for guns, he would have spent most of his time chipping paint and painting. His work was not hard. He was left alone. He felt the independence of a neighborhood ice-cream vendor, without the urgency of having to make a nut. If a night's liberty left him hung over or sleepy, there was always someplace to which he could crawl off and rest. He prowled the ship constantly, his box of light bulbs his passport to even restricted parts of the ship. Officers' and nurses' quarters were open to him. He could breeze right past the off-limits signs when the officers were at their duties. He was certain he knew the ship better than the chief engineering officer. He knew it the way he had come to know the alleys and backdoors of his own city. In that knowledge there was always a hideout, a way to turn and scramble through, to come out somewhere else looking as innocent as a starched shirt. Making his idle rounds, he got to know everyone and could tarry to take an interest in their work. He had become something of a joke, a character aboard, as every city has its character. Nurses teased him and offered him candies from boxes they had received from home.

"How old are you really, Muskrat?" was a question often asked.

"Old enough to know better and too young to care," was a ludicrous rejoinder that always made the nurses smile.

"Cocky little bastard, aren't you?" tougher nurses would observe.

But once, when a couple of the surgery nurses who were especially tough were teasing him, Lieutenant Wentz said something that made him feel very strange. She said, "Muskrat is ninety years old and still growing." She had said it in that soft, mocking way she had, and had never explained what she meant. But when she said it, she looked him right in the eye, not unkindly, but deeply, so he felt touched by fire. He knew she saw right through him and was a little frightened by it, though he was sure she meant him no harm.

For seamen he stood in contrast with their labor as the symbol of injustice or else was treated by the more kindly as a sort of mascot. If he had gone so far as to sew a rating on his sleeve, they might have mutinied.

"You know who has it *made* on this bucket?" they asked rhetorically as he passed with his box of bulbs and sectional bulb-snatching pole. *"Muskrat!"* they all chorused.

"Hey, Muskie, how you get that *clean* job?" they would wonder.

"Pure ignorance," he replied honestly.

"It ain't who you know, it's who you blow," they consoled themselves, slapping black grease on wire as thick as a man's arm.

So he grew a perverse pride in his rateless sleeve. His best buddies, Gorilla and Al, were about to go up for third class.

"You can't go home nothing more than a fireman, ace," they argued. It had been his papers from which they copied during boot camp.

But he could not see why not. That he had got in the Navy at all at his age was victory enough.

He was standing a rate's watches. He could check out a circuit, basically understood the difference between one hooked up in a parallel or series. Not even Egan made neater electrical splices. He wore his electrician's scabbard of tools without embarrassment, slung low across his loins like a gunslinger.

"Go for your Wiggy!" he often challenged, stepping into the electric shop and getting a drop with his voltmeter on more serious men overhauling a motor at the bench, to their exasperation and occasional amusement.

Nor was he any longer frightened of the invisible juice. He would happily link hands with others and see the big voltage tester in the shop run up while the tingle went through him, until one or the other in the chain had enough and broke off. He had never been the first to turn loose.

No, there was no desire to forge a career that led to crawling around between someone's ratty walls following an old cobwebby wire insulated with that crap like asphalt which had become brittle with age and fuzzed with grease and dust. If he was learning anything upon which he might base a career, it was as a movie projectionist. That he would not mind doing. At least while he went to school.

He had definitely decided to go back to school. He wasn't sure what he wanted to study. He wanted to study everything. Reading and the questions of China had done that. But he learned such an answer was not acceptable when he was asked, so one time he would say "art" and another "history," then for variation he might decide "architecture." That seemed to be everyone's favorite for him, though no one seriously believed he could achieve it. No one championed art. History was good only if he planned to be a teacher, it was explained. He had been sorry to hear that. He wondered how H. G. Wells got *his* start. So he refined his aims to *commercial* art or architecture.

"I wouldn't sleep a damn night in anything you ever architected, Muskrat," Division Chief Egan voiced one of his rare opinions.

"You know, Muskrat," Huffman confessed, studying him seriously, "sometimes when I look at your face, I just want to smash it."

Being none too pleased with it himself and having felt such an urge when looking at certain others, he was curious. Huffman had neither the size nor the character to fulfill his urge. "Yeow? Why is that?"

"Because . . . because you just don't give a shit about nothin! It gets on my nerves."

"Well, I do give a shit," Jack said quietly. "Maybe it seems like I don't. But I do. I just don't want to go up for third class."

"Crud!" Huffman wobbled away. He really wanted to go home, and the boy felt genuinely sorry for him. He had a face like a Peke, which was emphasized by the fact that he wore his cap on the back of his nob behind two carefully combed Pekinese-colored waves of hair. He wanted

353

to go home and study electrical engineering. He had been a Boy Scout, all that. His old man worked for GE.

Jack accepted he was something of a disgrace. But he wasn't going to commit suicide over it.

The officer below had completed his briefing and welcoming the new men. He asked if there were any questions.

"Yes, sir!" From the front rank Alfonso Castro's voice rose with an edge on it that made Jack cringe for the man's careless, truculent stupidity. "Where I go to put in for transfer? See, sir, the Navy make a big mistake with me."

The officer studied the small sailor puffing out his cockerel chest in the tailored blues, slowly appraising the expensive, special uniform. The levee had come aboard in dress blues though the fleet had already gone into whites.

"You haven't given the *Retreat* a chance," he said sadly.

"Yeah. But, see, I don't join the Navy to be on no hospital ship . . . sir. I'm the best gunner in boot camp. You see in my records. I got hawk eyes!"

The lieutenant leaned closer to peer into Alfonso Castro's wide-open dark eyes.

"You be sure to mention that when you put in for transfer," he suggested.

As the muster broke up, Alfonso Castro continued to complain for all the world to hear, "All you guys see. I don't stay on this thing! I go re-up today!"

Jack could hear him complaining as he was shepherded away between Peterson, who hung onto the man's sea bag, and Yablonski, who hoped to lure him into the engine room by toting his hand baggage and sword.

But before Castro could re-up, he had first to be processed and become an official member of the crew. It was a noxious technicality that only Peterson's calm assurance could convince the hot little tailor-made seaman to accept.

"Let me show you the engine room," Yablonski offered. "You'll like it down there. Very relaxed."

"I don't go in no black gang!" Alfonso drew himself up to swear. "You never see no enemies. Never!"

Yablonski gave him his bag and sword.

"No need to get yourself excited," Peterson soothed. "You know how the Navy is. I'm sure it'll be only a few days before they'll let you re-up."

And thus, in the meantime, Alfonso Castro was con-

354

vinced to proclaim himself a budding coxswain—no matter how temporarily. Peterson also arranged for him to get a liberty card on the same watch as his own, and he fixed him up with a bunk and locker as near him as possible.

Castro did not shut up through lunch. It was as if he alone had been insulted by being ticketed for that white ship. By implication, his new messmates were suspect in all naval and masculine arts. This, of course, did not dawn upon him as his voice cut above the clatter of knives, forks and stainless-steel trays.

"Sure, maybe it's OK for *you* guys," he ranted. "But me, I'm gonna be a career man. I don't join the Navy to be with no buncha peckercheckers. I shoot good, man!"

"Get up a petition! We'll *all* sign it!" Gorilla called out from where he sat beside Jack.

"Who's the wiseass that say that?" Alfonso Castro jumped to his feet to demand.

More than half the men in the mess stood up.

"OK. You guys laugh. I show you guys! They don't keep *me* on this thing!" He sailed out of the mess, his twenty-one-inch bells angry wings on his spit-shined heels. He alone of all the new men had not yet changed into work clothes.

Peterson carried both their trays to the scullery and hurried after his hot-blooded striker.

Pete was the only man aboard that Jack had never seen lose his temper. He had picked up the nickname Sister for the imperturbable calm which always surrounded him. There was nothing sissy about him, however. He was simply everyone's surrogate sister. There was no teasing he would not tolerate. Though six feet tall, he let smaller men bully him, play with his earlobes, kiss his neck, pat his ass and squeeze his not at all feminine breasts. He would just blush and chuckle at the others' craziness.

Once, upon encouragement of others, Jack had leaped on Pete's back as he lay in his bunk reading a book just before lights out, got his earlobe between his teeth and hunched his ass until he got a hard-on and Peterson began to protest a bit.

"Kiss Sister on the ear and you can fuck her," was the word on Pete.

And Jack had the feeling that had he tried to cornhole the guy, Pete's protest would have been secondary to his lazy acceptance of another's need.

No one had seen him even a little drunk. He hadn't an enemy on the ship.

As Pete and Alfonso Castro dressed for liberty, the small man confided, "See, I know it's gonna be a long time before I see some girl, so in Vallejo I give this big blonde pig Pedro nine times this night! Her ole pussy get sore, man. Puff up like something, until I can't even get my finger in. I wear her big old butt out. She never see no one like me."

"Ah'll bet she didn't," Pete drawled kindly. He was from back in the Everglades with the air of a 'gator sleeping in the sun.

Alfonso Castro had also had his whites cut down until they hugged his rooster knees.

"Goin to get you some Chink pussy tonight, Pedro," he promised his cock before buttoning it into his trousers.

"I was wonderin how he worked it," Yablonski said. "That's a microphone there, see. It's connected to his mouth. He talks through his cock, and the words come out his trap without ever passin through a brain."

"That's all you think!" Castro yelled. "Pedro's got more brains in his head than you got in yours!"

"That's quite possible, Yablonski," Huffman stirred himself to add.

"Hey, Pete," Jack observed, "when's the last time you went on liberty? Those whites don't look like they've been unrolled since you left boot camp."

He tugged at the wrinkles.

"You'll never get off the ship like that. Fuckin Fetterman is OD. He'd turn back his own mother if he couldn't see his kikey face in her shoes."

Peterson looked at his hopeless trousers. He was only twenty. He had grown since boots. His pants were two inches above the tops of his low cuts.

"Fetterman isn't Jewish," Swartz corrected. "He's some kind of Episcopalian."

"He is?" Jack was amazed. "Whatever he is, he looks like that little shrimp Hitler always had around."

"Goebbels," Keating supplied.

"Yeow. He looks just like him. You ought to see the shit this ugly girl of his writes him and always signs her letters with a big lipstick kiss. Can you imagine anyone kissin Fetterman?"

"Muskrat, you're going to get in trouble poking around

356

in officers' quarters one of these days. They'll hang your butt."

"Aw, Fetterman's a peter-puller," he claimed with authority. "None of the nurses will even give him a smell."

Keating, who was as tall as Peterson, finally lent him a pair of whites that would pass Fetterman's inspection.

Obviously, in combing his hair, Alfonso Castro could not wait until it grew to an approximation of its former pachuco glory. His cap, bent into wide wings, rested on the back of his head like a nesting cormorant. He would never get past the OD until he squared it. But let him find that out for himself.

"Maybe I set a new record tonight," he boasted, rubbing himself as he and Peterson went toward the ladder.

Peterson returned to the ship an hour after lights-out.

"*Yahoooooooooo!*" he bellowed from the top of the ladder and executed a perfect swan dive—splat!—onto the steel deck below.

Jack was certain he had killed himself. His landing seemed to jolt the entire compartment. He and Gorilla and Keating all scrambled out of their racks and hurried to where Pete lay like a conked supplicant before a cross.

He lifted his face across which spread a slothlike grin.

"I got drunk," he burbled happily.

"What else did you do?" Keating asked.

"I ate hamburgers—*urrrrrack!*" He heaved up on the deck.

"He ate hamburgers."

They hauled him up and dragged him toward his bunk.

"Where's your good buddy?"

"Hmmmmmm?"

"You didn't leave alone. There was that new little guy with you. Alfonso."

"Alfonso Castro," he corrected proudly.

"That's the one. Where is he?"

"Don know. He just disappeared . . . *pffft!*" He missed snapping his fingers.

"Did you go to a cathouse?"

"Noooooo." He shook his head. He did not think they had.

"Where were you?"

"American Bar. Then——" He began to laugh. "Then Alfonso Castro thinks this Sikh is givin him uh evil eye."

"What happened then?"

He could not say. Whatever he saw behind his drooping lids was very funny. "Set his whiskers on fire ..." he mumbled.

"Castro set the Sikh's whiskers on fire?"

He nodded affirmatively. "Funniest thing. . . ." Suddenly he sat bolt upright and said, "Alfonso Castro!" He looked terrified. Then he slumped over and fell asleep. Jack took off his shoes, and Keating got him out of trousers. There had been some kind of scuffle. Keating's trousers were filthy.

"Well, the SP's will bring him in tomorrow," Gorilla decided.

Pete was a silly drunk. They had always wondered. Even though puking in the compartment was unforgivable, everyone forgave Pete.

No one covered for Castro at muster the next morning. He was put down AWOL. When a week had passed, Jack brought a hacksaw from the electric shop and cut off the combination lock on the missing man's locker. It was in the evening. Everyone was lolling around the compartment. There was a box of letters in there with a photograph of a Mexican girl in white shorts and a peasant blouse off one shoulder. "Love, Raquel" was written across it. The back of each letter was sealed with a big smeary kiss. All of his personal things Jack gathered in a neckerchief to turn over to the personnel office.

"What do we do with the rest of his stuff?" he asked. "Anybody want anything?"

"Shit, no!"

"Are you crazy, Muskrat?"

Everything was marked with his name. Jack decided to keep the samurai sword. It was a real one, and Castro had to pay a hell of a lot for it, over a hundred bucks probably.

Then he pulled out the tailor-made dress blues. He unfurled the trousers and held them up to his waist. They looked to be a perfect fit. He skinned out of his dungarees and slid his legs into the smooth tailor-mades. The trousers were lined almost to the knee with black satin. Across the flap in yellow script was embroidered "Alfonso Castro."

358

"What the hell you doin, Muskrat?" Peterson raised up and inquired with horror.

"Tryin on these blues."

"Those are a dead man's clothes, man!"

"He won't miss them then. They just fit."

"Ghoul! That's what you are, Muskrat, a goddamned ghoul."

"You can't wear a dead man's blues," others assured him.

"Man, *I* wouldn't!"

"Not me!"

"Don't you know what kind of bad luck that is?"

"They're sure great blues." The jumper had a zipper up the left side, it was so form-fitting. They were a bit tight, but OK. He walked a little between the bunks getting the feel of the twenty-one-inch bells.

"No one else wants them?" he asked again.

"Hell, no!"

He put them and the sword in his own locker.

"Muskrat, you stay away from me, hear?" Peterson said with the only edge of anger in his voice Jack had ever heard.

But when fall came, he would wear those blues. And he never cared enough to bother trying to pick Alfonso Castro's name off the flap.

23

SUNDAY morning rose like a gong in the Shanghai sky. Beneath the canvas awnings the decks were holystoned and still damp. There was a cool summer smell in the air. A lassitude could be felt upon all the ships tied up at the jetties and strung on buoys out in the channel. It could have been Sunday at Pearl Harbor those several years ago.

This in contrast with the city beginning to stir, where Sunday was an imposed, foreign institution.

Across the jetty, huge Sikhs in khaki shorts of British issue, stripped to the waist, bearded and turbaned, wearing British Army boots, were doing calisthenics in their rubbled court. Above, in the window of their scabrous barrack, another was combing dry his long crow's-wing black hair, hanging it down out the window in the sun. He had shoulders like a very fit heavyweight, but his movements were graceful as a woman's.

And all the whores were sleeping, alone at last, in their beds beneath sheets that yet smelled of Saturday night. The dreams of fifty thousand whores rose from their shuttered houses and dens and lay over the city as palpable as the lethargy of the sailors tied up in the river.

Docked nearby was a Russian freighter on which many of the sailors were sturdy, broadassed women who seemed as tough as any man aboard. They returned the catcalls of American seamen with obscene gestures and clearly profane Russian expletives. Tompkins, the weight lifter from Portland, had fallen in love with a big blonde built along the lines of an Olympic shotputter. He mooned around the fo'c'sle for sight of his fancy. He begged her interest by throwing a pack of Luckies across the distance and gained a smile missing a few teeth.

When by elephantine sign he communicated a wish that they could meet off their ships for what appeared to be a walk and a ferocious hugging, she shrugged hopelessly and indicated she could not. Then glancing at the scowling rating supervising her work, she stooped to bending line on the Russian fantail. When the boss wasn't looking, she lifted her head, indicated her ample bosom and pronounced her name, "Tamara."

Astern was a British light cruiser upon which the seamen still slept in hammocks in compartments that were not air-conditioned. They made about eight cents per day, someone reported. The ship's hull was riveted and sported portholes, which had disappeared from U.S. military ships with the advent of welding and air conditioning. On the fantail under awnings the British officers in white shorts with knee socks were hosting a brunch for ladies from the international community-in flowered summer dresses, large garden hats and sensible white shoes. There was also a vicar in attendance. All balanced tea cups and ate biscuits. A few officers and nurses from the *Retreat* had gone over. The British, in turn, attended wardroom parties thrown by the Americans and toured the hospital ship, striding along, hands clasped behind their backs, full of correct interest.

Up on the navigation deck Jack Andersen took from his pocket a business card he had found on a dresser in one of the officer's compartments.

La Maison Blanche

Dedicated to the pleasures
Of gentlemen
Mme. Sophie de la Bresque

The card held promise for him beyond that of the ordinary two-dollar cathouses he most often visited. He had shown it to no one.

After lunch he took Tompkins' sea bag which was crammed with cigarettes from the electric shop storeroom and carried it up to the starboard quarterdeck. Tompkins had bought cigarettes from everyone who would sell them to him rather than risk black-marketing them himself. It seemed a crazy plan, but he had given Jack one hundred dollars to lower the bag to him.

Tompkins was right on time. He came alongside in a water taxi. Jack hooked the bag to a litter hoist and lowered it down to him. Then he ran the hoist back up as Tompkins' taxi wobbled away, him urging the young man at the stern sweep to greater speed. The operation took only a couple of minutes. Tompkins had several wristwatches in the sack as well. He stood to make quite a lot of money. What no one could understand was why he had done it that way, rather than piecemeal as did the others. Very few of the officers checking you when you went ashore showed a sign of finding cigarettes taped to one's body when they went through the motions of patting you down on the quarterdeck. Everyone was taking off a couple of cartons every liberty and an extra wristwatch every month or so. A twenty-five-dollar watch brought a hundred and twenty-five dollars on the black market.

Tompkins was a strange fellow. His favorite food was cold cuts. He could barely read or write, often asking Jack to help him with his letters or read an article in the exotic motorcycle books he had sent from home. His dream was to buy a bike called a BSA and climb a hill near Portland that he had only to close his eyes to see. He liked to come up behind the boy wherever he might be working,

361

snatching him up by the belt with his teeth and carting him off like a big dog with something he would bury. Everyone thought it amusing to see Tompkins carry the Muskrat around in this fashion. Jack found it annoying. It wasn't so much the interruption in what he was doing that he minded; it was the *idea* of the thing. To be carried about like a dog's bone with no say as to destination was inhuman!

Jack dressed for liberty. He lashed a carton of cigarettes in loose packs around his waist, securing them with electrician's rubber tape, and taped half a carton each to his lower legs beneath his trousers.

The OD patted him down, looked blankly in the boy's equally blank face and stepped back to return his salute. At the gangway Jack snapped a fuck-it-all salute toward the fantail and went ashore.

He passed the warehouse where the Japanese soldiers had lived with their women and children. It had since been repaired and was full of U.S. relief commodities. The enormous iron-studded doors were locked by a massive chain and three padlocks each the size of a plate. All the windows had been boarded up and fixed with bars.

Jack wondered where the Japs and their families had gone. He still occasionally saw one of the men around, distinguished by the star-emblazoned wool forage cap of imperial issue.

Across the International Bridge he passed the Shanghai Club on the Bund, a massive stone building that made him feel the entire history of British Empire. In the great windows of the reading room old men with pink faces peered out over copies of the London *Times* from the depths of enormous leather chairs.

He touched the card of Mme. de la Bresque, caterer to the desires of gentlemen, and felt something of being upon the brink of Empire himself. He whistled the first few bars of "Limehouse Blues" and had a vision of Hoagy Carmichael.

Off to the right, in front of the American Bar, a riot of some sort was in progress. Cars and bikes, pedicabs and rickshaws clogged the street. Atop it all, standing in a pedicab, was Tompkins, dealing from his sea bag. Chinese waved money at him, shook their fists at one another, pushed and argued. When someone tried to climb into the pedicab with him or get at the bag between his bollardlike legs, Tompkins swiped them away heels over head with the flat of his nearly fingerless hands.

He was crazy!

Yet the Shore Patrol trying to push through from the fringe of the mob were able to advance only inches a minute. By the time they reached the pedicab Tompkins, for all his lack of agility, had dropped down into the crowd and disappeared. Still, the crowd screamed threats and offers at one another in a hubbub of subsidiary transactions.

What the hell had happened? Probably the quantity of his goods had flashed through the district and when others came on the run he was forced from the small silk merchant's shop where most of the *Retreat* men sold their cigarettes into the street.

When the Shore Patrol left, Jack went up to the old silk merchant's place. Because of Tompkins, the price was down to eighteen dollars a carton. The old man excused himself to go find some cash.

While he was gone, Jack saw into a small adjoining room which was just large enough for eight people, including two small children, to sit around a table. Before each were bowls of white rice and a smaller bowl of soya sauce. In the center of the table was a single small fish no larger than a trout, from which each picked a tiny morsel. The margin of profit upon which the old man worked was not great.

Ten minutes later he saw Tompkins cruise past in the back of an old miniature Fiat taxi. He completely filled the tiny rear seat and was smoking a cigar.

Two blocks away Jack tarried before a Chinese cinema pretending to look at the stills outside, but truly arrested by the sight of the most beautiful Oriental woman he had ever seen. She stood before a jewelry shop beneath an umbrella in a pair of white Western high-heeled pumps. She was what he had always fantasized Chinese women would look like, delicate and perfectly formed but with a maturity that made every gesture and movement knowing, sensual as the essence of sandalwood and musk. Desire like a childhood fever swept through him, putting the slip on time, tilting the street, erasing memory and mission. He loved her totally and at a sign from her would have followed her wherever she led without question or fear. Sexuality, spirit, all grace and dreams were focused in the miracle of her breathing. The crook of her bare arm was heartbreaking, as was the lift of her chin, the shifting of her weight and the slight movement of her hips, the way her lips lay one against the other, the wisps of hair before her perfect ears that dangled earrings like miniature chandeliers. Her dark eyes slid beneath her mascaraed eyelids. Her fingernails, the color of pearls, were more than two inches long. She was flawless flesh and blood. She ate and slept and had had a childhood. She looked at the jewelry.

In her shadow awaited an old amah in a long asphalt-colored dress. She carried small purchases in a string bag. Her face was seamed and the color of the yellowed duck's carcasses across the sidewalk beneath an awning farther up the street. Eyes hard as an armed gunsel's drifted from her charge to every near passerby.

The beautiful woman felt the sailor boy's longing stare. At first she just blinked and shuddered as if bothered by a gnat. Then she glanced at him with a trace of fear that passed to annoyance. She twirled her umbrella slowly. Her delicate nostrils flared as if smelling something foul. She consciously lifted and slowly turned her face away. The old amah stepped up to shield her upon the side nearest to Jack.

He had never thought himself uglier. He felt sad and a very long way from home. But he knew it could have happened anywhere. *What was he? Nothing! A snaggle-toothed swabjockey. I don't even have a goddamned home!* he told himself, feeling even worse.

A pedicart loaded with bales of Chinese money, each bale made up of bills bound in tight cubes, made its way through the packed street, the ransom swaying precariously and unguarded.

Was the shit so worthless no one was even tempted to hijack the load or grab a handful? The fellow straining on the bike seat could have been freighting a load of heating blocks made from pressed coal dust. Somewhere, he imagined, *the beautiful woman he had fallen in love with fed a small fire in her room with blocks of the bills to heat water for tea.*

The world is crazy, or I am, or both, the boy considered.

He had noticed the trucks that had pulled up across each end of the street. He became aware of the panic of those around him. Then he noticed the trucks were mounted with machine guns. A young man in shorts and shower shoes jostled him in passing, wild-eyed and terrible, searching like an animal for a niche or doorway, a crack into which he might escape.

Armed soldiers of the Kuomintang were advancing with bayonets fixed on their rifles. Recruiters operated from the phalanx, grabbing every able-bodied man, checking his identification and herding those with improper papers and hastily adjudged good health back toward the trucks.

A young woman with a child lashed on her back engaged them in a tug-of-war for her husband. He was dressed in short pants and a short-sleeved white shirt. He had very muscular bowed legs and a bowl haircut that made his broad, frightened, country face seem all the more vulnerable. Jack had a feeling he and his wife had just come into town for a day's shopping and sightseeing. The soldiers yanked the youth away. His wife wailingly dropped to her knees behind their backs in a gesture of hand-wringing supplication. When he was thrown up on the truck, she began to tear her hair and beat her breast. Then she bashed her forehead repeatedly on the pavement. The sleeping child on her back bobbed about but did not awaken.

Jack stood in the cinema foyer tightly packed in among old people and women. The beautiful woman and amah had disappeared. Probably inside the jewelry shop. A young dodger crouched among them in the foyer, hunkering lower, his hands clasping his ankles, eyes wide and rolling with fear. When the recruiters spotted him, the old people pressed aside and let him be taken. The soldiers handled him roughly, but as far as Jack could see, they did not hit anyone or stick anyone with their bayonets.

Head and shoulders above everyone there suddenly appeared a young man with the curious dignity of Big Stoop out of *Terry and the Pirates*. He had simply been left in the street by the melting away of the crowd. He had not tried to hide. Being hustled toward a truck, he retained a presence, a pace that made the soldiers alter their own. A purely country boy, he wore knee breeches that would have been long trousers on any of the recruiters. On his feet were homemade cloth shoes. His faded denim jacket was burst at both shoulders. *Six four or maybe even six six,* Jack guessed. From so far out in the sticks, he still had a kind of fearless incorruptibility and offered neither excuse nor resistance.

The trucks roared away, and the people trickled back into the street. By the time he had reached the duck seller's life had become as it was before. When he tired of being jostled, he hailed a pedicab and handed the driver the card of Mme. de la Bresque.

The driver studied it, then glanced furtively at the sailor. He was an old man and had already cultivated the hairs of wisdom on his chin. The veins in his muscular legs were the size of angleworms and night crawlers. He pursed his lips but dutifully turned to the pedals to deliver the boy to the house dedicated to the pleasures of gentlemen.

Somewhere in Shanghai there was the Famous House of All Nations which lived in sailors' dreams as the heaven of whorehouses. In exotic rumor its international delights gathered from all the corners of the world rivaled the richest pornographic imaginings. Harems of slave girls, Nubian beauties, whore-nuns from Rome, cancan girls, Viking blondes with golden limbs, sultry Carmen Mirandas from South America, Indian houris with jewels in their noses, and elegant English dames—all under a single roof, connected by hanging gardens with an aviary of singing birds, peacocks and cockatoos, where miniature waterfalls tinkled and tiny streams babbled over rocks beneath arched bridges. A place where you were transported to the land of your dreams, where no sound of the city intruded. Though he had thought longingly of such a place and was sure it did exist, he had never actually spoken to an honest man who had ever been there or who could direct him to it. Every pedicab pimp who vowed absolute knowledge of it always delivered him and his buddies to a place far less exotic. Only when they stepped inside, of course, could they be certain the heaven for which they searched had not lain behind the ordinary façade.

It's reserved for officers and civilians, they decided. *It costs a fortune*, they consoled themselves.

In none of the places *he* had been had he ever seen an officer. They had to go somewhere.

He had lost count of the various houses he had visited, though he often tried to recall each woman with whom he had been. Most often he went to White Russian houses. He hardly ever went with Chinese women anymore. However, only the week before he had gone to a White Russian place where there had been a young Manchurian girl as tall as himself. *She would be a perfect match for that Big Stoop,* he suddenly thought. Of great sulking beauty, she had been wonderful. Stripped naked, her body was tawny and gorgeous. Her large, solid breasts had been especially fine. Her sex was young, smooth and muscular. She had refused to get on top or let him roll her onto her belly. But once she learned he was not a brute she was able to indicate her age was seventeen and that she came from far away. Unlike most whores, particularly Chinese, she was still fresh enough to react to being fucked, though not with any expression of pleasure. Her face reluctantly showed signs of excitement. The war between feelings physical and those emotional gave her a look of pain. When he had altered the angle of his cock to bring it in closer proximity with her clit, her heavy legs and wide hips jerked involuntarily. He had liked her a lot and sought to cheer her up. He told her if he could he would have taken her home with him, meaning the United States. But she did not understand. She glumly shrugged her big self into her cheongsam, stuffed her large feet into green satin pumps and went with him back to the sitting room. *Ding-how! You very ding-how!* he had told her. But she was not cheered by the news. She was a beautiful, big, slow, sad girl who would have made someone a wonderful wife.

There were others, so many others. He had counted up. He had fucked about a hundred different women.

They were on a street along the river that ran down to the International Bridge. From pictures he knew the street had been built to look like Paris. Formal stone houses of three and four stories topped with green copper mansard roofs with small garret windows stood shoulder to shoulder, with a view on the river. Wide chimneys with many chimney pots on them rose against the Sunday sky. The street was broad with clean walks and gutters. Not a Chinese was visible. River junks with their masts stepped to clear the bridges chugged upriver by the far bank and down on the near side. It was peaceful. He could hear the whirl of the pedicab's wheels, the pock-pock of the junks' tiny diesels and birds chattering. It had been a year since he had heard birds other than gulls. The sound was a tickle in his breast. He longed for something.

The pedicab man deposited him before number 43 and

blankly accepted his pay. An amah in clothes the color of shadows peeked from the door. He offered the card he had secretly hoarded. She seemed puzzled, hesitant, but decided to let him in off the street while she carried the card to a superior.

The room was dark, with a thick, though worn carpet, some heavy pieces of furniture, a table on which there was a single large Chinese vase. Before a prim, uncomfortable-looking dark velvet settee was a cold, clean-swept fireplace with brass lion firedogs and gleaming brass fire tools. He felt no one ever actually sat on the furniture or used the room. It suddenly occurred to him he might be in a private residence, that the old woman *had* never seen such a card and was at that moment transporting it to some Sunday-relaxed citizen who would boil in outrage. He removed his cap and edged closer to the door. A square wooden portico across the room framed a lateral hall down which a worn carpet runner protected a waxed, darkly varnished floor. There was a French river scene over another small polished table. There was not a sound in the house.

"Ah, non! Mais non, chéri!" a small woman in a soft black dress with white collar and cuffs exclaimed, bustling into the room so that he could hear the soft rustle of her clothes and hose. In her left hand she held the card while the fingers of her other toyed nervously with a rope of pearls that had been looped in an overhand knot upon her tailored breast. She had rings on several plump fingers. *"C'est incroyable! Ah, non!* Where you get this?" she demanded, lifting both hands on either side of her breast, palms outward in a gesture of confounded exasperation. The card hung idly between two fingers as if she might flick it away or drop the ugly thing. Behind her hovered the amah.

"I was given it by an officer on my ship, ma'am," he lied.

"Mais ce n'est pas possible!" She looked puzzled.

Something told him he hadn't barged in on citizens.

"What is your ship?" she asked.

"The *Retreat,* ma'am."

"La Retreat. . . ." She seemed to be thinking back.

"Yes, ma'am."

"So!" She lifted her hands and let them fall helplessly to her sides. She looked heavenward. "It comes to this."

368

Then she narrowly studied the boy shifting from one foot to another in her parlor, his cap held in both hands below his waist. She looked him over from head to toe. *"C'est incroyable,"* she sighed.

He wondered what was wrong with him. He looked down at himself to see.

She snorted softly. *"Non, chéri.* It is *un* mistake, *la maison est fermée.* Closed. You go somewhere else, yes?"

Then he recognized the old amah was the one he had seen on the street with the beautiful Chinese woman earlier. He was certain.

"Well, ma'am, I'll go. But I came here because the card says you cater to gentlemen. I wanted to go someplace nice."

"Ah, chéri, I am *soo* sorry. But we are closed now. The girls are sleeping. Maybe you come back later." She would have him know it was nothing personal.

"Well, I thought maybe if I came now, I wouldn't run into a lot of officers, you know. I understand how you don't want a lot of just sailors like me comin here. But I can pay."

"Ah, vous êtes très gentil. But you are *soo* young!" She stepped closer. "You are baby!"

He blushed and lowered his eyes demurely. She touched his arm, a mere whisper of fingertips against the cloth.

"Tell me, *chéri,* you have been with a girl before, *oui?"*

"Well . . ." he hedged, lowering his chin further.

"Ah! C'est très joli! Mon mignon! Perhaps. Yes. Maybe I have a beautiful girl for you." She seemed to be taking mental inventory for just the one.

"It is ten dollars short time, twenty long time," she broke out of her considerations to affirm.

"OK."

"C'est OK?"

"Yes," he confirmed and went for his wallet.

She ignored his efforts toward money. *"Ah, oui!"* She raised a finger, obviously having settled on the very girl for him.

"Uh, excuse me, ma'am. But you have a beautiful Chinese girl here . . ." He pointed at the old amah.

The madame was shocked. *"Non! Non!"* She waved her hands frantically. Her eyes looked terrified.

He realized she thought he wanted to screw the old servant.

He began to laugh. "No! I saw a beautiful Chinese girl in the street with this old woman. Earlier. In town."

"But we have no Chinese here. *Ah! Oui oui!*" She exclaimed a name that sounded like "New-Jean." *"Mais elle n'est pas Chinoise. Elle est* of Indochina.

"Could I meet her, please?"

She studied him again. She smiled gently. "But she is not for you, *chéri. Non. Peut-être* in a few years, yes? *Maintenant? Non.* If you please, put your trust in me. . . . Yes?"

"Yes, ma'am, but I would sure like to meet that New-Jean."

She made a little puff out of the side of her mouth. "I will speak with her. Perhaps. You go with the amah and I will send you a beautiful girl."

He followed the old woman down the hall and into a large bedroom that had a deep, shuttered window box. From the alley behind came the smell and sound of running water, the sound of feet passing and the muffled voices of Chinese. There was a large vase of yellow flowers on a bellied little stand beside the large, puffy-looking bed. The carpet was the color of the core of a sunflower. The walls were covered with a pale-yellow cloth that had lights of sunflowers in it. Then he discerned touches of blue in a seascape over the bed, in the vase, in faded flowers painted on the wardrobe and furniture. It was a sunny room though not a shaft of sunlight penetrated it, and it was cool and shady as a forest. The atmosphere felt magic. It seemed very clean.

He turned at the sound of the door opening hoping to see the beautiful girl from the street. But the girl that came smiling inside went with the room. She was golden, sunny circles, small and happy as the wallpaper. She wore a froth of net that floated around her like a cloud when she moved. Even her perfume was sunny, sweet and overpowering as honeysuckle. She looked very young.

"But you still have your clothings on," she exclaimed and pouted her little underlip. "Maybe you have embarrassment? You like me? You like to make love with me?" She advanced and put her smooth plump arms around his neck. Her perfume and the froth of her dressing gown enfolded him. Close she was not so young as baby-faced. "I don't bite you," she promised and began loosening his neckerchief. "You are just a baby. You are *la poupée*," she said.

He was a bit taken aback as he thought she was saying he was some kind of dumb baby shit. But the front of her gown was open and two lovely white pink-tipped tits were just peeking out. She looked up, laughed, then closed her blue eyes and gave him a slow, cool kiss, carrying his hands inside her gown that he could feel her smooth body. The top of her head came barely to his chin. Her kiss tasted sweet, as if she had been eating cherries.

"You give me your money now, please," she whispered against the corner of his mouth.

He quickly handed over his ten dollars.

"I will come back. You take off your clothings." She went out the door. When she came back, he was standing in just his socks beside the chair upon which he had placed his clothes after checking to make sure it was nowhere near the wardrobe which could have a trapdoor through which someone could snag his wallet.

She returned and stopped for a moment to admire him.

"You are almost pretty like a girl," she told him. "You are brown from the sun. I am not brown." She opened her robe and let it fall.

She was all pink and white circles and golden hair. She smiled and came toward him on yellow satin mules that had very high heels. She looked like a smaller, living version of Rubens' women. He had spent a lot of time in libraries looking at art books.

"You like me?"

"Yes."

"You want to make love with me?"

"Yes."

She smiled and pressed her body lightly against him, smoothed his shoulders with her hands, kissed his chest. He felt her rounded hips, her narrow waist, touched her breasts.

"I feel good to you?"

"Yes."

She kissed him, and her small hand trailed down to touch his penis. She gave it a squeeze and let him kiss her again.

He had never known whores that liked to kiss.

She slipped away and went to turn down the bed. The pillowcases were fresh as in a hotel. The sheets had been pressed. She got into bed and held out her right hand, patting the place beside her with her left. He took off his socks.

When he lay beside her and she was fondling his cock, he saw her quickly and surreptitiously check it for a drip. It had only been a moment's concentrated flicker; then she was all loving and running her thigh up over his own. He still had a foil-wrapped condom in his left hand. He showed it to her as if he did not know what to do with it. She took it and stuck it under a pillow.

"You think you give me a baby?" she laughed. Then she noticed his tattoo. "Why have an ugly thing put on you?" she asked crossly. He only shrugged and bent to suck her white breast. She ran her fingers through his short-cropped hair. "You think it makes you more a man? I will make you a man, baby. Hummn? Come. Come into my body."

Somewhere along the way she decided he hadn't been a virgin after all and accused him. "I am not the first woman you sleep with."

"I read a lot of books," he told her.

"Boulsheet!"

But she gave him his money's worth with kisses and touches.

By the end he had made her work. Beads of perspiration lay in the perfumed, powdered valley of her breasts. Her cheeks and his were red with her lipstick. Her little pink ears were bright red.

"How old you are?" she demanded when he lay exhausted upon her, his cock still twitching between her legs.

"Be sixteen in a month," he told her.

"How many?"

He showed her with fingers.

"Is all?"

"Is all."

"You are naughty boy, yes?"

He shrugged.

"You are fine *poupée* for me, *chéri*."

"What is *poupée*?" he wanted to know.

"Ah. *La poupée* is—how you say?—somethings the little girl play wiss." She laughed. "You my big *poupée*."

Then they became friends. She was not French but German, from someplace called Schwaben. "Maybe I am princess." She smiled. "Maybe. Anythings are possible."

Her name was Hannelore.

"What ship yours?" she asked.

"The *Retreat*."

"Oh, you on the beeg white elephants."

"Yes." He smiled.

"You go soon to Tsingtao, yes?"

If he did, it was the first he had heard about it.

"Yes," she insisted. "You go soon. Maybe one, two weeks, you go." She noticed the look on his face. "I am spy. I know somethings." She laughed. "Maybe I see you in Tsingtao."

"You go too?"

She stopped being mysterious. "I go for vacation. There is a house with the woman who is friend of the women here. We make the change sometimes. There is a nice beach by Tsingtao. I write on a paper for you. Maybe you come see me in Tsingtao. Maybe we go to the beach."

He liked that idea.

"What is your name, *poupée-line?*"

"Jack."

"Shack. OK. But you stay clean, boy. You don't go wiss ugly, dirty womans."

He would never think of such a thing.

"You give Hannelore one nice kiss."

She touched a button beside the bed. Presently the amah brought a basin and pitcher of warm water to the door on a tray. There was a washcloth, a soft fluffy towel and a bar of fragrant white soap. She poured the water for him, but let him do his own washing up as she turned up the bed. While he dressed, she discreetly squatted in the corner over the bowl and completed her toilet.

Where the parlor joined the hall, the madam met them, her bejeweled hands clasped patiently at her waist. Both he and she smiled broadly.

"The young gentleman enjoyed himself?" she inquired.

"Yes, ma'am."

She said something very quickly in French and adjusted his neckerchief.

373

The girl laughed. She patted his shoulder. *"Lui est la grande poupée."*

"You understand, *chéri*. It is not possible for you to speak of this place to your friends. If sailors come, they will be drunk and cause trouble and I will be placed off limits by the Shore Patrols. We are only for the pleasure of gentlemen. No one is permitted to enter without the card." There was the sound of a man's footsteps on a carpet overhead. "We are discreet." She gave him a fresh card. "I will trust you. But if you are not discreet, *c'est fini. D'accord?*"

"I won't tell a soul, ma'am."

Then he was outside. He decided to stroll down to the International Bridge along the street. He'd take a pro back aboard ship. It was just becoming dark; the lights of the city were aglow above the roofs of the stately houses. There was really nothing else to do.

Somethings little girls play with. He smiled, but he was not entirely happy.

24

IT WAS a heartbreaking, infuriatingly pathetic army, so patched and thin of bottom and shy of spirit only far-removed strategists who had lost all touch could have considered it the vanguard of a big spring offensive. More driven than moved, it already had the air of defeated troops.

"That's the saddest-lookin bunch of people God ever laid eyes on." Gorilla reflected the dispiritedness of the men strung out along the jetty below.

A Kuomintang light infantry division with a battery of mountain pack howitzers and some mortars had moved onto the jetty during the night and slept in place upon their packs. Their summer uniforms were every faded shade of poor-quality khaki, every one patched, some with blue denim: loose, bloused trousers above coarse tightly wrapped burlap puttees, a jacket and forage cap with the Nationalist buzzer. Some of the soldiers wore Chinese high-top tennis shoes, some rubber sneakers, most only their own homemade cloth slippers. Their personal weapons ranged from U.S. Springfields that might have been salvaged from the battlefields of previous wars through British Enfields and Spanish Mausers to long Jap Arisakas. Some men in the back ranks carried only bamboo lances tipped with bayonets. Others were unarmed porters. Men hauled the mountain guns for want of mules. Men carried the shells for them in canisters hung on the ends of balance poles. Their mess was a system of fifty-five-gallon oil drums under which fires were built with sticks carried by the porters. It was a foot army without good shoes.

Sailors called down obscenities and derision from the line of waiting ships. Some of the men on the dock reacted angrily. A banty NCO stepped forward, gesturing to offer fight. When Finn tauntingly made as if to climb over the rail and jump down, the soldier drew his pistol and everyone ducked.

But the body of the army merely shuffled glumly beneath the low peaks of their caps toward the steaming mess barrels. They returned with a single bowl of soup or tea. There was no grabass, no jokes, no laughter, little talk.

He stuck up like a tree, an incredible target among the porters, head and shoulders above the entire army.

"Look at that big sonofabitch!" Gorilla cried. "I never *seen* such a big gook!"

Big Stoop. The pieces of uniform he had been given went a long way to bend his natural dignity. At each end of a long bamboo pole as thick as one of his muscular calves, he balanced more than four rounds of 75 millimeter mountain gun ammo. His trousers and leg wraps did not quite meet. A large square patch of darker khaki cloth covered his seat. His jacket and cap made him look like an idiot.

"Hey, Finn! There's a match for you!" Gorilla called down the rail.

All the sailors began shouting at the tall man, calling him Big Stoop.

When he had to move his load, the thick pole across his

shoulders bent like a bow. He walked in a shuffling partial crouch, with the familiar rhythm of the burdened land sounding in the *shush-shush* of his slippers and in the grunts that escaped from him—*unh-unh-unh-unh*—the sound of a man moving the load of a beast. The entire time that Jack watched him, he never spoke to another, nor any to him.

Though NCO's and officers strode about excitedly shouting orders and haranguing the troops so there seemed to be a constant clamor of Chinese, it was spooky how few of the men spoke to one another. There was the feeling from above of standing over a pen of cattle in a slaughterhouse stockyard.

"Some army!"

"Madness!" Jack exclaimed.

"How's that?"

"It's nuts. Some asshole general or somebody's *blind*, man. Those poor fucks aren't going to whip shit."

Al came puffing up excitedly. "Muskrat, Egan wants to see you. Now!"

"What about?" He searched his memory for some forgetfulness, some failure.

"Some detail."

He hurried to the electric shop.

Egan was calmly sitting on the workbench, sipping a cup of coffee, idly swinging his tiny feet.

"You like guns, kid. Get up to the quartermaster. They got a detail for you."

"Guns? What kind of detail?"

"I don't know. They just called down for someone who knows something about guns. Get up there now."

A dozen men were in the passageway outside the quartermaster's. Lieutenant Fetterman was there wearing leggins as if he were going on Shore Patrol, with a .45 caliber pistol strapped around his waist. Fetterman with a pistol looked like a little Jewish kid come out to play cowboys. The way he wore it, if it went off in his holster he would shoot his right foot.

They said he is Episcopalian, Jack reminded himself. He didn't like to think he was what they called "anti-Semitic."

"What's this?" he whispered to Peterson.

"I don't know, they just asked could I shoot."

"All right, men, hold it down," Fetterman piped. "You

376

will all draw weapons and report on the fantail in leggins and dungarees in ten minutes."

"Leggins?" someone said. "Shit, I ain't had leggins on since boots!"

"What's this about, sir?" another wondered.

"I'll brief you on the fantail."

They stepped up to the window. The ship carried a small store of arms, enough for a landing party or to quell a mutiny: rifles, submachine guns, pistols and a couple of air-cooled .30 caliber machine guns. A bosun deuce with a short dark beard and nine years in the Navy was in charge of the weapons. Jack had helped him clean them once on deck, just because he liked guns.

"You know how to keep from mashing your thumb in one of these, squirrel hunter?" he asked Peterson, popping an M-1 rifle on the shelf of the half door.

"I reckon," Pete drawled. He signed for the weapon.

"Here you go, Muskrat. This about your style?" He laid a clip-fed Thompson submachine gun on the counter.

"What we doin, Boats?"

"The Merchant Marine won't carry gooks unless we guard them."

"You goin?"

"Yeah."

By the time the party mustered on the fantail for Admiral Fetterman's inspection, they had dubbed themselves Fetterman's Raiders.

"You guys ever heard of the Fetterman Massacre?" a wiseacre called down from the navigation deck. Lieutenant Fetterman spun to reprimand the wise guy, then saw it was Lieutenant Cheatham and managed a strained smile.

The riflemen wore cartridge belts of seventy rounds in clips. The four men with Thompson guns had four magazines of twenty rounds each in a pouch.

Fetterman made Peterson redo his dungarees and leggins to form a more military line. He had everyone square his cap over his brow.

"Jesus Christ, Fetterman, but that's a mean-lookin bunch!" Lieutenant Cheatham called down.

"If you want to be in command of this detail, Lieutenant, you can gladly come down here and take my place," Fetterman turned and snapped.

"My apologies, sir! No disrespect intended, I assure you."

"Sling arms, dammit!" Fetterman yelled when Pete misunderstood the command and shouldered his rifle, almost coldcocking the men beside and behind him.

Officers, nurses and men began whistling "Anchors Aweigh" as Fetterman moved out with the *Retreat*'s own.

On the dock as thousands of curious Chinese eyes followed their progress, Fetterman hissed, "Get in step, goddammit! Look sharp. One, two, three, four," he counted, so dragging the cadence he was out of step as well.

"Don't turn your back on that bunch, Fetterman," a wag called from the ship.

Three other armed details from other ships were mustered under a commander on the jetty before the lead freighter that was going to transport the Chinese to Tsingtao. Captains of the freighters were there, none of them looking very happy, slouching casually in contrast with Navy bearing. The officers conferred and then came running to move the details off to the other ships.

A tall Occidental in a Chinese officer's uniform came over, saluted the commander and said in perfect Southwestern English, "When can we move on these ships?"

"Right away. Soon as we get our people aboard."

"Well, this goddamned operation is three hours behind schedule now. The general is about to split a gut."

The Chinese staff was standing a few yards off, arms folded angrily on their chests, glaring at the Americans and the old Liberty ships.

"Let him split!" a stocky Merchant Marine captain in rumpled khakis full of a big beer gut barked, his greasy cap tilted over one ear. "We ain't lettin none of them gooks aboard until we have it in writin that none of them have bullets in their guns or pockets or anywhere handy. Our contract is for deck cargo, not a bunch of bastards that might shoot our butts off."

The American in Chinese uniform looked horrified. "You don't think *we'd* give them ammo until we got them so close they could smell the other people, do you?" He grinned.

"Well . . . we just want it in writing. The union ain't at all happy about it," the merchant captain snorted, eyeing his cargo stretched far up the jetty.

"You'll have it." The cowboy went back to confer with the Chinese staff. He sported a large Smith and Wesson revolver in a quick-draw shoulder holster and carried a Marine Reising submachine gun.

Only when the armed sailors were aboard and stationed at every ladder and hatch leading from the ship's deck to its interior did the Chinese begin to load.

Carpenters had built gates at the top and bottom of each ladder and a web of lines had been strung between to make climbing the steps inside the barriers difficult and very slow. They had also built poops of new boards over the ship's rail so the Chinese would not have to come inside to use the toilet. They looked like old-fashioned outdoor privies. As soon as the Chinese were ranked on the deck and their packs dropped, there was a double line formed in front of the latrine. The men seemed to have diarrhea.

"Who knows what kind of goddamn disease those bastards got?" the captain barked on the wing of the bridge where Jack was stationed with his tommy gun and could cover the entire foredeck. Another tommy gunner was on the other wing. Riflemen were on the deck below.

The Chinese cooks had come aboard first and had already set up their oil drum and built a fire under it. Porters brought up the rear followed by some officers and NCO's.

Suddenly a porter halfway up the gangplank dropped his pole and began clawing his way back down past the men behind. His face was wildly berserk, like a crazed calf's. He was not going on that boat. He tilted the loads of other porters, causing them to fall while their stores splashed in the water between the ship and the jetty.

NCO's on the jetty spread their arms as if to turn a wild animal. He burst through them, spinning a couple around so violently their caps flew off their heads. Behind them an officer, very young, in a rather natty uniform with polished Sam Browne belt and good British shoes beneath his leggins, shouted and drew his pistol.

The porter wasn't stopping. He began to sprint. The officer fired a warning shot. NCO's began to unlimber their arms. The officer fired again, and the porter faltered a step and began to weave.

He's hit, Jack thought.

Men not in line to shit rushed to the rail and leaned over to see what was happening.

The officer commanded the others on the jetty to open fire. One of the NCO's bent to retrieve his cap and put it on his head before shooting.

The captain of the ship tied up aft had a bullhorn. Peeking just over the wings of his bridge, he screamed for the men to watch where the fuck they were firing. Some of the rounds had dinged his ship.

Officers behind the loading party aft took kneeling positions and began shooting at the berserk man. He turned and doubled back toward the warehouse. He was hit several times, running now with his hands in the air, his body jerking from the impact of the bullets. He went down.

The officers rushed up ready to pump more bullets into him. Though he lay as still as a bag of rags, they approached him with the caution of a bunch of Pygmies coming upon a wounded rhino. A dark flood began to spread around him. It darkened his trousers, stained the deck. It flowed too fast for blood and was too copious to be urine. He was soon lying in a puddle. One of the NCO's bent and put a finger in it and tasted it—for christsake! Then he and those around the body began to laugh. From the man's clothes, the NCO hauled several riddled tins of pineapple juice.

When they had moved away, leaving the body uncovered on the dock, Jack could see the porter's face very clearly. He lay staring blindly at the boards beneath his slack cheek. He was just a boy, probably no older than Jack, and dead as a doornail. He was still there an hour later when they sailed. A cloud of flies buzzed around him, drawn by the sweet juice.

The *Retreat* was supposed to follow the little convoy up to Tsingtao to serve as medical support or evacuation hospital for the marine detachment and air squadron up there in case they became involved in the battle. A cruiser and some destroyers were also converging to lay off the coast if needed. Fetterman explained it. They were there to protect American lives and property. The Chinese, lacking any suitable ships of their own, had hired U.S. merchantmen to carry the troops. Three times they had unsuccessfully tried to clear the bandits out of the hills behind the city by approaching from land. Each time their army had melted to nothing through desertions and ambush.

"What about that American guy, sir?" Jack had asked.

Fetterman shrugged. "Could be OSS. They have some officers working with the Nationalists. Liaison. Or he could be a private soldier of fortune."

Soldier of fortune, the boy said to himself. That was it. That was how he should have gone. Something between Old Bill Miner and Clark Gable would do. He cradled the heavy Thompson gun on his knees, ran his fingertips over the wood and dull good steel. *But,* he guessed, *I'd have to learn to speak Chinese.* He regretted having wasted a year there and not learning more than a few words. There was always something to keep him from anything good.

"Our job is to provide security for this ship," Lieutenant Fetterman said.

"I thought we and them were on the same side," Peterson said.

"If one of those people tries to move off that fo'c'sle, you *will* consider him an enemy!" Fetterman glowered.

That Fetterman was a killer. He looked like a clerk in a nickel-and-dime savings and loan, but he'd shoot.

"And if I find any one of you goofing off, I'll have you on report. You will *not* forget you are representatives of the U.S. Navy. I will not have *any* fraternization with the civilians who run this ship. They have liquor aboard and a relaxed discipline. There will be no intercourse with them except in the line of strict duty. Is that clear?"

"Any *what*, sir?" Pete croaked.

"You will only *associate* with them in the line of duty, Peterson."

"Oh."

Captain Butts had got a stern line wrapped in the screw, trying to get away from the jetty in Shanghai, and the *Retreat* would be delayed until late that evening while a diver went down and cut it loose, Lieutenant Fetterman announced after reading a message from the radio shack.

Some captain.

That night it began to rain. Within an hour they knew it was a full-fledged Yellow Sea storm. They had not brought foul-weather gear. When the ship's captain found them standing watch in their shirt sleeves, he handed out waterproof parkas.

After dark they decided to move the men with tommy guns down to the head of the ladders a deck above the fo'c'sle. Jack stood pressed closely against the bulkhead, trying to stay out of the spray and wind. The sea broke over the side rail constantly. He thought of the poor bastards huddled down there.

They must be puking their guts out, he thought, feeling none too secure himself. It had been a long time since he had been on the open sea. He forced himself to feel hard, emotionless. *Fuckum!*

There was a commotion in the dark. Whipped back on the wind, he heard some yelling and a lot of chatter. It was eerie being aware of all those men but being unable to see them except as a kind of different heaving shadow. He sensed a large movement among them.

Faces appeared beneath the light over the barrier at the foot of the ladder. Water soaked the men's uniforms, wilted their caps and streamed down their utterly foreign young faces with those high, goony haircuts. Half a dozen men leaned into the light to chatter excitedly, gesturing forward in the dark. One more angry than the others rattled the wooden barrier. Jack lowered the submachine gun to point at them and clicked off the safety and waved them to get away from there with the muzzle.

"Scram! Amscray!" he commanded in a large voice. They faded back into the black behind them.

The boy felt an elated rush of power, of being able to get people to do what he wanted by waving a gun.

Fetterman had been in contact with the *Retreat* by radio. It had sailed but had also run into the storm.

A Liberty ship is a pig. This one, being lightly loaded and all the cargo on deck, bobbed around like an enormous loose buoy and made about as much headway. Chiang Kai-shek's big spring offensive was wallowing forward at about five knots.

Jack wiped the gun dry and oiled it with a patch he found in the ingenious little oiler behind a trapdoor in the butt plate. He showed Peterson where to look for one on his M-1.

"You know a lot about guns, don't you?" Pete admired.

"A little. I studied them. Maybe when I get out, I'll take up gunsmithing," he mused, cocking the action and pulling the trigger on the empty chamber. There was the sensation of smoothly milled metal parts. He cocked it again and sighted on a spot on the bulkhead.

"If them gooks tried to come up, would you really shoot them, Muskie?" Pete asked softly.

"Yeow, sure I would."

"I don't know if I could kill a man. That's why I joined the Navy. My people are real strong against war. And it ain't like we're in no war anyway."

"If they came up, they wouldn't be thinking like that about you."

"I reckon. It's funny, ain't it?"

"What is?"

"Us and them gooks. I thought they'd be nice and all— you know—after what we done for them, whippin the Japs and such. Man, they *hate* our guts! And I don't care for them neither. That's why I don't go on liberty much. I feel like they're blamin *me* for some damn thing. All I want to do is get my ass back into that swamp and find me some good ole girl and never leave home again."

"Yeow. It's all sorta been a big disappointment." He clicked the gun at the spot on the bulkhead.

By morning they learned one of the cooking barrels had tipped over during the storm, scalding several men. When the captain learned of it, he had a first-aid box lowered on a line to his passengers. They did not even have organized medics, at least not on that ship.

They were drying their gear; blankets and clothing were hung everywhere. Many men had stripped naked. Under the suddenly bright sun steam actually rose from the stuff on the deck. A lot of men were sick, moaning like large children. They were mostly country boys who had never dreamed of killing a man any more than Peterson had, or even of a sea voyage so far from the land to which they had been bound by indebted inheritances for generations.

"What a sorryass army!" the captain spat and went back inside the bridge.

Out of nowhere Jack had an instant whiff of spring-greening earth, trees, flowers, sweet clover grasses. It was so real, he searched the horizon for land. But they were still four days from Tsingtao and far beyond the coast.

The Chinese disembarked Friday morning after chow on deck. There were four extra packs on deck when the men were mustered to move off. Four had either hidden or had jumped off the ship at sea.

"No one gets off until those fuckers are found," the captain hollered. "Don't put down that plank until every last one is accounted for."

He stood on the open bridge while his men searched the fo'c'sle.

"Here's one!" a seaman cried.

A man was wedged in a big ventilator, clinging to the smooth sides with bare fingers and toes. He was hauled out, kicked and beaten by the NCO's. Another was found burrowed down beneath a four stack of life rafts. He'd had to work his way down through three rope-net layers to get to the bottom. The rafts had to be unstacked to haul his quaking, hungry-looking self out. A third was discovered clinging to the supports under the skirt of the plank shithouse, arms and legs wrapped around the shitty two-by-four's. The last man could not be found. The captain finally accepted he had been washed or jumped overboard.

Maybe he had smelled that fresh land smell and tried to swim for it, Jack thought.

After much yelling and reorganizing on the jetty, the army shuffled forward in a column of threes stretching off the docks and down the street—a long, slow, mustard-colored snake. Far up the line the tall porter who looked like Big Stoop stuck up higher than the rest.

The ships made way as soon as they disgorged the offensive. Men knocked down the makeshift poops, letting the boards fall into the bay. Deckhands were scrubbing down the decks with suds. The Navy details were gathered in front of an open shed while the commander went somewhere to find out what they were supposed to do.

Tied up across the end of the pier was a little coastal freighter not more than one-hundred feet long. It was the rustiest damn boat they had ever seen. Not a speck of paint was left on its sides or the deck or superstructure. It was solid rust. While they watched, two Japs in what looked like cotton breechcloths came out and hung up laundry. They decided the ship had surrendered after the war and had just been forgotten. The Japs had the air of men who had been waiting a long while for instructions. There were things in China that could not be fathomed.

384

After a while a marine colonel arrived in a jeep. All the marines were bearing weapons. A loaded .50 caliber machine gun was lowered in forward firing position on the hood. The colonel told the commander he would have some trucks sent to take the men to the Marine base.

The base was on full alert. All the marines wore battle gear, and the checkpoints were using a system of passwords. A flight of Corsairs, inverted gull-winged and mean, ripped low over the city and screamed over the green hills beyond.

They were billeted in an empty barracks on bunks and bare mattresses. They played cards after chow and lay around and listened to the sound of desultory shelling off toward the hills. A few rounds seemed to fall rather near the city. The marines got excited. There was bustling outside. Someone started the rumor that the Marine base might be attacked.

"I hope it is. I'd like a chance to see what this thing will do," Jack said, indicating the gun which he still had.

Over on the other side of the base a marine guard opened up on something in the dark with four short bursts of a water-cooled machine gun. In an hour or so, the boy decided it was a false alarm and went to sleep. At morning chow, rumor was some marine's gook cunt was trying to creep up to the wire to find out why her fella hadn't kept a date and got her little ass shot off.

The *Retreat* arrived in the harbor that afternoon and Fetterman's Raiders returned to ship and checked in their weapons and ammo. Life became as it had been before. No one had fired a shot.

The evening news broadcast in the mess reported that Chiang Kai-shek had launched a massive attack against Communist-inspired bandits. First reports from the scene indicated the force was making rapid progress into the contested area, and the commander said he expected to wipe out the Red rebels within a matter of hours. "If this is true," the commentator added, "it may be the key to the final collapse of the rebellion that has divided China since 1927."

Sunday morning more than five thousand of the troops they had transported went over to the other side, most of them taking their weapons and equipment.

The morning news reported the commander of the

army as declaring he had captured most of the rebel command and victory was imminent.

Jack rolled his Navy swim trunks in a towel and prepared to go on liberty.

25

THE earnest expression on Gorilla's face was one of a friend who could no longer not offer a word to the wise. Determined in his supposed folly, the boy was embarrassed by Gorilla's sincere concern.

"I'm not doin anything wrong," he protested.

"Well, yeah. But it ain't good for you to keep goin on liberty alone, Muskrat. You could end up in the drink with your belly slit like that little Castro fella did."

"I'm careful." It was true. He never got drunk when he went ashore alone, never helled around. He merely felt more himself rather than "Muskrat" when he was alone. And since he had discovered the house in Shanghai dedicated to the pleasures of gentlemen, he saw himself in a superior light. A calmness had settled over him. He was able to think of the books he read without an inherent suspicion of them and the guilt of a secret reader. Even among those on the ship who talked of going to college when they got home, books were divertissements or sources of information to be digested toward gaining a better job rather than ideas and scenes that might electrify their spirit, open their eyes. Novels other than those that read like a movie mystery or Western were a waste of time, dangerous to health and threatening to one's masculinity. His best buddies cut sidelong glances at the books he read with the same quiet disapproval that veiled their faces when one of the more swishy corpsmen pranced and squealed upon being goosed in chow line.

"What you want to read that shit for?" they could not sometimes resist asking.

"I've known people like these in this book," he insisted in the face of their disbelief.

"Well, I never by God have! And I don't want to!"

But they had grown up in the same sort of places, he thought. *Maybe they had had it a bit better in a lot of ways. But are they blind? Everyone really thinks Henry Aldrich is the goddamned standard. That we're all going to be illustrated by that Norman Rockwell. Shit! If I could draw like him, I'd make pictures so real it would break your heart. I'd paint pictures of people fuckin so real it would make your head swim. All the brothers are brave and all the sisters are virtuous—in a pig's ass! We live one way and our minds are always in a picture show. If the President eats, he shits. And so does Lana Turner.*

There was a frightening threat in his best buddy's concern. He did not understand, but it made him feel ... *beyond the pale. Was that from something he had read, or was it from a sermon?* He was both vulnerable and truculent. They were not going to make him feel guilty for doing something that made him in some way better than he had been before.

But it was a problem. He did not consider himself better than the others. The note in his pocket that got him into a place they could not go was no measure of his being in any way superior. It was a matter of luck in an unfair world. He wished they *all* could be treated like gentlemen. There was no bullshit about *earning* the right. If an asshole like Commander Robert Beloved Butts II could command a ship and dream of high political office, then everyone had a right to any goddamned thing they could get away with.

"I just feel you ought to know what everyone is thinkin," Gorilla said.

"What are they thinkin?"

"That you're, you know, goin Asiatic or something like that."

"Yeow?" He grinned.

"Well, shit yeow! You know, you gotta go home one day, Muskie. You don't want to go home weird or somethin."

"I'll try and watch it," he promised.

"Yeah. You do that." Gorilla gave up. He had tried; that's all anyone could do.

What the hell's everyone want from me? the boy truly

387

wondered. It was the same feeling he had with his grandfather, his stepfather, his uncle. They all wanted him to be different, to be them.

Maybe I am weird, he told himself.

On the jetty two urchins were engaged in a curious enterprise which he noted, though it did not fully register until he had climbed into a rickshaw and was being towed away. One of the kids had been prying the slugs of .50 caliber machine gun ammo from the brass case using two sticks as rudimentary pliers. The other, a lad about the size of a thin American four-year-old, was pouring the tiny black cellulose doughnuts of powder into a Coke bottle. Perhaps they sold the cases to the place where they were made into silver-plated, dragon-embossed salt and pepper shakers. He had bought a pair for his grandmother. They came in a fake lizard skin case with a padded blue silk lining. Maybe they sold the powder to the guerrillas up in the hills.

But you can't fuck with bullets and stuff like that, he thought of the boys, *and grow up just ordinary. Can you?*

He felt sorry for the little scavengers. He felt sorry for the boy he had been.

We're all weird, he decided.

Tsingtao smelled like San Diego. There was that same good beach smell, the balmy soft air of a resort, hot, bright sunshine, cool deep shadows. On the high rickshaw seat, he wore dark Air Corps sunglasses, crossed his knees and sat back.

What the hell should he do, get down and haul the gook just because he felt sorry for the poor bastard?

In the city, the rickshaw boy revealed the place Jack wanted to go was too far to reach by rickshaw.

"Rong way. Many li. You takee taxi."

He left him before a café, upon the terrace of which soldiers were drinking beer and Cokes. Parked at the curb was a battered tiny Fiat with the sign PRIMA TAXI painted on its side.

Jack had supposed the place would be in town. He showed the driver, a local gangster with a chauffeur's cap, the note with the address on it.

"Many li," he explained. "Two buck, OK, Joe?" He held

388

up two rather busted-looking fingers so that there would be no misunderstanding.

"OK."

The Fiat smelled of tobacco and a strangely sweet-scented gasoline that began to make the boy queasy before they had left the city. Behind, the little car laid down a thick blue smoke screen. The laboring bit of engine sounded as if every rod were loose. Frequent gear changes and slipping of the clutch were needed to keep moving at all. The thick-necked driver seemed not perturbed and whistled silently between concentrated shifts.

They passed houses set among trees behind stone walls that had heavy chained gates or big studded doors. Only the tops of the houses and small upper windows were visible. Off to the right, over the town, he could see the bay and sea and his ship, a small white child's boat on a silver pond.

The driver pulled over on the wrong side of the road and stopped, keeping his clattering engine running while Jack paid him.

Jack stood before a tall black iron gate that needed paint. It was set in a tall wall topped with broken glass. There was a bell pull next to the gate. He yanked it but heard nothing. When no one came immediately, he tugged the handle several times.

A pretty Chinese girl in a cheongsam trotted down the path of crushed shell and inquired without opening the gate, "Yes?" He showed her his note from the whore Hannelore in Shanghai and also offered the card of Mme. de la Bresque. She took his documents, bowed slightly and carried them back to the house.

"You come." The girl returned and opened the gate. He could tell nothing from her face. Her eyes demurely avoided his.

She showed him into a two-story bungalow with upswept Chinese eaves to send evil spirits back to from wherever they flew.

"You wait." She left him in the downstairs hall before a sort of hatcheck booth with a half counter, unmanned, with no hats or coats on the empty hooks. Large lacquered double sliding doors opened into a parlor. There was the sound of Chinese women speaking softly in a room farther down the hall. A big dog barked upstairs and was hushed in a language that sounded like German.

A slender woman came down the stairs, hanging onto the collar of the largest fuzzy white dog the boy had ever seen. She wore loose black trousers, high-heeled patent sandals that left her long toes with their red lacquered nails exposed and a black silk shirt cinched at the waist with a gold filigree belt set with colored glass jewels.

"Shh! Ajax!" She spoke to the dog sharply, tugging on his collar. He yawned. His goddamned mouth and throat looked like a tunnel! From nose to tail he must have been over six feet long. His footpads were large as a man's fist, and his coat made Jack think of a sheep or some kind of exotic goat. When he wanted to sniff the sailor, not even she could hold him. He went straight for the boy's genitals, his big wet black nose forcing Jack back against the wall. Then he got his wrist in his mouth.

"No. Bad dog! Ajax! No!"

He did not chew, merely covered Jack's arm with slobbers. But the monster had teeth in there like a lion. She got the dog back and encouraged him to sit in the hall, where he lay thumping the banister with his tail so it sounded like an enormous, ghostly heartbeat.

"You will excuse him, please. He is just puppy." She pushed a wisp of dark hair back from her temple. "What can I do for you?"

She was about thirty and had lovely, bony hands, a long neck and a way of carrying her small dark head that made it look longer.

He waved his note which the girl had given back to him. "I was looking for Hannelore. She said I should ask for her here. She said she might be here."

"Ah. No. I am sorry. She is not here." She spoke slowly, seeming clearly puzzled by the young man standing in her hallway.

"Well, she said she might be. Said she might go to the beach with me." He grinned and showed her the rolled towel which contained his swimming trunks.

She rubbed the skin in the open collar of her shirt with her fingertips. Her hair was almost black, coarse and wavy, parted in the center and turned under in a bun at the back. She looked a little like Joan Bennett. No. She more resembled a sister of Charlie Chaplin—a foreignness he could place.

She smiled. "You come here to go to the beach?"

"Uh, yes, ma'am."

"You don't come for a girl?"

"Well, I thought if Hannelore was here we might go to the beach first. There's a good beach."

"Yes. I know the beach very well." She smiled. She was very dark. "You don't want a girl? I have lovely girls." She clapped her hands sharply. The dog got up. "No! Ajax! Sitasay," she said, or something that sounded like that.

The girl who had shown him in and two others appeared in the hall, all smiling and slinking toward him.

"They are all very beautiful, yes? I have only the best girls. You like?"

"Well, sure. They are very fine. But, uh ... I just thought if Hannelore was here. I'm kind of tired of Chinese girls." He lowered his voice to almost a whisper. He didn't want to offend them.

"Well," the woman said sharply. "This is what I have. They are beautiful, accomplished girls," she declared testily, unable to discern by searching with her eyes any requirement *he* might have that one of them could not adequately handle.

"How about you?" he suddenly blurted.

"Me!" she exclaimed and began to laugh. She looked at him and laughed all the harder. She spoke to the girls in Chinese, and they began to laugh. "But you are just a *baby!*" she chuckled. She reached out and pinched his cheek.

"I can pay," he insisted, blushing, offended.

"Oh! You can pay! How much? How much you pay to sleep with me?"

He looked at her as fully as she had looked at him. She was not what he would have called pretty, but there was something—the hollow of her throat, her small chin, the mocking mouth that became amusedly pouting, large dark eyes.

"A hundred dollars is all I have," he said.

"You give me one hundred dollars?" she asked, her eyes growing both wide and softening. Then she laughed again. "Short time or long time?"

"Whatever you say," he swallowed, knowing he was entirely serious.

"Ah, you are serious," she said softly. She laughed

391

again, but her eyes became shiny. Then she laughed and laughed. "Oh, my dear!" she sighed. "You are serious, yes?"

"Yes, ma'am." He dug out his wallet.

"Put your money away, baby. I don't want your money. I don't sleep with you. I give you tea, OK. You take tea with me?"

"Uh, OK. Thanks." He hated tea, and he thought he ought to get to the beach if he was going.

The dog arose and came to sniff and lick him. She reprimanded it and hauled it away.

"What kind of dog *is* that?" he asked.

"He is Irish wolfhound." She patted the dog's neck hard, like a woman beating a cushion. His lower jaw just hung and slobbered as he closed his eyes at the pleasure of it.

"He's big as a pony," the boy observed.

She laughed. "Yes, he is my protection."

He thought it might be safer to keep a gun. "What do you feed him?"

"Ah! He must have five kilos meat in one day. It is very difficult. I buy horsemeat for him. But sometimes I think it is not horse. I do not ask. He must have meat." She thumped him soundly again.

The girls giggled and looked at the boy when the woman explained she was having him up to her rooms for tea. The biggest one flirted with him with her eyes. When she went back down the hall, her ass rolled like a Mexican *puta*'s.

The woman and the dog led the way upstairs, the dog bounding ahead, covering half the flight between forefeet and rear. She walked with a very straight back, head erect, nothing rolled. Her step was delicate, almost mincing.

"What is your name?" she asked over her shoulder.

"Jack."

"Jack? That is common American name, no?"

He grinned. "Pretty common."

"I am Zizi."

"Is that a name?"

She turned and shot him a wry smile. *"Touché!* You are not so stupid. You are Jack, and I am Zizi. OK." She offered him her hand.

It was cool and slightly trembling. The palm felt smooth

and damp. She merely gripped his once, pumped it and let go. Her fingers felt long and fleshless.

On the landing, the dog waited and sniffed her happily and reared up a little until she spoke to him and patted his bear-sized head. His tail thumped the wall resoundingly.

She led the way into a small, cluttered sitting room where in one corner a samovar sat on a table. Light filtered through a single window from which he could see a sliver of the sea. In the room it seemed already evening. The damn dog lay down by a dark overstuffed couch on which brocade shawls had been casually arranged. The walls were hung with watered cloth and Chinese scrolls.

"If I would stay here, I change this room. It is too dark, yes?" the woman said, watching him appraise her apartment. "I think so," she decided. "But now I do not care. It is finished here now, I think. Maybe one year, two, no more. It is all finished." She had to step over the dog to fool with the samovar. She had tea cups and a sugar bowl on a lacquer tray with a small can of U.S. condensed milk.

She placed the things on the low table before the couch, shooing the dog to find a place for her feet. He moved over to lie under the window where the curtain hung without movement.

Jack took his tea with just sugar. It tasted strong, sweet, flowery.

"Good," he said.

"Yes. We can get good tea," the woman said. "So!" She sat back and laced her long fingers around one lifted knee. "You make me—how you say—interesay?"

"Interested."

"Yes. Tell me of you."

He shrugged. "Nothing to tell. I joined the Navy, and here I am."

"But why do you join the Navy? You are baby. How old you are?"

He decided not to lie. "Sixteen. Or I will be soon."

"But you should be home with your mama and papa."

"I don't have any." He grinned. "No mama, no papa, no chow-chow."

"But in America everyone lives very well, no?"

"Some don't live so well. My people live in an alley

393

with black people. In a trailer—a caravan—one room only."

"It is true? No! I don't think so. I have uncle in America. In New York. You know New York?"

"Yes." He lied.

"He write me all is good in America. Everyone make *beaucoup* the money." She rubbed forefinger and thumb together deliciously. "Everyone have money. Many American officers tell me these things also. Always before only American officers come here. Many beautiful girls. No problems with the police. They tell me of America."

"Well, America isn't so good for some." He felt defeated by her enthusiasm.

"For my uncle it is paradise," she insisted. "Yes. He go to America from Amsterdam when the war begins. We are Jews. Many, many years ago our people come from Espagne to the Nederlands. Then when the Germans come, my uncle say we must go. My father say it will be OK. We stay. Then we hear they take some Jews away. My father wants to go then, but he cannot go to America. So we get on the boat—'orrible boat—and we come to Shanghai. Then the Japanese come, but they do not bother us. My father sells the jewels, you know? But then he die; then my mother die. And I have nothing. Madame de la Bresque, she ask me to come stay by her. So I become prostitute. I was only girl then. Only I am for gentlemen. For officers." She sipped her tea, looking back blankly over the rim. "Sometimes we have gala. Very nice. You know?"

He had only the vaguest idea. "For the Japs, too?"

"Yes. For Japanese also. Madame gives them money for them to let her do business. With money you can do anything in this world."

"What were the Japs like?" he asked.

"Yes. They are not so tall." She looked at his face and laughed. "What you think, baby? Men are so different? They are all the same. Nice ones and fools. Intelligent ones and brutes. The Japanese officers have good manners. Very loyal. They not so drunk like the Americans. Then when the Americans and English come back, Madame explain me there is a good chance here. I take my money and have this house. Now it is finished, I think. No one comes. I cannot keep the beautiful European girl, for there is nothing for her. I must make a house in town for the sailors or go somewhere else. The rebels win now, I think. Everyone say it is soon. Why don't the Americans stop the rebels?" she suddenly turned on him to demand.

"I don't know."

"But America is strong. They have the marines and many airplanes and the Navy. I don't understand." She shook her head. "No officer I know explains this to me."

"Maybe we are just tired of war. Maybe we are afraid to try and fight all of China. We haven't so many soldiers anymore. They put the Navy in mothballs. No sailors."

"But it is stupid!" she protested. "They will win here, like the Germans win. They are Communist, worse than Germans. They do not like my business. They do not like girls. Sometimes they come, you know. Yes. They are just there, in the street. They come and make propaganda and take a tax from some people. They don't trouble me. But they are there, and it makes everyone afraid. I must go." It was as if she kept making and unmaking the decision. Now she seemed about to get up and start packing.

"Where will you go?"

She shrugged. "Maybe Shanghai. Maybe Hong Kong. Maybe Singapore or Bangkok. I like to go to America. But it is very difficult. I am known to your government. One officer—a major—tell me he try to fix for me to go to America. He lives in Los Angeles. He say we can make business together. But he don't write me for long time now. My uncle tell me I must marry the American. But it is very difficult. You like to marry me? Yes? You marry me, and go to America and tell them, then they let me come. I give you money if you do this."

He looked shocked, so she laughed and pinched his cheek.

"So. You want to sleep with me, but you don't want to make marriage with me? You wish more tea?"

"Uh, no, thanks, ma'am." He fidgeted a bit, looked at his watch. He wondered if she could get him a taxi to take him back to the beach.

"I have not sleep with a man—" She thought a moment. "Three month!" She held up three fingers. She stood up and stretched, lifting her arms over her head and yawning. The dog got up and stretched as well. "This weather makes me sleepy." She let her arms fall to her sides. "OK. I sleep with you. You give me one hundred dollars."

He blinked. A hundred dollars suddenly seemed a lot.

She stood holding out her open pale palm.

"What? You change your mind? Now you don't think I am worth so much?" She shrugged and went to the door and placed her hand on the latch.

He got up. The dog came and began sniffing his towel and making as if to bite it. His muzzle was breast-high. He had bad breath.

"All right," he said.

She smiled with a sardonic downturning of her mouth. She put out her hand again. Very dark brows were plucked into perfect scimitars. There was Vaseline or something on her large, dark lids.

He drew out his wallet again and dropped all the bills in it into her palm. She folded it without counting it and slipped it in her breast pocket.

"A long time?" he squeaked.

"What you think?" She grinned.

He hadn't a notion.

She slipped her left hand in his right hand and interlaced her fingers. The goddamn dog was sniffing at their genitals. When he turned, he felt the dog's nose in his ass. She led him outside to the top of the stairs, folded his arm around her waist, keeping her fingers entwined, and called down in Chinese to the girls below. She turned to him, still holding his arm around her waist, leaning back, her loins and soft belly against him to look in his eyes. "Baby," she breathed. She gave him a quick kiss and began to laugh. He lunged forward to kiss her, but she averted her face, letting him kiss her cheek and neck. He could feel the laughter in her with his lips.

He did not know if she was making fun of him or not. The hundred he had given her seemed a foolish lot of money. He did not like feeling she thought him a fool. If he had offered her just fifty, it would have been generous. But a hundred was a fool's gift.

"Ajax!" She slapped at the dog, whose nose in her ass nudged her in a little hop against Jack.

He did not like that sniffing dog. Her room smelled of him, he noted, when they were back inside. Ajax went over toward the window, his high hindquarters moving stiffly. He had balls about the size of a man's, maybe a bit larger, and a large fuzzy dong swaying beneath his belly on a thin filet of flesh. He curled in an awkward pretzel position and began eagerly biting his penis, or sucking it, whatever, as if it itched. The woman ignored it.

There was a soft knock on the door. The young Chinese girl came in with averted eyes and set down a bucket with ice water and a bottle of champagne in it.

"We have a little wine, yes?" She smiled. "I go make pee-pee." She waved the glasses for him to take care of the wine.

He hauled the bottle out of the bucket and studied it with suspicion before peeling the foil from its crown. He had never tasted champagne. By rumor and movie he thought it could make you very drunk. Figuring out the wire bail over the knobbed cork, he untwisted and removed it. Then he began trying to unscrew the cork. Nothing. He put his thumbs under it, prying upward until he felt he was tearing the quick from his nails. The cork began to come out.

Pop! It went off like a shot. The cork ricocheted off the ceiling, hit the wall under the window, just missing the dog who leaped up and began barking at the boy—deep, chesty "Woof-woofs!" with the timbre of a goddamned lion.

"Oh, no!" The woman hurried into the room. "Shh! *Ajax!*"

The wine fuzzed from the neck of the bottle and ran over Jack's hands and made a small puddle on the floor.

"That is not the way," she clucked at him. With a napkin, she quickly squatted and wiped up the floor.

She had put on a red Dragon Lady dress with a round Chinese collar above a large lozenge-shaped hole which showed a lot of her caramel-colored bosom. Her breasts were not large, but were soft and quivered like gelatin molds in the frame made by the opening in her dress. The dress was slit up each side to her hips. When she squatted down, the front panel of the dress was caught between her thighs. Her shining thighs and calves were very slender, devoid of but only the softest muscle. All the intricate ankle and foot bones were touchingly visible. Her big toes were long and deformed from wearing pointed shoes, the nails actually canting toward the second toe. Her little toes

397

as well were bent under their neighbors. Yet her legs and feet were very sexy when she crouched down, bending sideways over her knees to wipe up the wine.

The tawniness of her skin and the exotic mystery of her blood made her seem alien. *Feline.* He had read that so often about women. To say it himself was curiously distasteful, as if the writers of books had missed it, but unless they had seen *this* one, they were misapplying the term. For she wore herself the way a cat does.

He thought of all the dicks that had been in her body. *There must have been hundreds and hundreds*, he thought, seeing an army of Japs lined up as far as the eye could see, seeing battalions of officers, British and American, in all shapes and sizes, all branches. *How could a body like hers take such treatment?* he wondered. Then he decided it might not be as difficult as being a wife. After all the pretty woman at his feet did not have to cook and scrub and go out and work. She fucked, did her accounts, then her time was her own. But how many had she had?

She rose, took the bottle from him and poured the wine. Behind her left ear she had pinned a sprig of tiny white flowers that looked like miniature bells in her dark hair. She had laved herself with perfume—a heavy night scent. When they touched glasses, she said, "To love," smiling mockingly over the rims.

He could taste her perfume in the wine. Looking into her eyes he thought, *One hundred dollars.* The foolishness of it made him feel good. He smiled, broadly, happily.

"Yes?" she wondered.

"Nothing."

"Yes. You think something. Tell me what you think."

"I think in a little while, soon, I'll be in your body. It's a strange feeling. It always feels strange to give a woman money and in a few minutes she lets you get into her."

"You think it is funny? You don't laugh. You look sad."

"Not funny, ha-ha. Strange. I like it. No mumble-mumble bullshit. But in a minute we will be fucking."

"You think about to fook me? You have naughty thoughts. You are baby." She slithered her arms around his neck and let him kiss her mouth, opening to offer him a taste of the place where her snaky, soft tongue lived. Her kiss was all but passive, yielding, enfolding. It was just

398

right. It made him feel very young, awkward in his thought, but not stupid or foolish.

Her cheek slid silkenly along his own. He squeezed her strongly in his joy.

"Don't break me," she warned with a small laugh. "We take the wine into the other room," she whispered against his jaw. When she said "other," it sounded like "usser."

Though it was still midafternoon, she had adjusted the draperies so there was the curious feeling of uncommonly bright twilight. An idle breeze shifted the curtains and gave him the sensation of being perched upon a pier above water. He felt the sparkle and insidious low lap of a tide within him.

Suddenly, he did not know how to proceed. He had never dreamed of paying a woman a hundred dollars before. It did not seem he ought to just jump out of his clothes. Awkwardness fit him like a pair of country overalls.

It was a larger room than the other, with a high double bed set upon a low carpeted platform.

She opened the bed, carefully folding a pale-blue damask cover. Turning, she found him standing in the same spot.

"You become tree?" She smiled. She patted the bed and had to make the whore's remark that always hurt him, cheapened his desire. "My workbench." She reached up and picked open the tiny knots that served as button loops on her dress. "You come to bed in your clothes?"

Quickly he began getting out of his whites. When he straightened up she was sliding down a zipper along her left side. The red gown was lifted away. She turned to drape it carefully over the foot of the bed. In the light her mellow skin seemed darker than his own, though he was tanner from the sun. Paler loins and breasts showed she also liked the beach. Two large dimples created shadows above her very soft-looking buttocks. When she turned again toward him, she carried her right arm across her breasts in a gesture of incongruous modesty.

She was not voluptuous if he knew the meaning of that word from pinup books, but very slender, yet with a definite softness and depth of flesh at breast, belly and hip. Her navel was set in a long dimple. The sooty smudge of hair beneath her belly drew his eyes, though he would not let himself stare at her there. The wedge of hair above her slender thighs looked long and thick.

"When I get married, if I get married, I want to be sure to marry a black-haired girl," he said.

She smiled. Coolness seeped from the twilight corners of the room and touched his naked skin causing slight gooseflesh, leaving the hairs on his body erect, sensitive to the least breeze.

"You are pretty boy," she said very softly, gazing over his body. "You will be my golden one." She put out both her hands, palms upward. Her breasts were tipped by dark coned nipples.

He stepped forward, putting out his hands to lay them palm down on her own. Her fingernails scuttled like beetles over his palms and up the bare bellies of his forearms, up over his forearms, climbing them as she came closer, until the fine electrified hairs upon his thighs and belly touched her skin—a moment of indefinite sensation—supercutaneous. Then he wrapped his arms around her. Her body came up against his own, yet still there was a sweet passivity in her. His penis beginning to stiffen, rose into the dark puff between her close thighs. She stood on tiptoe and tilted her head back onto her right shoulder to offer him her mouth as if it were a sexual flower. He felt enfolded juicily in lips, in a place with melting flesh walls and an incredible tongue. A mouth for nothing so much as to kiss, tutor him with kisses—the feeling a delicious other end of cockshaft and cunt wall.

She held him tightly by the hand and led him up onto her high bed.

Even then there was time to know the luxury of a good bed, each square inch supporting part of his weight. Linen sheets cool and glazed-feeling—*Deluxe* leaped to mind.

He leaned over her and kissed her again. His cock bore against her closed thighs, ranged upward against her soft belly. He mauled her left tit, bent from the kiss to take it into his mouth. She rolled it upward for him by pressing her arm tightly against her breast. Stroking his head idly, she traced a whorl of hair on the crown of his head with a fingernail. A quickening of her body and small cry warned him he had hurt her. He tried to gently kiss away the hurt, lifting his head to offer apology. The cone of her tit was slick with saliva.

She let him kiss her once again, not so passionately. The fingers of her left hand curled between them on his chest. She touched his paps, tickled them with a fingernail. He shivered. No one had ever done that. He hadn't known that he had such feelings there. Her long, narrow hand traveled down over his belly, just prowled the fringe of his pubic hair as he stroked her spine and the feathery cool globes of her bottom. She trailed her fingertips along his hard shaft, wrapped her hand around it as if it were precious. Her touch was slow and featherlight. Then she squeezed it and rubbed the pad of her thumb across its little mouth, feeling the tear of clear liquid she had drawn from it, rubbing the liquid back up over its head and around its ridge, causing him to shudder deliciously.

When he made a slight move to carry his desire to her, she turned in a way to lay her head on his chest. She trailed her tongue all around his face, lips—a deep kiss— neck, shoulders, chest, ringing his paps to send shivers through him, holding all the while his erect cock in her gently loving hand.

She had an incredible tongue. It was long and pointed, its tip as mobile as the joint of a little finger. Down the rill of his chest she trailed the flicking tip, beginning to double back upon herself.

He had seen a book on yogi where a woman in a leotard was sitting in a lotus position, staring straight ahead, with her tongue thrust out until it touched her chin. Zizi's face over his belly looked like that. The tip of her tongue darted in and out of his navel, described rings outward from it like the waves of a stone thrown into still water, until with large roundy-round sweeps of her dark head she was touching the tickling places at his sides, licking the hollows of his loins, the curly undergrowth out of which his cock stood. He could see the head of his prick over the wrap of her slender fingers, the long, lacquered nails.

Her back was infinitely woman to him. Nothing else could ever really approximate that soft curvature. The differences between her and himself were a source of overwhelming excitement. He trailed his fingers down along the opened gully of her bottom to touch the short black hairs. She made purring noises, slurpy sounds and hums. As she stopped a moment to look intently at the mouth of his penis, her fingers tightened at the base of it and drew

401

forward on the shaft of his penis, to see if there was a venereal discharge. Her expression was one of a woman objectively examining food. Only a clear tear glistened on its tiny guppy lips. She flicked it away with the tip of her pink tongue, rimmed the crown all around, then lowered her lips over it as if in an open-eyed kiss. Her eyes looked glazed, seeing and yet inward-looking. Then slowly, so he could not believe possible what he saw or felt, she slid down his cock until it all but disappeared. He thought of that story by Steinbeck about the woman who came once a week to feed the biologist's snake. He had seen a snake eat a white rat, more crawling upon it than by force of teeth and jaws gobbling it into him. He felt the head of his cock inside the ring of her throat.

Her fingers gently squeezed his testicles. She nudged apart his legs, stroked the root of his penis under his balls back to his asshole. His cock felt a foot long when she did that. He was aware of the hardness of it there for the first time. She made it so much more than just in and out and roundy-roundy.

She left it with a wet kissing sound to swivel completely around with her feet at a forty-five-degree angle to his head, her left knee slightly bent, the shiny cap he could have hidden in his palm pointing toward him, belly and breasts slewed over toward him, black puff of hair peeping from the pale belly of her curves.

Beginning again, she kissed his nuts and followed the string below, her head dipping between his legs, breasts mashed upon his loins, to lick him between the legs, run the tip of her tongue around and into his butthole.

Guys were always talking about an "Around the World." He supposed this was what they meant. But being uncertain, he was at a loss to know how to assure himself that was, indeed, what was happening.

Lifting her head from between his legs, scootching so her mouth was on more direct line over his cock, she held it at the base with her right hand and again took it into her mouth. He found her sex with the fingers of his left hand. She did not open for him. But soon he worked between her legs to find her slit and worked down and in until he found the liquid interior of her cunt. She was sucking him faster, not going so deeply, massaging him between the legs with her left hand contra to the motion of her mouth. She began to feel sweaty against him.

Could she like doing that? he puzzled. He had only thought of it before as a gift, a purchased performance, or queer.

More furiously he worked his fingers inside her, then switched to put his thumb in her, jabbing her between the legs with the blade of his hand. He could no longer remain so still and began thrusting upward into her mouth. Then he pushed her right hip flat onto the bed with his right hand, carrying his right leg over her to force her onto her back, and lay over her. She protested but accepted it, never letting his cock slip from her lips. He looked back between them to where his thighs were a low bridge over her up-turned face, his cock going in and out of her mouth, shiny with her saliva, pink with her lipstick.

He kissed her deep perfumed navel, belly, around the fringes of the coarse dark bush under which the skin looked so pale, as if it had never been touched by weather or sun. He pulled the hair with his lips, took a big bite and chewed it, pulling it a bit with his teeth. The dark lips were there, just before his eyes. They did not look so appealing to kiss, but he kissed them. Then he thought he smelled a faint doggy odor. Definitely dog beneath the perfume. He kissed all around her cunt without actually dipping between her lips. He chewed them. He inserted his fingers into her again, flicked her clitoris with his tongue. She parted her legs and began to move. He began to really fuck her face, not caring a damn for her, not caring if he did her some terrible damage. She tried to hold him off, from going so deep.

Still she moved her hips as if fucking too. He felt her jaws sort of crack, a distant little pop. It felt as if he were actually fucking her in the throat, his cock going completely into her mouth. He closed his eyes and plunged his face between her legs.

He began to swell to come, feeling the engorgement, the gathering, gathering as if to burst. She worked her forefinger into his ass and massaged the root of his penis in there.

He came, ramming himself into her, wanting her to die. Spurting into her mouth again and again. She sounded as if she were dying. Her hips jerked beneath her face, her soft inner thighs squeezed his head. Then she began to fight to get free. He quickly pulled himself out of her and fell limply across her body. A headache ripped through his brain. Before his eyes danced brilliant colors. He felt awful, exhausted, drained but unsatisfied. Her racking, deep gasps for breath were distant, of only indifferent concern to him.

"Whew! Whew! . . . Never . . . do . . . that," she breathed, scolding him with a kind of fear in her eyes. "You kill me, baby." Then she smiled and crawled up to lay beside him.

"No woman ever do you that?"

He admitted not.

"If you let me do, everything is better."

He looked at her and wondered how he had done what he did. How had he felt so willing to kill her if that had been the result?

Hitler, he said to himself, feeling very bad.

She kissed his mouth. He was not too eager for her kiss. It smelled and tasted of his cock. But after all, she had done it for him, hadn't she? Then he was lost in the wonder of her magic mouth. His prick felt cold and stiffing with saliva and come. There were two of her hairs in his mouth. When the kiss was done, he had to fish out the hairs with his finger.

"I never have so young boy," she confessed. "I like. Yes. I like!" She gave him a happy squeeze. She hopped up. "I go make pee-pees." She bounded off the bed and went trippingly into the small bathroom off the chamber. He heard her make water in the bowl, the flushing, then water running and minor bathing.

In the lighted doorway in dark silhouette with flesh-toned edges, she rested her chin on her chest to reach behind her head to withdraw half a dozen pins from her hair. It tumbled over her bare shoulders and down to her waist. Gathering it in her left hand she drew it forward over her left shoulder and began slowly brushing it with a curved brush that had metal teeth. Occasionally there were visible sparks in the dark cascade.

"The Egyptian Girl!" he exclaimed. That was who she looked like. Not quite so young. Not so slender, but that was how she was put together. Sargent's painting, he explained in an enthusiastic rush.

404

"Ah, chéri. C'est charmant. Vous êtes très gentil."

"You have beautiful hair," he said.

She made a face. Women with long hair always made a face. "One day I cut. Is too much trouble. Come, you wash now."

When they passed, he put out his arm and arrested her. She laughed and let him draw her against him and kiss her as if he had bought a perfect right.

They made love. Her cunt was not as good to fuck as her mouth, nor did she seem to like it so much. But she did not want to blow him again either. She merely let him use her, turning herself toward his pleasure. They slept.

When he awakened, it was dark and he knew he must go soon. So he willed himself hard against her sleeping ass and entered her from the back, though she gave only barest sign she was awake until he was inside her.

"Encore?" she asked over her shoulder without great joy, her voice sleepy, resigned.

Determined to get his hundred dollars' worth, he rolled onto his back, hauling her with him to sit upright upon him, astraddle, facing his feet. Moving her hips with his hands, he had her work that way for a while. He could tell she was trying hard to get him off as quickly as possible. She asked to turn around.

"I don't like. Your foots don't make me exciting," she explained. She sank back upon him. He clasped her hips with both hands and moved her the way he wished, virtually using her as a large machine with which to masturbate. She did not appear to be feeling anything especially pleasant. But her cunt began to feel good to him. She became very beautiful. Her hair fell on either side of him. Her face looked so young and helpless. She began to move more vigorously of her own accord and toward her own pleasure. The coarse hair of her cunt ground against his own. He fancied he could hear the rustling. He came before she had gotten well started on her own way. She sighed and gave him a long, perfunctory kiss, then bounded off once more to go into the can.

The goddamn dog began to bark in the next room. He could feel as well as hear the deep "woofs" through the building's structure. Leaping from bed, he stood at the window, peering between the gauze inner curtains. The lights of city were winking below, strung out along the beach. The *Retreat* was lit up like a Christmas tree, illuminating the water and dockside for yards around. He wondered why it had *all* the lights on. Broken by the breeze and distance he could hear a loudspeaker truck in the streets far below, but he could not make out what it was saying. Out in the bay, a large junk hung with kerosene running lights was making its slow way out to sea. Then he saw the dark lumps of men in the street. Some had lifted their faces toward the house at the dog's barking. They chattered in Chinese and laughed. The laugh was a shock. It made him instantly alert. He had never heard a Chinese laugh. It made him feel happy and curiously unsure of himself. It was a lovely, bubbling, hearty sound.

"What is it?" He felt her hand lightly at his waist.

"I heard a Chinese laugh," he explained, wrapping her in his arms.

"Ajax! Shh! Shh!" she shouted at the wall. "I must go make him be quiet. Every time they come he go crazy."

"Who?" he suddenly felt threatened.

"The Blue armies, darling. The Communists." The skirt of a flowered kimono swirled around her slim calves as she flipped into the other room.

"Those are rebels?" he squawked after her.

"Yes. I tell you before. When the Kuomintang comes to make war with them, the Communists always catch them, eh? Then they come into town to make the proof for the peoples they are still OK. Don't worry. They don't come in here. They stay in street. But I tell you. Business is impossible in these times. It is finished now. I go."

The dog broke away from her and bounded into the room, bent on Jack, bouncing around, shaking his enormous growly head like a puppy. He reared up and struck the boy in the chest with his paws, causing him to trip backward on the low stage of the bed and fall onto his back asprawl. The beast began to lick his genitals, its tongue like a swipe with a piece of warm, fresh liver. He was pinned by the bastard, trying to scramble up the side of the bed, his bare heels refusing to find purchase.

"Non! Non!" Zizi cried. "He don't bite. Don't worry," she offered Jack encouragement. Or was it for the dog?

She had to haul him off with both hands on his collar, heaving like a seaman hauling a wet line. Her kimono fell away prettily from her legs, though he was in no position to genuinely appreciate it. She gave the dog a couple of slaps on his big black, cold, wet nose.

"I wouldn't have that damn dog!" he told her flatly.

"Ah. He is *puppy!* I love him."

To ease the rebuke, the animal plunged his nose into her kimono, lapping at her cunt while she backed away, glancing uncomfortably at the boy and the back of the nosing animal. She tried to push him away with one hand, then the other.

The boy thought of the doggy smell there and thought bestial thoughts about the woman and her wolfhound.

Cunthound! he thought, seeing them together.

There was an excited rapping at the door in the other room. Zizi went with the dog beside her to open it. The young Chinese girl spoke quickly. She seemed frightened.

"Ah la!" Zizi cried, glancing at Jack. She ran back and began gathering up his clothes. She handed them to him. The dog tried to play with them. She slapped him away.

"Quick! Quick!" She opened a wardrobe, tripped a catch somewhere behind the clothes and the bottom half of the closet popped open on hidden upper hinges. She held it for him to crawl inside. "You will be safe. Make no sound," she said. She shut him in the dark.

Literally, he could not see his hand before his eyes. The floor felt dusty, rough beneath his bare ass. He stifled a sneeze. He could faintly hear her talking to someone downstairs. There could be goddamn spiders, scorpions maybe, any Chinese damn thing in there. He stretched out his foot to make himself more comfortable, felt something strange and quickly withdrew it. He clutched his clothes tighter in his arms.

As his eyes became more accustomed to the dark he saw he was in a small room too low to stand in, but large enough to sleep in if there had been a mattress. He was sitting among some boxes, dusty suitcases and baskets of stuff. The basket he had touched with his foot had a wicker lid like a picnic hamper. When a quarter of an hour passed, he hauled the wicker basket near with his toes, held his clothes in his lap and withdrew the dowel that fastened the lid.

It was full of bills in bound cubes. When he carried a cube near his face, he saw it was American dollars. There were cubes of U.S. script, English pounds, Chinese gold certificates. If each bundle were only a hundred dollars, she had thousands in that basket.

A rush of larceny flashed through him. He hadn't felt the urge so strongly since he was a small boy stealing toys from Kress'. His head felt full of blood. He racked his brain for a way to take some of it. There was no way to hide a cube in his whites. He peeled off the rubber bands and began filling his pockets with the flattened bills. The more he was able to get in, the more he felt it necessary to take. He tore loose a place along the hem of his jumper and began working the hole with his fingers until he could shove bills folded lengthwise into the opening, working against the fear the door might be opened on him at any moment, listening intently for the sound of footfalls. Sweat dripped from his face; he wiped it with the back of his sweaty arm. He got one bundle of bills stashed and opened a second. He flattened a quarter inch of bills into his shoes. He thought a moment he was making a mistake. He should have taken nothing, but come back with some-one and robbed her. But it would have taken a gun to get around that dog, he reasoned, searching for somewhere to hide the rest of the second cube. He put some in his sock, then put his sock neatly inside his shoe. He wondered if he might crinkle. But the bills felt limp from the humidity, and he guessed not.

Something crawled under his butt. He searched for it and squashed it.

He sat in there for the better part of an hour dreaming of all he could do with the loot in the basket. He considered tossing it out into the garden and trying to get it when he left. Curiously, his thought strayed to the woman and all they had done. A beautiful summer feeling came over him, and he giggled. He clapped a hand over his mouth.

She had not turned on the light in the room when she came to let him out. Instead she carried a candle in a holder.

"Is OK now."

When she snapped the door shut, he saw one of the broken rubber bands caught between the door and the floor of the closet—a tiny elastic worm, bent in a beckon-ing. His heart stopped. But she did not see it.

He stood holding his clothes, ready to get away as quickly as possible.

"They just come to see the dog. They are very shy, like peasants. They never hear such a dog. They think it is lion." She laughed.

He could understand their mistake perfectly.

"You look like chimney cleaner," she laughed. "You take bath."

He shot a look at his watch. It was nine thirty. "I ought to be going. I gotta get back to ship."

"You have time. I give you bath." She moved to take his clothes.

He quickly went and stowed them neatly beside a chair on top of his shoes, his cap mounting stern lookout on top of the bundle.

She clucked and cooed him into a bubble bath, pretending he had lost use of his hands. Then she tucked up her hair once more and climbed in with him. The bathroom was nice, with old-fashioned fixtures, a chain-pull toilet tank. The tub was big enough for two or for one to lie full out. He stood in the tub, and she washed him vigorously.

In turn he washed her, sluicing the airy froth from her glistening hips and legs with his hands, seeing the flesh compress under his touch. When she turned, her dark muff was covered with a sudsy beard. He kissed her there, carrying away a mustache and a goatee of bubbles which made her laugh.

They dried each other. She gave him a navy blue Japanese kimono with stylized flowers—rosettes—on the shoulders and back. It was very handsome. It felt wonderful.

"Ah, but it is you!" she cried stepping back to admire him. "C'est joli, Shack."

He lifted his arms to wave the loose sleeves. It was of dull, lined silk, heavy, yet sleek against his skin.

"I make you present. Yes, for you. You keep," she said.

"Really?" He flew around in place. "Hey! Thanks, Zizi."

Gentle laughter came from her. "I like you, Shack." The silk of their kimonos slithered together as they embraced.

But it was getting late. He picked up his watch and strapped it on.

"I gotta hurry."

"But you cannot, darling."

"What?"

"Is not possible."

"What do you mean?"

"You cannot leave this house when the soldiers are outside . . . do you think?"

At the window he looked out again. The men were beginning to settle down for the night, camping in the street.

"When they come, they always do that," she said beside him. "They do not bother. They just stay. One or two days. Then they leave."

A few had gone off somewhere, about half. The others remained, standing guard over their gear. It was a platoon, perhaps forty men. It was too dark to determine the kind of weapons they carried, but unlike the mustard-colored army, rifles in their hands did not seem incidental. Their uniforms were dark, and they wore soft caps like puffy round breads with short peaks. When one lit a pipe, his face in the match's flame was high-cheekboned and not young. There was a faded red star on the front of his muffin cap. The pipe was short with no more than a two-inch stem, which could be easily carried in a pocket. He shielded the bowl in his hands when he smoked.

"You must stay. There is nothing to do." She went to the bed and straightened it, plumped it with her hand. "We sleep, yes?"

"My ship's leaving!" he exclaimed.

The *Retreat* was slowly moving out toward the open sea. All its lights were ablaze.

"How can it just leave me?" he asked. He still had almost an hour before his liberty was officially up.

She came to the window and shrugged against him. "Maybe then you stay with me forever." She was not smiling. It sounded rather sad. When she sensed his recoil at the idea, she snorted, "You think that would be so bad?"

"No. I just. . . . Well, there goes my goddamned ship!"

She shrugged again and laughed. "So, fook them." Her using the word was so surprising he looked at her closely. The way she said it sounded like "fook zem." "Yes, maybe you be useful to me. You are not stupid. You are not genius either," she had to add lest he feel proud. "You are young. I teach you like puppy. Many things."

Thinking of what Ajax's duties might be, he said, "Everyone said my calling was for pan boy in a whorehouse."

She slapped his arm hard. "Not whorehouse! I run only nice place. You think I am *whore?* *No!* I was prostitute. I take money for to live. I take money from you. I don't need your money. I take for a lesson to you. I take for the joke. I give you kimono worth much more than one hundred dollars. I give you Japanese colonel's kimono. He never come for it when it is the last days of Shanghai. Maybe he is dead or prisoner now. He was good man. Very honorable. Many times a hero. I give you with my memories. I like you. You call me whore!"

He protested he did not mean it like that, that he was just making a joke.

"I don't like your joke."

But she let him come to bed.

"I guess when the people in the street go, I'll just turn myself into the Marine SP's and tell them what happened." He could see *that.* "Anyway, they can't eat me?"

"What you say?"

"Said they can kill me but they can't eat me."

"They don't kill you." She was certain. When she felt him become aroused again against her body, she said, "But I eat you. I eat you all up."

He wanted to fuck her.

"No, Shack. I don't like so much. I like use my mouse. You see. You let me. You just relax. That's good boy, ummm. . . ."

She used her "mouse."

She ought to have that patented, he thought somewhere along the way. He fingerfucked her to have some contact with her sex. She could have well lived without the pleasure. *Maybe she only likes fucking that goddamn dog*, he thought.

Whatever her real pleasure was, it somehow made robbing her all right.

Full of a good late breakfast of eggs and sweet rice cakes, with his rolled towel and a parcel containing his kimono under his arm he stepped out of the house. The money he had in his shoes he had stuck in the towel with his swimming trunks when she had not been looking. When he had awakened around nine, the rebels who had

411

been camped in the street had gone. There was very little litter where they had been. There was a darkened place on the street where they had built a fire to heat water for tea. A red star from one of their caps curled like a tiny starfish on the pavement. He bent and picked it up for a souvenir. Maybe he could offer it in evidence when he stood trial or whatever punishment might befall him. He did not see how they could do a hell of a lot. After all, his ship had left him. He turned at the end of the street to look up at her window, but she was not there. He tried to imagine her anger when she discovered he had taken some of her money. He had been tempted at the last minute to tell her and give back the dough.

Then he decided, *Fuck her. Start getting sentimental about people like her and there is no end to it.* He could wind up some tapped-out old Asiatic rumdum, shuffling along the back streets of that godforsaken land. But he would never forget her. *No one's perfect*, he decided.

And for all her being so insulted about the hundred he had given her under the impression she was a whore, she never did insist he take it back.

The line for Captain's Mast shuffled apprehensively forward in the passageway above the ladder down to the mess. When one came up the others asked against their own fears, "What did you get?" "How is he?"

Cheatham had a hair in his ass, was the consensus. Not at all himself. Ordinarily, Lieutenant Cheatham would have been lenient.

Jack had changed his plea half a dozen times in the passageway as he approached the down ladder. If he pleaded "not guilty," he would have to request a court-martial. That was no good. "Guilty as charged, no excuse" was the preferred response. But he did not *feel* guilty.

Standing before the table, he replied to the officer's question, "Guilty as charged, with excuse."

Lieutenant Cheatham looked up for the first time. "What is your excuse?" he sighed wearily.

"Sir, I was kept from returning to my ship by rebel soldiers in the street outside where I was."

Lieutenant Cheatham's neck seemed to stretch several inches from his collar. There had been a farewell party for Captain Hatten, the chief surgeon, the night before.

All the officers and nurses were hung over, still in quarters or, if abroad, grouchy as hell. They said Lieutenant Cheatham had thrown Lieutenant Fetterman out of the liberty launch into the Whangpoo, where they had been tied up since returning to Shanghai from Tsingtao. His swim necessitated his undergoing immediate supplementary inoculations against all the diseases of the Orient. The river was considered so deadly the sailors had come to shy from a single drop of it as if it were acid.

"I was in this house where there was a woman—a Dutch-Jewish woman . . . with a great big white Irish wolfhound. Out on the road from Tsingtao toward the hills. And the dog began barking. When we looked out there were these rebel troops camping in the street. So, she put me in a little trapdoor in her closet—"

Lieutenant Cheatham was holding his head up with his left hand, massaging his temples, nodding positively in a funny idle way.

"Then— Oh, before that, I saw the ship pulling out an hour before my liberty was up. I didn't hear the sound truck going around telling everyone to report back to their ships, see . . . sir?

So the lady said I couldn't go out. While I was in the trapdoor, they had come to the door to see what kind of dog was barking like that. He made a hell of a noise. *Woof! Woof!*" Jack approximated the wolfhound's roar.

Cheatham jumped clear of his chair. He blinked water from his eyes.

"Goddamn, son, don't bark!" he breathed. "You won't do that again, will you?"

"No, sir."

Cheatham looked down the table at the busy scribe. "You got all that?"

"Yes, sir."

"The captain goes over every word of this, you know?" he asked the young sailor. "He *loves* reading Captain's Mast proceedings."

"Anyway, sir—"

"No more barking or anything?"

"No, sir."

He lowered his eyes behind his hand and waved the boy onward.

"So, I stayed there with Zizi—"

413

Cheatham jerked erect again. "You can't put a name like that in the report!" he insisted.

"That was her name, sir," Jack insisted.

"Zizi . . ." Cheatham muttered, waving the boy on again with a gesture of "what-can-it-matter-now."

"So she said I should stay. She talked about my staying with her and helping her business. Deserting, sir. But I told her I wanted to get back to my ship. Then the next morning they were gone."

"Who was?" Cheatham asked sharply.

"The Chinese rebels, sir."

He nodded at that. Yes.

"And she fixed me a little breakfast and I left. She gave me a kimono that belonged to a Jap colonel. I could go get it, if you wanted it for evidence."

"No." Cheatham cleared his throat. "No. . . . Ah, this, uh, woman, she wasn't a prostitute, was she?"

"No, sir!"

Cheatham shook his head as if he had known that and seemed to wipe cobwebs from between him and the boy. "Of course not," he said.

"She was a madam."

"Oh! All the world of difference!"

"Yes, sir. And the place wasn't off limits or nothin. No sign anywhere. Cause only officers usually go there—"

"Strike that!" Cheatham ordered the scribe, leaning to make sure the offending words were crossed out.

"But no one goes there much now, see, sir, because the rebels keep coming down and camping in the street. They don't bother anybody, just camp and make some propaganda, Zizi said. But I didn't think it would be good to try to go through them. They were right there in front, sir. Then the ship had pulled out. . . ."

"That's it?"

"Uh . . . yes, sir—Oh! Then I turned myself into the Marine SP's, and when the ship came back, they escorted me to the quarterdeck."

"When you, uh, turned yourself into the Marine SP's did you tell them what you have told me?"

"Yes, sir. But all the guy wrote on the paper was 'subject says he fell asleep in a cathouse' . . . sir."

"That we can verify." Cheatham looked as if he had found the solution. He turned to the scribe. "Show the

414

man's excuse was heard and recorded and not accepted." Without looking up at Jack, he added, "Ten dollars to be deducted for three consecutive pay days, and thirty days' restriction to ship."

Jack took a backward step, thanked him and did a smart about-face.

As he marched toward the ladder he heard Cheatham ask the scribe, "What kind of dog did he say that was?"

"Irish wolfhound, sir," the man replied softly, consulting his notes.

"Irish wolfhound," Cheatham said wondrously as the boy began mounting the ladder.

The tip of Jack's bulb-snatching pole peeking knee-high around the edge of the hatch into nurses' quarters gave Lieutenant Wentz a start. She had not been completely sober for three weeks, since the night of the chief surgeon's farewell party. She had not received a letter and was beginning to accept the fact that she would never hear from him again. He had a beautiful wife and lovely children in South Carolina. In a drawer in the bureau in her cabin there was half of a fifth of Black & White, and she felt a need to go open the drawer. The chief nurse had put her more or less in permanent charge of quarters, beginning that morning when the new chief surgeon had complained about her in surgery. The chief nurse had been kind, but had suggested she better get hold of herself.

"Muskrat!" she exclaimed with relief when his face beneath his cocky white cap poked around the hatch opening.

Her reaction startled him. "Ma'am?"

"Aren't you supposed to call out or something before you come in here?" she asked angrily. "What *is* that?"

"My bulb snatcher, ma'am. For reaching overhead." He gave her a little demonstration.

"It looks absolutely obscene."

"Ma'am?" He regarded the pole. What else could it be? Lieutenant Wentz seemed funny. Everyone was getting funny. He wondered if he was getting funny too. He supposed he was.

"Aren't you supposed to give vocal warning before entering here?" she demanded again.

"Well, yes, ma'am. I did that for a long time." He lowered his voice almost to a whisper. "But the night duty nurses began complaining I was waking them up."

"Oh ... uh...." She looked helpless and began casting around at the overhead lights. She had never been in charge of quarters before. He had been surprised to find her there. When she looked up, the movement of her large breasts tugged her shirt a bit from the waistband of her skirt.

"I just go around and see if any bulbs are out," he explained helpfully.

"Do I go around with you?" she asked, wondering what was proper. No other men invaded the quarters regularly.

"You can if you want to, ma'am, but I know my way."

"Oh? You do?"

He looked at her more closely. She did not seem at all like herself. Forgetful or something. He wasn't sure. She sort of weaved when she walked too, as if aware of every slight movement of the ship tied up in the river. He followed her nice high rump as she tapped on closed doors and called out, "Man on the floor," before opening them so that he could flick the switch and see whether the overheads were working. He did not tell her that the charge of quarters usually asked for extra light bulbs and changed them herself.

When they had returned to where they had started, Lieutenant Wentz suddenly remembered, "Hey! The light over my bunk has been burned out for a week!" She held him personally responsible. "And I can't get the bulb out to change it. It's stuck or something."

"Let's have a look at it," he said professionally.

"In here."

Her cabin was the nearest one to the wardroom. She shared it with another surgery nurse. Two wide bunks fastened permanently to the bulkhead, upper and lower, with real inner-spring mattresses and light-blue coverlets over the blankets. Two bureaus side by side, a desk, a straight chair at the desk and a leatherette easy chair, and through a curtain a shower and toilet.

The boy thought the Navy would have been fine if he could live like that. Chiefs lived pretty good, but officers really had it made. Their quarters were almost like a hotel.

He could not budge the defective light bulb from its

socket. "I'll have to sit on the bunk, ma'am," he apologized.

She impatiently indicated that it was all right.

"Sometimes when they blow, they swell or sort of solder theirselves in the socket," he explained. "Good thing you didn't try too hard to take it out. That's how people cut their fingers."

"Um." She kept moving her eyes toward the top drawer of her bureau.

"Could I have that trash basket, please, ma'am? That way I won't get glass on the bunk."

"What? Oh! Yes, certainly," she said as if pulled back from a distant thought.

Carefully holding the basket beneath the bulb, he shattered the glass with a rap of his fuse pullers. With the pullers jammed inside the bulb's brass base he tried to use the leverage of the tool to twist it from the socket, but succeeded only in breaking off the glass stalk of the filament. It was soldered.

He replaced the fuse pullers in his holster and took out a pair of insulated long-nose pliers.

"It's really in there," he explained. "Going to take a minute or two."

While he worked, she got a tumbler from the washbasin and stood facing the open drawer of her bureau to pour herself a drink without taking the bottle from the drawer. Then she turned around suddenly and said, "Can I offer you a little drink, Muskrat?" as if she were addressing an equal.

"Uh, no, thanks, ma'am. Little early for me."

She smiled in that wry way she had and sipped from the glass. She cleared her throat. "How old are you, Muskrat?"

"Uh, almost eighteen, ma'am," he said.

"Like hell," she said, leaning back against the bureau and crossing her ankles.

"Ma'am?"

"I won't tell if you won't." She lifted the glass and dipped her head in its direction.

"I'll be sixteen the twenty-fourth of this month."

"You will! Hank's birthday." She caught herself. "Er, uh, I know someone whose birthday is the twenty-second."

It no longer seemed such a joyous recollection. She took another sip.

He had bent down the lips of the bulb base and was trying to break it loose, both bending and twisting. He had begun to sweat. Unless the individual compartments were left open, not much air conditioning reached them.

"Sixteen," she said. "And you are an old-timer already, aren't you?"

"Ma'am?"

"I mean, it seems like you and me are old-timers on here now. Everyone's going home."

"Yes, ma'am. I don't hardly recognize anyone anymore."

Egan had gone. There was a new chief electrician, young and busy, who kept everyone scurrying around like cats covering shit, full of ideas and all eyes. He wanted everything inventoried and painted. Jack had even had to paint the deck in the electric shop. Keating and Huffman were going home. There were a whole gang of new guys—all third class electrician's mates, right out of electricians' school with brilliant new ratings on their sleeves. Keating and Huffman resented their getting third class before they'd even been on a ship. On-the-job training was finished. It was the *new* Navy. No more old draftees like Egan and Pop Carter, who was about forty-five and a third class carpenter. Farmer Brown had been gotten rid of, some said to retirement. When he had gone, the boy strangely missed the evilly leering encounters in passageways. He had proved quite harmless after all, and he and the boy had developed a bantering fondness for each other. *"I'll blow you, you old bastard,"* the boy would promise as wickedly as the Farmer himself. *"I'll blow the back of your ugly neck while I fuck you in your rusty ass!" "Promises, lad, promises. That's all you give me."*

"Yeow. I guess we are sort of old-timers, ma'am." He smiled.

He got the bulb base out, dropped it in the can and wiped his face on his sleeve.

"Hot," Lieutenant Wentz said and flapped her collar a little in sympathy.

"Yes, ma'am." He peered into the socket. It was corroded, but not too bad. With an insulated screwdriver he reached inside and scraped at it to get at bright metal. He

418

decided she did not read much in bed. The bulb probably had been in there for years. He touched the contact in the base of the socket and leaned the screwdriver against the brass lip. A bright spurt of sparks made both Lieutenant Wentz and himself jump. It was live.

He took a fresh bulb from his box and tried to screw it into the socket. He tried another. It too would not go. Maybe the first thread was damaged. Sometimes he had to really force a bulb into a socket. This one would not go.

He looked up at the nurse who seemed far away again, staring blankly past him.

"Would you have a little Vaseline, ma'am?"

"What?" she asked as if she had not heard right.

"Some Vaseline. The bulb won't seem to go. Sometimes if you put a little Vaseline on it, you can get it started."

"You need some Vaseline?" she asked incredibly, her eyes crinkling up to laugh. The drink was shaking in her hand.

"Yes, ma'am, if you have some—" Suddenly the implications of his request hit him, and he blushed.

She said, "I think I have some." She turned her back and opened the drawer. He could see her shoulders shaking with controlled laughter. Then she looked up at him in the mirror above the bureau and burst out as if spewing water. "Here!" She giggled, handing him a Kleenex upon which she had squeezed some petroleum jelly from a tube. Their fingers touched when he took the tissue, and he blushed even more. "Muskrat, you are red as a beet!" She laughed.

"It works!" he insisted.

"On light bulbs?!"

"Yes, ma'am. You try it."

"Oh, I *will!*" She was bending over to watch the operation, holding her stomach with both arms crossed to contain her mirth. Her face was poked interestedly under the upper bunk. The faint odor of her breath, of booze, and her lemonly perfume touched his face. The whites of her eyes looked faintly blue, but were shot through with tiny red veins.

He pushed and cursed the damn bulb silently, sweating. He *had* to make it go now. Finally, he felt the first thread take hold. Gently, without any lessening of inward pressure he got the bulb engaged. He tightened it until he felt it against the contact. He gave it just a touch more, flicked the switch, and it lit.

"A masterful performance, Muskrat," she congratulated him.

He stood near her and wiped his face with his sleeve.

"Just a little Vaseline, ma'am." He grinned.

She was wryly nodding, yes. She laughed. "You're precious!" Then she quickly leaned forward and kissed his lips. He thought he heard her say, "I love you." He must have pulled back by reflex or blinked. When he looked again, there were tears in her eyes and she looked shocked and frightened by what she had done.

"Ma'am?"

"No. Forgive me," she stammered, staring at him with a wildly frightened, pained look.

"Are you all right, ma'am?"

She shook her head to clear it. "Yes. Yes." She wiped the corners of her eyes, touched the sides of her hair with her fingertips. "Just lost my head there for a second, Muskrat. Women are crazy, sometimes, you know. And in spite of the Navy, we *are* still women."

"Sure." He looked at the collar of her shirt, at the rise and fall of her bosom, thought for a moment what would happen if he just grabbed her and tried to pull her on to that bunk. The thought made him even dizzier.

She had control of herself now. "Well?"

"What, ma'am?" Behind her on her bureau he saw a beautiful jade rosary with a gold cross like ones he had seen in town. He knew it had been a good-bye present from the surgeon. Before, she'd had an old battered wooden one.

She inclined her head toward the door, indicating that they should step outside.

From the wardrobe table she lifted a large bowl of fresh fruit holding it before her with both hands. "Can't I give you some?" she said in a way that made him unsure the words might not have another meaning, but her eyes above the bowl were not teasing. He looked at the fruit. "Don't you see something you would like?" she asked. Again there was that small hit at the base of his skull.

"Ah, thanks, ma'am." He took an orange to be polite, though they got the same damn ones in their mess.

Stepping into the passage, he felt drunk. The passageway bent and veered. Then he realized that the question in her eyes had only to do with whether he would keep his mouth shut. He was sorry she felt so concerned. She should have known he would never breathe a word.

The ship moved out of the river into its old place at the jetty. The boy felt again the depression of being tied to China. He was breaking in a new projectionist to take Keating's place, a blond kid from Ohio named Englander, fresh from electricians' school, and already sporting a third class rating. The thing about him that vexed Jack most was the way he kept referring to anyone who had been on the ship longer than himself as "you old guys."

All the new men were Regular Navy, enlisted for four years with supposed guarantees that made them act as if everyone else were simply a supernumerary.

Jack had to sneak all his pornography out of the projection booth; certain Englander would report him if he found it or at least begin spreading ugly rumors. He dropped it over the side at night, watching the basis of several pleasant hours sink among the ugly river scavenger fish.

He was still sweating out the Tsingtao trip when he hadn't used anything, checking every morning for a drip, searching himself for the first sign of a chancre. If he *was* going to get something, it should have shown up by now. But he kept checking.

"If I ever get the clap," he confided in Gorilla, "I think I'd just re-up. I know I would if I got the syph." There was still debate among the men whether syphilis was ever really cured.

"Can't you see Muskrat?" Englander piped. "Thirty years in the Navy and *still* only a fireman ace!" He got a small laugh.

Gorilla stuck a finger in the wag's breastbone. "Listen, boot, that third class of yours don't mean shit with us. And only we who love him call him Muskrat. You call him Andersen."

All these new guys treat us like we have some kind of terrible infection, the boy thought. Then he remembered that was how he, Gorilla and Al had felt about the "old guys" when they had come aboard.

He went topside, pleased to think it was not such a

421

"new" Navy after all. *Maybe they'll loosen up later,* he told himself. Still there was something basically different about these new men from what they had been, even in the beginning.

He leaned on the rail to puzzle it out. *They all act like kids who don't know what being poor is! They got all the answers, and we don't even know the questions.* That was it. They seemed born with some asshole sense of superiority. *They see the Navy as a career, a job, not a means for getting away. They never talked about the war.* They almost seemed to make fun of or patronize the men who had actually been in action. Jack had never seen kids of seventeen and eighteen so goddamned serious, so smug. It was as if there were a law just for them that guaranteed them a good place and plenty to eat. Nor had he seen any so eager to squat and shit at the first suggestion of authority. *Hitler Youth!* he said to himself, in surprise, remembering newsreels and films he had seen.

She-it! They can have it! he decided.

It was his birthday! He had awakened early and gone forward to sit on the hold cover on the fo'c'sle to watch dawn come up out of the Yellow Sea. Just as a glow began to appear in the east, the rim of the big rising sun not yet in view, he saw small figures climbing out from under the jetty and onto the dock. There were dozens.

He saw they were children. All kinds and sizes of boys who evidently lived under the jetty on planks laid across the crosspieces between the pilings. He had seen them a hundred times before in twos and threes and half a dozens, but there were hundreds! A small army in rags, barefoot, the littlest bareassed. At first peep of the sun they hurried away in twos and threes to beg, steal, earn a few cents. Tots toddled off hand in hand with an older boy. There were cripples minus a foot or most of a leg, going off with a stick in their armpit on their lame side. An older boy and two smaller ones were left on the jetty, presumably to stand watch over their hideout. Jack had always seen three boys there on the jetty. Now, he realized, that they took turns.

He had always thought of the children as lepers, abandoned by parents. By light this morning he saw their disfigurement and scars for what they were—rat bites. The face on the right side of one of the little fellows was open back to his molars, his nose half gone, some fingers missing. He was hideous. The eyes that looked out beneath his close crop of black hair made Jack think the lad had not often seen himself in a mirror. The eyes were soft and without regret. His wounds, old and long healed, were a mere difference between him and his fellows.

A community of children whose every breath was to stay alive. He had rarely seen them playing, and then no real game. He had never heard them laughing. Nor did they cry except when hurt. When they fought, it was quickly settled by the older ones. He realized he had seen them a lot, but he had never really looked. None of them were older than Jack. He had never seen an obvious leader.

On the dock the tallest boy picked strands of jute from a large piece of ship's fender while the little ones, sitting facing him, solemnly wound the strands into balls as if there were no other measure of time. They were as serious of mind as the new men aboard the ship, but of a different order and utterly foreign tempo.

Watching them, Jack felt he had been there and was somehow more of them, whose language he did not understand, than he was of the new men aboard whom he understood even less, though he recognized every word. A question of meanings.

There was no sentimentality involved. Sympathy and charity had nothing to do with those on the jetty. *He* wouldn't have touched one of those rat-bitten little kids with a stick.

No. He was alone. What he had been nominally a part of for a while was coming apart. He had lived in the backwash of the big war and having missed the real thing was left feeling he had been but an inconsequential stopgap. Between what? For what purpose? He had no notion.

Suddenly he was ready to go home. To go back, more precisely, get a room of his own, return to school to gain the credentials that he thought were the only thing separating him from a position equivalent to an officer's. Dummies who knew algebra could command ships. He would study goddamned algebra. If there was another war against Russia, he wanted to be ready. *If you had been an Oberleutnant in even the Luftwaffe, it wouldn't have been bad while it lasted,* was his reasoning.

When he left the deck, he stopped in front of the bulletin board to check his points toward going home and began watching for *his* replacement.

Lieutenant Wentz began to tear long slivers of skin from her face, arms and legs sometime before dawn. Lieutenant Martin, who shared the cabin with her, said she felt the movement for quite a while from the lower bunk but that her roommate had been very upset and restless lately and had been drinking a lot, so she thought little about it. She had dozed off, then awoke again and looked down to see Lieutenant Wentz, her face torn to ribbons, her arms lacerated with scratches from her shoulders to the bleeding backs of her hands, lying staring fixedly overhead, her pajama bottoms off, scoring her thighs with her nails. When she spoke to her she did not answer or seem to hear.

The word went through the ship before the end of breakfast:

"Lieutenant Wentz went nuts last night."

"Tried to kill herself."

"She's pregnant, that's why she wanted to die."

"She had the DT's."

"She's full of the syph."

"Them nurses are all a bunch of whores or dykes. I wouldn't fuck one if I had the chance."

"You could see she was on the verge."

"Say she tore her cunt wide open."

"They crazy thing is, she would have gone home in a couple of weeks."

Jack pushed the bell outside the locked ward. The blank California face of one of the Muscle Beach boys who worked in there appeared in the strong-glass port in the door.

"Yes?" he said.

"Electrician. Tracing a short. The cable runs through here."

"Well . . . no one's admitted without authorization."

"Call the OD," Jack snapped.

In about ten minutes the lawnhead came back and opened the door. Tan, sun-lotioned muscles bulged from a white T-shirt two sizes too small for him. His white trousers fit like paint. Yet he swung his muscular ass when he walked and had pretty ways with his silly, useless hands. A blond crew cut like a brush had been mowed level as a putting green. He looked born of color advertisements. Anyway he posed he appeared one-dimensional.

"I don't know what you're looking for." He rolled his small blue eyes helplessly.

"I'll find it."

Jack had never been in there. It was a long room with four padded cells along the inside wall. Three stood open. Walls, floor and overheads were covered with thick quilted white canvas padding not unlike gymnasium mats. There was a desk for the keeper on which a paperback mystery was opened, text down. It was *The Black Dahlia Murders*. Jack had read it. It was about a nut in California, a sailor, who mutilated women, bit them in fits of sexual cannibalism, cut them up horribly. When he had read it, it had excited him. Now he resented its being there and the muscle-man's reading it.

He pretended to follow a cable along the overhead. He stuck the probes of his voltmeter in a live outlet so the meathead who was hovering near could see the little arrow jump in its slot. He shook his head in feigned puzzlement and sucked his teeth loudly.

"Hmmm," he said.

Turning, he walked back along the padded cells. In the second from the door he saw, through the narrow window, Lieutenant Wentz in a corner in a straitjacket. She was curled like a cat, or more like an old boobatch sleeping in a skid row doorway. Beneath the legs of the hospital pajamas her bare feet were crossed one upon the other as if they were cold. Her red polished toenails were the only points of color in the stark padded room. They were very vivid. She looked so harmless. Her short dark hair was tousled. He could only see one closed eye and a little of her left cheek. They had painted her wounds with Mercurochrome.

"If you are finished, you better go," the orderly said behind him.

"Yeow. Sure. She going to be all right?"

"Her?" He shrugged and made a face. He did not give a damn. "What business is *that* of yours?" he asked suspiciously.

"I just wondered. She's a good person."

"Good-bye." He shut the door and locked it.

He saw her once more being taken off the *Retreat* and helped into a military ambulance on the jetty by a husky nurse, the chaplain and one of the boys from the locked ward. The chaplain did not get into the ambulance with her. Though it was summer, she had her blue cape over her shoulders. It was fastened at the collar. Her white dress cap had been set upon her head. Beneath the cape, her hands were in restraints. In her fingers she ran her jade rosary. Her lips were moving in silent prayer.

Jack prayed she would look up—just once—but she didn't.

Everyone had gone. Only Al and Gorilla were left, and all they did anymore was make plans for the air-conditioning business they were going to open when they got home. They liked to huddle together and make notes as if their plans were a big secret which he was busting his butt to steal.

He supposed of all the men he had gone through boot camp with, he was the only one who hadn't risen a single notch in the better part of two years. Even in that he no longer took any pride.

PART THREE

26

EACH morning he expected someone to summon him to explain a terrible mistake had been made. The summoner would be very angry. *For, God! But life had become good,* he thought cautiously, wary of jinxing it, sticking the '36 red Ford roadster between a metallic blue '28 coupe and a little ice-box white Crosley.

He snatched his books off the adjacent seat. The hollows in the cracked, worn leather for a moment made him think of Sharon.

He saw others beginning to hurry and ran toward his seven forty class. He passed two freshmen in black and yellow beanies with the casual sense of superiority of a veteran exempt from that shit.

He was only a provisional freshman, though, taking high school French and math to come up to the university's standard. When he had told the Veterans Administration official he wanted to return to school, he was given a general educational development test to determine placement. It seemed they did not want anyone who had been tattooed going back to ninth grade. To his great surprise he was issued the equivalency of a high school diploma. With that in hand he went out on the hill to the university and took another battery of tests, after which he was offered enrollment as a provisional freshman, required to take a language and math for no credit. Still, he was sixteen years old and already in college, and in his family no one else had even graduated from high school.

When he turned the corner, he looked back and saw the parking lot of new gravel and student cars already shimmering in a heat sea. He wished he'd had time to put the top up on the car. The seats would blister his ass later.

He passed into the shade along one of the walks on the original part of campus. A black custodian was mowing the lawn with a power mower. The sweet smell of freshly

429

cut grass was also part of summer. Then he recognized the guy behind the mower.

"Hey, Ron!" he called, and faked throwing him a pass. Ron squinted and scowled at the provisional freshman in faded Navy dungarees and a sweat shirt hacked off at the sleeves worn, for some local reason, inside out. He made no move to snag the imaginary ball.

"Hey, man," Ron said tentatively. "What you doin here?"

"Goin to college, Ron."

"No shit? Who *you* foolin?"

Jack shrugged. "They didn't want me larkin about with that high school stuff, I guess. Anyway. Here I am. I gotta cut."

"You ain't goin to play football er anything here?"

"Naw. Gotta work."

"Glad to hear *that*. Maybe they have a good team then."

As Jack dashed on, he heard Ron Reed yell, "I'll be savin one of these mowers and suits for yuh, when they catch you up, man." And Jack felt frightened. The heat seemed suddenly intolerable. Beneath the sweat shirt his body was wet.

He slid into his seat just as the bell rang its final ding.

M. (Pére) Noel looked more like an old turtle than Santa Claus. Totally bald, his dome, dotted with liver spots and moles, was the color of Jack's old tan leather car seats. A long, fleshy wattle depended from the end of his chin to be gathered in wrinkles and folds by his collar. In the classroom he had hung the jacket of his slate-colored and shiny suit on the back of the chair in deference to the weather, exposing the elastic sleeve garters that kept his cuffs from falling over his spotted bookman's hands. His trousers were held up by an ancient belt about as wide and supple as an old, well-oiled gunsling. When he spoke, his head seemed to rise out of the folds of flesh at his collar just like an old turtle's. *Monsieur* Noel had been called out of retirement to tutor veterans taking the makeup courses. He hadn't been to France in thirty-five years, but he could recall the places as if it were yesterday. The boys encouraged his recollections to forestall the lessons, only to learn that no matter how long he reminisced, there was the same amount of work to be covered.

If the class had not been all vets, most as ignorant of the parts of speech as himself, Jack did not think he could have done it. The embarrassment would have been too great. *Voulez-vous couché avec moi?* After which the ability to count to ten might be of some use, was *his* thinking.

He'd asked to study Chinese against the time he might become one of those soldiers of fortune, but the school did not have such a course. He had been under the impression a university knew everything. A woman who appeared to sweat some dewy skin moistener had peered over the shelf of her lethal-looking, small, pointy boobs and convinced him, "French *is* the international language," in a way that intimated its mastery was the *only* thing standing between them and a very nice time.

Most of the guys were very serious, working hard as hell to get through their studies as quickly as possible and get on with their lives. Many were married, living in apartments or a Quonset hut village nearby. It was a community campus with a commuting student body except for those members of sororities and fraternities who had a row of nice houses along the eastern edge of the campus.

After class Jack wandered over to the grass above the stadium to have a smoke and watch the ROTC drills. When he was a junior, he could take the last two years of ROTC and graduate with a reserve commission as a second lieutenant.

Watching the meatheads hut-two-three-fouring around the gridiron made the back of his throat close in distaste, but he thought he would probably do it. A commission would always be a good thing to have. It looked as if the country would need an army and navy forever.

He sat on the grass, leaning forward to rest his forearms on his knees, squinting into the sun, smoking.

"What are you doing here?" a pretty brown-haired girl stepped into his sight line and challenged.

He saw a crisp, tight chino skirt above saddle shoes, rolled athletic socks and very nicely tanned calves. When he looked up, it was Jeanne Harris who had been a couple years ahead of him when he had gone away. Now he had caught up. She had been the keenest East High cheerleader, as well as a lettered diver, tumbler and golfer. Her short hair was streaked from sun and pool.

431

"Havin a smoke." He made as if to offer her his pack.

"No. I mean are you *enrolled?*"

"Yeow."

"I mean, *how?*"

He shrugged. She seemed flushed. Even rather angry.

"Took a couple of tests."

She had to swallow twice to accept this example of democracy in action. "I don't believe it," she muttered, rolling her big brown eyes.

"Oh, I've changed," he assured her. "Regular citizen now. Up, up and away." He zoomed his planed right hand into the wild blue yonder. "Why don't you have a beer with me this afternoon and see?"

"No! ... I mean, I can't. I'm pinned to Jerry Scardino. You know the new quarterback who transfered from Pittsburgh?"

He did not know the fellow. But she was still the same old Jeanne Jockstrap.

"I'm pledging Tri Delt," she announced as if that explained everything. He glanced at her left tit where pledge pin clung just above the precipice next to another more masculine tiny shield. He saw a swarthy Italian hand squeezing those nice knockers and wondered if Jeanne fucked. She had gone steady with a guard in high school who everyone said was getting into her, but none of his crowd was ever close enough to hers to know for sure.

She looked at her watch. "I gotta scoot. You have a nine forty?"

"English lit." He flipped his cigarette through the chain-wire fence and got up, gathering his books. Jeanne was a short, compact girl without being either muscular or chunky. He saw her measure his chest and shoulders approvingly. He had grown a lot since she had last seen him.

"Why don't you go out for football?"

Did he detect some personal fantasy in her suggestion. She was always a prickteaser. Now she stood so closely the pert tips of tits radiated warm spots on his chest. She smiled.

"I might," he said. "I've been thinking about it."

"Do!" she encouraged. "Hey, I'll see you."

"Right."

She scooted off, her cute little ass flipping away beneath the tight chino cloth.

Then he felt disgusted with himself for fawning after her, girls like her. It was a waste of time. He always felt somehow diminished after such an encounter.

Football. She-it! The school didn't have any black guys on their team. Going up to Pittsburgh to recruit Italians when the unofficial best halfback in the state, Ron Reed, was pushing a fuckin lawn mower around the yard. *Tri Delt. Scooter-roonie! She-it! What the hell did all of that have to do with what he had seen in the Pacific and China?* he would have just liked to know.

He had tried to pose the question in geology, first rock out of the box, and was advised it was really not in the field. Actually what he had questioned was the existence of God from a geological point of view. In English lit he wondered at the validity of Elizabeth Barrett Browning's romantic pastoral vision regarding a milkmaid and a farm boy, incurring the undiminishing wrath of the gnome with a withered right arm who taught the class and who seemed to resent the boy's experience as much as his question. From Jack's point of view, if that milkmaid didn't have angry red bumps on her prat, he was a monkey's uncle.

Well, love is blind and poets are forever, he wrote in lieu of subsequent notes on the head of a page in his notebook, knowing no more of what he truly meant than Mrs. Browning knew of country folk.

In recent U.S. history, he took a worm's-eye view. The teacher was icily droll, and when he spoke of the "muckrakers," it was with tones so pejorative that it was a week before Jack figured out that for his money they were heroes. When they got to the IWW and Jack announced he'd had an uncle shot in Tennessee by strikebreakers, the teacher looked at him as if he had crawled from under a rock. If kids like Jack were breaking into college, the lecturer's days were truly numbered.

Only in comparative religions did he feel at home. Dr. Hearn had been in China! He had taught at Soochow U. The son of missionaries, he had lived through the battles of the warlords and those of the Kuomintang and rebels from the twenties until the Japs invaded the country. Nominally a Methodist, he accepted Jack's avowed atheism with a genuinely warm smile and said, "Ah, but then you are a Hindu," when the boy had defined what he meant, granting that something cannot within the law of contingency come from nothing, but that the something everything came from did not reasonably seem to him to have ears, brains or actually give one good goddamn about anything within *our* lights. "That is a rough approximation of the Hindu concept of Brahma," Mr. Hearn explained. "They conceive of Brahma like the sea, all temporal time likened to but a single drop from a single wave and the duration it takes to break loose and return to the sea. If you tell a Brahmanist that you are an Atheist, a Baptist, a Catholic, or whatever, he will smile and tell you, 'Ah, yes. You are a Hindu.'"

Jack often stayed after class—it was his last of the day—and talked to Dr. Hearn. They made word equations, one writing the numerator and the other writing the denominator:

$$\frac{Life}{Death} + \frac{Time}{Eternity} + \frac{Experience}{Unconsciousness} + \frac{Good}{Evil} + \frac{Magnanimity}{Selfishness}$$

$$+ \frac{Love}{Hate} + \frac{Hope}{Despair} + \frac{Confidence}{Dependence} + \frac{Self}{Selfless} + \frac{Man}{Devil}$$

$$+ \frac{Superman}{God} + \frac{Knowledge}{Belief} = ?$$

They would cover the blackboard with such words. Jack was never certain what they were trying to accomplish, but the process made him feel that wisdom was not wholly beyond his grasp.

For his class project he decided to draw and mount a series of irreligious cartoons. The focal effort was a Sunday school rendering of the crosses on the hill to which Coca-Cola, Orange-Crush and beer signs had been tacked, the ground all around littered with bottles, Dixie cups, tobacco and hot-dog butts. It was not funny, but in color he was rather proud of it.

He lit another cigarette as he made his way to the parking lot. When he came home and found Sharon had begun to smoke in spite of her faith that it was a ticket to eternal damnation, he quickly learned to inhale, eager to explore the farthest extent of her fall from grace. It was not as deep as he had hoped. She had won the high school

"Sweater Girl" title, but when she had given him a copy of the winning photograph, she explained, "I looked so ridiculous, I cut them off." She had cropped the picture at mid-chest.

Still she would not consent to park with him and let him fondle her winning entries, and she had learned how to kiss somewhere. She did not like his efforts to discover the precise details of her experience.

The car seat was too hot to sit on. It burned him through his dungarees. Behind the front seat he found a square throw pillow that smelled of damp which he put under him. Even then he sat forward so that his back would not touch the hot leather.

His clutch slipped. He had been fucked on the Ford. He knew buying a secondhand convertible was buying trouble. But he wanted it. It was sitting on the raised platform of a South Broadway used car lot when he'd first seen it, tilted skyward like a great red jewel.

"A real cunt wagon," the salesman had whispered confidentially in his ear. "A real gem. Belonged to a guy in service. Been up on blocks in a garage since forty-two," he lied in his yellow teeth.

Against all cautioning good sense, Jack gave him four hundred dollars cash and was handed a title that showed at least three previous owners. If it had been on blocks, it was after the mileage counter had gone as far as it would go. The car was a fire-engine red with yellow wheels and dash, and he drove it away trying to catch its reflection in the plate-glass windows of buildings he passed. In the first month he had replaced the generator, starting motor and battery, bought two recapped tires and a new thermostat. Still the thing ran hot. And now the clutch was slipping badly.

At the corner of Hillside and Central he saw Glenn waiting in his '36 black two-door at the light. They faced each other across the street. Glenn stuck his head out and yelled, "Kau-Kau Korner!"

Jack waved OK and made a right turn, and Glenn tucked in behind him. At the drive-in Jack pulled up and Glenn followed. Since his old man had died, he had really fixed up his car.

He climbed out and walked around Jack's "cuntwagon" condescendingly pursing his lips.

"The clutch slips," Jack said, dogging after the other.

Glenn nodded wisely as if that were the least of its problems. "Think you got a rod knocking too, ace. That'll be trouble," he promised without hope. The car was no threat to him. "So! You still goin to college?"

"Sure. Doin pretty good, I think."

Glenn grinned wider. "Gettin any of that college pussy?"

"Had a weed with Jeanne Harris this morning."

"Yeow? We don't see you much anymore. Me and Buck were talkin about it the other night. Sort of feel like maybe you think your shit's too hot for us or somethin. With all this college crap, you know?"

"It ain't that," Jack quickly assured him. "I gotta work like a bastard to get this stuff, man. I gotta part-time job every afternoon. You know. I meet my ass comin and goin."

"Yeow. Well, that's what I told Buck. You'd gotten serious an all. But, you know, this college shit don't mean doodley if you lose your friends."

It sounded like a warning. He was incredible. Vain as a cunt. Jack was afraid of Glenn.

"I'll be around." he promised. "Just as soon as I get this routine solved. You flunk, you know, and they'll cut off your GI Bill."

"Someone said you were in love or something." Glenn slipped in, studying Jack with his yellow cat's eyes. "Going to church and all that."

Jack blushed. "Naw! Who said that? There's just this pud I wrote to in the Navy. She was Sweater Girl last year at East. Great knockers! It's nothin serious."

"Yeow. You oughta come wolfin with me and Buck. Now that I took over the old man's laundry route. I'm meetin all these *real* women. Great gash, man. Wives. Hillcrest rich bitches, man. All kinds of stuff. Just standin on my joint." But the idea made him reflective. He turned philosophical. "Seems like them handin over their underwear, dirty sheets and stuff gives you and them, uh . . . you know . . . sorta makes, uh. . . ." He waved his hands around as if directing a crane operator.

"Creates an intimacy?" Jack posed.

"That's it! Creates an, uh, intimacy! Hey! That's good.

That's just it." He looked proud of Jack. "That college shit's all right."

He stared into the distance where the hot sky was bleached almost to white, the color of very faded dungarees. "I was goin, you know. Went back to high. Would of graduated too. But the old man had a heart attack. Was carryin a hundred-pound sack of wet wash up four flights. Just—blips! And he fell ass-over the banister all the fuckin way to the bottom."

Jack shook his head sympathetically.

Glenn waved it away. "He was dead before he hit bottom. So I took over his route. You know it ain't like bein' no fuckin delivery boy." He wanted to make it clear. "It's a real business. I own the truck and got to roust up and service my own customers. It ain't no nine-to-five jolt or like fuckin school shit, man."

Jack looked impressed.

"I'm clearin well over a hundred a week." He reached under his T-shirt and rubbed his bare, flat belly.

The girl in a uniform of gold shorts with blue vest and a matching cap pinned to her bright red hair ambled up as if challenging the world to make her go faster. She chewed gum as lazily.

"Hi, Glenn," she drawled, cutting her slow eyes from time to time to the red car and Jack.

"You still puttin out, Jan-Jan?" Glenn asked.

She crowed and slapped him hard on the bare upper arm, which he tensed into a mighty example of Dynamic Tension. "You're just *aw*-ful," she squealed.

"You oughta take her out to the toolies," he offered Jack. "She'll go like a herd of turtles. Me, all them freckles makes my eyes go funny after a while. Got freckles on her . . . but she's pretty."

She drew back to slap him again. He grabbed his right wrist with his left hand and made a proper arm for her. She stung her hand, and he didn't even flinch.

"You guys *want* something?" she asked in a nasal snarl to show them she did not care.

The backs of her hands, arms, legs were freckled.

"Yeow. Jack here wants to punch you. I said you'd go out with him after work. OK?"

"I don't get off till, uh, ten."

"That's right. Ten's all reet, ain't it, Jack?"

He looked at the slow, freckled girl. Even her lips were freckled. Her hair was the color of a carrot. "Uh, sure."

Glenn waved his hand as if it were all set. "So, he'll come get you at ten, right?"

She looked at the red roadster and back at Jack. "You go to the U?" she asked, nodding at the decal on his windshield.

"Sure." Glenn spoke for him. "Ex-Navy. Vet and all. Been to China. Got a real samurai sword that long." He extended his arms wide in double meaning.

She laughed, shrugged. "OK," she said more to Glenn than to Jack.

When she went for their root beers, she arched her back and glided along in a pigeon-toed way that made her big butt go chung! chung!

"Cinch, man," Glenn said offhandedly. "Good pussy, that Jan-Jan. But, me I can't go them freckles. Get fuckin cross-eyed, man." He meant it.

Jack laughed.

"So don't say old Glenn ain't a buddy."

"Thanks," Jack quickly got in.

Glenn indicated it was nothing. "Let's just see more of your ass around, man. Go out wolfin. Hit some dumps. Buck's got this punchboard cased up in Cherryville. Figures it could be hit for a couple of C's. We might go up some afternoon. Want to come along?"

"Sure."

"Good. I knew you weren't goin to let that college shit go to your head. Bring this junker you bought over some evening and I'll see if it can be saved." He kicked a re-capped tire.

He copped a feel of Jan-Jan's left boob when she delivered their root beers. She flinched no more at that than Glenn had when she had slapped him. He hauled a pint of whiskey from beneath his car seat and laced their root beers.

When they pulled out, Jack waved at the girl. Glenn was OK. The university's codes were no more absurd than those by which Glenn lived, merely different. But in no way more free or even much more enlightened. The geologist who would not address himself to considerations of a god was, in an even more self-satisfied way, more rigid than Glenn, who *had* been happy to explain his connection through laundry with housewives as intimacy.

Glenn never gave away a thing he ever really wanted for himself. But then the way pedants guarded education, to acquire what Jack wanted of it already assumed the proportions of guerrilla warfare.

I could use some pussy, Jack realized. Sharon was a beautiful girl, but necking left him frustrated and feeling backlogged. Then he could only be with Sharon Wednesday, Friday and Saturday nights and for an hour or so after church Sunday night. Her parents accepted that she smoked, danced and was a sweater girl, but until she finished high school, she would keep hours.

She wanted to study music and fancied she had "a voice," though her singing made Jack's asshole pucker—all those high, pear-shaped tones. He could see her as a pouter-pigeon music teacher, making little kids keep time by bobbing their hands at the wrists like goose necks—*one,* two, three!

But where *had* she learned to kiss?

He was going to be late for work again. With the GI Bill, he had enough money for expenses, though not luxuries. He still had twelve hundred dollars left of his savings and mustering-out pay. He hoped to keep it to see him through his last year of college, if he got that far, for the GI Bill would not carry him completely to the end. If he did make it all the way, he would only be twenty. The idea made him giddy, but it was a very distant dream still, particularly in light of the D minus he'd had on his French quiz, the D in English and the fact he wasn't doing that much better in most of his other subjects. Only his B plus in art gave him hope he was not a total dummy. He did not know how to study, Sharon said.

Maybe he wouldn't go back for that girl later. He ought to go home and crack the books.

The heat was metallic in his throat with the smell of welding, hot asphalt, rusty piles of iron and the hint of fresh sawdust. High wire fences rose beside the sidewalks beyond which the ground was barren, discolored and sere. Dusty milkweed grew between the cracked concrete plates of sidewalk alongside nodding, anemic dandelions. The tar in the street was soft underfoot and instantly hot through the soles of his shoes. The doorsill of his car was too hot to touch. He swore and slammed the door with his knee. The water in the radiator was hissing. A rusty subterranean steam odor came from beneath the hood. The street was dominated by an old lumberyard and an iron foundry. On the corner was the Hangdon Tent & Awning Company, which had been there almost as long as the lumberyard. Old man Hangdon had made enough on military contracts to buy a Cadillac, air-condition his sewing and cutting room and move to Eastborough. Jack was his way of saying thanks, he had explained when taking the boy on part time in the frame shop.

He clocked in, conscious that he was fifteen minutes late and there was no way to hide the fact from the goddamn clock. Glancing quickly at the order on the top of the clipboard on the large scuffed table, he went to the racks on which lengths and sizes of pipe were laid, ascertaining in another glance there were no odd pieces against the wall long enough to bend into the frame. Laying the pipe, which had been pickled to prevent it from rusting, on the bending table, he measured the short leg from the outside curve of the jig, mentally calculating the additional length of the nipple eye with which it would be attached to the installation, bent the pipe at a neat ninety-degree angle, threaded the end and screwed on the fitting. He flopped it on the table to bend the other leg.

Seally, the shop foreman, limped alongside. He was a grouchy old fart with long hairs growing out of his ears. He had been with Hangdon Tent & Awning for forty years. Seally had bent so much pipe his arms were ellipses to his perpetually stooped body. Whatever life he'd possibly had beyond tents and awnings had become so negligible his every moment was defined by the time he spent on the work floor. That Jack made as much in three hours as he had made in a long week at Jack's age was an injustice that made the old man's youth seem to have been stolen.

"Veteran or not, boy, you keep on turnin up late and we're goin to let you go."

"I'm sorry, Seally." The boy bent the other end of the pipe and began cutting it to length with a hacksaw. "Got held up after class by a professor."

"You get held up a lot, don't yuh?" he grumbled. His voice had a way of skittering all around so it made Jack think of a bunch of pipes clattering onto the concrete floor—a sound that went to the quick inside his bones.

"Now you been warned before. This ain't no playhouse. We ain't in business to put you through college. Don't know why we taxpayers got to put all you fellas through college for anyhow."

"We made the world safe for tents and awnings, Seally," Jack cracked.

"You never made the world safe for nothin," he sniffed. "I wouldn't mind helpin out men who'd actually fought. But I don't see why we got to bend over backward for you all. If it hadn't been for the war, a lot of you wouldn't have gotten a job nohow."

"Isn't it good we had a war?"

"How's that?"

"Said why don't you write your Congressman." Jack raised his voice.

"No responsibility. That's you fellas' trouble. Don't care. Think the world owes you a livin. I never was late or missed a day in forty years," he added, as if that was a mark to which the world ought to be made to aspire.

"I've never *missed* yet," Jack reminded him.

Seally opened the place in the morning and stayed in the evening until everyone else was out. If Hangdon played golf in the afternoon and worked in his office until nine at night, Seally never left until the old man did or came back and ordered him to go home. He had varicose veins the size of garter snakes and wrapped his legs tightly from ankle to knee in elastic bandages.

Even with the big back doors open it was hot enough to make Jack feel a little sick. His belly growled with swallowed rage at the old foreman as he gimped away, his crookedy arms jumping like Walter Brennan doing his "grandpa" turn.

The smell of chemically impregnated canvas came drifting back from the front where little old ladies in housedresses and aprons and hairnets sewed their asses off, chattering back and forth over the motors of the machines. He had recognized two of them as acquaintances of his grandmother when she worked for the WPA overall factory during the Depression. They brought their lunches and got paid by the piece. The key, the boy figured out, was to get a humorless, stupid, insanely industrious lead

441

woman, who worked as if her every breath depended on it to keep the pressure on the others. Hangdon had the key in Old Sally, who stuck a yard of rump in a pair of slacks and never looked up from bell to break. A humorless black-haired bitch, she worked in an angry frenzy that made her face resemble that of a steelhead catfish. The other women gathered around their lunch sacks and laughed at Old Sally eating alone at her machine, her eyes dreamy with gluttonous consumption of sandwiches. There was never any question who would get the fifty-dollar bonus with her ham at Christmas.

But she and Sally didn't work that hard for fifty dollars extra. Jack could not understand it. They worked that way out of some kind of hatred. *They're insane!* he decided. Coming to that, he felt a kind of pity for them. He didn't think they had been born that way.

Jack went for another pipe. There was no way to make awning frames faster than he did. So why did he feel guilty all the time? Work was bullshit when it made you feel like that.

He stayed an extra fifteen minutes that evening to make up for the time he was late and clocked out. He had bent as much pipe as he would have if he had arrived on the money. But while he was washing up in the scummy crapper, Seally stuck his head in to warn him again.

"Mr. Hangdon says if you're late one more time, vet or not, we'll let you go."

"I'll be here. I made the time up," Jack protested.

"That don't cut no ice. You're supposed to be here at three o'clock. That don't mean no three fifteen."

"Fuck, Seally, you're a goddamned fascist."

He turned red, began shaking and stomped away. His big old fists were so tightly clenched they trembled.

He drove to Sharon's house and parked in front. It was an ordinary frame dwelling built before the war, with a real front porch and porch swing. A small foyer led into a living room dominated by a large upright piano. There was a dining room through French doors which were usually open. Off to the right was a parlor-study. Off the dining room was Sharon's bedroom. A large kitchen was straight back with Sharon's parents' bedroom off it. Until Sharon's sister, Sparkle, had gotten married, the front room had been her bedroom. Her real name was Ruth, but she had been called Sparkle since she was a baby. The basement had been converted into a game room. Sharon was down there.

"It's cooler," her mother explained as he passed through the kitchen where she was skewering bits of meat on wood dowels to make mock-chicken legs. Hot or not, a real Kansas woman never served her family a cold lunch or supper. She seemed to eye him and the bits of meat as if deciding whether there was enough to invite him to stay to eat. He ate there often. When she did not say the expected words before he turned to go down the cellar stairs, he guessed she had decided she hadn't enough.

Sharon's father was weeding around the back walk to the garage on his hands and knees. To see them in their home when he had only seen them in church was like seeing them naked. At home they were not so peppy. Her father's face looked grayer, older, his eyes less alive. Her mother was a pretty woman gone plump. Sharon would look like that when she was older. That was all right, he decided, noticing her mother's bare legs beneath the blue wide-legged shorts. She had a cloth over her hair and looked as if earlier she had been working outside. When she bent to pick up a dowel she had dropped on the floor, her wide bottom with her shorts hiked up tightly behind made him wonder what she was like in bed. It was hard to think of Sharon's parents having at it. Not her mother so much, but her father. He had asked Sharon if they still did it. Her room and theirs shared a wall. She had looked exasperated and said, "Sure. What a dumb question." He had tried to explain. "Well, I don't know. I don't know much about, you know, regular people." He had felt a fear in her then. And it worried him still.

Sharon was sitting at the end of the room on a padded lawn chaise in white shorts and a sleeveless cotton-knit pullover, with a book propped on an upraised knee, chewing a tendril of her dark brown hair. She seemed so grown-up, so large and womanly. That they had both grown from the little kids they had been in Sunday school was a constant marvel to him.

She did not look up until he crossed the room and stood beside her. She reluctantly closed the book, marking her place with a finger. He cut a look at the stairs before bending down to slip his right hand under her arm, between her back and the chaise and lift her slightly as she raised her face to be kissed.

He loved the way she kissed, the way she opened her lips just as his touched hers so he could feel the sweet givingness of it, her receiving him. She was passive, yet totally into it, juicy, not up to tricks or teasing. The only thing that bothered him was the way she sometimes had of crooking her hand behind his head with the palm outward, probably after some movie star she had seen. That and how, until he got her hot, there was a hint of her doing him a favor in it. He liked to hold the back of her small head in his hand as if to drink from her lips.

The kiss went on so long she cracked an eye to peek at the stairs. When he tried to share the chaise with her, she broke away to protest in whispers, "Don't! It squeaks like mad."

He wondered how she knew that, tugging her up and wrapping his arms around her. She no longer held her can out to keep her sex from touching his. She came tight up against him in the same coyless way she gave him her mouth to kiss. He rolled himself against the little mound beneath her belly until she could feel him getting hard. She put her hands under his sweat shirt to feel his bare back against her palms. He tensed his muscles until they felt like rocks beneath his skin. She loved his back and said he had a sexy bottom. He had resented that until she explained, "That's what girls look at first. Don't you know?" That had been such a revelation that when he had got home he had stood on the lid of his toilet to look at himself in the medicine cabinet mirror.

"Hunh-unh," she warned as he slid a hand down the back of her shorts under her pants against her cool white bottom. "Don't get me excited now. You just get yourself worked up and then feel bad." She reached back and hauled his hand out of there.

"I'm already worked up," he complained.

She smiled and bumped him once with her sex. "Tough."

"You don't care," he accused. "Look at that!" He stepped back enough for her to look down between them at the cockstand poking out the left leg of his dungarees.

"Poor old fella," she pouted and gave him a little pat.

He caught her hand and held it against him, making her fingers feel the shaft. "Do something, Sharon," he whispered in her ear. "It hurts later when you don't." He stuck his tongue in her ear, which usually drove her wild.

She jerked away. "Don't! Are you crazy?" She looked at the stairs and struggled to pull her hand away. "I can't help it if you get excited every time you kiss me."

"I can't help it if every time I kiss you I get excited."

"Well . . . I'm sorry. But if you haven't come to study, you'd better go. You know, since we've been going together, my grades have fallen so much I could miss the honor roll. And if I do . . . lover"—she pointed overhead—"they'll never let me go out with you again."

"OK. We study. One little kiss first?"

"Jack. You're *incorrigible!*"

"That's what my fourth-grade teacher told me."

"You know, the only reason they let me see you so much at all is because you're going to the U and attending church regularly. They're scared to death you're going to do something to me. That stupid tattoo you got didn't do you any good with them either. I wish you'd get it taken off or something."

"Well, I looked into it. Went to a plastic surgeon. He said he could do it for two hundred bucks. Do a skin graft. Slice it off and switch it with a clear piece of skin from somewhere else. Would you rather have the thing on my ass?"

"Well, at least we wouldn't have to *look* at it."

"Thanks a lot. But it would show when it counted most. When we do make love, I want the lights on. I want to see you, the whole beautiful bunch of you. I want to see me going *into* you. I want—"

She put her hand over his mouth though he had been whispering. A frown wrinkled completely across her brow.

"When you talk to me like that, you make me feel like a whore," she accused.

"Oh, no!" He didn't want her to feel that way. "I meant it would be beautiful. I love you. I want to see you and kiss you all over. I won't do it in the dark, like we were ashamed or something. Don't you understand?"

She shook her head as if she did not or didn't want to. She looked as if she might cry.

"What did I say?"

445

"Oh, it isn't that," she said angrily. "It's just all the things you have told me. All those women. I don't know how I can love someone who has done all the things you have done."

She looked at him pleadingly, angrily, frightened.

"Baby, baby, I told you because I wanted to be honest with you. All the way. I *love* you! Jesus Christ! You give me all that jazz about forgiving seven times seven—"

"Don't talk so loud," she whispered.

He whispered. "I didn't *have* to tell you. I could have kept my mouth shut. You would have never known."

"Yes, I would have," she said mysteriously. "And I'm not *perfect!* I'm only human. All those poor creatures—"

"They weren't poor creatures!" he cut in angrily. "I wish you'd can that crap. We aren't all so damned different from one another, you know. They were just women doin the best they could with what they had in a damned bad spot. You don't know what you would do in that place."

"I wouldn't do that! I'd die first!"

"OK. But they didn't want to die." He felt trapped again.

"I mean," she went on, "I could understand if you'd met some decent girl and fallen in love or something. I know how hard it is to control ourselves. I could accept *that.* But all those, those—*whores!*" She shuddered all over, stamped her foot and raised her book as if to throw it at him. Her face was wildly angry, her lips drawn back over her teeth. Then she collapsed in tears. "I hate it!" she cried, her face buried in her hands. He went to her and put his arms around her. She tried to shrug him away. He held her tight. "I hate that you did it." She wept softly in the circle of his arms. She turned and put her head on his chest, her hands between them under her chin like a child. "I know it isn't right to hate, but I can't help it. I wish you hadn't told me. I'd rather not know. I *would!*" She buried her face in his chest. He felt her sobbing in his arms.

"I'm sorry, honey," he said, kissing her hair.

"You don't know how many times since you told about those ... women, I've decided not to see you again."

He was shocked. He hadn't imagined the stuff he had told her would have made her feel that way. He panicked.

446

He did not want to lose her. Suddenly, he very much did not want to lose her.

"I love you!" he insisted. "It was just what the guys did," he begged.

"Not all of them." She looked up with narrowed eyes as if she had someone in particular in mind.

"OK. I'm a horny, no-good bastard. But I haven't *ruined* you, have I?"

"You would if I'd let you," she snapped.

"The hell I would! I love you. I want you. You aren't like those others to me. Oh, I want you so bad my back aches. But only if you really want me—heart, head, everything. I'm not a goddamned monster!"

She seemed to be weighing that suggestion a long while. There was such genuine fear in her pretty face he felt ugly.

Then she threw herself on him, clinging to his neck, kissing his face, eyes, mouth. "No, no, no, no, no! You are beautiful. Awful. Strong. Weak. Crazy. Wonderful. No. You are not a monster. I'm just very confused, Jack. I just wish you had waited until I graduated before you came home. I don't know! I want to go on to college. I *must*! I just didn't want to get seriously involved now." She looked unhappy again. "Don't you see?"

"Are you seriously involved?" he asked.

She hid her face on his chest. "I don't know."

She turned away, picked up her book and sat back on the chaise. "Study," she commanded, pointing at a table against the wall.

He felt fake opening the schoolbook. After he had read one page three times and still did not know what he had read, he looked over to where she sat with both knees up, her shorts cutting in beneath the soft inner bulge of her long, straight thighs, a crescent of her paler bottom showing. She had never said she loved him. No one had had her, he was almost absolutely certain. He hadn't ever really known anyone who hadn't been fucked.

She glanced up and met his eyes. Giving a little cry, she put out her arms. He covered the space between them in a single bound and landed as softly as possible on top of her. She opened her legs to let him lie between her thighs. They hadn't mouths enough for all the kisses they tried to give. He hunched her, just close, short, more tensing him-

447

self against than actually moving. She began to breathe hard in the way she had just before she became quite wild, thrashing her head back and forth, digging her nails into his head and back, rolling her mouth crazily around over his.

"I wish I were *in* you," he breathed.

"Me, too."

"You do?"

"Yes! Oh, yes!" For the first time, she let herself really move against him.

She would be fantastic! he realized. *Did she just move like that naturally?* He was amazed.

He heard her mother's first footfall on the stairs and was off there and bending over the chaise at the waist to hide his condition, while Sharon snatched up her book and looked up expectantly.

"Uh. . . . That word means to rise on wings of fire," he extemporized.

She pressed her lips tightly together to keep from laughing.

"Supper will be ready in ten minutes, Sharon," her mother announced icily, looking at them narrowly. She went back up the stairs. They weren't fooling her for a second.

Sharon exploded in stifled laughter. Jack clasped both hands over his mouth and rocked back and forth. Tears filled his eyes.

"Wings of fire, hell!" she laughed, trying desperately to control her voice. She leaped up, standing on the chaise, hugged his shaggy head to her breasts and said, "I love you, you nut."

He rolled his head between her prizewinning boobs, then took the end of one in his mouth, just dancing his teeth on it.

"Sweater girl, huh?" he humphed, the taste of sanforized cotton in his mouth.

"Ow!"

He suddenly bent down and clasped her tightly around her hips and kissed the cloth over her sex.

"Oh!" she cried softly on an intake of breath in a way touching, wondrous and beautiful. She clasped his head gently between her hands for a moment, then moved him away. "Don't, honey."

There was a damp spot on the tip of her right breast.

She covered it with her hand as they walked toward the stair, their arms around each other's waist.

"You're just the right size," he said.

"For what?" she shot back brightly.

"For me. For everything." The top of her head came to the lobe of his ear. There were glints of red and gold and darker walnut strands when the light touched the crown of her hair.

"Sorry you aren't staying for supper," she said. "I could ask Mom."

"Naw. I got a pot of spaghetti home on the stove I can warm up."

She made a face.

"Hey. I make good spaghetti. Great spaghetti! Why don't you let me fix *you* dinner Friday night?"

"You're *joking!*"

"I'm serious."

"No way! Ever since your grandmother let it slip out that you've got your own apartment, Mom and Dad have had conniptions. 'A young woman does *not* visit a young man alone in his apartment under any circumstances!' I asked, 'What if he's sick?' They said they hoped you had Blue Cross."

"So I'll fix dinner for them, too." He felt expansive, a real citizen magnanimous and without other motive.

"The thing to do, dear, is *forget* it! Cause this child will never see the inside of it, and that, chum, is de-eff-in-nate. . . . Whatever you rise on." She giggled.

The basement had been divided by a large plywood cabinet, about seven feet high and nine feet long, which served as his clothes and storage closet. He came in through the furnace room past his toilet and shower, which were right beside the door. The door opened into the kitchen. All the fixtures had come from a secondhand store. The Frigidaire stood on legs, as did the old gas stove with a high oven. The refrigerator had a cylindrical motor housing on top. When it started and stopped, it shuddered so much, in spite of the book of matches wedged under a short leg, it woke him in the other room when he had first moved in. There was also a cupboard, sink, and Formica dinette set with two chairs, all on tubular chrome legs. Pots and pans were kept beneath the sink behind a curtain. The place had been a mess when he rented it. It had been vacant since the end of the war. Before, it had been rented to aircraft workers. The cheap paint had flaked from the walls in great scars from the damp. The floor had been covered with such a layer of grease and dirt he had needed kerosene to get down to the linoleum. He had painted the walls a bright green with some expensive latex-based paint. The floors and doors of his closet he had painted with glossy white enamel. His grandmother said white floors showed the dirt too much, but she made him some bright red curtains for the little ground-level windows. He put the old bed that had been in there out in the furnace room and spent a hundred and a half on a bright-red studio couch that opened out into a double bed and another twenty-five on a matching red rug to put in front of the couch on the shiny white floor. He enameled the desk that was in there white, and also the wooden straight chair in which he sat and put a red cushion on it. His mother and her boyfriend gave him a white plastic club chair they had found somewhere secondhand, which hadn't looked bad after he had scrubbed it with kerosene. He built white bookshelves with boards and bricks. The walls were decorated with his drawings and a large Join the Navy and See the World poster he had cut from its standard outside the post office one night. Above his desk he hung the samurai sword he'd taken from Alfonso Castro's locker.

He kept the place neat, rarely leaving his bed unmade or clothes lying around. He liked the place. He had fixed it up so nice he had a feeling Mrs. Meens, the landlady, would like to raise his rent. It was the first place he'd ever had that was his own. If he sometimes awakened during the night with the sense of a great danger just beyond the walls, he would get up and check the door, then slip the samurai sword from its scabbard, trying to decide if it would be more strategic to lay it on the floor beside the bed or hide it under the covers. The floor seemed the place from which he could most quickly bring it into play. His fear was a small price to pay for a clean place of his own. Living alone, he talked to himself, often aloud. You could cut a man in two with that sword.

A sharp car, an apartment, going to college—no matter how provisionally—money in the bank: the world had been stood on its end. His luck had changed so drastically that the fear it could as easily shift back became a new, faceless bogeyman.

"When the hell does a guy feel safe?" he wondered to himself in the mirror, splashing on Old Spice to go pick up the girl at the drive-in.

She was the first girl he had brought to his place. He glanced up to see a light in Mrs. Meens' bedroom window. She thought she had cancer of the throat and talked in a deathly whisper. That was why she had decided, since losing her husband, to let the basement for seven dollars a week, plus utilities, which made it an even ten dollars. She didn't have separate meters. He took her word. He felt a little rotten handing the girl down into the furnace room. It was going against Sharon, but—goddamn! As soon as the slow freckled girl had gotten in the car, she had scooted over and put his arm around her, expecting him to play with her tit. When he had asked her if she'd like a Coke or something, she'd asked, "Are you nuts?"

For, indeed, what would Jan-Jan of the Kau-Kau want with another Coke? There was nothing, in fact, to offer her between the open door of the car and his desire. She understood that.

There was a note stuck in his door. He had a crazy notion Sharon had been there and felt wild that he had not been home.

It was from his mother.

> Hon, I just stopped by to say hello. You never come to see me anymore. You mad at me or something? I'll stop by again tomorrow about 9 after I get off work.
>
> Love, Mother
>
> P.S. Could you loan me $10 until pay day? I had to get a prescription filled and I don't want to ask the Chinks at work for it. I'm a little short—but I'm very lively—ha. ha. Love again.

He stuck it in his pocket.

"Bad news?" the girl asked.

"Huh? Aw, no. Just my mom."

He opened the door and steered her inside by one freckled elbow. Close, she smelled like French fries.

"I've never been in a guy's apartment before," she confessed, gawking around. "It's real nice." She turned and held out her arms and closed her eyes.

She kissed with a lot of phony little excitements, shoving her box right up there and rolling her big butt. She felt fatter than she looked, solidly congealed French fry and hamburger fat around the band of her shorts.

"How old are you?" he asked.

"Fifteen. Why? Fraid I'll get you for statutory rape?"

He hadn't thought about *that*. But, no sweat, he was sure he could find a platoon of guys who'd punched her.

"I'm goin to fuck your ass off," he vowed.

"I don't care if you talk dirty," she breathed into his mouth. "Just don't hurt me."

When he unfolded the bed, she began pulling her top over her head.

Why do redheads always insist on wearing pink? he wondered.

"This is a real nice place," she decided, turning around in the room in her panties and tatty white bra. She started to climb into bed that way.

"Unh-unh. I want you bareass."

"Turn the light off then."

He shook his head. "I like to see what I'm getting into."

"You're awful. You know it?" Without a semblance of grace she stripped off her bra and pants and let them fall beside the bed. She was freckled all over. In the light he thought she was orange-colored except for the paler stripes of her breasts, which were large but already sagging.

"I've never fucked a real redhead like you before," he told her when he was in her large, snotty cunt. He liked talking that way to her, saying "fuck" to her.

"You do it good," she said and crooked a meaty freckled thigh up along his side. "Don't come in me."

When he had done everything to her he could think of without completely disgusting himself, he got up and set the alarm for five-thirty. She was almost asleep in the slick dampness where he had withdrawn from her to ejaculate.

"Hey." He jostled her with his foot. "Don't you want to take a shower or something?"

"Hmmmmm? Inna morning. I'm tired."

Pig, he thought, going to the shower himself.

Soaping his cock under the warm spray, he thought of Sharon and closed his eyes and found himself jerking off in a handful of suds, seeing her on the chaise in her basement, knees drawn up, reading her book. She looked up and smiled. He came but a drop, but jerked and shuddered so violently he almost collapsed to his knees in the stall.

"You're crazy." He nodded at his face in the mirror. His expression seemed as slack and devoid of intelligence as that of the girl sleeping in the other room. "Yeow. You're really wack-o sometimes, man. A goddamned monster." He made a horrible monster face at himself in the glass, shooting out his lower jaw over his upper lip, contorting his features, bugging his eyes until he felt he had strained them.

He made her bacon and eggs while she was in the shower.

She came in dressed in her shorts and vest. She wanted a hug.

"You still smell like French fires," he said.

"I can't help it," she whined. "I didn't wash my hair. I can't go home with it wet." She touched her carrot top in a gesture that would be pathetic in a few years when she had blown up into a whining, sad, old punching bag.

In his dreams he had beat her big freckled ass with the flat of his samurai sword until she blubbered and begged. The grip had twisted in his hand, and he cut a big chunk out of her, right down into the red-red meat. Watching her eat, he was no longer hungry. She broke the yolks of her eggs with the corner of a piece of toast and dipped them out until her breakfast made him think of the faces of Brueghel's blind men.

She asked him to stop about a block from her house, mumbling something about telling her mother she'd stayed at a girlfriend's house.

She yawned. "You sure didn't sleep much."

He laughed.

"Will I see you again?" she wanted to know.

"Sure."

"I really like you. It's different doin it in a bed in a guy's own apartment. I like it. I can cook, you know," she offered.

"So next time, you cook." He grinned.

"Oh! I will! Gee, that'd be fun. Like playing house, only for real."

Forget it! he thought.

"I don't want you to think I do what we did with just anybody. I wouldn't do it with a guy I didn't like."

"That's what everyone says about you," he assured her.

She was happy, then. "Yeow?" She put her hand between her legs suddenly as if feeling a twinge. She frowned. "I sure hope you didn't come in me."

"I didn't. Not a drop."

"I sure hope so." She didn't truly seem that worried. She was angling for something else. Outside the car she hesitated for a moment. "See you, no foolin?"

"Sure. See you, Jan-Jan."

"OK then, bye."

After she had walked a few steps, he called, "Hey!"

She turned around.

"Thanks, Jan-Jan."

"Huh?" She screwed up her face.

"Thanks."

"What a dumb thing to say."

He could see the ticket on his windshield half a block away. How the hell could he get a ticket in the school parking lot?

"Crap!" he said aloud.

But it was a note from Sharon.

Je t'adore!

(That's French for I love you, in case you haven't your verb wheel handy.)

S.

She would have had to get off the College Hill bus to do that on her way to school and catch the next one. Or maybe someone had given her a lift. He tried to think of what bastard might be taking her to school.

Seally met him at the clock. His card was not in its slot. "Mr. Hangdon wants to see you in his office!"

He was only six minutes late. Surely they wouldn't can him for a lousy six minutes.

Mr. Hangdon was a small man with a peeny, neat, silver head. Mostly he was spotless white collar and cuffs sticking out of a sharply pressed gray summerweight business suit that seemed hinged at elbow and knee. He looked like an emaciated Herbert Hoover. A small squad tent with "Hangdon" printed on it decorated his large, old-fashioned desk covered with a sheet of beveled glass. His office, like the rest of the factory, had glass blocks instead of windows to let in the light so that operators would not go woolgathering. Jack could follow the cold logic of it. A sewing-machine operator or cutter could stitch or cut a hand in a second's slip in concentration. Still. . . .

On the wall over the little man's head was a wartime production efficiency pennant.

"I understand you called my foreman an obscene name." He minced no words, moving two yellow lead pencils a precise short distance on his desk top.

"Name, sir?" It had taken him by surprise. He couldn't think of having called Seally anything.

"Come, come! I'm not here to play games." He snapped his fingers. "There's no need to try and deny it. You called him a fascist."

"Uh . . . yes, sir. I guess I did. But—"

He cut him off with a tidy gesture. "We've put up with all we are going to from you." He had Jack's time cards on his desk. He picked them up. "I was willing to understand about your being late as long as you made up your time and the work got out, even if it did set a bad example for everyone else. You served our country, and I thought you were a serious lad honestly trying to get ahead. I like that. But you fooled me. No one fools me twice." He chucked Jack's time cards onto a far corner of his desk like a man folding a losing hand. He looked up and fixed the boy with his eyes. "I'm just curious why you thought you had the freedom to call a man who has worked for me loyally for forty years, and never once in that time missed a minute, such a dirty, filthy, despicable name?"

"Well, it isn't exactly a name, sir. I didn't mean it like a name. It's more of an attitude or persuasion, I reckon. I meant it to mean, uh, rigid, you know, unforgiving character."

"You did, did you? In my book to call a man what you did is worse than anything you could call him. I'd be mad as hell if you called me that. Calling names constitutes assault, did you know that? You could be put in jail."

Jack hadn't known that. "No, sir."

"Well, you can be," he sniffed. "If we were so rigid and unforgiving as you *think*, that's by God what I'd do to you!" His face had turned red.

Jack began to feel lucky there hadn't been a cop waiting for him in there.

"We took you on in good faith. You could of had a future here," he droned. He was no longer talking to Jack but toward a handsome leather bag of eighteen golf clubs standing in the corner. Jack had caddied for Hangdon the year before he went into the Navy. Hangdon didn't remember it. There wasn't a club in that bag that would help Hangdon break ninety. He'd need a mortar.

"Glad to help out a young veteran trying to get ahead. Nearly all our installers are veterans. Most of them with more impressive records than you, sonny. Now, I don't think one of those men would have said to my foreman what you did. No. I surely don't." He paused a moment before adding, "Here's what you have coming to you." He pushed a pale-green check that had been written by a machine across the desk. The sum was stamped in red perforations so no one could alter it. Hangdon wasn't taking any chances.

He walked through the factory, winked at old fat Sally, who sniffed at him. Stopping at the water cooler, he had three folding paper cups of ice water, though no one else ever went to the cooler except during breaks.

Passing through the frame shop, Seally turned his back and reached up to fuss with some pipe. There was already a new boy from the employment agency standing by the table expectantly, trying to look alert. Jack simply reached out and goosed the old man in his khaki-clothed crack. He jumped off the ground with both feet, waving his hands and hollering as pipe fell clatteringly around his ears. When he came down, he gave chase, modocking pretty good for a guy about seventy with bad pins. Jack had to sprint about fifty yards toward his car, laughing like a fiend, before Seally gave up and stood waving his clenched fist.

"You little . . . *pissant!*" he screamed as Jack drove past. Jack gave him a Nazi salute.

He had never actually been fired before. It frightened him. Those old dry men frightened him. *No joy in them*, he marveled. He would start looking for another job next week. In the meantime, he reminded himself to be sure to stick his swimming trunks in the car tomorrow before he went to class.

27

ON THE way out of the university parking lot he decided to go pick up Sharon at school. Since he lost his job, such a prospect seemed a great luxury.

It was her gym period, the next-to-last class she had that day. The driveway behind the high school passed one of the athletic fields and the gym. It was a big school, more than two thousand students attended, and it was run more like a college than a high school.

He saw her playing a woolgathering, or rather flower-picking, second base on a girl's softball team, idly making dandelion garlands and chatting with the shortstop who had come over as if a grounder hadn't been hit their way in a week.

He stopped in the drive to watch her. She did not see him until the shortstop called her attention to the bright-red car. Her hands went to her mouth in a touching, girl-ish gesture of surprise. She glanced toward the gym in-structress in a white gym suit and trotted over to the car. She ran with a lazy grace, elbows clamped tightly to her sides just under her breasts, thighs slipping silkily against each other with every stride. Her gym togs, by regulation of the Kansas State Board of Education, were institutional green sleeveless buttoned blouse and short bloomers. Tied back with a bit of white ribbon, her chestnut hair bounced in a ponytail off her neck. She tilted her head toward her left shoulder as she ran. A wide white smile, pretty face, tan limbs jogging in clean pointed sneakers and sparkling white gym socks made her look like an advertisement for a particularly feminine product. In her left hand she carried a crown of dandelions. Whatever it was that passed for love in him welled up like an enormous, fragile soap bubble. He felt so happy it made him sad. But his smile grew as wide as her own.

She hopped the low cable barrier to the field and dropped her garland crown at a rakish angle on his head.

"You look very pretty." She laughed just as he formed a similar compliment for her.

He kissed her arm that rested on the doorsill of his car.

"Don't," she warned, glancing toward where the stocky instructress was glaring at them.

"Think she's got the hots for you." He grinned. "That's naked jealousy."

"Um. Think you could be right."

"We're going swimming."

"Who we?"

"You and me."

"I can't cut art!"

"Everyone can cut art," he assured her.

"Jack, you're *ruining* me. I can't. I haven't a suit, anyway. Meet me after school."

"Ok," he reluctantly agreed.

"I got to go. Miss Quisenberry is turning red."

"Quisenberry?"

"That's nothing. Her first name's Quentin."

"Keep your back to the wall in the shower. Or ... I guess it's different for girls. Do whatever you have to do. I love you."

"You're awful." She laughed.

He turned her hand over and kissed her palm before letting her scamper back to second base. The taste was slightly bitter, of dandelion stems. When he went up the drive to turn around, he winked at Miss Quisenberry, the garland of dandelions falling over one eye.

To kill the hour, he drove to the small shop on East

Douglass, where Al and Gorilla had opened the AAAA Air-Conditioning Refrigeration & Electrical Repair Company. They called it AAAA to get a prominent alphabetical listing in the phone book. A small decal of a ruptured duck was visible in the lower corner of their single plate-glass show window. The place had been the home of a lot of things—the last Jack could recall, it had been a gypsy fortune-teller's den. In the small display window was a cut-out cardboard house with crepe paper streamers showing the flow of cool air that Gorilla and Al could provide. With the temperature on the big thermometer outside their place touching 103 degrees, it seemed business ought to be booming.

But they weren't out hanging air conditioners in anyone's windows. Al was in the half-glass little office going over papers with the tall reddish-blond woman he had married and who was the firm's secretary. Al had begun wearing glasses and was losing his hair. He did not look especially happy to see Jack, though he smiled.

"How'd you know I wasn't a customer?" Jack wondered.

"Customers for air conditioners don't walk in, Muskrat. They phone."

"Oh. Not even for portables?"

"Sometimes. You want to buy an air conditioner?"

"No. I figured with this heat wave you might need some part-time help after school with your installations."

"Yeah? So did me and Gorilla," he grumped, an edge of fear in his voice. "You've met my wife?"

"Sure. How are you?" He shook her hand, glancing at her belly for a sign of a pregnant rising. She seemed flatter, if anything.

They weren't having much fun, if Jack was any judge. She hovered defensively over Al's shoulder.

"Gorilla's in the back if you want to say hello," Al said. "We gotta go over this stuff."

"Sure. Don't let me interrupt you. Just popped in to see how you're gettin along. Waitin for my girl to get out of school."

"Good." He was already pouring over the papers. Most looked like bills. His wife pulled up a typist's chair on his side of the desk. There was a large ugly ledger on her knees.

Gorilla was working at a bench in the small repair shop beneath a fluorescent light, both hands inside an old window cooler that was part of a birdshit-dappled litter of like machines on the floor around his feet.

"Hey, Muskrat!" He looked and grinned. "How's college?"

"Rough, man. They resent tellin you anything you really want to know. Act like it's all a great secret you got to suck out of them. You feel they really hate you, man. Least they do me. There's a couple that are all right, though. You makin any money?"

"Shit, no! We got this crap on bid from the county hospital. Things are so damn old we're going to lose money on it."

"So tell them they're no good and sell them new ones," Jack suggested.

"Al's tryin to get them to replace some. Times are bad, Muskrat. It's the inflation. Only now nobody's got any money. Or they're scared to spend it. All this talk about a recession. It's just month to month, man. Al's been drivin a fuckin cab nights to keep up payments on his house. They're so scared of having a kid right now they don't hardly look at each other. I was goin to get married, but we decided to wait. I almost wish I'd stayed in the Navy for another hitch."

Their problems seemed remote to Jack, and depressing. They weren't fun anymore. Gorilla was getting a gut on him and had taken to smoking fat black cigars. His hairline had started to creep back at the corners. Jack would not have wanted to hook his future to grubbing around in the guts of the county's old air coolers.

Yet he tried to take the hopeful view. "You've fixed yourself up a good shop here." They had put a large door in the back of the place to handle the big units they might install. It opened onto an alley where they could bring in their truck. "Maybe if they build the air base they're talking about, things will open up," he offered.

"Yeow. That's a chance," Gorilla agreed. "Only they'll probably bring in some big outfit for that. The old man's talking about retiring and opening a joint out on North Broadway. I don't know. If things don't pick up, maybe I'll go in with him. I reckon Al and me could get out of this without getting hurt too bad. If the fuckin place wasn't connected to buildings with people livin in them, we could burn it down for the insurance," he joked, but not so heartily that it hadn't been an acual consideration.

"Want to duck out for a quick brew?" Jack offered.

Gorilla seemed tempted. He really looked at Jack for the first time and smiled. He licked his lips. Then he shook his head. "Naw. I gotta get this done. It wouldn't be fair to Al. He's sweatin out this month's accounts to see if we get paid. We'll probably have to work tonight on this crap. Me and Al."

Jack said he had to shove off then. Gorilla told him to stop by his house for supper sometime soon. Jack promised he would do that. He knocked on the glass and waved to Al and his wife on his way out.

They're getting worried and sadass like everyone else, he told himself gloomily as the sun shimmered around him like the sound waves of a constant great gong. *How the hell does anyone get old without becomin scared and sadass?* he asked himself.

"Stay mad!" he advised aloud, causing an old woman waiting for a bus to look at him curiously.

Sharon walked out along the arcade from the art annex toward the main building with a tall, good-looking kid named Alden Bright, whom Jack recognized from the recent sports pages as a junior tennis champion and captain of East's team. His dad had a photo supply company. Alden had printed up cards and went door to door selling his services as a baby photographer and had even taken pictures of a few weddings. He always had money and dressed as well as anyone in school. He was taking a special photography course for his art requirement. An expensive leather camera bag hung off his left shoulder. In his left hand he carried a folding tripod. His hair was so bleached by the sun it looked peroxided. In spite of the prevailing butch fashion vying with pachuco pomps, Alden's hair was combed neatly back on either side of a low left part so it looked like sheets of light gold. He was talking earnestly as they walked, a self-satisfied, mocking smile flitting at the corners of his mouth. Sharon listened as intently, staring at the walk before her feet, her chin almost on her chest. Jack saw the knuckles of the kid's right hand graze the back of Sharon's hand, and she looked up quickly to laugh at something he said. He was a sharp bastard, Jack had to give him that. A silky-looking light-blue shirt fitted his slender torso perfectly. He was one of only a few kids who wore a tie to school. He would have a sports coat in his locker for going after school to call upon ladies who might like to have their children's portraits made. Rumor was, the slick creep was getting plenty going door to door. The shirt was tucked neatly into houndstooth check slacks, pleated and pegged, held up by a good leather belt in the dropped belt loops. A real gold key chain of snaky links descended from the belt to the keys in his right pocket.

Sharon nodded her head as if complying with something and turned to wave once before he cut into the main building. Jack honked the horn, and she saw the car, smiled brightly and waved. She had combed her hair after gym. She *was* beautiful, he realized with a surprisingly sinking feeling. He could see how she could get more beautiful for the next dozen or so years and it made him feel inadequate, ugly, roughed-up, simple.

She tossed her books into the back seat and hopped in beside him, wiping her brow with the back of her wrist and blowing air up over her face.

"It's murder!" She sighed.

He gunned the car, spinning the wheels on the gravel to get her quickly to someplace cool. To please her.

She scooted down and lay her head on the back of the seat to catch some of the slipstream around the corner of the windshield. Her breasts were large hills beneath her blouse, yet not the stiletto-tipped cones most of the girls sported. A bosomy woman herself, her mother insisted a girl should spend as much as she could afford on a good bra. There was already a womanly softness to Sharon's breasts that made him ache for her. He suddenly wondered if that asshole Alden had taken the photo of her that won the school's Sweater Girl title.

"So," he demanded, "what were you doin with that punk?"

"What?" she asked lazily with her eyes closed. "Who?"

"That Alden schnoorp."

"Oh!" She hadn't been aware he had seen them. But it was OK he had. "Just talking. And he isn't a punk."

"Yeow? Looks like a punk to me. What were you talkin about?"

"He asked me for a date."

"He *did?* That bastard."

"Umm." She rolled her head away from him and looked up at the big trees that arched over the street.

"Didn't he know you go with me?" he asked.

"Well, no. I don't think it came up."

"Well, Jesus Christ! Didn't you explain it?"

"What do you mean exactly?"

"Well, shit, Sharon! About *us*. Me and you?"

She rolled her head back to look at him. "Jealous?"

"Of that punk! I'll break his face!"

"Don't be silly, Jack. Anyway, we aren't going *steady*, you know...."

"Well, same as! Only because your folks won't let you, we're not. I don't go screwin around with other girls," he lied self-righteously. "And it ain't easy." He rubbed the basket of his Levi's meaningfully.

She turned away and observed blandly, "Well, maybe you ought to then ... if it's so difficult for you."

"I didn't meant that," he insisted. "I don't like to think some punk like that can just come up and ask you out. I wish we were in the same school."

"So you could keep an eye on me?" she said bitterly.

"No. But so I could see you more...." He did not really wish they were in the same school. He liked the idea of being at the U and her still in high school. There was the freedom to flirt openly with others. And he trusted her. Oh, he wasn't, from what she had let him do, all that sure, but deep down, after his own sexual hysteria had passed, he trusted her.

"I love you, you know," he said. It sounded completely phony to him, though he truly meant it. He reached from the gearshift knob and patted the inside of her bare leg above the knee. Her skin was hot and damp.

She removed his hand when he presumed to move it a bit higher. "Don't, Jack. It's too hot."

They were racing out Hillside.

"Where are we going?" she asked.

"The sandpit."

She sat up. "I told you, I don't have a suit. I'm *not* going in naked." She frowned.

"I don't have my suit either," he lied.

"Well, I am not going in without one," she said firmly.

"Others do."

"I'm not."

"Wear your underwear then," he suggested.

"Don't be silly."

"So we'll just dangle our feet. It'll be cooler out there. There's always a little breeze."

They did not speak then until he turned in on the old road that had been used by the sand trucks when the place was a working pit. It was overgrown except for the twin ruts. Milkweed and tall timothy grass rattled under the car. The odor of the broken weed came to them.

A Model A four-door painted yellow and black with big fraternity decals on the front doors was parked behind the first dune, with clothes hung from the door handles and draped in the windows. Down by the water they had a big beer cooler. He wished he had thought to bring beer.

Stopping the car, he hopped out and ran down to the cooler.

"Sell me a couple of beers!" he hollered to the three guys and two girls splashing around about fifteen yards offshore.

After consultation one of the frat-rats called back, "OK." But he did not sound happy about it.

They had almost a case in that cooler. Jack took four cans and stuck a dollar under the corner of the cooler.

Someone hoisted a squealing co-ed out of the deep, cool water and flipped her. She was starkers.

"They don't have any suits either," Jack told Sharon, dumping the cans in her lap.

"Um."

"There's a church key in the glove compartment," he informed her, though she knew where it was.

He parked around a dune at the far end of the pit where they could not see the others. But the sounds of their joy made even the shade of the tree under which he spread their blanket seem oppressively hot. The blanket was a Navy one of wool. If they didn't go in, it was a lousy idea coming there.

Sharon slapped at flies around her ankles. She sat with her knees up. Hell, he could see her thighs and the white wedge of her perforated cotton panties. What difference would it make if they went in? He handed her an open can of beer.

"Let's go in," he begged.

"I wish we had brought suits," she said. She took a sip of the cold beer.

"I won't rape you," he argued.

"I know that!" she sniffed. "I didn't say you would."

"I've all but seen you naked anyway."

She looked at him over her can of beer and modestly lowered her legs. Then she lay back with one arm shading her eyes and kicked off her loafers. She raised one knee and again and skidded her skirt up off her legs.

Jack dropped to his knees beside her on the blanket, throwing his arms around her upraised leg, and kissed her knee, then tobagganed kisses down her thigh until his ear was pressed against her sex. He could hear the soft rustle of hair beneath the cloth.

She pulled his head up with both hands and gave him a deep, surprisingly hungry kiss. Something about her made him less careful than usual. He cupped her right breast, causing her to give a small cry in his mouth. She covered his hand with her own, but she did not try to remove it. With that confidence, he ran his hand down over her clothes, feeling the little jumps of her body in the passing of his touch. He caressed her sweaty thighs and cupped the soft, cotton-covered mound between them. She folded her right leg over his hand, holding it there. Her tongue was soft, flat and giving in her mouth.

"I just love you so much, Sharon, I don't know what to do," he told her breathlessly.

She smiled at him. "You better stop what you are doing, or I'll rape you."

He gave her a final squeeze. She closed her legs on his hand, licked her lips and raised herself against the pressure for a single delicious moment. She made a face as if in pain. It cleared. She sat up and looked at him with a stricken look in her eyes.

"We shouldn't ever see each other again," she said.

What? Are you crazy?! What?

"If we keep on like this, something is going to happen. I know it. It just isn't good, Jack." She laid a hand over his tattoo.

"Horseshit!" he exploded. "Haven't I promised you? Nothing's goin to happen."

"For God sake, do you think I'm made of stone?" she flashed angrily. "I have feelings, too!"

"I know." He tried to sound sympathetic, not really knowing of what he hoped to convince her. He touched her back and felt it stiffen beneath his hand.

"We can't go on like this. It's too hard on both of us."

"Well, what do you *want* to do?" he asked desperately.

"I don't *know!*" She flung herself facedown on the blanket. Her back moved as if she were crying softly.

He wanted to say something—some perfect thing that would make it all right. He did not understand. Yet, he could not help noting how her bottom shook so intriguingly as she sobbed. He wanted to leap on top of her, feel his dick in there while she wept.

"Baby, baby. Would it be any better if I was that Alden punk? That shutterbug sonofabitch?"

She shook her head. "I don't *know!* I don't know anything. I only know since you came home and we began seeing each other I'm miserable so much. I like to be with you. I *like* you to touch me. I shouldn't, but I do. But I can't stand it. We have so much time ahead of us. College. It seems impossible. I want to have fun. Go dancing and to parties. We never go dancing or anything like that. . . ."

"Well, I was workin before. We'll go out more now," he promised.

"We always seem to go somewhere and do just this. I don't want this now!" she insisted.

"Well, I'm sorry as hell! Do you think *I* wanted this? Hell, I just wanted to come home and go to school and have a nice time. Only now I want you. Only you. I don't know why—shit!"

They looked at each other helplessly for a moment. Both had gotten up on their knees on the blanket, hands on their thighs. "And he's a *Baptist!*" he shouted.

"Who?"

"That asshole Alden!"

She began to laugh. "You *are* jealous!"

They fell laughing and kissing into each other's arms.

"Let's do go in," she said, peeling away bits of hair stuck to her face.

"Yes?"

"You don't think anyone will see us?"

"No way." They could hear the others far down behind the dune.

"OK." She pushed him away. Her blouse was already out of her skirt. The upper half of her expensive bra was white nylon net, appliquéd with tiny flowers. He had played with her tits, kissed them, but had never actually seen them completely bare. When she saw the look on his face, she covered herself with her blouse.

"Don't look."

"For christ sake," he muttered, turning his back. He undid his Levi's and slipped out of them, pulling off his loafers and socks in the same motion. He turned around still wearing his jockey shorts.

Sharon stood on the blanket with her back to him. Her skirt and blouse were laid neatly at her feet. She had unfastened her bra in the back and held the cups modestly on her breasts for a second or two before slipping down the straps and laying it on top of her clothes. She began peeling down her panties.

God, she's beautiful, he thought. *Like a dream. I don't deserve somethin like that,* he had a sudden, sinking insight. But in the realization he became determined. *No one else, man! I want that.* Her butt at the end of a deep, supple spine looked so cool, clean and white he wanted to bury his face between those globes. Eat her. Devour her. In his desire there was nothing that did not seem beautiful.

Stripping off his shorts, he was aware his cock had begun to rise, arching out in a lazy, thickening curve.

When she turned, she covered her sex with her hand, her face young, wondering, full of questions, as her eyes flicked here and there about his body. He too tried not to look directly at any part of her. Her fine, sensitive hand did not entirely cover the wedge of dark hair between her closely held legs. Her breasts were large but shapely—like in a drawing by Petty in *Esquire*—that perfect, with small veins beneath the pale skin near her nipples that made them look swollen, almost bursting. Her glance darted to his cock. He tried to smile at her.

"It's OK," he said. He took a step toward her, putting out his hand.

"Don't, please," she asked.

She had jerked him off in the car into a handkerchief a

couple of times when he had begged her to and gotten her so hot she swore she did not know what she was doing. He had put a fingertip in her neat, firm slit, so smooth and slick. But standing before each other in daylight, naked, made them both hesitant, awed.

"Take away your hand. It looks silly," he told her gently.

Holding his eyes with her own, she removed the hand to her side and stood like a little soldier. As he deliberately looked away from her face and down at her, she stiffened as if in anticipation of a blow. Her belly jumped and tightened as if his gaze was tactile. He heard her catch her breath and whisper, "Jack...."

He thought of her monthly blood, that she urinated there. None of that mattered at all. It made him happy to look at her.

"But it's beautiful!" he cried. "You are beautiful! All of you." He threw himself on his knees before her, wrapped his arms round her hips and buried his face beneath her belly, kissing her there as happily as if it were her pretty face. "I love you!" he insisted into the center of her.

She was shocked and tried to push him away.

He got up laughing, hurt only by the look of terror in her eyes. He scooped her up in his arms and ran down the bank with her, with her squealing now in fear of being thrown in. He dove with her in his arms, carrying her deep into the cool pool—into a small, deep, blue, freshwater sea in the heart of the prairie.

A few feet below the surface the water was really cold. Fed from an underground spring it was almost as clear as a pool. He opened his eyes underwater and saw her, pale green and beautiful, floating at the end of his arm, asprawl, her cheeks puffed like a blowfish. He laughed underwater, towed her near and wrapped her in his arms and kissed her as they floated upward, tasting the alkaline water in their mouths, her lipstick, aware of how delightfully slippery her body and limbs felt against his.

They surfaced and she squealed and struggled away from him, laughing, kicking water in his face, scissoring away. She rolled on her belly and began swimming strongly, her bare bottom breaking the surface as she rolled from side to side.

"Beautiful!" he yelled after her. He put his head down and swam after her. He felt *good*!

Catching her ankle, he hauled her under. He held her close as she spluttered water and blinked it from her eyes. Her hair streamed over her face. Her breasts floated just below the surface, bobbing upon the slight wake of their bodies. He drew her slowly toward him until just her erect nipples touched his chest, then more slowly, until his cock was against the sea moss of her sex, her belly slick against his.

They played and laughed. He drew up his feet until only they and his head remained out of the water, paddling around her in circles, looking like a two-and-one-half-foot dwarf, spouting water from his mouth to make her laugh. He became a shark, diving beneath the surface, darting at her thrashing body to bite her legs and bottom. He caught her around the waist and kissed her sex underwater. She protested that real sharks hadn't hands. He explained he was a pool shark, and that they had hands. The next time he darted in he caught a knee on his lip. When he came up it was bleeding. She kissed the blood away. In the cool-cool water their bodies felt young, solid and slick as tunas.

"If we had gills, we could live in this pit," he exclaimed happily.

"Would we want to?" She laughed.

"Beat the housing shortage. Sure! Wouldn't you?"

"I don't know."

"It's great. Sometimes I think I haven't evolved very far from the sea creatures from which I stem."

"Heretic!"

"Listen. I tell you the truth, the only good thing I feel in your church is being close to you. Here, like this, I feel great. Really next to myself—with you—Hell! I'm not such a bad guy at all."

"You aren't?" She feigned surprise. "That's not what the girls tell me."

"What do you say?"

"I don't know." But she swam close to touch his face tenderly. "Sometimes, dear Jack, you lose me." She shook her streaming head. "I'm getting out, waterbaby. It's cold and I feel the beginning of a cramp." She swam toward the steep bank.

She slipped and fell squealing back into the water. He had to get out first and haul her up by both arms. She dug in her toes to climb. Large beads of water clung to her shoulders. Her right breast brushed his cock as he pulled her up. He felt very free, beyond petty gropings and passionate lies.

He carried her to the blanket. Laying her down, he kissed her chastely, determined to keep it merely fun, so he had control. She pulled his head down and wrapped her arms around his neck, pulling him over her. Their bodies were still cool and wet from the water. When he felt his cock rising between her legs to press against her sex, there was the incredible wonder in the proximity, a mere point on the world's surface.

She let him move against her for a moment, even responded by moving her hips as they sometimes did when clothed. Then there was the fear in her eyes.

He promised, "I won't go into you. I just want to feel myself against you there." After a few more moments, he asked, "Will you let me lie between your legs? Just let me be there for a moment."

Her eyes narrowed suspiciously, but she did as he asked.

"I won't do anything," he assured her. "Just practicing." He wanted to keep it from being serious. "Does it feel any kind of good to you?"

"Yes," she whispered. "But I'm afraid. . . ."

"Hush. Don't worry. I won't do anything. Oh! It feels so good to me, Sharon. You!" He made a great effort to control his excitement. "Sweetheart. Baby. Darling," he crooned. "You feel so good to me."

She wanted to be kissed. The shaft of his cock slid along the slick lips of her beautiful sex. She began to move so perfectly he thought perhaps with real Christians like her, maybe God did give them a special talent to compensate for lack of practice. For he had screwed chicks who had fucked dozens who hadn't a clue in comparison with Sharon.

In moving he caught the tip of his cock in the lower extremity of her sex in a way that made her flinch and cry out.

Cuddling her face, he kissed away the pain. He altered the angle to slide his cock against her clit and let the head just slip inside her.

"What are you doing?" she asked both in awe and suspicion, her eyes opening wide.

"Nothing."

"You're going in me," she accused.

"No. Just a little way. Just so I don't hurt you again. Doesn't it feel better?"

"I guess. But I wish you would stop it now."

"Just let me a little more, Sharon. It feels so wonderful. Just to be a little way in you is like heaven. God! I want so badly to be all the way in you. Feel you all around me. Know it feels good to you—"

"Don't!"

"Oh, I won't. Just this. But, please, please, Sharon, don't stop me. Tell me it feels good to you, too."

"Yes. Only you hurt a little. Ow! Be careful."

He determined not to touch her maidenhead.

"Let me come, darling," he begged. "Just like this."

"Not *in* me!"

"No. No. Trust me. Please."

"No. I don't want to. Please stop, Jack."

"I can't. . . ." Not even if she was dying. He began to fuck her faster, shallowly, going around, just the head of his cock in her. When he went too deep, she winced. She was breathing through her mouth. She still moved, but her eyes were terrified.

"Oh, Jack! Please, no more. Please don't come. JACK!"

"Darling, darling Sharon," he crooned. Only at the last possible instant did he yank his cock from her and plunge in down against the crack of her ass, collapsing upon her as his cock jerked and ejaculated against her cool bottom.

She was smiling bravely, tears in her eyes, brushing back the hair from his forehead.

"You're wonderful," he told her. "I'm so happy I could cry." He slid down and kissed her breasts and rubbed her belly while she stroked the top of his head.

"Did it feel good for you too?" he asked.

She seemed to be nodding her head affirmatively. "Too good," she said firmly. "We mustn't take a chance like that again."

"No chance," he assured her. "I was careful. I knew what I was doing."

"I know, dear. But I could feel in you and see in your face only the barest sort of thread kept you from going all the way. And if I had let *myself* go a single nother little bit, it would have been all over but the shouting."

Jesus Christ! he thought. *But the shouting? Let's get to*

471

*the shouting! Now she's feeling all superior and maternal
and strong. She-it. Man, if anyone's made for it, she is.
But I love her, man,* he added as if someone were monitor-
ing his thoughts. He didn't want any misunderstanding.

"I wouldn't have, Sharon. Never!"

"I know, dear," she purred with condescending wisdom,
twisting a finger in his hair. "But it is too great a responsibility to put on ourselves."

He just brushed the curling extremity of her pubic hair
with his palm, looking down over her belly, loving the
wide bones of her hips when she lay on her back.

"You wanted more?" he asked.

"Yes!" She yanked him up by the hair. "What do you
think I'm made of, for goodness sake?! I could have
just—my God, didn't you know?" It seemed a terrible accusation.

"Well, uh, sure. But I was so, uh, you know—happy to
be there, I. . . ."

"That's what I mean!" she insisted. "See! So, how about
another quick dip before we go?"

"Hell, yeow!" He leaped on her again, rolling his eyes
and waggling his tongue like Harpo Marx.

She squawled and fought. "No! To cool off, you *nut!*"

He hauled her off the blanket and they ran hand in
hand down to the bank. "Dive!" he yelled.

They lay side by side on the blanket, her head, wrapped
in his only towel, on his shoulder, letting the air dry their
bodies. He felt magnanimous within his sense of possession. If she would let him do that, he thought he would
not need another girl. They could have a couple of years
of college and get married. With part-time jobs and the
GI Bill they could make out OK. Others did it. The beautiful naked girl beside him extended intimations of citizenship he had never known, of a suburban-quiet possibility
he had never even dared to dream about. His dreams had
always been of glory and derring-do, of fame and adula-
tion. Now he thought of a GI home, a small lawn, Sharon
to love him and he would be faithful to her all of his days.
He saw brown-haired and blond children, well dressed,
well equipped with trikes and skates and a jungle gym,
and not a fear between the vision and the horizon. He
could be a political cartoonist for one of the papers,

work for Western Lithograph or one of the plants. He put his hand on her belly.

She tilted her head up to smile and kiss his chin. "I love you," he said.

She lowered her eyelids in acceptance of something her natural due.

He talked her into stopping for double cheeseburgers and milk shakes, though she was certain her mother would have a fit if she missed Thursday night supper. Jack was starved. He had two double-deck burgers.

He could not stop looking at her. It made him happy to see her in profile sucking her milk shake through a big candy-striped straw.

"So, what are we doing tomorrow night?" he asked. "There's a good show on at the Airport Drive-In. *Soldiers Three*. A Kipling story, I think." He hoped to deflect her thoughts from the possibility of getting into her pants a bit again.

"I have a date tomorrow night," she said in a precisely modulated voice, only turning to smile tentatively at him after she had spoken.

"You have a fucking what?" His mouth hung agape.

"Not a *fuckin* nothing," she shot back. "And don't yell at me."

"Well, *Jesus* Christ! I mean after—Who the hell with? That Alden cunt?"

"Yes," she said defensively. "And stop swearing, *please.*"

"Sonofabitch!" He bellowed so others in nearby cars looked at him. "You mean while I was waitin for you, you were makin a date with that cocksucker?"

"He is none of the things you say. You're just acting crazy, Jack. For your information he asked me two days ago. I only said yes today."

"Why'd you wait?" he wondered.

"Oh, *I* don't know!"

"Do you *want* to go?"

She got hold of herself in spite of the tears in her eyes. "Yes. Yes, I do!"

"And you knew all this when we were out at the pit— You *bitch!*"

"Jack!"

473

He pounded the steering wheel with his fist, causing the horn to honk.

"How the hell could you?" he wondered. "I mean we were the same as going steady."

"We were not! You know I told you I promised Mom and Dad I wouldn't until I was eighteen."

"Oh, they would rather you went out and screwed around with a lot of guys, hunh! Some fuckin big Christians *they* turned out to be."

"You're just talking stupid, Jack. I'm not going to sit here and listen to you say things about my parents."

"Piss on them," he muttered.

"You honk, honey?" The carhop came up and popped her gum. "You through here?"

"Yes!" Sharon snapped. "We're through."

He laid down rubber getting out of the drive.

They did not speak until they were near her home; then he asked, "You mean what you said?"

"What?"

"What you said. That we're through?"

She dropped her face into her hands on her knees. "Oh, I *don't* know! . . . Maybe it would be better." She sat up bravely then.

"What about this afternoon?" he squawked hysterically.

"That's what I *mean*." She looked so distressed, bent over her arms as if she had a bellyache, her hair stringy from swimming.

He wanted to hurt her. He wished he had ripped out her precious cherry and fucked her until she could not walk.

"We just can't go on like this, Jack. I'm not up to it. My grades have gone to hell." That meant she had got a couple of B pluses. "I'm not ready for you, if I ever will be. We aren't ready to be thinking about marriage. Oh!" She shook herself all over. "It's stupid to think about it. Don't you see?"

"So you want to be through?" he concluded cruelly.

"I don't know. No. Yes. I mean, I want to go to Alden's party, date other boys. Not a lot, some. I don't just want to go somewhere and park all the time. . . ."

"So it's Alden's party?"

"Yes."

"Beautiful! I know about those rich boys' fuckin parties. Folks not home. Then they put out the lights and pretty soon everyone's screwin all over the place. Maybe All-den will take flash pictures."

"You think everyone has as dirty a mind as you?!" she bristled. He had never seen her so angry. "Anyway, he's my second cousin."

"A *Baptist?*"

She just shook her head. "You ought to have pictures taken of yourself. If you could see and hear how crazy you are over nothing, you would say you're insane, Jack."

"OH, YEOW!" he bellowed. "I'll show you what's fuckin insane, baby! Don't be surprised if you don't have some very roughass uninvited guests at that goddamned party!"

"Don't you dare!" She was up in the seat on her knees. "Now that I've seen what you are really like, I'm glad this happened. My God! When I think of the mistake I *could* have made this afternoon!" She rolled her eyes at the horror of it.

"Oh, cram you and your goddamn *mistake!*" He sneered. "Who taught you to kiss like that, Cousin *All-*dean?"

"Yes, as a matter of fact, he did."

"He fingerfuck you, too?"

"Stop this car! I'll walk!" She stood as if to bail out.

He yanked her back into the seat. She sat in her corner of the seat, crying, staring straight ahead.

In front of her house, she grabbed her books from the back seat and bounded out, slamming the door.

"We're through, right? That's what you want," he called after her.

On the porch she turned to look back at him in the car. "I think you're sick. I really do, Jack." She went inside.

Sick? "Sick, *shit!*" he said aloud angrily. But he was scared. Maybe she was right. He dashed through his store of experiences. On evidence, he ought to be crazy, he had to admit. *Damn! Damn!* He banged the steering wheel with his fists. *Fuckin snotty goody-goody! Why didn't I stay with my own lousy kind anyway?* "I'm not good enough for her fancy ass," he mocked himself in falsetto. "But Cousin *Alden* is. PISS ON IT!" he hollered down the bricks and beneath the trees of the street.

He went to his place and opened a can of beer. He tried to study. He could not concentrate. The words on the page made no sense. He took down the samurai sword and whirled it around the room. Picking up one of the red throw pillows, he tossed it in the air and swung at it as though hitting flies with a bat. The cushion was sliced in two. A storm of feathers swirled about the room. He swung at individual feathers.

He stopped and studied the blade. That thing was sharp!

He thought of going to get the freckled redhead at the Kau-Kau Korner and bringing her back to the room. Then realized, Sharon had never once said she loved him. Or had she? He tried to remember. She had—once— maybe twice.

He glanced at the books on his desk. "Piss on it," he said aloud.

Opening another can of beer, he took it with him out to the car to go look for Glenn and Bucky.

28

IT WAS just a ramshackle little piece of gas station outside of town on a secondary highway that pumped something called Jet-Gas for 18-½ cents a gallon.

A pile of cement blocks sporting signs for off-brand oils, additives for those jackrabbit starts, tires, brake linings, shock absorbers, ice cream, beer and soda pop, the place was truculently doing business out of the main stream of motor commerce. Jack could not imagine how it got its supplies. He hadn't heard of any of them.

The man who came out to the pumps looked as though he knew of Standard Oil and bore it an irreconcilable grudge. He also looked prepared to brain the next wiseass who inquired after the pedigree of his products. Out to trim the trimmers, he seemed like the man who had started on a shoestring and was about at the end of his rope. Vet's Jet-Stop, anointed with the obligatory ruptured duck, was the sign over his dream, and the one under which he lumbered out now to pump gas with such a bitter chip on his shoulder that the boy began to wonder if it was a case of Standard Oil having turned down his request for a franchise. The biballs and Monkey Ward's shit kickers told you he was also doing some farming before and after hours to make ends meet. Moreover, he was a big, ugly bastard.

With the thermometer, a gift of Nehi-Cola, on the front of his place nudging 103, it suddenly seemed a long way to have come to hit the brute's punchboard.

Painted on the side of the place was the announcement that the Vet also offered sandwiches, cold drinks and ice cold beer.

Glenn told him to fill up the tank, check the oil and tires (he had stopped a mile up the road to lower the pressure in the two offside tires) and try to guess why the engine was overheating.

Before he had pumped the first gallon, they popped inside and called him in to lay on three ham and cheese sandwiches, uncap some beer and leave them with the punchboard on the counter.

He did not offer them the punchboard. He merely left it on the counter where cellophane packets of peanuts and Cheese-Ritz peanut butter snacks waited with stale appeal in a large lidded apothecary jar. The countertop had been surfaced with ordinary linoleum. Screwed to the oily wooden floor, the stools before the counter had feet that revealed their disparate parentage. On the flyspecked back wall next to a VFW member's pennant was an Army Corps of Engineers plaque and a photograph hanging at a dippy angle of the Vet standing in front of a bulldozer holding an M-1 stiffly at solemn port arms.

The Vet was not an intelligent man. There were only lights enough in his small, flat-backed skull to make him suspicious, mistrustful of even himself. His clumsy country hands handling prepacked sandwiches gave Jack the feeling he had when bears were made to roller skate.

"You fellas from Wichita?" he asked, his small eyes narrowing beneath the brim of a silver-painted pith helmet that was evidently a gift of D-A Products.

"Yeow, Wichita." Glenn grinned. "Hotter than a by-God, ain't it?" he offered in an effort to establish sympathy to country origins.

"It'll get hotter," said the glum Vet.

"How's the wheat look around here?" Jack asked as if he had interest.

The Vet shrugged. The seat of his biballs were shiny with grease.

"I'll have a look at your car," he said without enthusiasm, hesitating a moment as if wondering whether to collect for the sandwiches and beer first or not. Finally he decided it was safe to go outside.

Out of the white afternoon glare their eyes began to adjust to the dim interior. Tires, wheels, power mowers with bits of grass stuck in their blades and wheels, small motors, all sort of battered stuff were heaped along one wall. Behind were tiers of cans of those funny oils and auto accessories. The lunch counter ran parallel to the stuff from halfway along the adjacent wall. Abutting it was a sales counter cluttered with loose and spindled bills, receipts and manifests, all smudged by greasy fingers. The sales countertop was as greasy as a workbench, as was the small adding machine and the ornate, old, secondhand cash register hung with a placard:

> NO CREDIT
> NO CHECKS
> NO REFUND

The Vet was a hard man.

Glenn and Buck were busily punching out the board in search of the four-hundred-dollar jackpot. They shoved the losing numbers along to Jack, who ate them with bites of the sandwich and swigs of beer. They kept only enough of the tightly folded bits of numbered crepe paper they shoved from their little cells in the honeycombed board with the provided key, to make them look like players.

They were about twenty dollars to the good when a big dusty dump truck roared up, braking to a halt on the gravel between the station and the pumps. Before the dust of their arrival had settled, Billy Bell piled out of the cab and came hobbling into the station.

They recognized Polio Paul Kiefer at the wheel and Sherman Workman and Henry Blass up in the dump bed. Kiefer kept the engine running and the door on Billy's side open. It was Kiefer's dad's truck. But there was a brown

478

paper taped over the sign on the door. The two in the dump bed moved to the side of the truck above where the Vet was bent over Glenn's car. They appeared to be holding something just out of sight in front of them in the bed.

For a single beat, Bell stopped cold, his little drop-seat mouth hanging open in surprise at finding the other boys there.

"Hey, Billy—" Glenn started a grin, then realized Bell did not want to leave his name. He looked high on bennies or something. He darted behind the sales counter and came up with a Roi-Tan cigar box, which he stuck under his shirt beneath his left arm, and turned for the door.

That told them he had cased the place better than they.

Billy had a funny way of walking, for he wore cowboy boots several sizes too large into which he wadded rags in the toes and bent small condensed milk cans into the heels to make him a couple inches taller than his natural five three. Above a small Huckleberry face he had dyed his carrottop jetblack. He had also dyed his eyebrows, but the paleness of his lashes made him appear perpetually surprised rather than mean.

The boys looked at each other, questioning whether they should bolt themselves, when Billy lurched out the door, piled in the cab and sped off, throwing up gravel as he left.

Glenn began to laugh.

"Jesus Christ! Who but Billy Bell and Polio Paul would go to hold up a gas station in a goddamn dump truck?" Buck put word to it.

"They gotta be high on somethin!" Jack was sure.

"That Bell and his gang smokin pot, gobbling bennies, all kinds of bad shit," Glenn said with authority.

The Vet stood up from checking Dale's tires when the truck roared away without waiting for service. It was still laying a little dust cloud down the highway when it struck him.

"Goddamn!" he cried, dropping the air hose and lumbering toward the store. He lunged behind the sales counter and came up empty and angry and leveling a sawed-off pump gun at the only customers he had left.

"Goddamned bastards, robbed my ass," he said, as if accusing them.

"Listen, we ain't part of this," Glenn tried to explain.

479

"We've seen those crazy guys around. But we don't know them, man!"

"Don't you by-God move. I'm callin the police."

Good as his word, he lost a few seconds finding a nickel for the greasy pay phone by the door. But once he found one he wasted no time in stabbing out the short number.

"Listen, this is Will out on the turnpike. I just been robbed. Some Wichita sonsabitches came in here in a dump truck and ran out with my cashbox. A Jimmy, I think. Yeah, a Jimmy. Blue cab. Dusty. I didn't see no name on it. Right! No, I didn't get no number." He sounded less hopeful. But he perked up. "I got three others here from Wichita who *say* they ain't in on it, but they know the fuckers that got away. Yeah, I'll hold um. It was headed out of town, headed north. Had over five hundred in that box, Jake. I sure hope so. Goddamn if it ain't one damn thing after another. Yeah. You can sure as hell say that again." He hung up the earpiece.

"Listen, pardner, you got us all wrong," Glenn said, trying to ignore the big hole in the shotgun. "We've seen them guys around. But we don't *know* them. We just stopped in on our way to see some girls in Cherryvale. Look, we got twenty dollars' winners on your punchboard." He held out the winning papers in his sweaty palm.

The man cut a quick look at his board. A frown wrinkled his brow as if he couldn't decide if there were more holes in the board than ought to be represented by the punches in Glenn's palm. The gun wavered a moment. Then he decided.

"It don't count less I'm watchin'," he said, tightening his grip on the gunstock.

If he had pulled that before things had turned bad, they would have threatened to call the police. Everyone knew the boards were illegal in Kansas. But in view of his shotgun and how he called the police chief Jake, their contention seemed at the moment a very foolish one.

"Look, we'll pay for our punches," Glenn offered. "We'll help you chase them bastards. While we're standing here, they're gettin away."

The old Army dozer driver blinked as if trying to understand. They could feel he was just on the brink of going along. But he shook off the temptation, squaring himself stubbornly between them and the door.

"We'll just wait for the cops. I ain't playin and I ain't payin."

Jack thought he ought to add *that* to his sign on the cash register.

"Them little cocksuckers got my whole week's take in that box."

They had to give Bell credit. They hadn't known of the cigar box.

Soon a police car with siren going sped through the heat mirage out on the asphalt. The driver lifted his hand as he passed.

Then a second car skidded up in the drive, and a man as large as the Vet got out, left the car door open so he could hear the police calls on the radio and minced toward the station on tiny, brightly polished brown Acme cowboy boots, lifting his stag-handled .357 Magnum pistol from its holster.

"Howdy, Will. Sorry about this." He appraised the three boys as if they were a species other than his own, and he was looking for a sign on them that would tell him what they were. He ambled across the space between them and slapped Jack beside the head with his free hand, making the boy's knees buckle. It had been a slow, deliberate slap, heavy as a ton, which they had all seen coming, but which none could believe, because there was no reason for it. The chief's blank country face had held Jack so transfixed he hadn't moved.

He felt a trickle of blood from his right nostril down over his lip. There was a buzzing in his head.

"Now. What do you boys know about this?"

"Nothin, honest, Chief," Glenn pleaded. "We just stopped cause we were overheatin and two tires were low. We don't *know* them crazy bastards. We've *seen* them around Wichita. But we don't know them. We'll help you chase them, sir," he offered.

"What are their names?"

"Uh, ah." He looked at the others. "The little one's called Billy somethin, I think. Yeah. And then one's named Fred or Red. I mean, sir, we see them around, but they aren't from our side of town, see. We didn't go to school with them er anything."

"Um. What are you doin here?" the cop demanded of Jack.

481

No one had ever slapped him openhanded that hard. He sniffed up the trickle of blood. "We were goin to Cherryvale to look up these girls we met at the skating rink a couple weeks back."

The cop slapped him again on the other side of the head. This time he went to his knees and slumped forward.

"Liar!" the cop said calmly.

Jack had a close look at the tiny, stiletto-toed boots on which the big man was perched. He thought of Babe Ruth—all that belly on those little spindly legs. He had a vision of one of those glassy toes taking out his front teeth. He was hauled up by his collar and stood on his feet. His pain was clearly reflected in his buddies' eyes.

"We ain't got no skatin rink in Cherryvale."

"Oh, not here!" Glenn leaped in to help. "No, sir. In Wichita. We met them in Wichita. They said to come down and see them. So we decided we would."

"What are the girls' names?"

"Sue. Yeow. And one was named Sally and—" He looked at Buck. "What was the name of the one you were with?"

"Ruth."

"Yeow! Ruth, she said. Brunette, sort of short and real cute," Glenn supplied.

"What did they say their last names were?" the cop asked.

"Uh. They didn't. Anyway, I don't think they did," Glenn said. "You know, you don't ask shit like that anymore. We just figured we'd come find them. You know. Find the kids' hangout and ask. There's a place where kids go."

The chief shot a disgusted look at the Vet. "How old are you?" he asked Glenn.

"Twenty." He reached for his wallet to show his draft card. The chief almost put the barrel of his pistol under Glenn's nose.

"Keep your hands where I can see them. You call yourself a kid?" he wondered incredulously, as if they were indeed of another planet.

"Well, uh, sorta." Glenn blushed. "I work. I gotta laundry route, run my own truck. I'm independent," he said with no little pride. "Buck here, he's got a good job with a printer. And Jack, he goes to college. *On the GI Bill!* You got the wrong guys, Chief!"

"S'at so? Then why in hell ain't you back where you belong stead of down here chasing after fourteen-, fifteen-year-old goddamn girls you met at some skatin rink? Put out your hands."

He snapped cuffs on Glenn and Jack, linking them together with the single pair. At the car, his deputy gave him another pair, and he joined them all three together and shoved them into the back seat.

"Don't worry, Will. I radioed the state patrol. There ain't a chance in hell those little fuckers will get away in a dump truck."

Under the brim of his silver pith helmet, Will's eyes looked as dark and depthless as two holes onto pitch-black space.

"What are you chargin us with, Chief?" Glenn asked as casually as a bystander when they drove off.

"Suspicion of grand larceny or disturbin my lunch. Take your choice."

Just at the edge of town, he lifted one cheek of his ass and farted resoundingly. "Chili for lunch," he explained to his grinning deputy. "Ever time I eat that chili I get the farts."

"You never thought about givin up the chili then?" the deputy asked as the wind reached him and his expression changed.

The chief studied him a moment. "Why, no, I never did. I like that chili a lot. Reckon I'd get me a new deputy, Ralph, before I gave up that chili."

Ralph grinned again and looked at the big man out of the corners of his eyes. The chief had a large, square initial ring on his left hand.

Jack, who was linked outside Glenn, reached up and searched his jaws for indents of that initial.

In the station they turned out their pockets and removed their belts and shoelaces.

"Put them down for 'Vagrancy,'" Ralph instructed the clerk. "For now."

"But we ain't Vag," Glenn offered. "We got money, a car. We got jobs. We're regular citizens."

"We'll have to check that." Ralph grinned.

The clerk laughed.

"We just come here lookin for a little fun," Glenn protested to the man at the typewriter.

"Cherryvale?" He looked at the thin young man as if he were nuts. "Reckon you looked in the wrong place, boy."

The turnkey took them back to the piss-smelling cells and locked them all in together.

"You're gettin in too late for dinner," he advised them as if they should have planned their visit better, meaning lunch, but said it in such a way they knew there would not be any Saturday supper either.

"How's my face look?" Jack asked, feeling his cheeks tenderly.

"Not bad." Glenn gave it a glance. "A little puffed. Not bad. Man, can you imagine what was in that fuckin crazy Bell's head pullin somethin like that in broad daylight in a dump truck?!"

They could not.

"He's wild, man! Screwy! Jacked off his brains or somethin."

"Yeow. He's a freak-o all right," Bucky put in. "Dyin his hair like that. You know. Glenn set him up with old Vanda Hardasty once out in Sim's Park. We screwed her, and then he was goin to, only he couldn't get a hard on. He slugged the shit out of her when she laughed at him and went runnin off. We waited to take him home in the car, but he didn't show. Shit, we ain't seen him a dozen times since."

They spent the afternoon speculating on the other gang's tastes and how in the petty pool hall world of Wichita word of the Vet's place had become such common knowledge. Had Glenn overheard one of them or had it been the other way around was a puzzle. That punchboards were illegal did not loom in their minds as the basis for much of a defense, they decided.

Jack became more morose as the day wore on and he thought of Sharon and school. The prospects of an easy hundred and twenty-five dollars in the face of his recent unemployment looked like small potatoes now. *Kid's shit!* he thought, hating Glenn and Buck stretched out on the bare bunks trying to look like lifers.

About sundown the highway patrol brought in Bell and his gang. Kiefer was protesting loudly they had nothing on them. He demanded to call his dad.

484

Kiefer looked like a benny-eating cousin of Abe Lincoln. His left leg was in a metal brace attached to a special shoe. What puzzled Jack was why Kiefer and Blass needed to rob a thing. Kiefer's old man had plenty of money. Paul had one of the first really sharp Model A hot rods in town. He drove a truck for his old man in the summer. Blass' family was even better off. Hell, he lived out on the hill, in one of the city's fine old houses where the trees had been there for generations, not the little sticks on the lawns of some new forty-thousand-dollar ranch thing out in Eastborough. His old man was an electrical contractor. Once Jack had gone to his house with him, and their black cook made him smoked salmon and cream sandwiches with the crusts trimmed off the bread and served them on a plate with potato chips and deckled pickle slices and radish roses just like in a fancy restaurant. Blass had poured their beers into real pilsner glasses. The whole house was air-conditioned. In the basement there was all kinds of sports equipment.

Jack could not understand guys like that.

"They like to think of themselves as badasses," Glenn tried to explain. "They like to run with guys like us."

The cops laid a .38 pistol and a German submachine gun in perfect working order on the booking desk. The German gun was one Blass' brother had brought home from the war.

"Maybe they feel bad cause they missed the war," Jack suggested.

"You dumb bastards seen too many movies!" they heard the chief voice his opinion in the other room.

"You don't have to shove!" they heard Bell complain.

"Get your ass in there, boy, or I'll break your crazy back." The chief hustled Bell and Kiefer into a cell himself.

Finally, the turnkey came back and opened the cell and said, "OK. We're lettin you bunch go."

Passing Bell's cell, Glenn cracked out of the side of his mouth, "Keep your pecker up, Billy. Hang tough."

The chief would not let them go without warning:

"I know you guys were here lookin for trouble. If it hadn't been that bunch back there, it woulda been you. You show yourselves around here again and you'll get more damned trouble than you'll be able to stand. You stay up there in the city where you belong. Don't come down here tryin to fuck up our country. We don't want your kind here. You're all no damn good, and you never will be. An honest day's work would kill you. One day we're going to clean up this whole damn country of scum like you, and I hope I live to see it." He leveled a sausage-sized finger at them like a gun. "Get out of here. And don't look back until you see Wichita."

Glenn guessed it wouldn't be a good idea to stop and try to collect on the punchboard winners.

Buck laughed.

Jack sat in the corner of the back seat watching the prairie zip past while night-flying grasshoppers and moths died in exploded patterns against the windshield.

29

IT WAS Sunday morning, and in a tousled, acrid sweat he saw himself a crablike old boobatch scuttling between skid row bars, flashing his tattered discharge papers in pursuit of a drink, a tolerant word, lying his ugly head off about long-gone battles and victories he had never attended to men who did not believe a word of it; the lies leaving a hollowness in him no amount of drink could ever fill. He did not even *like* booze, yet the vision was so immediate that the schoolbooks on his desk and the desire to brush his teeth seemed a pose.

You're no good and never will be, a chorus of kith and kin spoke from all quarters of his folding bed. Even Glenn and Bucky were there. *By what right?* he wondered. Yet he knew, by their standards, he was less than they. Nowhere now did he see a welcoming smile, an offered hand. The university sent him hurrying in terror along the cool halls. He showed up, kept his mouth shut and found his teachers' eyes sliding over him as if he were not there. Education seemed the inalienable right only of those who would have been cared for by the achievement of their parents in any case.

486

Nor did he feel one with his fellow veterans, who in the main took dead aim on a specific niche in business administration, engineering, advertising, medicine, or science. In the student union and along the walks they spoke to each other in confident terms of exclusivity. The whole fucking system was one of shutting others out. Eyes all around him harbored intricate secrets. Clever bastards playing games to which only they and a chosen few knew the rules. *Shit on that!* he raged within himself. *They are no different than goddamn criminals. It's the same thing!* he was certain.

Then why did he feel always guilty?

Eager curiosity was a waste of the university's time. He had quickly discovered that. Purpose was the rule. To the boy's surprise, poverty in human terms was never broached in a discussion of economics, or wealth either.

Even the books he was required to read seemed to him to be based on foregone conclusions, so unanimously held that the questions the books begged in his mind made him feel he was either morally inferior or crazy. He refused to accept the possibility he was stupid. He had an IQ at the last checking five points higher than General Eisenhower's. If that meant anything in the general's case, it had to mean something in his.

The bells of St. Francis a few blocks away began tolling to commence the eleven o'clock elevation of the Christ. He would be sent up once more at two. The idea of such a yo-yo God made him too tired to get out of bed. He fell back on the pillow with his hands behind his head, staring at the cheap acoustical-tile ceiling.

His grandmother would be mad because he hadn't come to drive her to church, though she said she was embarrassed to be seen in his bright-red car. She said it looked like a tart in the parking lot among the sedate sedans.

He imagined Sharon surreptitiously looking around the church for him, aware of the space beside her he had religiously filled since coming home from the Navy. He fancied the others asking her after services if he was sick.

Finally he had to get up and piss. When he came back he put on soft Levi's without bothering about underwear. The nice thing about living in a basement was that it was always cool. In the kitchen a small roach tickled a little gray roly-poly bug like a tiny armadillo which turned itself into a wee ball smaller than a pea. He lifted a cobweb out of the corner behind the refrigerator where a nearly transparent spider had expired for want of flies and promised himself to give the place a good cleaning.

Staring into the refrigerator, he decided eggs and bacon were too great an effort. He felt very hollow, however. He tilted up a quart carton of milk and drank from the spout, tasting the wax and feeling the cold, chalky liquid slide soothingly down to his stomach. Then he had a little, ordinary hunger. A cold loaf of bread half gone, the milk, an opened plastic bottle of Kraft cheese and a small jar of mayonnaise were balanced on his arm, stacked against his bare chest. On the way to the table, he reached out and snagged a knife from the drainboard of his sink. He sat down, wiped the blade on his Levi's and made a cheese sandwich. There was a kind of extravagance in eating the processed food his mother had always claimed was unhealthy. The white bread and cheese stuck in his throat and had to be washed down with large sips of the milk.

With breakfast done and the confidence that Christ had safely ascended again, Jack turned determinedly to his books.

> Alas, alas, who's injured by my love?
>   What merchant ships have my sighs drowned?
> Who says my tears have overflowed his ground?
> When did my colds a forward Spring remove?
>   When did the heats which my veins fill
>   Add one man to the plaguy Bill?
> Soldiers find wars, and lawyers find out still
>   Litigious men, which quarrels move,
>   Though she and I do love.

Or do we? he asked himself.

The knock on the door made him jump. There was a mad hope it was Sharon. Then he dreaded it was Glenn and Buck. Maybe it was only the landlady, though he had paid his rent.

It was his mother, come dressed for her work at MacFarlane's Chinese restaurant, carrying her low-heeled shoes in a paper sack. Her vanity portal-to-portal required white stiletto-toed pumps with four-inch high heels.

"You never come to see me, so I came to see you." She smiled reprovingly. "Didn't you get my note?"

"Note? Uh, no," he lied. "What note?"

She brushed past him and dropped her sack on his table. "I put a note in your door." She knew he had gotten it.

"Must have fallen down," he mumbled.

Quickly, she turned around and wrapped arms around his neck in a move so slick he hadn't actually seen it coming at all. He permitted himself a sardonic smile of admiration but braced himself for the blues that were to follow. Her head nestled on his shoulder.

"Oh, I'm just so sick and tired of working at that awful place. They don't pay me anything, and tips aren't very good. It's such long hours, and you never feel the Chinks who run it have blood like you and I. I wish I could find something better."

Rather than stand there like a crying post, he put his arms around her. Resentment and disgust made his mouth cruel. He knew her every turning. She was going to con him for some money. He was going to let her have it. Yet he could not resist letting her run through her scheme, evilly curious to see where it would lead. He could feel the whorish plaint empty her of all else. He was someone to be worked like any other.

"You try any of the plants?" He fed her a line.

"I don't want to work in a plant. And they're laying off, not hiring. Anyway, they wouldn't hire someone with a prison record."

He sensed the cold gray walls and steel doors opening.

"I would like to have a cosmetic counter. But maybe I don't look good enough anymore."

He tightened his arms around her. She looked fine. He told her so. She had lost weight in jail which she had not put on again. She used makeup well. Her dark eyes behind thick, modern lenses were enormous and liquid. The glasses made her look young and kooky. Whatever her need for money, she was able to go to a hairdresser regularly and always kept her nails perfectly manicured. Her clothing was fresh, her shoes were whitened, and he had never seen her with a run in her stockings. She would go bare-legged first. She was a woman with soft edges and small bones, and he could not imagine her ever as old.

"Mom, did you ever think we might be nuts?" he asked.

She leaned back to look at him. "No! What makes you ask that?"

"I don't know. Sometimes I feel I really am."

"Well, I don't." She was certain.

"Neither do I down deep. But just sometimes I'm sure either I am or almost everyone else must be. And I do believe in democracy."

She hugged him tight and put her head back on his shoulder.

"I don't think you are nuts, baby. You've had a rough way to go. You may be warped a bit, but you aren't cracked."

He laughed.

"You feel strong as a tree." She squeezed him again. "I need someone strong to hold me."

"How's Blackie?" he asked of her boyfriend.

"Oh, Blackie is good, you know. He isn't very smart, but he's OK. They put him on nights at the factory now. I hardly ever see him."

They did not actually live together, he guessed because their landlady would not permit it or something. She had her kitchenette apartment, and he had a room down the hall.

Her uniform was of nylon through which he could see the straps and lacy bodice of her slip, the skin tint of her shoulders. Wash and wear, it felt cool against his bare skin. He slid his arms and hand slowly up and down her back to sense her softness beneath the plastic cloth.

"I thought you were mad at me or something," she said like a little girl.

"No."

"Then why haven't you come to see me? I would like to make dinner for you or go to a movie or something."

"I've been busy. This college stuff is tough for me. I have to work my tail off because I never learned how to study. Then I had this part-time job."

"Mom said you lost it."

"Yeow ... assholes. I'll get another. I still got some dough." He regretted letting the slip the moment the words were out of his mouth.

"I thought you did," she purred. "Maybe you could let me have ten or so until next week. I really need it, honey.

I have to see this doctor, and it's ten each visit. I have to go every week."

"What the hell for?"

She tightened her arms around him and moved closer, kissing his neck. "Oh it's probably nothing," she said bravely. "I just get so weak and feel washed-out. The treatments help me."

"What kind of treatments?"

"I go to Dr. Martinez who gives me adjustments."

"A *chiropractor?*"

"He's an osteopath!" she insisted testily. "I don't care. It works! He always makes me *feel* better. Isn't that what you go to a doctor for?"

"Horseshit! If something's wrong with you why don't you see a real doctor?"

"Well, I did, and they can't find anything wrong with me. He's in a clinic with three other doctors, and he was recommended by the one I saw."

He didn't want to give her his money to pay some greaser quack, but he could see no way out of it.

"You need more than ten?" he asked resignedly.

"Well, I could use it if you could spare it," she admitted.

He reached in his pocket and pulled out three fives.

"I'm an easy mark." He grinned at her.

She patted his face. "Not so easy, baby."

Their eyes met for an electric second of recognition and kinship.

At the door she gave him a peck. "Work hard, dear, and take care of yourself," she advised. "If you *want* to come over for a nice dinner or a show, you know I'd love to see you."

"I will," he promised. He gave her a pat on the bottom.

He stood in the furnace room and watched her go up the stairs. Before emerging into the sun, she clipped tinted plastic lenses over her glasses. Outside she straightened her back and lifted her chin. She always walked as if she had a place to go.

Around seven he left his books and went out in the car to bring back two cheeseburgers, a thick choc shake and a pint of chili in a carry-out carton. He took a book to the table to study as he ate.

491

At ten, he was lying on the bed with his back propped against the cushion trying to puzzle ten French sentences into passable English and ten English ones into plausible French. There was another knock on the door, so timid he at first did not hear it for what it was. He was afraid it was his mother returned to tell him she had chucked her job and intended to move in with him.

It was Sharon! Dressed for church. She threw her arms around him and kissed his face all over before finding his mouth.

"I'm sorry about the other night," she said. "I just had to come by after church and tell you. Carol Whiteside drove me. She's waiting in the car." The words bubbled out of her.

He was so happy he could not speak. She had never looked more lovely to him or felt so altogether fine.

"I'm glad—OH! I'M GLAD, SHARON!" He lifted her off her feet in the wrap of his arms and swung her inside. "I'm sorry, too. I wanted to die." He kissed her again.

When he set her down, she peered around the place. "I can't stay, sweetheart. Carol's waiting . . . I wish I could."

"So do I."

"At least, you finally got me *in* your apartment," she joked. She looked around beyond him.

"It's a mess right now," he apologized. "I usually keep it pretty neat. I've only been out once today to get some chow."

She glanced at the carry-out papers and cartons on the table.

"Been in here studying like a bear," he said.

"Poor baby. Maybe I'll come over next Saturday and help you give it a good cleaning."

"That would be great!"

She looked at him out of the corners of her eyes. "You'd have to promise to behave."

"I would." He raised his hand like a scout.

"Um. We'll see." She put her arms over his shoulders again and the tip of her nose against him. "I gotta go. I wish I could stay and fix you a decent supper and tuck you in like a good little boy."

"And give me a bath first?"

Her eyes shot heavenward for strength.

"I love you, Sharon."

"I love you, too," she said.

492

They hung together kissing until Carol honked and Sharon had to run.

"*Love* you!" he whispered loudly through the furnace room. She threw him a kiss.

30

THE job with Emerson's Market and Wholesale Meat Company paid only seventy-five cents an hour. He worked after school and Saturdays. But it was not hard, and there was no bullshit about his ever going to make it a career. He worked wherever he was needed and also drove the delivery truck. And whenever he helped make up the orders, he would always stash an extra pound of "hotel" bacon, butter, cheese, chops or eggs to drop off at his grandparents' place. Hotel bacon was cut specially to get more slices per pound. All restaurants and institutions ordered it. There were dozens of little tricks like that.

Most of his deliveries were commercial, though he did deliver at a few homes who bought in great bulk or were friends of old man Emerson. He liked being out in the blue and yellow truck and looking down at stoplights into cars where women had hiked their dresses high to catch a breeze, stopping for an ice cream or quick beer whenever he felt like it. He liked blowing into the kitchens of hotels, hospitals, schools, restaurants, old folks' and children's homes, the jail, country clubs and the wonderful world of hamburger joints. He knew who got the best and who, not knowing the difference, paid the price of the best for something less. Those who could afford best got the best deals. Mama Gomez paid more for her hamburger than did the country clubs, but she also had pride enough to send it back if it did not meet her exacting requirements. She always paid cash and broke a patty or dug into an order of bulk before handing over a dime. She would smell

493

it, look into the soul of the steer, taste a pinch. He could spend half an hour by Mama Gomez to get rid of a ten-dollar order. But when he wanted to eat better for thirty-five cents than he might elsewhere for three fifty, Mama Gomez's was the place. She also patted out her own tortillas by hand and ground her own coffee. She had gone through five husbands in sixty years, and her present one was in the hospital. Not because of her cooking, Jack decided, but because Mama was a small, round woman of exquisite parts and likely as thorough in all things as she was in inspecting meat. She opened at six, closed at midnight and was always there. She had the energy of a dozen.

He knew one of the most popular and expensive restaurants in town, the El Matador, could not fill a taco beside Mama Gomez. Out past the Veterans Hospital, with reservations suggested for those who could dine at ten because they did not have to get up and go to work the next morning, the El Matador bought the cheapest sort of meat cubed with suet to bubble in its chili con carne and stuff in its tacos.

Hospital kitchens made him determined to stay well, and he always drove more carefully after those deliveries. He left the children's home with a sadness that left him wondering if any of this work-study shit was worth the effort. It took a cold beer in a joint where the blowzy barmaid had an ass that rolled on ball bearings to inspire him to finish his route. The jail's kitchen wasn't so bad, but it was bologna or franks most every day.

As he went up the drive of the country club beneath a tunnel of trees, he could see Cadillacs, Lincolns, Packards, Buicks and Chryslers lined up in the parking lot—a million dollars' worth of ice-cream and candy-colored iron. In the boy's mind, with its wide porches and glassed-in dining room, the club resembled an enormous white landlocked riverboat. The splashing and calls of young country clubbers in the pool had the effect of a paddlewheel. It was an institution absolutely predicated on slavery, no matter what the boys on the tractors and the white-coated black waiters were getting.

Leaving a large order at a café across from Beechcraft, he learned the company was really on its ass, trying to keep going by stamping out refrigerator trays while they got the bugs out of a corn picker which had yet to suc-

494

cessfully pick corn. The café owner did not sound hopeful.

Then he had a final box to drop off over in Eastborough. Houses there now cost a minimum of forty thousand dollars, he had been told, but no one wanted to be the one to put up a house for the minimum. Figuring on about fifty dollars a week after he got out of school, he would not have been able to pay off the principal of a twenty-year mortgage on an Eastborough minimum with every cent he made. Even if he was willing to do without a swimming pool and rumpus room, it seemed sheer folly for someone like him to even dream of getting a toehold on the top. If Sharon taught for a while after she graduated, they might handle something for around twenty thousand dollars.

There were no sidewalks in Eastborough. If he parked his meat wagon and got out for a walk, he would be savaged by every kind of Nazi hound in creation and *then* arrested on suspicion of uttering or some damn thing. He did not know for certain what, if anything, that meant, or if it was a criminal offense, but it was what Eastborough made him want to do. "Utter against them!" was his cry. It sounded properly Biblical and official. "Go ye and utter against them," the Lord commanded. Or if He hadn't, He ought to have.

The house was as blind from the street as a prison wall. A sheer sweep of shiny white brick with contrasting black exposed girders, within which the owners were sure enough of their power to offer no lights up front to the world. Only a single wrought-iron *M* marked the façade. Deliveries were discreetly directed to the rear by a tasteful drive-side plaque.

He parked the truck in front of a four-car garage with black doors. The nearest door was open. Inside sat a custom Kurtis-Kraft sports car, semenly pearlescent, with lipstick-red upholstery.

Jay Mossbacker made it in diverse ways. He had pieces of a lot of things. The keystone was a local oil company and more recently a bank. Only his second wife, his home and the handmade car were newer acquisitions than the bank. His first wife had the old Mossbacker house over in the park and drove a conservatively green Olds 88 convertible.

In the box on Jack's shoulder were special aged Omaha filets and porterhouses old man Emerson had selected himself just this side of personally interviewing the donor steer. There were no figures indicating cost on the ticket in the box.

As closed as the place was in front, the rear was entirely of glass overlooking a patio and large L-shaped pool with an old tree, grass and flowers inside the angle. Sentinel cypresses stood shoulder to shoulder around the inside of a high shiny white wall. Those trees hadn't had time to grow there. They had to have been hauled in and transplanted full-grown. The boy figured he could live very well for ten years off what those fucking trees alone must have cost.

Jesus Christ! There was another old tree growing through the roof of the living room—or whatever they call it in a house like that. With that hole in the roof it must cost a fortune to air-condition the place. Or there was some trick Jack did not understand. Rain could fall in and around the tree onto the flowering jungle out of which it grew. How did they keep bugs out? was a question. Probably had some kind of electronic barrier, he decided! Too much!

But electronic marvels were nothing. Sitting on the kitchen table in a short terry-cloth robe, eating cottage cheese and pineapple from the carton, was the sexiest woman Jack had ever seen. She looked like a movie star. White taffy hair good enough to eat spilled around a small face that warped between hints of Little Rock and glints of Hollywood.

"Emerson's" he announced.

"What?"

"I brought your meat."

"Oh!" She giggled. "Just put it in the cooler." She pointed at a brushed steel door across the kitchen with her foot and wiggled her toes.

If war ever came and the Mossbackers were not bombed, they could hold out for the duration on the stuff in that cooler. Next to it was a door of equal size which was a freezer. In the freezer were pheasant, duck, venison and even bear meat. Mossbacker was a hunter.

The kitchen, large enough to harbor a little echo, had a floor of black and white tiles. Its ovens were built into the walls.

"Sure a nice place you got here," he observed.

"Beats camping out," she agreed dryly. She rummaged in the pockets of her robe. "Afraid I don't have a tip," she apologized. "I never see any damned money. You like a beer or something?"

"That's OK. It's good to get out of the heat."

"Um." She pointed to the built-in refrigerator with her foot. "Help yourself to anything you want."

"Thanks."

There were beers from Mexico, the Philippines and Europe, as well as domestic brands. He had lived on the Mexican border. He selected a bottle of Carta Blanca, popped the top into a wall-mounted opener.

"You want a glass?" he asked.

"No, ma'am. This is fine." He wiped off the neck with his hand and drank from the bottle.

She winced at "ma'am" but did not flinch at seeing someone drink from a bottle. A smile of wry memory moved her Hollywood mask slightly. "You look a lot like my brother."

He smiled back with his eyes in the middle of a gulp.

"You aren't from Arkansas."

"No, ma'am."

"Stop saying that. Come here."

He moved closer. "I was born here, but I've lived all over," he reported. "Was over in China for more than a year."

"China?"

"Yes, ma'am."

"Don't call me ma'am. Makes me feel like an old bag. How the hell old do you think I am?"

"I don't know. I mean you look so much like a movie star I can't tell."

"Shit!" She reached out and took his bottle, drank from it and handed it back. "I like that Mexican beer. I drink champagne now, but I still *like* beer. If I get fat, he'll fire me. Someday I'm going to lay on my duff and blow up like a balloon and get me a gang of those skinnyassed Italians to take care of me." She snapped her fingers. "I've got it coming," she said. On her robe was embroidered the word "Honey."

"Everyone's called me Honey since I was a little girl," she explained. "Because I'm sweet," she added sardonically, the words so bitter he felt the alum in his own mouth. "I've never been to anything but model and secretary school, but I can count as quick as Mr. Mossbacker or anyone," she said as if challenging him to try her. He realized that whatever she liked to drink she had been at something besides cottage cheese and pineapple.

"You sure put me in mind of my brother, though."

He finished the beer and put the bottle on the counter. He felt proud so sexy a woman would think he resembled her brother. She seemed to like her brother a lot.

"Don't you wind up like him."

"How's that?"

"Dead. Fellow shot his ass off in a trailer outside of Little Rock. Bullet went right through him and killed the man's wife as well. He was only twenty, but it would have been how he would have wanted to go. They should have been buried together that way, but they weren't," she said sadly.

"I can think of a lot worse ways to go," he said.

"Yeow. . ." she drawled and looked him over from head to toe twice.

"How old are you?"

"Sixteen," he said.

"And you've been to China?"

"I lied about my age."

She smiled. "Me, too." Then she looked away and stared at the wall until he decided he had better go.

"Well, thanks for the beer."

She did not reply. When he was at the door, she called, "Hey, what's your name?"

"Jack."

"That was his name, too." She stubbed her cigarette out in the cottage cheese carton.

Outside, he felt at home enough then to duck into the garage and look at the car. He saw beneath the doorsill in real gold letters the name "Honey."

He felt he had caught old Jay Mossbacker in his underwear. He felt a living part of the asshole world as he had not all that day.

The old man wondered, "You don't reckon you could get us some more of that *good* coffee, do you? We're plumb out. That's sure good coffee."

"Well, I'll try," Jack promised. "I don't make up regular grocery orders, Grandpa. Unless a restaurant or something wants groceries with their meat, it's kind of hard to do. Most places buy coffee in bulk from the coffee companies."

"I know that," the old man said. "I just meant if it wasn't any trouble. I like that coffee. Then what I like don't matter much nowhere, I guess."

"It ain't that, Grandpa. I gotta *take* the stuff, you know. They don't give it to me."

"I just asked," the old man snapped.

"I'll see," Jack promised.

"Well, if you can get into trouble, we don't want it," his grandmother insisted. "Do we, Daddy?"

The old man only grunted. They had come to expect the frequent grocery drop. It was not saving them much money. For the kind of stuff he left was not the quality they usually bought. So, though he might drop off ten dollars' worth of stuff a week, it was only taking the place of what would have cost them at best three dollars. Still, three dollars was a lot in their budget, and they did like the "fancy" better than the "economy."

Give someone something better than he's had before and then don't keep it up and he is going to blame you more than if you gave him nothing. It seemed a law more powerful than blood.

"Still goin to that college?" the old man always asked.

"Yeow. Still goin."

"You learnin anything?"

"Some, I guess."

"What they teach you at that college besides how to skin some other sonofabitch for a living?"

"They haven't got to that. Anyway, I'm not goin into law or business administration."

"What you going into anyway? I misforget."

"Art or maybe architecture. Somethin like that."

"What the hell good is that goin to do you? Shit, we figured you went into the Navy to learn a trade and when you got back you'd go to work and make somethin of yourself. Maybe help me and Mama out a little around here."

He evidently didn't feel the groceries and meat were of any help. "Looks like you would be glad I had a chance to go to college."

"That shit don't teach you nothin about what's right and wrong. Seem the same fella you always been to me. It don't teach you what's what. It never did, and it never will. Folks like us got no more business in it than a nigger. If they put the money they spend on them fuckin colleges

499

and churches into somethin for the people and stopped the big boys from skinnin us, we wouldn't need all them goddamned doctors and lawyers and specialists to try and straighten things out every inch of the lyin way. They ain't really tryin nohow. They're just in it for the goddamned money. Not a one of them specialists knows his ass from Newton, Kansas. Them specialists is just a way of doublin the price of everything. They don't care a fart for folks! None of them! Don't need no goddamned specialist anywhere. Need some decent, sensible men who can see the nose before their face. That's what this goddamn country needs!"

Yet he believed in Harry Truman.

It was all a kind of skin, is how Jack saw it. Preachers no longer reminded anyone that it was easier to hike a camel through the eye of a needle than it was for a rich man to enter the kingdom of heaven. Rich men were on a too short-range profit basis to look toward the hereafter.

There was absolutely nothing in either the economics or the history Jack was reading that offered any long-range hope even for the rich. The way it read, the only logical thing to do *was* to get it while the getting was good. As far as Jack could see, the United States was an industrial oligarchy every bit as much as any of the banana republics.

Nor did a free-enterprise economy seem particularly desirable to him. It was such a waste, one company killing off another, when it would seem if they cooperated in full view of the public they might together cut the price of a thing twice . . . and still live. Well, he didn't understand it, and from what he could tell neither did the President, the Secretary of the Treasury or his professor of economics. The old man was right: the thieving at the top came down faster than prosperity trickled, turning all men into thieves.

The old man's enthusiasm for Truman could be explained by his disappointment in all previous and present alternatives. He was getting on toward ninety, and he hadn't in all that time had a political choice worthy of a bedbug.

"Maybe what this country needs is another war," he suggested to the old man.

"Now that's the goddamnest stupidest thing I think I ever heard! We don't need no goddamned war to pull our nuts out of the fire. We need to stop the lyin and stealin and stop dealin with those who do and there won't never be no more wars. That the kind of shit they teach you in that college?"

"Not exactly. But I thought when the war was over, Beechcraft, say, would build a little plane that we might all be able to fly."

"Don't need no goddamned planes. Need some decent way common folks like me and your grandmother can get our asses to town and back, to get out into the country for a breath of air. What you just said about war is like this sonofabitch told me the other day. He told *me* if I didn't like it here, I ought to move to Russia. *Me* goddamn! I told that cocksucker! I told him, I made this country what it is in the best sort of way while the Rockefellers, Carnegies, and Mellons, and DuPonts and Astors, and Goulds, and Rothschilds were stealing the place blind. And they're still doin it too! And this sonofabitch—why, I've known him for years, used to be a president of a Townsend Club, still *calls* himself a Townsendite and good Democrat—tells *me* I ought to go to Russia. Shitfire. This country has completely lost its bearings. Friends can't trust friends. Nobody helps anybody anymore. Nobody cares. It's every poor ass for himself and the devil take the hindmost. Rockefeller and that crowd did that. The oil crowd did it. The money-interest crowd. They'll kill a man—anybody—lock him up, buy a congress or a country, do any damn thing, and call it bein in the national interest. Horseshit! These are no good sonsabitches. Every one of them. And nobody cares. Next thing I won't be surprised they elect a Hitler. Goddamn country don't even provide a means for old folks to get to town easy or out into the country anymore. That's the history of this country, if you read it. Don't need no schoolbooks. It's in the papers for anyone who has brains enough to read. Don't guess they teach you that in that college."

"No."

"No. I didn't reckon they did. They're all in cahoots, too, you know. But that's still what it's all about. You go on to college if you think it's doin you some good. But until we face up to the fact we been cheated and lied to from the start and do what's necessary to change it, all the rest is just fartin on the wind."

The old man was about all done. More and more his face and body failed to rise with the old inner merriment.

501

Only anger seemed to stir him, leaving him sagged and bent when it had been exhausted so he never quite stood straight now. The boy was taller than he, though he had been a bigger man than the boy would ever be.

His grandmother had become a fussy, addled, chubby, clucking shadow, given to heaving great sighs.

School was nothing like he had supposed it would be. He had thought it would be a bunch of people helping each other, everyone learning something new every minute. It was the same thing as any place he had ever worked and far more competitive and closed-mouth than the Navy.

He wasn't sure how Honey got where she was, but headed toward his basement apartment with the leaky top of the car down, he found himself wishing he were a woman. Then he imagined having to fuck Jay Mossbacker, and knew there was *no* way to win without getting on top. He was already too tired to begin the climb.

31

HIS car was in the Ford Garage for a new clutch and valve and ring job. The cost of that canceled out every cent he had earned working after class since he came home from the Navy. It made getting down and punching in at the time clock as hard as if he were dragging the goddamned car after him.

There *was* no way to get ahead. Keeping up was enough to kill a man. If it was the same dogass way every day until he was thirty, forty, sixty—shit! It just didn't seem worth it.

He hopped off the Thirteenth Street bus and sprinted. Still, he arrived fifteen minutes late. The old butchers looked up disapprovingly. Their cleavers, splitting ribs, came down with a single, exceptionally vicious chop. Sweat from his hands smeared his time card. He began dragging the boxes and pans of orders to the back door.

He mentally arranged his route and put the duplicates of the bills on a clipboard in the order of delivery, then loaded his truck according to his plan.

It was after seven thirty when he finished. Everyone had gone when he got back. The place was closed. He locked the truck and dropped the keys through a flapped slot in the rear door where they fell into a cheese box.

He loitered near a phone booth at the Shell station across the street, hoping to bug the zoot-spade-cat inside into hurrying it up.

The black kid didn't even see him, though their eyes met several times. He was taller than Jack, blade thin, with waist and hips like a snake in high-rise drapes of soiled white windowpane check. He sported stiletto-toed yellow shoes that looked like money and a Hawaiian print sports shirt with belled sleeves. On the back of his long, narrow head he had nailed a black fedora with white satin band.

Jesus Christ! It was *Arthur!*

When he finished his animated conversation, he oozed out of the booth and started to turn away.

"Arthur?" Jack asked.

The cat turned as if he were on bearings, his face willfully devoid of the slightest expression.

"Don't you recognize me, man?"

"Hey, Jackson." He put out his hand to give him some skin. His hand was long and elegant, the pale palm smooth and yellow. He wasn't hauling anything heavy for a living. He looked Jack up and down. "You looked better in your sailor suit. You out now?"

"Yeow. Going to college."

"No shit!"

"No. What're you doin? You look real sharp?"

"Yeah. Well, I just got me into town ten, eleven days ago, see. You know, just doin what I can."

Jack figured Arthur would be about fourteen. "Well, you're lookin good."

"Gettin by. You know. Got me a little thing goin."

"How was Buffalo?"

He took out a gold penknife on his zoot chain and twirled it like a golden propeller. "It was cool. You know." He shrugged.

"You've grown like hell! Ought to play basketball."

"That's what you think?" Arthur asked coldly. "I got

me some little somethin goin. You know. Don't worry about me."

"You goin to school?"

He studied Jack tolerantly, but his eyes kept sliding up the street so Jack had to exercise considerable will to keep from turning and looking behind him. "Naw. I finish school," he said as if he had graduated with honors. "I'm in business for myself. Look, I gotta split now." He consulted a gold watch with an expansion bracelet on his elegantly held wrist. "I got me an appointment. I catch you later, OK?"

"Sure. See you, Arthur."

Arthur went up to the next corner and flagged taxis until one stopped.

Jack called Sharon and told her he would be late for their date. They would have to catch the last show.

He could not get over how Arthur had grown. He was about six feet tall. Riding the bus past the part of town that was almost totally black, seeing the signs for the Four Aces Café and Sweet Sister Brown's Beauty Parlor, he felt Arthur had left him behind, even though *he* had been to China and back. He wondered what Arthur had going. Then, seeing a tall, juicy dark woman with straightened hair coming out of Sweet Sister's in a skintight dress, clipping along on white platform heels, her long legs outlined through her frock, the cheeks of her ass rolling together as if they were buttered between, he wished he *were* Arthur.

After they were out of the black area, suddenly there were no more people on the porches, no kids playing in the gutters and yards. When he had been little, there had been kids there, men on the porches in undershirts, women pouring lemonade. Where had they gone? He felt suddenly he was of the last generation of white kids who would ever know what it was like to open a hydrant in July, what the mysteries of the neighborhood were, its dangers, what made the old town tick. It had all turned to money-making in a world where kids were growing up taking watermelon for granted, or not at all.

That was all right, he was certain. But there ought to be some way for them to know what it had been like before. A navigational fix. Unless you shot your angles truly, you'd never know where in the fuck you were.

He and Sharon hardly ever went to any movie but the

504

drive-in. Now, with his car laid up, he felt old-fashioned and funny going into the big theater with its gilt and blue and green and red Egyptian decor. The carpets hushed their steps, and they automatically lowered their voices. There was a sad elegance about the theater that had once rivaled for Jack the wonder of the ocean he had never seen. Now the feeling was like going into an old, abandoned, once-grand house, slated for demolition. They rushed to get popcorn and Cokes and chocolate bars before the movie began.

Settling down in the first balcony, they felt committed to an intimate experience. That MGM lion roared your ass tight in the seat in a theater the way it never did at a drive-in. Jack stuffed another handful of popcorn in his mouth. A couple of kernels fell into his lap. Sharon ate her popcorn, piece by damn piece.

He clamped the box between his knees and dipped lefty so he could slip his arm around the back of Sharon's seat. She lifted the back of her hair over his arm and settled onto his shoulder. He dropped his right hand down on her arm where it pressed lightly against the curve of her breast. She no longer looked at him disapprovingly or otherwise acknowledged it other than to snuggle happily a little closer. Being in love was nice.

But it was all downhill after the roar. A pirate film with Virginia Mayo in Technicolor. As much as he lusted for the body of Virginia, the movie was so transparent and predictable it made him angry. He had seen it—God!—a hundred times. They would make the thing as long as the crummy ship sets held up. Before giving up on it completely, he amused himself by picking out props he recognized from other, similar epics. No wonder row upon row of seats were empty on a Friday night. Everyone was out at the drive-in playing smash-body where it didn't matter what kind of crap was up on the screen. Some cop wasn't going to shove a light in your car window and run you in for statutory rape or illegal cohabitation, and you weren't being bushwhacked by guys from the other side of town, beat to shit while they gangbanged your chick. Even if the sound track was tinny through the speaker hung on the window, it beat two hours in a theater watching Virginia Mayo swing on ropes.

He leaned over and kissed Sharon, pushing her head

back on his arm, finding bits of popcorn in her mouth, slipping his fingers under her breast.

She snuggled down farther, with her knees against the back of the seat in front, creating a kind of isolation in which he caressed the bare underside of her legs with his left hand. With Virginia laying to with a cutlass, her skirt slit up to her hip to show off her chorus girl's thighs, he slipped a finger under the elastic of Sharon's panties and found her sex was wet. She did not help him, but she did not stop him until he touched her clit. Then she asked, "Please, Jack. Not *here*."

"I love you," he said and withdrew his finger, feeling very honorable. He gave her cunt a little squeeze.

She closed her eyes ecstatically. When he removed his hand, she said, "That's a good boy, darling."

"You feel ready," he whispered, though he knew she did not want him to talk about it. She no longer minded necking, but she didn't like to talk about it, either before or afterward.

"I can't help it," she said as if he had been insulting her. "I'm human, you know."

"I know." He grinned. "That's what I like about you."

"Well, I wish you didn't so much."

"Sharon?"

"Shh. Watch the show."

"Let's go to my place."

"*No!*"

"It's a bullshit show. Come on. We won't do anything there we don't do in the car."

"No. Be still. You're disturbing everyone."

"Bull. We're the only ones here. Those others are just dummies the theater sticks in to make everyone think there's an audience."

"Don't be silly."

"It's true!" he insisted. "They do that."

"They do not!"

"They do. *EVERYONE HERE NOT A DUMMY STAND UP AND HOLLER!*" he yelled.

"Jack!" Sharon hissed.

"Nobody here but us dummies!" a strong voice from another part of the balcony echoed. "Only a dummy would pay good money to see this crap." Nervous giggles and rumbles of protest rose from other seats.

506

They caught a College Hill bus and held hands but talked very little. A few blocks from Sharon's stop, he said, "Let's get off and walk."

"OK."

He reached up and pulled the bell cord.

Passing Fairmount Elementary School, he tugged her into the playground. "I always envied you kids here," he told her. "You had the only hill for sledding in town."

Off the back and side of the playground was about the longest slope he had ever seen in Kansas, falling away to the end of the property, perhaps a fifty-to-seventy-five-foot drop in elevation. But to him when he was little, it was a mountain.

He pushed her on a swing, running underneath as he carried her high to make her squeal. But for some reason, she did not react. She seemed quiet, thoughtful. "What's the matter, honey?" he asked.

She shook herself and smiled. "Nothing. Why?"

"I don't know. You seem sort of quiet."

She smiled bravely again. They teetered for a while, her skirt hiked high over her bare thighs, her white panties a soft blaze in the dark.

In the shadow of the building where the windows all around looked on with mute disapproval, he pulled her to him and kissed her. He had expected her to be cold and disinterested. Instead, she threw herself tightly against him. Her arms on his neck were strong and trembling with an intensity he had never felt in her before. Her mouth was hot and so eager he was momentarily taken aback. His mind had half been on something else.

She sat on his lap on the fire escape, one kiss feeding the next. Her hair fell like curtains around his face so he could see nothing but her face so near. It looked swollen, babyish, beautiful.

His cock was tangled in his clothes and cramped. He shifted a bit.

"Hurting you, honey?" she asked, and slipped down on the next lower step between his legs, smothering the hard-on in his slacks against her fine breasts. He rolled himself gently back and forth against her until he was very hard, pressing her breasts from the side. They felt bursting with her bra. She did not say anything. She simply found the zipper of his trousers, and tugged open his fly, then reached in with her fingers and dug out his cock. He had never felt larger. It looked enormous even to him as she held it in her hand, studying it almost sadly. He could not understand it, but he sensed something happening in her. She was different from the way she had ever been. She had often jerked him off or let him make it by just fucking her very shallowly and pulling out to come on the seat between her legs. These practices had become virtually routine any time they were alone.

She stared at his cock as if looking at it for the first time. She gave a little cry and dropped her head to kiss it tenderly. He cried out and felt he might swoon. She took the head into her mouth and then tried to take in all of it she could. He moved and thrust up into her mouth where she sucked him lovingly until he was about to come. Then it was he who pulled her head away. She had gone after it until her hair was flying around on her head. Her eyes looked as if they no longer focused. Then she looked at him and seemed to think he would disapprove of her. Her face was blotched and swollen. She had never been more beautiful in his eyes. She looked both younger and yet more a woman than she ever had before. He lifted her up into a kiss. It was deep and long, tasting in her always sweet-tasting mouth the flavor of his own cock. He reached under her skirt and hauled her panties down from the back. She raised up to let him pull them off.

Wondrously, they studied each other's faces, each transmitting unspoken questions regarding the other, as he guided her up and astraddle of him. He wished they had gone to his apartment, but the moment could not have been better. With her own hand she placed his cock in herself. He supported her hips with his hands. She was more wide open and wet than she had ever been. The lips of her sex around his cock were hot and seemed to close upon it in the gentlest of kisses.

The steel edge of the steps above against his back could have been knives and it would not have mattered. All love filled him until his toes tingled, his lips felt swollen, until he felt there was no more room in him. He did not care for life, ideas, dreams, another moment. He was so happy there was no comparison in his memory.

"This girl," he said aloud as much to himself as to her. "Only this girl. And she loves me."

She kept coming down on him, catching herself and her breath when there was a pain.

"Sharon!" he exclaimed.

"Yes," she said softly.

"Sharon!"

She cried out, catching and letting out her breath, but the voice sounded like the end of the world to him.

And he was truly in her. Then came a sense that she was suddenly sorry or perhaps utterly lonely for the first time in her well-ordered life. He felt the sudden fear she would regret and blame him.

She was crying. Yet it was too delicious, awesome, feeling good, to put word to it. His body felt as engorged as his penis. All the feelings came within the catch of her breath as he penetrated her and the first tear.

"It's all right," he assured her.

"No!"

"Yes. It is." He moved and made her move, made her ride up and down upon him.

"It hurts."

"It's all right. I love you. Do you love me?"

"Oh, yes! I *love* you. I must. Oh, Jack—Stop! . . . Please."

"I can't—*Sharon!*"

"No!"

He came. Too late. So he locked his arms around her hips and hauled down, thrusting deep into a place he prayed all love lived. It felt so good. More than coming. An exquisite surrender of himself. He belonged to her as he had never belonged to anyone or anything—not even himself.

She was crying hysterically, deep sobs racking her entire body. Her sex was sobbing around him, he felt. Her tears wet his collar and neck.

"Why did you *do* it?" she blubbered.

"I didn't mean to. I couldn't help it. I just loved you so much."

"What good is all this experience you're always bragging about when the one time you—Oh, shit!"

"It will be all right," he insisted.

"No, it won't. I'll be pregnant. What kind of all right is that?"

"I'm sorry. But you won't be pregnant. You don't get pregnant every time you do it. Take a douche when you get home."

"I never!"

"Doesn't your mother? Use hers."

"I couldn't."

"Don't worry. It will be OK. I promise you."

"Oh, Jack, Jack." She began kissing his face. "I do love you! It's as much my fault as yours. I should have controlled myself."

"No. I'm glad you didn't. It was the most beautiful thing for me."

She looked at him tenderly, wiped his face with her hand. "Really?"

"The most beautiful. Really."

She kissed him passionately, grabbing a handful of the back of his hair until it hurt.

"Didn't feel good to you, too?" he asked her.

"Um. Some."

"It will get better for you."

"I'm not going to do it again."

To be certain he did not mean to do it again then, she moved to dislodge his still-erect penis. He gave her a couple of sweet, loving moves as he helped her get off to remember him by, and she sank down once more and clung to his neck, rocking him deeply within her. Then as quickly, just as he knew she was feeling something nice, she pulled herself up.

He had never encountered such innocence before. Everyone called it innocence. It wasn't that. It was more a different system of transactions. He loved her, so he loved the idea of going all the way in her and was humbled by the courage it must have taken her to do what she had done. He wondered if he would have been so brave if he'd had been born with a maidenhead. She was what her grandmother and people like her pointedly called "a *good* girl." And out of her own desire, she had blown him and ridden his cock all the way home.

He could not imagine why. Looking back over the evening, he could not think of a thing that would have inspired her. In fact, until the moment she had opened his fly, he had felt she was about to announce one of her periodic decisions not to see so much of him in the future. He knew she did not have much of a social life with him, and he had even decided not to make a big deal out of it this time.

He wasn't doing well in school. He had been thinking of trying to transfer to an art school in San Francisco. He could not hack that French grammar—or English grammar either, for that matter. Every idea he put forth in classroom discussions was rammed back down his throat. Everyone said San Francisco was where everything was happening. Even Bucky was trying to get Glenn to sell his laundry route and take off for California. He thought he could transfer to art school and not lose his GI Bill.

Sharon wiped herself with her panties and threw them under the fire escape. When he was in first grade at Washington, he and some of his little friends had found a pair of woman's panties under the fire escape. The memory sponsored a new flow of tenderness toward this amazing girl. He caught her beautiful face between his hands and kissed her.

"Your pants are ruined," she told him.

"It's OK." But he could never go home on the bus like that. She hadn't bled a lot, though.

Walking toward her house, he put his arm around her and slid his hand down to her hip. It excited him to be walking beside her knowing she hadn't any panties on beneath her skirt. Along a dark hedge, he stopped and turned her to him and kissed her again, skidding up her skirt in back to caress her bare bottom with both hands.

"Don't!" she said angrily.

Walking on, he thought of all the whores and others he had his dick in, and now Sharon. It made him determined, in spite of the fear he could not do so, to change however it was necessary to be worthy of this girl. He told himself he needed no other than her.

But she felt so distant, walking beside him, more so than she had before, when they first went into the playground. He began babbling as he often did when he had nothing to say but was afraid he was about to be discounted.

On her porch, she wearily turned and plunked her arms on his shoulders like any other girl offering her date the obligatory good-night kiss.

He snatched her furiously against him. "I *love* you, Sharon! I love you!"

"OK. Good night."

"Say it. Say you love me."

"I'm too tired."

"But you do?"

She nodded her head slightly, affirmatively.

"I'll call you in the morning before school. OK?"

She shrugged.

"It will be all right. You'll see. Just take a douche. Warm water with some vinegar in it."

She said nothing. She gave him his kiss.

"Good night." She turned to go in the dark house.

"I really love you, Sharon," he told her once more.

He walked a long way, first beneath trees where their leaves dappled the walks in shadow, then through meaner streets where trees had been cut down to create a boulevard. Finally, he hailed a cruising cab.

In his bed in the basement room, he determined, it would be all right. He loved her. He would never let her down. In dream, he saw himself zooming around on all sides of her, punching out guys who were trying to get at her until he had no time for work or anything else until he just wore his ass out. He awoke before it was light—exhausted.

He called her at ten when he took his truck out on his route. He worked all day Saturday.

"How are you?" he asked.

"OK." Her voice sounded bitter, distant.

"Can you talk?"

"Yes."

"You take a douche?"

"I couldn't. Mom wasn't asleep."

"Well, it'll be OK. Don't worry."

"Sure."

"I love you," was all he could think to say to help her.

"OK. I gotta go if you're through," she said.

"See you tonight?"

"I don't know."

"Don't you want to? Christ! We have a date."

"For what?" she asked sarcastically. "Mom and Dad may go over to my sister's for dinner. I might go with them."

"Don't you want to see me?"

"I don't know."

"I'll call you when I get off."

"OK."

"It's all right, Sharon. Don't worry." But he heard her hang up before he had finished. He wanted to call her back. Then he got angry. *Fuck her! Goddamn virgins, anyway! Think their precious asses are gold!* He heard his nickel fall into the bottom of the phone box.

He worried his entire route around.

32

THE building was a heavy, old, architectural confection, its shoulders, turrets and sills blackened with grime, frosted with bird lime. The elevator had a collapsible metal gate rather than a door. It shuddered upon starting. They could see the weights and cables through the wire cage overhead. He took Sharon's hand, feeling the elevator would fall and they would die.

She stared straight ahead and did not answer the squeeze of his hand. They paused before an opaque glass door in a dark, varnished frame on which was painted:

STERLING LABORATORY
(Please Push Bell)

The door buzzed, and they went in. She hesitated in the open door until the pressure of his hand in the small of her back moved her ahead.

The room had been divided by a plyboard wall painted white in which a service window had been cut and a sliding glass pane installed. Four plastic tubular-legged chairs on which there were several dog-eared magazines. The place needed dusting.

A young woman with pancake so dark and heavy her neck looked anemic opened the glass and gave them a card to fill out.

"I can't do this," Sharon whispered.

"Sure you can. What's the problem?" Jack leaned across to study the card over which she poised her pen. "Write 'Sharon Andersen.' There you check 'married.' "

513

"I feel so cheap." Her face was sad. She had worn a nice dress in expectation the lab would be like a doctor's office. It made her seem vulnerable and cheated.

"It doesn't matter," he assured her. "They don't care, or check, or anything. They just do the test. Put my address in there. That's it."

Each bit of bogus information she wrote on the card seemed to diminish her. She actually shrank as he watched until she bent low over the card like a little girl. Her eyes were wet.

He rubbed her back and assured her it was all right.

"What do I put here where they want the name of the doctor?" she asked in a panicky, small voice.

"None."

"Won't they think something?"

"They don't care. Long as they get paid. They do this all the time."

"I feel so *cheap*."

What worried Jack was the indefiniteness of the test. If it was positive, it was almost certain, but if it was negative, it did not necessarily mean she was not pregnant.

He passed the card through the window and paid the girl fifteen dollars for the rabbit.

"Could I have brought my own and saved the money?" he asked.

"No. The rabbits have to be bred specially." She did not think it was funny.

Neither did Sharon. She had turned away.

"Do you wish us to send the report to this address?" the girl asked. "You don't list a doctor."

"We don't know if we need one yet," he said. "Can't we telephone you?"

"We don't give out our information on the phone." She sniffed righteously.

"OK. We'll come back. When will you have the results?"

"Tomorrow." Clearly they were not up to the standard of her regular customers.

He wanted to reach over and yank her ass out of there and make her kiss Sharon's feet. She wasn't worth what Sharon spent on underwear.

"We'll be back after"—he had started to say, "after school"—"four."

"You taken anything on your stomach today?" she asked Sharon.

"No."

When Jack had called for the appointment, he had been instructed to be sure Sharon ate or drank nothing for breakfast.

"Very well. If, uh"—she glanced at the card—"Missus Andersen will step in please." She buzzed open a door in the partition.

Sharon had surreptitiously turned her birthstone ring around with the gem in her palm. He loved her for that. But he could not go in with her.

When they were outside, Sharon put her head on his chest and cried. He was glad there was no one in the disinfectant-smelling corridor.

"What did they do?" he asked.

"Nothing. I had to pee in a bottle and they took some blood."

"I'm sorry."

In the elevator she dried her eyes.

"Hungry?" he asked.

She shook her head she was not and sniffed.

"But you've got to eat."

She shook her head again. "I've got to get to school."

"Hell, why don't you forget about school today? We can go to my place or take a drive out into the country."

"No!"

But she let him lead her into the Hotel Lassen coffee shop. He felt on holiday, rich, having a late breakfast in a hotel. It was as if she *were* Mrs. Andersen. He loved her very much.

The menu did not interest her. She would not look at it.

"How about number three? Hotcakes, ham or bacon," he suggested.

She actually gagged.

"How about some fresh fruit? Strawberries and cream!" No one could eat strawberries and stay in a lousy mood.

She shrugged listlessly.

He ordered scrambled eggs, bacon, toast *and* strawberries for himself and a double order of strawberries and cream for her.

Halfway through the bowl she picked up a wedge of his toast and nibbled it.

Afterward she felt better but insisted he drive her directly to school.

Sharon was pregnant. He had known she would be. Looking back, he realized he had known from the moment of pure love when he had come in her that she would be.

That was what it was all about, I guess, he told himself.

She sat far over in the corner of her seat crying. He had driven out a shady road and parked in an old lovers' lane where the katydids were already sawing up the evening.

He had to force her to come over and lay across his lap. He smoothed her hair away from her brow and traced her eyebrows with a fingertip in a soothing way she always liked.

"This doesn't happen to girls like me." She wept. "To others, but not me."

"I know. I'm sorry, Sharon. Really, I'm sorry."

"That doesn't do any good."

"I'll marry you. I love you. I have some money to help us get started. I can get a good job. It'll be OK. We'll make out. I do love you more than anything."

"No! I don't *want* to get married!"

"Do you want to get rid of it then?"

"What do you mean? How?"

"You know, find some doctor."

"NO!" She buried her face in his chest and sobbed so hard it shook her whole body.

He held her tight. He had never been more aware of her body. It felt large and lovely in his arms. No little girl, Sharon. He looked down her hip to her legs so long, tanned, shaved and glistening. He stroked her back down to her buttocks.

"Sometimes if you do it again, it brings it on," he suggested softly, trying to keep desire out of his voice.

"What?"

"Sometimes. I heard, if you do it again, it will bring it on."

"I don't believe that."

"I don't know. That's just what I heard." He put his hand on her leg beneath her skirt. "My aunt brought it on that way," he lied.

516

"You just want to," she accused as his hand touched her sex.

He kissed her. "I love you, Sharon."

She let him remove her pants and enter her in the front seat of the car in broad daylight. She wept quietly, only reluctantly returning his kisses, as he moved in her so furiously the car springs complained. Her arms were resolutely over his back. He told her repeatedly he loved her, telling himself it might work. It might work. And came deep and hopelessly within her.

Through her tears she watched him with the fear and coiled wariness of a wounded animal.

Then whatever love he had left for her dissolved in his own great fear.

33

THERE was a jackass braying in the back of his mind, a mocking laugh on him that was part of his own voice and a chorus out of which the predominant sound was that of his college adviser. *I told you you would never graduate from here, Mr. Andersen.* The voice was righteous with fulfilled prophecy. He could see the little man's babyish pink lips redden and glisten as if he had just popped a lemon drop.

A stiff dick has no conscience, Jack rationalized, swinging the truck around a dairy van he almost hit for his musing.

There was no question but that he would marry the girl. That was how he explained it to himself—impersonally, as if he dared not any longer think of her by name.

One day the world had been especially good. Then it was all over for him. Oh, he knew for Sharon it was worse. But that was her, and this was him. For the wonder of a few minutes in the place where all love lived he was now a slave to Sharon and the baby that was growing each day inside her.

They had gone to visit her sister, Sparkle, one afternoon in the GI home where she and her certified public accountant husband lived. Sparkle looked like Sharon, only taller and very thin. She had been lying out in the backyard in the sun and wore white cotton shorts and a halter with the straps tucked into the cups. She was very brown. She was not as pretty as Sharon, nor did she have as fine a body. In the dim living room where a floor fan blew on a two-year-old sleeping in the bottom of a folding play pen among plastic and stuffed toys, she sat on the couch and cocked up one leg in a careless way that allowed Jack to see her panties and the dark pubic hair caught outside the elastic. She lit a Pall Mall and leaned back to study them. Though she was skinny, Sparkle was a looser, sexier young woman than Sharon. Maybe being married and having the kid did that. He had only seen her in church with her husband, a tall, pale, dark-haired fellow in no-nonsense specs, with bookkeeper's hands, who belonged to a chess club. He sang hymns in a deep voice, as if taking an oath.

"So what are you going to do?" Sparkle asked.

"What do you mean?" Sharon replied.

"About it. You're knocked up, aren't you?"

"*Yes!*" Sharon cried and dropped down on her knees beside the couch and began crying in Sparkle's arms. Sparkle stroked her hair and murmured that it would be OK. Then she looked up with pursed lips and studied Jack from head to toe, as if he were a species different from her own.

"Does Mother know?" she asked.

Sharon nodded her head that she did not.

"You have any money?" she asked Jack.

"Some."

"How much some?"

"Little over a thousand dollars."

Sparkle raised her eyebrows and seemed rather impressed.

"Want me to get you the name of a doctor?"

"I thought ours was OK."

"I mean to get rid of it for you."

"You mean have an abortion?" Sharon sat up on her knees and stared at her sister.

"The girl next door, Pat, has two kids. Her husband is a draftsman out at Beech and had to take a pay cut to stay on. She got pregnant again, and they just couldn't afford another. So she went to this doctor in Joplin and had it taken care of. Cost three hundred. But he is a regular doctor with his own clinic. She said it wasn't any worse than having your tonsils out."

"But I *couldn't!*" Sharon's face was very pained.

Jack stood quietly, hoping her sister would convince her to do it, yet curiously proud that Sharon did not want to. He looked at her back and bottom and thought of his seed growing inside her. There was no sound other than the fan and the baby in the playpen sucking on a rubber pacifier in small bursts of noise.

Sparkle suddenly looked up and challenged Jack. "Didn't you care enough about her to use something?"

"Well, it was really the first time," he managed. "I mean we didn't intend it to happen. It just did."

"And you were in service?" she was incredulous.

"Well, yeow. . . . But I was never in love. You know."

She looked disgusted. "What the hell does *that* have to do with it?"

At that point, the boy really could not say. Since Sharon knew she was pregnant, love seemed the slightest consideration in their problem.

"Why don't you let me fix it up with this doctor? I'll take care of it. You won't have to do anything but go see him."

"No! I can't!" Sharon began crying again.

"Well, you've got to do something. Do you want to marry him?"

The way she said it made Jack feel as if he were a Robert Hall suit hanging on its plain pipe rack.

"I don't know," she blubbered.

"I could quit school and get a regular job," Jack offered. "We could manage."

Sparkle looked at him with doubt he could manage to find his way to the door without directions. Yet she also looked at the bulge of his cock in his faded Levi's and unconsciously licked her lips. She bent and kissed the top of Sharon's head and stroked her. She looked up at him again. He knew she was wondering what he was like. In spite of all else the moment contained, he could sense the woman's curiosity so strongly he hooked his thumbs in his hip pockets, rolled his shoulders forward and shifted his weight onto his left leg the better to show himself off. And he relaxed. He knew then where he was. Between

519

Jack and Sharon's big sister was the knowledge that he had fucked the girl. For a moment Sharon was only a despairing accessory to that knowledge. When he looked directly at her and met her eyes, her mouth was parted slightly, though she continued to stroke the chestnut crown of the girl's head in her lap. Then she shook herself. "Well, we will have to go to Oklahoma, unless you want to try and get Mom and Dad's consent."

"NO!" Sharon cried.

"Okay. This is Wednesday. I guess if you are going to do it, there is no use waiting. You can get your blood tests, and Cliff and I will drive down with you Saturday."

Sharon began weeping again.

"Come on, let's go wash your face," Sparkle suggested.

The girl let her sister lead her away to the bathroom.

Jack could hear their talking, muffled by the door and the distance down a short hall, but he could not make out what they said. He liked the sound of their voices. He felt a part of them.

He tiptoed over to the playpen. The little boy was puffy and hot in spite of the fan. He wore only a terry-cloth cover over his diapers. He had dark hair like his father and very white skin. He was not a cute kid. The pacifier would hang in his slack pink lips; then he would go after it and haul it in for a moment of intense sucking during which his little forehead wrinkled into a frown and his hands and feet twitched.

Jack found himself seeing his and Sharon's child. A golden-haired little boy—or girl—with tan, golden skin like their own. A baby out of an advertisement. Then he saw them getting rich, from money they got for letting pictures of the kid be used for advertisements. After all, he had won a Beacon Baby Contest when he was a baby. And Sharon was truly beautiful. They wouldn't have some little white, hairy Clifford Junior kind of kid like the one in the pen. They would have a world-beater of a kid.

Getting through college and all that had just been a dream anyway. *I had no right to expect to make it,* he told himself.

Sharon did. She had every right in the world. He felt bad that he had messed up her tidy, happy life. But she had wanted it as much as he. If she didn't know it, her body damn well did. She could graduate. Others in her fix had. She was an honor student; probably they would just give her a diploma. Then when the kid was born, she could go on to college. It wouldn't be easy, but hell, she could do it if she wanted to. She could have everything she wanted and him too.

What was wrong with that? he wondered. *I mean she was there when the scrontchin was done.* But his tough pose faded when he heard her crying again in the bathroom.

When they came out, Sharon walked behind her sister, and Jack had the feeling she had changed her mind and was going to have an abortion. He hated Sparkle then for having talked her into it.

Fuckin skinny bitch married to that meathead. She'd like a bit of hot young cock herself. Clifford was ten years older than she. An ex-corporal in Air Corps accounting. A dodo bird. A wingless wonder. *She-it!*

But then she winked at him and smiled. She looped her arm in his and tugged him to her side, reaching back to haul Sharon up along the other side.

"Come on, brother-in-law," she said. "Let's go have a glass of iced tea and cool off."

34

HE HAD moved all morning with the self-consciousness of wearing a new blue suit. It was an Eagle. He had paid a hundred dollars for it at Henry's men's store and spent another sixty dollars on shoes, socks, shirt, tie and cuff links.

In the car, he drove with regard for his creases. They followed Sparkle and Clifford's Plymouth coupe. The cloth top on the Ford drummed on its stays as they ran along around sixty. He had put the top up to keep them from getting windblown.

Sharon wore a soft gray suit with a short jacket, pink gloves and small matching hat that was merely an open lattice on the crown of her head through which her hair shone. It had a sort of turned-up soft visor-looking thing from which depended a veil masking her eyes.

He wondered silently who dreamed up such things to set on women's heads. More, why women were so eager to wear them. But it was cute, and her effort at looking grown-up was sweetly touching. It made him feel protective. Her hands were folded loosely in her lap. She had sat the same way since she had got in the car. She had sneaked her clothes over to her sister's and had dressed there. They had not spoken much. To the point of the trip, not at all. An orchid corsage he had bought for her, along with a smaller one he had purchased for Sparkle, was in a florist's box on the seat between them.

Out of the corners of his eyes he watched the gentle rise and fall of her belly as she breathed and thought of the living fetus they had made inside her.

Windmills of wheat farmers gave way to sucking, mantislike pumps of oil wells as they neared the border.

"I love you, Sharon," he pledged very seriously and reached out toward her with his right hand.

She took his hand between the gloved palms of her own and patted it in an abstract maternal way. "OK," she said.

"It will be all right," he said determinedly.

She did not answer.

Sparkle pinned the flowers on Sharon's shoulder in the vestibule of the minister's old prairie-Gothic two-story house. She had white carnations for Jack and her husband.

They stepped into the parlor where the minister met them before a dark oak table on which there was his record book. It said "Record Book" on the cover. And there was a large family Bible opened upon a passage, the pages marked by a faded ribbon of wine satin.

A spare man, slightly stooped in an old iron-gray suit, he had the furtiveness of one who did what he did against the echo of a questioning consciousness. He introduced his wife who would stand their witness. She was a heavy, jolly woman who had been called from her canning, Jack decided, judging by the smells of bubbling fruit pectin that wafted from time to time from the rear of the house.

There was no question that Jack and Sharon had come from Kansas because they were underage and the girl was pregnant. Still, the minister's wife beamed at them with the professional pretense they were youngsters she had known all their lives.

Jack wondered how many times they had stood there with strangers in their parlor, performing a cheap ceremony to legalize the consequences of sex. The sexual power in the room was so real Jack fancied he could smell everyone's individual odor. This awareness made him feel dizzy. The old woman smelled acrid and strong beneath her lilac, like his grandmother. The minister's scent was dusty and neuter. Sparkle and Clifford shared an antiseptic blend in which their sexual smell was all but neutralized by shaving lotion and Lysol. Then, from the orchid closeness of his bride, came the smell of crushed milkweed and wild honey so suddenly familiar all memory of others before her was moved to a place of remote and impartial recall. He felt a twinge in his cock and had the giddy fear he might get a hard-on while he stood there.

He hadn't touched Sharon since the time in the park right after they were certain she was pregnant. He had tried to a couple of times, but his efforts had only made her sad and cold, though she had suffered his kisses and gropings as if they were now his right, responding to a degree he felt she had calculated would please him. He found himself courting her with a solicitude so unnatural to his nature and so tentative in light of their previous relationship that he felt stupid, awkward and increasingly unattractive in her eyes. To counter that feeling, he became a loutish parody of himself, strutting and preening and posing until he wondered if he would find her or himself again. Or, indeed, if he would ever know again the intensity of what he thought must be what you call love.

He realized he was scared, that he had been scared from the moment after he had come in her. All this marriage-preacher-brother-sister-mother-father business scared the shit out of him. He didn't want to be there doing this.

Clifford gave the minister the license. He read the service, peering over his glasses to charge them with the importance of the words in a way that seemed like an indictment to Jack. It hit him: no one there believed for a moment that what they were consecrating would last. He even suspected Sparkle had counseled Sharon to do it to give the child a name. He felt angry and that he was being had. The only thing anyone there truly gave a damn about was Sharon and her belly.

On the girl's left hand was the diamond solitaire engagement ring that had seemed all right in Zale's window, but now looked small and cheap on her lovely, trembling hand. He wanted to snatch it off her and hide it. He silently cursed Zale's for selling such cheesy damned diamonds, and himself for calculating one hundred twenty-five dollars was enough to spend. He didn't give a damn about diamond rings, though the really big mothers were fascinating. Only a really big one was worthy of her.

He slipped the plain gold band on her finger, feeling the tremor that ran through her entire body. Sharon then put a matching band on his finger. He had not worn a ring since his last Captain Midnight code ring. It felt enormous and made him nervous. Her eyes were brimming with tears. He too felt like crying. He had never felt so unhappy, trapped, nowhere.

Then he kissed her. There was the taste of her carefully applied lipstick and the familiar softness of her lips. *Mine,* he thought, as the physical possibilities of their future crept up from his loins. His own mouth felt dry, as if in the corners there was white dust.

The minister, his wife and Clifford all shook his hand in a professional way. While they were giving Sharon a peck on the cheek, Sparkle stopped her post-wedding banter and kissed him warmly in a way that belied the thinness of her lips. In her quick, exuberant embrace his cock bumped her belly and it felt as if she purposefully rolled herself up against him for an instant. It puzzled him, for her eyes never gave away a thing. There was a desperate let's-all-have-fun sheen that recalled the rah-rah days when she had been a cheerleader.

"That's five dollars, please," the minister's wife whispered, a receipt book in hand. "We *do* wish you every happiness."

Walking out behind Sparkle, Jack wondered what it would be like to get between those long, skinny legs, bend them back to her pierced ears. Clifford hadn't bent her, Jack felt sure.

He couldn't understand why, now that the ceremony was over and he and Sharon had everyone's permission to fuck, he was curious about her sister, who he was sure was not as passionate as Sharon, and certainly no way as beautiful. It was funny. There really must be something wrong with me, he concluded, and consciously strove to shift his thoughts exclusively to the girl who felt so soft and alive and near beneath his hand as they followed, his arm around her waist.

Sparkle had brought a little packet of rice and threw it at them when they got in the car. Then she leaned in and kissed Sharon again and said, "Buck up, baby. I was two months pregnant when I married Cliff. Mom and Dad knew. It will be all right."

Sharon was surprised. She hadn't known. They had told her Sparkle's baby had come early.

In the car she snuggled close to him, scootching over until she was sitting uncomfortably on the division between the front seats. She was clinging to his right arm so tightly that he turned to look at her and found her studying him in a soft, objective way in which barkless, mongrel questions chased one another aimlessly.

He patted her knee and smiled. She leaped up, threw her arms around his neck and kissed him with a passion he was not prepared for and did not meet. But for the first time that day he was no longer aware of his new suit. She took off her dippy hat, shook out her hair and relaxed. Once again she was so beautiful he was filled with joy and heartbreaking tenderness. The physical reality of her was overwhelming, a feast he wanted to both nibble at and devour in one impossible gulp.

She rolled her head toward him on the seat. "What is it?"

"We're married. Goddamn." He shook his head.

She turned away. It was not a reaction compatible with his own. "Um," she said. And lit a cigarette and leaned her head back on the seat and stared at nothing.

The desk clerk was a snide young man who looked as if he had worked nights all his life and was barely able to contain the secrets of his profession. A junior manager kind of ass, he certainly had some little rackets going with the bellhops, Jack thought as he filled out the "guest card."

He held the card with his left hand, though it was offered in a weighted leather holder, to flash his new wedding band beneath the punk's supercilious nose. He had been afraid the bastard would ask him for their license. Out of the corner of his eye he noticed Sharon had also idly laid her hand on the marble to show her rings. He saw the clerk's gaze flick to them and disdainfully appraise the small stone, the barest flicker of a sneer pulling at the corners of his mouth.

What did the crumb make? Forty, maybe forty-five a week.

He weighed their scant luggage with his eyes, glanced at the card and asked loudly, "You will be staying only the one night?"

"That's right," Jack managed, feeling he ought to sign up for a week just to be regular.

"That will be twelve fifty in advance, please."

"Oh, sure." Jack reached for his back pocket, then, remembering he had put his wallet in his jacket, embarrassedly switched his search after an instant of panic that he had lost it. He laid a five and a ten on the desk and waited as the clerk made change in a way that was even an insult to the boy's money.

Jack tried to think whether it was proper to tip the desk clerk in such fancy hotels. You could not deal in common currency with the sonofabitch. Tip, shit! Jack wanted to jerk his snide ass out over the desk and stomp his face.

He was a snoop. A secret underwear sniffer and laundry prowler after the odd pubic hair. A worm incredibly taken with his dinky night clerk's power. A kid who could hustle up a whore good enough looking to walk through the lobby of the second-best hotel in town, he had measured his success in tips and palmed percentages so long his entire character was formed of dog-sniffing knowledge of his betters. That he always wore a starched white shirt and necktie at work seemed to him success enough.

He lifted his castanet grandly to the level of his ear and clacked it. A bellboy appeared behind them. He had been hiding in the thick carpet all the time. There was no other explanation. He and the clerk held unfathomable communication of eyes.

"Ten fourteen, please. For Mr. and *Missus* Andersen." He trusted the jockey-sized man with the key.

Jack could not accept the necessity of someone carrying their baggage when he could have done it with one hand. Luxury made a lot of wasteful intrusions on a person, he decided. The bellman glided along in front of them, Sharon's white overnight case in one hand and Jack's blue soft Navy PX handbag with the anchor on it in the other.

He put his arm around Sharon's waist. She looked at

him as if they were running a gauntlet of disapproving eyes and shifted his arm to hook through hers. In her other hand she carried her little pink wedding hat.

At least the bellhop looked the way Jack thought he ought. A regular little Johnny Morris in short jacket with three rows of brass buttons, stripes down his trousers and a cocky little pillbox cap strapped over one ear. When he held the elevator open for them, Jack began feeling expansive, imagining himself a success, and he and Sharon checking into such hotels anywhere in the world as if it were nothing.

All the doors to the rooms were off the main corridor in softly lit little private halls. There was a hush of thick carpet and indirect light that made their steps almost churchly. The brightness of the prairie afternoon never penetrated the long air-conditioned maze they followed, which led them so far from anything like home they truly felt out-of-town. There was the delicious, stolen hours feeling of cutting school and going to see a matinee. And the loneliness.

The hop deposited their luggage in a folding rack beside the door so that one need never stoop and busied himself flipping the door on the air-conditioner control, flicking on lights in the bathroom and other useless business that brought him back to the open door where he awarded Jack with the key.

"Will there be anything else, sir?"

Jack already had his hand in his pocket. "Uh, yeah, uh. I would like a bucket of ice and a couple of glasses. Do you handle that?"

"I'll tell room service. Anything else in beverages or food you can order by dialing room service."

"Uh, thanks."

"Will that be all?"

Jack turned to the girl. "You want anything else. A sandwich or something?"

"No."

"I guess that's all." He laid a quarter in the young man's gloved hand. He looked at it so long, Jack sort of leaned over to peek and see if he had inadvertently slipped the guy a slug. No. It was a quarter.

"Thank *you*," the bellhop said icily, already spinning away.

Hadn't a quarter been enough, for christsake? Jake wondered. He would have gladly carried their two bags that far for two bits.

"Fuckim!" he said, closing the door.

Turning, he saw Sharon collapse facedown on the bed, sobbing so quietly but strongly it shook and jiggled the soft hump of her bottom. He lay down in his new suit beside her and stroked the crown of her head.

"What's the matter, honey?"

"I feel so cheap," she squeaked.

He felt the same way but would never have given in to it as she had.

"Aw, those assholes just think they are smart. They don't respect anything but money." That they had made her cry made him see himself going down to the lobby and wiping out all of them. "I've known a lot of creeps who work in hotels. They're like something that lives under a rock." He found a kernel of rice in her dark hair. She turned to see what it was.

"Rice." He showed her the luminous white grain. Then popped it into his mouth and played with it with his tongue.

She gave a little cry and threw her arms around his neck. The kernel went back and forth between their mouths in a long kiss that blended into other kisses. He put his hand beneath her right breast, then moved it up to cover the large globe that swelled beneath layers of soft blouse, slip and brassiere. Her underthings felt so crisp he was sure she had bought them for her wedding. He felt the small roundness of her belly. It was nice to feel so free to touch her. Now he might any time he wanted. He balanced that wonder against the fear of all the rest of it. Sliding his hand down her passive body along her thigh, he inched up her skirt and slipped his hand under it, up over the sheer skin of her new stockings, excited by the uniquely feminine harness. When they necked, her thighs always felt hotter where they touched each other than those of any other girl he could think of. He had just touched the smoothly encased mound between the tiny lace fringe of her panties when there was a knock on the door. She leaped up and darted into the bathroom. The bed cover was dented where they had lain.

The bellhop was a different one, older, taller. He set the bucket of ice and glasses on a tray down on the bureau without a glance at the bed.

"Will there be anything else?" he asked.

"No. Thanks. That's fine." Jack gave him a quarter, and he seemed happy to get it.

He found the pint of Old Granddad in his bag, uncapped it and made them each a bourbon and water with plenty of ice. In the movies it was always champagne. In Kansas, as far as he knew, it was bootleg whiskey, 3.2 beer or nothing.

"I made us a couple of drinks, honey," he called.

The toilet flushed. She came out and carefully hung her jacket in the closet before turning to take the glass he held out to her.

"Well"—he smiled—"here's to us." And touched her glass with his.

She sipped her drink, watching him over the rim with large, questioning eyes.

The whiskey tasted too strong and smoky for what he had hoped to convey. After the first sip he was frightened again. He set their glasses down and took her in his arms. She was yielding but felt sort of dead, tired or something. The only time she had felt that way before was when she was in one of her moods in which she thought she should not see so much of him. He tried to stir her by sheer power, crushing her so tightly she gave a small cry of pain and accused, "You hurt me."

"I'm sorry!" he promised. "I don't mean to hurt you. I don't ever want to hurt you, Sharon. I'd rather die first."

She was looking flatly past him. She had fallen into that way of responding with "um" and "uh" that passed for communication when her mind was really on something else. He tried to follow her gaze. There was an empty vase on the bureau. He wished he had ordered a dozen roses. White roses. There was a florist in the lobby. He hadn't any idea what a dozen would cost. Probably twenty-five bucks at least. He could not go to the phone and make the gesture. Twenty-five was a lot for flowers. After all, he had bought her an orchid. What would more flowers prove?

Life ahead of them suddenly seemed so long that he could not imagine them ever making it together to the end. *What the hell have I done?* he asked himself. He felt she was comparing the day against a more perfect, girlish dream she would now never know. If roses would help, he thought, I would get her roses. And knew it was in the necessarily considered cost of roses that the day was irrevocably cheapened. She should have married a guy who didn't ever have to calculate. In her dreams, he was sure there had been such a guy.

Families.

If it weren't for the kid in her, her parents would have their marriage annulled. If she hadn't become pregnant, they would not have been married at all. So what did it mean? Where in the process had their love gone?

For all that, she could not look at him for longer than a second at a time. He had worried so about what he had been giving up that only then did the full force of what she felt she was losing really hit him. Christ! He was really more willing to try and make the best of it than she, he realized.

"I'm sorry, Sharon," he said very seriously.

She flashed at him for an instant, then looked away. "So am I," she muttered.

With his hands on either side of her waist he gently shook her. "But we can make a go of it if we try. I know we can."

She reached over and picked up her drink and knocked back most of it in a long gurgle, set the glass definitely back upon the tray and turned to look into his eyes.

"OK," she said.

It was still light outside. Too early for dinner. There was really nothing else to do. He took her tenderly in his arms and kissed her. She responded dutifully, then slipped from his arms, picked up her overnight bag and went into the bathroom and closed the door.

He finished his drink and made them a couple of more. He lifted a slat of the turned venetian blind and peeked out into an alley down which the bright late-afternoon sun cast big chunky shadows above the freight entrances and delivery trucks below. Some view that weasel at the desk had sold them. He had delivered meat to that very hotel only two days before, parking his yellow and blue truck down there in the alley. When he had told them at work he wanted the day off to get married, they did not greet the news with congratulations but with a kind of fear he was not nearly as responsible as he had seemed. They reluctantly granted him permission when he swore he would be in on time the next evening. He wondered what José, the hotel chef, would say if he knew he was up there with

his bride. He had a notion to take Sharon down and introduce her to José. He was a tough, but a nice guy. Maybe
he would make them a great, special dinner. Then he rejected the idea. His thoughts made him feel that he had
broken into the place, that the whole deal was somehow
so illegal someone might come any moment and snatch
Sharon away and arrest him.

He hadn't any pajamas. He had thought about buying a
pair but decided since she would never see him in them
again, it would be too extravagant. Probably her old man
slept in pajamas. Taking off everything but his trousers, he
hung the stuff in the closet beside her jacket which smelled
nicely of her perfume.

To be sitting out there naked or in his jockeys trying to
look casual when she came out did not seem such a good
idea either. He wished he had brought his Jap kimono.
Why hadn't he thought of it? It would have been real
sharp. *Stupid bastard!* he damned himself. He wondered if
he ought to put on his shirt. Glancing in the mirror, he
sucked in his gut, tensed his muscles and guessed he
looked all right. He was young, lean. He smoothed the
back of his hair with his hand and splashed on some more
Old Spice.

She came from the bathroom in a nightie-peignoir outfit
that rustled in at least three layers. She had combed her
hair until it shone, falling just right to her shoulders. A
white ribbon was tied to hold it off her face. She had redone her makeup, pancake, mascara—everything. That
was what had taken her so long. She could spend half an
hour on her face. There was more rouge on her cheeks
than she had ever worn before. He did not really like it. It
made her look different. It made him think of a young
Chinese whore.

But she was beautiful. The sleeves of her peignoir were
like white honeysuckle bells just before they open.

"You're beautiful."

"Thank you. Sparkle got it for me." She looked down
and shook out a wrinkle.

"I don't have any pajamas. I just don't wear them," he
explained.

"I see."

He took her hand. "I love you, Sharon."

She did not reply. Nor did she say another word as he
led her to the bed and began to make love to her. Only

when he worked to truly excite her did she speak. "You might as well just do it. I don't think I'm going to get any hotter."

When he tried to excite her when he was in her by movement and rhythm, she reached down and began playing with his balls. She had never done anything like that before. It was a move she had read about or been told. Probably Sparkle had had a little talk with her. He resented that. Trying to hurry him up and make him come.

He resisted for a moment. Then he decided to hell with it. He slipped his left hand under her ass, kissed her roughly, smearing her lipstick all around, and came in her—in there—laying every drop. What did anything matter now?

She was crying in his arms.

"What's the matter, Sharon?"

"I don't think I love you at all," she squeaked.

A terrible pain ripped through his brain, made him sick at the stomach.

"Why?"

"I don't know."

"It'll get better. You're just upset and nervous. You liked it before. You will again."

She shook her head, waving all that away as if it had nothing to do with what she meant.

"What do you want to do?" he asked desperately.

Slowly, sadly, she nodded her head. "I don't know."

"For christsake, Sharon. I love you. I'll do the best I can. Won't you try?"

Turning to look at him, she asked bitterly, "I don't have much choice, do I?"

BELLY.

Everytime he looked at her he said to himself—*Belly*.

Wearing a short blue quilted satin housecoat with the sleeves shoved up her forearms, her hair held back with a scarf tied in a bow on the top of her head, she moved barefoot around the old stove. There were grease spots and coffee stains on the robe. The belt was tied over the melon of her belly in a way that made him think of the statuettes that were sold during the war of a very pregnant little girl standing dolefully on a pedestal that proclaimed "Kilroy Was Here!"

He did not find the Belly unattractive, though it made her waist thicker and had flattened her pretty ass a bit, altering the natural bow of her spine. But it did call to itself a certain constant regard. And now that he could place his hand or face on the taut melon and feel the soft jabs and eerie liquid turning of life inside, Belly began to live with them as a genuine personality around which both orbited. When he brought her a small gift after work, he also brought one for Belly.

But Sharon was not happily pregnant. She would see only her closest friends or her family. Everyone knew she had dropped out of school when she began to show. She was permitted to do her assignments at home and, having been an honor student, was assured of receiving her diploma. When they did meet her former friends by chance in the street, for all their eager enthusiasm and promises that she never looked more beautiful, she would haul him into a store to avoid them if she could do it without their seeing her. She was often sad, hardly communicative. They rarely talked about anything. She would respond only to direct questions or listen tolerantly, resisting every effort to bring her to express or elaborate on a judgment or idea. Often she seemed sad and cried by herself. Though she did not feel good in the mornings and he insisted she should stay in bed, she got up and fixed him eggs. She had an unshakable belief in the beneficence of eggs every morning. He did not like the way she fried his eggs, but he never said anything about it. She cooked them on too low a flame. He liked them cooked quickly on high heat so the whites had a slight lacy fringe while the yolks remained mostly liquid. The way she did it the whites were rubbery while the yolks sat in a little puddle of uncooked albumen. A bowl of Rice Krispies and coffee would have been better, but he did not want to criticize her. There was more duty in her care of him than enthusiasm, and he felt a constant sense of imposing on her. When she made up their laundry to take to her mother's, she always handled his shorts with thumb and forefinger, a distasteful set to her lips.

Still, he persisted in trying to catch her interest, asking how her lessons were going, hoping to get into a discussion about history, government, English—something. But she did them quickly and did not talk about them. In the evenings he related everything that had happened at the plate-glass company where he worked, speaking of his plans and possibilities with such a forced effort to inspire her to share his enthusiasm no matter how inflated, he ended up feeling foolish, awkward, a fucking magpie, until words became dry and stuck in his throat. He left at eight and came home at six. She was glad he had a good job.

For her part, she and Belly spent much of their time curled up on the couch, reading one of the book club novels that were handed on to her by her mother. Even so, she would not discuss what she was reading with him. It was as if he were trying to pry into a world especially her own and she resented it. It was Frank Yerby's world that was big with the book club that year. It was a world into which she would eagerly escape as soon as he was out of the door.

When he began working out of the shop, he had stopped by on an impulse to surprise her. Suddenly excited by the increased possibilities of freedom from supervision, he had been driving down the main street at ten in the morning and wanted suddenly to pop in on company time and make love to his wife. That was how he had seen it.

She was curled on the couch, smoking a Pall Mall, her robe loose and revealing her long bare legs, the breakfast dishes still on the table, an ashtray of cigarette butts, a cloudy empty milk glass and half a cup of cold coffee on the floor at hand, the big novel propped on her knees. He had laid aside her book, opened her robe, as she stubbed her cigarette out in the ashtray, lifted the short gown over her belly and fucked her passionately on the couch, all the more delicious for the fucking of his superiors. Though she had responded as passionately, shuddering and gulping in the strange lonely way she had when coming, eyes open but not really seeing, he felt more instrument of her private pleasure than personal blend of it. He had the feeling she was imagining him to be the hero of the goddamned book and glanced at it with silently seething jealousy thereafter. He sneaked a peek or two at it when she wasn't looking, but he wouldn't have read the thing on a bet. He had come home a couple of other times on the spontaneous urge to get a little. And though she was always willing, even more eager than at other times, he felt he had intruded, a stranger in his own rooms.

It was only through sex he felt she cared about him at all. It was the only way he could penetrate the amorphous swamp of ennui in which she moved slowly behind her Belly. But the more pregnant she became, the more care she took of making up her face before he came home, the more passionate she became in sex. He could touch her, turn her anytime from whatever she was doing and find her eager to fuck. Frontwards, backwards, sideways, in a chair, sitting on the table, on hands and knees, 69 with her slick cunt open over his face, her sucking as enthusiastically on his cock, and looking like a sexy Buddha, on the floor of the shower, the water and her hair streaming down above his face—he figured out they fucked an average of nine and a half times a week. Only when he tried once to fuck her in the ass had she balked. And she did not like him to touch her there. Three times a day she oiled her body with a super lanolin lotion to keep from getting stretch marks. Often he lovingly applied the oil and gave her a back rub, which she adored. When her now very heavy breasts were taut and oily, she liked him to crouch above her, being careful of the Belly, and slide his cock between them as she pressed them together until he was achingly hard, the head swollen and dark as a plum. She would watch with her chin on her chest like a puppy watching a harmless snake, her hips moving behind him in her own excitement, her small nipples growing into

535

little pink raisins. Yet they made love with hardly a word of endearment passing between them. She seemed to prefer it that way. The sounds of their breathing, cries and rutting were the only accompaniment to the milling of the bed. The landlady obviously heard them at it so often, particularly startling in light of Sharon's condition, she always looked at them disapprovingly when they chanced to meet, her lips thinning primly. Since the day they were married, Sharon had not volunteered a verbal expression of any love for him. He had to ask if she loved him. To which she would reply, "Sure," or become flip or coy. She had more than once changed the subject by grunting "um" or beginning to suck his cock rather than answer his question.

What did it matter? What the hell did it mean anyway? When he was in her, he thought he would never want any other. Only at climax when every atom of him strained, leaning over a chasm of stretching for her love, did the way she moved into herself—so far back he could never touch her—leave him empty, wanting as much emotionally as he had physically when they had begun.

"You have any complaints?" she had snapped when he had haltingly tried to talk to her about it. "I thought I was a *great* piece of ass for you." She threw back his own words exclaimed in passion and wonder only a few minutes before.

"I just would like to feel you love me too," he had mumbled humbly.

"Well, we can't have everything, can we?" she had flipped back, slapping her bare ass and striding off behind the Belly to the shower.

Shit. Shit. Shit, he groaned to himself on the bed, looking down at his limp dark dong left lying back at an angle on his pale loins like a thing with a separate reality from himself—like the Belly on her. *I do love her,* he argued silently. *I really do.* He just didn't know what the hell more he could offer.

Different strokes for different folks, he mentally chirped, stepping out of Sanderson's hole-in-the-wall hardware store. The older black guys in the alley where he had lived used to say that. It was perfect explanation of the glass business.

In Jack's pocket was a small ring binder—strictly confidential—which told him what kind of discount Sanderson got on orders. What Sanderson didn't know was there were places who got an even better break. What glass actually cost no one but the boss and his wife and Pittsburgh Plate really knew. Though they were divorced, the boss' wife remained a partner and bookkeeper of the business. Their divorce was recent and still a tender thing around which everyone crept.

It was a mysterious business, though after six months it no longer held the fascination for Jack, fired by ambition and need, it had during his training period. He had gone as far as he could and had only future possible raises and a rumored Christmas bonus to look forward to. He had slipped into the routine of the company's junior salesman.

There were two others. Being senior, they naturally called upon and serviced the big accounts and large building contractors. Jack handled the retail hardware stores and individual houseowners who wanted a mirror wall or thermopane picture windows.

R. "Bob" Wheeler, the boss, had taken him on after interviewing half a dozen young men the State Employment Service had sent over. He had shoved his application and other papers aside with barely a glance, saying, "What I want to know about is what kind of man are you?"

Wheeler was tall and fit, with wavy graying hair, and wore an expensive lightweight medium-tone suit and slightly pink tinted glasses in clear plastic frames. Jack's mother would have found him handsome.

And Jack had leveled with him as much as he could. He described his life knocking around oilfields with mother and stepfather. He told him his stepfather was doing time in Lansing, and his mother had also done some time for forgery.

"You ever been arrested?"

"Only for throwing a two-inch salute under a sleeping cop's car out on Harry on the Fourth of July. I paid a fine."

Mr. Wheeler grinned.

"Oh, and a few months back some guys and I were in a gas station when some other guys we knew stole the cash box. But we were only held for questioning."

"What were you doing there?"

"Well, we went there to hit the guy's punchboard," he confessed.

Again the man grinned, only not so broadly. He cleared his throat. "You're married, right? I guess you have that kind of crap out of your system."

"Yes, sir. I've sort of outgrown those guys, I guess. The stuff they do doesn't make much sense to me anymore."

"Good. Why did you get married so young? Why didn't you stay and finish college? It looks like coming from as far back as you have, you would have welcomed the opportunity. You knock her up?" He glanced quickly and penetratingly at Jack.

"Yes, sir."

"You love her?"

"Very much."

"It's going all right?"

"Well, it's difficult. It's hard on her. She was an honor student and had dreams, you know. I guess I was sort of a comedown to her."

"How's the bed part of it?"

"Sir?"

"Sex. You get along OK that way?"

Jack grinned and crossed one ankle over his knee. "That's about the only thing we *do* seem to completely agree upon."

The boss smiled. "Good. You know all this modern psychology that's going around now about the adjustments people have to make is a lot of bull. What it comes down to is bed. If that's going good, a woman will put up with short money and a long shift. Now my wife and I—if you're going to work here you're going to hear about it, so you might as well get it from the top, so there's no misunderstanding—that good-looking blond lady you saw in the other office is *Missus* Wheeler. I and my two top men call her Lucille. To everyone else she is *Missus* Wheeler. We're divorced. Got married when we were kids. It's all my fault. She's good as gold. Always was. But a man gets a certain age. . . ." He lifted his hand palm upward in a helpless gesture. "We're all like dogs. Slaves to our meat. It's the women like Lucille who are the strength of our nation. I don't know, maybe if we'd had children. . . ." He cleared his voice and straightened himself. "Next to myself, she is the boss here. I still have more respect and love for her than any other woman on earth. Whatever you hear and see, you remember that."

538

"Yes, sir." Jack uncrossed his legs and sat up straighter in the chair.

He got Jack to speak of his dreams and hopes. Jack told him about his interest in art and saw him take it without wincing, but with a flatness of interest. Jack did not elaborate.

Wheeler cleared his throat again when the boy had finished.

"We've all had our dreams. Mine was inventing the perpetual-motion machine. Drove my dad and everyone crazy about it."

Jack grinned at the man.

"I hope you've put your dreams behind you. Glass is a creative business in many ways. You will find me open to ideas and suggestions. My two top men call me Bob. I like the way you handle yourself and how you speak up and don't flinch when someone cuts close to where you live. You can have a good job here and a good future if you give a shit and work. You'll start at a dollar ten an hour for the first month, during which you will be learning the business and we'll be learning what you are made of. All the men in the shop are older, and you will have to earn their respect. If you work out, I'll put you up for membership in the Junior Chamber of Commerce. Later on, if you work out and you want to buy a house or something, you come see me, and I'll see what can be done. Both my other salesmen have gotten their own homes while working for me. One of the fellows, Harry Green, started here like you a few years ago. Just out of service, a beginning family, rough background like you, not too good prospects, not much education, and now he is chairman of the Jaycees' Youth Committee, has a nice home and is as good a citizen as you will find anywhere. It makes me feel this business is something more than just a glass shop. If it doesn't work for us all who work for it, what good is it?"

Jack cocked his head respectfully at the man's wisdom.

"I've been over some bumps myself. I've been in my share of trouble. But that's crap. There's no percentage in it. You just scuffle for pennies and buck the tide."

He picked up the phone and dialed the employment service and told them the position had been filled.

"The sales staff is in as close to eight thirty as possible. The rest come in at nine. You got anything to take care of before you begin?"

539

"No, sir."

"See you in the morning then."

They shook hands as if sealing a life bond.

He was a funny guy, Wheeler. Jack had gone in looking for a job and had left feeling the imposing weight of the entire business and the delicate personal relationships of a "family" whose names he had yet to learn. On top of that was the mysterious process of glassmaking and distant great rolling mills—Pittsburgh—Brussels—the meaning of American and international trade. . . . It seemed a lot to shoulder for a buck ten an hour.

And he would need another suit or two.

To celebrate he took Sharon out for charcoal barbecue ribs in a spade joint because she did not want to go somewhere they might run into their old friends.

She did not know if a dollar-ten-an-hour to start was good or not. Nor did she have much interest in the glass business or his strange interview with Mr. Wheeler. They had been married five days. She was just glad he had found a job.

Parked in the drive-in theater, the first time they had been out together since they were married, they fell into each other's arms, freed by the legality of their situation. Kisses not being enough, they put their fingers deep into each other's mouths and sucked them greedily, awed by the power of their mutual desire. It was as if after the first few days of anxiety in which they used their bodies in a sexual totem against their fears, they were free. They had dressed up a bit for their evening out and were tugging at each other's clothes, she as eagerly as he. They fucked in the front seat. When they left the drive-in before the film was over, it smelled like a comewagon. Her thighs above her stockings were slick with their fluids.

They raced home in virtual silence and went into the house with their arms around each other's waists.

Sharon showered and voiced the hope it would not be too long before they were able to move to a place with a real bathroom and tub. She missed long soaks in a tub of bubbles. He promised it would not be long.

Before she was dry, he sat her on the terry-covered lid of the stool and knelt between her open legs and ate her. After her initial shock of seeing his head and feeling his mouth there, she really liked it and wrapped her long legs over his bare shoulders. He felt so full of love for her,

540

what had before seemed a perverted and rather nauseating act became a delicious, heartbreakingly tender giving of love. He carried her to the bed and went down on her again and again, for hours it seemed, until repeated orgasms caused her to begin to shudder and weep hysterically, begging him to stop. Then he gently mounted her, his cock seeming to have grown extracutaneous nerve endings. Each touch was like an electrical shock, and he cried out softly with the contact. He fucked her long and lovingly while she shuddered and whimpered like a child after a tantrum.

"I love you more than God," he vowed, holding her in his arms until she fell into sleep.

The first week he had spent riding around with Harry Green, the number two salesman, getting a general picture of the business. The second week he was told to wear work clothes and spent his time in the shop, filling orders for window lights, cutting the glass to size on the smaller of two big cutting tables, helping out in the silvering room where mirrors were made, installing auto glass with the tough little mechanic whose main job was handling the large number of insurance orders for car-glass replacements. A hailstorm had kept him very busy. The kid had been a paratrooper but had not fired a shot. He wore army surplus fatigues to work with a PFC stripe still on the shirts and chutist's wings on his cap. He had a mocking, watching approach to Jack whom everyone took to calling Jaycee after Jack had stupidly revealed some of the boss' plans for his future. To counter that, Jack found himself dropping back into GI profanity and coarse service humor to convince the shopmen and glaziers he was not the prima donna they supposed. He also worked his ass off. Trying to assert some sign of natural leadership, he was always lending a hand elsewhere when the auto-glass kid was content to lean against a wall and have a smoke. He was careful not to overdo it but moved with the conviction of one who had a deep personal interest in the business, akin to the boss' own.

He even held the shovel for the old black custodian, Imo Sacks, who had been his grandfather's hired man when Jack was just a baby and his grandfather had had a little farm out on Ninth Street. Imo had a cataract on his left eye, and his hair was worn on top like threadbare carpet, turning to a frizzy gray around his ears. Yet he remembered the boy and his family and recalled "Ole John MacDairmid" as "the fairest white man I ever knew."

"If you turn out to be half the man he is, boy, you'll be somethin," he advised.

Imo still had arms like a steel driver. His son Cleo had been a promising boxer whose career was curtailed by a stretch he did for the murder of a wife. Everyone testified on the boy's behalf that the bitch had it coming, so he only did about five. The last Jack had known of Cleo he was setting pins for the Playmor Bowl. When he asked Imo about his son, the old man bristled.

"He ain't no good. Never was. Fistfightin. No brain about the women. That's what Joe Louis did to me."

For the first few nights he worked in the shop, he offered the old sweeper a ride home. It was only a bit out of his way and in the same direction.

Wheeler called him in and spoke to him about it.

"Imo is a good old nigger. But he's uppity. Give him an inch and he starts thinking he runs the business. Some of the men think you are a little soft, and if you are going to work in a capacity superior to them, you have to have their respect. If you didn't treat Imo fairly, I would be the first to fire your ass out of here. But you don't have to goddamn hold his dustpan or cater to him. If he couldn't do the work he was hired for, he wouldn't be here. That goes for everyone else. The difference between a good business and a bad one is often how those in authority bear their responsibilities and maintain the respect of those beneath them. It's not only important in business but in the family. Between men and women, fathers and their kids—it's the same thing. Everyone deserves fair and considerate treatment. But someone has to be in charge. The glaziers and shop boys are good men, or I wouldn't have them. But they are basic men. They like their beer and their pussy, and you have to be able to get down there in overalls and work beside them. But they have to never forget who's boss. Marty, you know, he's the best damn glazier I got. But he's from the East. And he got the idea a couple of years back of making this a union shop. He came in here and told me what he planned to do and that he and the others were going to strike if they didn't get the union. Glass breaks, you know. I mean if they had a

542

union and I fired them and brought in some others, window lights and storefronts we did all over town might start breaking. I told him: 'You think you and the boys are worth more money, you come to me. You want a union, get your ass out and go over to Pittsburgh where they got one, if you think they have a better deal.' Well, they don't, and Marty knows it. They don't have any more benefits over there. But some guys feel more secure if they have a piece of paper. I said there would be no goddamn union. He then said maybe if I would let them see the books to prove I was paying them as much as I could. I said no way. Well, he stomped out of here and stewed around for a week, but in the end he decided I was right. Now I respect Marty all the way, I *like* him—has a beautiful little Italian wife that gives you a hard-on just to see her walk. Marty's a good man. And he could have caused me a lot of grief. But there's times you just have to sit tight. Business is the biggest poker game around. He had to figure and realize in the long run I probably hold a stronger hand and have a bigger bankroll than he has. He might have taken a pot, but he couldn't afford to back his chances to the limit. If he'd had the slightest inkling I was soft, he could have caused me a hell of a lot of trouble. In the end, he had to find a way back down and still hold *his* authority over the others. That's why he's the best glazing foreman in town. He's younger than some of the other men, too. Oh, it's a great game." He leaned back in his chair and clasped his hands behind his head.

"You've got to learn to play it or get out of it. But I'll tell you, not the goddamn service or anything else compares with it for seeing what yourself and others are made of. The goddamn Army is a snap compared to the conduct of regular American business."

Wheeler had been a staff sergeant in the Corps of Engineers. He had not liked the Army. He said he could have been an officer but turned it down.

When a shipment—a carload—of glass arrived on the siding behind the warehouse, he came in on Saturday and Sunday in overalls with the rest and helped unload it, taking his lunch beside the men, passing as much rough teasing banter as the next—only they always knew he was the boss.

Jack tried to see how he could model himself on the man but felt deep inside he did not have the same kind of stuff. He still had so many questions, while the boss and most of the men dealt in and quarreled over the rightness of a whole lot of answers. He harbored the constant doubt that he was by their measure "man enough." It had so much to do with something other than the job.

The day they unloaded the freight car, he had pissed beside Wheeler in the shop toilet. Though the boss cupped his hand over the top of his cock in a kind of backhanded way as some men do, Jack saw he had a big one, and turned slightly to shield his own, standing close to the urinal. He felt mistakenly effeminate, inferior. All men ought to be born with the same size cocks. A god that would permit such disparity was a mean sonofabitch! was his thinking.

That night he dreamed of the boss fucking Sharon, his big dong frothing her tight, slick cunt. And she had walked away with him arm in arm, a look of contentment and love on her face such as he had never seen. When he called after her, she turned and treated him as coldly as she would a bothersome boy.

He had awakened in a panic, his body slick with cold sweat. Looking at the head of the girl sleeping on the pillow beside him, seeing her face twitch slightly and her lips move, he begrudged her the dream. Shaking her softly awake, he began to make love to her, though she mumbled protests. "Jack, please, let me sleep." He fucked her hard, entering her before she was quite ready, hauling both legs back in the crook of his arms, pounding her cunt until his balls throbbed from smacking her bottom. When he had finished, he asked her, "Am I good enough for you?"

Her reply, "I hardly can make comparisons, can I?" left him feeling no more sure than before.

"Would you like to?" he persisted. "Do you think about it?"

"Oh, for *God sake*, Jack, go to sleep! Let me sleep."

"I'll let you sleep!" he snapped, grabbing his pillow and bounding out of the bed, giving her an intentional sharp nudge in the process.

"What are you doing?" She sat up as he began to make his bed on the cushions that fit on the couch when it was closed.

"Letting you sleep," he sneered.

"What's the matter with you? Why are you acting so crazy?"

"I'm letting you sleep."

"You aren't satisfied?" she asked. "You want to do it again. You wake me up from a sound sleep, and I wasn't hot enough for you?" She threw off the covers and whipped her gown up and off and threw it away. "Come on. Fuck me again. If that's what you want. I'm awake now. I'll cry and whimper and roll my eyes." She spread her legs. "Come and get it." She lifted her breasts with both hands and lowered her eyelids sexily and winked like a droop-mouthed puppet in a way she had that usually made him laugh. Now it shriveled him, made him want to bust her in the face.

He went toward her. "I don't want that, Sharon. I just want. . . ."

"What do you *want?*" she snapped, a sneer tingling her voice.

He stood beside her and put his hand on the top of her head. "Just you. I want you."

"Well, of course." She reached up and skinned back his dick. "And I want *you.*" Her voice dipped huskily. She stuck out her tongue and touched the end of his cock with it, just teased it with the tip of her tongue, then rimmed it around the head, jacking him with her fingers. "Ummm." She smacked her lips greedily and sucked him until, in spite of the knowledge she was mocking him, he became hard.

When he got between her widely spread legs and felt himself going into her, she said sadly, "That's what you wanted."

"I just want you to love me," he protested. "I *love* you! I love you, Sharon! Why don't you love me?"

"I don't know," she confessed matter-of-factly, rather in puzzlement.

"Isn't it all right with you?" he heard himself asking in a voice higher than his own normally was, a whining little boy's voice. A punk's voice.

"It's bigger than both of us." She threw one of his own lines mockingly back at him. "Come on, *do* it! Do it good. I feel like coming."

He fucked like an engine. Doing it for her. For Sharon, he told himself.

"Do it, darling. Do it, baby. Really get it. Give it to me,

Sharon. Give it to me!" he breathed against her closed eyes.

And she was sensational. For the first time, he felt he had tapped again that purely liquid place of warm, incredible wonder, where all love lived, that he had felt the first time with her. Out of love, hatred, disregard, whatever, he did not care. He was there and so was she. THERE! ... Where all love lived. They came together.

He was ecstatic. He had seen comets, pinwheels and millions of colored lights in the air like electronic confetti. Even minutes after, the little dancing, colored lights were there. He wanted to love her, talk about it, snuggle his enthusiasm against her own.

All she said was, "Whew! That was nice." And went to the bathroom. When she returned, she wanted to sleep.

Leaning on one elbow in the dark, he stared at her hair fallen over her cheek, lifting it and bending to kiss her as he might a child.

"Sharon?"

"For *God sake!*" she erupted. "What is *wrong* with you? I don't *want* to do it again. It was fine. I came. *Now* will you go to sleep?"

"Why don't you ever want to talk to me? What's wrong with me?" he demanded.

Up she popped again. Mad now. "That's what *I* would like to know!" She snatched up her pillow and swung out of bed, her gown flipping up over her bare bottom. "When you figure it out, let me know. If I'm around." She pounded her pillow into shape on the cushions and quickly went to sleep.

He got up and covered her with the blanket.

He lay in the dark feeling he was the least sonofabitch on earth.

If it was all a game, as the boss said, he felt it was one there was no way for him to win.

36

AFTER the training period, when Jack was out there every day trying to cut the mustard, he knew again that at this rate there weren't days enough in life to gain anything but a cut-rate facsimile of the Great American Dream. Seventy-five dollars a week, seven and a half cents per mile car allowance and a promise of being put up for membership in the Jaycees had never been his idea of success.

Oh, when he was handed the plans during his training for the quarters of the new air base and told to figure an estimate for a glazing contract, there were intimations of glory. There had been pride in having the boss check and accept his figures. That another company won the bid was irrelevant. But when it was going door to hardware store door and doing the expected talk, cracking the joke, making the other person feel like a customer, he began to think of himself as a glass-nattering magpie. He had to catch his reflection in a sheet of polished plate to recall what he looked like.

"Fuck, fuck, fuck," he hummed carelessly. That and work were all there really was. And selling glass was not what he called work.

Past the new tract of Shady Acres Ranch Estates, he drove along through a kind of no-man's-land where a wheatfield still stood golden as in an ad for local beer. Then a golf course and country club to mark the outpost of the wealthy.

He parked the car deep into the Mossbacker drive where it fanned out to the size of a small parking lot. Honey Mossbacker's semenly pearlescent Kurtis-Kraft roadster was parked at a careless angle. The door on the driver's side was ajar. He adjusted his necktie, shifted the plastic zipper folder in his arm, centered his jacket button and nudged shut the door. A friendly act. He went along

547

the back flagstones where he had last come as butcher's delivery boy.

He was let in by a middle-aged black woman in white nurse's uniform, white stockings and low rubber-soled shoes. But she also wore a white hairnet and an apron. Probably the cook, he decided.

"I'm Mr. Andersen from Western Glass. I'm here to give an estimate on some mirrors."

"Um. You wait here. I go see. I don't know nothin about it," the black woman instructed him. She walked slowly, as if her feet hurt. Her ankles bulged over the tightly laced shoes.

After being announced, he found himself knocking at a door at the end of a very long hall.

"Come in." The voice triggered the same kind of slightly nervous, heightened expectation he had felt entering a first-class Shanghai whorehouse. Ridiculous in light of his mission, but nevertheless, the same feeling.

She was reclining on a white chaise before an expanse of sliding thermopane that opened onto a small private garden. She was reading a paperback novel with a lurid cover, a pair of horn-rimmed glasses perched on her nose. She wore tight white slacks and a red halter top. The splash of red was the only color in the room.

It was an enormous room, low and long, a kind of ultramodern cave.

She lowered her book and tilted her head back to peer through her glasses. "Yes?"

"I'm from Western Glass. I have an appointment to discuss some mirrors you are thinking about."

"He wants them," she corrected.

"Yes, ma'am." When as a delivery boy, he had called her ma'am, she had flinched and asked him to call her Honey. In his Robert Hall second-best suit, he saw her accept his deference as her due.

"Where were you thinking of putting the mirrors?" he asked when she did not seem interested in volunteering anything more and had in fact begun to hunt for her place in the book.

She looked up again through her glasses. "He didn't tell you?"

"No ma'am."

"He wants the whole goddamn wall and the one behind the bed and the ceiling covered with mirrors." She waved her hand in a great circle as if painting the area in a single swipe.

Jack's face turned red. He cleared his throat. "Yes, ma'am."

"Yeah. And that wall there too."

There were flush doors there, probably closets. They wouldn't be a problem.

"If I may, I would like to show you some of the installations we have done to get an idea of what type of mirrors you would like."

"Want it like that one there." She pointed to her dressing table glass. It was a perfectly polished plate of lightly golden-pink tint with a seamed rather than beveled edge, fastened with clips, no screws or rosettes. It was the kind of glass that made everyone look healthy, tan and as beautiful as he could ever be. His head reeled with the cost of covering the walls and ceilings with such expensive mirrors. His commission would run several hundred dollars. Maybe even a thousand! He felt cold and dry and clearheaded as a snake looking at a white mouse.

"If I may take some measurements then, I can put together an estimate for you. I can have it by tomorrow."

"No estimate. Just do it."

Wow! Found money. He took out his tape measure and began making measurements, writing the figures down on a page in his zipper book. The bed was a custom-built job, low and as wide as it was long. Above it, like a strange crucifix of a pagan religion, the long bit end of a water-well-drinking rig was mounted vertically on the shiny white wall. They would probably want that there when they had mirrors if they wanted it there at all, he figured.

Then he sat down and began to make a sketch in his book.

She got up and came over.

"Hey. You're a pretty good drawer."

He looked up and smiled. "I studied art for a while in college."

"Yeah? I used to draw all the time. Had a natural talent for it. But no one cared."

He smiled at her again. "I know what you mean."

"You do?"

"Sure. I got that all the time. "What good is that stuff going to do you?' " He mocked his detractors.

She laughed. "That's right! You've *been* there."

"Um." He nodded his head.

"But you went to college. I didn't get that chance."

"Only a few months. On the GI Bill."

"Why'd you stop?"

"Got married." He held up his ring.

"Why, for God sake?"

"Had to."

She blew out a flume of breath. "Phooey! Nobody *has* to anymore."

"I did."

"You don't *look* dumb." She looked at him closely, tilting up her chin to peer through her glasses. "I've seen you somewhere before. I know because you look like my brother. A whole lot."

"I delivered meat here once. You gave me a beer."

"Oh, yeow." But she did not remember. "Sure look like my brother. He could draw a little, too. But not so good as you. Nor me neither."

"You still draw?" he asked. She was bending close. He was aware of her boobs in the red halter just out of the corner of his eye, the way her white slacks fit so tightly between her legs that the seam divided the lips of her cunt. Large, heavy lips. Big cunt. Not so big a woman. She wore high-heeled strapped sandals that left her perfectly manicured toes bare. Her toes were devoid of hair, the skin as softly white as her arms.

"How about a drink?" she asked.

"Thanks. I would."

"What would you like?"

"Oh, uh. . . ."

She went to a cabinet that was a refrigerated bar. "How about some bubbly?" She hoisted a bottle of champagne from the depths.

"That would be fine."

"Good. I like a little bubbly when it's so hot out. Funny weather for this time of year, isn't it?"

"Yes, ma'am."

"Of course, I like it when it's cold out too." She grinned crookedly. "I think I like it best of all for breakfast." She poured them two glasses and carried them over. They were tall, like little pilsner glasses, rather than the wide ones he had always associated with champagne.

"Your name's Jack. Same as my brother's," she remembered.

She clicked glasses. "To art."

"You should still draw if you like it," he suggested, finishing up his work.

"I do," she confessed shyly. "But I never let anyone look at it."

"I would really like to see it."

"Would you?" She suddenly tried to look very sexy but found her glasses an impediment. She whipped them off and glared at them. "Damn doctor sold me some glasses. I was always backing into things in the car." She threw them on the chaise beside her novel, then turned and gave him the full treatment with her eyes as if to prove she could.

He felt everything inside of him had melted and turned to warm champagne. He felt a little sick.

"Would you really like to see my drawing?"

"I sure would."

"Well, it isn't very good. You won't laugh?"

Never in the world would he.

"OK," she decided. She went to one of the closets and got down on hands and knees to haul out a big cheap scrapbook.

Her ass was like a movie star's. He felt weak. Doris Day maybe. Fantastic ass.

She put the book on the bed and plumped down and sat cross-legged next to it. She patted the place beside her.

"Don't laugh," she warned coyly and opened the book.

The drawings were like a child's. The figures were developed in a flat, stiff way, with much concentration on makeup, hairstyle and clothing. But there was something terrible in childish expressions and the groupings against stark basic landscapes on which grew one or a few trees that looked like a child's effort to copy Rousseau. Every leaf was there, though the grass might be but a few careless patches. Ladies posing on the edge of the world. For whom? For the artist, the viewer? It was like looking in upon the creatures looking out and no way to pass a word between. Even smiling, they looked desperately screaming.

"Munch," he said.

"What?"

"Edvard Munch. He is a very great Norwegian painter. This reminds me a little of his work."

"Bull. Now you're just trying to make me feel good. I know they're no good."

"Well, they do make me think of his stuff."

"Really?"

"Really."

"He can't be much good then."

"He's all right."

"I'll have to check him out."

He grinned and looked at her. "When you do, you won't think I was so flattering."

"Why?"

"He was crazier than hell."

She laughed. She roared. A real Little Rock beer joint pearl of laughter ripped out of her. She held both ankles with her hands and rocked back and forth. Then she stopped, reached over her book and took his head between both her hands and kissed him. Her lips opened seductively upon her mouth which seemed filled with honeyed, champagne-flavored come. He was dizzy as hell. He was dribbling in his pants immediately. She hauled him back as she fell sideways onto the bed. The second kiss was even better than the first. He had never had that experience. The first was always the inspiring one, the others were fine, but always slightly tinged with a consciousness of technique. Even as he touched her breast, knowing that he could, he could not believe what he was about or harbored any notion that it would go beyond just that. Yet he knew that they were going all the way.

She seemed another species altogether—star or something—not just woman. When he dared remove her halter and she arched her back to make it easier for him, his head was swarming. Then she was bare, squeezing her tits together by pinching them between her arms, rolling them slightly.

"What's the matter, baby?" she asked. "You look so sad. Don't you like me?"

"Oh! Yes! YES! You're just too beautiful." He plunged his face into the soft pale flesh, found the nipple that was still pink and had never been suckled by offspring. While he sucked, she held his head with one hand and reached down with the other to unfasten her shoes. When he unsnapped her slacks and ran down the zipper, she watched him and moved her ass around gently, wantonly, and lifted herself again to help him slide them over her hips. Her cunt was a dark wedge in contrast with her champagne-colored hair. In the center of her pale belly was a

552

fine little scar down in the pubic hair. He kissed the scar, her belly, her body, as she turned and moaned and encouraged him with her hands.

She lay on the bed watching him as he hurriedly undressed, squeezing her boobs together again as if posing for a photograph, writhing slightly as if she could not wait, her hands in a prayerful position before her sex.

There was nothing in his experience with which to compare her. Her cunt was large, soft, but muscularly trained to grip, hold, soothe, nip. She fucked with a frenzy and a change of rhythms and angles, using everything, all of her aswirl around her sex, until he felt a beginner and was just hanging on. When he thought he would come, she would do a twist with her sex that was the same as popping him out, stopping the ejaculation, yet holding him fast. He had never gone so long in his life. She was puffing, screaming, biting his shoulders, face, ripping his back with her nails, literally ripping it, and he did not care.

Fuck, fuck, fuck, fuck, his brain screamed. *Don't care if I do die, do die, do die.*

He screamed. She had bitten deeply into his shoulder. The pain zinged through him worse than any electric shock. It enraged him. He rose up and slapped her goddamned face. She laughed, hollered and looked as if she would kill him, then went all funny, liquid, mad, and kissed his lips until they felt bruised. He came in her all the way from his asshole. Everything came. When it was over, he was trembling, too weak to support himself with his arms. He lay on her with his face in her tangle of artificially candied hair and felt all the places of pain with which she had marked him. Lips, back, shoulders, rump, cheek. He ached inside and out. She caressed him with hands and feet, still gently pulling on his joint with her sex.

When he lay beside her, she held his genitals in her lovely hand, soothing, tickling gently, incredibly bringing him to a hard again.

"You're beautiful—so beautiful, Honey," he crooned. "I love you, I love you," he babbled incoherently.

When he tried to turn toward her again, she pushed him back flat on the bed, poured the rest of the champagne on his cock and went down on him. She got very excited doing it. She worked her forefinger up his tight ass while he had all of his hand except his thumb in her gaping cunt. He would have eaten her too if she wanted him too. But when he tried to move her closer, she shook her head no with his cock in her mouth.

When he had come, she slid up his body and opened her mouth on his and slipped the little oyster of his semen into his mouth.

"Swallow your own. I'll get it back later," she said as if feeding a nestling of her own.

There was no part of him that did not hurt. He stood in the shower while she soaked in a big tub of bubbles, her head wrapped in a towel. He looked as if he had been beaten with a cat-o'-nine-tails. Inflamed scratches latticed his back, ran in long runs from his neck to below his buttocks.

What a senseless fuckin thing to do! he thought. And wondered what in the hell he would tell Sharon. He couldn't hide a mess like that.

Honey lifted a toe free of the bubbles and traced the course of one of the angrier rills on his back in the air.

"I can't help it," she explained. "Hope you don't mind too much."

"Honey, hell!" he observed, examining the perfect set of tooth marks on his left shoulder. "More like trying to screw a mountain lion."

Her laughter bubbled through the big tile room, shattering off the walls. Tiny rubies of blood seeped from the scratches and the bite.

"You always do that?" he wondered.

"The first time with someone—yeow."

He blotted his back with the large velvety towel. "What the hell will I tell my wife?" he asked aloud.

She laughed. "Be sure to let me know."

"You keep a diary or something?"

She laughed again, loudly and freely. "No. But I really should. I never thought of it before. But what they tell their wives ought to be priceless. Anyway, be honored. That is one of my better works. . . . Come here."

She pulled him to his knees beside the tub and twined a soapy arm around his neck and kissed. It was like the last bit of too much cake and ice cream. He felt sick. She offered him her hand to help hoist her out of the tub. She padded over to the shower and adjusted it to rinse her below the neck.

She was a beautiful woman. He had no idea how old

554

she was. She seemed barely mortal. He could regard her openly as he might any of the fixtures in the house. Perhaps it was because she had absolutely no self-consciousness. When she came out of the shower, he was sitting on a white stool. She plopped her foot onto his knee and dried her leg, her dripping dark bush on the level of his face. She fluffed it with a towel, saw his solemn expression as he stared at it and reached out to touch his face tenderly.

"It's beautiful." He looked up to tell her.

"Thank you." She laughed. "Sometimes I get to feeling it's just a hole. But Jay says it takes three hundred barrels a day to keep it filled." She turned around. "Make yourself useful." He dried her flawless white back and fancy bottom. He could not believe all the things they had done, nor could he reconstruct how it happened.

She went into the other room and sat naked before the mirror to repair her face while he dressed.

"You even put your pants on like my brother," she told him via the tinted glass.

He sat on the rumpled bed and watched her. She winked at him in the mirror.

"I can't believe it happened," he admitted.

"Um."

He wanted to do something more to her. Yet he was completely drained. What more could he do? Tie her to the bed and literally eat her alive? That had a passing flash of appeal, though he really did not want to hurt her. It was just what they had done had nothing much to do with what he had felt about sex before. It was somehow even more defeating than fucking an indifferent whore. At least there was understanding in that. He felt he hadn't touched Honey.

She slithered into her clothes. He loved seeing her work her tight pants up over her ass and pop it inside. She walked him to the bedroom door.

"I can bring a drawing and estimate around tomorrow," he said.

"Oh—sure. For the mirror deal."

"Yes. What time would be most convenient?"

She seemed reluctant to think about it. She frowned. "Oh—anytime." She waved it all away and plunked her arms over his shoulders. He winced when she hit the place

555

where she had bitten him. "Sorry," she apologized. "Come early in the morning. Before lunch."

"OK. . . . I sure want to thank you . . . for everything."

She laughed. "My pleasure, baby. My pleasure. *Do* come again."

"Don't think I could." He ducked his head and grinned.

"Pity." She lowered his head between her hands and kissed him on the forehead. "I want Jay to meet you," she said. It struck him as a strange thing to say. The last person on earth *he* wanted to meet was her big damn husband.

"*Ciao!*" she trilled after him in the corridor from her door.

"What?" he turned to ask.

"Good-*bye!*"

"Oh." He grinned and waved.

He felt he had truly come up in the world or was on the brink of doing so. He enthusiastically told Sharon all about the Mossbacker house and his big mirror job. She was cautious about spending the bonus he expected until she saw it. But she touched his head lovingly as he sat at his desk and got out his price books and graph paper for making a plan. He would do an impression as well on drawing paper. When it was all set, only then would he spring it on the boss. Racing on in fantasy, he saw himself a great glass contractor or even an architect. When the kid was born, he would go back to school nights.

"What's wrong with your back?" Sharon asked.

"What? Oh. Nothing."

"It's *bleeding!*"

"Naw?" He put his hand behind him.

"It's bleeding right through your shirt. Take it off. Let me see."

"It's OK. I fell against something in the shop. Just a scratch."

"You ought to put something on it."

"It's nothing. I want to do this now. Go fix dinner."

"Yes, sir, Mr. Bumstead." She bent and kissed the top of his head.

From the kitchen, where there were comfortable domestic sounds, she called, "When you get the bonus, can I get a new pair of shoes? My feet are swelling. The only thing I can get them in are my sandals."

"Sure."

"Thanks. Boy, I'll sure be glad when I can get rid of Sir Belly, I feel so horrid. Like a wienie about to split."

"You never looked more beautiful." It was true. Her face had begun to glow. He had seen the quality in the faces of pregnant women before. Sometimes they were so milky beautiful he could get a hard-on just looking at them. In spite of how awful she had felt in the beginning, Sharon had become like one of the pretty ones.

"Gagh. . . ." She rejected his contention.

"Soup's on," she called presently.

She had begun to dress up their table. She had bought some avocado and orange napkins and matching table cloth that made the white Melmac dishes look nice. She also often had a flower from the yard in a thin vase in the center of the table. It pleased him and made him feel luxurious.

Before serving him, she made him pull out his chair and sat on his lap. He nuzzled her very full breast where it peeked above the top of her maternity jumper.

"Get you *two* pair of shoes," he muttered.

She squeezed him so tightly he worried about her belly and kissed him long and passionately.

"Wow," he breathed when she broke off. Her chest was heaving. He slipped his hand familiarly beneath her smock and patted her bare thigh. She felt very voluptuous. Much larger than she had been before. She had gained twenty pounds. Her broadened bottom on his lap, the sheer new bulk of her felt good. "What was *that* for?"

She blushed and glanced away, then back. "Because I feel happy."

They wrapped their arms around each other. It was the first time she had said so. The very first since she knew she was pregnant.

The soup bubbled up under the lid of the pot and she said, "Damn!" And hopped up to tend to it.

As she ladled her specially doctored cream of tomato soup into the square white bowl, he fondly ran his hand up the back of her leg beneath her smock.

"Careful there, buster. You'll get hotter stuff in your lap than you're groping for." Sometimes her voice became sort of boyish and gravelly. It could almost make him cry for the tenderness he felt for her.

Where he had been that day and what he had done was

as remote from what he was feeling as if it were a rumor he had heard about some other person. It was like all the places he had been and all the things he had done before he met her—totally unrelated. There was no way he could ever square them with what he felt staring at pink soup in a square white bowl—too frightened for the wonder of the love he felt to form a phrase to communicate it.

"I love you, Sharon. I love you very much," he told her solemnly when she had seated herself across the small table from him.

Her lips narrowed as if stopping a reply. But the edges turned up toward dimples. Her eyes were very liquid and dark—shiny. "Eat your soup."

"You won't work all night?" she asked, getting into the bed that was a couch by day.

"No. I just have to finish this. They want to see it in the morning. I'll move this shit into the kitchen."

"No. I like to have you there. The light doesn't bother me." Before she turned over with her back to the light, she said, "You can wake me up when you come to bed if you want to." She waggled her bottom invitingly beneath the covers.

"I will," he promised.

She waggled her bottom again—good-night.

She was becoming such a real woman he felt boyish and anxious that she would leave him behind—becoming more of a woman than he might a man. Now it was he who was the frightened one every day, while Sharon became more and more secure with her belly, the apartment, the idea of being married. There was the same kind of enduring quality in her he had seen in his grandmother. It was a solid plateau of strength from which men might sail their silly kites.

She was snoring lightly, her mouth slightly open on the pillow. He did not wake her. Slipping on a sweat shirt to sleep in, he got into bed beside her. Neither had he removed his shorts. She turned and snuggled her head onto his shoulder, laying her right arm and leg across his body. Against his side he could feel the tiny movements of her womb. He slept on his back, holding her like that all night.

Bending over her big belly, she lifted his sweat shirt to

kiss his stomach. He awakened. His cock was stretching his shorts up into a white tepee. Slipping her long fingers beneath the elastic waistband, she crawled them down to encircle his penis gently.

She put both their pillows under her bottom, and he crouched between her spread legs with sweet regard for her belly, moving slowly and lovingly in her body. They held each other in wondrous gaze, licking each other with their eyes, smiling in the gentleness of morning while the day was still their own.

She glided the smooth palms of her hands over his hips and up his sweat shirt. He winced when she lightly raked a scratch with her nails.

"Sorry." She frowned tender concern.

"Nothing." He began fucking her to finish. After the initial reaction of disappointment in his changing the tempo from exquisite slowness to orgasmistic purpose, she adjusted her emotions like a hen settling her feathers and closed her eyes. He watched a frown grow again between her eyes as she concentrated on getting off too. He came before she, but continued until her knees began twitching uncontrollably on either side of him and he knew she was going to make it. Though what had begun so sweetly ended with a touch of loneliness, he had never loved her more.

"I wish I had a prick as big as a ball bat," he confessed.

The very notion caused her to clasp either side of her belly protectively.

"Whatever for?" she wondered.

"I'd just like to fill you with me," he explained.

"Looks like you have done a pretty good job with what you got."

They laughed.

"Anyway, Mom says we shouldn't be doing it very much. She stopped at the beginning of her seventh month."

"Better ask the doctor about it."

"I will. But it doesn't hurt when you are so gentle. I like it."

"Me too." He kissed her. "I like you. I like you more than watermelon, bananas, spotted pups, new tennis shoes, corduroy pants, your mother's Black George cake, Ferris wheels, freak shows, Fourth of July, pommie-granites and everyone else I know."

559

She was laughing. "What are pommie-granites?"

"Chinese apples. You know. All little red seeds you eat inside, if you like them. Lots don't like them. Pommie-granites."

She was laughing very hard. "You don't mean pomegranates?"

"Same thing," he insisted innocently.

"Oh, you are such a lovely dummy." She hugged him. "Pommie-granites," she said to herself again.

"Yeow. ... Well, I'll tell you the truth. I don't really like pommie-granites. But I like to say the word. It just sort of popped into my mind."

"You're *terrible!*"

"How's that?"

"Who can trust you when you do something like that in the middle of sweet-sweet nothings in the ear of your beautiful, passionate, loving, *good*, honest, loyal, all-American girl wife, who you knocked up higher than a box kite? Get off me!"

When he rolled out of the bed, she sniggered and muttered to herself, "Ball bat."

In the toilet he fastened the door's hook and eye.

Presently Sharon came and rattled the little plyboard cubicle.

"I'm in the shower."

"Well, reach out and unhook the door, stupid. I have to *pee!*"

Reaching around the wet plastic curtain, he let her in the door.

"God!" she exclaimed, hoisting her short gown, her bare bottom slapping the toilet seat. "When did you get modesty?"

There was the strong, cowlike rush of her urine into the bowl, a stillness when it stopped, then the quick, very efficient sounds of her with the paper and the way she wiped herself. The flushing.

She was doing something else. He saw her standing in rippled shadow against the greasy-feeling plastic curtain of the stall.

"I'm coming in," she announced, slipping around the side of the curtain, coming up naked against him, her hair tucked under a hideous red plastic shower cap that was supposed to look like a big strawberry.

Petrified with fear, his back against the wall, he felt her wet belly push coolly against him, her hands on his upper arms. There was a look in her eyes as if she were about to ask him very seriously if he loved her. Then she saw the tooth marks on his shoulder.

At first her expression was one of curiosity, concern. The corners of her lips still curled upward as the mist began to fill the corners of her eyes. The shower drummed on her plastic cap.

"What is that?"

He looked at it as if he had never seen it before. "Uh. . . ."

"It's a bite!"

"Uh . . . yeow. . . ."

"Tooth marks. I didn't do that," she told herself.

"No. Uh . . ." A thousand lies ricocheted crazily through his brain from all directions.

There was the sound of the shower on her plastic cap. Rivulets of water coursed down the slopes of her heavy, swollen breasts and off the easy big mound of her stomach. Her navel pointed at the center of him accusingly.

"How did you get that thing, Jack?" Her voice was thinned by the strain of holding it under control. "Who bit you?" There was still a sad, hopeful look in her eyes under the lid of her plastic hat, a wish to believe.

A fight, he thought. . . .

"Fight?" She wanted to believe him. He could feel her straining toward belief until the tension in her voice was finer than Munch's silent shriek. She yanked him around in the shower, saw his back and groaned as if she had been kicked in the belly. Her knees buckled, but she did not go down. Questions flitted crazily between anger, fear and sympathy for him in her eyes.

"I got in this fight," he said. "I don't want to talk about it." He pushed past her out of the shower. It was too stupid, too self-depreciating for him to explain.

She trailed him out of the shower into the other rooms, leaving puddles on the floor where she stepped.

"Tell me!" she demanded hysterically. The words were thin, pitiful. Her ignorance, need to trust, her naked big belly and tits and the shower cap made her seem so vul-

561

nerable he had to stifle the cruel laugh that for a moment rose out of his own terror.

"To hell with it. I just got into a fight with a guy."

"What guy? Why?"

"A guy. He thought I had made a pass at his wife."

"You what?"

"It was a misunderstanding." His words were a buzz in his ears. He felt he was pleading for his life.

Turning, she yanked the curtain of the clothes closet back on its rod and hauled out the suit he had worn the day before. She looked at it, turned it, searching for some sign that would support the scratches and bite on his body. Her eyes became terribly hurt, filled with tears—then flaring with some maddening vision. She flung the suit at his face with all the force she was able. A button clicked against a tooth.

"YOU BASTARD! YOU ROTTEN, LYING BASTARD! OH! OH! NO! NO! NO!" She ran screaming from the room, blindly, bumping a kitchen chair and knocking it over, yanking open the door. He ran after her.

Where could she go? What could she do?

"Sharon! *Sharon!*"

"NO!" She shook her head wildly from side to side as she seemed to claw her way through an invisible clinging barrier.

It was like moving through water. He strained every muscle toward reaching her. Just as she opened the outside door, he felt his fingers brush, but not grasp her bare hip.

"NO!" She twisted free.

He caught her just at the top of the cellar stairwell and hauled her down into a bed of purple iris that had yellow tongues and throats. She fought him, begging him to let her go.

"Let me *go!* Don't *touch* me! You BASTARD! Bastard! Bastard! Bastard. Bastard. Bastard. Bastard . . ." she wept.

"Sharon, please. Just listen—"

"NO!"

"Sharon. Nothing happened. Come inside. Just listen to me." He was aware that they were in the yard naked in a flower bed while cars were going by in the street. People were going to work. What if the landlady came and looked out her back door? A man in khaki, carrying a lunch bucket on which there were Mickey Mouse decals, stopped on the sidewalk to stare at them. He seemed to be making up his mind what it was he saw, a blank, unbelieving expression on his face. Then he got it. His mouth opened, then closed primly, and he hurried on, looking back twice before he was too far down the block to see.

"Come inside." He shielded her body with his own and began to lift her. There were bits of grass and dead leaves from the flower bed plastered to her skin. The shower cap had been wrenched off. In rolling her head, she had smudged her face with dirt. Dirt and bits of foliage clung to her wet skin. He got up and, with both arms wrapped around her, began leading her down the stairs. She still resisted, called him every filthy name she could think to call.

Back in the room she began dressing quickly while he spun out his lie.

"The truth is, darling, I almost did—uh—you know— get into something with this woman. A goddamned whore! A nympho. Went there to measure some mirrors for the bedroom. She just went after me. Gave me champagne. Rich bastards. They don't give a damn about anything. She was real pretty—glamorous, sort of. I didn't know what happened. Next thing we got our clothes off and I'm thinking, *What the hell am I doing? I love my wife. I don't want this! This garbage.* Then in comes her husband and jumps me. And I'm blasting him in the face. Only I can't get leverage, see. Then he bites my shoulder and his goddamn whore begins clawing at my back like a wildcat. . . ."

She flipped her hair back angrily and hauled her medium white suitcase out of the bottom of the closet.

"What are you doing?"

"What does it look like?" she snapped.

"Aw, Sharon. . . . Listen. I told you the truth. I didn't do anything. I wouldn't have. I was just—uh—you know—overwhelmed for a minute. . . . I—"

"Poor, poor *you*."

"Naw. *Listen!* That's bullshit, baby. I love you. *I love you!* Stop that crap. You aren't going anywhere. I told you the truth. I really did, Shar. I love you."

She looked up from putting things from the closet into the case. "Jack"—her eyes wide and bright—"I don't care."

"What do you mean?"

She closed the case.

"What do you mean?" he repeated.

Without looking at him, she flipped the back of her hand in his direction as if dismissing him from the human race. "I just don't care." Her voice went up almost joyously, it seemed, as if she were about to laugh. "Don't care about you, your lies, your truth. Simple, Jack. I-do-not-care." She took a light coat out of the closet and laid it on the suitcase.

"Where are you going?"

But she was through speaking to him. She moved around him and picked up the phone and dialed a taxi number. When he realized what she was doing, he lunged for the phone and cut off the call.

She turned coldly, sneering at him, the left corner of her mouth twitching. Lifting her head, eyes straight ahead, she hauled the case off the bed and began humping it toward the door.

"If you want to go to your mother's, I'll drive you," he offered. "Wait, Sharon. Please. *Please!* Goddammit, Sharon! Don't go. . . ."

She never looked back. He followed her to the outer door. He hadn't dressed. He saw her drag the heavy case to the curb and stand looking expectantly for a cab.

He slammed the door, rattling the entire house.

Fuck her! Just goddamn fuck her! he cried inside himself.

He hadn't meant for it to happen. What did it mean anyway? He loved her. He really did love her. He did not know what to do. Most of her clothes were still in the closet. He plunged in and wrapped his arms around the clothes, smelling her scent, remembering her dear big belly, the way she kissed. He slid to his knees in the closet and cried into the hems of her clothes.

Then there was nothing left to do but go to work. She would be back. He would go over to her mother's that evening. She was just hurt and angry. It was something that happened to lots of people. She would come back when she settled down. Holding fast to that thought, he got up, made himself feel hard, knowing, experienced. A man of the world. A man of business—like the boss. They understood such things. *A stiff dick has no conscience.*

He shaved his face. He thought he looked old. He looked as though he had been out all night. He splashed

shaving lotion on lavishly, dressed in the same suit he had
worn the day before and combed his hair. He got together
the plans for the Mossbackers' mirrors and went outside.

"What was all that commotion down there?" his landlady opened her back door to inquire.

"Nothing. Just a little family spat." He grinned.

"Hmm. Well I told you. You can't keep the place after the baby is born. I don't want no kids or pets."

"Don't worry," he promised.

37

HONEY'S sports car stood in the garage, its gleaming
white rear as voluptuous as her own.

The black woman in the kitchen asked him to wait
while she went to the phone and rang.

"She say she be right out," she informed him coldly.

He wondered what all she knew.

"You wait in there," the black told him as if not
deigning to share the same room with him. Maybe it was
his imagination, but that was how she made him feel.

His back felt stiff, plastered with memory of pain, from
Honey having marked him. He wondered why she hadn't
asked him to be sent in but instead had him kept waiting
in some kind of living room filled with plants.

Then she came striding in. She wore a plain pink shirt
dress that fit tight across her bottom, accentuated all the
more by a wide white belt that matched her shoes. She
had a soft white little coat sweater buttoned beneath the
collar of her dress but just shrugged over her shoulders.
She looked very young, very country club, curiously innocent. In her left hand she carried a small white bag and
trailed a white chiffon scarf.

"Oh, hi!" she said coolly in the teeth of his smile. He
felt like a stranger.

"You're beautiful," he vowed.

"Um. I'm sorry. I'm in a hurry."

"Oh. I have the sketches for the mirrors and the esti-mate."

"Huh?" She was digging in her purse for something.

"The mirror job. I worked late last night to get it ready. I have it." He hoisted his case slightly before him.

"Oh. Fine!" She turned to yell into the kitchen, "Mary! Have you seen my keys?"

"No, Miz Honey, I ain't."

"Shit!" she spat and turned on her heel.

He followed her as she loped back through the other room and turned down the long corridor toward her bed-room.

"I can never remember where I put my keys either." He lied to make conversation. He had to really walk to keep up with her.

He trailed her into the bedroom and joined her in her search, while she ripped open her dressing-table drawer.

"There they are!" He spied them beneath the table against the wall and dropped down on all fours to retrieve them.

When he handed her the keys, their fingers brushed and he felt a tingle that raised gooseflesh on his lacerated back, causing him to shiver a bit.

"Thanks. Now I really must run."

He noticed the bed was unmade and rumpled. He reached out to touch her arm.

When she stopped and turned half toward him, he dropped his case and wrapped his arms around her and tried to kiss her.

She drew back violently and snapped. "Don't be *silly!*"

He wondered if he were the same fellow who had been there the day before; if she were the same woman he'd had three ways to teatime on that big rumpled bed.

She extricated herself easily in the face of his wonder and strode from the room.

He swept up his case and hurried after her.

"Would you like me to leave the stuff with you or could I stop by later?"

"That's fine," she trailed over shoulder.

"Which?"

They were through the room of plants and passed on through the kitchen.

"Mary." She stopped to speak to the cook. "There will be about twelve I think tonight. Just one of your big famous salads. And maybe some melon. Jay wants to barbecue. Rufus will be along to help and serve."

"Yes, Miz Honey."

"How's your daughter?"

"She OK. Doctor say it not malignant."

"That's *good!* Everything was all right with the hospital?"

"Yes, Miz Honey. Mr. Mossbacker, he took care of evrything all right. We sure do thank you and remember you in our prayers. Sar-uh do, too."

"That's all right. You don't have to thank us ... ever, Mary. You are like our family."

"Yes, Miz Honey," the woman said wearily.

At the garage he asked again while she wrapped a scarf around her head the way he had seen in pictures of Greek and Russian peasant women. She was gorgeous. "Could I come back again later?"

"Why don't you give me a call later? We have people coming. There are so many things to do. You understand. ..." She was in the racy low car with its lipstick-red leather interior. She reached up and patted his arm and smiled fully on him.

"Sure. I can do that."

"Beautiful! You *are* a lover."

The special engine roared to life beneath the hood of the custom-built machine. She depressed the clutch and slipped into reverse and turned to watch rearward over her other shoulder to back out the drive. Her legs were parted slightly, her skirt over her knees. Above the tops of her hose would be her full white thighs. Before he could follow the thought further, she had let go of the clutch, and the car leaped out of the garage like a startled animal. In the drive she got control of it and began backing carefully.

He took a few quick steps after it.

"My wife saw my back and went home to her mother!" he blurted.

She glanced at him and smiled and gestured she hadn't heard.

"See you!" she called.

Then she was out of the drive and into the street. Changing gears neatly, she laid down a brief strip of rubber when she let out the clutch.

He was standing in the drive beside his old red Ford

with his zipper case containing the plans for the expensive mirror installation, feeling like a chump.

He thought of Sharon and how frightened and hurt she had looked when she had seen his back where Honey had ripped him with her nails and the marks of her perfect, capped teeth on his shoulder.

"Fuckin-hardassed-bitch!" he muttered loudly to himself and kicked the right front tire of his car—hard.

"Where have *you* been?" Sheila, the display room counter and phone girl, asked when he came in and slid into a chair behind the service counter and reached for a phone. He had made a few other calls and wanted to write them up before seeing the boss. He had thought all day he had ought to call in but hadn't had the heart to attempt an explanation over the phone. He had rung the Mossbacker house twice in the last hour and once an hour earlier.

"I have this big mirror deal working," he snapped at the girl impatiently. "I had to be there first thing this morning."

She looked skeptical. "You better go tell the boss. He's mad as hell."

"I will."

He dialed the Mossbacker home number again. He had it memorized by now.

"No. Miz Mossbacker ain't back yet," the woman on the other end snapped and hung up on him.

He replaced the receiver, then picked it up again and dialed Sharon's mother's number.

Her mother answerd.

"Hello, Mom. May I speak to Sharon, please?"

"Hello, Jack," she said warily. "Well, I'm very sorry, Jack. But Sharon is resting now. She's been crying all day."

"I'm sorry. It is really a misunderstanding. If I can just talk to her and explain it calmly, I'm sure she will understand."

"I'm not going to bother her now. She said she didn't want to talk to you if you called anyway. She needs time to think. Surely you can understand that. She's been through a great deal because of you, you know. We *all* have!"

"Yes, ma'am. I know. And I'm sorry. But if I could just come by this evening and *explain....*"

"I don't think this is the time for explanations. But if you insist, you can call back later and I'll speak to her."

"OK. I will. Thanks, M—" He could not bring himself to call her Mom again. He hung up. He felt like crying. Her voice had been so cold and acid it had reached right inside him and plucked some cord that made him feel he was going mad.

"More troubles?" Sheila asked.

"Yeow."

"When it rains, it pours."

He looked up Jay Mossbacker's number at his office and dialed it.

"What do you wish to speak to Mr. Mossbacker about, Mr. Andersen?" his secretary inquired in studied business college tones.

"I designed a mirror installation for his home at his wife's request and I would like to show it to him and deliver the estimate for his approval."

"Just a moment, please."

About five minutes passed. He watched a tiny, lone ant hauling a relatively enormous crumb of Sheila's lunch across the counter. If it hadn't been for the size of its load, he would never have seen the ant.

"I'm sorry, Mr. Andersen. But Mr. Mossbacker is in conference now. I will give him your message, and he will, of course, contact you if he is interested."

"Well. . . . Listen. Be sure he understands I have design and estimate ready and that his wife knows all about it."

"Very well, Mr. Andersen. Thank you for calling."

"Thank you." He hung up.

The ant got too near the edge with his big crumb and both went over the side.

He gathered up his orders, his sketches and estimate to go in and see the boss.

38

SHARON had been at her mother's a week.

The greasy skillet and pans he had cooked in were piled in the sink. He hadn't made or closed their studiocouch since she had left. His suit, shirt and tie hung over the back of the chair to his desk. Newspapers, orange peelings, a box of graham crackers, a milk-clouded glass and a deck of pornographic playing cards he had got in the Navy and cached in the box of his Chinese mementos were scattered around the floor beside the unmade bed.

She hadn't come or called for the rest of her clothes. He did not like opening the closet curtain and seeing them there. Yet he felt their presence was hopeful hostage for her eventual return. At least she had not decided absolutely she would not.

But the perfume she had left on her pillow had faded to a memory that haunted him through the acrid smell of his own nightmare sweat. He had awakened several times and sat bolt upright in the bed when in dream he thought he heard her call his name—as clearly as if she were in the room.

She had permitted him to visit her one evening after dinner and offer again his explanation in the presence of her parents. They had listened without interruption but with obvious distaste as he described his attempted seduction by the glamorous wife of one of the city's most prominent citizens. That he altered the facts to say that he did not have sexual relations with the woman and that the scene had ended in a free-for-all with her husband during which she also attacked him did not enhance his moral position in their eyes.

When he had finished and Sharon had agreed to sit with him for a while in their backyard to speak privately, her father said to her mother, "I don't believe a darn word of it! He would lie just to keep from telling the truth. He was messing around with some trash of his own kind."

"What do you think we ought to do?" his wife wondered.

"We don't have to do anything. Sharon's here, and I hope she stays here."

"What about the baby?"

"It will have a name. She's young. She can meet a forgiving, Christian young man. What kind of life will someone like Jack give them?"

"But I do think he truly loves her."

"His kind don't know what love is." He popped out his evening paper and felt of a distinctly minority breed—an insister that Jesus was not a Jew because He was the Son of God, and everyone knew what God thought of the Jews—assailed by devils like his son-in-law on one hand and Harry S. Truman on the other. Things were so bad and prospects so dim that the only thing that kept him from praying for the Day of Judgment now was the rumor that the deacons and elders of the church were talking about asking him to join them at the First Federal Savings and Loan.

When Jack had tried to take Sharon's hand, she had coolly moved it away. "Just talk if you want to," she advised.

"I only want you to know I could give an arm and a leg easier than being away from you."

She looked at him disgustedly. He wasn't missing any limbs.

"I love you. I've never loved anyone before. Not like this. I want you to come back, Sharon. I want to prove to you I will never do anything like that again. I love you. I love the baby we're going to have."

"I'm going to have," she amended.

"Don't think like that, Sharon."

"Oh, I've thought a lot about you and everything the last few days."

"What?"

"Oh, like maybe our parents aren't such stupid-os after all."

"What do you mean, honey?" The word stuck in his throat.

She too, having been told the name of the "other woman," also visibly winced.

"I don't love you, Jack. I don't think I ever did. It was just all sex with us really. I couldn't stand how you spent such time combing your hair, and didn't bathe every day, and always made everything seem dirty."

"I didn't!"

"You *do!* Everything! I never heard language like you use every day. 'Fuck. Shit.' Having been away from you it seems to me like a nightmare. I can't believe it was me."

"I'm sorry!" he begged. "Really. I don't know. I can change. You can help me. I want to be what you think is good."

"Do you?" She looked at him icily.

"Yes! I *do,* Sharon. I really do. I'll do anything."

She seemed to weaken for a second and then flared. "How can I believe you? Goddamn! The first chance you get—or was it the first? Or have you been screwing everybody you can all along? Oh, NO! How can I believe you? And when I was like *this!* You really stink, Jack! You really do, boy!"

"I told you the truth, Sharon. It wasn't the first chance. I could have had others." Then, sensing that hadn't helped him much, quickly added, "I didn't—don't—want anyone else. I honestly haven't. She wasn't like a real person. I was overwhelmed. The fancy house and all. It didn't seem real. It was like a dream. You are all I want, darling. You are all I need. I *love* you."

"Don't touch me! I don't believe you, I don't *want* to believe you. I could never go back to that—that—basement! I couldn't!"

"You won't have to. I'll find us a good apartment. I'll ask the boss about helping us get a house. He has helped other guys. We could have our own house, Sharon, and a yard for the baby to play in." Carried away by his vision, he became generous. "You don't have to come back to the apartment. Stay here until I can get the house set. I'll speak to the boss about it right away. Tomorrow. Just let me court you. Call on you the way we did when we were dating. We'll go for walks and see a show. Let me prove I love you. I know you can love me, too. Sharon?"

She cautiously granted the remote possibility it might

work. But she vetoed dates. "You can take me to church and come back here for a little while afterward." She laid down her ground rules.

"Can't we at least go for a drive or take in a drive-in movie?" he wheedled.

"*No!* There's only one place where that would lead with you, and you know it. . . . Anyway, we shouldn't do it anymore now until the baby is born. The doctor said."

The last note gave him hope. It meant she at least thought about and probably wanted him that way. He snatched at the revelation and cached it without comment or visible sign of its importance. He left that evening a hopeful and dedicated young man, promising to show her spartan proof of his love.

The boss had listened to him explain why he wanted to buy a house, then rocked back in his chair and said, "To be perfectly frank with you, son, you just haven't shown me the stuff that would make me want to help you at this time."

Jack paled.

The boss noted that and went on. "It isn't that your work is unsatisfactory. There have only been a couple of complaints from customers. It's more a matter of character, let's say. Some of the fellows in the shop laugh about you behind your back. Know what they call you? 'First of May.' That's an old carnival term for someone who comes out in the spring but doesn't last through the winter. They don't think you have the stuff to stick, to make a good glass man. I concede that you are young. But there's an indefinable quality in those that can be a success, and so far none of us has seen it in you. Now I don't know why or what the troubles with your wife are. But it would seem to me, whatever they are, this would not be a promising time to be investing in a house. I'm willing to ride along with you a bit further. But unless you show us more than you have. . . ." He raised his palms upward helplessly.

Jack didn't know what the hell he was talking about. He worked as hard as the other salesmen. He didn't screw around any more than they. Dammit! He really tried.

"I'm serious about this job, Mr. Wheeler. I intend to keep it and advance in it. I'm not a fuck-off or a fool either, I don't think. I love my wife, and I intend to keep her too. I work as hard as anyone here."

"I believe you," Wheeler admitted. "If I didn't, I would

573

have had your ass out of here. But you must develop natural qualities of leadership. That's important. I was going to put you up for membership in the Junior Chamber of Commerce, where you could develop some of these qualities. But then I heard about your wife leaving you—from someone else, I might add. No. We have a considerable investment in you. So far you aren't making your way. I expected that. That doesn't matter. What matters is, I hired you on my instinct ahead of better qualified people. I don't want to think my instinct is wrong. I don't think that it is." He smiled a bit for the first time. "Let's give it another six months. You come back then, and we'll talk about a house." He stood up and extended his hand. Jack took it, prepared for the crushing squeeze that was intended to be taken for utmost sincerity.

What the boss had felt about him had come as yet another shock. He hadn't imagined the shopmen and other salesmen gossiping and giggling like old faggots about him.

It was the same old "Prove you are a man" bullshit.

Goddammit, if *they* were men, he didn't want to be one. He would be whatever he was. He could outthink, outfuck, outwork, and outhustle any of them. But as soon as he made the brag, he was insecure on all scores. Maybe they were right. Maybe he was an oddball.

When he called Sharon, he told her the boss had promised to help them get into a house in six months. "By then, I won't have been there quite a year. He's made everyone else wait until they had been there a year." Sunday he would explain that the boss would be much more agreeable to helping them if they were back together. He would look for a better, regular apartment for them. He felt it was only a matter of a few rough days before she returned.

He gathered up the pornographic playing cards, twisted a rubber band around them and hid them in the back of his desk drawer.

39

THEY caught him eating a can of chili, breaking the crackers into the saucepan in which he had heated it to save dirtying a bowl. The sink was piled with dishes he had promised himself he would wash after his supper.

They came in without knocking. Glenn swung a half-gone fifth of Cascade by the neck. They stood in the low cellar room like two gunslingers come to hurrah a sodbuster. Both wore Levi's low on their slender hips. Both wore sports shirts rolled on their arms to show off their muscles and tattoos.

"Look at him!" Glenn cackled. "Our old little buddy livin like a mole er somethin. We heard you and your old woman split up. So we come by to cheer you up." He swung the bottle like a bell.

Jack could not imagine how he had heard. Maybe he had run into his grandmother in the street. "We had a little spat. It's only temporary," he explained. "I'm looking for another place. She just couldn't go this basement any longer. You know how pregnant women are."

"Sure." Glenn understood.

Maybe if Bucky hadn't been there, Jack would have told Glenn about Honey Mossbacker. But he realized his urge to do so was bragging. In fact, he resented their intrusion upon his and Sharon's life. That they should even think about Sharon was a shocking affront to him. He wished they would go.

Glenn opened the refrigerator and took out two cans of beer as if they were his property and went to the sink to search through the dirty dishes for an opener.

"How did you hear?" Jack asked.

"What? Oh. You know, word gets around. How'd we hear, Buck?"

He shrugged his disinterest. It seemed he had just come along at Glenn's insistence and was anxious to get on to where they were going. As he glanced around the apartment, his face looked as though he found it all scornfully amusing. He picked up Sharon's old Raggedy Ann from the easy chair and examined it casually, finally lifting up its apron and dress and grinning at its bloomers.

"Yours?" he asked. Then dropped it on its head into the chair in a jumble of stuffed cloth arms and legs.

Glenn plugged holes in the cans and passed around the bottle.

"Well, we just came around to see how you were," Glenn said again. "See if maybe you'd like to go out bummin with us a little. You know, like *old* times. We ain't seen you much since you got married and got that *white*-collar job. Sort of felt like you didn't think we was good enough to meet your old lady er somethin."

Jack hastened to explain that was not what he felt at all. "I wanted to have you guys over. I really wanted to. But it's been rough. Sharon has been upset. In the beginning she felt real bad about havin to leave school and get married. She didn't want to see anybody. Not even her best friends. Then, just when it seemed to be gettin all right, you know. Zap! This shit happened. I was just thinking the other day about havin you over for dinner or somethin. I was goin to mention it to her."

"Yeow. That's how I figured it was," Glenn said. "I mean, I sort of *wondered* when I didn't hear from you after you got married. I mean I really thought there for a little you were ashamed of your old buddy. But I said, 'She-it, no! He ain't like that.' Naw, I knew it was somethin. But, shit, man, you could of called or somethin. Like I woulda understood."

"I'm sorry as hell I didn't. Honest. I don't know. I just didn't want to bother anyone with my shit. You know."

"Well, it made me think some shit for a long time, man. I mean, you don't know how close I was to comin over and throbbin your goddamn ass." He said the last with such genuine venom Jack knew it was so.

He felt humbled and ashamed, cheap. For indeed he would never have asked Sharon to feed them. She did not like them. And there was nothing he had ever been able to say to convince her Glenn was not a menace. Still, where was she? And who was it who had come to cheer him up?

"But I'm goin to overlook all that," Glenn advised Jack

magnanimously. He visibly wiped out his previous feelings with a swipe of his knobby hand.

"You guys sound like a couple of old queers," Buck sneered.

"Yeow?" Glenn turned on the lean dark-haired boy. "That's *your* ass!"

He grinned crookedly. "I thought we came here to take him out, not get all sentimental."

"Sentimental, shit!" Glenn seemed flustered. It was as if he had forgotten their mission.

Seeing him cast about with his narrowed yellow eyes, physically writhing in his skin, Jack suddenly wondered if Glenn's brain was going. Or maybe he was seeing him through Sharon's eyes. Maybe that was the way he had always been. There was menace there, too. It made him feel very, very tired.

"Yeow. Come on. Let's get the hell out of here!" He came around and took Jack roughly by the arm. "Forget that scum you're eatin." He hauled Jack to his feet. His hands were like talons. The spoon rattled in the pan.

"I don't know, guys." Jack hesitated. "I don't feel much like bummin around. I got to get up early tomorrow and go look for another apartment. My boss is goin to help us get a house in six months, but I want to find a good place for Sharon and the baby that's comin in the meantime."

"Fuck the *mean*time, man!" Glenn insisted. "Naw. You aren't going to chicken out on us?"

There was no question. Jack sensed Glenn's feelings were getting dangerously back to the place where he thought Jack had rejected him.

"Should I change clothes?"

"Naw, naw. You're fine. We're just goin to do some bummin."

Jack had on dirty Levi's and a Navy chambray shirt with his name stenciled on the back. The cloth had faded to the color of an August sky. It would be OK to have a couple of beers. He owed them that much. Their friendship was no longer imperative, but it was easier to go along than to say no.

He wondered why he felt shaky, frightened, shanghaied. No one was joking and laughing. All the grimness of former forays they had made together came back, and he felt enraged. What goddamn stupid right had they to come barging in on his life? His problems—his fucking *sad-*

ness—were worth more than the bullshit they brought, however sympathetic their intention. It was all he could do to drag his ass along with them to the car. Yet, with Buck hovering along behind and Glenn almost crowding him at his side, Jack could not shake the feeling that he had no option but to go with them. They did not speak all the way to the car.

Jack heard himself saying, "I guess it would do me good to get out for a couple of beers. But I can't stay out very late."

Glenn just grunted.

As soon as he was in the back seat, he thought he heard a telephone ring. If it was Sharon and he was not there— He forced himself not to think about it. He could say he went out to eat. Went to see an apartment for rent. It was all right. But if she was calling, he would like to be there.

Poor goddamn clowns, he thought.

"So what you guys been doin?" He leaned forward with his elbows on the back of the front seat.

But now they did not seem to want to talk. Glenn had to swallow before he could say with surprising bitterness, "Not some white-collar salesman's shit like you."

Jack's elbow touched Bucky's shoulder as they turned the corner, and he shrugged it off the back of the seat.

"Sorry."

He stared straight ahead.

Glenn took a drink from the bottle and handed it wordlessly to Bucky. They had put the top back on before Glenn remembered and handed it back.

"Here."

"Thanks," Jack managed.

Fuck these people! his mind screamed. *Just goddamn to hell with them!* It was the same old shit. They weren't any fun. It was hard for him to remember when they had been. Maybe Glenn before Bucky came along. It had been fun before it got mean. He wished he were back in the apartment. The idea of running a sink of hot soapy water and washing the dishes, sweeping and mopping, and making the place look good loomed as a great luxury. He longed for the lonely solitude of the cellar—the pornographic playing cards even. This was nowhere!

"You want to tell him about the cunt we ran into?" Glenn turned to ask Buck.

"You tell him."

"Found this old whore—well, not so old—like thirty-five or forty. Say she's about that, Buck?"

Bucky agreed as to the woman's age.

"But still good-lookin. With the prettiest goddamned snatch you ever saw, man!"

Bucky found that particularly hilarious, which set Glenn to laughing. They laughed so hard Jack found himself laughing as well, though he had no notion what the joke was.

"Oh, yeow! Great pud on her. And she gives you your money's worth. Got some liquor in her and me and Buck just stood on our joints. Like she don't get such young cock like us *too* often. I mean, she liked it, didn't she, Buck?"

Buck was not talking.

"She liked it," Glenn was certain. "I mean I had her puffing over my old pajonk. Only her snatch opened up like a goddamn airplane hangar. You could of rammed your head in there. Like you can't hit the sides! So we put this ketchup bottle up her twat to see how big that thing *is,* man. And she could take the whole damn thing."

"King size or regular?" Jack wondered.

They could not speak for a while for laughing. "King size or regular?" Glenn kept repeating, feeding their laughter.

"Regular. Yeow it was a regular," he decided breathlessly. "Only she got kind of upset about us doin that and tellin her what a big box she had. 'I thought you were nice boys,' " he mocked the woman.

Jack could see a sleeping room-kitchenette apartment somewhere and the poor woman being made a fool. Still, he was fascinated and no little envious. There was a fullness in his loins. The full body of a mature woman. A commodity—a pleasure—all the more exciting for the transaction. Not of the real world somehow. Going to fuck. That was what they were there for. No pretense. A world in which a woman sold her cunt gave some ultimate human dimension to business. There was little question in *his* mind, if he had a cunt, he would sell it before he would do a lot of the stuff people did to make a living. Then even the commonest whore reacted to you personally. They asked you your name, what you did, how you got this or that scar or tattoo. Unless they were working some kind of smile-a-minute operation with a pimp waiting to rap on the door, there was no way they could lay back and open their legs without touching and being touched somehow. Guys who said whores felt nothing were wrong.

They cruised around for a while, drinking from the bottle and using the cans of beer for chasers. The new bright streetlights made the downtown seem shadowless. It was curiously more frightening than the old mellow lights with the alley and doorway shadows. Every discarded cigarette pack stood out like a boulder.

Moving along Broadway, slowly past the Airway Recreation and the Chinese restaurant where Jack's mother worked, he looked inside to see if he could see her. She was not there. Maybe she had gone on days. He hoped so. She did not like working nights. It was hard for her to sleep during the day.

"That her?" Glenn asked.

"Yeah. That's her," Bucky said.

Jack felt a quickening. Maybe they would pick her up again.

Ambling slowly along on slender, good legs was a high-hipped white woman still perched on summer high heels though the city had gone into fall fashions a few weeks past. An out-of-fashion short tight skirt twitched nicely beneath a short boxy jacket. She wore a head scarf and carried a summer sling bag on her left shoulder.

Glenn slowed down and pulled over near the no-parking zone along which the woman angled. He tooted the horn, and she slowed her steps, glancing over her shoulder. Jack could not see what she looked like from the back seat, but he thought she had smiled slightly. He tightened his ass and felt his balls come up nice and solid.

She continued very slowly, glancing again over her shoulder. Glenn made a motion for her to come to the car. She glanced up and down the street quickly and turned to come over.

Jack wanted to scream. He could not move or speak. Buck had turned to watch him. The bastard's expressionless face swam before him. His dark eyes seemed to open onto the night sky beyond the city's new bright lights. Jack felt as he had when he had gone under ether. He could barely hear.

"Yeow, it's his old lady," he seemed to hear one of

them say. He could no longer sort out the differences in their voices.

"He looks *sick,* man!"

"Hey, honey, we told our ole buddy how good you are, and he would like to boff you too."

She was still smiling slightly when she looked into the back seat.

Jack met her eyes. Her hand with the cheap wedding and engagement rings rested on the doorsill. He had to give her credit. She did not more than bat her eyes twice.

"Sorry, boys. I think you've made a mistake. You must be looking for someone else. I thought you were my ride. I just got off work."

"You big cunt, you got off work!" Glenn yelled. He jammed the car in gear and sped away.

Jack could not move. Their voices came to him as over water.

"She wouldn't even recognize him," Buck snarled.

"That's his goddamn mother, man! I know it! I seen her ass around before. Look at him. He's like he seen a ghost. That was *her,* man!"

Bucky leaned over and poked at Jack with a finger. Then slapped his face hard. "Wake up!"

"You miserable pieces of shit," Jack said sadly, the slap having unlocked his jaw. "You really don't give a damn about anything, do you?"

"Listen! We don't want no fuckin lectures from you, you *sonofabitch.* You been goin around puttin on airs around me ever since we were kids. Like you were better than me or somethin. Well, she-it, man, we plowed your old mother's ass—me and Buck—and she liked it too. I mean when we realized who she was, we *told* her we knew you. But that didn't stop her. So don't lecture us no more, you sonofabitch—*ever!* Readin books and them big words don't mean shit. You and your old lady are both cunts as far as we are concerned."

"You don't understand anything, and you don't know anything," Jack said flatly.

"Yeow? Well, we're goin now to see about that."

Jack did not care where they went. It didn't matter. He felt cold and very calm. He saw the familiar buildings and signs slide past. He did not want a cigarette. He did not want a thing.

Glenn spun the car in behind the civic fountain, which

581

was supposed to look like a waterfall along the river. He wheeled it as if he were on some great caper. It skidded to a halt. He was leaping out as soon as the engine was cut off.

"Get your ass out of there!" he demanded, his fists already clenched.

"Why do you want to whip my ass?" Jack wondered.

"Because, boy, I've wanted to bust your goddamned face ever since I could remember. I can't explain it, man. I *feel* it! Come on. Fight!" He busted Jack hard in the mouth. He didn't even raise his hands.

"You fuckin yellow bastard! *Fight* my ass!"

"I'm not going to, Glenn. I love you."

"You—" He hit him again, spinning him almost completely around.

"He *loves* you," Buck mocked.

"Love this!" He set himself and brought one up squarely on Jack's chin which made him see stars. His knees buckled, but he did not go down.

"Let me have some of his ass," Bucky begged. "Save some for me."

"This is *mine!*" Glenn hissed. "FIGHT, YOU YELLOW SONOFABITCH!"

Jack shook his head that he would not.

Glenn became a fury. He could not wait to set himself to throw punches. He looked as though he were frothing at the mouth. When they fell in close, Jack could feel the other's spittle spraying from his lips. Then he was pushed away and felt as if he were being hit from all sides. He was down on the ground and could taste the grass and earth. All sound was inside his own head. It felt secure and indestructible inside. He was yanked up by the hair and hit while he knelt on his knees.

Only when he washed in and out of unconsciousness, no longer able to really focus on the other boy, did the rage he felt earlier start to come back. What was he taking a beating from them for? he wondered. There was no sense in it. He did not love Glenn. That was bullshit. That was a coward's goddamn con. He hated the evil little bastard. Stupid! He tried to claw his way off the ground. His left eye was completely closed. He searched for him with his good eye. He began to growl like an animal. He could hear and feel the rumble inside himself. Nothing mattered, least of all himself.

He launched himself at the old-young face around which the elaborate arrangement of curls had fallen. He saw his left fist hit the large-toothed mouth and was amazed at the flash of joy that flared in the other's rage. There was a look of genuine pride in Glenn's yellow eyes. Was he smiling? Jack felt his own puffed and split lips stretch to smile. There was a trickle of blood from Glenn's lip. He wiped it on the back of his hand, looked at it.

"Yeow! Fight! *Fight me!*" Glenn yelled, hanging his hawky face out, a pleading look in his eyes. Jack stumbled toward him, taking the now sharply aimed jabs as the other boy moved neatly backward, on his toes, feinting to one side, then weaving back again. Jack followed him as if on a lead, taking the punches, not even blinking now, his right cocked for one delicious punch, seeing the punch land over and over again like a movie being replayed. He might have followed that way forever.

But he never got to throw the punch.

He sank down into a sweet, sweet night, embracing it as if he thought it was death and death was rest. Lonely, stupid, but if that was dying, it was OK.

He saw a star, high, alone.

"He don *look* dead," a frightened night voice said.

He ran his tongue over his lips. They felt dry and feverish. Beneath his head he could feel the earth, grasses, small stones.

"Look! He openin his eye!" another voice exclaimed.

"Les cut!" Someone kicked his head. Another kicked his side.

"Les *mo*-dock, mutha!"

They had turned his pockets out. His wallet was gone. He watched them scramble up the riverbank and race along the drive toward the bridge. There were three of them. Just little kids. On the bridge they slowed to a walk, huddling together, their young black faces eager in their search of his wallet. They took money from it and sailed the leather envelope off the bridge into the water. He did not care.

He sat up on the riverbank and thought it was lucky he hadn't rolled in and drowned. He wondered if Glenn and Bucky had rolled him down there or if the little boys had.

Curiously he did not blame Glenn and Buck. He felt a warm sympathetic glow toward the little kids who had rolled him. It was all over. Sharon, dreams, the illusion he was like everyone else—it was finished. Jack Andersen was no more. I'm dead, he thought. He did not feel any particular pain, merely an enclosing warmth.

The buttons had been ripped off his shirt. A long rent ran along the placket. His shoes felt full of dirt. From the ornamental strap over the arch of the loafers he dug out a dime. He got up, went to the bank laboriously, stopped in the street to tuck in his shirt as best he could and brushed his clothes a little with his hands. His hands were scraped and swollen. Going along the drive, he kept making himself aware of the dime in his right fist lest he lose it. He made it across the bridge and leaned against a building at the nearest bus stop.

The driver stared at him and looked as if he were about to refuse Jack passage as he climbed aboard and carefully tilted his good eye to make sure he got the dime in the hopper.

A couple holding hands on the seat behind the driver leaned together and whispered at the shocking state of Jack's face and clothes.

Others looked at him as he weaved down the aisle. He was sorry he offended them. There was just no other way he could get back across town.

A well-dressed black couple, middle-aged, primly ignored him, staring out the window; he was the passing of ugliness in an ugly world. They did not choose to see, but they were nevertheless aware.

"—All this fightin an all!" he heard a heavy white woman exclaim. "I just don't know what the world's comin to. Do you?" she asked a man holding his hat in his lap.

"Oh, it's the same, missus. Here, there, everywhere. It's the same."

He had to force himself to concentrate on every stop to be certain he recognized the one before his own so that he could ring the bell. He felt he had only enough energy to do what he must and could not afford to make a mistake. An illuminated clock in a shopwindow told him it was past 11 P.M.

It was four blocks to his apartment. He counted every step of it to a hundred, then counted again. The breeze that had come up in that part of town rustled the leaves

584

of the trees, made the shadows on the walk wavery, felt good on his face.

It hurt to raise his left arm so he tore off the rest of his shirt and batted pans and dishes away from the tap to sluice cool water over his face and torso. He looked at his reflection in the mirror above the sink. Glenn had done a good job on him. He had wanted to ever since they began to give up bikes and think about girls. Jack did not care why. He hoped Glenn got something out of it. He felt he had. It did not matter.

In the other room he opened the closet to look for a clean shirt. He scooped up Sharon's clothes in his right arm and plunged his battered face into the cool folds for a moment to breathe the perfume and the hint of her. The cloth felt cool against his lips. He wanted to cry but could not. It didn't matter.

"Pretty girl. Pretty dresses. I love you, pretty girl. I'm sorry."

He was able to get into a denim Navy jumper. Turning, he went to his desk, reached above it and lifted the souvenir samurai sword from the nails driven into the wall. He let the scabbard slide off the blade and clatter to the floor. The sword felt light, perfectly balanced.

"Think I'm going to commit suicide?" he turned and addressed an imaginary inquisitor sitting in the big chair with Raggedy Ann. "Don't be stupid," he said pityingly.

He saw three bodies stretched out on a mortician's slab.

No regret, no meaning.

Here, there, it happens everywhere.

"They will say I am crazy," he argued. "I'm not going to say a thing." He had a wonderful vision of remaining forever mute after what he was about to do. "I will from this night never speak a word again," he vowed.

"Now what you call yourself doin?" he mocked himself in high black falsetto. "Whatchou goin do wif that ole ssward? You lookin for to *kill* somebody, honey?"

"I reckon," he said in his own voice.

"You some kinda *fool,* lover. You ain't goin to kill *no*body!"

"We'll see."

He took his car keys and the sword and went out and got into the car.

He missed an overhead stoplight at an intersection and hit the brakes, swerving on his bald tires as another car slewed around him and got through. The other driver leaned out of his window and yelled, "Drunken sonofabitch!"

The side of the old frame house seemed as large as a ship. It had been the mansion of some long-gone magnate in its day, two stories high and long and wide as a steamboat, with full width, deep balconies across the front on each floor. Since it had been cut up into sleeping rooms and kitchenette apartments, the front door was never locked.

Smells of food filled the lower hall. Two rows of standard black mailboxes hung at the foot of the stairs. A Christian Science newspaper poked out of the top of one of the boxes. The large round knob of the balustrade felt familiar in his hand. He began climbing.

It was the first door to the right at the top of the stairs. Trying the knob, he found the door locked on the bolt. He rattled it. It was very still inside. He rattled it again.

"Yes?" his mother's voice asked, contriving to sound sleepy. He was both charmed and angered by her dramatics.

"Open up."

"Who is it?" The voice yawned. She knew who it was.

"Me. Jack."

It was quiet for a few seconds. He was certain he heard whispering. He grinned through his disgust.

"Jack! What do you want at *this* hour?"

"Open the door."

"It's late. . . ." She yawned again. "I'm tired, honey,"

"Open the door."

"I'm in bed. What's wrong? Can't it wait?"

"No."

"Listen. . . ." More whispering. Rustling sounds.

He rattled the door hard just to shake her up.

"*Shhh!*" she hissed. "Listen, baby. I don't see what's so important it can't wait." She sounded pissed off. "But OK. But give me a few minutes. Go have a cup of coffee or something and come back."

"Open the door."

After another whispered consultation, she said, "I *can't.* Go have a coffee and come back. Use your head."

"Just tell him to get his ass out of there. I'm coming in."

"Look. I don't want no trouble," he heard a man's voice say.

"Jack. Will you *please* go take a walk or something?"

He stepped back and raised the sword and brought it down on the upper right panel of door, splitting it. Four inches of blade went through the wood. He felt he could chop the house down with that sword.

"Jesus Christ!" the man inside exclaimed. "He's crazy or somethin."

Jack almost giggled. The guy was shitting his pants.

"Get-ass-out-of-there!" he ordered in a deep voice.

"Well, listen. I don't know who you are, but I'm not lookin for no trouble. Hear? I just come here at this lady's invitation. I don't know nothin about her or you. I never met her before tonight. Honest."

"Open the door."

"Jack. What is wrong with you? Are you *drunk?*" He heard her whisper to the man, "He's drunk."

"He's got an ax or somethin," the man said.

Jack raised the sword and put it through the other panel of the door.

"Goddamn!" the man exclaimed.

"Stop it, Jack!" his mother hissed. "I'll let you in. Just stop it."

"Open the door."

"I *will.* Just be a little patient."

"Maybe you ought to call the cops," the man suggested.

"The phone is in the hall." She offered him directions.

There was the creaking of the bed and sounds of them hurriedly dressing.

"I'm going to open the door, honey. Just a minute."

"Yeah. She's going to open it," the guy promised.

Then nearer to the door, but still safely back into the room, the guy said, "Now listen out there. I want to come out. I'm just an ordinary fella who met this lady in a joint and come up here cause she seemed lonely and I was lonely. I don't know her situation, and I sure ain't lookin for no trouble from you or nobody. See? I *want* to come out. And I'm goin to if you'll let me. But I don't want to get hit with no ax or nothin. I sure didn't intend to slight you no way. You let me come out safe and I'll just go my way. What do you say?"

"Come on."

"You won't hit me with that ax or whatever it is? I want to feel real secure about that."

"You come on out."

"Well ... all right. Here I come." The bolt was withdrawn. The door opened a crack. An eye appeared in it about even with Jack's head. He was not a short man. "Now, boy, if you're going to jump me, you'll be makin a big mistake. I don't mean you or this lady, whatever she is to you, no harm. I just want to come out and go my way."

"Come on, man."

"Well. . . . He's got some kind of sword," he whispered back to the woman. "Listen. Why don't you step back a-ways along there or somethin so I feel better about it, son?"

Jack moved far enough away to give the man confidence that he had a chance for the stairs.

He opened the door and slipped around the edge into the hall. At the top of stairs he ducked his head and split. A tall man in a two-toned Western cut jacket and low-heeled scuffed boots, he carried a cheap stockman's hat in his hand. A heap of a shambling man with a long, doleful face behind a drinker's bulbous horn. His dangling old earlobes flapped in his hurry to get on his way.

His mother was furious. She had wrapped herself tightly in a faded chenille robe as if it were armor. The bed was rumpled. Odor of cigarette smoke was thick in the room. Most of a fifth of Four Roses was on the nightstand with two glasses.

"What is the meaning— My *God!* What's happened to you? You been in a fight? Was it those stupid boys?" She had put on her glasses. Her eyes were dark and bright behind the thick lenses. "What are you doing with *that* thing?"

"I come to cut off your head."

"*What?*" Her fear was an electrical charge in the room. He felt as if he had touched a live wire. It almost sapped his strength. Suddenly they were total strangers. Her right hand strayed to her throat, pulling closer the top of her robe as if she felt a chill. She smiled tightly. Then forced herself to laugh. "Oh, Jack! Why do you want to scare me like that? You funny boy." She reached out to touch him. He slapped the back of her hand with the flat of the sword. "*Jack!*" She backed a step, rubbing her hand. "That *hurt*, damn it! If you want to tell me what's troubling you, I'll be glad to listen. But stop acting nuts."

He reached out with the tip of the sword and loosened

the tie of her robe. Then he prevented her from retying it by flicking at her hands with the blade when she made the effort.

"Stop it, Jack!" she protested angrily. "I *mean* it! If you are going to act like this, you can just leave."

He almost laughed. "What are you going to do, call the police?"

"If I have to."

"Shit." He flicked open one side of her robe with the sword tip, revealing her left breast. Below she snatched at the flies to keep herself from being further exposed. Fear and hatred and a search for some way to con him darted behind her lenses.

"Please, honey. Just tell me what's wrong. What happened to you. I'll help you. You know I will, if you'll only tell me."

Could she not know? He raised the sword up across his body and heard a kind of low cry come from himself. She screamed and tried to get around him to the door. He gave her a shove and sent her sprawling on the bed. Again he raised the sword to cut her in two. She screamed again, just like the first time and curled into a ball on her back, arms and knees raised to shield herself. Her bare buttocks were white and waxy-looking.

"You let Glenn and Buck fuck you," he said sadly, suddenly so full of tears he could not see clearly. "You fuckin no-good *whore!* You let them fuck you. Didn't you *know?* Didn't you care?"

"*What?* What are you talking about?"

"You know what I'm talking about, damn you!"

"I do not!" She had lowered her arms and legs when he lowered the blade and was scooting on her back across the bed toward the wall.

"The hell you don't, you fuckin cunt! They screwed you. My best buddy and Bucky. They plugged your ass, and you liked it!"

"Is that what they said? Well, it isn't *true!* It *isn't!* Honest, honey! Would I do something like that? They were just trying to get your goat. Baby baby. Come here. Come here." She put out her arms toward him, around one upraised bare knee.

He slapped them away with the sword.

"Stop that!" she cried. "It *hurts.*"

"I'm going to slit you open like a pig," he told her solemnly. He whistled the blade within an inch of her nose, and she flattened on the bed, her head canted up against the wall awkwardly.

"I *didn't*, Jack! I *didn't!*"

Slowly he lifted each side of her robe with the blade and laid them back. She held her breath, flattening herself even more into the bed. He lifted the nipple of one of her breasts with the tip of the sword and her scarred, soft stomach heaved. He traced a line between her breasts down over her belly, watching the soft flesh indented by the tip's passing, seeing the gooseflesh rise on her arms and legs.

"Oh, please, *don't*, Jack! Listen to me, honey. I *didn't!* I don't care what they say. They're lying to you. Kill me if you don't believe me. Just stop this. KILL ME!" she commanded.

He yanked up the sword high over his head with both hands. He could feel his battered face twitching uncontrollably. She was writhing around on the bed, her eyes about to pop out of her head.

"*DON'T!*" she screamed. "OH! Please . . . don't. . . ." She seemed to faint for a second. Her belly was racked with sobbing.

He couldn't do it. The pain in his left side was like a stab. He dropped the sword and grabbed his side and reeled where he stood. He could not see. His face became twisted into a big fist. He lurched first one way, then the other.

She came to the edge of the bed on her knees and clasped her arms around him. "There, there. It's all right. It's all *right!*" She pulled him down to sit on the edge of the bed as she knelt and wrapped her arms around him, pulling his head to her bare breast. "Just let me hold you. That's it. Poor, poor baby."

"I'm not a poor baby!" he protested through his tears. "You don't really care anything about me. You never have."

"I don't see how you can say that. I do. Don't you know how much I care?"

"No."

"Well, I *do!* I almost wish you had killed me," she said. "I don't blame you. I'm no good anymore. I wish you would. It doesn't matter. I'm dying anyway. Too sick to keep a job. You're all I have left in the world, and you

590

think such awful things about me. Just look what I've caused you. Your poor face." She kissed his bumps and cuts.

"It will heal," he said.

"I know it will, dear. I wish I would." She sighed.

"What's the matter?" he asked, sure he was being conned.

"Oh, they aren't sure. I have an enlarged spleen. And my blood's no good. I get so *weak*. They've been giving me a pint of blood, and that makes me feel better. But they say it could get worse. I can't afford the treatments. I don't know what I'm going to do. I can't live and take a treatment each week too on what I make at the Chink's."

That explained why she had been hooking on the street, he guessed. But he only half believed her about the treatments. She went to some damn chiropractor or what was it—an osteopath?

"They said they screwed you," he said.

"Well, they *didn't!*" She sounded definite.

It did not matter really. They knew she was a whore. It would be all over town. It would be common knowledge.

"I really wanted to kill you," he said, as much to examine his own amazement as to inform her of how serious his intention had been.

"I understand," she said, smoothing back his hair with her hand.

"It doesn't matter," he said. "I can't stay here any longer. Sharon's gone. Nothing matters. I had no business with a real girl like that."

"Oh! You did too! You're good enough for any girl!"

He looked at her dreamy woman's-magazine-reader of a face.

"Shut up. You don't know what the hell you're talking about." He did not blame her. He just didn't want her to open her mouth again. He reached for the bottle of whiskey, uncapped it and took a big drink.

"That's it. You just drink all you want. Then you lie down here and I'll get some ice water and put a cold washrag on your face."

He stood up. He hurt all over now.

"What do you want?" she asked.

"Going."

"Where?"

He did not answer.

"Don't go, honey. Please. You shouldn't be out. Stay here. I'll take care of you. I want to. I love you. I can't stand to see you go out alone like that."

"It's all over for me, Mom." He picked up the samurai sword. "I wanted to make a go of it with Sharon," he insisted. "I really did. I love her, really love her. But all I did was mess her up. That's what our love does—yours and mine—we mess the hell out of people. We aren't fit to live with regular people."

"Let me tell you about *regular* people sometime," she said.

But he was not listening.

"Stay with me. Let me take care of you. Let me make you well."

"You can't."

He lifted the sword at the balance and hurled it like a javelin through the back of her only overstuffed chair. He was finished with souvenirs ... snapshots ... dreams of all kinds.

He looked back. She was sitting on the side of the bed, her stomach puddled in her lap, staring at the sword stuck through her chair, worrying how she would pay for the damage.

"You can stay here," she said barely audibly. "You could stay."

"I hope you don't die," he told her. "I really do."

He took the whiskey with him. When he was partly down the stairs, he heard her bolt the door.

He drove by Sharon's house, turned and drove back past it. She was sleeping in there in a nice clean bed, her belly swollen with their child. Tears again filled his eyes. He cried aloud, racing through the streets, hitting potholes and bumps without a care for the car, being thrown about behind the wheel. He drank from the bottle.

"I DON'T WANT TO KILL ANYBODY!" he shouted up at the trees.

"Yea-uh, you some kinda sissy's ass," he mocked himself, in black dialect. "Maybe you some kinda faggot too."

"No, man. No. But all this killing, hurting. Man, I told you, I DON'T WANT TO KILL ANYBODY!"

"Bull! They's *lots*-o-people you *like* to kill. You jes don have that kinda craw."

"I don't know," he had to admit.

He was on the new road they were building west of

town. It was wide but not yet paved. He twisted the wheel back and forth, skidding the back end around on the loose gravel. Going to drive the car's guts out. He was doing over sixty. The engine was hammering away.

"Where you goin?" he asked himself aloud.

"Goin west, man. Goin to Californ-I-ay."

"You'll never see Sharon or your little baby."

He began to cry again. He floorboarded the car. And hit the bridge abutment head on. He never saw it. His mouth smacked the top of the windshield. He felt the steering wheel bend in his hands. The engine came through the fire wall and pinned his right leg against the brake. Hot oil and gasoline burned his foot and leg.

Four men running trout lines along the river after cat-fish heard the crash and saw the fire.

The fire was mostly in the floor of the front seat. The men wet empty cement bags in the river and got the boy out of the car. They tore off his trousers. His sock was still burning on his right foot. He came around while the men held him and saw the subcutaneous fat of his lower leg afire, the skin peeling back like cracklings. They wrapped the leg and foot in a wet cement bag and put him in the back of their pickup truck and drove to the county hospital.

Jack felt every lie and pretense had been forever canceled.

40

THERE was snuggling warmth in the aftermath of the chill of shock. Jack burrowed into the warmth, feeling clean, confident and wanting for nothing. The dressing on his foot and leg was tight and secure, containing the pain in a sterile wrap as delicious as love. The old county hospital bed was high, important, for the time his own. The sheets, smelling faintly scorched from the hospital laundry, had been pulled up and tucked beneath his chin. Toward dawn it rained, and he slept on his back with his head on two plump pillows, hearing the rain in the trees in the yard, smelling it through the open windows of the ward. The snores of the other men and the one who cried out cursing a woman did not bother him or cause him much to wonder. He slept well, smelling the rain.

He awoke when the large practical nurse came to wash his face for breakfast and give him another shot. In the next bed was a county prisoner called Taxi. He never explained why.

"They're just butchers in here," Taxi said out of the corner of his mouth as if planning to bust out. "An old man died the other night and nobody came until the shift changed. Get out of here as fast as you can."

"What are you here for?" Jack wondered.

"Mashed my hand in a manure spreader." He lifted his bandaged right paw.

A homeless man with an empty middle distance in his eyes, Taxi had gotten himself on the Pea Farm to lie out the winter. He took his family where he found it and offered Jack a small county orange from his breakfast tray.

Jack declined with thanks and offered the man in return a tailor-made cigarette. He accepted it gratefully, though he could roll his own with one hand, and lit it by striking the match with a flick of his thumbnail.

Taxi was Jack's stepfather and all the old petty cons Jack had always feared he would one day become. He saw his own future in the gray old bottle boy and turned away and slept again.

Awakening, he found his grandmother and Taxi chattering together. She sat patiently on the hard chair beside his bed. She handed him a small greasy paper sack.

"I didn't have time to do anything else so I brought you a big chocolate-covered doughnut. I know you always liked them."

He sat the bag on his chipped enamel taboret.

"Well, I just don't know how to tell you," the old woman fussed. "But Sharon had her baby this morning. About nine o'clock. A nice healthy boy, though it was a little early. Doctor misjudged a month, I guess. Anyway, congratulations. . . . I suppose that is in order. But you sure picked a fine time to get yourself banged up."

"Sharon had the baby?"

"Yes. That's what I just told you. She named him Mark."

He didn't want any son named Mark. They had talked about it. She had liked Mark and he hadn't and they had settled on Luke. Mark was an asshole name. He had never known a Mark he hadn't disliked. Mark Andersen. Luke Andersen. Luke was a *name*. Mark was just something everyone called their kids instead of calling them Kent. The world was going to be covered with Marks and Kents and Debbies and Sherrys. He wondered why she had done that. It frightened him.

"They tried to call you all evening. Said no one answered the phone. Soon as she went into labor. Guess you were already out hellin around." She shook her old head. Her hair, frizzed from years and years of cheap permanents, was all the shades of birdshit. As if sensing his thoughts, she reached up and idly gave it a poke. "Well, I stopped by before I came here. Had to change busses three times. She and the baby are fine. But it just makes me see red to see a new mother sittin up in bed smokin a cigarette."

The vision sent a warm flood of longing over him. The pain and bandage that had been so securely enfolding became a trap.

"I've got to get out of here," he said.

"Well, I don't reckon it will be today," the old woman said. "I talked to the doctor, and he said you'd have to be here at least two days, and rest for a couple of weeks anyway, and see how the hurt comes along."

"Will you go to her, Grandma, and tell her what happened and that I love her and I'm sorry? You've got to make her understand."

"I don't know what to say, son. I don't understand all this. Looks to me like if you loved her or whatever you call it, you'd of both been home where you belonged. I just don't understand it. She knows you got drunk and wrecked your car. It was in the papers. I don't know what else there is to tell."

What else, indeed, could he offer in explanation? He was driven into a corner where he had to suffer the superficial facts as a lesser evil than the truth.

"I guess you'll just have to tell her what you want to yourself." The old woman sighed. "When you can. It seems like there's no way for any of our offspring to grow up and live right. If it isn't one of you, then it's the other." Though she had no tangible evidence, she somehow seemed to blame her husband. "It's like a curse been put on us by God," she said. "Maybe if Daddy had believed in the church instead of spending all his time railin about politics, things would have been different. After Roosevelt, he just didn't care no more," was how she saw it.

"Will you call in work for me?" he asked.

"Well, all right. But I don't like to do it. I don't know them people, and they don't know me. I don't know what to say."

"Just tell them I'll be out in a couple of days, and it isn't so bad."

"But how are you goin to work if you have to lie around for a couple of weeks? How you goin to work anyway without the car?"

"I've got a little money saved up. I can get another car. Just call them, will you?"

"All right. I only wished you had someone else to do these things for you. And who's goin to look after you when you get out? You can bet Sharon's folks aren't goin to want you lyin around the house." She was almost ready to weep desperate tears. She wiped the corners of her eyes with her finger. "I thought and hoped when you and Sharon got married that you were goin to make a go of it. You had a good job and everything seemed all right. Then this. . . . I just don't know what's goin to happen. I can't never count on a thing."

When she had gone, waddling out in shoes that had been someone else's, her swollen ankles inflamed with eczema seeping through the mismatched hose, Taxi said, "It's hell if you do and hell if you don't, ain't it, kid?"

"Yeow. That's about it."

"I know. Well, I been there and back. Just tough it out, kid. Tough it out."

He couldn't eat the doughnut. The mere thought of it closed his throat. He offered it to Taxi.

"Naw. Thanks, kid. I gave up sweets a long time ago. They weaken you. Make you want things you ain't got. Worse thing for you there is. I'd go hungry first. Sweets can kill you in this hard old life. I learned that a long time ago. I learned that the hard way."

He went up the wide hospital steps on his crutches, a cellophane of roses in his left hand. He felt thin and weak. His eye hurt for some reason. He stopped at the visitors' desk and got a card for the maternity ward.

Sharon was sitting up in bed near the window with a yellow bedjacket over her gown and her dark chestnut hair tied back prettily with a yellow ribbon. She was reading a novel. Behind the screen another woman was just coming out of ether. There was one empty bed, then a chubby brunette of about thirty-five with big milk breasts peeping through her blue nightie was doing her nails in the bed next to Sharon's. Both looked up when he hobbled in the door. Only the other woman smiled.

He extended the flowers to Sharon, who took them and laid them on her table amid the clutter of cards and bottles and other things. There were more flowers along the windowsill. A truly lush bunch of long-stem roses from her parents made Jack's bouquet look secondhand.

She turned her head when he tried to kiss her. The dark-haired woman got out of bed, slipped into a robe and left the room.

"Want a Coke, honey?" she asked Sharon from the door.

"No, thanks. Not now."

"Right-o."

"You look beautiful," he told her.

She would not look at him, studying her hands on her book, having marked her place with a card.

"I'm sorry, Sharon. I just couldn't stay in that place any longer without you. I got drunk and. . . ." He shrugged down at his bandaged foot. "I love you."

She was shaking her head no. "It's no use!" She turned her eyes on him furiously. "I don't care! Jack . . . I mean it. I really don't care. I didn't cry for you. I cried for myself and for my baby. And now I'm not going to cry anymore. When I think of the time I lived with you, it seems like a nightmare. It seemed like I must have been nuts. Now I feel like me. And you aren't going to worm your way into me again."

"I didn't worm my way. Did I?" he truly wondered.

"There's just no use to talk about it. Like I said, I don't care." She shook herself out a cigarette and did not offer him one. She lit it before he could fumble around his crutches for his Zippo.

"I was wrong, Sharon, about a lot of things. But I loved you. I love you. I want us to make a go of it. I know we can."

"Mother said you lost your job."

"Yeow. But I want us to leave here." He became excited with the plans he had made in desperation in the last couple of days. "This place is no good for us. We can go away and make a new start. Leave all the heartaches behind. California. There are good jobs out there. Sunshine and the ocean. You'll love it. Just the place to raise kids. I've thought it all out. I'll go on ahead and get a job and a good place for us to live, have it all ready, and in a few weeks you and the little fellow can come along."

"I'm going to get a divorce, Jack."

He sat in the chair and heard the birds outside the window, the hospital's soft call bells, people in the corridor shuffling by on rubber soles and slippers and the woman behind the screen muttering and calling a name dreamily. He had expected nothing more. He had known his hope was desperate fantasy all along. Then the reality that he would never again touch her, know her, gutted him. At the same time he was enraged with jealousy at all those who might. He felt emasculated, turned into a hopeless little boy. She was woman among women and he was a—what?—a goddamn thing on sticks.

"Don't say you're sorry again," she warned, hard as hell but hanging on tight to keep from ever being soft again. "I don't care, and there is nothing to talk about. I don't love you, Jack."

He sat for a long time without speaking. Then he said, "I guess I better go."

She looked at her watch. "They will be showing the babies in five minutes if you want to see him."

"Oh. Sure. I do." He thought of something else to say. She had opened her book again, though he did not think she was reading. "Grandma said you had a pretty hard time of it."

"Yes. I did."

"I wish I could have been with you."

"I don't."

When the five minutes had passed, he hauled himself up on the crutches and looked down at her. She had never seemed more beautiful. Her breasts were full and heavy.

"You going to nurse him?" he said.

"Yes." It was a challenge.

"I just wondered."

"The nursery window is open now," she said, and turned to her book.

At the door he looked back and said, "You're very beautiful, Sharon. Very beautiful."

"His name is Mark," she said.

"Yeah. I know."

The woman from the bed next to Sharon's was in the hall in her robe and fuzzy slippers. She had a body like Anna Magnani. Four other children between the ages of fourteen and three waved at her from a glassed-in lounge where kids who were not permitted on the floor could wait. A tall man with a horselike face that made Jack feel better just for looking at it stood with his arm around the small, voluptuous, slatternly woman. From his clothes, Jack knew they didn't have much, but goddamn, they looked happy. They stood at the viewing window of the nursery with their arms around each other, she sipping a Coke through a straw from the bottle and laughing at the ugly little fish of a fellow the happy nurse held up to the window. Two inches of soft black hair grew every damned way on the baby's head. The father smiled and drew his wife near, and she reached up quickly and kissed his long jaw.

He put his card in the window and waited while another nurse went to wheel the basket over. She glanced at Jack without much pleasure and went away.

Well, it did look a lot like him. Same frown and widow's peak in the front. Hardly as much light hair as a honeydew. He opened his eyes, and Jack wondered if he could see him. "Hello, baby," he muttered to himself and smiled at the little fellow. He looked like a good one. A little thin, but the same deep chest as his old man. The fact they would never know each other made him feel like crying. He left the card in the window and turned away before the nurse came back.

By dark that night he was standing down in Oklahoma along the edge of Route 66 with his Navy handbag at the foot of his crutches and his thumb hopefully in the air.

41

"IF you're from out of state, you're out of luck," the young black man ahead of Jack offered. "I been here every day for two weeks, and if you ain't from California, they won't even let you sweep the street."

The pale man behind the counter reluctantly accepted Jack's card of application for employment. His manner corroborated the black's prediction. He acted as though the lack of work were the direct result of Jack's having been born.

"Why did you come out here without a job?" the man demanded angrily, as if no one had the right to enter California without being sent for.

It's a free country, isn't it? Jack thought, but he said nothing.

"Well, my advice to you is go back where you came from. I don't have anything for you. If you were a tool and die maker or had some skilled trade. . . . Sorry." He filed Jack's card as if aware of the waste of the paper it represented.

Yet Jack was not angry at the man. There he was, as pale as the belly of a fish in Los Angeles, in a crummy office, in a cheap Penny's shirt and tie.

Many men, white and black and Mexican, sized up the defeating scene and left without filling out a card. The lines of men at the stand-up tables waiting for a shot at the chained ball-point pens slumped hopelessly.

"Fuck it!" a black man about forty said to no one in particular, dropped his newspaper with only two men between him and making an application, and went off with his hands in his pockets, head high, eyes angry as hell.

In the neighborhood men slept in the doorways with flies blowing empty wine bottles, and the dead Sterno cans would not have made even a Christian fool wonder where the picnic had been.

Out of state, out of shoe, out of pants, out of luck.
Thank God it was not cold. It was June in January.

California was a freak show. Ordinary, prosperous citizens wore clothes that would have got them stopped on suspicion in Wichita. Grown men walked down the street eating ice-cream cones. Whole families went along licking Fudgicles.

Where mid-America had moved and never grown up, Jack thought in charmed amazement, strolling along Hollywood Boulevard, eyes agog, a cynical smile flirting at the corners of his mouth. Did someone have in mind a perpetual carnival? Yet no one looked as though he was having all that much fun. Jack began to wonder what his chances were of being discovered—seriously! Crossing Vine, he looked at others, boys like himself dressed as cowboys, girls with more tit and ass than he had seen outside a *Sad Sack* cartoon strip, parading endlessly, going where? ... pausing expectantly on the corners whenever a Jaguar or other ritzy open car was caught at the lights. Well, why not? It happened every day. Hadn't someone told him he looked a little like Guy Madison? He stopped in front of Schwab's, hauled out a piece of comb and touched up his pompadour in the glass.

By Pershing Square he followed the most fantastic whore he had ever seen. Or maybe she worked in a burlesque house and had stepped out in her costume for a malt. In her yellow and green high heels she was as tall as he. She wore a yellow, short, tight jacket just bursting with boobs and a tight fuchsia skirt of satin that was costume, not clothes. On her head was a matching little satin hat. And my-great-God-almighty-didn't-her-big-ass-roll? It made him feel seasick. Tits larger than Kathryn Grayson's! He had followed her less than ten yards before he had a hard-on he had to mask by jamming one hand in his pocket. Oh, he would have followed her anywhere. He could hardly breathe. The sexual rush obliterated and tilted all purpose toward an insane and hopeless desire as he hustled along behind her, one hand in his pocket, staring passersby a blur, gray as the buildings—everything he owned, his life, for one time with something like that.

At a stoplight, he cruised alongside and shakingly made his move. "Excuse me, miss—"

"Get lost, crumb!" she snapped with barely a sidelong glance.

The light changed, and he stood like a fool, feeling ugly and shrimpy on the curb.

From the opposite corner an old spook in sneakers and pants rolled to the knees, sporting a sailor's cap, popped out and dogged her across the intersection with a query, in an impeccable British accent, "Can you direct me to the Venutian consulate?"

Jack shook his head to see if it would rattle. Then he went in a drugstore, bought an ice-cream cone and walked down the street eating it. Drugstore Cowboy. He passed a tall dude in a rodeo rider's elaborate outfit coming in the opposite direction. The guy was perched on a pair of Monkey Ward's three-toned boots, opening his gap to lick drippings from a double dip pistachio and chocolate cone. Jack, unable to resist the impulse, lifted his hat and said, "Howdy, pardner!"

You'd have to be nuts to take California seriously, he concluded. Where Painless Parker and Madman Muntz could make fortunes and grown men walked Irish wolfhounds down for a chocolate soda, it was more than a lot of people running around with a screw loose—the whole machine was tilt.

On the street one hot rodder eyed another's machine like the improbable act of passing strangers measuring dicks. One twist gripper sniffed at another's bike with superiority or hoped to sneak by without too much loss of pride, depending on how he was mounted. What had started as an avocation of displaced wheat shockers and corn huskers had become an entire generation's reason to be. And a lot of them were not kids any longer either. The taffy-toned rods with naked chromed heads and pipes and Iskenderian cams prowled the streets like so many show dogs, the single greatest investment in their owners' lives. Going nowhere in particular.

It made Jack feel old.

Pasadena was easier to take. It seemed a more understandable place, even though the things in the stores and the middle-aged men in white shoes and crested blazers who strolled dogs on leashes continued to challenge his sense of time and effort. The junior college looked so much like East High in Wichita he thought of enrolling if he could find a job and room nearby. In Pasadena he thought California might be solved.

He found the address of a former shipmate he had hoarded in a small address book. He hardly knew the fellow, but in the shape he was in he saw him as a great buddy.

Pausing in front of a small red brick cottage, so solid after all the stucco all around Hollywood, he took a deep breath and felt hopeful as he went up the walk. A neat but not gaudy hot rod—a '32 chopped and channeled Ford coupe, metallic blue with moon caps, and tucked and rolled white naugahyde upholstery—sat in the driveway with a FOR SALE sign in the rear window.

The woman, about fifty, who answered the bell wore an apron over her lemon slacks. A sleeveless sweater revealed the tanned, clabbered flesh of her upper arms. She thought he was there about the car, and it took him awhile to get through to her he was an old Navy buddy of her son's.

"Oh! . . . Well, Bud isn't here. He reenlisted over a month ago."

"Reenlisted?"

"Yeah. Lots of fellas are. There ain't any good jobs, you know."

"Yes, ma'am." He loitered there, hoping she might invite him in for lunch. He suddenly had the wild notion of fucking her old Pasadena ass. Seeming to sense the danger, she put one hand firmly across the door as if to bar it.

He said, "Well, thanks. Tell Bud I stopped when you write him," and turned and went down the walk.

He wondered why he had suddenly wanted to bust in and rape that old cunt. Tear off those lemon slacks, mess up that dyed hair and put it to her. It was a frightening puzzle. He would have to watch it. *You could really go nuts in a place like this,* he warned himself.

He sat down at a bus stop to watch kids coming out of the junior college. They were beautiful, healthy-looking, like kids in Wichita, only more so. Surely there had never been a healthier, happier, prettier race on the face of the earth. He wanted to be one of them. He hoped to be mistaken for one of them. Then he remembered how he was dressed, and that he couldn't afford to take one of those girls out even if she came up and swore he looked just like Guy Madison.

He watched misfit men come into the YMCA with pinup magazines folded and stuck in their hip pockets, was aware of the pinup magazine in his own little cell and felt misfit himself. Everyone sneaked sandwiches and drinks past the disapproving glance of the old gym fag behind the registration desk.

He turned to the want ads in the YMCA edition of the L.A. *Times* on the desk in the reading room.

The ad read:

> Presentable yng man free to travl wanted by exec to dr new Cad cross-cntry. $60 week + expns.

There was the number of a hotel to call before 5 P.M.

Jack dialed the number from the hall pay phone. The man who answered had a pleasant, carefully neutral voice. Jack told him the essential facts about himself. The man suggested he come up that afternoon for an interview and after seeming to check appointments, suggested a time.

Jack took his blue suit out to have it pressed and got his boots shined. From a drugstore he bought a ten-cent bottle of white shoe polish. Back in his room he painted the collar and cuffs of his only white shirt. He hacked at his long hair with a razor blade and shaved his neck. He wet and combed his hair carefully, then studied the effect to see if he could pass for a salesman or clerk or chauffeur. He did not dress until just before time to leave for the appointment. His socks had big holes in them, but in his boots they would not show. The white polish on his collar left marks on his neck which he erased with a wetted fingertip. He tried to walk without moving his head.

It was a good hotel but not one of the best. He went up in the elevator feeling everyone on the staff was looking at him suspiciously.

A well-dressed man in his thirties opened the door, glanced at Jack quickly but carefully, and waved him inside in a businesslike way. He indicated Jack could sit on the couch and seated himself in a facing comfortable chair. He wore a conservative business suit with a vest, horn-rimmed glasses, neat socks and glistening shoes. Jack tried to hide his worn boots beneath the couch, but the guy wasn't missing a thing. Jack was glad he'd had them shined, though he had resented dropping the dime at the time.

The man did not offer his name so Jack just called him Sir. With neatly barbered, curly dark hair and trimmed mustache, he looked as if he meant business.

"What did you do in the Navy?" he asked.

When Jack told him, he seemed disappointed. "Not a clerk or medic?"

"No, sir."

"Do you type?"

"Only hunt and peck, sir."

He seemed even more impatient. But he hadn't asked any of that on the phone. "You do have a valid driver's license?"

"Yes, sir!"

"Any accidents?" The man's eyes narrowed.

"Uh, no, sir," he lied and felt certain the man knew he had.

"You said on the phone you were free to travel. What about your family?"

"I really don't have any. Just a grandmother and grandfather. They are very old."

"Where did you telephone me from?"

"Uh, the Y."

"You staying at the Y?" The man smiled for the first time.

"Yes, sir."

The man relaxed back and made a steeple of his fingers just before his lips over which he peered steadily at Jack's eyes. "What about girlfriends and things like that?"

"Not right now." Jack grinned, flashing that the guy probably had a raft of real slick stuff and that he might somehow get in on it if the man took him on.

The man thought for a moment, his eyes never leaving Jack's face. "I see," he said finally. "Well, you might just do."

Jack's heart leaped. Suddenly he looked forward to blowing his last bit of money on a feast of hamburgers and chili and a double-thick shake and maybe top it off with a banana split and coffee.

"The young man I am looking for must be able to drive for me. I have a new air-conditioned Cadillac. I travel more or less constantly. Coast to coast and my business may soon expand to take me overseas as well. The person I am looking for must be a kind of personal secretary and companion with a desire to make himself useful to me. It

605

is a position with genuinely educational possibilities for the right young man. You would be meeting all kinds of very successful and *very* clever people."

Jack was ready. His tongue was all but hanging out. That was how he wanted to go—with those clever and successful types. Maybe *this* was his big break.

"You are quite rough around the edges. You will need clothes ... *and* manners ... but I might be willing to give you a trial. ..." He studied the boy thoughtfully. "You aren't lying about your family. I mean, you *actually* have no ties?"

"No, sir. No ties?"

"Very well. ... Oh. I'm a homosexual, of course. You understand that?" He hadn't moved a muscle. His eyes were as bland and blue as the sky outside the window.

"Well, that's your business," Jack said as neutrally as *he* could. But all those visions of pretty girls began slipping away.

The man smiled, lizardlike, wryly. "Well, not exactly. But I'm afraid, my dear, you would have to make it *yours.*"

Jack sat there a moment, staring at the top of the coffee table, the man's glistening black shoes, weighing the implied opportunities, that chance for foreign travel, against the vision of having to do something about that guy's cock.

"I'm afraid I can't take the job then," he said. "I mean all the rest. ..." He looked up pleadingly.

The man waved away the apologetic note in the boy's voice. "Pity. Well, there's no use in discussing it further." He uncrossed his legs and stood up. He did not offer his hand or walk the boy to the door. Jack had the feeling the man was making a disgusted, amused face behind his back. He hesitated a moment at the door, almost turned, but went out and was in the hall, feeling empty, gliding past the numbered, impartial doors on the silent carpet.

At the corner of Hollywood and Vine the old weird-o in high top sneakers with his pants rolled to his knees and the dippy sailor's cap on his head popped out and inquired of Jack in his perfect British accent, "I say! Can you direct me to the Venutian consulate?"

"Get-away-you-crazy-sonofabitch!" Jack snapped at the harmless nut.

"Don't hit! Don't hit me!" the man screamed pleadingly, covering his face with his arms. Other people on the street looked to see what was happening but did not stop. As Jack hurried on, he heard the man moan to disinterested passersby, "This is such a *violent* planet!"

He crawled out from beneath the boardwalk at Long Beach where he had slept for three nights with his bag for a pillow and his suit jacket for a coverlet. He had long since sold the winter stuff he had brought with him to provide him with a couple of days more at the Y while he had looked in vain for something to do. He had become so scruffy-looking that going for a soda jerk's job or one in a parking lot or car wash had become as hopeless as any grander ambition. He had lasted one hour in a hamburger joint washing dishes and been told, "Kid, you can't do the work." He was amazed at how many men there were who *had* good experience washing dishes. Nor did he think he could steal as he had as a boy. Oh, he could hook a piece of fruit, and he had lifted a camera from a tourist's car seat which had been left unlocked. He had got two dollars at a hock shop—it wasn't much of a camera—but he no longer had the sense of invisibility and daring that would permit him to enter a store and walk out with a power tool or something that would go for real money. Besides, the stores had become much more careful since he was a kid. They *chained* their display stuff down! And hardly anyone was leaving his car unlocked anymore.

Each morning he awoke beneath the boardwalk with a terrified start, no longer knowing what day it was. The night before a boy and girl had crawled under the boards and started to make out. Noticing him curled in the sand, they had crept farther along so they could have some privacy. Even so, in the moonlight filtering through the boards, he could see the girl's bare white legs on either side of the boy on top of her and he had felt very lonely.

He dreamed terrible, frustrating dreams beneath the boardwalk and awoke once crying in his sleep.

In the early-morning beach smell, he was aware of how crummy he had become.

The muscle boys were already working out. Half a dozen incredibly developed men who seemed to have no other interest or need of employment—or maybe they were all night clerks—were using the bars and rings, lifting weights, striking poses of Dynamic Tension, hoisting each other around gymnastically. They were there every day. *What the hell are they going to do with all those muscles?*

If I was a cannibal, I could live off the carcass of one of those bastards for a month, he considered. But how would he keep him without refrigeration? Every possibility had a catch in California.

He washed up in a public toilet, combed his hair and turned a cold eye on an aged man who looked as if he wanted to ask him something.

Breakfasting on a hot dog and a paper cup of water on the boardwalk, he watched old-age pensioners arrive and stake out their places on benches, hiking up their trouser legs and hems to sun their eczema.

He had tried to get a job at every concession and ride along the boardwalk.

After sizing up a fat woman reading a racing paper on a bench to which was tied an equally fat white mongrel bitch, he went over and patted the overfed beast.

"Nice doggy," he told the woman. "I had a dog like that when I was a little boy. In fact, you look so like my mother I just had to stop." He placed his hand respectfully over his heart.

The woman had about two dozen plastic hair rollers in her blue-dyed hair and looked so little like his mother he felt a rare sense of sin in his lie. The woman had peeled a banana she had taken from a closely guarded sack and bit into it, glancing warily from her paper.

"I wonder, ma'am, if you could spare me a quarter. I've been promised a job, but I haven't got bus fare to get there."

Chewing the banana so he could barely understand her words, she said, "Go fuck yourself."

He laughed. He threw back his head and laughed. He turned and walked away, laughing until his eyes filled with tears.

Off the boardwalk he wandered up the street past an abandoned tattoo parlor. How did anyone manage to live? He wasn't going to get any job in California. His lethargy had become so great he wasn't sure he would be able to take the simplest job unless someone led him to it by the hand.

Passing a store front Navy recruiting office, he started

to turn in before he realized it had been deactivated. Peering through the glass he saw the abandoned space, an eye chart and poster still on the walls.

In the center of the wide street a portable Army recruiting office had been set up. It was simply a small hut that could be carried about on the back of a truck.

He had his Navy discharge in his handbag. Empty with the fear of ultimate rejection, he crossed the street and went inside.

Any port in a storm, he told himself to buck himself up.

Not only would the sergeant take him, but he could enlist as a private first class and not have to take basic training as result of his having had previous military service. But it was a regular three-year enlistment.

Three years, Jack thought, filling out the necessary forms, his belly growling around the hot dog. He gave his last address in Kansas.

"Where are you staying out here?" the sergeant asked, eyeing Jack's handbag.

"At the Y in L.A. . . . But I had to give up my room. I'm flat broke, Sergeant."

That did not bother the recruiter.

"You had breakfast?"

"Uh, not exactly." Jack grinned.

"Here, take this. There's a restaurant up the street that will honor it. It ain't bad." He issued Jack a meal ticket. "You go chow down and come back, and I'll have your papers all set. Guess you want to get in as soon as possible."

"Yeow."

"Well, go chow down. I'll get you a ride out to the fort, where you can be processed."

The sergeant told him to leave his bag there. Only on his way to the restaurant did he realize the sergeant was holding his bag ransom for his return. It made him feel cheap.

The surly waitress with a broken front tooth gave him watery scrambled eggs with a single strip of barely cooked bacon, toast and coffee, which was only one of two choices they honored for the meal ticket. When he bummed a cigarette off her to enjoy with his coffee, she let him have it but exclaimed loudly, "Jesus Christ! *Some* people!"

He had an impulse to get up and just walk out and

leave his stuff at the recruiting office. But then thought probably he could get in trouble. They had his name and his copy of his discharge. Yet he wasn't sworn in or anything. . . .

"Aw, what the hell. . . ."

The sergeant looked up and smiled when Jack came in. "All set." He pushed the papers across the desk and held out a pen. "Sign all copies."

Jack signed. Before signing the last copy, he looked up at the sergeant and sighed. Three years seemed like a hell of a long time.

PART FOUR

42

HE left his duffel bag in the flight operations office at the air base in Wichita and took a taxi directly to the hospital. The woman he had spoken to on the phone said he had better hurry.

The Red Cross had got in touch with him at his battalion headquarters in Mannheim the day before, and by that evening he was on a MATS flight out of Frankfurt to Boston, then on to Wichita. He felt as if he had been awake for a week. It had been strange to get out of the plane in Wichita and be hit by the prairie smell of Kansas as familiar as his mother's favorite perfume. Boston hadn't smelled all that different from Frankfurt.

Dropping his handbag in the hospital corridor outside the room, he went in while an old nursing sister searched his mother's wrist for a pulse. She then bent over and reached under the covers with a stethoscope to listen for a heartbeat. It was strange to see a nun using a stethoscope. It was strange to see his mother in a Catholic hospital. His mother looked very flat in the tight little hospital bed. The nun closed the woman's eyes.

"You can stay just a few minutes alone," she told the soldier. "I'm sorry." She rustled out of the room.

He stood beside the bed, looking at the waxy dead face of his mother. In a way he was relieved there had been no time for last words. What would they have said? He wondered what had been her last thought. There seemed no regret in the small, still, soft-looking face. Her short, dark red hair was lifeless, stringy and damp, as if she'd had to work a bit to die. But there was yet a girlish softness to her cheeks and chin, that incredible innocence—or guiltlessness of one who never had time for rooted commitments, unqualified pledges. If her soul still lived, it was back out on the street somewhere—hustling.

The nun returned and drew the covers over his mother's face. There was a certain impatience in the old woman with the corpse. Jack wondered if they had tried to wring a confession from his mother before she died and convert her to Catholicism. He wondered if they *had*.

He had telephoned his grandmother from the air base as soon as he had spoken to the hospital. She had said she and his uncle and aunt would come as soon as his uncle got home from work. She had said she would call his mother's boyfriend, Blackie, and let him know.

Jack was puzzled why none of them had been alerted to be with her in her last moments.

He sat on the foot of the bed with his arms around the little tent of his mother's feet beneath the covers. The old nun had gone out again. He pressed his forehead against her toes, but no tears came.

Shortly, another, younger nun came in, a tall, sturdy girl, with a pretty, sympathetic face.

He looked up. She smiled gently, though her eyes were all pity. She crossed and laid her hand on his head. Then he cried. She held his head against her belly for a moment, until he became aware of her body beneath the many-layered habit, and she seemed to become aware that he was not a child and stepped back with a final pat on his shoulder to give him heart. He was through crying. It had been like one of those little Kansas rainstorms that seem to come out of a single small dark cloud in an otherwise clear sky and be over in a couple of minutes.

The nun asked him if he would please step into the corridor for a few minutes. He got up, patted his mother's knees where they were small bumps beneath the taut covers. The nun closed the door behind him.

Blackie was outside the door, crying helplessly. Jack's lips tightened at the sight of the stocky, graying, simple worker with his Cessna night shift badge on his belt, crying behind his hands as shamelessly as a child. Perhaps he was envious of the man's ability to show more emotion at his mother's death than he had. Yet he did not trust it, was suspicious of its depth, felt the guy had really known very little of her.

"Why didn't you come in?" he asked.

"I didn't know if it would be right," the man managed. "I was afraid to look. To see her dead." He erupted again into uncontrolled sobbing.

Jesus Christ, man! Dummy up! Jack wanted to tell him. _She was tougher than anyone. You poor clod, it's too late for that. She's gone. Alone. With strangers to hold her hand. Why hadn't some of you been here?_

A young woman in a blue pleated skirt with a white hospital jacket over it hovered nearby. When Jack turned toward her, she said, "When you can, they would like to speak to you at the desk."

He glanced at the closed door. "I can go now."

"There's no rush. Just before you leave, OK."

"I can now."

The middle-aged woman at the desk explained wearily, as if his mother had been a terrible problem for her, "She refused to give her correct name or the names of her next of kin when she came in or we would have been able to locate you and them sooner. It was only after we discovered Mr. Poole we were able to begin to straighten things out." She looked up with a downturned mouth. Blackie had gone along to the desk with Jack rather than remain alone outside the dead woman's room. Jack realized whatever decisions had to be made, he was going to have to make them.

"We find now she has a husband . . . a Mr. . . . Wild?" She peered up over glasses at Jack.

"He's in the can," he said. Then explained. "The penitentiary."

"Oh . . . I see. . . ."

She didn't really see shit, but it didn't matter.

"She made me promise not to tell anyone anything when she came into the hospital," Blackie explained to Jack. "I didn't have no idea she was so sick. I don't think she wanted anyone to know. I don't think she knew she was going to die . . . do you?" he begged.

"Yeah. I think she knew."

"Then why didn't she? It was only when they caught me here and told me she was dying did I break my promise to her. I had a hell of a time getting ahold of your grandmother. She's washin dishes somewhere during the day and the old man must of been out. No one answered the phone. I told them you was in the Army in Germany somewhere and they said they would get the Red Cross to find you. Why do you think she didn't want nobody to know?"

"She didn't want anyone to get stuck with the bill," Jack

615

said. It was obvious. Then he had a doubt. Maybe she simply wanted nothing to do with any of them. . . . No, he decided. She just didn't want anyone to be stuck with the bill. Then he was very proud of her. She had been herself right to the end. He was sure there had been no deathbed confession or conversion to a thing.

"Well, listen, I ain't got no money now. You know she hadn't been working for a while and I sorta supported her, you know. But I'll be glad to pay my share of this," Blackie offered.

"It's OK. You've done enough," Jack told the sad, older man, who he sensed wanted nothing more than to get the hell out of there.

"Well. Listen. I gotta go on shift pretty soon. But you let me know if there's anything I can do."

"Sure. I will, Blackie. Thanks." He put out his hand and they shook hands.

"Well, OK. I just don't know how to say what I feel. But I want you to know, I loved her too."

"Yeah. It's OK."

They shook hands again, and the not very bright last lover of his mother scurried away down the corridor to the night shift at Cessna.

He was smoking in the corridor when his grandmother, aunt and uncle and two cousins came in a small pack, the old woman in the front, no one holding her arm, coming in her kind of Groucho Marx crouch with which she could really cover ground, even at her age.

"Is she gone?" she asked.

"Yeow."

His cousins and aunt burst into tears.

"When?" the old woman asked, not crying herself. Only her mouth drew a bit thinner. Her son put his arm around her shoulders.

"Mom?"

"I'm all right," she insisted.

"Just now," Jack said. "A little ago."

"Well, I guess MacGown's will handle the funeral," she said, staring past Jack down the corridor. "Daddy wouldn't come," she explained. "He said he didn't see no sense in seein her die. But I think he was pretty hurt. I think he wanted to be alone. He hasn't been feelin well either. It's his stomach, but he won't go to the doctor. Now this. I just don't see why she didn't want to let any of us know she was here," she said rather angrily.

"I think she didn't want us to be stuck with the hospital bill," Jack offered his theory.

"Well, we are stuck with it anyway, ain't we? It just looks like she would have wanted her mother or someone with her at the end." The old woman sniffed, and for the first time her eyes filled with tears. She reached a little wadded handkerchief up beneath her spectacles and wiped them and blew her nose. "Well, I guess we're too late to see her at all."

"I don't know. They chased me out, and a nun has been in there. They have to do a lot of stuff right after someone dies."

"I'd just like to see her face," the old woman mused. "But then I guess it's just as well to wait for the funeral."

"Was she . . . peaceful?" his Aunt Elfie asked hesitantly. She was still a cute little black-haired woman with a fabulous butt. But he noticed she was going gray.

"Yeow, I think so," he reported.

"Was she able to recognize you. Say anything?"

"No. They closed her eyes just as I got in the room."

His aunt and the cousins began weeping again.

The girl from the desk returned, looking apologetic. She spoke to Jack. "I'm sorry to bother you, but if you could spare another minute, the doctor would like to speak to you."

The doctor was a very beautiful woman about thirty who looked Spanish. She asked him several questions about the incidence of cancer or leukemia in his family, making notations on a form on a clip board.

"Are you South American?" Jack asked.

"What?" She frowned. "Oh. Yes, I am Argentinian."

"Can't imagine you being a doctor," he said, looking at her tiny well-manicured hands.

She was reluctant to let the conversation become at all personal. "Your mother died of leukemia. We don't know much about this disease," she said earnestly as if speaking to a child or stupid-o. "Medicine needs to do much more research into it. What I want to ask you is a very hard thing. . . ." Her accent was charming. "We would like to do a complete autopsy. If we can do that and make some tests, we might discover a clue to what causes this disease and perhaps do something about helping to stop it in others."

"Sure. Go ahead," he said.

She seemed rather surprised at the quickness of his response.

"If you want to think it over or talk it over with the others," she suggested, rather shocked. "But for it to be effective, it *should* be done as soon after death as possible."

"It's OK," he assured her.

"Then, if you will just read and sign this release." She showed him another form and put it on the high ward desk for him to study and sign. "An autopsy isn't as bad as people say," she said, leaning close to see that he filled the form out correctly. Her perfume was good. "There is nothing visible or any reason to, uh, make any change in plans for a funeral or anything."

She was a very beautiful woman in her white medical jacket, tight green skirt, high heels and sheer stockings. He was very aware of her nearness. He thought, they could have sent a male doctor. It was a gentle con, too. It did not matter. His mother would have appreciated the ploy. *We're all whores of some kind, aren't we, doctor-baby?* he thought, looking up and finding the woman's dark eyes so close. She had to turn away. There had been a moment of understanding, almost electric, from which they had both retreated.

"Uh, your mother was entered as a charity patient," the doctor said, tucking the release form away on her board. "I think I can arrange for it to just remain like that, if you like. There need be no charges."

"Thanks," Jack said genuinely. He didn't think the hospital could make him pay anyway, his being in service. But he was afraid they might try to get something from his grandparents or his uncle.

The doctor offered him her hand. It was very small, warm and moist. He thought of it groping around in his mother's insides and held it a bit too long, until a questioning look grew on the pretty woman's face. He let go quickly.

She turned and went away purposefully, high heels tapping on the hospital corridor, small shoulders, South American hips so womanly. He saw her naked for an instant. She must have thought he was nuts.

He felt rather nuts. He wasn't sad about his mother's death. There was even a kind of juicy intimacy in it that made him aware of his sexuality. Nor did he feel guilt about not feeling, as thought, "normal," about it. He was sorry her life had been so hopeless. But he was not sad she was dead beyond the personal regret he would never see her alive again.

Yet he chided himself, looking after the little Argentinian doctor, *Cunt-crazy bastard.*

Doctors and nurses, nuns, kith and kin, they were all gathered for the moment at the death of a pretty good woman who, by circumstances and ignorance and superficial vulnerability, had to trade on her sex. She had given him all she had to give. And in giving that which she held to be of so little value herself, maybe she saved something intrinsically her own. She had to know something to die so calculatedly alone.

He loved her very much. He admired her, too.

43

THE taxi drew up at a tidy, stone-faced ranch home in one of the new housing developments. It was about seven o'clock. He had telephoned and was expected. He had to sit the large gift-wrapped carton he was carrying on the curb to pay the driver.

When the cab went away, he realized the development was on land that had once been farmed by his grandfather. The people inside the house did not know that, and he knew it would mean nothing to them if he told them.

The entire city, though it had grown enormously since the time he had played in fields where the neat little house now sat, his head no taller than the stalks of grain that were the color of his hair, seemed smaller than he remembered—just another place now. He felt very old, of his grandfather's generation, but he did not feel tired.

His heart was beating fast when he rang the bell.

The man who owned the house was in accounting at Boeing and had been one of the fortunate ones to hang onto his job when they had made their cutbacks.

Sharon came to the door. She was taller, more full-bodied, prettier than he remembered. He wanted to kiss her. All the intimacy and words they had said only to each other came back like a packet of stuff that had been put away while he was gone, a bit out of date but very real. She wore a soft gray dress with tight three-quarter sleeves. He remembered how he used to brush his lips softly along the light hair of her arms for insane lengths of time as she had sat up in their bed reading. A wide leather belt with a large, ornate buckle of double eagles girdled her waist tightly and emphasized her hips. Her hair was shorter, stiff with lacquer as if she had been to the hairdresser that afternoon. She had on stockings and brown pumps that matched her belt. She extended her hand, which was very cool.

"Hi, Jack. Come in."

He towed the large package into the house.

"My goodness! What is that?" she exclaimed.

"Just something for the boy."

"You shouldn't have!" she insisted, frowning slightly in a way that made him feel the present was an intrusion upon some system of values she strictly followed regarding the boy. He stood uneasily in the small living room and looked for his son.

The boy was standing beyond the living room in the part that formed a dining area. Sharon's parents also stood there side by side, smiling nervously, clearly apprehensive. The very blond child was dressed in short, bibbed suspender trousers, a short-sleeved shirt with yellow ducks on it and little blue and white sneakers. He was entwined shyly around his grandmother's knees as she gently urged him forward. All his fingers except his thumb were stuffed into his mouth. Large brown eyes studied the tall soldier warily, unblinkingly.

Jack acknowledged the others, but he could not take his eyes off the boy. He smiled and set the package out as an offering.

"I brought you something," he smiled.

"Come here, Mark," his mother encouraged. "See what. . . . Here's a surprise for you, honey!" She kneeled down on the carpet beside the gift and held out her arms, wiggling her lovely fingers invitingly. The curve of her body in the soft dress, the way the cloth grew taut over her beautiful buttocks sent a rush through Jack that made his ears seem to fill.

Sharon's mother gave the lad a little push, casting him loose from the security of skirt and knees, and he dashed across the space into his mother's arms as if it were a shaky bridge over a crevasse of terror. He clung to Sharon's neck and peered at the soldier like a little monkey.

"Hi, little fellow," he smiled and reached out to touch the boy's arm. It tightened more strongly around his mother's neck.

"Now, Mark," she chided gently. "He's just a little shy. He's never seen a soldier before, I don't think. He's really a friendly, open child," she explained. The words went deep into Jack. He was a stranger there. He had to be told about his own son. They were all uncomfortable, making the best of a difficult situation to get it over with.

"Of course, when he is older, we will explain everything," she said sincerely to Jack. "Now I think it is best to—you know—say nothing. He wouldn't understand."

"Sure."

"Look! Look at the nice *big* present he has brought you!" She squatted again and sat the clinging lad on the floor facing the brightly wrapped gift to which his eyes had strayed repeatedly even as he clung to his mother's neck. "Shall we open it and see what it is?" she enthused. The blond head nodded affirmatively.

Jack thought, *Christ, he looks a lot like me!* As they tore at the gay wrapping, he happily reached out and tousled the boy's shaggy straw-colored locks which curled around over his ears and onto the back of his neck. Sharon looked up and smiled.

"My hair was like that," Jack said.

"Everyone wants me to cut it, get him a 'boy's' haircut, but I just can't. It's so lovely. When he runs, it bounces and it sort of tickles me inside, you know?"

Jack was nodding eagerly. "Yes." He saw it. He knew. God, he loved her. And that little boy. He should be *with* them. They should be with him. He knew things about her and their son no one else could ever know. "Yes-yes-yes" things. For a moment he felt Sharon and he would leap into each other's arms. He felt tears welling up in him. Tears of great joy and relief.

"But I guess we will have to cut it soon. People think he is a little girl. Peter—" She cut herself off and covered by exclaiming at the big red fire engine she and the little boy spied in the box. "OH! My goodness, Mark! What *is* it."

"Fire engine!" The little boy was all eyes and wonder, as Jack bent to help haul it from the box and set it on its genuine rubber tires on the carpet, shiny with bits of packing dust clinging to its bright paint.

Sharon's reference to her husband had made him sick, wrenched him from the moment when he had felt so tied again to her and the boy. He watched his hands doing the things with the truck that were necessary. Hanging the two little ladders on the back and arranging the plastic firemen's hats. There was a real little hose on a reel on the back that pumped water from a tank that could be filled. It was a great fire engine.

On the low, modern, upright piano were wedding pictures of Sharon and her new husband. *Peter*, for Christsake! He was tall, taller than Jack, angular, a dark-haired fellow who in the photos looked like an accountant who had just been promoted. No, in all honesty, he and Sharon looked very happy, clean, remote from all the shit he carried around with him. On the church steps ... all those clean, smiling, got-all-the-answers faces. A vision of Sharon and that guy fucking swarmed before Jack's eyes. *How could they? How could she fuck a guy like that?* It was unfathomable to him. What the hell did they say? Did she ever think of him then?

He helped lift the now-eager little boy into the seat of the fire engine. His feet did not reach the pedals necessary to make it go. He looked up frustratingly at his mother.

"I'm afraid it's too big for him," she said. "He's just a baby."

Jack felt stupid. It was much too big for such a small boy. The little boy sat in the thing and could not use it. Jack gripped both his little shoulders reassuringly.

"You'll grow!" he promised. "Hang on."

The little boy grasped the steering wheel even tighter in his chubby fists.

Love, longing, something more powerful than anything those words had ever meant to him before, went deep inside him where he knew they would remain as long as he lived, to haunt him in the lonely times, to make even the best of occasions touched with loneliness.

"Rrrrrrrrrrrooooowwwwwwwww!" Jack imitated a siren and pushed the little fellow in the engine around the living room. The boy's expression flitted between terror and delight, the pedals he could not reach whirring inside the machine.

"Rrrrrrrrrooooooooooowww! Out of the way, lady!" He careened the lad and engine around the room. "You wanta get run over?" Then hauled it to a stop before Sharon.

"Like it?" Jack asked, kneeling to speak to the boy.

He looked up at his mother and nodded his head solemnly, in cautious affirmation.

"We can put it up for when he is older," Sharon said. "It's really great!"

"I always wanted one of those when I was little," Jack explained. "Never did get one. Guess I figured he was bigger."

"It's fine. We'll put it up until he's big enough. Thanks, Jack." For a moment she touched his sleeve tenderly, then turned quickly. "Say, 'Thank you,' darling," she instructed the boy.

He ignored the suggestion, turning the steering wheel vigorously back and forth, off on a big alarm of his own imagination.

"That's all right," Jack said as she was about to insist, and touched the kid's head again in a friendly way. In his mind, when he had bought the toy, he had envisioned a scene in which the boy would wrap his arms happily around his neck the way he had around Sharon's.

"We want him to get the habit of saying, 'please' and 'thank you,' " she insisted.

Aw, fuck it! he suddenly wanted to exclaim and sweep her in his arms and kiss the slight hardness away from the corners of her mouth.

"It's OK. He's tired."

Still she insisted, "Say, 'Thank you,' dear." It was a command.

"Fank you," the boy muttered almost inaudibly, glancing up quickly at the strange man in a uniform and shiny boots with the badges on his jacket.

Sharon scooped the boy out of the fire engine and hugged and kissed him. "*That's* a dear boy," she crooned.

"That's Mama's *big* man!" She looked at Jack as the boy snuggled his head on her shoulder and put his thumb in his mouth, staring at Jack in a blissful, satisfied way that said, "I got mine."

Jack smiled at the little devil.

"We've stayed up to see you. Now we must get our jammies on and say night-night." She kissed the boy again as her mother came from the other room to take him. Impulsively Jack bent and lightly kissed the boy's cheek, brushing Sharon's hair, smelling both her lightly perfumed scent and the good sunshine smell of the boy. The boy accepted it as his due. She handed him over to her mother, who called him a "little scamp" and clearly loved him a lot. Sharon touched up her hair tenderly.

"Mom and Dad are baby-sitting for us tonight," Sharon explained. "We have to go to some people's house for dinner." She looked at her watch. "Pete will be here any minute. . . . Well! . . ." She turned and smiled fully at Jack, seeming to size him up for the first time. "The Army seems to be doing all right by you. You seem *enormous* in this room. You look fine."

"You too! You're more beautiful than ever."

She looked away and made a nervous movement. "I'm getting fat." She patted a hip. "Have to watch it." She sort of giggled but did not look at him.

"You look good," he told her sincerely.

"Well! It's really been nice seeing you, Jack." She turned again and shifted her weight a bit toward the door.

"Yeow. I guess I better be running along."

Then the boy burst out of the kitchen bareass, astride a small trike, wearing a fireman's hat at a crazy angle, shooting glances at Jack as to show him how damn well he *could* wheel. He looped the dining-room table, his sturdy legs going like pistons on the pedals of the tiny, battered trike, with his grandmother hustling after him, brandishing a pair of sleepers, laughing, "Come back here, you little rascal!"

Jack laughed. It was the first time he had been happy since entering that house.

"See you, pardner!" he called as the naked rider was towed back into the kitchen.

At the door Sharon said, "You haven't said what you think of your—of Mark."

"He's great. Maybe he'll survive." He grinned.

"What do you mean?" she asked suspiciously.

"What? . . . Oh, nothing. He's fine, Sharon."

"Pete is very good to him. They love each other very much," she added defensively. Then in a rush: "I wanted to talk to you about our adopting him. Then, when your mother died, we decided this might not be the time. But it would complete our happiness. Your grandmother told me you are thinking of staying in the Army and making it a career, that you have put in for officers' school or something. I know if we had a chance to talk about it, I think I could make you see how good it would be for Mark. We would tell him the truth, of course, when he is older. It would mean so much to *us!*" Her eyes were pleading.

He didn't give a damn what it meant to *them.* "What does it mean to *you?*" he asked, feeling sick, yet some strength growing out of the hurt.

"Oh, Jack, it would mean *everything* to me!" She almost reached out her hands and put them on his chest or might have hugged him.

"OK," he said.

"*Yes?*" Her face became again the face of the girl he had loved more than anyone, more than life, more than himself. "Oh, God! Thank you! Thank you!" Then she did throw her arms around him and squeeze him tight and kissed his cheek. He held her lightly, his hands trembling on the small of her back, so aware of her body. He just grazed the corner of her mouth with his lips. His face felt on fire. Her color was high too, beneath her going-out-for-dinner makeup. She pushed herself away, made a sound like *ahh*, clasped a hand over her mouth tremblingly, then dabbed at the corners of her eyes with a fingertip. "We've prayed that you might let us. . . ." She sniffed.

"You're happy then?" He grinned, though his eyes were narrowed.

"Oh, yes." She sighed and clasped her bosom.

"He better in bed than me?"

She recoiled a moment, then crumpled and looked away. "Don't, please, Jack."

"You're right. I'll see you, Sharon." He turned to go out. He started to tell her he loved her but did not.

"Thank you *so* much, Jack. We will remember you in our prayers."

She closed the door before he was off the low porch. To

go tell her parents the good news, he supposed. He would guess she would send him the necessary papers through the Red Cross as she had done for the divorce. Well, that would end the deductions from his pay for the kid's allotment, he thought bitterly.

Leaning at the bus stop at the corner, he saw a new small Oldsmobile sedan stop in front of the house—the least expensive model—and a tall man in a suit unfold from it and go up the walk carrying a briefcase. Light glinted off a pair of glasses. In the wedding pictures he hadn't been wearing glasses. Vain accountant. *Asshole!* He spat unfairly. *Fuck it,* he told himself. What the hell did love mean when it had to be bungalowed so damned defensively, so wrapped up and snug? Got it all balanced. Big accountant's ass! Sharon was gone. The boy he would have called Luke was gone. But his blood was in that boy, the blood of *his* people, and he did not think the future would be as simple as they all supposed in that snug house. In fact, he felt their constant awareness that boy was also of his blood. That could have been one of the reasons they were so defensive, so in need of making it all legal and formal and wrapped up. They would have to watch the little fellow forever. He smiled wryly to himself.

44

THE girl behind the post librarian's desk had the most beautiful hands Jack had ever seen. It seemed a long time since he had noticed a *real* girl. Unlike most of the other men, he did not keep a German shack-baby. Instead, he went down on "Goodmanstrasse" and got a whore when he needed sex. Humping shit from the PX every weekend off to some dreary Kraut *Shatzi* in a nearby room seemed somehow less appealing to him than the straight deal with the girls of "Goodmanstrasse." And the guys took damned snapshots of their *Shatzis* and hung them in their lockers, though they had no more respect for the conniving cunts than the girls had for them. Both sides were dealing from a disadvantage and both felt superior to the other. To hell with that!

The girl behind the desk clicked through the narrow drawers of library cards with rapid efficiency. He had always been attracted to girls with lovely hands. She wore a class ring from a university. A heavier man's military ring nestled in the open throat of her white blouse against soft tan skin that seemed lotioned. She had a nice face with a kind of funny little potato nose and a wide, full-lipped mouth. Her hair was almost black. She was very meticulous about her makeup, which she used rather heavily. Long, sooty lashes rimmed large brown, luminous eyes behind black-rimmed glasses which were pushed down on her nose. In her man-tailored blue uniform of the Special Services Organization, she had shoulders like Esther Williams.

So Jack laid the stack of books before her and asked, "You swim?"

"I'm sorry?" She looked up and smiled cautiously, marking her place in the tray of cards with a finger.

"You swim?"

"Why . . . yes." Cautious, curious.

"Can I buy you a cup of coffee or Coke or something?"

She stiffened a bit, blinked, squinted, unable to see what *that* had to do with his opening. Service club girls were uniformed civilian employees of the Army under civil service and were for all social purposes equivalent to commissioned officers. Yet, in running the clubs, acting as hostesses, they would occasionally have a soft drink or snack with a lonely soldier. But the librarian was not working in a hostess capacity. And there was an intensity in the young corporal's way of looking at her and his strange come-on that made her wary. She looked at her wristwatch.

"Well, I'm not due for a break for twenty minutes, Corporal. One of the hostesses downstairs is probably free." She smiled and turned back to her filing.

"Good. I'll wait," he said cheerfully. He sat down at the first reading table facing her desk. He opened an English translation of Clausewitz's *Vom Kriege*, on top of a copy of Waugh's *Men at Arms*. When he looked up and saw she was glancing at him, he smiled broadly. She sort of rolled her eyes to heaven and went back to her filing, but she too was smiling slightly.

The other men in the club were in Class-A uniforms, their leather billed garrison caps at casual angles on the tables. Jack wore his tanker's jacket and bloused trousers over his boots, and his overseas cap lay on the table like a limp envelope. He was no service club commando. He rarely went there except to visit the library or have a snack. In the snack bar and library Class-A uniforms were not required. After five, in the lounge when it was officially open, soldiers had to wear dress uniforms. He did not like YM-YWCA atmosphere and the like attitudes of the hostesses. Though obviously endowed with tits and cunts, and quite aware of the fact, they might as well have been behind plate glass as far as an enlisted man was concerned. He had never had a sister and was not looking for a casual, surrogate one. He would pass the anxious, animated puppies in uniform who yipped around the hostesses, wagging their goddamned tails for a smile they could call their own, with a narrow-eyed scorn that made his face almost a sneer. He was a field soldier. *Fuck such shit*. The former librarian, a Miss Sanders, had been a small, older red-haired woman with a withered right leg on which she wore a brace.

Presently the new one stood up, tugged down her jacket and looked toward Jack, who closed his book and rose. She was taller than he supposed. In her shiny black "Red Cross" pumps she was only a couple of inches shorter than he. Long of leg and comfortable of hip, her bare calves slender and glistening, feet mature and sexy, he wasn't sure what the hell he was going to do, but it was going to be *something*.

"Still want that coffee?" She smiled.

"Yes, ma'am."

On the stairs he firmly gripped her arm just above the elbow. She looked at him out of the corners of her eyes and lifted the near brow quizzically at the gesture of possession.

Jack straightened to his full height and saw her across the floor of the main club room as if he had been absolutely charged with her safety and every other GI in the place were fanged monster and convicted rapist.

"Hey! Miss Wisdom! Judy!" An almost albino young corporal with the face of a skinny Van Johnson and an evident IQ of 2 jived up, snapping his fingers, to beg promise of a dance some two hours later. He looked and acted as if a 45-rpm record spun continuously in his dome and Miss Wisdom's promise was the thing he had lived for all week. Jack scowled at him.

The geek was all whirly blue eyes and yammering wet red lips. Jack was sure he was a good dancer. What else could he have been? Miss Wisdom called him Roy and promised to save a dance for him.

"I thought you were the librarian," he said when the jerk jived away.

"I'm just filling in until they get a regular one," she explained, rather as if it was none of his business, glancing around professionally to see who was in the club. Jack was just another soldier to her. But he only released her arm when she was safely deposited in a booth in the snack bar.

"Cream, sugar?" he asked.

"Black, please. Always!" she emphasized, rolling her eyes as if she really *needed* black coffee.

He went directly to the coffee end of the line. A clerical sergeant complained, "Hey! No bucking the line!"

Jack did not even look at him. Clerks of any rank were not to be taken seriously.

Without a tray he carried the two cups of coffee back to the booth. He sloshed a bit in his saucer. When he sat down, he poured the coffee from his saucer back into his cup. He felt she disapproved of that move and raised the cup to her in a silent toast. "I come from pretty far back." He grinned in explanation. She shrugged.

"That guy called you Judy." He tried to get a word from her.

"That's right." She smiled professionally again. She had large white teeth. The eyetooth on the left side was, touchingly, a bit crooked.

"Well, I think I'm going to marry you one day soon, if I can," he said levelly.

She choked on her coffee and sat back in the booth fast. She coughed and had to clear her throat.

"*Corporal!*" she squeaked hoarsely. "Don't *ever* use that line again on a girl when she's drinking GI coffee. . . ." She smiled, though. "I don't know what success you have had with it before, but I must say it *is* a stopper." She looked at him sideways, clearly wondering how she attracted all the nuts.

Suddenly he was very sincere. "I don't think it is a *line* . . . ma'am."

629

His face was so serious she could not help laughing. It was lovely, absurd laughter. She cocked her head toward her shoulder a bit to see what he would say next, her lips pursing and playing with one another.

"I don't mean *tomorrow*," he assured her, smiling now himself and blushing a bit. "Though I think I would if I could. I've taken the ten- and twenty-series extension courses for rank up through captain from the Army General School. I've passed the OCT and I'm in for OCS—on the waiting list—I want to be an officer. I don't waste my time. I've taken a Usafi test that gives me the equivalent of two years' college, and I took a course at night in Heidelberg run by the University of Maryland in political science and got a B plus in it. . . ."

She was smiling at his earnestness and had widened her eyes to indicate she was impressed.

"Yeow. I want to make it. It may take another year. If OCS doesn't open up, I can put in for a direct commission. But the Army is up to its a—loaded with brass, and it might take a year. You in love with the guy who gave you that ring you have around your neck?"

"Now just a minute. . . . Really! I think it is great you are so ambitious. Really. But I don't even know your *name*."

"Oh. Andersen. John, but everyone has always called me Jack."

"Happy to meet you . . . John." She stressed the name as if making certain to set herself apart from whomever he considered "everyone." She extended her hand. It was cold and trembled slightly. His own felt warm, dry, strong.

He turned her hand over and studied the back of it. The skin was fine over the bones, but not drawn. The ring was from the University of Wisconsin. He smiled when she gave a little tug to take her hand back.

"How old are you?" he asked.

"Are you *always* so direct?" she asked, becoming a bit annoyed.

"I guess. But I hardly have any choice in this case, do I? If things were equal, if I *were* an officer, I would ask you to go to Heidelberg with me and have dinner in a great old place across from the university where Sigmund Romberg is supposed to have gotten the idea for *The Student Prince*. I would take you for a boat ride on the river up to where the Lorelei used to sing from a dangerous rock. And though I'm *not* a good dancer—I've just never had much time to learn—I'd take you dancing, because I think I could dance very well with you. . . ." He took a deep breath for all the words had just tumbled out. "But I can't do any of those things." Then he waved that away. "It doesn't matter," he assured her. "It will come to the same thing . . . as far as I am concerned anyway."

"But you can't just see someone and be sure about such a thing. You don't know me at *all!* And *I've* surely never come across anything quite like you." But she was not angry. Instead, she seemed amused and flattered. He did not appear truly dangerous.

"Well, I just know," he insisted. Then grinned widely. "We would be just fine . . . I think."

"Oh, you *do*?" She had her doubts, clearly. "How old are you?"

"I'll be nineteen in May."

She smiled tenderly, her eyes became soft and she said gently, "I'm twenty-three."

"Oh, that's OK," he assured her. "I've lived enough to be thirty anyway. No. It's true," he insisted. "I was a sailor in China when I was fourteen. I've hustled and worked and—yeah—stole since I can remember. I come from poor people, you would say 'bad' people. I've been pretty badass myself. Really. Now that will be a problem. You'll have to try and understand that. There's stuff I wouldn't even tell you . . . but I don't think I'm such a bad guy. I'm trying to be something. Oh, yeow. I've been married. I've got a little son, but his mother remarried and they wanted to adopt him and I let them."

She winced at that.

He had to try to make her understand. "I loved his mother very much. Always will love her. I mean she thinks love starts and stops, that people 'fall in and out of love.' I don't believe that. I mean there may be a lot of reasons people can't go on together, but you don't stop *loving* them, do you?"

She shook her head that she did not know, blinked, now truly amazed by the earnest corporal.

"Well, she made me know what it is to love, I guess. And the little boy will be all right. He's a great kid. . . . Or he won't," he added thoughtfully. "Anyway. It doesn't matter what his last name is. From the little I know of him, he gave me something else, like a different love that will never go away. I don't know how to explain. But I'll try my best not to lie to you."

"Are you always so *serious?*" It was almost a plea.

"No, ma'am. I laugh a lot. I also use very bad language. Like I said, I come from a long way back. . . . In a very profane line."

She batted her eyes and cleared her throat. "Well . . . I just don't know what to say. You *are* something, Corporal." She pressed her hands together in a prayerful attitude and sighed. "Now, can we *please* talk about something else?"

"Sure." He smiled. "What did you study at Wisconsin?"

"English lit," she barely managed and repeated it more firmly. "Oh, and I *was* on the swimming team."

"Thought you could swim. What about the guy who gave you the ring on the chain?"

She ignored his question, looked at her watch. "I must get back. I'm *late!*" She stood up, facing him.

He popped up. "I'll see you," he promised, looking into her eyes.

"Are you attending the dance tonight?" she asked.

"No. I don't hang around the club much."

"Oh, you don't approve of us?" she teased, and squinted one eye menacingly.

"It's not that. I don't like standing around to say hi or dance with a girl who sees me as just another GI. It's OK for some guys, though."

"You don't believe in platonic relationships, I take it."

"Uh . . . no, ma'am."

"Maybe you don't know what you are missing," she continued to tease.

"That's just it. I *do.*"

"Touché," she conceded.

"I'll walk you back. I left my books and cap upstairs."

This time he took her arm more gently, and this time she did not seem to mind.

Later she confided in the club director, a rather dykey-looking older woman with short graying hair and a compact athletic body, "I've met the darnedest young man. I don't know if he's crazy or what. He proposed to me! My knees have been shaking ever since."

"Well, if he becomes a bother, let me know."

"I will."

She went into the staff rest room and took a small pill

box from her shoulder bag. She popped a pale-pink Dexedrine between her lips, cupped her hand beneath the tap, took a sip of water and swallowed. It was hard for her to swallow pills. She smoothed each eyelid with her fingertip, leaning close to the mirror to see without her glasses, touched up her makeup, put on a smile and went out, cheering herself silently: *Full-of-pep! Full-of-pep!*

Most of the men not on pass were still in their sacks when Jack returned from an early-morning foray into Mannheim. The guard on the main gate had eyed the musette bag he had carried with some curiosity. Andersen wasn't known to have a steady shack-baby, and nine o'clock of a Sunday morning was a weird hour to be going to town. But Andersen was a weird cat. Maybe like some of the guys said, he was CID. Half the guys in the Army thought the other half were CID or CIC or some such shit. Everyone was spying on everyone else, it seemed. No one was certain for what. There was an ex-first lieutenant in Jack's room, a personnel clerk, who said he had been cashiered as an officer for misappropriating French francs while a liaison officer with the French during the war, but everyone knew he was a CID man. The asshole even dreamed in French, walked around on the balls of his feet like a tennis nut and had a most annoying habit of bounding out of bed at reveille and vigorously fluffing up his goddamn pillow until Jack and his other roommate, Bruffey, wanted to kill the bastard. Bruff's own brother was a code expert with an Army Security Agency unit listening to Russian radio transmissions in Berlin. The Army was full of spooks. But Andersen was always studying, wanting to be an officer, and that made him under suspicion. And he was the colonel's "golden boy" of the moment. The guard guessed Andersen was straight enough. He had dropped forty bucks to Andersen in a crap game last payday. Bastard got hot as a spade when he shot craps. Believed in his fuckin self. "Sonofabitch *ought* to be a goddamned officer," was the guard's opinion.

When Jack was back within the hour, the empty bag rolled in one hand, the guard had observed leeringly, "That was a quick trip, ace."

"I was in a hurry!"

"Yeah, that's what everybody says about you."

"Maneuver, shoot, communicate. Maneuver, shoot, communicate."

"When I get ass-off this fuckin post, I'm goin to maneuver me into town and communicate this to my ole pig-ass *Shatzi*." He had grabbed his cock with his free hand, the other holding onto the sling of the carbine hanging on his shoulder.

"How's she receive you?" Jack ran out the chatter.

"She gets me five-by-five, man! *Five*-by-five."

The guard's *Shatzi* was a dumpy *Kartoffel* ball with lank blond hair of whom "pig-ass" was an honest description.

There were only a couple of guys in the main room of the service club, playing ping-pong. A Special Services PFC was pushing a long custodian's broom around the dance floor. A young Italian-looking private was answering a letter at one of the writing desks. A picture of a cute dark-haired girl was propped before him. Only one hostess was on duty downstairs. She sat in the small office applying polish to her nails. There were a few men in the snack bar having breakfast after sleeping in and missing it in the mess. There was the stale smell of cigarette smoke from the dance. In the corner of one of the couches was a balled Kleenex smeared with lipstick.

He went up to the library. She was bent over her desk, checking in a stack of books, stamping the cards and card pockets with a librarian's date stamp on the eraser end of a yellow lead pencil. The sweet, solid curve to her back and the dip of her short, curly dark hair gave him a rush of desire, made him short of breath as if the climb had been difficult, and caused him to tighten his ass. *Beautiful! But substantial*, he thought. She was not a small woman.

There was no one else in the library. That was the best of luck. Her pencil stamp went from inked pad to book fly to pad with delicate efficiency. He resented her pretty hands touching books that had been held by others. He worried about her catching some disease.

She looked up when his steel-rimmed heels hit the linoleum tile floor that was waxed to a high shine, the sunlight refracting off it as off water. The sunlight put deep auburn lights in the corona of her hair. Her expression was completely neutral, perhaps a trifle wary. So was his own as he crossed to her desk, his right hand in his pocket. She peered up through her glasses, which were always halfway down her funny little nose. A chain from the bows went around her neck. She looked a little tired, her makeup extra thick. The dance must have been exhausting. Or maybe she'd been out on a date with an officer afterward. She did not look as if she had got a lot of sleep.

He reached across her desk with his left hand and picked up her own left, took his right from his pocket and, before she knew what was happening, slipped an emerald-cut diamond in a platinum setting on her finger.

"What?" She stared at the ring. "You're *crazy!*" she exclaimed, scooting back on the little wheels of her chair. "What-do-you-think-you-are-doing?'" she demanded angrily, tugging at the ring.

He had tried it on his little finger and knew she would not get it off without soap.

"I can't take *this!* It's just—" Her face was twisted in a deep frown of consternation. Her eyes blazed.

"It doesn't have to mean anything to you," he explained. "I don't have one of those class rings. Just wear it. Maybe you will get used to it." He grinned.

Not even in dreams had she leaped into his arms.

"It's just crazy! I can't. It's an *engagement* ring! I won't!" She tugged futilely on the ring. When she could not get it over her knuckle, she looked a little helpless. Then she sort of relaxed and looked at the ring. "It's beautiful." She looked up helplessly, a slight desperate madness flickering in her large dark eyes before she shook her head vigorously. "No!" And tried again to get the ring off her finger. Finally she gave up and held out her hand to him. "Please, take it off. You can't give someone you don't even know something like this."

"It cost me nothing much. I won most of the money shooting craps. Tossed in a few cartons of cigarettes. Call it a friendship ring."

She extended her fingers and turned it to try the lights. "It's really lovely. It must have cost a fortune." Then she became serious. "But I am *not* accepting this from you. I'll get it off.... I am flattered ... I guess.... But it is quite insane. Things don't happen this way. You've seen too many movies," she lectured him sincerely. "We don't know one another. And I'm too old for you in any case. Oh. . . ." She sighed and shook her head, then put the hand with ring on it on her brow as if feeling for fever. "I

635

don't know how I get into things like this. . . ." she thought aloud. He thought there was the start of tears in her eyes.

"Rough night?" he said sympathetically.

"Very."

"Sorry. . . . Look, I told you, it's nothing, I wanted to do it. I did it. OK?" He smiled.

"But it's ridiculous. . . . I can't accept it." Her voice had a touch of hysteria in it. Then a light went on in her head. "Besides, it is absolutely against regulations for me to accept any sort of real gift from the men."

"Well, it's yours, ma'am. Have it cut off if you like. Throw it away. You know—fuck it." He turned and walked out the door, his heels sounding on the tiles.

"Wait!" she rose and called after him.

He had skipped lunch to lie on his bunk reading Waugh's book. He was amused by the description of the commanding officer diving under a table every time an airplane flew overhead while Waugh was reporting for duty with the CO's unit, and how he had stayed there during the entire conversation. Only in understanding the "club" attitude of the British command and the incredibly false French sense of military superiority in the early years of the war could he see how the Germans could have rumbled out of a small land—he had been amazed at how small Germany was compared to the United States, where it was still highly agricultural—to terrorize a complacent merchant Europe and then the world. Hell, there was no one but the Germans and Japanese ready to begin to fight a war until after '42. The politics of a military organization were defeating. There was something very wrong with the military he could not quite put his finger on. In the field where officers squatted over slit trenches to shit just like the men, it seemed simple—maneuver, shoot, communicate. . . . Still, he wanted to go as far in it as he could. It was the only place he had ever been where it seemed his brain and abilities were properly weighed and valued.

Whitman, who was in charge of quarters in the orderly room, blew into the room without knocking. "There's some cunt on the phone for you," he spat. He seemed suspicious and angry at having to have to come call Jack. With all the CID-CIC shit, no one trusted anyone except in the field.

Jack raced downstairs and across the quadrangle to the other wing of the barracks and picked up the phone on the first sergeant's desk.

"Corporal Andersen speaking."

"Listen, I'm sorry." Her voice was gorgeous over the phone, heavy, a little tremulous with all she had been thinking since that morning. "I would like to talk to you. Are you free this afternoon?"

"Yes."

"Would you like to take a little ride?"

"Sure."

"Well, look, meet me outside the gate, OK?"

"OK."

"At the place where the bus stops. In about half an hour. Is that all right?"

"Sure."

"OK.... Bye...."

He replaced the receiver. Whitman was canted in the company clerk's chair, reading a comic book. "What the fuck was all that about?" he demanded suspiciously.

"Nothin."

"Yeah? You may be the colonel's golden ass right now, but you better be fucking CID, because if you ain't, there's goin to be a day...."

Jack was surprised at Whitman's bitterness. Maybe he was worried about who was with his crummy *Shatzi* while he was pulling weekend duty. He had a living fear of her going with one of the GI's from one of the black units. There was a rumor the girl had had a black soldier lover before Whitman. Whitman was a hillbilly, and though he and Jack had never had much to do with each other, he hadn't supposed the guy bore him any grudge. He could not understand why he did, though he searched his memory for a clue. Nothing. Yet, the man's words haunted him through his joy in going to meet Miss Wisdom outside the gate. Sometimes those dumb hillbilly fucks saw things and knew things others missed. They live with all those haunts and fears and superstitions. "Shit! Screw it," Jack decided.

He stood in front of the bus shelter. It was a bright, soft day. He realized it was the first of May. Birds were singing in the leafy tops of the linden trees. He would be nineteen that month. It meant nothing to him. He thought he felt about as old as he would ever feel. He could not imagine himself an old man.

A new tan Morris Minor convertible pulled up at the stop, and Miss Wisdom leaned over and opened the door near the curb.

"Hi." She smiled pleasantly. "Sorry I'm a little late. I had to get someone to take my place for a while."

"It's OK. . . . Great." He smiled. The little car smelled new inside. The seats were leather.

She looked like a college girl, though her makeup was heavier and more expert. She had changed into a muted tan plaid skirt, soft brown sweater and a short suede jacket. She drove neatly. Her feet on the car's little pedals were in highly shined loafers. Clean white athletic socks were turned down in neat cuffs above her trim ankles. She held the wheel lightly with both hands and sat very erect. Whoever had taught her to drive had been a sane, careful person. He saw she had got the ring he had given her off her finger, so he waited for her to speak first.

"Where would you like to go?" she asked.

"I don't care," he said.

"Why don't we go along the river?" she suggested cheerfully.

"Fine."

She smiled at him and made a mocking little pout.

At a railroad crossing he told her, "This is where General Patton was killed in an accident . . . I think."

"Really?" She glanced at him. Before starting up again, she reached over and lifted his cap off his head and ran her hand over his short haircut. "At ease, soldier," she commanded.

Mannheim had had the shit bombed and shelled out of it. Block after block of buildings stood gutted against the soft sky. Here and there spring flowers bloomed in the debris. Some even grew in the rubble on lightless windowsills. Destruction had turned the street into a meandering path. The Ludwigshafen bridge to the French zone was a temporary steel job, courtesy of the U.S. Army Engineers. In the center of town a former underground bomb shelter had become the Pradplatz Hotel, where you could get filet mignon served by a tailcoated waiter while the average German was living on *Kartoffel* balls and a square ounce of sowbelly, when he could get the sowbelly.

"You love the Army, don't you?" she asked.

"Huh?" He laughed. "No, ma'am. I don't love it. It's something I seem able to do ... pretty well. One day I had fifteen cents in my pocket. I was sleeping on a beach. I couldn't find a job. I blew the fifteen cents. Tried to reenlist in the Navy. The office was closed. I joined the Army. It has been OK. I've learned a lot. Maybe I've found a home. I've learned what I've always known—I don't want just a job—ever. I'm in for sergeant as soon as the freeze on promotions ends. I'm willing to work for something I want. I would like a commission. I *want* to be an officer and a gentleman." He grinned wryly. "Marry you —and live happily ever after."

She reached over quickly and squeezed his hand without taking her eyes off the meandering road through the rubble.

"I'm sure you will," she said with genuine confidence in him that made him feel his dream might be around the next bend. "Realize what you want," she added.

Then they had cleared the city streets beside the river and were poking along above the wide, fast-moving water. After a while, she stopped the car. Deliberately, she set the hand brake and hopped around in the seat with her back against the door and her knees tucked neatly toward him. She put her hand in her pocket, took it out, reached across, unsnapped his blouse pocket, dropped the ring he had given her in it, resnapped the flap, patted it, smiled, sighed and sat back again, satisfied.

"There. Now let's start over. . . . OK?"

"Yes, ma'am."

She gave him both her hands. He held them tight as he explained, "It was the only way I could think to do it. To get through all those gawking other guys and the regulations. It was the only way I could think to do it. I had to."

She smiled softly. "But what if I had reacted differently?"

"You didn't. I think I do love you, ma'am." He waved away the beginning of a protest and held her hands tight. "I love the way I felt when I saw you, see you *now*. I like the way you are. Just are. You don't have to know so much about a person to know how they are. Anyway, I don't think I do. You're just fine, ma'am. I know I've done more really bad stuff than anyone you could have ever known. I know if we had lived in the same town you would have nothing to do with me. . . . Or not much." He grinned. She raised her eyebrows. "Well, *some* of the nice girls sort of liked us wild ones ... a little. Anyway, I'll be as good to you and for you as I can be.... Which I know will be a hell of a lot better than most guys would be. I don't have a paper to prove that. But you can count on it. I love you the same as I loved the girl I was married to. Only better. That is over. Gone. And now I know it. Then I was always anxious, scared all the time. I don't know why. With you, I'm not. I know I can take care of it ... you ... you would be good to me in every way. I know that too. I would never want another. I don't keep some shack-baby. I never have. It's too damn dreary. Guys humping off every weekend with a bag of crap like little lost husbands.... I like women. I mean I really like them. I like them better than men, even for company. Anyway, when I have to have sex, I go to a prostitute." He saw her wince. "It's a straight deal, nobody is bullshitting anyone. Oh, they run their line of crap, but the sex part is straight. Sometimes we can have a few laughs. And they are more interesting than anyone's little shack-baby I've ever met. I've never had VD. From China to here, I've always been very careful...." He tried to think of what else he should tell her. She pressed her fingers against his lips to stop him.

"Enough," she begged. "You go so fast."

"I'm not very romantic, I guess." He grinned. "Like dancing, I've never had time to really learn."

"You do just fine," she breathed, staring at him, frowning slightly, holding his hands in her lap. He was aware of the warmth and softness of her thighs beneath the wool skirt. He leaned toward her. He knew he could.

"You're so sweet ..." she whispered as he leaned close.

He could feel her warm breath, faint tobacco smell but sweet. His lips just touched her own.

"This is crazy, you know?" she said.

Then they both gave a pained cry and leaped into each other's arms. It was the most electric moment either had ever lived. So powerful was it, they would talk about it often later with wonder. For as fine as it would always be after, there was nothing like that moment. There was no dimension, sense or breath.

"Like a *bomb!*" she exclaimed when they had fallen apart and then back into each other's arms. She looked at him wide-eyed, stunned. She shivered all over. So did he.

"I feel like I'm going to cry or something," he confessed.

"Me too. Let's get out of here and walk," she begged.

They walked with their arms around each other along the darkening river. He told her honestly as much about himself and his past as he could manage. He left out only that which he knew there was no way for her to understand, that which he did not understand himself.

When he had finished, she stopped, turned him toward her and gently pressed the full length of her body against him during a long, tender, deep kiss.

"I don't care," she admitted out of a kind of dreamy wonder that she did not. "I don't *care* if it is crazy. I really don't care." She laughed, and he held her and smiled happily.

"Maybe it isn't so crazy," he insisted. "If it *is*, it's better than however it was the other way."

"Oh, yes!"

They kissed again and then walked.

"I'm afraid my life has been terribly ordinary," she said. "I'm just a little girl from Oconomowoc. I'd never been much farther from home than Milwaukee and Chicago, except to attend my brother's wedding in South Carolina, until I finished school. I fooled around for a couple of years, then joined Special Services. I was stationed for a year at Fort Sheridan, which was almost like being at home, and finally got sent here. I guess there isn't much to tell about me, is there? I have great parents, had a *good* home, have a handsome hero brother who is with Northwest Orient Airlines. He's married to a sexy little Southern belle who would flirt with herself if there were no one else around. But they have two beautiful children and a great new home on Puget Sound, and Dad has just about gotten to where he can like Divinna—some name, huh? I have a sister married to an Army major. They have three kids. Probably the best thing would be for me to show my photo album. I was in the Badger marching band at Wisconsin. I played the oboe."

The vision of her in the uniform of a marching band playing an oboe made him smile.

"I was a fat little girl," she said as if it were a warning. "I weighed a hundred and fifty *pounds*. I have to take pills to keep slim."

He could not imagine her fat.

"I'll show you pictures. I was horrible. I wasn't in a sorority. Swimming club, band and Spanish club were my activities. B-average scholar."

"Are you a virgin?" he asked.

"Well! I must say you continue to be blunt, don't you? Sex was not one of my extracurricular activities. I don't know honestly if I am or not. I think I am. I never slept with anyone. . . . Well"—she touched the lump of ring on the chain beneath her sweater—"I was having a pretty torrid romance with a first lieutenant at Sheridan. I mean I've necked a lot. And especially after I lost weight and found I wasn't an ugly duckling with a waddle and really good-looking fellows seemed to find me attractive."

"You're beautiful," he promised her.

"*Anyway*. . . . One night we got pretty blasted . . . the lieutenant Don—and he slept on the couch in my quarters with me all night. It seemed like I felt something, but he swore in the morning he hadn't really done anything . . . you know? We didn't take off our clothes."

"Um."

"Does it matter?"

"What?"

"Whether I am or not?"

"Jesus Christ! Hell, *no!*" He had been seeing the scene of the officer and her sleeping the night together on her couch. But her virginity had been a matter of curiosity rather than importance.

"So big a *no*, Cyrano?" she teased.

"Huh?"

"Don't you know *Cyrano de Bergerac?* Oh, it's so beautiful! That is what I have been thinking about ever since yesterday. We'll have to read it together. You can read Cyrano's part and I'll read Roxanne's."

The notion made him blush. "Yeow. Well, we'll see."

"No. Listen. Cyrano was a great soldier, a musketeer, a great swordsman. Very independent. Oh, you'll like him. You make me think of him. He had this great enormous nose—"

"I don't have a big nose," he pointed out.

"We'll fake it! We'll fake it!" she cried happily. "Let's run!" She towed him along by the hand; then they really ran, him in the lead, towing her, laughing, until they were out of breath and flopped down on the grassy bank and looked long and close at each other in twilight and kissed many, many times, trying to figure out what was happening, really happening. She let him touch her breasts, which were not large, but very soft, and run his hand over her body, over her clothes, all of which he did with gentle wonder rather than passion, as a blind man might in trying to see her, feeling all love for her, not wanting to frighten or hurt. Wordlessly she understood that and did not stop him when he felt her belly and laid his hand on her sex outside her clothes. Her hips were wide. . . . "Made for having kids," he told her. Her pelvis was a strong, wide arch.

"But not right this minute," she teased, and removed his hand and lifted it to her cheek. "You are very gentle. I'm glad."

"Not always," he warned.

"We'll cross *that* bridge when we come to it," she said. "Now, suddenly, I'm famished. I didn't have lunch."

"Me neither," he admitted.

They laughed. She wrapped her arms around him very tightly and kissed his cheek a thousand small times.

"I'm scared. Really scared," she said very seriously. "I can't believe this is happening. That I am so happy. I don't feel myself at all. I feel all jumbled up and half sick and wonderful. I keep thinking, 'But I'm four years older than he is.' But I feel like a little girl again. And you don't seem like a boy at all, somehow. I don't know. I don't care. But I'm very, very scared, Corporal Andersen."

"I love you," he said. He did not tell her that suddenly he was quite scared, too.

They had *Wienerschnitzel* with an egg on top, and a salad, and two cups of strong coffee each in a little *Gasthaus* in the suburbs where they hoped they would not run into anyone either of them knew. Yet, already, the fact they had to be careful not to be seen together was a depressing intrusion upon their pleasure.

Four black GI's came in from some trucking company and ogled them and whispered among themselves over beers. It was evidently an unspoken spade-trooper joint.

She leaned near and said, "They think I'm your *Fräulein*. I never realized how those poor girls must feel to be looked at like that." She shuddered.

"*Du bist ein prim Schatzi!*" he said loudly and smacked her thigh beneath the table.

The black soldiers smirked and turned away. He winked at her. Her face was scarlet.

"I feel like meat," she said.

It was about ten when they went back to the post. She refused to let Jack out to walk through the gate. They were waved through by the guard, who mistook Jack for an officer and snapped a smart salute and must have cursed the sonofabitch in the car for not returning it.

She led him up the outside stairs near the parking spaces to the quarters she shared with another hostess, Miss Janine Smith.

"She has a big thing going with a medical captain in Heidelberg and probably won't be back tonigh—" She caught herself. "She sometimes stays out all night."

"Will you get in trouble if she comes back and finds me here?"

She shrugged. "Janine's OK. She'll understand. She'll just have to."

She made them each a scotch and water in a small pull-man kitchen in a closet and asked him to excuse her. She sure seemed to have to go to the john a lot, he thought.

In the bathroom she shook two Dexedrines into her palm, ran a glass of water and swallowed them. She was taking about six a day.

She was in there for a long time, more than half an hour. He had begun to get worried. When she returned, she had on a long, loose burgundy corduroy robe that zipped up the back from her waist. She had him do the last few inches of zip.

"I was getting worried about you."

"Had to put on a new face." She smiled.

So she had. She had also slipped on her black pumps.

She punched on an expensive transoceanic portable and tuned it from AFN to an all-night Italian station.

They sat together on the couch and drank their drinks with her heavy photo album on their knees. She had been a fat little girl—not as a child—but from about puberty on. If he had known her in high school and college, he would have not paid her any notice. In her marching band uniform with the dizzy cap on her head, her dark hair sticking out all around, oboe at port arms, she looked so dumpy he was embarrassed for her. It made him sad and hurt to see her that way, knowing what the smartass cats said behind her back. He looked at her beside him and wondered that so pretty and sexy a woman could have come out of that poor dumpling. In the back row of the swimming team her wide smile and open face made him aware of how she had relied on her personality to compensate for her then vexing shape.

He caught her hand gently on the album and said, "I *love* you."

She blushed and quickly turned the page, knowing exactly how he felt.

Her parents were pleasant-looking, tempered American Gothic, who had moved to town within their generation, standing before a neat, stone, English-looking, comfortable two-story bungalow at the end of a lane on a nice lake. They were surprisingly old. She explained she had been born when her mother was forty-one. Her father was a small man, smaller than her mother, who was built much like Judy, comfortable body perched on long, slender legs. They made Jack think of Jack Sprat. Both wore rimless glasses. She said her father ran one of the two movie houses in town. He also had the family farm up near Green Lake on which he had a tenant. It was only a quarter of a section and barely made its expenses, but he was very tied to it and would never sell it, though everyone encouraged him to do so. Campbell's and Libby's had made him good offers. They had bought all the land around it, torn down the fences and farmed with modern methods that the old man said were ruining the country and resulted in tasteless produce. In the side yard of their property in town, he still had a vegetable garden, and grew most of their vegetables. They were Congregationalists. Jack liked her parents very much. When he told her so, she was pleased.

There was her dog; their dock and rowboat; her handsome brother in Air Force uniform and in civies; her sister and her husband, a pudgy career Army quartermaster major; their two teen-age daughters, one a real little sexpot with enormous boobs of which she was much aware. There was her brother's wife, the Southern belle, sexy in white shorts that showed her cute cheeks perched on a bike. Judy lifted her eyebrows and began tapping her fingers on the album when he looked a bit longer at the page than he had at the others.

Stuck loosely in the back of the album was a retouched,

matte studio photo of a rather handsome first lieutenant of artillery on which was written: "To my darling Judy, with all my love! Don."

She closed the album. "Well, there I am."

"I wish I were an officer already." He spoke his thought. "It would make everything so much simpler."

Laying her palm along his face, she smiled. "You are so *serious!*"

"Oh. It's just I can't see you as an equal. Take you out openly. . . . Court you properly, ma'am." He grinned crookedly.

"But I feel just fine, sir. No complaints. It has been a lovely day." She relaxed in the crook of his arm, her right hand cool on his neck, and turned her face to offer her wide, delicious mouth to kiss. The margins of her lipstick left lines of red above and below her lips when he finally drew away.

When he laid her back on the couch, she did not resist, smiling softly, a slight look of query in her eyes, curling her arms around his neck, then feeling the hard wedge of his back as if marking every muscle with both hands. Nor did she protest later when he brought his left hand beneath her loose robe.

"I want you," he breathed, his brow wrinkled as if in pain. "I want you!" he repeated loudly and strongly.

"I want you, too," she replied gently, her eyes half-lidded, her voice unclear as to what exactly she meant. "I think I do. . . ."

It was that easy. *I'm going to fuck her*, he realized. *I can.* It suddenly seemed improbable—too quick—his dream a crazy drama he had constructed—and now she was going along with it. He hadn't intended to fuck her. It had not been his pure intent. She was a beautiful twenty-three-year-old woman who in the ordinary course of events he would have never known. But what the hell was the ordinary course of events anymore? He suddenly felt very young, bumptious, not at all full of the confidence he had when he put the ring on her finger. *But she wants it too*, he argued.

"I love you," he said.

Her breasts were small and soft. Her sex was large, hairy and very soft. He knelt on the couch and reached under her robe to pull down her white nylon panties. She lifted her hips to facilitate the move. Behind her dark lids fringed with the long sooty lashes, her eyes flickered nervously, though her body remained placid. Carefully, he worked the underwear over her ankles and her shiny black pumps. Between her legs, he slipped the catch on his brass belt buckle, tore open his fly and skidded his trousers and faded olive drab GI shorts down to his thighs, lifting his shirttails to feel her soft white belly against his own.

He entered her very carefully, gently, barely breathing. The back of his head and sinuses felt congested. His lips and fingertips tingled. Then he was aware there was no need for his caution. The lieutenant was a liar. She was prepared for pain and did not realize he was fully into her until he began to move slowly, roundly, deeply, lovingly.

She opened her eyes full of questions.

"You're beautiful," he told her. "Sooooo beautiful."

She wrapped her arms fiercely around his neck and squeezed tears from the corners of her eyes. "Am I all right?" she squeaked.

"Yes, Oh, *yes!*" She had a very big cunt. But she was just fine. "You are beautiful. Do I feel good to you?"

She nodded her head vigorously, affirmatively.... "Yes."

No bones in there, he told himself. She was large, wet and all velvet. She began awkwardly to try to move with him. He lifted her right leg back onto the back of the couch, aware of the long, gleaming length of it, the shiny pump in the air above them. She opened her eyes wide, her lips parted as if to speak, then kissed him passionately, her hands crawling all over his back beneath his shirt, finding his bare buttocks. "Oh, God!" she breathed. "*Oh, God!*" She came with a delicious violent shudder, almost as if against her will. She looked puzzled when he did not stop but began to do it even more violently. He felt he could go on forever. He had begun to breathe. He could hear his breathing deep and loud in the room above the sound of her own shallow panting, as if reacting from blows. She was all liquid. His pelvic bone rubbed hard, constantly against the internal shaft of her clitoris. He felt froth all around his penis, and the slickness on her bottom and his thighs. He fucked her harder and harder. He had never gone so long. And she hung on, taking it, liking it.... She was marvelous.

He felt about to come, swelling enormously. He was dizzy, faint. His head ached painfully.

"I love you! I love! I LOVE YOU!" she was crying.

"Oh, goddamn!" he cried back. "GODDAMN!"

It gathered somewhere back at his spine and crept forward painfully, then became a rush. At the last second as the rush felt at the very end of his penis, he yanked himself out of her. She screamed, "NO!" and clawed at his back, rising herself against him, tugging his buttocks with both hands, her belly and thighs slick against him. He came down against her slick-slick bottom as she ground her sex against him, writhing and crying and gulping for breath.

He lay still on her completely limp body for a very long time. He could feel his heart beating furiously against her and knew she could feel it too. After a while their breathing became synchronized, and he was aware of the satisfied stillness within her into which he seemed to continue to flow. He thought she was the only woman he had ever so satisfied and he wanted never to lose her, and wanted no other—ever.

"Are you all right?" he asked.

She smiled without opening her eyes, extended her arms as if floating and said, "Wooooooo. . . ."

"Me too," he told her. "You sure are good in there, ma'am."

He scooted down and kissed her belly.

When he lay again beside her, she said, "Thank you."

"Thank *you!*" he insisted.

"I mean for not—you know—uh, coming inside me. I wanted you to. I really wanted you to."

"I wanted to. There was a place where I was sure I was going to."

"I know." She scootched around and snuggled in his arms. "I love you, Jack."

"I love you too . . . ma'am."

She raised her head and saw he was grinning. "When are you going to stop calling me that?" she demanded.

"After we are married. I'll call you 'hey you.' "

"The hell you will! You'll call me 'darling, dearest, sweetheart, honey, lover,' all those things."

He tried them all. "Pretty easy."

She kissed him long and lovingly.

"I wasn't, was I?" she asked.

"What wasn't you?"

"A virgin."

He shrugged. "It's all in the mind anyway. You were a virgin, Judy." He fished the ring from his blouse pocket, found her finger and slipped it on. "We were both a couple of virgins this time."

She popped up, kissed his mouth happily, then whispered, "Will you excuse me for a minute, darling? I have to go to the john real bad."

"It's those damn pills you take," he said as she crawled over him, her robe falling over pale bottom, and tripped toward the other room.

"Would you rather I get fat?" she called.

"Bring me a couple," he called after her.

She had redone her makeup again and brushed her hair. She reluctantly gave him two of the Dexedrine tabs, which he knocked back with the rest of his diluted drink rather than the plastic bathroom glass of water she had brought. The heat had gone down in the club. It was well after midnight. She was dragging a down-filled comforter by one ear. He wondered why they did not go into her bed but did not say anything. She asked, "You don't have to be back before reveille, do you?"

"No."

"I didn't think so. Good. I would hate it if you had to go now. I would understand, but I would hate it."

She knelt on the floor and removed his boots. She helped him off with his trousers, shirt and underwear and tossed them in a club chair. She studied his naked body shyly, but happily.

"Want a pair of my PJ's? They would be a bit tight, but you could probably get into them."

"You keep me warm."

"I will," she promised. "Want me to keep this on or take it off?" She plucked her robe.

"Off."

Dutifully she lifted the wine-colored robe up and over her head. Beneath she was bare. Her torso was pale where it had been covered by a swimming suit, but her limbs were very brown. Her bush was abundant, dark but not tatty. A few single long black hairs climbed up toward her deep navel. She saw him looking at her and blushed. "I've never been naked with a man before. I feel ugly."

"You aren't. You're beautiful," he assured her.

Nevertheless, she quickly hopped over him onto the

small couch, drawing the comforter about them and tucking it around him.

The chain with the lieutenant's ring was gone. He kissed her body from the tip of her nose to the soles of her feet. He went down on her so full of love for her he was again dizzy, drunken, unaware of time, wanting only to give her pleasure, great, exquisite pleasure. She was hesitant about what he was doing, then relaxed and gave herself to it languorously, opening her thighs wide and pushing her sex up toward him, beginning to move her bottom. He rubbed the base of her clitoris that he could feel running back toward her pelvis bone with his thumb while he tongued the button within the lips. When she came, he pushed his face between the large lips of her sex and sucked the liquidy, tender tissue for a long time, wiping his face in the copious fluid that flowed from her, smearing it over her thighs, belly, breasts, mouth and face, until the entire room smelled of come, sweet, clean, healthy come. They made love until dawn lightened the window shade above the couch and the light that burned in the room became pale, washed-out. They had dozed only a few minutes all night long.

When they heard reveille sounding over the post—no bugler, it was a recording played by the battalion charge of quarters over the PA system—she clasped him tighter.

"I don't have to stand reveille in headquarters company," he explained. "Just so I show up in the office around eight."

She reached down and took his cock in her hand. "I never want to let him go."

"Forever," he promised.

They made love once more. She bit her lower lip and requested, "Easy, darling. I'm sort of sore."

She made them coffee and toast in the little kitchen in the closet and sat it prettily on the coffee table. She put a pillow under her when she sat across from him. "Uh ... being new at this, I would just like to know. . . . We *do* sleep sometimes, don't we?"

Showered, dressed and feeling wonderfully weary, he laughed. "We'll just lay in a barrel of those pills you take and never sleep."

She would later tell him that she had asked Janine about it. All the roommate had done was to laugh and

war tuxedoes began pumping out a polka. The German girls began dragging their men to the party.

No one seemed particularly disturbed by the news. Judy was determined to have a good time. "Come on, I'll teach you how to polka."

He grasped her waist, remembering its naked suppleness, and whirled her around the floor. The German girls' skirts lifted gaily. They loosed happy yodels. Jack and Judy laughed in each other's faces.

They were having drinks at the bar when the MP's roared up to the hotel and stormed in to announce that all leaves were canceled and all personnel were to report back to their units immediately.

Everyone groaned and groused at the order.

"That thing will be over before we get back!" someone argued.

"Get lost!" a German girl shrieked.

"You ever heard of that fuckin island?" the red-haired corporal asked Jack.

"It's a peninsula," Jack told him.

"Who the fuck *cares!*" the kid wanted to know.

"Do you think we will get involved?" Judy asked him.

"I reckon," he said. There had been a troop information and education lecture about how we were containing "Communism" with a series of bases ringing Russia and China. He seemed to remember that Korea was not included in the places we would without question go to war for, but South Korea was some sort of ally. "I hope so," he added.

"You do? Why, for God sake?" She looked at him as if he were mad.

"OCS will open up. I can become an officer. We can get married."

That hardly seemed worth a war to her, and she said so, but she held him and kissed him right in the bar.

They took the boat back across the lake, staring at the flat back of the German driver's head. He had told them he had been a submariner in the North Sea during the Second World War. His war was over. He whistled lightly, racing along a moonshaft on the cold lake water.

Silently they packed their bags in the tiny room in which they happily bumped into each other when out of bed. When they were finished, she took his hand and drew him with a look toward the bed.

"Once more before we leave," she begged.

"Sure. Of course," he said, unbuttoning her light sweater.

46

"THEY'RE kicking our ass off over there!" the colonel roared, dashing between his car and headquarters. "Our people aren't standing and fighting. They are just picking up and running, leaving their equipment, rifles, everything! This is sickening!"

He and all the West Pointers were already packing, plaguing division, EUCOM headquarters and Washington for orders to Korea.

The battalion was being cannibalized for men. There were new levees posted every day. In the States they were calling up the reserves.

Jack hounded the sergeant major for word of his application to officers' candidate school. The two other men who had qualified and been notified they were on a waiting list had already been assigned classes and were on orders. Jack had scored higher than either of them and had more military experience. His promotion to sergeant came through, but the sergeant major continued to shake his head negatively every morning when dispatches came down from division.

To celebrate his promotion, Jack and Judy went to an expensive restaurant in Heidelberg filled with officers and EUCOM civilian employees. They no longer cared who saw them. It was only a matter of time before he was one of them. He had watched her to see which of the array of cutlery was appropriate for whatever the snobbish German waiter slid before him.

Janine was in quarters that night, so they made love in the car in the parking lot, sucking each other's fingers for some crazy, delicious reason until they were so excited they had to have one another, she wriggling out of her panty girdle and hose, then finding it impossible to manage things except with her sitting on his lap.

Yet, even in making love to Judy, there was always in the back of his mind the dream that soon—any day now—he would have an OCS class and everything he really wanted, had worked so hard for, would begin to come true.

They figured out that as soon as he was on orders she would resign her job and get a place near Fort Benning, even if they could only see each other occasionally while he was in OCS. The day he was commissioned, they would get married.

"And *that* night I'm not wearing this damn diaphragm!" she vowed.

They had discussed it. They wanted to have a baby right away, especially as he would surely be going to Korea.

"I want to feel it inside me growing while you are gone," she said.

He was certain Korea would not last very long once the United States got organized, and men like the men of his battalion, the marines, real field soldiers got there. Perhaps their being so close to the Russians in Germany had made them sharper, better trained, more aware of the possibility of having to fight. He knew if his battalion had been there, they would not have bugged out. But MacArthur was committing his units piecemeal, probably full of the shit that as soon as the North Koreans saw a few Americans they would cut and run. They hadn't. They had chewed up Task Force Smith in the first meeting, a small band of American GI's hauled out of bed in Japan and loaded on a plane and rushed up to stop a North Korean Army that was well trained and driving Russian T-34 tanks. The task force's weapons were a battery of 105's and six rounds of HEAT antitank ammo which was nearly *all* the antitank ammo *in* Japan. They had no mines, and their antiquated communications equipment went out in the first fire fight. The North Koreans were so amazed at their easy victory they paused to wonder at all the materiel and weapons the Americans had left on the battlefields. They did not pursue the fleeing, absolutely disorganized U.S. troops. One survivor walked completely across the Korean peninsula; another made his way to the Yellow Sea, commandeered a bum boat and went by water all the way down to Pusan. But they had gotten their ass kicked good. Worse, they abandoned their wounded, leaving some unknown hospital corpsman who volunteered to stay with them. No one had taken the time to learn his name, that he might be put in for a medal. MacArthur continued to speak for publication like a man dictating the text for an elementary-school history book. Jack did not like or trust MacArthur. He had studied every important American general since the Revolutionary War. (In that one for sheer genius *and* ability to fight, he had to take Benedict Arnold—never mind how he turned out—a stiff dick has no conscience; then Mad Anthony Wayne, who was a fighter, and after him, Nathanael Greene, who was a great strategist. But MacArthur had never been, in Jack's judgment, more than an adequate division commander and a good colonial administrator. In the Second World War in the Pacific, it was all the Marines and Navy. In Europe, it had been Patton's Third Army which showed the others how to run a modern mobile war while Montgomery was straightening up his lines and pivoting on this or that point until it became a dirty joke. Montgomery was ranked with MacArthur in his category of much "overrated" generals.

The all-black 24th Infantry Regiment had bugged out scandalously in Korea, even adopting the pop song "Bug-Out Blues" as its unofficial regimental theme, which fed racist sentiment among the men of Jack's all-white, mostly Southern tank battalion. The Army was still segregated except in leaders' courses and the OCS, but not many dark faces were to be seen in either. In Jack's leadership school class there had been one black man, who had become his friend. In fact, it was after Tommy had come down from Kitsingen that they had put Morris, the ex-first lieutenant, in his and Bruffey's room. When he thought back on it, he was certain now Morris *was* a CID man. If Jack were black in a segregated army, he wasn't sure he wouldn't bug out too. Why the fuck not?

Still, he never thought of Korea as a personal danger of any consequence in relation to the personal opportunity it represented. He did not think he would get killed there. "Most soldiers don't," he pointed out to Judy.

He liked the idea of having a baby with her; a son he

658

could call his own—or a daughter, it really didn't matter that much. If it was a boy, they thought they would name it John after his grandfather and after himself. Before, he would never have considered such a thing. Now it was possible he could make it a name not to be ashamed of. Sometimes when they made love, they pretended they were conceiving the baby and they became very tender. She never failed to have an orgasm when they played making a baby.

The sergeant major had held a wartime commission of captain. He had stayed in the Army at his permanent rank of master sergeant. In Burma he had been with some kind of British commando outfit, and he now spoke with a slight British accent when he was feeling good. He was taken to bracing a trooper with a button undone and bellowing, "SOLDIER, YER NAKED! STARK STARIN 'ORRIBLE NAKED!" When he was not feeling good, he would fall into silent introspective depression for days that would always culminate in his going for a weekend to some distant town, where he would take a room, lock the door and drink himself senseless, returning precisely on time to be his curious self again for a month. The colonel liked him, and so did the men. It was the sergeant major who had told Jack about the extension courses for officers he could take by correspondence. That was how he had become an officer.

"Think you will go back to a commission, Sarge?" Jack had asked him when the Korean thing broke out.

"No. That's all behind me. I don't want any more of it. You go taste the bitter fruit of command, my boy. I've had it, and they can keep it."

He was a bachelor or had been divorced. There was a WAC in Heidelberg, but it seemed more companionship and a mutual interest in booze than any kind of romance. She was even uglier than the sergeant major.

Jack stopped at the sergeant major's desk as he did every morning. He could see his papers on top of the stack of dispatches from division. He recognized all the photostats and everything in quadruplicate he had made. His heart leaped. It was there!

"They don't have a class for you," the sergeant major said, without looking up.

Jack thought for a second he was joking, but only for a

second. He heard the sergeant's words echo through his brain as the finality of it sank in.

"When will they?" he managed.

"It's a turndown, son. You'll have to start all over and put in again." He did not sound hopeful.

"Why, Sarge?"

"How the hell do I know?" He shoved the papers over to Jack.

There was a short covering letter stating that after careful review the subject was not accepted for placement in an officer candidate class.

"I had higher scores and efficiency ratings than those other two guys. I want to know why," Jack insisted.

The sergeant major shrugged. "Sometimes you can want a thing too much. I don't *know*, Andersen. Maybe they could tell you at division."

"Do I have your permission to go see?"

"Go. . . . Here, drop this off for me." He gave Jack a dispatch routing envelope to take with him. "I'll tell anyone who asks I sent you."

Jack was already on his way toward the door.

"And take your time getting back," the sergeant major advised.

There was a *Gasthaus* along the highway that they always stopped at for a beer or two when they had to go to division.

It was about a sixty-mile trip by jeep. It was a beautiful day, the kind of day it had been when he had first gone out with Judy for a drive. The full weight of his being turned down hit him as he was barreling at the maximum the governed jeep would go past woods on either side of the highway. He felt crushed. He felt as he had so many times as a little boy. "It all had been a fucking dream. A stupid dream," he berated himself. "Turned down, man!" He blamed his mother, his stepfather, his grandparents. It had to do with something like that. What else could it be? He had qualified in every way. He had demonstrated his seriousness by working for it on his own time. It wasn't fair. He knew he would be a damned good officer. He knew it!

The clerk who had handled his application and tests came to the window in the School Section of headquarters.

"I want to know why my application for OCS was bucked back," Jack demanded.

"Well, Sergeant, we don't have that information. They never tell us." He was a pale young man and rather girlish. He hadn't worn field boots since basic training, but he had always been conscientious about helping Jack take care of all the paper work and had always seemed truly interested and confident that Jack would make OCS.

"Where can I find out?" Jack persisted.

He shook his head that he could not. "Probably S-two could tell you something, but they won't."

"Goddammit! It isn't fair to turn a man down and not tell him why!" Jack exploded.

The corporal clerk blinked. "Just a minute." He went and made a telephone call. Then he found a copy of Jack's papers in one of the file baskets and returned to the window. "I called a friend. He said the application was turned down on 'psychological grounds.' "

"What do you mean?"

"Well, that means they don't consider you psychologically sound officer material." He noticed the look on Jack's face and said quickly, "Oh, don't let that upset you. It could mean anything, nothing. That's a kind of catchall." He riffled through Jack's papers, stopping here and there to study an entry or document. "It could be just an accumulation of a lot of little things. Something you told the psychiatrist . . . or, something one of the people you gave as references said about you . . . your schools. . . . They check all that. The FBI makes a standard investigation in your hometown. Then there's the fact you ran away and went to the Navy at fourteen, and got married and divorced so young. . . ." Now that the clerk looked at it that way, he seemed to see how hopeless Jack's effort had been from the start. "I'm sorry, Sarge. That's all I can tell you."

"Thanks." He turned and walked out. He felt silly and preposterous now in his cocky tanker's jacket with the new sergeant's stripes, bloused trousers over his boots and cunt cap like a centurian's crest over his brow. He passed a small WAC private who looked at him as if he were "big" and essayed a weak wolf's whistle after him. Another time it would have made him feel good, thinking of Judy and what he had in her that he could never know with some little WAC. Now he walked as if stunned, repeating the words in his mind until he wanted to yell, *"Psychologically unfit. . . ."*

Oh, yeow, I'm a crazy bastard! he told himself.

At the *Gasthaus* halfway back to the post, he stopped the jeep in the parking lot and walked to one of the outdoor tables beneath gay Cinzano umbrellas. The waiter wanted to know if he desired lunch. He asked for a large beer and a shot of *Schnapps*. When the *Schnapps* was gone, a good-looking young whore came out in good high-heeled shoes, stockings, a short skirt that cupped her ass and a soft white blouse open at the throat. She stopped at his table, striking a pose, holding a cigarette, and asked, "You have *Feuer* for me, *bitte?*" He lit her cigarette. "I sit down, *ja?*" She was already pulling out a chair, sitting in it and crossing her legs provocatively. He noted to himself that the whores in Germany were getting younger, better-looking and better-dressed all the time. She was a pretty girl with one of those strange medieval, utterly corrupt baby faces. He knew she would have almost hairless skin, smooth and deep, though she was in no way fat—a kind of moist, half rotten whore-child who looked about sixteen and was about twenty-four.

She prattled in broken English, asking if he had a girlfriend, where he was stationed, would he buy her a drink. He bought her a drink. She found reason to touch him often as she told some boring long story about a girl she knew who had gone with a black man and gotten pregnant. She described the issue as if it were a monster. She thought Jack was a Southerner. "I never go with no night fighter!" she swore, putting her hand on her left breast as if making a pledge. "I like you. You are nice. You like me." She pawed his stripes kittenishly. "You are so sad, *Schatz*. I bet Karin make you happy ... huh?" She pulled at his lower lip playfully. He jerked away. "What's the matter you?" she demanded.

"I'm psychologically unfit." He grinned.

"Was?"

He stood up and fished some money out of his pocket and put it on the table.

"You give me a lift?" the girl called after him.

He got in the jeep and backed it around in the drive. He saw her speak to the waiter, shrug and tap back into the place, waggling her cute ass.

He parked the jeep in the service club lot and went up to the library. Judy was there as he had first seen her, at her desk, checking in books. She looked up and smiled, both pleased to see him and curious as to what he was doing there at that hour. He hadn't come over for lunch or called, but everything was moving so fast since Korea broke out, she figured he had some important duty. There was no one in the library, so she got up and crossed to meet him and kissed him fully on the lips, then laughed and reached for a Kleenex on her desk to wipe the lipstick from his mouth, peering over his shoulder at the door like a naughty girl.

"I was turned down for OCS," he told her.

She looked at him for a moment and saw he was not joking. She started to ask him why, then saw the look on his face.

He heard her say, "Come on. Come on, baby." She led him by the hand out of the library and around the balcony to her quarters. As soon as they were inside, she threw herself fiercely into his arms and kissed his face and eyes and neck and hands, pledging, "I love you! It doesn't matter. I don't care. I *love* you!"

He pushed her gently away. "Yeow, it matters, Judy." He turned, put his hands in his pockets and walked over to the window. He never put his hands in his pockets. His shoulders rolled forward as he let his weight rest in his hands deep in his GI pockets. "I'm psychologically unfit to be an officer," he said, grinning out the window.

She pressed herself against his back, laying her lips softly along his neck. "Come to bed with me," she whispered. "Please. Now."

He turned around. "You're on duty."

"I want you now. Please, darling." There were tears in her eyes. He grabbed her tightly and kissed her mouth and began to cry.

"Yes. Yes. I love you so," she soothed. She led him into her bedroom. They had never made love in her bedroom. She drew the shades. Then she picked up the phone and called downstairs. She asked whoever it was on the phone to close the library. Then after listening, said, "It's *important*, Janine." Then she listened again and said, "Well, if she comes back, tell her I'm sick. *Yes!* Thanks, Janine. Thanks a lot." She went and locked the door and came back, taking off her jacket and blouse. He began to take

663

off his clothes. She stripped naked in the small room, whipped back the covers of the bed and lay down and drew him to her. She made love to him. His dejection was too great for him to become genuinely excited, and he felt he was using her as he might have a whore, seeing her body around and beneath him and feeling the same kind of loveless, superficial excitement he would have felt with a whore as she worked very hard to make it better than it had ever been. He felt he had no right to be fucking that good, loving girl. Before he came, his erection began to fail, but she held him all the closer and moved so innocently and eagerly beneath him he felt himself begin to come, then remembered, though she hadn't mentioned it, that she did not have her diaphragm in. He had felt the soft cone of her naked cervix. He withdrew, though she tried to hold him fast.

"I wanted you," she said, tears again in the corners of her eyes. "I wanted to prove to you it doesn't matter, darling. I'm glad! I mean, I'm sorry, because it was so important to you, but I don't care about it, really. I don't want you to have to be away from me, go to wars and maybe get killed. You can do anything! I believe in *you!*" She shook him. *"I believe in you!* I don't care what you do. Be a farmer, work in a gas station, I don't give a damn. Just love me and take care of me and let me take care of you and love you. I *want* you."

He was lying beside her, staring up at the ceiling blankly, unblinking, until his eyeballs felt cold. "Looks like I can't even do that." He snorted. "Not even psychologically fit to fuck!" he spat.

"Oh! Stop being stupid!" She raised up angrily. "Stop being stupid!" She reached down and took hold of his cock and started to go down on him to induce another erection. He stopped her.

"Don't."

"Well, it just makes me mad to see you act like the world has come to an end because some stupid Army asses somewhere don't think you should be an officer. People who have never *met* you, for christsake, Jack! You know you got high marks from the board here and that the colonel gave you the top rating possible. Maybe it's just a mistake. Maybe you'll get a class tomorrow."

"It was no mistake. Look!" He sat up and faced her. "My mother was a whore and jailbird. My stepfather's

664

doing twenty to life as a habitual criminal—When I think about what the preacher and all those assholes back home probably said about me . . . teachers. . . . Shit, I must have been nuts! I mean, I must have really been *nuts!* I've been kidding myself ever since I got in the goddamn Army. *There's no place for me, Judy!"*

"There's a place with me," she said very coldly, angry too. "If you want to make one."

"I don't want to be a farmer or work in a gas station."

"I don't give a damn what you do. You want to go back to college? I'll work. Be a doctor, or lawyer, or architect, be an artist. I'll help you."

He knew how much she would hate going back to a college campus. She had said how miserable she had been there. And she would be almost thirty when he finished something like law, not that he had ever thought about being a lawyer. And how could he ever be anything like that? There were always boards to stand before. Whatever the Army found out would come up for as long as he lived.

"I've got to pee," she said, rolling out of the small bed and padding into the toilet. The sound of her strong stream in the bowl made him smile. He had never known anyone who had to piss as much as she did. He knew he loved her more than anything. He swung his feet over the side of the bed and began putting on his socks. The toilet flushed. In his mind's eye he saw her fluff up her pubic hair because he had told her how pretty it was when it was fluffy. The pain of his love for her was sweet inside him.

She stood in front of him and pulled his face against her bare belly. He wrapped his arms tight around her bottom and squeezed her until he could hear the gurglings inside her. He kissed her cunt. She tenderly stroked his crewcut head and then, with both hands, made him look up at her. "Do you love me?" she demanded.

"Yes."

"Will you marry me? Now?"

"You know we can't. I've got another year almost to go on my enlistment."

"I'll quit. I have a little money saved. I can probably get a job with an American company in Heidelberg or Frankfurt."

"And what if I go to Korea?"

"I'll go home and wait."

"No."

"No what?"

The pain inside him was solid as tungsten steel armor-piercing pain. "Look! I love you too much!" he shouted. "Think I'm going to marry you and drag you to some goddamn fucking dump where the pans are behind a curtain under the sink and see you turn into some ugly, beaten, bitter woman like my grandmother, like every damn body I know? NO!"

She was still standing naked, beautiful, rigid, her fists clenched at her sides. Suddenly she exploded and rushed at him, beating him with her fists. *"You sonofabitch! You sonofabitch!* I LOVE YOU!" she screamed. Her fists beat off his shoulders and chest. As abruptly, she turned and flung herself facedown on the bed and wept. "You sonofabitch, I love you." The words were small and muffled in the bed, and she kept repeating them.

He bent and stroked her bare back and told her, "I love you, too. I really do. And that's why, Judy."

"GO!" she turned her head and cried. "Go ON!"

"I'm sorry." At the door he said again, "I love you, Judy."

They did not stop seeing each other. They continued to meet as often as before. They continued to make love, but it was not the same, and they both knew it. When she had an orgasm, she went deep within herself, no matter how strongly she clung to him. Afterward they both felt a little lonelier.

Then he was on orders for Korea. He hadn't wanted to go to Korea after being turned down for OCS. He hadn't cared who he had to fight if he could gain what he wanted. But now he didn't want to go clear around the world and kill Koreans. His interest in the war had been personal, not political. He didn't give a damn if Korea was Communist. Anyone who, like him, had been in China after '45 and had eyes could see the "rebels" were going to take it. Maybe the Americans could have stopped it from happening, but they did not try very hard. Chiang had no stomach for war, only for butchering dissenters. Maybe the U.S. didn't think they could get anyone to fight there so soon after the Second World War. Now they were trying to stop the same thing from happening in Korea and getting their asses kicked. Jack really didn't want any part of it. He wanted now to do his time and get out of the Army. He knew there was no chance of winning a battlefield commission. Even if he were put in for one, it would be bucked back. Or at best be temporary, as the sergeant major's had been. If he had taken a change in MOS when he went to headquarters as acting operations sergeant, he might not have been put on orders for Korea. But he had insisted on keeping his tank commander's MOS number. Somewhere in the Army system his number had come up. Field soldier.

The night before he left, he and Judy did not make love. They did not say anything about it; they just knew they would not. They walked along the river where they had walked that first time. He talked about probably going back to college when he got out. He had come to that decision simply because there was nothing else he wanted to do and he would be eligible for the GI Bill. "Maybe I'll study art and go build me a house in the desert like Georgia O'Keefe. I've been reading about how to make adobe," he joked. She listened to him talk, but was sort of humoring him, not wanting to point out how self-pitying and self-centered she thought his plans were. She had stopped trying to show him they might do anything he wanted together. Yet there was always an implication in their talk that they would try to get together when he got out of the Army, and promises to write to each other were often pledged. It began to rain, and they ran for the car.

She let him out in front of his barracks. She took a package from the back seat and handed it to him after he kissed her for the last time and was about to get out of the car.

"Open it later, please," she begged.

"OK."

They really pretended it was not the last time they would see each other. "I love you," she said.

"I love you too . . . always."

They kissed once more, quickly, and she cried. He closed the door and walked without hurrying through the rain toward the barracks. After a bit she got the car going and turned around. He watched it drive away.

The present was an expensive fitted toilet kit in good

leather. Inside was the ring he had given her and a short note:

> Maybe one day you will put this back on my finger— for keeps. Then we will read *Cyrano* together. In the meantime, please, please, do take care of yourself— for me. I love you, Judy

He went back out into the rain and walked over to the service club and stood at the foot of the outside stairs and looked up to where there was light behind the drawn draperies in the living room. He could faintly hear her radio tuned to a music station. He stood with one foot on the first step for a moment, the rain running down his collar. He looked up once more, then turned and walked back in the rain.

47

IN THE small square in Masan, Jack watched an old woman put a dog in a sack and methodically beat it to death to make it tender enough to eat.

The tanks were drawn up alongside the square. Men were having their ration of beer in spite of people back in America writing Congress deploring giving young soldiers beer. The wounded had been taken from the tanks, mostly infantrymen who had ridden in on the back decks. Dark runs of their blood marked the dusty sides of the armor.

A correspondent with a tape recorder over one shoulder was going among the men, asking them questions, while another correspondent was filming the interview for the news. The battalion had been reduced to little more than company size. Jack's platoon leader was dead in his tank some miles up the road. Jack, now a sergeant first class, was in charge of the three tanks left in his platoon.

"You just came back from up there, Sergeant." The

man put the microphone in front of Jack's face. "Tell us, what happened?"

"Well, we went up to support the Twenty-fourth at Chinju. They broke through on the left, then the right. Then they were all over and had gotten people behind us like they always do. Some regiments broke down and took off. We had to fight our way out of there."

"Did the North Koreans have tanks?"

"Yeow. T-Thirty-fours. Our shells bounce off them. Theirs don't off of us."

"Are they good soldiers, Sergeant?"

"Who? The gooks? Yeow. They're good enough."

"One more question, Sergeant. Why are *you* here?"

"They sent me."

"No. I mean, why do you think we are fighting here? Everyone is asking that question. I'd like to hear why you think *you* are fighting here in Korea?"

"You tell *me*."

"Well. . . . Do you believe we are fighting to save this small country from Communism?"

"Me! I fight to stay alive. Your chances of getting killed are more if you don't fight. That's the only thing I've learned about war that is true here."

"Thank you very much, Sergeant. Would you like to say hello to anyone back home?"

"No."

"OK. Thank you and good luck." He went to another group of men, shoved the mike beneath some trooper's nose and asked him, "Tell me, soldier, why are you in Korea?"

"I don't know, sir," the young man said earnestly. "No one told me."

The old lady continued to flog the mess in the sack. Jack thought she could have been *his* grandmother, if he had been Korean. She had the same kind of determined little face and timeless way of working. Bareass kids and old men hunkered on the curb among their loaded A-frames and refugee bundles, watching the old woman, waiting to eat.

When the correspondent had gone, Jack thought of all he could have said, but ever since he had been turned down for OCS, he had determined to speak only when spoken to, and then with the economy of a miser and words ten cents each. He would become like his uncle, who had never "conversed" in his life. "Cop a mope," was how Jack's stepfather would have put it. The fact was neither he nor that correspondent could ever go over and find out what was on the mind of that old woman tenderizing that pup.

What the newspapers called the United Nations Forces were compressed into the Pusan perimeter, a rectangle about fifty by one hundred miles long on the toe of Korea. Outside the perimeter were some seventy thousand North Korean troops, still fighting like hell, but now suffering from constant pounding by the superior UN air forces, their supply lines riddled daily. North Korean prisoners complained of being hungry and not having enough ammunition. Wherever there had been ten enemy T-34 tanks, there were now perhaps two.

On September 15, the Marines led the Army 7th Infantry Division ashore in a landing around the coast of Inchon. It was a great success. The next day, after delaying twenty-four hours to pass the word of the landing to the men in the perimeter, General Walker launched his breakout.

At first it was hard to tell if it *was* a breakout. In many places along the line, it was the North Koreans who were attacking. Then, as Seoul was falling up north to the troops who had landed at Inchon, the North Koreans began to withdraw. But it was not a rout. The North Koreans fought well, every day and every night, conducting a series of delaying actions and orderly retreats that were textbook-sharp in their execution until finally, when they were outgunned six to one and outnumbered two to one, lacking air cover, the pace of their retreat picked up.

It became a tankers' and engineers' war, a war of breakout, rapid exploitation, bypassing pockets of the enemy, supply trucks running night and day to keep the tanks in ammo and gas. It was Walker's kind of war. An old Patton man, he had taken part in Third Army's dash to the Rhine, across it and beyond. Now it was the thirty-eighth parallel that was the Rhine, and there was no trooper who believed that, once they had the Koreans on the run, anyone was going to stop at the thirty-eighth. They were going to drive the gooks across their own half of the Land of the Morning Calm and then across the goddamned Yalu. ROK commanders promised South

Korean President Syngman Rhee they would wash their swords in the Yalu. Rhee talked of "unifying" his country under his "democratic" rule, as had Kim Il Sung, Premier of North Korea when he had sent his people south three and a half months before. Winning is heady stuff. Patton always said, "The greatest builder of morale is victory."

The Army didn't bother about straightening out communications behind them or worry about the tangled supply net from Pusan. "Go hog! MODOCK!" was the cry. MacArthur said something about having the boys home for Thanksgiving. That was good, because old *papasans* with their horsehair hats tied beneath their chins shook their heads, pulled their scraggly whiskers and said it was going to be an early winter.

Jack wasn't aware when they crossed the thirty-eighth parallel. They kept rolling. The new platoon leader had known nothing of Korea before the breakout. A second lieutenant, straight from the armored school at Fort Knox, a distinguished military ROTC graduate, he kept pumping his arm for the column to close up and speed up. He was having fun. Oh, it was great to be a young officer on the point with the miles tumbling beneath your tracks. Back at the end of the platoon, eating dust, Jack tucked a wet handkerchief under the sponge goggles and into his collar and thought of doing the rest of *his* time back in some cushy place like Knox, if MacArthur was right.

On October 25 in support of the 1st ROK Division about fifteen miles northwest of the Chongchon River, with a spanking new first lieutenant's bars on his collar, Jack's platoon leader riding on the point, standing in the hatch, took an antitank shell ricochet off the bow plate of his tank just under the chin. His head was severed, his body thrown out of the turret and off the back deck into the road. Jack had by then seen headless men, but the sight never failed to sicken and fascinate him. The body just lay there without a head, blood and juices oozing out of the neck.

Jack ordered the platoon off the road and radioed that they had been hit by what seemed a very strong roadblock. The battalion commander came up and concurred. The battalion deployed and began a fight that lasted all that day and into the night. They moved forward a bit as the enemy seemed to weaken. An enemy soldier was found crouching in his hole badly shaken by a nearby

671

shellburst. He was not Korean, but Chinese. The word was radioed throughout the army. In the hours that followed other Chinese were taken prisoner. All along the advance, units were encountering Chinese.

The Chinese fought differently from the North Koreans. They put up a bright flash of resistance such as the one Jack's platoon had encountered, then let the Americans fight through if they could, retreating well, until the attacking forces were sucked into what they called their fish-trap defense. They trapped the 8th Cavalry Regiment, leading the division advance, on November 1. The night was filled with the sound of bugles, whistles and cymbals, which the individual Chinese units used to keep in contact and communication for want of radios and telephones. In the night the cavalrymen, who had never been astride an army horse, were attacked by mounted, saber-swinging Chinese on little Mongolian ponies.

In the dark, the wild honking of runaway camels which the Chinese had used in their supply train added even greater unreality to the scene. The 8th lost six hundred men that night. One battalion was completely isolated. The 5th Cavalry Regiment directly behind the 8th tried desperately to get through a Chinese roadblock to rescue the trapped troopers, but could not do it. General Hobart Gay, the division commander who had made the decision three months before to blow the bridge over the Naktong when it was filled with Korean refugees, now had to make another and withdrew the 5th Cavalry and left the battalion to fight its way out or perish.

General Walker decided then to order all units to pull back to the Chongchon to consolidate.

As suddenly as the Chinese appeared, they seemed to evaporate. By November 7, Eighth Army patrols were hardly able to find a trace of them.

Then the Korean winter came down out of the mountains. The October orders to proceed to the Yalu still stood. The experience of being hit by Chinese had been like a nightmare, and like a nightmare, it had passed. MacArthur explained that his intensified air attacks had effectively kept enemy supplies and reinforcements from reaching the battlefield. No one believed the Chinese would actually get deeply involved in the Korean War.

Still, General Walker was certain he would see some of the Chinese again, and he prepared his new offensive to be stronger. He also tried to get his tangled supply situation straightened out, delaying the attack set for the fifteenth until November 24. The snow was bright with sun breaking through the clouds every now and then. The enemy resistance was very light. For twenty-fours the leading units could roll in spite of the cold which sapped strength of the men and vehicles.

On the morning of the twenty-fifth, the Chinese struck back. Air observers reported hundreds of Chinese streaming toward Tokchon.

Major General Keiser, commanding the 2d Division to which Jack's battalion had been shifted, told his men the main Chinese effort would be directed against ROK II Corps on the right flank. He was wrong. Instead, the Chinese aimed directly down Chongchon Valley at the 2d as it moved north from Kunu-ri.

The new platoon leader was a Lieutenant Neal, a Notre Dame man, who had given the platoon a pep talk about killing Communists the night before they rolled out. The lieutenant's holy war was over by the next night. As the battalion rolled back, fighting all the way, Jack saw the lieutenant burning in the open turret of his tank like a dummy atop a football rally bonfire, his arms extended in a kind of feeble surrender. After forty-eight hours of continuous fighting the "offensive" in Jack's sector had lost two miles.

The fighting around Kunu-ri continued for five more days. Beside his tank, Jack watched a medic heat morphine ampules in his mouth to prepare them to relieve the pain of a gut-shot infantryman. Men were coming down with enteritis from eating frozen rations. Jack and Hinajosa, his Mexican-American gunner, developed a routine. Every time one or the other felt his feet beginning to get frostbitten, they got down inside the tank and opened their pile jackets and underclothing and warmed each other's feet on their bellies. Hinajosa thought of a great bellied uncle who had hair all over like an ape. "I give one year's fuckin for that uncle now," Hinajosa vowed. "I give any year you like," he tried to strike a deal, rolling his eyes heavenward. A fire at night was out of the question. It was colder inside the tank than it was outside, where men could burrow into little snow caves.

On December 1 they were told the division was moving back to Sunchon, about ten miles farther south. The

Chinese were in an arc around the entire division area. Almost half of Jack's battalion was gone, much of the loss owing to breakdowns and equipment made useless because of the cold. The infantry had hundreds of cases of frostbite as they began loading onto the division's trucks. Some seven thousand men loaded up. The division had been about ten thousand. The tanks were put in the lead and in the rear for the withdrawal. Jack's tank was the last one in the lead column.

What division intelligence had not been able to discover was that along a five-mile stretch of the road out of Kunu-ri, an entire Chinese division had set up the most hellish roadblock in the history of the war. The road ran through high ground on either side. The Chinese put their guns and mortars on the heights. When they opened up on the column, some of their positions were as close as one hundred yards from the road. No division scout, no recon platoon had spotted them. At the end of the pass the road cut for a narrow quarter of a mile between high cliffs of loose rock on either side. When the lead tanks were in the cut, the Chinese let it *all* fly. In the face of the holocaust, the column accordioned and came to a halt. Trucks were exploding from shells dropped by Chinese mortars. Jack looked back and saw the bodies of men thrown up from the trucks like ugly broken dolls into the air. His driver tried to move the tank off the road so Hinajosa could place the big gun in a firing position. He had succeeded in getting it crosswise in the road before a shell knocked off the right track and the engine stalled, probably throwing all the fan belts.

"Give me a target!" Hinajosa kept shouting over the intercom. Jack could not *see* a target. He hit the tank commander's override control and elevated the gun toward the high cliffs.

"I don't see nothin! Give me a target, Sarge!" Hinajosa screamed.

Jack was peering over the lip of the open TC's hatch. The glassed viewing slits were frosted and useless.

"H.E. FIRE!" he yelled, and reached up to close the hatch. Bullets were pinging off the turret like high-velocity hail. He was just reaching for the handle of the hatch when something hit the side of the turret just below and in front of him, about where Hinajosa's eager gunner's head would be bent into his sight. Maybe it was an antitank shell or a captured bazooka rocket. Jack was blown out of the turret. He felt himself bounce off the right fender on which he landed in the middle of his back. The noise around him was incredible. His right leg hurt suddenly, as if it had been bitten by a big wildass dog. Right through the boot. Then again in the thigh. He knew he had been shot. He was rather amazed. Getting shot hadn't been all that much to be afraid about. He thought, *A man could get shot a lot like that before it killed him.* He also thought the fact the bullets were probably of foreign manufacture, maybe from some factory in China where Chinese girls packed them in wax-paper-lined crates—the vision was very clear, very real—a little factory in China where it was springtime, girls packing bullets in boxes. . . .

He was on the ground a few yards from the tank. He tried to get farther away from it in case it blew up. Attempting to stand, he fell. Men stumbled over him. There was snow and dirt in his mouth. Everywhere he looked, bullets were augering into the ground, kicking up little geysers. He glanced back to see if anyone else was getting out of the tank. The loader was twisted awkwardly half out of the loader's hatch, his clothes and body jumping every now and then like a sand-filled practice dummy as the odd bullet whacked into his corpse. Jack did not see anyone else.

There was no way for a vehicle to move either forward or backward along the road. Ammunition in the burning vehicles was exploding. The din was incredible. No war film Jack had ever sat through came close.

There was a man lying facedown in the ditch with his mittened hands over both ears, screaming at the top of his lungs. Jack watched fascinated until a bullet hit the man and he was still. Somewhere near he could hear another whispering, "Water. Water. Water. Water. Water," as if he could not stop saying it. Hardly anyone in the road was firing back. Those not already hit either clung to the cold earth or stumbled around as in a dream, not knowing where to go or what to do. Also as in a dream, Jack saw his own hand take his pistol from his shoulder holster, click off the safety, point it in the direction of the top of the cut and pull the trigger until the pistol was empty and the slide caught in the open position. Then he got the giggles. A .45 wouldn't reach up there by half. He had a flash of Big John Wayne grabbing a machine gun in his bare hands and scaling the cliff and killing all the Chinese up there. The sound of his own pistol in the din had seemed unreal, mysterious, hopeless.

The only other man he saw firing anything was a sergeant who had taken an 81 millimeter mortar from his 3/4-ton weapons carrier, set the bastard up in the road all alone and was firing the thing on line of sight at the top of the south end of the pass.

A man sat on the hood of a jeep with bullets smacking all around him trying to bandage the foot of another soldier braced against the windshield. The foot had been blown away at the ankle.

Down in the ditch with Jack, a wounded soldier was trying to drag an even more seriously wounded man to cover behind a clobbered jeep. "Now get your goddamned leg around the corner of that jeep. Do it, I say! That's the way. Goddamn it, I knew you could make it."

General Keiser had to leave his division commander's jeep and make his way on foot up along the column. The men he spoke to responded to nothing, saw nothing and seemingly heard nothing. He would report later that it was "hallucinating." Men neither sought better cover nor cried out. Their facial expressions were set, masklike with dust and dirt, distorted by the drooping of their jaws. By the time the general got there they were no longer speaking. Not a word. They were doing nothing. A few shuffling aimlessly about seemed to reel in their tracks. The general went from group to group even as the enemy fire kicked around him, barking questions, trying to startle the men back to consciousness. "Who's in command here?" he demanded repeatedly. "Can you *do* anything, soldier? Can you do anything?" He got not a single response. He stopped at the shallow ditch where Jack lay holding his empty pistol. He had other clips in his pocket, but he had not reloaded.

"Who are you?" the general leaned near to ask. "Are you hurt badly? Can you do anything, Sergeant?"

Jack felt his lips move. They were tingly, as if he had been doped. "I don't know, sir. War's an impersonal thing. We get lost in it." He wasn't sure he had actually spoken. Perhaps it was only a thought.

"Can you do anything?" the general asked again. Jack could see pity and disgust in the man's eyes.

Jack did not answer. Maybe he shook his head. He did not know. The general moved on.

Jack saw him trudging up the hill. He looked tired too. His feet seemed almost as leaden as the men who were staggering around. Directly in his path, crosswise in the road, lay a dead soldier. The general tried to step over the dead man but, failing to lift his boot high enough, caught the man in the belly. The dead man sat bolt upright and yelled, "You damned sonofabitch!"

The general was so astonished he replied only, "My friend, I'm sorry," and went on.

Finally air support arrived and began working over the enemy positions on either side of the pass. Some of the infantry began to rally behind officers, often behind sergeants, corporals, even privates who took over squads and platoons. There were some good soldiers that day. Jack did not feel he was one of them. He wondered if he would have been if he had been an officer or if the Army had been right about him after all.

As night began to close, he busied himself in putting a tight bandage around his lower leg, right over his boot. He could feel blood inside it, but neither it nor the wound in his thigh seemed to have bled very much. He put another bandage around his thigh, after crawling over to a corpse and taking its first-aid pouch. Each infantryman had taken to carrying two on his cartridge belt. He also took the man's canteen and sipped some of the half-frozen water.

He jumped so at the ugly, filthy face that loomed over his left shoulder out of the dark that he hurt his wounded leg. "Drink," the man demanded hopefully, gesturing with a dark bare hand toward his reeking mouth. "Drink. . . ." Jack handed the man the canteen. He wore a woolly British type overcoat almost to the ankles. He looked as mean and smelled as bad as a junkyard dog. About a week's beard grew on his swarthy chops. A cut along one cheek was closed with clotted blood. His left hand was bound in a bloody bandage. His feet were wrapped in strips of blanket over his boots, from which bits of dried grass stuck as if he had been stuffed for a scarecrow.

"Come," he said after he had drank. "Come!" He gestured they should go along the road.

"I don't think I can walk," Jack said, pointing to his leg.

"You come," the man insisted. He reached with his bare hand and hauled Jack to his feet. He put his rifle beneath

Jack's arm for a crutch. He had the bayonet on it, so it was about the right length. He grinned and nodded his head approvingly. Then he took the dead infantryman's rifle for their protection and looped Jack's left arm over his shoulders. They started along the road.

They passed burning vehicles and vehicles burned out, sitting at tragic angles. Traces still crisscrossed the pass in the dark.

"Turk!" the ugly little man explained, nodding.

"American," was all Jack could think to reply.

The Turk grinned and nodded that he knew as much. He felt a solid, little, bandy-legged man beneath his stuffed clothes. He smelled like hell, but Jack was beginning to like him a lot.

After a while the man spoke again. "You like girls?"

"Yeow," Jack admitted.

"I like." The Turk established their common interest.

"You like boys?"

"No," Jack said.

"Umm," the Turk said, then he smacked his lips evilly. "Sometimes a boy is better," he said with authority.

"You like donkeys?" Jack asked.

"Huh?"

"Donkeys, *burros*. Mexican boys tell me donkeys are the best there is."

"Huh?" And he spouted a lot of Turkish.

Suddenly, as they neared the end of the cut, they heard a strange, wailing music.

"It's a fucking *bagpipe!*" Jack decided.

The Turk grinned and picked up their pace a bit.

It screamed and moaned, a music that did not need words or the sentiment of anyone's ridiculous language. It was the whole thing—all together. It was everything that was true that no one could say well enough—about living, dying, soldiering, or—shit, just living on this earth and knowing in the silent areas of your brain that the greater part of it is *lonely*, uncharted, and that the rest is mostly bullshit.

The Scots held open the bottom of the pass. Three thousand of the seven thousand men who had gone in five miles back came out of the south end.

Jack sat in the aid station, feeling nice from the morphine in his veins. Some of the men in the battalion had gotten into the morphine and shot it for the buzz. He could understand that, as the world became quiet, nice, cozy. He was smiling from the litter upon which he was propped while waiting for evacuation. Japan certainly, maybe even Stateside. That morphine was nice.

The station was just some tarps put up next to a truck, with a flap for a roof. He watched soldiers moving Chinese prisoners into an area across the road. They were made to hunker on the ground with their hands locked behind their necks. Then he saw the tallest Chinese on earth prodded apart from the rest and made to hunker all alone outside the others.

"Big Stoop!" he cried aloud. When the interpreter with the prisoners asked the squatting taller man something and he did not reply immediately, the guard popped him in the mouth with his rifle butt, causing his felt-booted feet to slip from under him and him to fall awkwardly on his ass. The guard set him up again, prodding him with his bayonet, and the interpreter spoke to him again. His face was bloody, his mouth split. When the guard started to buttstroke him again for his continued silence, the interpreter, an officer, restrained him.

Jack wasn't certain it was the coolie he had seen dragooned into Chiang Kai-shek's army as a pissant ammo bearer, but if it wasn't, this one could have been his twin brother. He stared across the road and felt the morphine warm and cozy inside him and fell asleep. When he woke, the prisoners were gone. At dark he was loaded on a jeep that had racks for two stretchers and driven away over a bumpy road that became a highway after a while.

In the hospital in California all his mail caught up with him. There were dozens of letters from Judy. At first she had written every day. Then she wrote less frequently. She complained of getting only three letters from him. She worried he had been "lost," as she put it. Then, there was quite a break between letters, and one in which she said she had decided what they had had together was really just her first "serious love affair." She went on about how beautiful it had been and she would never forget him as long as she lived, and that he would always be a special person to her. But she had met another man, a captain in the medical corps, not a career man, just fulfilling his military obligation, and they were going to be married. He was a marvelous, good, loving man, she assured him, and she knew if he met him, he would like him and be happy for them. She was sure he would find a sweet, "passionate," girl who would be proud to accept his beautiful ring one day, even if he told her about the girl who had worn it before. She signed it: "May my love for you be a part of all your happiness—always, Judy."

"What'sa matter, ace? You get a 'Dear John'?" the kid from Arkansas in the next bed cracked.

"Well, yeow," Jack grinned. "It's like getting shot. Not all that much to get scared about."

He wrote her a long letter, describing what had happened to him, and wished her the best happiness in her marriage to the captain. He really meant it, "But," he added, "I will love *you* too, as long as I live."

The nurse came in as he was leaning out of the bed to dump the letters in the wastebasket.

"They will be in here in the morning to give you two goldbricks purple hearts and take your pictures. So comb your hair and"—she turned to the Arkansaser—"get those filthy girlie magazines out of sight. I know something they could of shot off and done the world a favor," she snorted.

"Hey, Sarge," the kid asked, "if they *did* shoot your dick off, would you get hundred percent disability, you reckon?"

"Whoo!" the nurse crowed. "If they got you both, you two wouldn't get ten percent between you!" She went out laughing.

"I'd like to show *her* somethin!" the kid protested.

"I can teach you to wiggle your ears," Jack offered.

When he was released from the hospital, Jack was stationed at Fort Leonard Wood, where he ran a combat training course until his enlistment was up. The recruiters asked him if he would like to re-up, promising promotion to master sergeant, pointing out he would be one of the youngest master sergeants in the Army since the Civil War. Jack declined the honor. While awaiting discharge, he enrolled at the nearest university, bought a 1951 Ford convertible and began classes two days after he was discharged.

His faculty adviser was a teacher of English who had been a bomber pilot during the Second World War and wore a neat graying crew cut. "Why did you want to return to school?" the man asked Jack during their first meeting.

"I want to try to learn somehow to live sort of alone, sir."

The man raised both eyebrows. "Yes?"

"I mean, I've got to learn how to do something I care about outside of business and working for someone, stuff like that."

"Why?"

"Well, I'm psychologically unfit for anything else."

"Are you so sure?"

"Yes, sir."

"You haven't thought about becoming a teacher?"

"No, sir."

The man looked very relieved to learn that. He wished Jack the best of luck in whatever he decided to do, shook hands and told him he should come and see him any time he had a problem. "Let us hope not a psychological one." The man smiled.

48

THE old man was dying.

Snow intermittently swirled up the alley, forming little whirlwinds in the drafts between the houses that fronted on the streets.

When the old man's daughter-in-law telephoned to ask about him, his wife spoke softly into the receiver, thinking he was asleep, whispering in a way that enabled Jack to hear her false teeth sucking and clacking loosely.

"Well, the doctor can't say, Elfie. It could be anytime. I just don't know. He hurts so bad, I think it would be a blessing. It's been so *hard*. I don't think *I* can stand it much longer. I have to be up all night with him. He's like a baby now, you know. Can't control himself at all. Jack's here. Yes. That let's me get out a little and take care of what I have to do. I've just let everything else slide. I did

go to prayer meeting last night. I think it did me good. ....
Oh, I *know* you would if you could. I know that." Then,
seeing the old man on the narrow couch, which had once
been Jack's bed in the trailer, was awake and staring at
her, she lifted her voice cheerfully. "Daddy, it's Elfie! She
wants to know what you want for Christmas."

The old man's strong features were sharper for the skin
being drawn more tightly over the big bones. "Tell her I
won't be here Christmas," he barked, and rolled painfully
upon his side. He plunged his hands down between his
wasted old thighs beneath the covers and lay staring
blankly at the fire in the gas heater next to which Jack sat
on a straight chair.

"Oh, Jack got here day before yesterday." The old
woman spoke into the phone. "He's got a car. Drove from
Missouri. I don't know what he's doin. Goin to college is
all I know. Nobody tells *me* nothin. I can't understand
him anymore. Guess he's quit goin to church. None of my
children give a hoot for Christ. It just makes me feel like
nothin I ever wanted or tried to do was worthwhile. I
wonder why I ever try. .... Well, yes. You know Daddy
always likes a nice tie." She lowered her voice and glanced
at the old man. "But just between you and me, Elfie, I'd
wait until the last minute. .... *Me?*" She brightened. "Oh,
you know *me.* Anything you want to get me pleases me. I
ain't particular." She giggled. "I *could* use a steam iron.
I'm still sprinklin. But I don't want you to think you and
Son should get me one. Whatever you want to get me is
fine with me. .... Well, thanks, Elfie. But don't think you
have to. ... That's awfully good of you. But I know
you're both workin now. Jack's here. He really don't seem
to mind sittin with him. He hasn't gone out or called any
of his pals since he got here. Maybe he's growin up. But I
hoped when he got back from Korea, he would settle down
and do somethin. I just can't make head nor tail of what
he's after. But then I hardly understand nothin
anymore. ... OK. I'll tell him. Bye."

She put down the phone and stood a reflective moment
as if trying to remember something she should have said
but had forgotten. Her fingers fussed at the neck of her
housedress. Then she turned. "Elfie says hello. They are
looking forward to seeing you Christmas. You'll be able to
meet your cousin Jerry's wife. They have a little boy now
and another on the way. Real little scamp, too. He's as

hardheaded and stubborn as Jerry, and *he's* gettin more like his grandpa every day. Jerry might not have gotten along with the teachers at school, but he's doin good, you know. He's the best body and fender man Yingling's have. And he's a year younger almost than you. He only works on the Cadillacs," she added with great pride.

Jerry had left school at fifteen to marry a girl about fourteen. Jack remembered at the beginning, his grandmother had whispered the girl was half-Mexican.

"Well"—the old woman sighed—"I reckon I ought to do somethin about supper." She looked without enthusiasm at the end of the trailer where the little stove sat beneath the end window with a battered tea kettle on it.

"I'm not hungry," Jack said.

The stench in the trailer was terrible. After he had first arrived, Jack had almost gagged from the smell. He had opened the window, and his grandmother had protested, "Daddy always complains he's cold. I got to keep the gas on all day and all night. I got the electric blanket on him, but it's old and only heats a little. I think some of the little wires in it are broke. I washed it in Elfie's machine. The man who sold it to me at Sears *said* you could wash it."

But Jack had put another blanket on the old man and kept the window open a crack.

When the old man looked at him, it was often as if he were trying to place the boy in his memory. A small light of seemingly angry fear in his pale gray eyes indicated that he thought Jack might hurt him. The look gave Jack such a rush of tenderness he lay his hand on the old man's grizzled cheek and offered, "In a day or so, when you feel better, Granddad, I'll give you a shave."

"I ain't gonna feel no better, and I know it," he said, looking the boy unblinkingly in the eyes.

"Sure you don't want somethin to eat?" his grandmother asked again. "I'll fix somethin."

"No. I'll go out after a while and get a hamburger. You ought to get out yourself, Grandma. Why don't you go down to the corner and have something at the White Castle? It'll do you good."

"I don't like to spend money to eat in restaurants. Everything's so blamed high nowadays. Anyway, it's snowin."

"It's about stopped. Just little wisps anyway."

"Aw. . . . There's always a bunch of smart-alecky colored boys in there."

"Do they bother you?"

"No. . . . But I just don't feel comfortable."

"Go *on*. I'll give you some money."

"Well, I reckon you *need* your money. And I don't *like* eatin alone," the old woman said childishly. "And it's cold out. I'm always afraid I'll slip. I did last winter. I was cripplin around for two weeks. I coulda broke my hip. Opal Hightower's mother slipped and broke *her* hip, you know. On the way to church. Right on her front steps. She died. But they do *do* miracles today. Missus Brown at church, she slipped and broke her hip when you were in Korea, and they put in a metal one as good as new. She says it cured her rheumatism, too. They can do miracles, if you got the money. . . ." She was lost in a reverie of unlimited spare parts.

"Go on, Grandma," Jack persisted. "Don't try to cook. Go on. Here." He held out a couple of dollars.

She was reluctant to take it, and she was a bit flustered in being made to go out when she did not really want to. "That's too much! I could never eat that much. I'll take one and bring you change."

"OK."

"You never were any better at managin money than your grandpa. You always did have a hole in your pocket."

He held her old coat with a fox collar so worn he could see the dead, doggy hide through the fur. Someone she had worked for had given it to her. She had shortened it once to make it more fashionable.

"I just don't see how goin to college for art or whatever you call it is goin to do anything to help you make a livin," she rambled on. "I don't see there's any money in it. You know the fat lady who took the trailer of that little hunchback next door who worked at Ball's, after his wife left him? She married an artist."

"The hunchback's wife?"

"No! The fat lady. Vivian. She's Missus Dean now, though she lived with him without bein married until the caseworker caught her and threatened to cut off her relief. I don't see how she can *look* at him, let alone *marry* him. He just came up the alley one day, and next thing you know he'd moved in. He don't have no nose. He said he lost it in the last war, but I know he wasn't in no war. If he did, he would have a pension, wouldn't he? Well, he don't have no pension. But now he's got a false nose he sticks on that looks almost real. But, of course, he can't hold no job where he has to meet the public. He talks through his nose so you can hardly understand him. *He's* an artist! Goes door to door out in the rich part of town seein if they will let him decorate their kid's room or the playroom or somethin. He can paint anything you want on a wall. I see pictures of his work. He did a place out in Eastborough, all Mickey Mouse and Donald Duck and all them Disney characters, *life size!* . . . in a kid's room. But he don't make much. It ain't steady. If they weren't on relief, they would be in a fix. I don't understand why you didn't stay in the service!" she blurted so out of the blue and with such force it made Jack's head jerk. "You went in so young, you could of stayed in and *retired* at thirty-four or five with a good pension."

"You should be a recruiting officer," he told her.

"Well, you could of! Elmer Steegers is stayin in. He's got a good job as a chief cook in the Air Force. He was home to see his mother. He's a sergeant. He said he likes it. He's got six years in already. He asked what you were doin. He would have liked to see you. But you can't even go to school here. He said he's goin to stay in for thirty years and he'll be only forty-seven when he gets his pension. And then he could still get a job cookin somewhere if he wants to. The cook at the airport when I was washin dishes there got his start in the service. I never understood why *you* didn't get into somethin in service that woulda helped you later."

"I don't either, Grandma," he teased her a bit.

"Oh, you think you're so smart. Better than the rest of us. You can laugh at Elmer. But he knows where *he's* goin!"

He tucked her ratty collar up close beneath her stubborn little chin and peered for a second through her bifocals into her small frosty blue eyes. There was nothing to say.

"Take a flashlight," he reminded her, and got one for her. He leaned out the door to hand her down the rickety steps.

"Take your time."

"I'll probably slip and break my hip. Then won't we be in a fix with nobody to do nothin?"

He sat there with just the gas fire for light, watching the old man sleep, seeing the hump of his shadow on the cracked, ply-faced wall. There was ice on the small window above his head. He had always looked so large to Jack. Now he seemed like an ordinary-sized old man who was dying. He groaned as a wave of deep, gut-ripping pain washed over his face. His lips trembled. A tear or two were squeezed from his eyes.

"Mama!" he called, panic touching his voice.

"She went for a bite to eat, Granddad. It's me. Jack."

"Mama!" he called as if he hadn't heard.

Jack touched him. "I'm here, Grandpa. It's me, Jack. Can I help you?"

The old man rolled his head toward the young man. His eyes found him and focused weakly. "Where's Mama?"

"She went to get something to eat. She'll be right back."

His large, now shaking hand reached out, and Jack took it. The old man's hand gripped fiercely—he was still remarkably strong—and bore down as the crab's claws bit painfully into his bowels.

"Lord-Lord!" he cried when the pain began to pass. Using breath that might be his last, he swore, *"Goddamn!"* Such a goddamned way of doin! I just got no control over myself. It's just as well I'm dyin. I don't want to go on no more like this." He looked sheepishly apologetic—yet angry too. "I just messed all over myself," he confessed.

They came for the old man in the morning—two young men who worked on the county's ambulance—to take him to the hospital to die. They were OK. They tried not to breathe in the trailer, and in their glances between each other, Jack could see they were appalled at the way some people lived, but they handled the old man gently.

"You won't have to bring me back," the old man joshed with the boys. When they made perfunctory sounds of protest at his contention, he said, "Shit, I know it. It's OK. I outlived that goddamned Roosevelt!" He chuckled at his favorite joke. "But that Ike's another one. Truman was the only goddamned decent man we've had in the White House since Lincoln. And I ain't all that sure about Lincoln. But Harry was all right, by God!"

The boys weren't interested in politics.

At the door he reached up and touched his wife's hand. "Mama."

"What, John?"

"I can't go like this."

"What is it?"

He whispered shyly. "I don't have no breetches on."

"It's OK, old-timer," one of the boys said.

"No. Hold it," Jack said. He got the old man's everyday pants—patched as a coolie's—and rolled them into a bundle. The cloth felt soft as velvet. He tucked them beneath the blanket where the old man could feel them.

"I love you, Grandpa," he said, touching the old man's face. He had never said that to the old man before. He wanted him to know it.

About the Author

Earl Thompson was born in Kansas, served in the armed forces, has held a wide variety of manual jobs, attended the University of Missouri, and for the past several years has been living in Europe.

Thompson served in the U.S. Navy in 1945–46 and in the U.S. Army from 1948–54. He was a Sergeant First Class, Tank Commander, and First Sergeant. He attended the University of Maryland in 1949–50, the University of Missouri from 1954–57, and Columbia University in 1959–1960.

Among his jobs, he includes fried-pie salesman, paperboy, roustabout and roughneck, gandydance for the Santa Fe Railway, truckdriver, cattle slaughterer for Cudahy Packing Company, newsman, editor, cartoonist, commercial artist.

He twice received the Mahan Short Story Award at the University of Missouri, an award for fiction from Columbia, and best actor of the year award from the University of Missouri in 1956.

A Garden of Sand, his first novel, was nominated for a National Book Award in 1971. *Tattoo* was chosen by the Book-of-the-Month Club as an alternate selection.

"Oh, *sure!*" She snapped her left shoulder around as if slamming a door in his face.

He'd come back and visit school in his uniform. He'd show those know-it-alls.

Jeanne squealed, "There's your mother!" They took a last suck at their shakes and bounded off the stools, leaving half in their glasses. A maroon '40 Lincoln Continental Cabriolet had pulled up in the no parking zone out front. A pretty woman leaned over to look inside the kitchen and honked the horn. He had caddied for her. He remembered her swing, the way her tits leaped when she drove, the way her skirt fit her nice rump, the slender brown legs above socks that left her ankles bare. He could remember her perfume, how her manicured hands looked, one bare, the other in a perforated golf glove, how their fingers had touched when he handed her a club. She had dubbed a drive into the deep and exclaimed, "Shit!" and then had tipped him fifty cents. He had carried her clubs to the Lincoln and put them in for her. She sat on the seat to change her shoes and he'd caught a flash of her shiny brown thighs. She must shave her legs all the way up, he remembered.

He wondered what it would be like to be rich. He had delivered groceries to the houses of people like them. They bought whole boxes of stuff at one time. The Ferrells had a refrigerator like a cold storage room you could walk into. Hoarders. They had enough stashed away to last for the duration. *They* didn't fuck around with ration stamps. How'd they do it? he wondered. What would it be like to always wear new stuff? Cashmere? She-it. It wasn't a world he knew or ever would know. They were different. Tightass little cunts. You couldn't tell him that hot stuff like that Mrs. Ferrell wasn't gettin something on the side. All those rich bitches fucked like minks—only not guys like him. He often dreamed of jumping in one of their bigass cars with a gun and making the bitch drive them to some lovers' lane where he would make her suck his cock, tear off her fancy clothes while she cried and begged for mercy.

Vanda had gone outside with her gob, then pretending she had forgotten something, she came back and quickly asked Jack, "You seen Glenn?"

"Not since last night."

"Well, if you see him, tell him he can come over tonight. I'd really like to see him."

"What about the sailor?"

She made a face. "Anyway, he's got to catch a bus back to base. You'll see him, won't you?" she insisted.

"I don't know. I'm goin into the Navy myself tomorrow mornin."

"You're *kidding*!"

"Naw. Changed my birth certificate and they accepted me."

"That's double-jointed! *Too* much!"

"Yeow."

"Listen, will you tell him?"

"Maybe I'll just come over myself," he said quietly.

She cocked her head at the idea for a moment. "OK. If you want to."

"I gotta go to church first, though. I promised my grandma. My last night. You know. So it would be sorta late."

"Oh, that's all-reet, Jack. My folks go to bed early. We can listen to the radio downstairs . . . undisturbed."

"Great. Maybe I'll see you then."

"I'll be waiting," she said trying to be sexy. "If you see Glenn you can both come," she had to add, her greed—or was it some kind of frantic need?—so obvious it made something curl up inside of him. In some ways, she reminded him of his mother. Vanda fucked guys like eating popcorn. And in between she bit her fingernails to the quick.

He used to bite his fingernails like that; then he heard he might be turned down for the service because of it and quit.

He was torn between the desire to fuck Vanda and the feeling that it would somehow reduce him to a stupid remark in her diary—Glenn said she kept a diary about every guy who had ever pronged her. He had seen it. She said *he* was the best—that he could just look at her and she wanted to do it. Stupid cunt. Jack decided he would just see how things went. Maybe he would. Maybe he wouldn't.

He felt cool. . . . Reet! He left a nickel for the soda jerk on the old-fashioned marble counter.

In front of the Wichita two skinny little black girls with

108